The Asimov Chronicles
Volume One

Fifty Years of Isaac Asimov

THE ASIMOV CHRONICLES
Volume One

Edited by
Martin H. Greenberg

CENTURY
A LEGEND BOOK
LONDON SYDNEY AUCKLAND JOHANNESBURG

First published in Great Britain in 1991 by
Legend, an imprint of Random Century Group
20 Vauxhall Bridge Rd,
London SW1V 2SA

Century Hutchinson South Africa (Pty) Ltd
PO Box 337, Bergvlei 2012
South Africa

Random Century Australia Pty Ltd
20 Alfred St, Milsons Point, Sydney, NSW 0261
Australia

Random Century New Zealand Ltd
PO Box 40–086, Glenfield, Auckland 10
New Zealand

British Library Cataloguing in Publication Data
Asimov, Isaac
The Asimov chronicles: Vol 1. – (Legend books)
I. Title II. Series
813[F]

ISBN 0–7126–4770–8

Printed and bound in Great Britain by
Mackays of Chatham PLC, Chatham, Kent

Table of Contents

Acknowledgements

The Publishers would like to express their gratitude to the following people. Thank you: Dawn Austin, Kathy Jo Camacho, Stan and Phyllis Mikol, Wayne Sommers, Dr Stan Gurnick PhD, Tony Hodes, Bertha Curl, Kurt Scharrer, Gary Fronk, Linda Solar, Ken Morris, the people of the All American Print Center, Dick Spelman, Maureen Austin, Luis Trevino, Raymond, Teresa and Mark Stadalsky, Tom Pas, Ken and Lynda Fotos, and Ann Cameron Williams.

And, of course, special thanks go to: Martin H. Greenberg, Isaac Asimov, Ron Lindahn and Val Lakey Lindahn.

Marooned Off Vesta

"Will you please stop walking up and down like that?" said Warren Moore from the couch. "It won't do any of us any good. Think of our blessings; we're airtight, aren't we?"

Mark Brandon whirled and ground his teeth at him. "I'm glad you feel happy about that," he spat out viciously. "Of course, you don't know that our air supply will last only three days." He resumed his interrupted stride with a defiant air.

Moore yawned and stretched, assumed a more comfortable position, and replied. "Expending all that energy will only use it up faster. Why don't you take a hint from Mike here? He's taking it easy."

"Mike" was Michael Shea, late a member of the crew of the *Silver Queen*. His short, squat body was resting on the only chair in the room and his feet were on the only table. He looked up as his name was mentioned, his mouth widening in a twisted grin.

"You've got to expect things like this to happen sometimes," he said. "Bucking the asteroids is risky business. We should've taken the hop. It takes longer, but it's the only safe way. But no, the captain wanted to make the schedule; he *would* go through"—Mike spat disgustedly—"and here we are."

"What's the 'hop'?" asked Brandon.

"Oh, I take it that friend Mike means that we should have avoided the asteroid belt by plotting a course outside the plane of the ecliptic," answered Moore. "That's it, isn't it, Mike?"

Mike hesitated and then replied cautiously, "Yeah—I guess that's it."

Moore smiled blandly and continued, "Well, I wouldn't blame Captain Crane too much. The repulsion screen must have failed five minutes before that chunk of granite barged into us. That's not his fault, though of course we ought to have steered clear instead of relying on the screen." He shook his head meditatively. "The *Silver Queen* just went to pieces. It's really miraculously lucky that this part of the ship remained intact, and what's more, airtight."

"You've got a funny idea of luck, Warren," said Brandon. "Always have, for as long as I've known you. Here we are in a tenth part of a spaceship, comprising only three *whole* rooms, with air for three days, and no prospect of being alive after that, and you have the internal gall to prate about luck."

"Compared to the others who died instantly when the asteroid struck, yes," was Moore's answer.

"You think so, eh? Well, let me tell you that instant death isn't so bad compared with what we're going to have to go through. Suffocation is a damned unpleasant way of dying."

"We may find a way out," Moore suggested hopefully.

"Why not face facts!" Brandon's face was flushed and his voice trembled. "We're done, I tell you! Through!"

Mike glanced from one to the other doubtfully and then coughed to attract their attention. "Well, gents, seeing that we're all in the same fix, I guess there's no use hogging things." He drew a small bottle out of his pocket that was filled with a greenish liquid. "Grade A Jabra this is. I ain't too proud to share and share alike."

Brandon exhibited the first signs of pleasure for over a day. "Martian Jabra water. Why didn't you say so before?"

But as he reached for it, a firm hand clamped down upon his wrist. He looked up into the calm blue eyes of Warren Moore.

"Don't be a fool," said Moore, "there isn't enough to keep us drunk for three days. What do you want to do? Go on a tear now and then die cold sober? Let's save this for the last six hours when the air gets stuffy and breathing hurts—then we'll finish the bottle among us and never *know* when the end comes, or *care*."

Brandon's hand fell away reluctantly. "Damn it, Warren, you'd bleed ice if you were cut. How can you think straight at a time like this?" He motioned to Mike and the bottle was once more stowed away. Brandon walked to the porthole and gazed out.

Moore approached and placed a kindly arm over the shoulders of the younger man. "Why take it so hard, man?" he asked. "You can't last at this rate. Inside of twenty-four hours you'll be a madman if you keep this up."

There was no answer. Brandon stared bitterly at the globe that filled almost the entire porthole, so Moore continued, "Watching Vesta won't do you any good either."

Mike Shea lumbered up to the porthole. "We'd be safe if we were only down there on Vesta. There's people there. How far away are we?"

"Not more than three or four hundred miles judging from its apparent size," answered Moore. "You must remember that it is only two hundred miles in diameter."

"Three hundred miles from salvation," murmured Brandon, "and we might as well be a million. If there were only a way to get ourselves out of the orbit this rotten fragment adopted. You know, manage to give ourselves a push so as to start falling. There'd be no danger of crashing if we did, because that midget hasn't got enough gravity to crush a cream puff."

"It has enough to keep us in the orbit," retorted Brandon. "It must have picked us up while we were lying unconscious after the crash. Wish it had come closer; we might have been able to land on it."

"Funny place, Vesta," observed Mike Shea. "I was down there two-three times. What a dump! It's all covered with some stuff like snow, only it ain't snow. I forget what they call it."

"Frozen carbon dioxide?" prompted Moore.

"Yeah, dry ice, that carbon stuff, that's it. They say that's what makes Vesta so shiny."

"Of course! That would give it a high albedo."

Mike cocked a suspicious eye at Moore and decided to let it pass. "It's hard to see anything down there on account of the snow, but if you look close"—he pointed—"you can see a sort of gray smudge. I think that's Bennett's dome. That's where they keep the observatory. And there is Calorn's dome up there. That's a fuel station, that is. There's plenty more, too, only I don't see them."

He hesitated and then turned to Moore. "Listen, boss, I've been thinking. Wouldn't they be looking for us as soon as they hear about the crash? And wouldn't we be easy to find from Vesta, seeing we're so close?"

Moore shook his head, "No, Mike, they won't be looking for us. No one's going to find out about the crash until the *Silver Queen* fails to turn up on schedule. You see, when the asteroid hit, we didn't have time to send out an SOS"—he sighed—"and they won't find us down there at Vesta, either. We're so small that even at our distance they couldn't see us unless they knew what they were looking for, and exactly where to look."

"Hmm." Mike's forehead was corrugated in deep thought. "Then we've got to get to it, eh?"

Brandon suddenly exploded, "Will you two stop this infernal chitter-chatter and do something? For God's sake, do something."

Moore shrugged his shoulders and without answer returned to the couch. He lounged at ease, apparently carefree, but there was the tiniest crease between his eyes which bespoke concentration.

There was no doubt about it; they *were* in a bad spot. He reviewed the events of the preceding day for perhaps the twentieth time.

After the asteroid had struck, tearing the ship apart, he'd gone out like a light; for how long he didn't know, his own watch being broken and no other timepiece available. When he came to, he found himself, along with Mark Brandon, who shared his room, and Mike Shea, a member of the crew, sole occupants of all that was left of the *Silver Queen.*

This remnant was now careening in an orbit about Vesta. At present things were fairly comfortable. There was a food supply that would last a week. Likewise there was a regional Gravitator under the room that kept them at normal weight and would continue to do so for an indefinite time, certainly for longer than the air would last. The lighting system was less satisfactory but had held on so far.

There was no doubt, however, where the joker in the pack lay. Three days' air! Not that there weren't other disheartening features. There was no heating system—though it would take a long time for the ship to radiate enough heat into the vacuum of space to render them too uncomfortable. Far more important was the fact that their part of the ship had neither a means of communication nor a propulsive mechanism. Moore sighed. One fuel jet in working order would fix everything, for one blast in the right direction would send them safely to Vesta.

The crease between his eyes deepened. What was to be done? They had but one spacesuit among them, one heat ray, and one detonator. That was the sum total of space appliances after a thorough search of the accessible parts of the ship. A pretty hopeless mess, that.

Moore shrugged, rose, and drew himself a glass of water. He swallowed it mechanically, still deep in thought, when an idea struck him. He glanced curiously at the empty cup in his hand.

"Say, Mike," he said, "what kind of water supply have we? Funny that I never thought of that before."

Mike's eyes opened to their fullest extent in an expression of ludicrous surprise. "Didn't you know, boss?"

"Know *what?*" asked Moore impatiently.

"We've got all the water there was." He waved his hand in an all-inclusive gesture. He paused, but as Moore's expression showed nothing but total mystification, he elaborated, "Don't you see? We've got the main tank, the place where all the water for the whole ship was stored." He pointed to one of the walls.

"Do you mean to say that there's a tank full of water adjoining us?"

Mike nodded vigorously, "Yep! Cubic vat a hundred feet each way. And she's three-quarters full."

Moore was astonished. "Seven hundred and fifty thousand cubic feet of water." Then suddenly: "Why hasn't it run out through the broken pipes?"

"It only has one main outlet, which runs down the corridor just outside this room. I was fixing that main when the asteroid hit and had to shut it off. After I came to I opened the pipe leading to our faucet, but that's the only outlet open now."

"Oh." Moore had a curious feeling way down deep inside. An idea had half-formed in his brain, but for the life of him he could not drag it into the light of day. He knew only that there was something in what he had just heard that had some important meaning but he just could not place his finger on it.

Brandon, meanwhile, had been listening to Shea in silence, and now he emitted a short, humorless laugh. "Fate seems to be having its fill of fun with us, I see. First, it puts us within arm's reach of a place of safety and then sees to it that we have no way of getting there.

"Then she provides us with a week's food, three days' air, and *a year's supply of water*. A year's supply, do you hear me? Enough water to drink and to gargle and to wash and to take baths in and—and to do anything else we want. Water—damn the water!"

"Oh, take a less serious view, Mark," said Moore in an attempt to break the younger man's melancholy. "Pretend we're a satellite of Vesta—which we are. We have our own period of revolution and of rotation. We have an equator and an axis. Our 'north pole' is located somewhere toward the top of the porthole, pointing toward Vesta, and our 'south' sticks out away from Vesta through the water tank somewhere. Well, as a satellite, we have an atmosphere, and now, you see, we have a newly discovered ocean.

"And seriously, we're not so badly off. For the three days our atmosphere will last, we can eat double rations and drink ourselves soggy. Hell, we have water enough to throw away—"

The idea which had been half-formed before suddenly sprang to maturity and was nailed. The careless gesture with which he had accompanied the last remark was frozen in mid-air. His mouth closed with a snap and his head came up with a jerk.

But Brandon, immersed in his own thoughts, noticed nothing of Moore's strange actions. "Why don't you complete the analogy to a satellite," he sneered, "or do you, as a Professional Optimist, ignore any and all disagreeable facts? If I were you, I'd continue this way." Here he imitated Moore's voice: "The satellite is at present habitable and inhabited but, due to the approaching depletion of its atmosphere in three days, is expected to become a dead world.

"Well, why don't you answer? Why do you persist in making a joke out of this? Can't you see—*What's the matter?*"

The last was a surprised exclamation and certainly Moore's actions did merit surprise. He had risen suddenly and, after giving himself a smart rap on the forehead, remained stiff and silent, staring into the far distance with gradually narrowing eyelids. Brandon and Mike Shea watched him in speechless astonishment.

Suddenly Moore burst out, "Ha! I've got it. Why didn't I think of it before?" His exclamation degenerated into the unintelligible.

Mike drew out the Jabra bottle with a significant look, but Moore waved it away impatiently. Whereupon Brandon, without any warning, lashed out with his right, catching the surprised Moore flush on the jaw and toppling him.

Moore groaned and rubbed his chin. Somewhat indignant, he asked, "What was the reason for that?"

"Stand up and I'll do it again," shouted Brandon, "I can't stand it anymore. I'm sick and tired of being preached at, and having to listen to your Pollyanna talk. *You're* the one that's going daffy."

"Daffy, nothing! Just a little overexcited, that's all. Listen, for God's sake. I think I know a way—"

Brandon glared at him balefully. "Oh, you do, do you? Raise our hopes with some silly scheme and then find it doesn't work. I won't take it, do you hear? I'll find a real use for the water—drown you—and save some of the air besides."

Moore lost his temper. "Listen, Mark, you're out of this. I'm going through alone. I don't need your help and I don't want it. If you're that sure of dying and that afraid, why not have the agony over? We've got one heat ray and one detonator, both reliable weapons. Take your choice and kill yourself. Shea and I won't interfere." Brandon's lips curled in a last weak geature of defiance and then suddenly he capitulated, completely and abjectly. "All right, Warren, I'm with you. I—I guess I didn't quite know what I was doing. I don't feel well, Warren. I—I—"

"Aw, that's all right, boy." Moore was genuinely sorry for him. "Take it easy. I know how you feel. It's got me too. But you mustn't give in to it. Fight it, or you'll go stark, raving mad. Now you just try and get some sleep and leave everything to me. Things will turn out right yet."

Brandon, pressing a hand to an aching forehead, stumbled to the couch and tumbled down. Silent sobs shook his frame while Moore and Shea remained in embarrassed silence nearby.

* * *

At last Moore nudged Mike. "Come on," he whispered, "let's get busy. We're going places. Airlock five is at the end of the corridor, isn't it?" Shea nodded and Moore continued, "Is it airtight?"

"Well," said Shea after some thought, "the inner door is, of course, but I don't know anything about the outer one. For all I know it may be a sieve. You see, when I tested the wall for airtightness, I didn't dare open the inner door, because if there was anything wrong with the outer one—blooey!" The accompanying gesture was very expressive.

"Then it's up to us to find out about that outer door right now. I've got to get outside some way and we'll just have to take chances. Where's the spacesuit?"

He grabbed the lone suit from its place in the cupboard, threw it over his shoulder and led the way into the long corridor that ran down the side of the room. He passed closed doors behind whose airtight barriers were what once had been passenger quarters but which were now merely cavities, open to space. At the end of the corridor was the tight-fitting door of Airlock 5.

Moore stopped and surveyed it appraisingly. "Looks all right," he observed, "but of course you can't tell what's outside. God, I hope it'll work." He frowned. "Of course we could use the entire corridor as an airlock, with the door to our room as the inner door and this as the outer door, but that would mean the loss of half our air supply. We can't afford that—yet."

He turned to Shea. "All right, now. The indicator shows that the lock was last used for entrance, so it should be full of air. Open the door the tiniest crack, and if there's a hissing noise, shut it quick."

"Here goes," and the lever moved one notch. The mechanism had been severely shaken up during the shock of the crash and its former noiseless workings had given way to a harsh, rasping sound, but it was still in commission. A thin black line appeared on the left-hand side of the lock, marking where the door had slid a fraction of an inch on the runners.

There was no hiss! Moore's look of anxiety faded somewhat. He took a small pasteboard from his pocket and held it against the crack. If air were leaking, that card should have held there, pushed by the escaping gas. It fell to the floor.

Mike Shea stuck a forefinger in his mouth and then put it against the crack. "Thank the Lord," he breathed, "not a sign of a draft."

"Good, good. Open it wider. Go ahead."

Another notch and the crack opened farther. And still no draft. Slowly, ever so slowly, notch by notch, it creaked its way wider and wider. The two men held their breaths, afraid that while not actually punctured, the outer door might have been so weakened as to give way any moment. But it held! Moore was jubilant as he wormed into the spacesuit.

"Things are going fine so far, Mike," he said. "You sit down right here and wait for me. I don't know how long I'll take, but I'll be back. Where's the heat ray? Have you got it?"

Shea held out the ray and asked, "But what are you going to do? I'd sort of like to know."

Moore paused as he was about to buckle on the helmet. "Did you hear me say inside that we had water enough to throw away? Well, I've been thinking it over and that's not such a bad idea. I'm going to throw it away." With no other explanation, he stepped into the lock, leaving behind him a very puzzled Mike Shea.

* * *

It was with a pounding heart that Moore waited for the outer door to open. His plan was an extraordinarily simple one, but it might not be easy to carry out.

There was a sound of creaking gears and scraping ratchets. Air sighed away to nothingness. The door before him slid open a few inches and stuck. Moore's heart sank as for a moment he thought it would not open at all, but after a few preliminary jerks and rattles the barrier slid the rest of the way.

He clicked on the magnetic grapple and very cautiously put a foot out into space. Clumsily he groped his way out to the side of the ship. He had never been outside a ship in open space before and a vast dread overtook him as he clung there, flylike, to his precarious perch. For a moment dizziness overcame him.

He closed his eyes and for five minutes hung there, clutching the smooth sides of what had once been the *Silver Queen*. The magnetic grapple held him firm and when he opened his eyes once more he found his self-confidence in a measure returned.

He gazed about him. For the first time since the crash he saw the stars instead of the vision of Vesta which their porthole afforded. Eagerly he searched the skies for the little blue-white speck that was Earth. It had often amused him that Earth should always be the first object sought by space travelers when stargazing, but the humor of the situation did not strike him now. However, his search was in vain. From where he lay, Earth was invisible. It, as well as the Sun, must be hidden behind Vesta.

Still, there was much else that he could not help but note, Jupiter was off to the left, a brilliant globe the size of a small pea to the naked eye. Moore observed two of its attendant satellites. Saturn was visible too, as a brilliant planet of some negative magnitude, rivaling Venus as seen from Earth.

Moore had expected that a goodly number of asteroids would be visible—marooned as they were in the asteroid belt—but space seemed surprisingly empty. Once he thought he could see a hurtling body pass within a few miles, but so fast had the impression come and gone that he could not swear that it was not fancy.

And then, of course, there was Vesta. Almost directly below him it loomed like a balloon filling a quarter of the sky. It floated steadily, snowy white, and Moore gazed at it with earnest longing. A good hard kick against the side of the ship, he thought, might start him falling toward Vesta. He *might* land safely and get help for the others. But the chance was too great that he would merely take on a new orbit about Vesta. No, it would have to be better than that.

This reminded him that he had no time to lose. He scanned the side of the ship, looking for the water tank, but all he could see was a jungle of jutting walls, jagged, crumbling, and pointed. He hesitated. Evidently the only thing to do was to make for the lighted porthole to their room and proceed to the tank from there.

Carefully he dragged himself along the wall of the ship. Not five yards from the lock the smoothness stopped abruptly. There was a yawning cavity which Moore recognized as having once been the room adjoining the corridor at the far end. He shuddered. Suppose he were to come across a bloated dead body in one of those rooms. He had known most of the passengers, many of them personally. But he overcame his squeamishness and forced himself to continue his precarious journey toward his goal.

And here he encountered his first practical difficulty. The room itself was made of non-ferrous material in many parts. The magnetic grapple was intended for use only on outer hulls and was useless throughout much of the ship's interior. Moore had forgotten this when suddenly he found himself floating down an incline, his grapple out of use. He grasped and clutched at a nearby projection. Slowly he pulled himself back to safety.

He lay for a moment, almost breathless. Theoretically he should be weightless out here in space—Vesta's influence being negligible—but the regional Gravitator under his room was working. Without the balance of the other Gravitators, it tended to place him under variable and suddenly shifting stresses as he kept changing his position. For his magnetic grapple to let go suddenly might mean being jerked away from the ship altogether. And then what?

Evidently this was going to be even more difficult than he had thought.

He inched forward in a crawl, testing each spot to see if the grapple would hold. Sometimes he had to make long, circuitous journeys to gain a few feet's headway and at other times he was forced to scramble the slip across small patches of non-ferrous material. And always there was that tiring pull of the Gravitator, continually changing directions as he progressed, setting horizon-tal floors and vertical walls at queer and almost haphazard angles.

Carefully he investigated all objects that he came across. But it was a barren search. Loose articles, chairs, tables had been jerked away at the first shock, probably, and now were independent bodies of the Solar System. He did manage, however, to pick up a small field glass and fountain pen. These he placed in his pocket. They were valueless under present conditions, but somehow they seemed to make more real this macabre trip across the sides of a dead ship.

For fifteen minutes, twenty, half an hour, he labored slowly toward where he thought the porthole should be. Sweat poured down into his eyes and rendered his hair a matted mass. His muscles were beginning to ache under the unaccustomed strain. His mind, already strained by the ordeal of the previous day, was beginning to waver, to play him tricks.

The crawl began to seem eternal, something that had always existed and would exist forever. The object of the journey, that for which he was striving, seemed unimportant; he only knew that it was necessary to move. The time, one hour back, when he had been with Brandon and Shea, seemed hazy and lost in the far past. That more normal time, two days' age, wholly forgotten.

Only the jagged walls before him, only the vital necessity of getting at some uncertain destination existed in his spinning brain. Grasping, straining, pulling. Feeling for the iron alloy. Up and into gaping holes that were rooms and then out again. Feel and pull—feel and pull—and—a light.

Moore stopped. Had he not been glued to the wall he would have fallen. Somehow that light seemed to clear things. It was the porthole; not the many dark, staring ones he had passed, but alive and alight. Behind it was Brandon. A deep breath and he felt better, his mind cleared.

And now his way lay plain before him. Toward that spark of life he crept. Nearer, and nearer, and nearer until he could touch it. He was there!

His eyes drank in the familiar room. God knows that it hadn't any happy associations in his mind, but it was something real, something almost natural. Brandon slept on the couch. His face was worn and lined but a smile passed over it now and then.

Moore raised his fist to knock. He felt the urgent desire to talk with someone, if only by sign language, yet at the last instant he was refrained. Perhaps the kid was dreaming of home. He was young and sensitive and had suffered much. Let him sleep. Time enough to wake him when—and if—his idea had been carried through.

He located the wall within the room behind which lay the water tank and then tried to spot it from the outside. Now it was not difficult; its rear wall stood out prominently. Moore marveled, for it seemed a miracle that it had escaped puncture. Perhaps the Fates had not been so ironic after all.

Passage to it was easy though it was on the other side of the fragment. What was once a corridor led almost directly to it. Once when the *Silver Queen* had been whole, that corridor had been level and horizontal, but now, under the unbalanced pull of the regional Gravitator, it seemed more of a steep incline than anything else. And yet it made the path simple. Since it was of uniform beryl-steel, Moore found no trouble holding on as he wormed up the twenty-odd feet to the water supply.

And now the crisis—the last stage—had been reached. He felt that he ought to rest first, but his excitement grew rapidly in intensity. It was either now or bust. He pulled himself out to the bottom-center of the tank. There, resting on the small ledge formed by the floor of the corridor that had once extended on that side of the tank, he began operations.

"It's a pity that the main pipe is pointing in the wrong direction," he muttered. "It would have saved me a lot of trouble had it been right. As it is . . ." He sighed and bent to his work. The heat ray was adjusted to maximum concentration and the invisible emanations focused at a spot perhaps a foot above the floor of the tank.

Gradually the effect of the excitatory beam upon the molecules of the wall became noticeable. A spot the size of a dime began shining faintly at the point of focus of the ray gun. It wavered uncertainly, now dimming, now brightening, as Moore strove to steady his tired arm. He propped it on the ledge and achieved better results as the tiny circle of radiation brightened.

Slowly the color ascended the spectrum. The dark, angry red that had first appeared lightened to a cherry color. As the heat continued pouring in, the brightness seemed to ripple out in widening areas, like a target made of successively deepening tints of red. The wall for a distance of some feet from the focal point was becoming uncomfortably hot even though it did not glow and Moore found it necessary to refrain from touching it with the metal of his suit.

Moore cursed steadily, for the ledge itself was also growing hot. It seemed that only imprecations could soothe him. And as the melting wall began to radiate heat in its own right, the chief object of his malediction were the spacesuit manufacturers. Why didn't they build a suit that could keep heat *out* as well as keep it *in?*

But what Brandon called Professional Optimism crept up. With the salt tang of perspiration in his mouth, he kept consoling himself, "It could be worse, I suppose. At least, the two inches of wall here don't present too much of a barrier. Suppose the tank had been built flush against the outer hull. Whew! Imagine trying to melt through a foot of this." He gritted his teeth and kept on.

The spot of brightness was now flickering into the orange-yellow and Moore knew that the melting point of the beryl-steel alloy would soon be reached. He found himself forced to watch the spot only at widely spaced intervals and then only for fleeting moments.

Evidently it would have to be done quickly if it were to be done at all. The heat ray had not been fully loaded in the first place, and, pouring out energy at maximum as it had been doing for almost ten minutes now, must be approaching exhaustion. Yet the wall was just barely passing the plastic stage. In a fever of impatience, Moore jammed the muzzle of the gun directly at the center of the spot, drawing it back speedily.

A deep depression formed in the soft metal, but a puncture had not been formed. However, Moore was satisfied. He was almost there now. Had there been air between himself and the wall, he would undoubtedly have heard the gurgling and the hissing of the steaming water within. The pressure was building up. How long would the weakened wall endure?

Then so suddenly that Moore did not realize it for a few moments, he was through. A tiny fissure formed at the bottom of that little pit made by the ray gun and in less time than it takes to imagine, the churning water within had its way.

The soft, liquid metal at that spot puffed out, sticking out raggedly around a pea-sized hole. And from that hole there came a hissing and a roaring. A cloud of steam emerged and enveloped Moore.

Through the mist he could see the steam condense almost immediately to ice droplets and saw these icy pellets shrink rapidly into nothingness.

For fifteen minutes he watched the steam shoot out.

Then he became aware of gentle pressure pushing him away from the ship. A savage joy welled up within him as he realized that this was the effect of acceleration on the ship's part. His own inertia was holding him back.

That meant his work had been finished—and successfully. That stream of water was substituting for the rocket blast.

He started back.

If the horrors and dangers of the journey to the tank had been great, those of the way back should have been greater. He was infinitely more tired, his aching eyes were all but blind, and added to the crazy pull of the Gravitator was the force induced by the varying acceleration of the ship. But whatever his labors to return, they did not bother him. In later time, he never even remembered the heartbreaking trip.

How he managed to negotiate the distance in safety he did not know. Most of the time he was lost in a haze of happiness, scarcely realizing the actualities of the situation. His mind was filled with one thought only—to get back quickly, to tell the happy news of their escape.

Suddenly he found himself before the airlock. He hardly grasped the fact that it *was* the airlock. He almost did not understand why he pressed the signal button. Some instinct told him it was the thing to do.

Mike Shea was waiting. There was a creak and a rumble and the outer door started opening, caught, and stopped at the same place as before, but once again it managed to slide the rest of the way. It closed behind Moore, then the inner door opened and he stumbled into Shea's arms.

As in a dream he felt himself half-pulled, half-carried down the corridor to the room. His suit was ripped off. A hot, burning liquid stung his throat. Moore gagged, swallowed, and felt better. Shea pocketed the Jabra bottle once more.

The blurred, shifting images of Brandon and Shea before him steadied and became solid. Moore wiped the perspiration from his face with a trembling hand and essayed a weak smile.

"Wait," protested Brandon, "don't say anything. You look half-dead. Rest, will you!"

But Moore shook his head. In a hoarse, cracked voice he narrated as well as he could the events of the past two hours. The tale was incoherent, scarcely intelligible but marvelously impressive. The two listeners scarcely breathed during the recital.

"You mean," stammered Brandon, "that the water spout is pushing us toward Vesta, like a rocket exhaust?"

"Exactly—same thing as—rocket exhaust," panted Moore. "Action and reaction. Is located—on side opposite Vesta—hence pushing us toward Vesta."

Shea was dancing before the porthole. "He's right, Brandon, me boy. You can make out Bennett's dome as clear as day. We're getting there, we're getting there."

Moore felt himself recovering. "We're approaching in spiral path on account of original orbit. We'll land in five or six hours probably. The water will last for quite a long while and the pressure is still great, since the water issues as steam."

"Steam—at the low temperature of space?" Brandon was surprised.

"Steam—at the low pressure of space!" corrected Moore. "The boiling point of water falls with the pressure. It is very low indeed in a vacuum. Even ice has a vapor pressure sufficient to sublime."

He smiled. "As a matter of fact, it freezes and boils at the same time. I watched it." A short pause, then, "Well, how do you feel now, Brandon? Much better, eh?"

Brandon reddened and his face fell. He groped vainly for words for a few moments. Finally he said in a half-whisper, "You know, I must have acted like a damn fool and a coward at first. I—I guess I don't deserve all this after going to pieces and letting the burden of our escape rest on your shoulders.

"I wish you'd beat me up, or something, for punching you before. It'd make me feel better. I mean it." And he really did seem to mean it.

Moore gave him an affectionate push. "Forget it. You'll never know how near I came to breaking down myself." He raised his voice in order to drown out any further apologies on Brandon's part, "Hey, Mike, stop staring out of that porthole and bring over that Jabra bottle."

Mike obeyed with alacrity, bringing with him three Plexatron units to be used as makeshift cups. Moore filled each precisely to the brim. He was going to be drunk with a vengeance.

"Gentlemen," he said solemnly, "a toast." The three raised the mugs in unison, "Gentlemen, I give you the year's supply of good old H_2O *we used to have*."

Robbie

"Ninety-eight—ninety-nine—*one hundred.*" Gloria withdrew her chubby little forearm from before her eyes and stood for a moment, wrinkling her nose and blinking in the sunlight. Then, trying to watch in all directions at once, she withdrew a few cautious steps from the tree against which she had been leaning.

She craned her neck to investigate the possibilities of a clump of bushes to the right and then withdrew farther to obtain a better angle for viewing its dark recesses. The quiet was profound except for the incessant buzzing of insects and the occasional chirrup of some hardy bird, braving the midday sun.

Gloria pouted, "I bet he went inside the house, and I've told him a million times that that's not fair."

With tiny lips pressed together tightly and a severe frown crinkling her forehead, she moved determinedly toward the two-story building up past the driveway.

Too late she heard the rustling sound behind her, followed by the distinctive and rhythmic clump-clump of Robbie's metal feet. She whirled about to see her triumphing companion emerge from hiding and make for the home-tree at full speed.

Gloria shrieked in dismay. "Wait, Robbie! That wasn't fair, Robbie! You promised you wouldn't run until I found you." Her little feet could make no headway at all against Robbie's giant strides. Then, within ten feet of the goal, Robbie's pace slowed suddenly to the merest of crawls, and Gloria, with one final burst of wild speed, dashed pantingly past him to touch the welcome bark of home-tree first.

Gleefully, she turned on the faithful Robbie, and with the basest of ingratitude, rewarded him for his sacrifice, by taunting him cruelly for a lack of running ability.

"Robbie can't run," she shouted at the top of her eight-year-old voice. "I can beat him any day. I can beat him any day." She chanted the words in a shrill rhythm.

Robbie didn't answer, of course—not in words. He pantomimed running, instead, inching away until Gloria found herself running after him as he dodged her narrowly, forcing her to veer in helpless circles, little arms outstretched and fanning at the air.

"Robbie," she squealed, "stand still!"—And the laughter was forced out of her in breathless jerks.

—Until he turned suddenly and caught her up, whirling her round, so that for her the world fell away for a moment with a blue emptiness beneath, and green trees stretching hungrily downward toward the void. Then she was down in the grass again, leaning against Robbie's leg and still holding a hard, metal finger.

After a while, her breath returned. She pushed uselessly at her disheveled hair in vague imitation of one of her mother's gestures and twisted to see if her dress were torn.

She slapped her hand against Robbie's torso, "Bad boy! I'll spank you!"

And Robbie cowered, holding his hands over his face so that she had to add, "No, I won't, Robbie. I won't spank you. But anyway, it's my turn to hide now because you've got longer legs and you promised not to run till I found you."

Robbie nodded his head—a small parallelepiped with rounded edges and corners attached to a similar but much larger parallelepiped that served as torso by means of a short, flexible stalk—and obediently faced the tree. A thin, metal film descended over his glowing eyes and from within his body came a steady, resonant ticking.

"Don't peek now—and don't skip any numbers," warned Gloria, and scurried for cover.

With unvarying regularity, seconds were ticked off, and at the hundredth, up went the eyelids, and the glowing red of Robbie's eyes swept the prospect. They rested for a moment on a bit of colorful gingham that protruded from behind a boulder. He advanced a few steps and convinced himself that it was Gloria who squatted behind it.

Slowly, remaining always between Gloria and home-tree, he advanced on the hiding place, and when Gloria was plainly in sight and could no longer even theorize to herself that she was not seen, he extended one arm toward her, slapping the other against his leg so that it rang again. Gloria emerged sulkily.

"You peeked!" she exclaimed, with gross unfairness. "Besides I'm tired of playing hide-and-seek. I want a ride."

But Robbie was hurt at the unjust accusation, so he seated himself carefully and shook his head ponderously from side to side.

Gloria changed her tone to one of gentle coaxing immediately, "Come on, Robbie. I didn't mean it about the peeking. Give me a ride."

Robbie was not to be won over so easily, though. He gazed stubbornly at the sky, and shook his head even more emphatically.

"Please, Robbie, please give me a ride." She encircled his neck with rosy arms and hugged tightly. Then, changing moods in a moment, she moved away. "If you don't, I'm going to cry," and her face twisted appallingly in preparation.

Hard-hearted Robbie paid scant attention to this dreadful possibility, and shook his head a third time. Gloria found it necessary to play her trump card.

"If you don't," she exclaimed warmly, "I won't tell you any more stories, that's all. Not one—"

Robbie gave in immediately and unconditionally before this ultimatum, nodding his head vigorously until the metal of his neck hummed. Carefully, he raised the little girl and placed her on his broad, flat shoulders.

Gloria's threatened tears vanished immediately and she crowed with delight. Robbie's metal skin, kept at a constant temperature of seventy by the high resistance coils within felt nice and comfortable, while the beautifully loud sound her heels made as they bumped rhythmically against his chest was enchanting.

"You're an air-coaster, Robbie, you're a big, silver air-coaster. Hold out your arms straight.—You *got* to, Robbie, if you're going to be an air-coaster."

The logic was irrefutable. Robbie's arms were wings catching the air currents and he was a silver 'coaster.

Gloria twisted the robot's head and leaned to the right. He banked sharply. Gloria equipped the 'coaster with a motor that went "Br-r-r" and then with weapons that went "Powie" and "Sh-sh-shshsh." Pirates were giving chase and the ship's blasters were coming into play. The pirates dropped in a steady rain.

"Got another one. —Two more," she cried.

Then "Faster, men," Gloria said pompously, "we're running out of ammunition." She aimed over her shoulder with undaunted courage and Robbie was a blunt-nosed spaceship zooming through the void at maximum acceleration.

Clear across the field he sped, to the patch of tall grass on the other side, where he stopped with a suddenness that evoked a shriek from his flushed rider, and then tumbled her onto the soft, green carpet.

Gloria gasped and panted, and gave voice to intermittent whispered exclamations of "That was *nice!*"

Robbie waited until she had caught her breath and then pulled gently at a lock of hair.

"You want something?" said Gloria, eyes wide in an apparently artless complexity that fooled her huge "nursemaid" not at all. He pulled the curl harder.

"Oh, I know. You want a story."

Robbie nodded rapidly.

"Which one?"

Robbie made a semi-circle in the air with one finger.

The little girl protested, "*Again?* I've told you Cinderella a million times. Aren't you tired of it? —It's for babies."

Another semi-circle.

"Oh, well," Gloria composed herself, ran over the details of the tale in her mind (together with her own elaborations, of which she had several) and began:

"Are you ready? Well—once upon time there was a beautiful little girl whose name was Ella. And she had a terribly cruel step-mother and two very ugly and *very* cruel step-sisters and—"

* * *

Gloria was reaching the very climax of the tale—midnight was striking and everything was changing back to the shabby originals lickety-split, while Robbie listened tensely with burning eyes—when the interruption came.

"Gloria!"

It was the high-pitched sound of a woman who has been calling not once, but several times; and had the nervous tone of one in whom anxiety was beginning to overcome impatience.

"Mamma's calling me," said Gloria, not quite happily. "You'd better carry me back to the house, Robbie."

Robbie obeyed with alacrity for somehow there was that in him which judged it best to obey Mrs. Weston, without as much as a scrap of hesitation. Gloria's father was rarely home in the daytime except on Sunday—today, for instance—and when he was, he proved a genial and understanding person. Gloria's mother, however, was a source of uneasiness to Robbie and there was always the impulse to sneak away from her sight.

Mrs. Weston caught sight of them the minute they rose above the masking tufts of long grass and retired inside the house to wait.

"I've shouted myself hoarse, Gloria," she said, severely. "Where were you?"

"I was with Robbie," quavered Gloria. "I was telling him Cinderella, and I forgot it was dinner-time."

"Well, it's a pity Robbie forgot, too." Then, as if that reminded her of the robot's presence, she whirled upon him. "You may go, Robbie. She doesn't need you now." Then, brutally, "And don't come back till I call you."

Robbie turned to go, but hesitated as Gloria cried out in his defense, "Wait, Mamma, you got to let him stay. I didn't finish Cinderella for him. I said I would tell him Cinderella and I'm not finished."

"Gloria!"

"Honest and truly, Mamma, he'll stay so quiet, you won't even know he's here. He can sit on the chair in the corner, and he won't say a word,—I mean he won't *do* anything. Will you, Robbie?"

Robbie, appealed to, nodded his massive head up and down once.

"Gloria, if you don't stop this at once, you shan't see Robbie for a whole week."

The girl's eyes fell, "All right! But Cinderella is his favorite story and I didn't finished it.—And he likes it so much."

The robot left with a disconsolate step and Gloria choked back a sob.

* * *

George Weston was comfortable. It was a habit of his to be comfortable on Sunday afternoons. A good, hearty dinner below the hatches; a nice, soft, dilapidated couch on which to sprawl; a copy of the *Times*; slippered feet and shirtless chest;—how could anyone *help* but be comfortable?

He wasn't pleased, therefore, when his wife walked in. After ten years of married life, he still was so unutterably foolish as to love her, and there was no question that he was always glad to see her—still Sunday afternoons just after dinner were sacred to him and his idea of solid comfort was to be left in utter solitude for two or three hours. Consequently, he fixed his eye firmly upon the latest reports of the Lefebre-Yoshida expedition to Mars (this one was to take off from Lunar Base and might actually succeed) and pretended she wasn't there.

Mrs. Weston waited patiently for two minutes, then impatiently for two more, and finally broke the silence.

"George!"

"Hmpph?"

"George, I say! *Will* you put down that paper and look at me?"

The paper rustled to the floor and Weston turned a weary face toward his wife, "What is it, dear?"

"You know what it is, George. It's Gloria and that terrible machine."

"What terrible machine?"

"Now don't pretend you don't know what Im talking about. It's that robot Gloria calls Robbie. He doesn't leave her for a moment."

"Well, why should he? He's not supposed to. And he certainly isn't a terrible machine. He's the best darn robot money can buy and I'm damned sure he set me back half a year's income. He's worth it, though—darn sight cleverer than half my office staff."

He made a move to pick up the paper again, but his wife was quicker and snatched it away.

"You listen to *me*, George. I won't have my daughter entrusted to a machine—and I don't care how clever it is. It has no soul, and no one knows what it may be thinking. A child just isn't *made* to be guarded by a thing of metal."

Weston frowned, "When did you decide this? He's been with Gloria two years now and I haven't seen you worry till now."

"It was different at first. It was a novelty; it took a load off me, and—and it was a fashionable thing to do. But now I don't know. The neighbors—"

"Well, what have the neighbors to do with it? Now, look. A robot is infinitely more to be trusted than a human nursemaid. Robbie was constructed for only one purpose really—to be the companion of a little child. His entire 'mentality' has been created for the purpose. He just can't help being faithful and loving and kind. He's a machine—*made so*. That's more than you can say for humans."

"But something might go wrong. Some—some—" Mrs. Weston was a bit hazy about the insides of a robot, "some little jigger will come loose and the awful thing will go beserk and—and—" She couldn't bring herself to complete the quite obvious thought.

"Nonsense," Weston denied, with an involuntary nervous shiver. "That's completely ridiculous. We had a long discussion at the time we bought Robbie about the First Law of Robotics. You *know* that it is impossible for a robot to harm a human being; that long before enough can go wrong to alter that First Law, a robot would be completely inoperable. It's a mathematical impossibility. Besides I have an engineer from U. S. Robots here twice a year to give the poor gadget a complete overhaul. Why, there's no more chance of anything at all going wrong with Robbie than there is of you or I suddenly going looney—considerably less, in fact. Besides, how are you going to take him away from Gloria?"

He made another futile stab at the paper and his wife tossed it angrily into the next room.

"That's just it, George! She won't play with anyone else. There are dozens of little boys and girls that she should make friends with, but she won't. She won't go *near* them unless I make her. That's no way for a little girl to grow up. You want her to be normal, don't you? You want her to be able to take her part in society."

"You're jumping at shadows, Grace. Pretend Robbie's a dog. I've seen hundreds of children who would rather have their dog than their father."

"A dog is different, George. We *must* get rid of that horrible thing. You can sell it back to the company. I've asked, and you can."

"You've *asked*? Now look here, Grace, let's not go off the deep end. We're keeping the robot until Gloria is older and I don't want the subject brought up again." And with that he walked out of the room in a huff.

* * *

Mrs. Weston met her husband at the door two evenings later. "You'll have to listen to this, George. There's bad feeling in the village."

"About what?" asked Weston. He stepped into the washroom and drowned out any possible answer by the splash of water.

Mrs. Weston waited. She said, "About Robbie."

Weston stepped out, towel in hand, face red and angry. "What are you talking about?"

"Oh, it's been building up and building up. I've tried to close my eyes to it, but I'm not going to any more. Most of the villagers consider Robbie dangerous. Children aren't allowed to go near our place in the evenings."

"We trust *our* child with the thing."

"Well, people aren't reasonable about these things."

"Then to hell with them."

"Saying that doesn't solve the problem. I've got to do my shopping down there. I've got to meet them every day. And it's even worse in the city these days when it comes to robots. New York has just passed an ordinance keeping all robots off the streets between sunset and sunrise."

"All right, but they can't stop us from keeping a robot in our home.—Grace, this is one of your campaigns. I recognize it. But it's no use. The answer is still, no! We're keeping Robbie!"

* * *

And yet he loved his wife—and what was worse, his wife knew it. George Weston, after all, was only a man—poor thing—and his wife made full use of every device which a clumsier and more scrupulous sex has learned, with reason and futility, to fear.

Ten times in the ensuing week, he cried, "Robbie stays,—and that's *final!*" and each time it was weaker and accompanied by a louder and more agonized groan.

Came the day at last, when Weston approached his daughter guiltily and suggested a "beautiful" visivox show in the village.

Gloria clapped her hands happily, "Can Robbie go?"

"No, dear," he said, and winced at the sound of his voice, "they won't allow robots at the visivox—but you can tell him about it when you get home." He stumbled all over the last few words and looked away.

Gloria came back from town bubbling over with enthusiasm, for the visivox had been a gorgeous spectacle indeed.

She waited for her father to maneuver the jet-car into the sunken garage. "Wait till I tell Robbie, Daddy. He would have liked it like anything. —Especially when Francis Fran was backing away so-o-o quietly, and backed right into one of the Leopard-Men and had to run." She laughed again, "Daddy, are there really Leopard-Men on the Moon?"

"Probably not," said Weston absently. "It's just funny make-believe." He couldn't take much longer with the car. He'd have to face it.

Gloria ran across the lawn. "Robbie! — Robbie!"

Then she stopped suddenly at the sight of a beautiful collie which regarded her out of serious brown eyes as it wagged its tail on the porch.

"Oh, what a nice dog!" Gloria climbed the steps, approached cautiously and patted it. "Is it for me, Daddy?"

Her mother had joined them. "Yes, it is, Gloria. Isn't it nice—soft and furry. It's very gentle. It *likes* little girls."

"Can he play games?"

"Surely. He can do any number of tricks. Would you like to see some?"

"Right away. I want Robbie to see him, too. —*Robbie!*" She stopped, uncertainly, and frowned, "I'll bet he's just staying in his room because he's mad at me for not taking him to the visivox. You'll have to explain to him, Daddy. He might not believe me, but he knows if you say it, it's so."

Weston's lips grew tighter. He looked toward his wife but could not catch her eye.

Gloria turned precipitously and ran down the basement steps, shouting as she went, "Robbie— Come and see what Daddy and Mamma brought me. They brought me a dog, Robbie."

In a minute she had returned, a frightened little girl. "Mamma, Robbie isn't in his room. Where is he?" There was no answer and George Weston coughed and was suddenly extremely interested in an aimlessly drifting cloud. Gloria's voice quavered on the verge of tears, "Where's Robbie, Mamma?"

Mrs. Weston sat down and drew her daughter gently to her, "Don't feel bad, Gloria. Robbie has gone away, I think."

"Gone *away?* Where? Where's he gone away, Mamma?"

"No one knows, darling. He just walked away. We've looked and we've looked and we've looked for him, but we can't find him."

"You mean he'll never come back again?" Her eyes were round with horror.

"We may find him soon. We'll keep looking for him. And meanwhile you can play with your nice new doggie. Look at him! His name is Lightning and he can—"

But Gloria's eyelids had overflown, "I don't want the nasty dog—I want Robbie. I want you to find me Robbie." Her feelings became too deep for words, and she spluttered into a shrill wail.

Mrs. Weston glanced at her husband for help, but he merely shuffled his feet morosely and did not withdraw his ardent stare from the heavens, so she bent to the task of consolation, "Why do you cry, Gloria? Robbie was only a machine, just a nasty old machine. He wasn't alive at all."

"He was *not* no machine!" screamed Gloria, fiercely and ungrammatically. "He was a *person* just like you and me and he was my *friend.* I want him back. Oh, Mamma, I want him back."

Her mother groaned in defeat and left Gloria to her sorrow.

"Let her have her cry out," she told her husband. "Childish griefs are never lasting. In a few days, she'll forget that awful robot ever existed."

But time proved Mrs. Weston a bit too optimistic. To be sure, Gloria ceased crying, but she ceased smiling, too, and the passing days found her ever more silent and shadowy. Gradually, her attitude of passive unhappiness wore Mrs. Weston down and all that kept her from yielding was the impossibility of admitting defeat to her husband.

Then, one evening, she flounced into the living room, sat down, folded her arms and looked boiling mad.

Her husband stretched his neck in order to see her over his newspaper, "What now, Grace?"

"It's that child, George. I've had to send back the dog today. Gloria positively couldn't stand the sight of him, she said. She's driving me into a nervous breakdown."

Weston laid down the paper and a hopeful gleam entered his eye, "Maybe— Maybe we ought to get Robbie back. It might be done, you know. I can get in touch with—"

"No!" she replied, grimly. "I won't hear of it. We're not giving up that easily. My child shall *not* be brought up by a robot if it takes years to break her of it."

Weston picked up his paper again with a disappointed air. "A year of this will have me prematurely gray."

"You're a big help, George," was the frigid answer. "What Gloria needs is a change of environment. Of course she can't forget Robbie here. How can she when every tree and rock reminds her of him? It is really the *silliest* situation I have ever heard of. Imagine a child pining away for the loss of a robot."

"Well, stick to the point. What's the change in environment you're planning?"

"We're going to take her to New York."

"The city! In August! Say, do you know what New York is like in August? It's unbearable."

"Millions do bear it."

"They don't have a place like this to go to. If they didn't have to stay in New York, they wouldn't."

"Well, *we* have to. I say we're leaving now—or as soon as we can make the arrangements. In the city, Gloria will find sufficient interests and sufficient friends to perk her up and make her forget that machine."

"Oh, Lord," groaned the lesser half, "those frying pavements!"

"We have to," was the unshaken response. "Gloria has lost five pounds in the last month and my little girl's health is more important to me than your comfort."

"It's a pity you didn't think of your little girl's health before you deprived her of her pet robot," he muttered—but to himself.

* * *

Gloria displayed immediate signs of improvement when told of the impending trip to the city. She spoke little of it, but when she did, it was always with lively anticipation. Again, she began to smile and to eat with something of her former appetite.

Mrs. Weston hugged herself for joy and lost no opportunity to triumph over her still skeptical husband.

"You see, George, she helps with the packing like a little angel, and chatters away as if she hadn't a care in the world. It's just as I told you—all we need do is substitute other interests."

"Hmpph," was the skeptical response, "I hope so."

Preliminaries were gone through quickly. Arrangements were made for the preparation of their city home and a couple were engaged as housekeepers for the country home. When the day of the trip finally did come, Gloria was all but her old self again, and no mention of Robbie passed her lips at all.

In high good-humor the family took a taxi-gyro to the airport (Weston would have preferred using his own private 'gyro, but it was only a two-seater with no room for baggage) and entered the waiting liner.

"Come, Gloria," called Mrs. Weston. "I've saved you a seat near the window so you can watch the scenery."

Gloria trotted down the aisle cheerily, flattened her nose into a white oval against the thick clear glass, and watched with an intentness that increased as the sudden coughing of the motor drifted backward into the interior. She was too young to be frightened when the ground dropped away as if let through a trap-door and she herself suddenly became twice her usual weight, but not too young to be mightily interested. It wasn't until the ground had changed into a tiny patchwork quilt that she withdrew her nose, and faced her mother again.

"Will we soon be in the city, Mamma?" she asked, rubbing her chilled nose, and watching with interest as the patch of moisture which her breath had formed on the pane shrank slowly and vanished.

"In about half an hour, dear." Then, with just the faintest trace of anxiety, "Aren't you glad we're going? Don't you think you'll be very happy in the city with all the buildings and people and things to see? We'll go to the visivox every day and see shows and go to the circus and the beach and—"

"Yes, Mamma," was Gloria's unenthusiastic rejoinder. The liner passed over a bank of clouds at the moment, and Gloria was instantly absorbed in the unusual spectacle of clouds underneath one. Then they were over clear sky again, and she turned to her mother with a sudden mysterious air of secret knowledge.

"*I* know why we're going to the city, Mamma."

"Do you?" Mrs. Weston was puzzled. "Why, dear?"

"You didn't tell me because you wanted it to be a surprise, but *I* know." For a moment, she was lost in admiration at her own acute penetration, and then she laughed gaily. "We're going to New York so we can find Robbie, aren't we? —With detectives."

The statement caught George Weston in the middle of a drink of water, with disastrous results. There was a sort of strangled gasp, a geyser of water, and then a bout of choking coughs. When all was over, he stood there, a red-faced, water-drenched and very, very annoyed person.

Mrs. Weston maintained her composure, but when Gloria repeated her question in a more anxious tone of voice, she found her temper rather bent.

"Maybe," she retorted, tartly. "Now sit and be still, for Heaven's sake."

* * *

New York City, 1998 A.D., was a paradise for the sight-seer more than ever in its history. Gloria's parents realized this and made the most of it.

On direct orders from his wife, George Weston arranged to have his business take care of itself for a month or so, in order to be free to spend the time in what he termed "dissipating Gloria to the verge of ruin." Like everything else Weston did, this was gone about in an efficient, thorough, and business-like way. Before the month had passed, nothing that could be done had not been done.

She was taken to the top of the half-mile-tall Roosevelt Building, to gaze down in awe upon the jagged panorama of rooftops that blended far off in the fields of Long Island and the flatlands of New Jersey. They visited the zoos where Gloria stared in delicious fright at the "real live lion" (rather disappointed that the keepers fed him raw steaks, instead of human beings, as she had expected), and asked insistently and peremptorily to see "the whale."

The various museums came in for their share of attention, together with the parks and the beaches and the aquarium.

She was taken halfway up the Hudson in an excursion steamer fitted out in the archaism of the mad Twenties. She travelled into the stratosphere on an exhibition trip, where the sky turned deep purple and the stars came out and the misty earth below looked like a huge concave bowl. Down under the waters of the Long Island Sound she was taken in a glass-walled sub-sea vessel, where in a green and wavering world, quaint and curious sea-things ogled her and wiggled suddenly away.

On a more prosaic level, Mrs. Weston took her to the department stores where she could revel in another type of fairyland.

In fact, when the month had nearly sped, the Westons were convinced that everything conceivable had been done to take Gloria's mind once and for all off the departed Robbie—but they were not quite sure they had succeeded.

The fact remained that wherever Gloria went, she displayed the most absorbed and concentrated interest in such robots as happened to be present. No matter how exciting the spectacle before her, nor how novel to her girlish eyes, she turned away instantly if the corner of her eye caught a glimpse of metallic movement.

Mrs. Weston went out of her way to keep Gloria away from all robots.

And the matter was finally climaxed in the episode at the Museum of Science and Industry. The Museum had announced a special "children's program" in which exhibits of scientific witchery scaled down to the child mind were to be shown. The Westons, of course, placed it upon their list of "absolutely."

It was while the Westons were standing totally absorbed in the exploits of a powerful electro-magnet that Mrs. Weston suddenly became aware of the fact that Gloria was no longer with her. Initial panic gave way to calm decision and, enlisting the aid of three attendants, a careful search was begun.

Gloria, of course, was not one to wander aimlessly, however. For her age, she was an unusually determined and purposeful girl, quite full of the maternal genes in that respect. She had seen a huge sign on the third floor, which had said, "This Way to the Talking Robot." Having spelled it out to herself and having noticed that her parents did not seem to wish to move in the proper direction, she did the obvious thing. Waiting for an opportune moment of parental distraction, she calmly disengaged herself and followed the sign.

* * *

The Talking Robot was a *tour de force*, a thoroughly impractical device, possessing publicity value only. Once an hour, an escorted group stood before it and asked questions of the robot engineer in charge in careful whispers. Those the engineer decided were suitable for the robot's circuits were transmitted to the Talking Robot.

It was rather dull. It may be nice to know that the square of fourteen is one hundred ninety-six, that the temperature at the moment is 72 degrees Fahrenheit, and the air-pressure 30.02 inches of mercury, that the atomic weight of sodium is 23, but one doesn't really need a robot for that. One especially does not need an unwieldy, totally immobile mass of wires and coils spreading over twenty-five square yards.

Few people bothered to return for a second helping, but one girl in her middle teens sat quietly on a bench waiting for a third. She was the only one in the room when Gloria entered.

Gloria did not look at her. To her at the moment, another human being was but an inconsiderable item. She saved her attention for this large thing with the wheels. For a moment, she hesitated in dismay. It didn't look like any robot she had ever seen.

Cautiously and doubtfully she raised her treble voice, "Please, Mr. Robot, sir, are you the Talking Robot, sir?" She wasn't sure, but it seemed to her that a robot that actually talked was worth a great deal of politeness.

(The girl in her mid-teens allowed a look of intense concentration to cross her thin, plain face. She whipped out a small notebook and began writing in rapid pot-hooks.)

There was an oily whir of gears and a mechanically-timbred voice boomed out in words that lacked accent and intonation, "I—am—the—robot—that—talks."

Gloria stared at it ruefully. It *did* talk, but the sound came from inside somewheres. There was no *face* to talk to. She said, "Can you help me, Mr. Robot, sir?"

The Talking Robot was designed to answer questions, and only such questions as it could answer had ever been put to it. It was quite confident of its ability, therefore, "I—can—help—you."

"Thank you, Mr. Robot sir. Have you seen Robbie?"

"Who—is—Robbie?"

"He's a robot, Mr. Robot, sir." She stretched to tip-toes. "He's about so high, Mr. Robot, sir, only higher, and he's very nice. He's got a head, you know. I mean you haven't, but he has, Mr. Robot, sir."

The Talking Robot had been left behind, "A—robot?"

"Yes, Mr. Robot, sir. A robot just like you, except he can't talk, of course, and—looks like a real person."

"A—robot—like—me?"

"Yes, Mr. Robot, sir."

To which the Talking Robot's only response was an erratic splutter and an occasional incoherent sound. The radical generalization offered it, i.e., its existence, not as a particular object, but as a member of a general group, was too much for it. Loyally, it tried to encompass the concept and half a dozen coils burnt out. Little warning signals were buzzing.

(The girl in her mid-teens left at that point. She had enough for her Physics-1 paper on "Practical Aspects of Robotics". This paper was Susan Calvin's first of many on the subject).

Gloria stood waiting, with carefully concealed impatience, for the machine's answer when she heard the cry behind her of "There she is," and recognized that cry as her mother's.

"What are you doing here, you bad girl?" cried Mrs. Weston, anxiety dissolving at once into anger. "Do you know you frightened your mamma and daddy almost to death? Why did you run away?"

The robot engineer had also dashed in, tearing his hair, and demanding who of the gathering crowd had tampered with the machine. "Can't anybody read signs?" he yelled. "You're not allowed in here without an attendant."

Gloria raised her grieved voice over the din, "I only came to see the Talking Robot, Mamma. I thought he might know where Robbie was because they're both robots." And then, as the thought of Robbie was suddenly brought forcefully home to her, she burst into a sudden storm of tears, "And I *got* to find Robbie, Mamma. I *got* to."

Mrs. Weston strangled a cry, and said, "Oh, good Heavens. Come home, George. This is more than I can stand."

That evening, George Weston left for several hours, and the next morning, he approached his wife with something that looked suspiciously like smug complacence.

"I've got an idea, Grace."

"About what?" was the gloomy, uninterested query.

"About Gloria."

"You're not going to suggest buying back that robot?"

"No, of course not."

"Then go ahead. I might as well listen to you. Nothing *I've* done seems to have done any good."

"All right. Here's what I've been thinking. The whole trouble with Gloria is that she thinks of Robbie as a *person* and not as a *machine*. Naturally, she can't forget him. Now if we managed to convince her that Robbie was nothing more than a mess of steel and copper in the form of sheets and wires with electricity its juice of life, how long would her longings last? It's the psychological attack, if you see my point."

"How do you plan to do it?"

"Simple. Where do you suppose I went last night? I persuaded Robertson of U. S. Robots and Mechanical Men Corporation to arrange for a complete tour of his premises tomorrow. The three of us will go, and by the time we're through, Gloria will have it drilled into her that a robot is *not* alive."

Mrs. Weston's eyes widened gradually and something glinted in her eyes that was quite like sudden admiration, "Why, George, that's a *good* idea."

And George Weston's vest buttons strained. "Only kind I have," he said.

* * *

Mr. Struthers was a conscientious General Manager and naturally inclined to be a bit talkative. The combination, therefore, resulted in a tour that was fully explained, perhaps even overabundantly explained, at every step. However, Mrs. Weston was not bored. Indeed, she stopped him several times and begged him to repeat his statements in simpler language so that Gloria might understand. Under the influence of this appreciation of his narrative powers, Mr. Struthers expanded genially and became ever more communicative, if possible.

George Weston, himself, showed a gathering impatience.

"Pardon me, Struthers," he said, breaking into the middle of a lecture on the photo-electric cell, "haven't you a section of the factory where only robot labor is employed?"

"Eh? Oh, yes! Yes, indeed!" He smiled at Mrs. Weston. "A vicious circle in a way, robots creating more robots. Of course, we are not making a general practice out of it. For one thing, the unions would never let us. But we can turn out a very few robots using robot labor exclusively, merely as a sort of scientific experiment. You see," he tapped his pince-nez into one palm argumentatively, "what the labor unions don't realize—and I say this as a man who has always been very sympathetic with the labor movement in general—is that the advent of the robot, while involving some dislocation to begin with, will, inevitably—"

"Yes, Struthers," said Weston, "but about that section of the factory you speak of—may we see it? It would be very interesting, I'm sure."

"Yes! Yes, of course!" Mr. Struthers replaced his pince-nez in one convulsive movement and gave vent to a soft cough of discomfiture. "Follow me, please."

He was comparatively quiet while leading the three through a long corridor and down a flight of stairs. Then, when they had entered a large well-lit room that buzzed with metallic activity, the sluices opened and the flood of explanation poured forth again.

"There you are!" he said with pride in his voice. "Robots only! Five men act as overseers and they don't even stay in this room. In five years, that is, since we began this project, not a single accident has occurred. Of course, the robots here assembled are comparatively simple, but . . ."

The General Manager's voice had long died to a rather soothing murmur in Gloria's ears. The whole trip seemed rather dull and pointless to her, though there *were* many robots in sight. None were even remotely like Robbie, though, and she surveyed them with open contempt.

In this room, there weren't any people at all, she noticed. Then her eyes fell upon six or seven robots busily engaged at a round table halfway across the room. They widened in incredulous surprise. It was a big room. She couldn't see for sure, but one of the robots looked like—looked like—*it was!*

"*Robbie!*" Her shriek pierced the air, and one of the robots about the table faltered and dropped the tool he was holding. Gloria went almost mad with joy. Squeezing through the railing before either parent could stop her, she dropped lightly to the floor a few feet below, and ran toward her Robbie, arms waving and hair flying.

And the three horrified adults, as they stood frozen in their tracks, saw what the excited little girl did not see,—a huge, lumbering tractor bearing blindly down upon its appointed track.

It took split-seconds for Weston to come to his senses, and those split-seconds meant everything, for Gloria could not be overtaken. Although Weston vaulted the railing in a wild attempt, it was obviously hopeless. Mr. Struthers signalled wildly to the overseers to stop the tractor, but the overseers were only human and it took time to act.

It was only Robbie that acted immediately and with precision.

With metal legs eating up the space between himself and his little mistress he charged down from the opposite direction. Everything then happened at once. With one sweep of an arm, Robbie snatched up Gloria, slackening his speed not one iota, and, consequently, knocking every breath of air out of her. Weston, not quite comprehending all that was happening, felt, rather than saw, Robbie brush past him, and came to a sudden bewildered halt. The tractor intersected Gloria's path half a second after Robbie had, rolled on ten feet further and came to a grinding, long-drawn-out stop.

Gloria regained her breath, submitted to a series of passionate hugs on the part of both her parents and turned eagerly toward Robbie. As far as she was concerned, nothing had happened except that she had found her friend.

But Mrs. Weston's expression had changed from one of relief to one of dark suspicion. She turned to her husband, and, despite her disheveled and undignified appearance, managed to look quite formidable, "*You* engineered this, *didn't* you?"

George Weston swabbed at a hot forehead with his handkerchief. His hand was unsteady, and his lips could curve only into a tremulous and exceedingly weak smile.

Mrs. Weston pursued the thought, "Robbie wasn't designed for engineering or construction work. He couldn't be of any use to them. You had him placed there deliberately so that Gloria would find him. You know you did."

"Well, I did," said Weston. "But, Grace, how was I to know the reunion would be so violent? And Robbie has saved her life; you'll have to admit that. You *can't* send him away again."

Grace Weston considered. She turned toward Gloria and Robbie and watched them abstractedly for a moment. Gloria had a grip about the robot's neck that would have asphyxiated any creature but one of metal, and was prattling nonsense in half-hysterical frenzy. Robbie's chrome-steel arms (capable of bending a bar of steel two inches in diameter into a pretzel) wound about the little girl gently and lovingly, and his eyes glowed a deep, deep red.

"Well," said Mrs. Weston, at last, "I guess he can stay with us until he rusts."

Nightfall

"If the stars should appear one night in a thousand years, how would men believe and adore, and preserve for many generations the remembrance of the city of God?"

EMERSON

Aton 77, director of Saro University, thrust out a belligerent lower lip and glared at the young newspaperman in a hot fury.

Theremon 762 took that fury in his stride. In his earlier days, when his now widely syndicated column was only a mad idea in a cub reporter's mind, he had specialized in "impossible" interviews. It had cost him bruises, black eyes, and broken bones; but it had given him an ample supply of coolness and self-confidence.

So he lowered the outthrust hand that had been so pointedly ignored and calmly waited for the aged director to get over the worst. Astronomers were queer ducks, anyway, and if Aton's actions of the last two months meant anything, this same Aton was the queer-duckiest of the lot.

Aton 77 found his voice, and though it trembled with restrained emotion, the careful, somewhat pedantic phraseology, for which the famous astronomer was noted, did not abandon him.

"Sir," he said, "you display an infernal gall in coming to me with that impudent proposition of yours."

The husky telephotographer of the Observatory, Beenay 25, thrust a tongue's tip across dry lips and interposed nervously, "Now, sir, after all—"

The director turned to him and lifted a white eyebrow. "Do not interfere, Beenay. I will credit you with good intentions in bringing this man here; but I will tolerate no insubordination now."

Theremon decided it was time to take a part. "Director Aton, if you'll let me finish what I started saying, I think—"

"I don't believe, young man," retorted Aton, "that anything you could say now would count for much as compared with your daily columns of these last two months. You have led a vast newspaper campaign against the efforts of myself and my colleagues to organize the world against the menace which it is now too late to avert. You have done your best with your highly personal attacks to make the staff of this Observatory objects of ridicule."

The director lifted a copy of the Saro City *Chronicle* from the table and shook it at Theremon furiously. "Even a person of your well-known impudence should have hesitated before coming to me with a request that he be allowed to cover today's events for his paper. Of all newsmen, you!"

Aton dashed the newspaper to the floor, strode to the window, and clasped his arms behind his back.

"You may leave," he snapped over his shoulder. He stared moodily out at the skyline where Gamma, the brightest of the planet's six suns, was setting. It had already faded and yellowed into the horizon mists, and Aton knew he would never see it again as a sane man.

He whirled. "No, wait, come here!" He gestured peremptorily. "I'll give you your story."

The newspaper man had made no motion to leave, and now he approached the old man slowly. Aton gestured outward. "Of the six suns, only Beta is left in the sky. Do you see it?"

The question was rather unnecessary. Beta was almost at zenith, its ruddy light flooding the landscape to an unusual orange as the brilliant rays of setting Gamma died. Beta was at aphelion. It was small; smaller than Theremon had ever seen it before, and for the moment it was undisputed ruler of Lagash's sky.

Lagash's own sun, Alpha, the one about which it revolved, was at the antipodes, as were the two distant companion pairs. The red dwarf Beta—Alpha's immediate companion—was alone, grimly alone.

Aton's upturned face flushed redly in the sunlight. "In just under four hours," he said, "civilization, as we know it, comes to an end. It will do so because, as you see, Beta is the only sun in the sky." He smiled grimly. "Print that! There'll be no one to read it."

"But if it turns out that four hours pass—and another four—and nothing happens?" asked Theremon softly.

"Don't let that worry you. Enough will happen."

"Granted! And, *still*—if nothing happens?"

For a second time, Beenay 25 spoke. "Sir, I think you ought to listen to him."

Theremon said, "Put it to a vote, Director Aton."

There was a stir among the remaining five members of the Observatory staff, who till now had maintained an attitude of wary neutrality.

"That," stated Aton flatly, "is not necessary." He drew out his pocket watch. "Since your good friend, Beenay, insists so urgently, I will give you five minutes. Talk away."

"Good! Now, just what difference would it make if you allowed me to take down an eyewitness account of what's to come? If your prediction comes true, my presence won't hurt; for in that case my column would never be written. On the other hand, if nothing comes of it, you will just have to expect ridicule or worse. It would be wise to leave that ridicule to friendly hands."

Aton snorted. "Do you mean yours when you speak of friendly hands?"

"Certainly!" Theremon sat down and crossed his legs. "My columns may have been a little rough, but I gave you people the benefit of the doubt every time. After all, this is not the century to preach 'The end of the world is at hand' to Lagash. You have to understand that people don't believe the *Book of Revelations* anymore, and it annoys them to have scientists turn about-face and tell us the Cultists are right after all—"

"No such thing, young man," interrupted Aton. "While a great deal of our data has been supplied us by the Cult, our results contain none of the Cult's mysticism. Facts are facts, and the Cult's so-called mythology *has* certain facts behind it. We've exposed them and ripped away their mystery. I assure you that the Cult hates us now worse than you do."

"I don't hate you. I'm just trying to tell you that the public is in an ugly humor. They're angry."

Aton twisted his mouth in derision. "Let them be angry."

"Yes, but what about tomorrow?"

"There'll be no tomorrow!"

"But if there is. Say that there is—just to see what happens. That anger might take shape into something serious. After all, you know, business has taken a nosedive these last two months. Investors don't really believe the world is coming to an end, but just the same they're being cagy with their money until it's all over. Johnny Public doesn't believe you, either, but the new spring furniture might just as well wait a few months—just to make sure.

"You see the point. Just as soon as this is all over, the business interests will be after your hide. They'll say that if crackpots—begging your pardon—can upset the country's prosperity any time they want, simply by making some cockeyed prediction—it's up to the planet to prevent them. The sparks will fly, sir."

The director regarded the columnist sternly. "And just what were you proposing to do to help the situation?"

"Well"—Theremon grinned—"I was proposing to take charge of the publicity. I can handle things so that only the ridiculous side will show. It would be hard to stand, I admit, because I'd have to make you all out to be a bunch of gibbering idiots, but if I can get people laughing at you, they might forget to be angry. In return for that, all my publisher asks is an exclusive story."

Beenay nodded and burst out, "Sir, the rest of us think he's right. These last two months we've considered everything but the million-to-one chance that there is an error somewhere in our theory or in our calculations. We ought to take care of that, too."

There was a murmur of agreement from the men grouped about the table, and Aton's expression became that of one who found his mouth full of something bitter and couldn't get rid of it.

"You may stay if you wish, then. You will kindly refrain, however, from hampering us in our duties in any way. You will also remember that I am in charge of all activities here, and in spite of your opinions as expressed in your columns, I will expect full cooperation and full respect—"

His hands were behind his back, and his wrinkled face thrust forward determinedly as he spoke. He might have continued indefinitely but for the intrusion of a new voice.

"Hello, hello, hello!" It came in a high tenor, and the plump cheeks of the newcomer expanded in a pleased smile. "What's this morgue-like atmosphere about here? No one's losing his nerve, I hope."

Aton started in consternation and said peevishly, "Now what the devil are you doing here, Sheerin? I thought you were going to stay behind in the Hideout."

Sheerin laughed and dropped his tubby figure into a chair. "Hideout be blowed! The place bored me. I wanted to be here, where things are getting hot. Don't you suppose I have my share of curiosity? I want to see these Stars the Cultists are forever speaking about." He rubbed his hands and added in a soberer tone, "It's freezing outside. The wind's enough to hang icicles on your nose. Beta doesn't seem to give any heat at all, at the distance it is."

The white-haired director ground his teeth in sudden exasperation. "Why do you go out of your way to do crazy things, Sheerin? What kind of good are you around here?"

"What kind of good am I around there?" Sheerin spread his palms in comical resignation. "A psychologist isn't worth his salt in the Hideout. They need men of action and strong, healthy women that can breed children. Me? I'm a hundred pounds too heavy for a man of action, and I wouldn't be a success at breeding children. So why bother them with an extra mouth to feed? I feel better over here."

Theremon spoke briskly. "Just what is the Hideout, sir?"

Sheerin seemed to see the columnist for the first time. He frowned and blew his ample cheeks out. "And just who in Lagash are you, redhead?"

Aton compressed his lips and then muttered sullenly, "That's Theremon 762, the newspaper fellow. I suppose you've heard of him."

The columnist offered his hand. "And, of course, you're Sheerin 501 of Saro University. I've heard of you." Then he repeated, "What is this Hideout, sir?"

"Well," said Sheerin, "we have managed to convince a few people of the validity of our prophery of—er—doom, to be spectacular about it, and those few have taken proper measures. They consist mainly of the immediate members of the families of the Observatory staff, certain of the faculty of Saro University, and a few outsiders. Altogether, they number about three hundred, but three quarters are women and children."

"I see! They're supposed to hide where the Darkness and the—er—Stars can't get at them, and then hold out when the rest of the world goes poof."

"If they can. It won't be easy. With all of mankind insane, with the great cities going up in flames—environment will not be conducive to survival. But they have food, water, shelter, and weapons—"

"They've got more," said Aton. "They've got all our records, except for what we will collect today. Those records will mean everything to the next cycle, and *that's* what must survive. The rest can go hang."

Theremon uttered a long, low whistle and sat brooding for several minutes. The men about the table had brought out a multi-chess board and started a six-member game. Moves were made rapidly and in silence. All eyes bent in furious concentration on the board. Theremon watched them intently and then rose and approached Aton, who sat apart in whispered conversation with Sheerin.

"Listen," he said, "let's go somewhere where we won't bother the rest of the fellows. I want to ask some questions."

The aged astronomer frowned sourly at him, but Sheerin chirped up, "Certainly. It will do me good to talk. It always does. Aton was telling me about your ideas concerning world reaction to a failure of the prediction—and I agree with you. I read your column pretty regularly, by the way, and as a general thing I like your views."

"Please, Sheerin," growled Aton.

"Eh? Oh, all right. We'll go into the next room. It has softer chairs, anyway."

There were softer chairs in the next room. There were also thick red curtains on the windows and a maroon carpet on the floor. With the bricky light of Beta pouring in, the general effect was one of dried blood.

Theremon shuddered. "Say, I'd give ten credits for a decent dose of white light for just a second. I wish Gamma or Delta were in the sky."

"What are your questions?" asked Aton. "Please remember that our time is limited. In a little over an hour and a quarter we're going upstairs, and after that there will be no time for talk."

"Well, here it is." Theremon leaned back and folded his hands on his chest. "You people seem so all-fired serious about this that I'm beginning to believe you. Would you mind explaining what it's all about?"

Aton exploded, "Do you mean to sit there and tell me that you've been bombarding us with ridicule without even finding out what we've been trying to say?"

The columnist grinned sheepishly. "It's not that bad, sir. I've got the general idea. You say there is going to be a world-wide Darkness in a few hours and that all mankind will go violently insane. What I want now is the science behind it."

"No, you don't. No, you don't," broke in Sheerin. "If you ask Aton for that—supposing him to be in the mood to answer at all—he'll trot out pages of figures and volumes of graphs. You won't make head or tail of it. Now if you were to ask me, I could give you the layman's standpoint."

"All right; I ask you."

"Then first I'd like a drink." He rubbed his hands and looked at Aton.

"Water?" grunted Aton.

"Don't be silly!"

"Don't you be silly. No alcohol today. It would be too easy to get my men drunk. I can't afford to tempt them."

The psychologist grumbled wordlessly. He turned to Theremon, impaled him with his sharp eyes, and began.

"You realize, of course, that the history of civilization on Lagash displays a cyclic character—but I mean, *cyclic!*"

"I know," replied Theremon cautiously, "that that is the current archaeological theory. Has it been accepted as a fact?"

"Just about. In this last century it's been generally agreed upon. This cyclic character is—or rather, was—one of the great mysteries. We've located series of civilizations, nine of them definitely, and indications of others as well, all of which have reached heights comparable to our own, and all of which, without exception, were destroyed by fire at the very height of their culture.

"And no one could tell why. All centers of culture were thoroughly gutted by fire, with nothing left behind to give a hint as to the cause."

Theremone was following closely. "Wasn't there a Stone Age, too?"

"Probably, but as yet practically nothing is known of it, except that men of that age were little more than rather intelligent apes. We can forget about that."

"I see. Go on!"

"There have been explanations of these recurrent catastrophes, all of a more or less fantastic nature. Some say that there are periodic rains of fire; some that Lagash passes through a sun every so often; some even wilder things. But there is one theory, quite different from all of these, that has been handed down over a period of centuries."

"I know. You mean this myth of the 'Stars' that the Cultists have in their *Book of Revelations.*"

"Exactly," rejoined Sheerin with satisfaction. "The Cultists said that every two thousand and fifty years Lagash entered a huge cave, so that all the suns disappeared, and there came *total darkness all over the world!* And then, they say, things called Stars appeared, which robbed men of their souls and left them unreasoning brutes, so that they destroyed the civilization they themselves had built up. Of course they mix all this up with a lot of religio-mystic notions, but that's the central idea."

There was a short pause in which Sheerin drew a long breath. "And now we come to the Theory of Universal Gravitation." He pronounced the phrase so that the capital letters sounded—and at that point Aton turned from the window, snorted loudly, and stalked out of the room.

The two stared after him, and Theremon said, "What's wrong?"

"Nothing in particular," replied Sheerin. "Two of the men were due several hours ago and haven't shown up yet. He's terrifically short-handed, of course, because all but the really essential men have gone to the Hideout."

"You don't think the two deserted, do you?"

"Who? Faro and Yimot? Of course not. Still, if they're not back within the hour, things would be a little sticky." He got to his feet suddenly, and his eyes twinkled. "Anyway, as long as Aton is gone—"

Tiptoeing to the nearest window, he squatted, and from the low window box beneath withdrew a bottle of red liquid that gurgled suggestively when he shook it.

"I *thought* Aton didn't know about this," he remarked as he trotted back to the table. "Here! We've only got one glass so, as the guest, you can have it. I'll keep the bottle." And he filled the tiny cup with judicious care.

Theremon rose to protest, but Sheerin eyed him sternly. "Respect your elders, young man."

The newsman seated himself with a look of anguish on his face. 'Go ahead, then, you old villain."

The psychologist's Adam's apple wobbled as the bottle upended, and then, with a satisfied grunt and a smack of the lips, he began again. "But what do you know about gravitation?"

"Nothing, except that it is a very recent development, not too well established, and that the math is so hard that only twelve men in Lagash are supposed to understand it."

"*Tcha!* Nonsense! Baloney! I can give you all the essential math in a sentence. The Law of Universal Gravitation states that there exists a cohesive force among all bodies of the universe, such that the amoung of this force between any two given bodies is proportional to the product of their masses divided by the square of the distance between them."

"Is that all?"

"That's enough! It took four hundred years to develop it."

"Why that long? It sounded simple enough, the way you said it."

"Because great laws are not divined by flashes of inspiration, whatever you may think. It usually takes the combined work of a world full of scientists over a period of centuries. After Genovi 41 discovered that Lagash rotated about the sun Alpha rather than vice versa—and that was four hundred years ago—astronomers have been working. The complex motions of the six suns were recorded and analyzed and unwoven. Theory after theory was advanced and checked and counterchecked and modified and abandoned and revived and converted to something else. It was a devil of a job."

Theremon nodded thoughtfully and held out his glass for more liquor. Sheerin grudgingly allowed a few ruby drops to leave the bottle.

"It was twenty years ago," he continued after remoistening his own throat, "that it was finally demonstrated that the Law of Universal Gravitation accounted exactly for the orbital motions of the six suns. It was a great triumph."

Sheerin stood up and walked to the window, clutching his bottle. "And now we're getting to the point. In the last decade, the motions of Lagash about Alpha were computed according to gravity, and *it did not account for the obit observed*; not even when all perturbations due to the other suns were included. Either the law was invalid, or there was another, as yet unknown, factor involved."

Theremon joined Sheerin at the window and gazed out past the wooded slopes to where the spires of Saro City gleamed bloodily on the horizon. The newsman felt the tension of uncertainty grow within him as he cast a short glance at Beta. It glowered redly at zenith, dwarfed and evil.

"Go ahead, sir," he said softly.

Sheerin replied, 'Astronomers stumbled about for years, each proposed theory more untenable than the one before—until Aton had the inspiration of calling in the Cult. The head of the Cult, Sor 5, had access to certain data that simplified the problem consider-ably. Aton set to work on a new track.

"What if there were another nonluminous planetary body such as Lagah? If there were, you know, it would shine only by reflected light, and if it were composed of bluish rock, as Lagash itself largely is, then, in the redness of the sky, the eternal blaze of the suns would make it invisible—drown it out completely."

Theremon whistled. "What a screwy idea!"

"You think *that's* screwy? Listen to this: Suppose this body rotated about Lagash at such a distance and in such an orbit and had such a mass that its attraction would exactly account for the deviations of Lagash's orbit from theory—do you know what would happen?"

The columnist shook his head.

"Well, sometimes this body would get in the way of a sun." And Sheerin emptied what remained in the bottle at a draft.

"And it does, I suppose," said Theremon flatly.

"Yes! But only one sun lies in its plane of revolution." He jerked a thumb at the shrunken sun above. "Beta! And it had been shown that the eclipse will occur only when the arrangement of the suns is such that Beta is alone in its hemisphere and at maximum distance, at which time the moon is invariably at minimum distance. The eclipse that results, with the moon seven times the apparent diameter of Beta, covers all of Lagash and lasts well over a half a day, so that no spot on the planet escapes the effects. *That eclipse comes once every two thousand and forty-nine years.*"

Theremon's face was drawn into an expressionless mask. "And that's my story?"

The psychologist nodded. "That's all of it. First the eclipse—which will start in three quarters of an hour—then universal Darkness and, maybe, these mysterious Stars—then madness, and end of the cycle."

He brooded. "We had two months' leeway—we at the Observatory—and that wasn't enough time to persuade Lagash of the danger. Two centuries might not have been enough. But our records are at the Hideout, and today we photograph the eclipse. The next cycle will *start off* with the truth, and when the *next* eclipse comes, mankind will at last be ready for it. Come to think of it, that's part of your story too."

A thin wind ruffled the curtains at the window as Theremon opened it and leaned out. It played coldly with his hair as he stared at the crimson sunlight on his hand. Then he turned in sudden rebellion.

"What is there in Darkness to drive *me* mad?"

Sheerin smiled to himself as he spun the empty liquor bottle with abstracted motions of his hand. 'Have you ever experienced Darkness, young man?"

The newsman leaned against the wall and considered. "No. Can't say I have. But I know what it is. Just—uh—" He made vague motions with his fingers and then brightened. "Just no light. Like in caves."

"Have you ever been in a cave?"

"In a *cave!* Of course not!"

"I thought not. *I* tried last week—just to see—but I got out in a hurry. I went in until the mouth of the cave was just visible as a blur of light, with black everywhere else. I never thought a person my weight could run that fast."

Theremon's lip curled. "Well, if it comes to that, I guess I wouldn't have run if I had been there."

The psychologist studied the young man with an annoyed frown.

"My, don't you talk big! I dare you to draw the curtain."

Theremon looked his surprise and said, "What for? If we had four or five suns out there, we might want to cut the light down a bit for comfort, but now we haven't enough light as it is."

"That's the point. Just draw the curtain; then come here and sit down."

"All right." Theremon reached for the tasseled string and jerked. The red curtain slid across the wide window, the brass rings hissing their way along the crossbar, and a dusk-red shadow clamped down on the room.

Theremon's footsteps sounded hollowly in the silence as he made his way to the table, and then they stopped halfway. "I can't see you, sir," he whispered.

"Feel your way," ordered Sheerin in a strained voice.

"But I can't see you, sir." The newsman was breathing harshly. "I can't see anything."

"What did you expect?" came the grim reply. "Come here and sit down!"

The footsteps sounded again, waveringly, approaching slowly. There was the sound of someone fumbling with a chair. Theremon's voice came thinly, "Here I am. I feel . . . *ulp* . . . all right."

"You like it, do you?"

"N—no. It's pretty awful. The walls seem to be—" He paused.

"They seem to be closing in on me. I keep wanting to push them away. But I'm not going *mad!* In fact, the feeling isn't as bad as it was."

"All right. Draw the curtain back again."

There were cautious footsteps through the dark, the rustle of Theremon's body against the curtain as he felt for the tassel, and then the triumphant *ro-o-osh* of the curtain slithering back. Red light flooded the room, and with a cry of joy Theremon looked up at the sun.

Sheerin wiped the moistness off his forehead with the back of a hand and said shakily, "And that was just a dark room."

"It can be stood," said Theremon lightly.

"Yes, a dark room can. But were you at the Jonglor Centennial Exposition two years ago?"

"No, it so happens I never got around to it. Six thousand miles was just a bit too much to travel, even for the exposition."

"Well, I was there. You remember hearing about the 'Tunnel of Mystery' that broke all records in the amusement area—for the first month or so, anyway?"

"Yes. Wasn't there some fuss about it?"

"Very little. It was hushed up. You see, that Tunnel of Mystery was just a mile-long tunnel—with no lights. You got into a little open car and jolted along through Darkness for fifteen minutes. It was very popular—while it lasted."

"Popular?"

"Certainly. There's a fascination in being frightened *when it's part of a game.* A baby is born with three instinctive fears: of loud noises, of falling, and of the absence of light. That's why it's considered so funny to jump at someone and shout 'Boo!' That's why it's such fun to ride a roller coaster. And that's why that Tunnel of Mystery started cleaning up. People came out of that Darkness shaking, breathless, half dead with fear, but they kept on paying to get in."

"Wait a minute, I remember now. Some people came out dead, didn't they? There were rumors of that after it shut down."

The psychologist snorted. "Bah! Two or three died. That was nothing! They paid off the families of the dead ones and argued the Jonglor City Council into forgetting it. After all, they said, if people with weak hearts want to go through the tunnel, it was at their own risk—and besides, it wouldn't happen again. So they put a doctor in the front office and had every customer go through a physical examination before getting into the car. That actually *boosted* ticket sales."

"Well, then?"

"But you see, there was something else. People sometimes came out in perfect order, except that they refused to go into buildings—any buildings; including palaces, mansions, apartment houses, tenements, cottages, huts, shacks, lean-tos, and tents."

Theremon looked shocked. "You mean they refused to come in out of the open? Where'd they sleep?"

"In the open."

"They should have *forced* them inside."

"Oh, they did, they did. Whereupon these people went into violent hysterics and did their best to bat their brains out against the nearest wall. Once you got them inside, you couldn't keep them there without a strait jacket or a heavy dose of tranquilizer."

"They must have been crazy."

"Which is exactly what they were. One person out of every ten who went into that tunnel came out that way. They called in psychologists and we did the only thing possible. We closed down the exhibit." He spread his hands.

"What was the matter with these people?" asked Theremon finally.

"Essentially the same thing that was the matter with you when you thought the walls of the room were crushing in on you in the dark. There is a psychological term for mankind's instinctive fear of the absence of light. We call it 'claustrophobia,' because the lack of light is always tied up with enclosed places, so that fear or one if fear of the other. You see?"

"And those people of the tunnel?"

"Those people of the tunnel consisted of those unfortunates whose mentality did not quite possess the resiliency to overcome the claustrophobia that overtook them in the Darkness. Fifteen minutes without light is a long time; you only had two or three minutes, and I believe you were fairly upset.

"The people of the tunnel had what is called a 'claustrophobic fixation.' Their latent fear of Darkness and enclosed places had crystalized and become active, and, as far as we can tell, permanent. That's what fifteen minutes in the dark will do."

There was a long silence, and Theremon's forehead wrinkled slowly into a frown. "I don't believe it's that bad."

"You mean you don't want to believe," snapped Sheerin. "You're afraid to believe. Look out the window!"

Theremon did so, and the psychologist continued without pausing. "Imagine Darkness—everywhere. No light, as far as you can see. The houses, the trees, the fields, the earth, the sky—black! And Stars thrown in, for all I know—whatever *they* are. Can you conceive it?"

"Yes, I can," declared Theremon truculently.

And Sheerin slammed his fist down upon the table in sudden

passion. "You lie! You can't conceive that. Your brain wasn't built for the conception any more than it was built for the conception of infinity or of eternity. You can only talk about it. A fraction of the reality upsets you, and when the real thing comes, your brain is going to be presented with the phenomenon outside its limits of comprehension. You will go mad, completely and permanently! There is no question of it!"

He added sadly, "And another couple of millennia of painful struggle comes to nothing. Tomorrow there won't be a city standing unharmed in all Lagash."

Theremon recovered part of his mental equilibrium. "That doesn't follow. I still don't see that I can go loony just because there isn't a sun in the sky—but even if I did, and everyone else did, how does that harm the cities? Are we going to blow them down?"

But Sheerin was angry, too. "If you were in Darkness, what would you want more than anything else; what would it be that every instinct would call for? Light, damn you, *light!*"

"Well?"

"And how would you get light?"

"I don't know," said Theremon flatly.

"What's the *only* way to get light, short of a sun?"

"How should I know?"

They were standing face to face and nose to nose.

Sheerin said, "You burn something, mister. Ever see a forest fire? Ever go camping and cook a stew over a wood fire? Heat isn't the only thing burning wood gives off, you know. It gives off light, and people know that. And when it's dark they want light, and they're going to *get* it."

"So they burn wood?"

"So they burn whatever thay can get. They've got to have light. They've got to burn something, and wood isn't handy—so they'll burn whatever is nearest. They'll have their light—and every center of habitation goes up in flames!"

Eyes held each other as though the whole matter were a personal affair of respective will powers, and then Theremon broke away wordlessly. His breathing was harsh and ragged, and he scarcely noted the sudden hubbub that came from the adjoining room behind the closed door.

Sheerin spoke, and it was with an effort that he made it sound matter-of-fact. "I think I heard Yimot's voice. He and Faro are probably back. Let's go in and see what kept them."

"Might as well!" muttered Theremon. He drew a long breath and seemed to shake himself. The tension was broken.

* * *

The room was in an uproar, with members of the staff clustering about two young men who were removing outer garments even as they parried the miscellany of questions being thrown at them.

Aton bustled through the crowd and faced the newcomers angrily. "Do you realize that it's less than half an hour before deadline? Where have you two been?"

Faro 24 seated himself and rubbed his hands. His cheeks were red with the outdoor chill. "Yimot and I have just finished carrying through a little crazy experiment of our own. We've been trying to see if we couldn't construct an arrangement by which we could simulate the appearance of Darkness and Stars so as to get an advance notion as to how it looked."

There was a confused murmur from the listeners, and a sudden look of interest entered Aton's eyes. "There wasn't anything said of this before. How did you go about it?"

"Well," said Faro, "the idea came to Yimot and myself long ago, and we've been working it out in our spare time. Yimot knew of a low one-story house down in the city with a domed roof—it had once been used as a museum, I think. Anyway, we bought it—"

"Where did you get the money?" interrupted Atom peremptorily.

"Out bank accounts," grunted Yimot 70. "It cost two thousand credits." Then defensively, "Well, what of it? Tomorrow, two thousand credits will be two thousand pieces of paper. That's all."

"Sure," agreed Faro. "We bought the place and rigged it up with black velvet from top to bottom so as to get as perfect a Darkness as possible. Then we punched tiny holes in the ceiling and through the roof and covered them with little metal caps, all of which could be shoved aside simultaneously at the close of a switch. At least we didn't do that part ourselves; we got a carpenter and an electrician and some others—money didn't count. The point was that we could get the light to shine through those holes in the roof, so that we could get a starlike effect."

Not a breath was drawn during the pause that followed. Aton said stiffly, "You had no right to make a private—"

Faro seemed abashed. "I know, sir—but frankly, Yimot and I thought the experiment was a little dangerous. If the effect really worked, we half expected to go mad—from what Sheerin says about all this, we thought that would be rather likely. We wanted to take the risk ourselves. Of course if we found we could retain sanity, it occurred to us that we might develop immunity to the real thing, and then expose the rest of you the same way. But things didn't work out at all—"

"Why, what happened?"

It was Yimot who answered. "We shut ourselves in and allowed our eyes to get accustomed to the dark. It's an extremely creepy feeling because the total Darkness makes you feel as if the walls and ceiling are crushing in on you. But we got over that and pulled the switch. The caps fell away and the roof glittered all over with little dots of light—"

"Well?"

"Well—nothing. That was the whacky part of it. Nothing happened. It was just a roof with holes in it, and that's just what it looked like. We tried it over and over again—that's what kept us so late—but there just isn't any effect at all."

There followed a shocked silence, and all eyes turned to Sheerin, who sat motionless, mouth open.

Theremon was the first to speak. "You know what this does to this whole theory you've built up, Sheerin, don't you?" He was grinning with relief.

But Sheerin raised his hand. "Now wait a while. Just let me think this through." And then he snapped his fingers, and when he lifted his head there was neither surprise nor uncertainty in his eyes. "Of course—"

He never finished. From somewhere up above there sounded a sharp clang, and Beenay, starting to his feet, dashed up the stairs with a "What the devil!"

The rest followed after.

Things happened quickly. Once up in the dome, Beenay cast one horrified glance at the shattered photographic plates and at the man bending over them; and then hurled himself fiercely at the intruder, getting a death grip on his throat. There was a wild threshing, and as others of the staff joined in, the stranger was swallowed up and smothered under the weight of half a dozen angry men.

Aton came up last, breathing heavily. "Let him up!"

There was a reluctant unscrambling and the stranger, panting harshly, with his clothes torn and his forehead bruised, was hauled to his feet. He had a short yellow beard curled elaborately in the style affected by the Cultists.

Beenay shifted his hold to a collar grip and shook the man savagely. "All right, rat, what's the idea? These plates—"

"I wasn't after *them*," retorted the Cultist coldly. "That was an accident."

Beenay followed his glowering stare and snarled, "I see. You were after the cameras themselves. The accident with the plate was a stroke of luck for you, then. If you had touched Snapping Bertha or any of the others, you would have died by slow torture. As it is—" He drew his fist back.

Aton grabbed his sleeve. "Stop that! Let him go!"

The young technician wavered, and his arm dropped reluctantly. Aton pushed him aside and confronted the Cultist. "You're Latimer, aren't you?"

The Cultist bowed stiffly and indicated the symbol upon his hip. "I am Latimer 25, adjutant of the third class to his serenity, Sor 5."

"And"—Aton's white eyebrows lifted—"you were with his serenity when he visited me last week, weren't you?"

Latimer bowed a second time.

"Now, then, what do you want?"

"Nothing that you would give me of your own free will."

"Sor 5 sent you, I suppose—or is this your own idea?"

"I won't answer that question."

"Will there be any further visitors?"

"I won't answer that, either."

Aton glanced at his timepiece and scowled. "Now, man, what is it your master wants of me? I have fulfilled my end of the bargain."

Latimer smiled faintly, but said nothing.

"I asked him," continued Aton angrily, "for data only the Cult could supply, and it was given to me. For that, thank you. In return I promised to prove the essential truth of the creed of the Cult."

"There was no need to prove that," came the proud retort. "It stands proven by the *Book of Revelations*."

"For the handful that constitute the Cult, yes. Don't pretend to mistake my meaning. I offered to present scientific backing for your beliefs. And I did!"

The Cultist's eyes narrowed bitterly. "Yes, you did—with a fox's subtlety, for your pretended explanation backed our beliefs, and at the same time removed all necessity for them. You made of the Darkness and of the Stars a natural phenomenon and removed all its real significance. That was blasphemy."

"If so, the fault isn't mine. The facts exist. What can I do but state them?"

"Your 'facts' are a fraud and a delusion."

Aton stamped angrily. "How do you know?"

And the answer came with the certainty of absolute faith. "I know!"

The director purpled and Beenay whispered urgently. Aton waved him silent. "And what does Sor 5 want us to do? He still thinks, I suppose, that in trying to warn the world to take measures against the menace of madness, we are placing innumerable souls in jeopardy. We aren't succeeding, if that means anything to him."

"The attempt itself has done harm enough, and your vicious effort to gain information by means of your devilish instruments must be stopped. We obey the will of the Stars, and I only regret that my clumsiness prevented me from wrecking your infernal devices."

"It wouldn't have done you too much good," returned Aton. "All our data, except for the direct evidence we intend collecting right now, is already safely cached and well beyond possibility of harm." He smiled grimly. "But that does not affect your present status as an attempted burglar and criminal."

He turned to the men behind him. "Someone call the police at Saro City."

There was a cry of distaste from Sheerin. "Damn it, Aton, what's wrong with you? There's no time for that. Here"—he bustled his way forward—"let me handle this."

Aton stared down his nose at the psychologist. "This is not the time for your monkeyshines, Sheerin. Will you please let me handle this my own way? Right now you are a complete outsider here, and don't forget it."

Sheerin's mouth twisted eloquently. "Now why should we go to the impossible trouble of calling the police—with Beta's eclipse a matter of minutes from now—when this young man here is perfectly willing to pledge his word of honor to remain and cause no trouble whatsoever?"

The Cultist answered promptly, "I will do no such thing. You're free to do what you want, but it's only fair to warn you that just as soon as I get my chance I'm going to finish what I came out here to do. If it's my word of honor you're relying on, you'd better call the police."

Sheerin smiled in a friendly fashion. "You're a determined cuss, aren't you? Well, I'll explain something. Do you see that young man at the window? He's a strong, husky fellow, quite handy with his fists, and he's an outsider besides. Once the eclipse starts there will be nothing for him to do except keep an eye on you. Besides him, there will be myself—a little too stout for active fisticuffs, but still able to help."

"Well, what of it?" demanded Latimer frozenly.

"Listen and I'll tell you," was the reply. "Just as soon as the eclipse starts, we're going to take you, Theremon and I, and deposit you in a little closet with one door, to which is attached one giant lock and no windows. You will remain there for the duration."

"And afterward," breathed Latimer fiercely, "there'll be no one to let me out. I know as well as you do what the coming of the Stars means—I know it far better than you. With all your minds gone, you are not likely to free me. Suffocation or slow starvation, is it? About what I might have expected from a group of scientists. But I don't give my word. It's a matter of principle, and I won't discuss it further."

Aton seemed perturbed. His faded eyes were troubled. "Really, Sheerin, locking him—"

"Please!" Sheerin motioned him impatiently to silence. "I don't think for a moment things will go that far. Latimer has just tried a clever little bluff, but I'm not a pychologist just because I like the sound of the word." He grinned at the Cultist. "Come now, you don't really think I'm trying anything as crude as slow starvation. My dear Latimer, if I lock you in the closet, you are not going to see the Darkness, and you are not going to see the Stars. It does not take much knowledge of the fundamental creed of the Cult to realize that for you to be hidden from the Stars when they appear means the loss of your immortal soul. Now, I believe you to be an honorable man. I'll accept your word of honor to make no further effort to disrupt proceedings, if you'll offer it."

A vein throbbed in Latimer's temple, and he seemed to shrink within himself as he said thickly, "You have it!" And then he added with swift fury, "But it is my consolation that you will all be damned for your deeds of today." He turned on his heel and stalked to the high three-legged stool by the door.

Sheerin nodded to the columnist. "Take a seat next to him, Theremon—just as a formality. Hey, Theremon!"

But the newspaperman didn't move. He had gone pale to the lips. "Look at that!" The finger he pointed toward the sky shook, and his voice was dry and cracked.

There was one simultaneous gasp as every eye followed the pointing finger and, for one breathless moment, stared frozenly.

Beta was chipped on one side!

The tiny bit of encroaching blackness was perhaps the width of a fingernail, but to the staring watchers it magnified itself into the crack of doom.

Only for a moment they watched, and after that there was a shrieking confusion that was even shorter of duration and which gave way to an orderly scurry of activity—each man at his prescribed job. At the crucial moment there was no time for emotion. The men were merely scientists with work to do. Even Aton had melted away.

Sheerin said prosaically, "First contact must have been made fifteen minutes ago. A little early, but pretty good considering the uncertainties involved in the calculation." He looked about him and then tiptoed to Theremon, who still remained staring out the window, and dragged him away gently.

"Aton is furious," he whispered, "so stay away. He missed first contact on account of this fuss with Latimer, and if you get in his way he'll have you thrown out the window."

Theremon nodded shortly and sat down. Sheerin stared in surprise at him.

"The devil, man," he exclaimed, "you're shaking."

"Eh?" Theremon licked dry lips and then tried to smile. "I don't feel very well, and that's a fact."

The psychologist's eyes hardened. "You're not losing your nerve?"

"No!" cried Theremon in a flash of indignation. "Give me a chance, will you? I haven't really believed this rigmarole—not way down beneath, anyway—till just this minute. Give me a chance to get used to the idea. You've been preparing yourself for two months or more."

"You're right, at that," replied Sheerin thoughtfully. "Listen! Have you got a family—parents, wife, children?"

Theremon shook his head. "You mean the Hideout, I suppose. No, you don't have to worry about that. I have a sister, but she's two thousand miles away. I don't even know her exact address."

"Well, then, what about yourself? You've got time to get there, and they're one short anyway, since I left. After all, you're not needed here, and you'd make a darned fine addition—"

Theremon looked at the other wearily. "You think I'm scared stiff, don't you? Well, get this, mister, I'm a newspaperman and I've been assigned to cover a story. I intend covering it."

There was a faint smile on the psychologist's face. "I see. Professional honor, is that it?"

"You might call it that. But, man, I'd give my right arm for another bottle of that sockeroo juice even half the size of the one you hogged. If ever a fellow needed a drink, I do."

He broke off. Sheerin was nudging him violently. "Do you hear that? Listen!"

Theremon followed the motion of the other's chin and stared at the Cultist, who, oblivious to all about him, faced the window, a look of wild elation on his face, droning to himself the while in singsong fashion.

"What's he saying?" whispered the columnist.

"He's quoting *Book of Revelations*, fifth chapter," replied Sheerin. Then, urgently, "Keep quiet and listen, I tell you."

The Cultist's voice had risen in a sudden increase of fervor: " 'And it came to pass that in those days the Sun, Beta, held lone vigil in the sky for ever longer periods as the revolutions passed; until such time as for full half a revolution, it alone, shrunken and cold, shone down upon Lagash.

" 'And men did assemble in the public squares and in the highways, there to debate and to marvel at the sight, for a strange depression had seized them. Their minds were troubled and their speech confused, for the souls of men awaited the coming of the Stars.

" 'And in the city of Trigon, at high noon, Vendret 2 came forth and said unto the men of Trigon, "Lo, ye sinners! Though ye scorn the ways of righteousness, yet will the time of reckoning come. Even now the Cave approaches to swallow Lagash; yea, and all it contains."

" 'And even as he spoke the lip of the Cave of Darkness passed the edge of Beta so that to all Lagash it was hidden from sight. Loud were the cries of men as it vanished, and great the fear of soul that fell upon them.

" 'It came to pass that the Darkness of the Cave fell upon Lagash, and there was no light on all the surface of Lagash. Men were even as blinded, nor could one man see his neighbor, though he felt his breath upon his face.

" 'And in this blackness there appeared the Stars, in countless numbers, and to the strains of music of such beauty that the very leaves of the trees cried out in wonder.

" 'And in that moment the souls of men departed from them, and their abandoned bodies became even as beasts; yea, even as brutes of the wild; so that through the blackened streets of the cities of Lagash they prowled with wild cries.

" 'From the Stars there then reached down the Heavenly Flame, and where it touched, the cities of Lagash flamed to utter destruction, so that of man and of the works of man nought remained.

" 'Even then—' "

There was a subtle change in Latimer's tone. His eyes had not shifted, but somehow he had become aware of the absorbed attention of the other two. Easily, without pausing for breath, the timbre of his voice shifted and the syllables became more liquid.

Theremon, caught by surprise, stared. The words seemed on the border of familiarity. There was an elusive shift in the accent, a tiny change in the vowel stress; nothing more—yet Latimer had become thoroughly unintelligible.

Sheerin smiled slyly. "He shifted to some old-cycle tongue, probably their traditional second cycle. That was the language in which the *Book of Revelations* was originally written, you know."

"It doesn't matter; I've heard enough." Theremon shoved his chair back and brushed his hair back with hands that no longer shook. "I feel much better now."

"You do?" Sheerin seemed mildly surprised.

"I'll say I do. I had a bad case of jitters just a while back. Listening to you and your gravitation and seeing that eclipse start almost finished me. But this"—he jerked a contemptuous thumb at the yellow-bearded Cultist—"*this* is the sort of thing my nurse used to tell me. I've been laughing at that sort of thing all my life. I'm not going to let it scare me *now*."

He drew a deep breath and said with a hectic gaiety, "But if I expect to keep on the good side of myself, I'm going to turn my chair away from the window."

Sheerin said, "Yes, but you'd better talk lower. Aton just lifted his head out of that boc he's got it stuck into and gave you a look that should have killed you."

Theremon made a mouth. "I forgot about the old fellow." With elaborate care he turned the chair from the window, cast one distasteful look over his shoulder, and said, "It has occurred to me that there must be considerable immunity against this Star madness."

The psychologist did not answer immediately. Beta was past its zenith now, and the square of bloody sunlight that outlined the window upon the floor had lifted into Sheerin's lap. He stared at its dusky color thoughtfully and then bent and squinted into the sun itself.

The chip in its side had grown to a black encroachment that covered a third of Beta. He shuddered, and when he straightened once more his florid cheeks did not contain quite as much color as they had had previously.

With a smile that was almost apologetic, he reversed his chair also. "There are probably two million people in Saro City that are all trying to join the Cult at once in one gigantic revival." Then, ironically, "The Cult is in for an hour of unexampled prosperity. I trust they'll make the most of it. Now, what was it you said?"

"Just this. How did the Cultists manage to keep the *Book of Revelations* going from cycle to cycle, and how on Lagash did it get written in the first place? There must have been some sort of immunity, for if everyone had gone mad, who would be left to write the book?"

Sheerin stared at his questioner ruefully. "Well, now, young man, there isn't any eyewitness answer to that, but we've got a few damned good notions as to what happened. You see, there are three kinds of people who might remain relatively unaffected. First, the very few who don't see the Stars at all: the seriously retarded or those who drink themselves into a stupor at the beginning of the eclipse and remain so to the end. We leave them out—because they aren't really witnesses.

"Then there are children below six, to whom the world as a whole is too new and strange for them to be frightened at Stars and Darkness. They would be just another item in an already surprising world. You see that, don't you?"

The other nodded doubtfully. "I suppose so."

"Lastly, there are those whose minds are too coarsely grained to be entirely toppled. The very insensitive would be scarcely affected—oh, such people as some of our older, work-broken peasants. Well, the children would have fugitive memories, and that, combined with the confused, incoherent babblings of the half-mad morons, formed the basis for the *Book of Revelations*.

"Naturally, the book was based, in the first place, on the testimony of those least qualified to serve as historians; that is, children and morons; and was probably edited and re-edited through the cycles."

"Do you suppose," broke in Theremon, "that they carried the book through the cycles the way we're planning on handing on the secret of gravitation?"

Sheerin shrugged. "Perhaps, but their exact method is unimportant. They do it, somehow. The point I was getting at was that the book can't help but be a mass of distortion, even if it is based on fact. For instance, do you remember the experiment with the holes in the roof that Faro and Yimot tried—the one that didn't work?"

"Yes."

"You know why it didn't w—" He stopped and rose in alarm, for Aton was approaching, his face a twisted mask of consternation. "*What's happened?*"

Aton drew him aside and Sheerin could feel the fingers on his elbow twitching.

"Not so loud!" Aton's voice was low and tortured. "I've just gotten word from the Hideout on the private line."

Sheerin broke in anxiously. "They are in trouble?"

"Not *they*." Aton stressed the pronoun significantly. "They sealed themselves off just a while ago, and they're going to stay buried till day after tomorrow. They're safe. But the *city*, Sheerin—it's a shambles. You have no idea—" He was having difficulty in speaking.

"Well?" snapped Sheerin impatiently. "What of it? It will get worse. What are you shaking about?" Then, suspiciously, "How do you feel?"

Aton's eyes sparked angrily at the insinuation, and then faded to anxiety once more. "You don't understand. The Cultists are active. They're rousing the people to storm the Observatory—promising them immediate entrance into grace, promising them salvation, promising them anything. What are we to do, Sheerin?"

Sheerin's head bent, and he stared in long abstraction at his toes. He tapped his chin with one knuckle, then looked up and said crisply, "Do? What is there to do? Nothing at all. Do the men know of this?"

"No, of course not!"

"Good! Keep it that way. How long till totality?"

"Not quite an hour."

"There's nothing to do but gamble. It will take time to organize any really formidable mob, and it will take more time to get them out here. We're a good five miles from the city—"

He glared out the window, down the slopes to where the farmed patched gave way to clumps of white houses in the suburbs; down to where the metropolis itself was a blur on the horizon—a mist in the waning blaze of Beta.

He repeated without turning, "It will take time. Keep on working and pray that totality comes first."

Beta was cut in half, the line of division pushing a slight concavity into the still-bright portion of the Sun. It was like a gigantic eyelid shutting slantwise over the light of a world.

The faint clatter of the room in which he stood faded into oblivion, and he sensed only the thick silence of the fields outside. The very insects seemed frightened mute. And things were dim.

He jumped at the voice in his ear. Theremon said, "Is something wrong?"

"Eh? Er—no. Get back to the chair. We're in the way." They slipped back to their corner, but the psychologist did not speak for a time. He lifted a finger and loosened his collar. He twisted his neck back and forth but found no relief. He looked up suddenly.

"Are you having any difficulty in breathing?"

The newspaperman opened his eyes wide and drew two or three long breaths. "No. Why?"

"I looked out the window too long, I suppose. The dimness got me. Difficulty in breathing is one of the first symptoms of a claustrophic attack."

Theremon drew another long breath. "Well, it hasn't got me yet. Say, here's another of the fellows."

Beenay had interposed his bulk between the light and the pair in the corner, and Sheerin squinted up at him anxiously. "Hello, Beenay."

The astronomer shifted his weight to the other foot and smiled feebly. "You won't mind if I sit down awhile and join in the talk? My cameras are set, and there's nothing to do till totality." He paused and eyes the Cultist, who fifteen minutes earlier had drawn a small, skin-bound book from his sleeve and had been poring intently over it ever since. "That rat hasn't been making trouble, has he?"

Sheerin shook his head. His shoulders were thrown back and he frowned his concentration as he forced himself to breathe regularly. He said, "Have you had any trouble breathing, Beenay?"

Beenay sniffed the air in his turn. "It doesn't seem stuffy to me."

"A touch of claustrophobia," explained Sheerin apologetically.

"Ohhh! It worked itself differently with me. I get the impression that my eyes are going back on me. Things seem to blue and—well, nothing is clear. And it's cold, too."

"Oh, it's cold, all right. That's no illusion." Theremon grimaced. "My toes feel as if I've been shipping them cross-country in a refrigerating car."

"What we need," put in Sheerin, "is to keep our minds busy with extraneous affairs. I was telling you a while ago, Theremon, why Faro's experiments with the holes in the roof came to nothing."

"You were just beginning," replied Theremon. He encircled a knee with both arms and nuzzled his chin against it.

"Well, as I started to say, they were misled by taking the *Book of Revelations* literally. There probably wasn't any sense in attaching any physical significance to the Stars. It might be, you know, that in the presence of total Darkness, the mind finds it absolutely necessary to create light. This illusion of light might be all the Stars there really are."

"In other words," interposed Theremon, "you mean the Stars are the result of the madness and not one of the causes. Then, what good will Beenay's photographs be?"

"To prove that it is an illusion, maybe; or to prove the opposite; for all I know. Then again—"

But Beenay had drawn his chair closer, and there was an expression of sudden enthusiasm on his face. "Say, I'm glad you two got onto this subject." He eyes narrowed and he lifted one finger. "I've been thinking about these Stars and I've got a really cute notion. Of course it's strictly ocean foam, and I'm not trying to advance it seriously, but I think it's interesting. Do you want to hear it?"

He seemed half reluctant, but Sheerin leaned back and said, "Go ahead! I'm listening."

"Well, then, supposing there were other suns in the universe." He broke off a little bashfully. "I mean suns that are so far away that they're too dim to see. It sounds as if I've been reading some of that fantastic fiction, I suppose."

"Not necessarily. Still, isn't that possibility eliminated by the fact that, according to the Law of Gravitation, they would make themselves evident by their attractive forces?"

"Not if they were far enough off," rejoined Beenay, "really far off—maybe as much as four light years, or even more. We'd never be able to detect perturbations then, because they'd be too small. Say that there were a lot of suns that far off; a dozen or two, maybe."

Theremon whistled melodiously. "What an idea for a good Sunday supplement article. Two dozen suns in a universe eight light years across. Wow! That would shrink our world into insignificance. The readers would eat it up."

"Only an idea," said Beenay with a grin, "but you see the point. During an eclipse, these dozen suns would become visible because they'd be no *real* sunlight to drown them out. Since they're so far off, they'd appear small, like so many little marbles. Of course the Cultists talk of millions of Stars, but that's probably exaggeration. There just isn't any place in the universe you could put a million suns—unless they touch one another."

Sheerin had listened with gradually increasing interest. "You've hit something there, Beenay. And exaggeration is just exactly what would happen. Our minds, as you probably know, can't grasp directly any number higher than five; above that there is only the concept of 'many.' A dozen would become a million just like that. A damn good idea!"

"And I've got another cute little notion," Beenay said. "Have you ever thought what a simple problem gravitation would be if only you had a sufficiently simple system? Supposing you had a universe in which there was a planet with only one sun. The planet would travel in a perfect ellipse and the exact nature of the gravitational force would be so evident it could be accepted as an axiom. Astronomers on such a world would start off with gravity probably before they even invented the telescope. Naked-eye observation would be enough."

"But would such a system by dynamically stable?" questioned Sheerin doubtfully.

"Sure! They call it the 'one-and-one' case. It's been worked out mathematically, but it's the philosophical implications that interest me."

"It's nice to think about," admitted Sheerin, "as a pretty abstraction—like a perfect gas, or absolute zero."

"Of course," continued Beenay, "there's the catch that life would be impossible on such a planet. It wouldn't get enough heat and light, and if it rotated there would be total Darkness half of each day. You couldn't expect life—which is fundamentally dependent upon light—to develop under those conditions. Besides—"

Sheerin's chair went over backward as he sprang to his feet in a rude interruption. "Aton's brought out the lights."

Beenay said, "Huh," turned to stare, and then grinned halfway around his head in open relief.

There were half a dozen foot-long, inch-thick rods cradled in Aton's arms. He glared over them at the assembled staff members.

"Get back to work, all of you. Sheerin, come here and help me!"

Sheerin trotted to the older man's side and, one by one, in utter silence, the two adjusted the rods in makeshift metal holders suspended from the walls.

With the air of one carrying through the most sacred item of a religious ritual, Sheerin scraped a large, clumsy match into spluttering life and passed it to Aton, who carried the flame to the upper end of one of the rods.

It hesitated there awhile, playing futilely about the tip, until a sudden, crackling flare cast Aton's lined face into yellow highlights. He withdrew the match and a spontaneous cheer rattled the window.

The rod was topped by six inches of wavering flame! Methodically, the other rods were lighted, until six independent fires turned the rear of the room yellow.

The light was dim, dimmer even than the tenuous sunlight. The flames reeled crazily, giving birth to drunken, swaying shadows. The torches smoked devilishly and smelled like a bad day in the kitchen. But they emitted yellow light.

There was something about yellow light, after four hours of somber, dimming Beta. Even Latimer had lifted his eyes from his book and stared in wonder

Sheerin warmed his hands at the nearest, regardless of the soot that gathered upon them in a fine, gray powder, and muttered ecstatically to himself. "Beautiful! Beautiful! I never realized before what a wonderful color yellow is."

But Theremon regarded the torches suspiciously. He wrinkled his nose at the rancid odor and said, "What are those things?"

"Wood," said Sheerin shortly.

"Oh, no, they're not. They aren't burning. The top inch is charred and the flame just keeps shooting up out of nothing."

"That's the beauty of it. This is a really efficient artificial-light mechanism. We made a few hundred of them, but most went to the Hideout, of course. You see"—he turned and wiped his blackened hands upon his handkerchief—"you take the pithy core of coarse water reeds, dry them thoroughly, and soak them in animal grease. Then you set fire to it and the grease burns, little by little. These torches will burn for almost half an hour without stopping. Ingenious, isn't it? It was developed by one of our own young men at Saro University."

After the momentary sensation, the dome had quieted. Latimer had carried his chair directly beneath the torch and continued reading, lips moving in the monotonous recital of invocations to the Stars. Beenay had drifted away to his cameras once more, and Theremon seized the opportunity to add to his notes on the article he was going to write for the Saro City *Chronicle* the next day—a procedure he had been following for the last two hours in a perfectly methodical, perfectly conscientious and, as he was well aware, perfectly meaningless fashion.

But, as the gleam of amusement in Sheerin's eyes indicated, careful note-taking occupied his mind with something other than the fact that the sky was gradually turning a horrible deep purple-red, as if it were one gigantic, freshly peeled beet; and so it fulfilled its purpose.

The air grew, somehow, denser. Dusk, like a palpable entity, entered the room, and the dancing circle of yellow light about the torches etched itself into ever-sharper distinction against the gathering grayness beyond. There was the odor of smoke and the presence of little chuckling sounds that the torches made as they burned; the soft pad of one of the men circling the table at which he worked, on hesitant tiptoes; the occasional indrawn breath of someone trying to retain composure in a world that was retreating into the shadow.

It was Theremon who first heard the extraneous noise. It was a vague, unorganized *impression* of sound that would have gone unnoticed but for the dead silence that prevailed within the dome.

The newsman sat upright and replaced his notebook. He held his breath and listened; then, with considerable reluctance, threaded his way between the solarscope and one of Beenay's cameras and stood before the window.

The silence ripped to fragments at his startled shout: "*Sheerin!*"

Work stopped! The psychologist was at his side in a moment. Aton joined him. Even Yimot 70, high in his little lean-back seat at the eyepiece of the gigantic solarscope, paused and looked downward.

Outside, Beta was a mere smoldering splinter, taking one last desperate look at Lagash. The eastern horizon, in the direction of the city, was lost in Darkness, and the road from Saro to the Observatory was a dull-red line bordered on both sides by wooded tracts, the trees of which had somehow lost individuality and merged into a continuous shadowy mass.

But it was the highway itself that held attention, for along it there surged another, and infinitely menacing shadowy mass.

Aton cried in a cracked voice, "The madmen from the city! They've come!"

"How long to totality?" demanded Sheerin.

"Fifteen minutes, but . . . but they'll be here in five."

"Never mind, keep the men working. We'll hold them off. This place is built like a fortress. Aton, keep an eye on our young Cultist just for luck. Theremon, come with me."

Sheerin was out the door, and Theremon was at his heels. The stairs stretched below them in tight, circular sweeps about the central shaft, fading into a dank and dreary grayness.

The first momentum of their rush had carried them fifty feet down, so that the dim, flickering yellow from the open door of the dome had disappeared and both above and below the same dusky shadow crushed in upon them.

Sheerin paused, and his pudgy hand clutched at his chest. His eyes bulged and his voice was a dry cough. "I can't . . . breathe . . . Go down . . . yourself. Close all doors—"

Theremon took a few downward steps, then turned. "Wait! Can you hold out a minute?" He was panting himself. The air passed in and out his lungs like so much molasses, and there was a little germ of screeching panic in his mind at the thought of making his way into the mysterious Darkness below by himself.

Theremon, after all, was afraid of the dark!

"Stay here," he said. "I'll be back in a second." He dashed upward two steps at a time, heart pounding—not altogether from the exertion—tumbled into the dome and snatched a torch from its holder. It was foul-smelling, and the smoke smarted his eyes almost blind, but he clutched that torch as if he wanted to kiss it for joy, and its flame streamed backward as he hurtled down the stairs again.

Sheerin opened his eyes and moaned as Theremon bent over him. Theremon shook him roughly. "All right, get a hold on yourself. We've got light."

He held the torch at tiptoe height and, propping the tottering psychologist by an elbow, made his way downward in the middle of the protecting circle of illumination.

The offices on the ground floor still possessed what light there was, and Theremon felt the horror about him relax.

"Here," he said brusquely, and passed the torch to Sheerin. "You can hear *them*-outside."

And they could. Little scraps of hoarse, wordless shouts.

But Sheerin was right: the Observatory was built like a fortress. Erected in the last century, when the neo-Gavottian style of architecture was at its ugly height, it has been designed for stability and durability rather than for beauty.

The windows were protected by the grillwork of inch-thick iron bars sunk deep into the concrete sills. The walls were solid masonry that an earthquake couldn't have touched, and the main door was a huge oaken slab reinforced with iron. Theremon shot the bolts and they slid shut with a dull clang.

At the other end of the corridor, Sheerin cursed weakly. He pointed to the lock of the back door which had been neatly jimmied into uselessness.

"That must be how Latimer got in," he said.

"Well, don't stand there," cried Theremon impatiently. "Help drag up the furniture—and keep that torch out of my eyes. The smoke's killing me."

He slammed the heavy table up against the door as he spoke, and in two minutes had built a barricade which made up for what it lacked in beauty and symmetry by the sheer inertia of its massive-ness.

Somewhere, dimly, far off, they could hear the battering of naked fists upon the door; and the screams and yells from outside had a sort of half reality.

That mob had set off from Saro City with only two things in mind: the attainment of Cultist salvation by the destruction of the Observatory, and a maddening fear that all but paralyzed them. There was no time to think of ground cars, or of weapons, or of leadership, or even or organization. They made for the Observatory on foot and assaulted it with bare hands.

And now that they were there, the last flash of Beta, the last ruby-red drop of flame, flickered feebly over a humanity that had left only stark, universal fear!

Theremon groaned, "Let's get back to the dome!"

* * *

In the dome, only Yimot, at the solarscope, had kept his place. The rest were clustered about the cameras, and Beenay was giving his instructions in a hoarse, strained voice.

"Get it straight, all of you. I'm snapping Beta just before totality and changing the plate. That will leave one of you to each camera. You all know about . . . about times of exposure—"

There was a breathless murmur of agreement.

Beenay passed a hand over his eyes. "Are the torches still burning? Never mind, I see them!" He was leaning hard against the back of a chair. "Now remember, don't . . . don't try to look for good shots. Don't waste time trying to get t-two stars at a time in the scope field. One is enough. And . . . and if you feel yourself going, *get away from the camera*."

At the door, Sheerin whispered to Theremon, "Take me to Aton. I don't see him."

The newsman did not answer immediately. The vague forms of the astronomers wavered and blurred, and the torches overhead had become only yellow splotches.

"It's dark," he whimpered.

Sheerin held out his hand. "Aton." He stumbled forward. "Aton!"

Theremon stepped after and seized his arm. "Wait, I'll take you." Somehow he made his way across the room. He closed his eyes against the Darkness and his mind against the chaos within it.

No one heard them or paid attention to them. Sheerin stumbled against the wall. "Aton!"

The psychologist felt shaking hands touching him, then withdrawing, and a voice muttering, "Is that you, Sheerin?"

"Aton!" He strove to breathe normally. "Don't worry about the mob. The place will hold them off."

Latimer, the Cultist, rose to his feet, and his face twisted in desperation. His word was pledged, and to break it would mean placing his soul in mortal peril. Yet that word had been forced from him and had not been given freely. The Stars would come soon! He could not stand by and allow—And yet his word was pledged.

Beenay's face was dimly flushed as it looked upward at Beta's last ray, and Latimer, seeing him bend over his camera, made his decision. His nails cut the flesh of his palms as he tensed himself.

He staggered crazily as he started his rush. There was nothing before him but shadows; the very floor beneath his feet lacked substance. And then someone was upon him and he went down with clutching fingers at his throat.

He doubled his knee and drove it hard into his assailant. "Let me up or I'll kill you."

Theremon cried out sharply and muttered through a blinding haze of pain. "You double-crossing rat!"

The newsman seemed conscious of everything at once. He heard Beenay croak, "I've got it. At your cameras, men!" and then there was a strange awareness that the last thread of sunlight had thinned out and snapped.

Simultaneously he heard one last choking gasp from Beenay, and a queer little cry from Sheerin, a hysterical giggle that cut off in a rasp—and a sudden silence, a strange, deadly silence from outside.

And Latimer had gone limp in his loosening grasp. Theremon peered into the Cultist's eyes and saw the blankness of them, staring upward, mirroring the feeble yellow of the torches. He saw the bubble of froth upon Latimer's lips and heard the low animal whimper in Latimer's throat.

With the slow fascination of fear, he lifted himself on one arm and turned his eyes toward the blood-curdling blackness of the window.

Through it shone the Stars!

Not Earth's feeble thirty-six hundred Stars visible to the eye; Lagah was in the center of a giant cluster. Thirty thousand mighty suns shone down in a soul-searing splendor that was more frighteningly cold in its awful indifference than the bitter wind that shivered across the cold, horribly bleak world.

Theremon staggered to his feet, his throat constricting him to breathlessness, all the muscles of his body writhing in an intensity of terror and sheer fear beyond bearing. He was going mad and knew it, and somewhere deep inside a bit of sanity was screaming, struggling to fight off the hopeless flood of black terror. It was very horrible to go mad and know that you were going mad—to know that in a little minute you would be here physically and yet all the real essence would be dead and drowned in the black madness. For this was the Dark—the Dark and the Cold and the Doom. The bright walls of the universe were shattered and their awful black fragments were falling down to crush and squeeze and obliterate him.

He jostled someone crawling on hands and knees, but stumbled somehow over him. Hands groping at his tortured throat, he limped toward the flame of the torches that filled all his mad vision.

"Light!" he screamed.

Aton, somewhere, was crying, whimpering horribly like a terribly frightened child. "Stars—all the Stars—we didn't know at all. We didn't know anything. We thought six stars in a universe is something the Stars didn't notice is Darkness forever and ever and ever and the walls are breaking in and we didn't know we couldn't know and anything—"

Someone clawed at the torch, and it fell and snuffed out. In the instant, the awful splendor of the indifferent Stars leaped nearer to them.

On the horizon outside the window, in the direction of Saro City, a crimson glow began growing, strengthening in brightness, that was not the glow of a sun.

The long night had come again.

Runaround

It was one of Gregory Powell's favorite platitudes that nothing was to be gained from excitement, so when Mike Donovan came leaping down the stairs toward him, red hair matted with perspiration, Powell frowned.

"What's wrong?" he said. "Break a fingernail?"

"Yaaaah," snarled Donovan, feverishly. "What have you been doing in the sublevels all day?" He took a deep breath and blurted out, "Speedy never returned."

Powell's eyes widened momentarily and he stopped on the stairs; then he recovered and resumed his upward steps. He didn't speak until he reached the head of the flight, and then:

"You sent him after the selenium?"

"Yes."

"And how long has he been out?"

"Five hours now."

Silence! This was a devil of a situation. Here they were, on Mercury exactly twelve hours—and already up to the eyebrows in the worst sort of trouble. Mercury had long been the jinx world of the System, but this was drawing it rather strong—even for a jinx.

Powell said, "Start at the beginning, and let's get this straight."

They were in the radio room now—with its already subtly antiquated equipment, untouched for the ten years previous to their arrival. Even ten years, technologically speaking, meant so much. Compare Speedy with the type of robot they must have had back in 2005. But then, advances in robotics these days were tremendous. Powell touched a still gleaming metal surface gingerly. The air of disuse that touched everything about the room—and the entire Station—was infinitely depressing.

Donovan must have felt it. He began: "I tried to locate him by radio, but it was no go. Radio isn't any good on the Mercury Sunside—not past two miles, anyway. That's one of the reasons the First Expedition failed. And we can't put up the ultrawave equipment for weeks yet—"

"Skip all that. What *did* you get?"

"I located the unorganized body signal in the short wave. It was no good for anything except his position. I kept track of him that way for two hours and plotted the results on the map."

There was a yellowed square of parchment in his hip pocket—a relic of the unsuccessful First Expedition—and he slapped it down on the desk with vicious force, spreading it flat with the palm of his hand. Powell, hands clasped across his chest, watched it at long range.

Donovan's pencil pointed nervously. "The red cross is the selenium pool. You marked it yourself."

"Which one is it?" interrupted Powell. "There were three that MacDougal located for us before he left."

"I sent Speedy to the nearest, naturally. Seventeen miles away. But what difference does that make?" There was tension in his voice. "There are the penciled dots that mark Speedy's position."

And for the first time Powell's artificial aplomb was shaken and his hands shot forward for the map.

"Are *you* serious? This is impossible."

"There it is," growled Donovan.

The little dots that marked the position formed a rough circle about the red cross of the selenium pool. And Powell's fingers went to his brown mustache, the unfailing signal of anxiety.

Donovan added: "In the two hours I checked on him, he circled that damned pool four times. It seems likely to me that he'll keep that up forever. Do you realize the position we're in?"

Powell looked up shortly, and said nothing. Oh, yes, he realized the position they were in. It worked itself out as simply as a syllogism. The photo-cell banks that alone stood between the full power of Mercury's monstrous sun and themselves were shot to hell. The only thing that could save them was selenium. The only thing that could get the selenium was Speedy. If Speedy didn't come back, no selenium. No selenium, no photo-cell banks. No photo-banks—well, death by slow broiling is one of the more unpleasant ways of being done in.

Donovan rubbed his red mop of hair savagely and expressed himself with bitterness. "We'll be the laughingstock of the System, Greg. How can everything have gone so wrong so soon? The great team of Powell and Donovan is sent out to Mercy to report on the advisability of reopening the Sunside Mining Station with modern techniques and robots and we ruin everything the first day. A purely routine job, too. We'll never live it down."

"We won't have to, perhaps," replied Powell, quietly. "If we don't do something quickly, living anything down—or even just plain living—will be out of the question."

"Don't be stupid! If you feel funny about it, Greg, I don't. It was criminal, sending us out here with only one robot. And it was *your* bright idea that we could handle the photo-cell banks ourselves."

"Now you're being unfair. It was a mutual decision and you know it. All we needed was a kilogram of selenium, a Stillhead Dielectrode Plate and about three hours' time—and there are pools of pure selenium all over Sunside. MacDougal's spectroreflector spotted three for us in five minutes, didn't it? What the devil! We couldn't have waited for next conjunction."

"Well, what are we going to do? Powell, you've got an idea. I know you have, or you wouldn't be so calm. You're no more a hero than I am. Go on, spill it!"

"We can't go after Speedy ourselves, Mike—not on the Sunside. Even the new insosuits aren't good for more than twenty minutes in direct sunlight. But you know the old saying, 'Set a robot to catch a robot.' Look, Mike, maybe things aren't so bad. We've got six robots down in the sublevels, that we may be able to use, if they work. *If* they work."

There was a glint of sudden hope in Donovan's eyes. "You mean six robots from the First Expedition. Are you sure? They may be subrobotic machines. Ten years is a long time as far as robot-types are concerned, you know."

"No, they're robots. I've spent all day with them and I know. They've got positronic brains: primitive, of course." He placed the map in his pocket. "Let's go down."

* * *

The robots were on the lowest sublevel—all six of them surrounded by musty packing cases of uncertain content. They were large, extremely so, and even though they were in a sitting position on the floor, legs straddled out before them, their heads were a good seven feet in the air.

Donovan whistled. "Look at the size of them, will you? The chests must be ten feet around."

"That's because they're supplied with the old McGuffy gears. I've been over the insides—crummiest set you've ever seen."

"Have you powered them yet?"

"No. There wasn't any reason to. I don't think there's anything wrong with them. Even the diaphragm is in reasonable order. They might talk."

He had unscrewed the chest plate of the nearest as he spoke, inserted the two-inch sphere that contained the tiny spark of atomic energy that was a robot's life. There was difficulty in fitting it, but he managed, and then screwed the plate back on again in laborious fashion. The radio controls of more modern models had not been heard of ten years earlier. And then to the other five.

Donovan said uneasily, "They haven't moved."

"No orders to do so," replied Powell, succinctly. He went back to the first in the line and struck him on the chest. "You! Do you hear me?"

The monster's head bent slowly and the eyes fixed themselves on Powell. Then, in a harsh, squawking voice—like that of a medieval phonograph, he grated, "Yes, Master!"

Powell grinned humorlessly at Donovan. "Did you get that? Those were the days of the first talking robots when it looked as if the use of robots on Earth would be banned. The makers were fighting that and they build good, healthy slave complexes into the damned machines."

"It didn't help them," muttered Donovan.

"No, it didn't, but they sure tried." He turned once more to the robot. "Get up!"

The robot towered upward slowly and Donovan's head craned and his puckered lips whistled.

Powell said: "Can you go out upon the surface? In the light?"

There was consideration while the robot's slow brain worked. Then, "Yes, Master."

"Good. Do you know what a mile is?"

Another consideration, and another slow answer. "Yes, Master."

"We will take you up to the surface then, and indicate a direction. You will go about seventeen miles, and somewhere in that general region you will meet another robot, smaller than yourself. You understand so far?"

"Yes, Master."

"You will find this robot and order him to return. If he does not wish to, you are to bring him back by force."

Donovan clutched at Powell's sleeve. "Why not send him for the selenium direct?"

"Because I want Speedy back, nitwit. I want to find out what's wrong with him." And to the robot, "All right, you, follow me."

The robot remained motionless and his voice rumbled: "Pardon, Master, but I cannot. You must mount first." His clumsy arms had come together with a thwack, blunt fingers interlacing.

Powell stared and then pinched at his mustache. "Uh . . . oh!"

Donovan's eyes bulged. "We've got to ride him? Like a horse?"

"I guess that's the idea. I don't know why, though. I can't see—Yes, I do. I told you they were playing up robot-safety in those days. Evidently, they were going to sell the notion of safety by not allowing them to move about, without a mahout on their shoulders all the time. What do we do now?"

"That's what I've been thinking," muttered Donovan. "We can't go out on the surface, with a robot or without. Oh, for the love of Pete"—and he snapped his fingers twice. He grew excited. "Give me that map you've got. I haven't studied it for two hours for nothing. This is a Mining Station. What's wrong with using the tunnels?"

The Mining Station was a black circle on the map, and the light dotted lines that were tunnels stretched out about it in spiderweb fashion.

Donovan studied the list of symbols at the bottom of the map. "Look," he said, "the small black dots are openings to the surface, and here's one maybe three miles away from the selenium pool. There's a number here—you'd think they'd write larger—13a. If the robots know their way around here—"

Powell shot the question and received the dull "Yes, Master," in reply. "Get your insosuit," he said with satisfaction.

It was the first time either had worn the insosuits—which marked one time more than either had expected to upon their arrival the day before—and they tested their limb movements uncomfortably.

The insosuit was far bulkier and far uglier than the regulation spacesuit; but withal considerably lighter, due to the fact that they were entirely nonmetallic in composition. Composed of heat-resistant plastic and chemically treated cork layers, and equipped with a desiccating unit to keep the air bone-dry, the insosuits could withstand the full glare of Mercury's sun for twenty minutes. Five to ten minutes more, as well, without actually killing the occupant.

And still the robot's hands formed the stirrup, nor did he betray the slightest atom of surprise at the grotesque figure into which Powell had been converted.

Powell's radio-harshened voice boomed out: "Are you ready to take us to Exit 13a?"

"Yes, Master."

Good, thought Powell; they might lack radio control but at least they were fitted for radio reception. "Mount one or the other, Mike," he said to Donovan.

He placed a foot in the improvised stirrup and swung upward. He found the seat comfortable; there was the humped back of the robot, evidently shaped for the purpose, a shallow groove along each shoulder for the thighs and two elongated "ears" whose purpose now seemed obvious.

Powell seized the ears and twisted the head. His mount turned ponderously. "Lead on, Macduff." But he did not feel at all light-hearted.

The gigantic robots moved slowly, with mechanical precision, through the doorway and cleared their heads by a scant foot, so that the two men had to duck hurriedly, along a narrow corridor in which their unhurried footsteps boomed monotonously and into the air lock.

The long, airless tunnel that stretched to a pinpoint before them brought home forcefully to Powell the exact magnitude of the task accomplished by the First Expedition, with their crude robots and their start-from-scratch necessities. They might have been a failure, but their failure was a good deal better than the usual run of the System's successes.

The robots plodded onward with a pace that never varied and with footsteps that never lengthened.

Powell said: "Notice that these tunnels are blazing with lights and that the temperature is Earth-normal. It's probably been like this all the ten years that this place has remained empty."

"How's that?"

"Cheap energy; cheapest in the System. Sunpower, you know, and on Mercury's Sunside, sunpower is *something*. That's why the Station was built in the sunlight rather than in the shadow of a mountain. It's really a huge energy converter. The heat is turned into electricity, light, mechanical work and what have you; so that energy is supplied and the Station is cooled in a simultaneous process."

"Look," said Donovan. "This is all very educational, but would you mind changing the subject? It so happens that this conversion of energy that you talk about is carried on by the photo-cell banks mainly—and that is a tender subject with me at the moment."

Powell grunted vaguely, and when Donovan broke the resulting silence, it was to change the subject completely. "Listen, Greg. What the devil's wrong with Speedy, anyway? I can't understand it."

It's not easy to shrug shoulders in an insosuit, but Powell tried it. "I don't know, Mike. You know he's perfectly adapted to a Mercurian environment. Heat doesn't mean anything to him and he's built for the light gravity and the broken ground. He's foolproof—or, at least, he should be."

Silence fell. This time, silence that lasted.

"Master," said the robot, "we are here."

"Eh?" Powell snapped out of a semidrowse. "Well, get us out of here—out to the surface."

They found themselves in a tiny substation, empty, airless, ruined. Donovan had inspected a jagged hole in the upper reaches of one of the walls by the light of his pocket flash.

"Meteorite, do you suppose?" he has asked.

Powell shrugged. "To hell with that. It doesn't matter. Let's get out."

A towering cliff of a black, basaltic rock cut off the sunlight, and the deep night shadow of an airless world surrounded them. Before them, the shadow reached out and ended in knife-edge abruptness into an all-but-unbearable blaze of white light, that glittered from myriad crystals along a rocky ground.

"Space!" gasped Donovan. "It looks like snow." And it did.

Powell's eyes swept the jagged glitter of Mercury to the horizon and winced at the gorgeous brilliance.

"This must be an unusual area," he said. "The general albedo of Mercury is low and most of the soil is gray pumice. Something like the Moon, you know. Beautiful, isn't it?"

He was thankful for the light filters in their visiplates. Beautiful or not, a look at the sunlight through straight glass would have blinded them inside half a minute.

Donovan was looking at the spring thermometer on his wrist. "Holy smokes, the temperature is eighty centigrade!"

Powell checked his own and said: "Um-m-m. A little high. Atmosphere, you know."

"On Mercury? Are you nuts?"

"Mercury isn't really airless," explained Powell, in absent-minded fashion. He was adjusting the binocular attachments to his visiplate, and the bloated fingers of the insosuit were clumsy at it. "There is a thin exhalation that clings to its surface—vapors of the more volatile elements and compounds that are heavy enough for Mercurian gravity to retain. You know: selenium, iodine, mercury, gallium, potassium, bismuth, volatile oxides. The vapors sweep into the shadows and condense, giving up heat. It's a sort of gigantic still. In fact, if you use your flash, you'll probably find that the side of the cliff is covered with, say, hoar-sulphur, or maybe quicksilver dew.

"It doesn't matter, though. Our suits can stand a measly eighty indefinitely."

Powell had adjusted the binocular attachments, so that he seemed as eye-stalked as a snail.

Donovan watched tensely. "See anything?"

The other did not answer immediately, and when he did, his voice was anxious and thoughtful. "There's a dark spot on the horizon that might be the selenium pool. It's in the right place. But I don't see Speedy."

Powell clambered upward in an instinctive striving for better view, till he was standing in unsteady fashion upon his robot's shoulders. Legs straddled wide, eyes straining, he said: "I think . . . I think—Yes, it's definitely he. He's coming this way."

Donovan followed the pointing finger. He had no binoculars, but there was a tiny moving dot, black against the blazing brilliance of the crystalline ground.

"I see him," he yelled. "Let's get going!"

Powell had hopped down into a sitting position on the robot again, and his suited hand slapped against the Gargantuan's barrel chest. "Get going!"

"Giddy-ap," yelled Donovan, and thumped his heels, spur fashion.

* * *

The robots started off, the regular thudding of their footsteps silent in the airlessness, for the nonmetallic fabric of the insosuits did not transmit sound. There was only a rhythmic vibration just below the border of actual hearing.

"Faster," yelled Donovan. The rhythm did not change.

"No use," cried Powell, in reply. "These junk heaps are only geared to one speed. Do you think they're equipped with selective flexors?"

They had burst through the shadow, and the sunlight came down in a white-hot wash and poured liquidly about them.

Donovan ducked involuntarily. "Wow! Is it imagination or do I feel heat?"

"You'll feel more presently," was the grim reply. "Keep you eye on Speedy."

Robot SPD13 was near enough to be seen in detail now. His graceful, streamlined body threw out blazing highlights as he loped with easy speed across the broken ground. His name was derived from his serial initials, of course, but it was apt, nevertheless, for the SPD models were among the fastest robots turned out by the United States Robots and Mechanical Men Corporation.

"Hey, Speedy," howled Donovan, and waved a frantic hand.

"Speedy!" shouted Powell. "Come here!"

The distance between the men and the errant robot was being cut down momentarily—more by the efforts of Speedy than the slow plodding of the ten-year-old antique mounts of Donovan and Powell.

They were close enough now to notice that Speedy's gait included a peculiar rolling stagger, a noticeable side-to-side lurch—and then, as Powell waved his hand again and sent maximum juice into his compact head-set radio sender, in preparation for another shout, Speedy looked up and saw them.

Speedy hopped to a halt and remained standing for a moment — with just a tiny, unsteady weave, as though he were swaying in a light wind.

Powell yelled: "All right, Speedy. Come here, boy."

Whereupon Speedy's robot voice sounded in Powell's earphones for the first time.

It said: "Hot dog, let's play games. You catch me and I catch you; no love can cut our knife in two. For I'm Little Buttercup, sweet Little Buttercup. Whoops!" Turning on his heel, he sped off in the direction from which he had come, with a speed and fury that kicked up gouts of baked dust.

And his last words as he receded into the distance were, "There grew a little flower 'neath a great oak tree," followed by a curious metallic clicking that *might* have been a robotic equivalent of a hiccup.

Donovan said weakly: "Where did he pick up the Gilbert and Sullivan? Say, Greg, he . . . he's drunk or something."

"If you hadn't told me," was the bitter response, "I'd never realize it. Let's get back to the cliff. I'm roasting."

It was Powell who broke the desperate silence. "In the first place," he said, "Speedy isn't drunk—not in the human sense—because he's a robot, and robots don't get drunk. However, there's *something* wrong with him which is the robotic equivalent of drunkenness."

"To me, he's drunk," stated Donovan, emphatically, "and all I know is that he thinks we're playing games. And we're not. It's a matter of life and very gruesome death."

"All right. Don't hurry me. A robot's only a robot. Once we find out what's wrong with him, we can fix it and go on."

"*Once*," said Donovan, sourly.

Powell ignored him. "Speedy is perfectly adapted to normal Mercurian environment. But this region"—and his arm swept wide—"is definitely abnormal. There's our clue. Now where do these crystals come from? They might have formed from a slowly cooling liquid; but where would you get liquid so hot that it would cool in Mercury's sun?"

"Volcanic action," suggested Donovan, instantly, and Powell's body tensed.

"Out of the mouths of sucklings," he said in a small, strange voice, and remained very still for five minutes.

Then, he said, "Listen, Mike, what did you say to Speedy when you sent him after the selenium?"

Donovan was taken aback. "Well damn it—I don't know. I just told him to get it."

"Yes, I know. But how? Try to remember the exact words."

"I said . . . uh . . . I said: 'Speedy, we need some selenium. You can get it such-and-such a place. Go get it.' That's all. What more did you want me to say?"

"You didn't put any urgency into the order, did you?"

"What for? It was pure routine."

Powell sighed. "Well, it can't be helped now—but we're in a fine fix." He had dismounted from his robot, and was sitting, back against the cliff. Donovan joined him and they linked arms. In the distance the burning sunlight seemed to wait cat-and-mouse for them, and just next to them, the two giant robots were invisible but for the dull red of their photoelectric eyes that stared down at them, unblinking, unwavering and unconcerned.

Unconcerned! As was all this poisonous Mercury, as large in jinx as it was small in size.

Powell's radio voice was tense in Donovan's ear: "Now, look, let's start with the three fundamental Rules of Robotics—the three rules that are built most deeply into a robot's positronic brain." In the darkness, his gloved fingers ticked off each point.

"We have: One, a robot may not injure a human being, or, through inaction, allow a human being to come to harm."

"Right!"

"Two," continued Powell, "a robot must obey the orders given it by human beings except where such orders would conflict with the First Law."

"Right!"

"And three, a robot must protect its own existence as long as such protection does not conflict with the First or Second Laws."

"Right! Now where are we?"

"Exactly at the explanation. The conflict between the various rules is ironed out by the different positronic potentials in the brain. We'll say that a robot is walking into danger and knows it. The automatic potential that Rule 3 sets up turns him back. But suppose you *order* him to walk into that danger. In that case, Rule 2 sets up a counterpotential higher than the previous one and the robot follows orders at the risk of existence."

"Well, I know that. What about it?"

"Let's take Speedy's case. Speedy is one of the latest models, extremely specialized, and as expensive as a battleship. It's not a thing to be lightly destroyed."

"So?"

"So Rule 3 has been strengthened—that was specifically mentioned, by the way, in the advance notices on the SPD models—so that his allergy to danger is unusually high. At the same time, when you sent him out after the selenium, you gave him his order casually and without special emphasis, so that the Rule 2 potential set-up was rather weak. Now, hold on; I'm just stating facts."

"All right, go ahead. I think I get it."

"You see how it works, don't you? There's some sort of danger centering at the selenium pool. It increases as he approaches, and at a certain distance from it the Rule 3 potential, unusually high to start with, exactly balances the Rule 2 potential, unusually low to start with."

Donovan rose to his feet in excitement. "And it strikes an equilibrium. I see. Rule 3 drives him back and Rule 2 drives him forward—"

"So he follows a circle around the selenium pool, staying on the locus of all points of potential equilibrium. And unless we do something about it, he'll stay on that circle forever, giving us the good old runaround." Then, more thoughtfully: "And that, by the way, is what makes him drunk. At potential equilibrium, half the positronic paths of his brain are out of kilter. I'm not a robot specialist, but that seems obvious. Probably he's lost control of just those parts of his voluntary mechanism that a human drunk has. Ve-e-ery pretty."

"But what's the danger? If we knew what he was running from—"

"*You* suggested it. Volcanic action. Somewhere right above the selenium pool is a seepage of gas from the bowels of Mercury. Sulphur dioxide, carbon dioxide—and carbon monoxide. Lots of it—and at this temperature."

Donovan gulped audibly. "Carbon monoxide plus iron gives the volatile iron carbonyl."

"And a robot," added Powell, "is essentially iron." Then, grimly: "There's nothing like deduction. We've determined everything about our problem but the solution. We can't get the selenium ourselves. It's still too far. We can't send these robot horses, because they can't go themselves, and they can't carry us fast enough to keep us from crisping. And we can't catch Speedy, because the dope thinks we're playing games, and he can run sixty miles to our four."

"If one of us goes," began Donovan, tentatively, "and comes back cooked, there'll still be the other."

"Yes," came the sarcastic reply, "it would be a most tender sacrifice—except that a person would be in no condition to give orders before he ever reaches the pool, and I don't think the robots would ever turn back to the cliff without orders. Figure it out! We're two or three miles from the pool—call it two—the robot travels at four miles an hour—and we can last twenty minutes in our suits. It isn't only the heat, remember. Solar radiation out here in the ultraviolet and below is *poison*."

"Um-m-m," said Donovan, "ten minutes short."

"As good as an eternity. And another thing. In order for Rule 3 potential to have stopped Speedy where it did, there must be an appreciable amount of carbon monoxide in the metal-vapor atmosphere—and there must be an appreciable corrosive action therefore. He's been out hours now—and how do we know when a knee joint, for instance, won't be thrown out of kilter and keel him over. It's not only a question of thinking—we've got to think *fast!*"

Deep, dark, dank, dismal silence!

Donovan broke it, voice trembling in an effort to keep itself emotionless. He said: "As long as we can't increase Rule 2 potential by giving further orders, how about working the other way? If we increase the danger, we increase Rule 3 potential and drive him backward."

Powell's visiplate had turned toward him in a silent question.

"You see," came the cautious explanation, "all we need to do to drive him out of his rut is to increase the concentration of carbon monoxide in his vicinity. Well, back at the Station there's a complete analytical laboratory."

"Naturally," assented Powell. "It's a Mining Station."

"All right. There must be pounds of oxalic acid for calcium precipitations."

"Holy space! Mike, you're a genius."

"So-so," admitted Donovan, modestly. "It's just a case of remembering that oxalic acid on heating decomposes into carbon dioxide, water, and good old carbon monoxide. College chem, you know."

Powell was on his feet and had attracted the attention of one of the monster robots by the simple expedient of pounding the machine's thigh.

"Hey," he shouted, "can you throw?"

"Master?"

"Never mind." Powell damned the robot's molasses-slow brain. He scrabbled up a jagged brick-size rock. "Take this," he said, "and hit the patch of bluish crystals just across that crooked fissure. You see it?"

Donovan pulled at his shoulder. "Too far, Greg. It's almost half a mile off."

"Quiet," replied Powell. "It's a case of Mercurian gravity and a steel throwing arm. Watch, will you?"

The robot's eyes were measuring the distance with machinely accurate stereoscopy. His arm adjusted itself to the weight of the missile and drew back. In the darkness, the robot's motions went unseen, but there was a sudden thumping sound as he shifted his weight, and seconds later the rock flew blackly into the sunlight. There was no air resistance to slow it down, nor wind to turn it aside—and when it hit the ground it threw up crystals precisely in the center of the "blue patch."

Powell yelled happily and shouted, "Let's go back after the oxalic acid, Mike."

And as they plunged into the ruined substation on the way back to the tunnels, Donovan said grimly: "Speedy's been hanging about on this side of the selenium pool, ever since we chased after him. Did you see him?"

"Yes."

"I guess he wants to play games. Well, we'll play his games!"

* * *

They were back hours later, with three-liter jars of the white chemical and a pair of long faces. The photo-cell banks were deteriorating more rapidly than had seemed likely. The two steered their robots into the sunlight and toward the waiting Speedy in silence and with grim purpose.

Speedy galloped slowly toward them. "Here we are again. *Whee!* I've made a little list, the piano organist; all people who eat peppermint and puff it in your face."

"We'll puff something in *your* face," muttered Donovan. "He's limping, Greg."

"I noticed that," came the low, worried response. "The monoxide'll get him yet, if we don't hurry."

They were approaching cautiously now, almost sidling, to refrain from setting off the thoroughly irrational robot. Powell was too far off to tell, of course, but even already he could have sworn the crack-brained Speedy was setting himself for a spring.

"Let her go," he gasped. "Count three! One—two—"

Two steel arms drew back and snapped forward simultaneously and two glass jars whirled forward in towering parallel arcs, gleaming like diamonds in the impossible sun. And in a pair of soundless puffs, they hit the ground behind Speedy in crashes that sent the oxalic acid flying like dust.

In the full heat of Mercury's sun, Powell knew it was fizzing like soda water.

Speedy turned to stare, then backed away from it slowly—and as slowly gathered speed. In fifteen seconds, he was leaping directly toward the two humans in an unsteady canter.

Powell did not get Speedy's words just then, though he heard something that resembled, "Lover's professions when uttered in Hessians."

He turned away. "Back to the cliff, Mike. He's out of the rut and he'll be taking orders now. I'm getting hot."

They jogged toward the shadow at the slow monotonous pace of their mounts, and it was not until they entered it and felt the sudden coolness settle softly about them that Donovan looked back. "*Greg!*"

Powell looked and almost shrieked. Speedy was moving slowly now—so slowly—and in the *wrong direction.* He was drifting; drifting back into his rut; and he was picking up speed. He looked dreadfully close, and dreadfully unreachable, in the binoculars.

Donovan shouted wildly, "After him!" and thumped his robot into its pace, but Powell called him back.

"You won't catch him, Mike—it's no use." He fidgeted on his robot's shoulders and clenched his fist in tight impotence. "Why the devil do I see these things five seconds after it's all over? Mike, we've wasted hours."

"We need more oxalic acid," declared Donovan, stolidly. "The concentration wasn't high enough."

"Seven tons of it wouldn't have been enough—and we haven't the hours to spare to get it, even if it were, with the monoxide chewing him away. Don't you see what it is, Mike?"

And Donovan said flatly, "No."

"We were only establishing new equilibriums. When we create new monoxide and increase Rule 3 potential, he moves backward till he's in balance again—and when the monoxide drifted away, he moved forward, and again there was balance."

Powell's voice sounded thoroughly wretched. "It's the same old runaround. We can push at Rule 2 and pull at Rule 3 and we can't get anywhere—we can only change the position of balance. We've got to get outside both rules." And then he pushed his robot closer to Donovan's so that they were sitting face to face, dim shadows in the darkness, and he whispered, "Mike!"

"Is it the finish?"—dully. "I suppose we go back to the Station, wait for the banks to fold, shake hands, take cyanide, and go out like gentlemen." He laughed shortly.

"Mike," repeated Powell earnestly, "we've got to get Speedy."

"I know."

"Mike," once more, and Powell hesitated before continuing. "There's always Rule 1. I thought of it—earlier—but it's desperate."

Donovan looked up and his voice livened. "*We're* desperate."

"All right. According to Rule 1, a robot can't see a human come to harm because of his own inaction. 2 and 3 can't stand against it. They *can't* Mike."

"Even when the robot is half cra— Well, he's drunk. You know he is."

"It's the chances you take."

"Cut it. What are you going to do?"

"I'm going out there now and see what Rule 1 will do. If it won't break the balance, then what the devil—it's either now or three-four days from now."

"Hold on, Greg. There are human rules of behavior, too. You don't go out there just like that. Figure out a lottery, and give me *my* chance."

"All right. First to get the cube of fourteen goes." And almost immediately, "Twenty-seven forty-four!"

Donovan felt his robot stagger at a sudden push by Powell's mount and then Powell was off into the sunlight. Donovan opened his mouth to shout, and then clicked it shut. Of course, the damn fool had worked out the cube of fourteen in advance, and on purpose. Just like him.

* * *

The sun was hotter than ever and Powell felt a maddening itch in the small of his back. Imagination, probably, or perhaps hard radiation beginning to tell even through the insosuit.

Speedy was watching him, without a word of Gilbert and Sullivan gibberish as greeting. Thank God for that! But he daren't get too close.

He was three hundred yards away when Speedy began backing, a step at a time, cautiously—and Powell stopped. He jumped from his robot's shoulders and landed on the crystalline ground with a light thump and a flying of jagged fragments.

He proceeded on foot, the ground gritty and slippery to his steps, the low gravity causing him difficulty. The soles of his feet tickled with warmth. He cast one glance over his shoulder at the blackness of the cliff's shadow and realized that he had come too far to return—either by himself or by the help of his antique robot. It was Speedy or nothing now, and the knowledge of that constricted his chest.

Far enough! He stopped.

"Speedy," he called. "Speedy!"

The sleek, modern robot ahead of him hesitated and halted his backward steps, then resumed them.

Powell tried to put a note of pleading into his voice, and found it didn't take much acting. "Speedy, I've got to get back to the shadow or the sun'll get me. It's life or death, Speedy. I need you."

Speedy took one step forward and stopped. He spoke, but at the sound Powell groaned, for it was, "When you're lying awake with a dismal headache and repose is tabooed—" It trailed off there, and Powell took time out for some reason to murmur, "Iolanthe."

It was roasting hot! He caught a movement out of the corner of his eye, and whirled dizzily; then stared in utter astonishment, for the monstrous robot on which he had ridden was moving—moving toward him, and without a rider.

He was talking: "Pardon, Master. I must not move without a Master upon me, but you are in danger."

Of course, Rule 1 potential above everything. But he didn't want that clumsy antique; he wanted Speedy. He walked away and motioned frantically: "I order you to stay away. I *order* you to stop!"

It was quite useless. You could not beat Rule 1 potential. The robot said stupidly, "You are in danger, Master."

Powell looked about him desperately. He couldn't see clearly. His brain was in a heated whirl; his breath scorched when he breathed, and the ground all about him was a shimmering haze.

He called a last time, desperately: "*Speedy!* I'm dying, damn you! Where are you? Speedy, I *need* you."

He was still stumbling backward in a blind effort to get away from the giant robot he didn't want, when he felt steel fingers on his arm, and a worried, apologetic voice of metallic timbre in his ears.

"Holy smokes, boss, what are you doing here? And what am *I* doing—I'm so confused—"

"Never mind," murmured Powell, weakly. "Get me to the shadow of the cliff—and hurry!" There was one last feeling of being lifted into the air and a sensation of rapid motion and burning heat, and he passed out.

* * *

He woke with Donovan bending over him and smiling anxiously. "How are you, Greg?"

"Fine!" came the response. "Where's Speedy?"

"Right here. I sent him out to one of the other selenium pools—with orders to get the selenium at all cost this time. He got it back in forty-two minutes and three seconds. I timed him. He still hasn't finished apologizing for the runaround he gave us. He's scared to come near you for fear of what you'll say."

"Drag him over," ordered Powell. "It wasn't his fault." He held out a hand and gripped Speedy's metal paw. "It's O.K., Speedy." Then, to Donovan, "You know, Mike, I was just thinking—"

"Yes!"

"Well,"—he rubbed his face—the air was so delightfully cool, "you know that when we get things set up here and Speedy put through his Field Tests, they're going to send us to the Space Station next—"

"No!"

"Yes! At least that's what old lady Calvin told me just before we left, and I didn't say anything about it, because I was going to fight the whole idea."

"Fight it?" cried Donovan. "But—"

"I know. It's all right with me now. Two hundred seventy-three degrees Centigrade below zero. Won't it be a pleasure?"

"Space Station," said Donovan, "here I come."

Death Sentence

Brand Gorla smiled uncomfortably, "These things exaggerate, you know."

"No, no, no!" The little man's albino-pink eyes snapped. "Dorlis was great when no human had ever entered the Vegan System. It was the capital of a Galactic Confederation greater than ours."

"Well, then, let's say that it was an ancient capital. I'll admit that and leave the rest to an archaeologist."

"Archaeologists are no use. What I've discovered needs a specialist in its own field. And you're on the Board."

Brand Gorla looked doubtful. He remembered Theor Realo in senior year—a little white misfit of a human who skulked somewhere in the background of his reminiscences. It has been a long time ago, but the albino had been queer. *That* was easy to remember. And he was still queer.

"I'll try to help," Brand said, "if you'll tell me what you want."

Theor watched intently, "I want you to place certain facts before the Board. Will you promise that?"

Brand hedged, "Even if I help you along, Theor, I'll have to remind you that I'm junior member of the Psychological Board. I haven't much influence."

"You must do your best. The facts will speak for themselves." The albino's hands were trembling.

"Go ahead." Brand resigned himself. The man was an old school fellow. You couldn't be *too* arbitrary about things.

Brand Gorla leaned back and relaxed. The light of Arcturus shone through the ceiling-high windows, diffused and mellowed by the polarizing glass. Even this diluted version of sunlight was too much for the pink eyes of the other, and he shaded his eyes as he spoke.

"I've lived on Dorlis twenty-five years, Brand," he said. "I've poked into places no one today knew existed, and I've found things. Dorlis was the scientific and cultural capital of a civilization greater than ours. Yes it was, and particularly in psychology."

"Things in the past always seem greater." Brand condescended a smile. "There is a theorem to that effect which you'll find in any elementary text. Freshmen invariably call it the 'GOD Theorem.' Stands for 'Good-Old-Days,' you know. But go on."

Theor frowned at the digression. He hid the beginning of a sneer, "You can always dismiss an uncomfortable fact by pinning a dowdy label to it. But tell me this. What do you know of Psychological Engineering?"

Brand shrugged, "No such thing. Anyway, not in the strict mathematical sense. All propaganda and advertising is a crude form of hit-and-miss Psych Engineering—and pretty effective sometimes. Maybe that's what you mean."

"Not at all. I mean actual experimentation, with masses of people, under controlled conditions, and over a period of years."

"Such things have been discussed. It's not feasible in practice. Our social structure couldn't stand much of it, and we don't know enough to set up effective controls."

Theor suppressed excitement, "But the ancients *did* know enough. And they *did* set up controls."

Brand considered phlegmatically, "Startling and interesting, but how do you know?"

"Because I found the documents relating to it." He paused breathlessly. "An entire planet, Brand. A complete world picked to suit, peopled with beings under strict control from every angle. Studied, and charted, and experimented upon. Don't you get the picture?"

Brand noted none of the usual stimgata of mental uncontrol. A closer investigation, perhaps—

He said evenly, "You must have been misled. It's thoroughly impossible. You can't control humans like that. Too many variables."

"And that's the point, Brand. They weren't humans."

"What?"

"They were robots, positronic robots. A whole world of them, Brand, with nothing to do but live and react and be observed by a set of psychologists that were *real* psychologists."

"That's mad!"

"I have proof—because that robot world still exists. The First Confederation went to pieces, but that robot world kept on going. It still exists."

"And how do you know?"

Theor Realo stood up. "Because I've been there these last twenty-five years!"

* * *

The Board Master threw his formal red-edged gown aside and reached into a pocket for a long, gnarled and decidedly unofficial cigar.

"Preposterous," he grunted, "and thoroughly insane."

"Exactly," said Brand, "and I can't spring it on the Board just like that. They wouldn't listen. I've got to get this across to you first, and then, if you can put your authority behind it—"

"Oh, nuts! I never heard anything as—Who is the fellow?"

Brand sighed, "A crank, I'll admit that. He was in my class at Arcturus U. and a crack-pot albino even then. Maladjusted as the devil, hipped on ancient history, and just the kind that gets an idea and goes through with it by plain, dumb plugging. He's poked about in Dorlis for twenty-five years, he says. He's got the complete records of practically an entire civilization."

The Board Master puffed furiously. "Yeah, I know. In the telestat serials, the brilliant amateur always uncovers the great things. The free lance. The lone wolf. Nuts! Have you consulted the Department of Archaeology?"

"Certainly. And the result was interesting. No one bothers with Dorlis. This isn't just ancient history, you see. It's a matter of fifteen thousand years. It's practically myth. Reputable archaeologists don't waste too much time with it. It's just the thing a book-struck layman with a single-track mind *would* uncover. After this, of course, if the business turns out right, Dorlis will become an archaeologist's paradise."

The Board Master screwed his homely face into an appalling grimace. "It's very unflattering to the ego. If there's any truth in all this, the so-called First Confederation must have had a grasp of psychology so far past ours, as to make us out to be blithering imbeciles. Too, they'd have to build positronic robots that would be about seventy-five orders of magnitude above anything we've even blue-printed. Galaxy! Think of the mathematics involved."

"Look, sir, I've consulted just about everybody. I wouldn't bring this thing to you if I weren't certain that I had every angle checked. I went to Blak just about the first thing, and he's consultant mathematician to United Robots. He says there's no limit to these things. Given the time, the money, and the *advance in psychology*—get that—robots like that could be built right now."

"What proof has he?"

"Who, Blak?"

"No, no! Your friend. The albino. You said he had papers."

"He has. I've got them here. He's got documents—and there's no denying their antiquity. I've had that checked every way from Sunday.

I can't read them, of course. I don't know if anyone can, except Theor Realo."

"That's stacking the deck, isn't it? We have to take his say-so."

"Yes, in a way. But he doesn't claim to be able to decipher more than portions. He says it is related to ancient Centaurian, and I've put linguists to work on it. It can be cracked and if his translation isn't accurate, we'll know about it."

"All right. Let's see it."

Brand Gorla brought out the plastic-mounted documents. The Board Master tossed them aside and reached for the translation. Smoke billowed as he read.

"Humph," was his comment. "Further details are on Dorlis, I suppose."

"Theor claims that there are some hundred to two hundred tons of blueprints altogether, on the brain plan of the positronic robots alone. They're still there in the original vault. But that's the least of it. He's been on the robot world itself. He's got photocasts, teletype recordings, all sorts of details. They're not integrated, and obviously the work of a layman who knows next to nothing about psychology. Even so, he's managed to get enough data to prove pretty conclusively that the world he was on wasn't . . . uh . . . natural."

"You've got that with you, too."

"All of it. Most of it's on microfilm, but I've brought the projector. Here are your eyepieces."

An hour later, the Board Master said, "I'll call a Board Meeting tomorrow and push this through."

Brand Gorla grinned tightly, "We'll send a commission to Dorlis?"

"When," said the Board Master dryly, "and if we can get an appropriation out of the University for such an affair. Leave this material with me for the while, please. I want to study it a little more."

* * *

Theoretically, the Governmental Department of Science and Technology exercises administrative control over all scientific investigation. Actually, however, the pure research groups of the large universities are thoroughly autonomous bodies, and, as a general rule, the Government does not care to dispute that. But a general rule is not necessarily a universal rule.

And so, although the Board Master scowled and fumed and swore, there was no way of refusing Wynne Murry an interview. To give

Murry his complete title, he was under secretary in charge of psychology, psychopathy and mental technology. And he was a pretty fair psychologist in his own right.

So the Board Master might glare, but that was all.

Secretary Murry ignored the glare cheerfully. He rubbed his long chin against the grain and said, "It amounts to a case of insufficient information. Shall we put it that way?"

The Board Master said frigidly, "I don't see what information you want. The government's say in university appropriations is purely advisory, and in this case, I might say, the advice is unwelcome."

Murry shrugged, "I have no quarrel with the appropriation. But you're not going to leave the planet without government permit. That's where the insufficient information comes in."

"There is no information other than we've given you."

"But things have leaked out. All this is childish and rather unnecessary secrecy."

The old psychologist flushed. "Secrecy! If you don't know the academic way of life, I can't help you. Investigations, especially those of major importance, aren't, and can't be, made public, until definite progress has been made. When we get back, we'll send you copies of whatever papers we publish."

Murry shook his head, "Uh-uh. Not enough. You're going to Dorlis, aren't you?"

"We've informed the Department of Science of that."

"Why?"

"Why do you want to know?"

"Because it's big, or the Board Master wouldn't go himself. What's this about an older civilization and a world of robots?"

"Well, then, you know."

"Only vague notions we've been able to scrabble up. I want the details."

"There are none that we know now. We won't know until we're on Dorlis."

"Then I'm going with you."

"What!"

"You see, I want the details, too."

"Why?"

"Ah," Murry unfolded his legs and stood up, "now *you're* asking the questions. It's no use, now. I know that the universities aren't keen on government supervision; and I know that I can expect no willing help from *any* academic source. But, by Arcturus, I'm going to get help this time, and I don't care how you fight it. Your expedition is going nowhere, unless I go with you— representing the government."

* * *

Dorlis, as a world, is not impressive. Its importance to Galactic economy is nil, its position far off the great trade routes, its natives backward and unenlightened, its history obscure. And yet somewhere in the heaps of rubble that clutter an ancient world, there is obscure evidence of an influx of flame and destruction that destroyed the Dorlis of an earlier day—the greater capital of a greater Federation.

And somewhere in that rubble, men of a newer world poked and probed and tried to understand.

The Board Master shook his head and then pushed back his grizzling hair. He hadn't shaved in a week.

"The trouble is," he said, "that we have no point of reference. The language can be broken, I suppose, but nothing can be done with the notation."

"I think a great deal has been done."

"Stabs in the dark! Guessing games based on the translations of your albino friend. I won't base any hopes on that."

Brand said, "Nuts! You spent two years on the Nimiam Anomaly, and so far only two months on this, which happens to be a hundred thousand times the job. It's something else that's getting you." He smiled grimly. "It doesn't take a psychologist to see that the government man is in your hair."

The Board Master bit the end off a cigar and spat it four feet. He said slowly, "There are three things about the mule-headed idiot that make me sore. First, I don't like government interference. Second, I don't like a stranger sniffing about when we're on top of the biggest thing in the history of psychology. Third, what in the Galaxy does he want? *What is he after?*"

"I don't know."

"What *should* he be after? Have you thought of it at all?"

"No. Frankly, I don't care. I'd ignore him if I were you."

"You would," said the Board Master violently. "You would! You think the government's entrance into this affair need only be ignored. I suppose you know that this Murry calls himself a psychologist?"

"I know that."

"And I suppose you know he's been displaying a devouring interest in all that we've been doing."

"That, I should say, would be natural."

"Oh! And you know further—" His voice dropped with startling suddenness. "All right, Murry's at the door. Take it easy."

Wynne Murry grinned a greeting, but the Board Master nodded unsmilingly.

"Well, sir," said Murry bluffly, "do you know I've been on my feet for forty-eight hours? You've *got* something here. Something big."

"Thank you."

"No, no. I'm serious. The robot world exists."

"Did you think it didn't?"

The secretary shrugged amiably. "One has a certain natural skepticism. What are your future plans?"

"Why do you ask?" The Board Master grunted his words as if they were being squeezed out singly.

"To see if they jibe with my own."

"And what are your own?"

The secretary smiled. "No, no. You take precedence. How long do you intend staying here?"

"As long as it takes to make a fair beginning on the documents involved."

"That's no answer. What do you mean by a fair beginning?"

"I haven't the slightest idea. It might take years."

"Oh, damnation."

The Board Master raised his eyebrows and said nothing.

The secretary looked at his nails. "I take it you know the location of this robot world."

"Naturally. Theor Realo was there. His information up to now has proven very accurate."

"That's right. The albino. Well, why not go there?"

"Go there! Impossible!"

"May I ask why?"

"Look," said the Board Master with restrained impatience, "you're not here by our invitation, and we're not asking you to dictate our course of actions, but just to show you that I'm not looking for a fight, I'll give you a little metaphorical treatment of our case. Suppose we were presented with a huge and complicated machine, composed of principles and materials of which we knew next to nothing. It is so vast we can't even make out the relationship of the parts, let alone the purpose of the whole. Now, would you advise me to begin attacking the delicate mysterious moving parts of the machine with a detonating ray before I know what it's all about?"

"I see your point, of course, but you're becoming a mystic. The metaphor is farfetched."

"Not at all. These positronic robots were constructed along lines we know nothing of as yet and were intended to follow lines with which we were entirely unacquainted. About the only thing we know is that the robots were put aside in complete isolation, to work out their destiny by themselves. To ruin that isolation would be to ruin the experiment. If we go there in a body, introducing new, unforeseen factors, inducing unintended reactions, everything is ruined. The littlest disturbance—"

"Poppycock! Theor Realo has already gone there."

The Board Master lost his temper suddenly. "Don't you suppose I know that? Do you suppose it would ever have happened if that cursed albino hadn't been an ignorant fanatic without any knowledge of psychology at all? Galaxy knows what the idiot has done in the way of damage."

There was a silence. The secretary clicked his teeth with a thoughtful fingernail. "I don't know . . . I don't know. But I've got to find out. And I can't wait years."

He left, and the Board Master turned seethingly to Brand, "And how are we going to stop him from going to the robot world if he wants to?"

"I don't see how he can go if we don't let him. *He* doesn't head the expedition."

"Oh, doesn't he? *That's* what I was about to tell you just before he came in. Ten ships of the fleet have landed on Dorlis since we arrived."

"*What!*"

"Just that."

"But what for?"

"That, my boy, is what I don't understand, either."

* * *

"Mind if I drop in?" said Wynne Murry, pleasantly, and Theor Realo looked up in sudden anxiety from the papers that lay in hopeless disarray on the desk before him.

"Come in. I'll clear off a seat for you." The albino hustled the mess off one of the two chairs in a state of twittering nerves.

Murry sat down and swung one long leg over the other. "Are you assigned a job here, too?" He nodded at the desk.

Theor shook his head and smiled feebly. Almost automatically, he brushed the papers together in a heap and turned them face down.

In the months since he had returned to Dorlis with a hundred psychologists of various degrees of renown, he had felt himself pushed farther and farther from the center of things. There was room for him no longer. Except to answer questions on the actual state of things upon the robot world, which he alone had visited, he played no part. And even there he detected, or seemed to detect, anger that *he* should have gone, and not a competent scientist.

It was a thing to be resented. Yet, somehow, it had always been like that.

"Pardon me?" He had let Murry's next remark slip.

The secretary repeated, "I say it's surprising you're *not* put to work, then. You made the original discovery, didn't you?"

"Yes," the albino brightened. "But it went out of my hands. It got beyond me."

"You were on the robot world, though."

"That was a mistake, they tell me. I might have ruined everything."

Murry grimaced. "What really gets them, I guess, is that you've got a lot of first-hand dope they didn't. Don't let their fancy titles fool you into thinking you're a nobody. You and I—I'm a layman, too, you know—have to stand up for our rights. Here, have a cigarette."

"I don't sm— I'll take one, thank you." The albino felt himself warming to the long-bodied man opposite. He turned the papers face upward again, and lit up, bravely but uncertainly.

"Twenty-five years." Theor spoke carefully, skirting around urgent coughs.

"Would you answer a few questions about the world?"

"I suppose so. That's all they ever ask me about. But hadn't you better ask *them?* They've probably got it all worked out now." He blew the smoke as far from himself as possible.

Murry said, "Frankly, they haven't even begun, and I want the information without benefit of confusing psychological translation. First of all, what kind of people—or things—are these robots? You haven't a photocast of one of them, have you?"

"Well, no. I didn't like to take 'casts of them. But they're not things. They're *people!*"

"No? Do they look like—people?"

"Yes—mostly. Outside, anyway. I brought some microscopic studies of the cellular structure that I got hold of. The Board Master has them. They're different inside, you know, greatly simplified. But you'd never know that. They're interesting—and nice."

"Are they simpler than the other life of the planet?"

"Oh, no. It's a very primitive planet. And . . . and," he was interrupted by a spasm of coughing and crushed the cigarette to death as unobtrusively as possible. "They've got a protoplasmic base, you know. I don't think they have the slightest idea they're robots."

"No. I don't suppose they would have. What about their science?"

"I don't know. I never got a chance to see. And everything was so different. I guess it would take an expert to understand."

"Did they have machines?"

The albino looked surprised. "Well, of course. A good many, of all sorts."

"Large cities?"

"Yes!"

The secretary's eyes grew thoughtful. "And you like them. Why?"

Theor Realo was brought up sharply. "I don't know. They were just likable. We got along. They didn't bother me so. It's nothing I can put my finger on. Maybe it's because I have it so hard getting along back home, and they weren't as difficult as real people."

"They were more friendly?"

"N-no. Can't say so. They never quite accepted me. I was a stranger, didn't know their language at first—all that. But"—he looked up with sudden brightness—"I understood them better. I could tell what they were thinking better. I— But I don't know why."

"Hm-m-m. Well—another cigarette? No? I've got to be walloping the pillow now. It's getting late. How about a twosome at golf tomorrow? I've worked up a little course. It'll do. Come on out. The exercise will put hair on your chest."

He grinned and left.

He mumbled one sentence to himself: "It looks like a death sentence"—and whistled thoughtfully as he passed along to his own quarters.

* * *

He repeated the phrase to himself when he faced the Board Master the next day, with a sash of office about his waist. He did not sit down.

"Again?" said the Board Master, wearily.

"Again!" assented the secretary. "But real business this time. I may have to take over direction of your expedition."

"What! Impossible, sir! I will listen to no such proposition."

"I have my authority." Wynne Murry presented the metalloid cylinder that snapped open at a flick of the thumb. 'I have full powers and full discretion as to their use. It is signed, as you will observe, by the chairman of the Congress of the Federation."

"So— But why?" The Board Master, by an effort, breathed normally. "Short of arbitrary tyranny, is there a reason?"

"A very good one, sir. All along, we have viewed this expedition from different angles. The Department of Science and Technology views the robot world not from the point of view of a scientific curiosity, but from the standpoint of its interference with the peace of the Federation. I don't think you've ever stopped to consider the danger inherent in this robot world."

"None that I can see. It is thoroughly isolated and thoroughly harmless."

"How can you know?"

"From the very nature of the experiment," shouted the Board Master angrily. "The original planners wanted as nearly a completely closed system as possible. Here they are, just as far off the trade routes as possible, in a thinly populated region of space. The whole idea was to have the robots develop free of interference."

Murry smiled. "I disagree with you there. Look, the whole trouble with you is that you're a theoretical man. You look at things the way they ought to be and I, a practical man, look at things as they are. No experiment can be set up and allowed to run indefinitely under its own power. It is taken for granted that somewhere there is at least an observer who watches and *modifies* as circumstances warrant."

"Well?" said the Board Master stolidly.

"Well, the observers in this experiment, the original psychologists of Dorlis, passed away with the First Confederation, and for fifteen thousand years the experiment has proceeded by itself. Little errors have added up and become big ones and introduced alien factors which induced still other errors. It's a geometric progression. And there's been no one to halt it."

"Pure hypothesis."

"Maybe. But you're interested only in the robot world, and I've got to think of the entire Federation."

"And just what possible danger can the robot world be to the Federation? I don't know *what* in Arcturus you're driving at, man."

Murry sighed. "I'll be simple, but don't blame me if I sound melodramatic. The Federation hasn't had any internal warfare for centuries. What will happen if we come into contact with these robots?"

"Are you afraid of one world?"

"Could be. What about their science? Robots can do funny things sometimes."

"What science can they have? They're not metal-electricity supermen. They're weak protoplasmic creatures, a poor imitation of actual humanity, built around a positronic brain adjusted to a set of simplified human psychological laws. If the word 'robot' is scaring you—"

'No, it isn't, but I've talked to Theor Realo. He's the only one who's seen them, you know."

The Board Master cursed silently and fluently. It came of letting a weak-minded freak of a layman get underfoot where he could babble and do harm.

He said, "We've got Realo's full story, and we've evaluated it fully and capably. I assure you, no harm exists in them. The experiment is so thoroughly academic, I wouldn't spend two days on it if it weren't for the broad scope of the thing. From what we see, the whole idea was to build up a positronic brain containing modifications of one or two of the fundamental axioms. We haven't worked out the details, but they must be minor, as it was the first experiment of this nature ever tried, and even the great mythical psychologists of that day had to progress stepwise. Those robots, I tell you, are neither supermen nor beasts. I assure you—as a psychologist."

"Sorry! I'm a psychologist, too. A little more rule-of-thumb, I'm afraid. That's all. But even little modifications! Take the general spirit of combativeness. That isn't the scientific term, but I've no patience for that. You know what I mean. We humans used to be combative. But it's being bred out of us. A stable political and economic system doesn't encourage the waste energy of combat. It's not a survival factor. But suppose the robots are combative. Suppose as the result of a wrong turn during the millennia they've been unwatched, they've become far more combative than ever their first makers intended. They'd be uncomfortable things to be with."

"And suppose all the stars in the Galaxy became novae at the same time. Let's *really* start worrying."

* * *

"And there's another point." Murry ignored the other's heavy sarcasm. 'Theor Realo liked those robots. He liked robots better than he likes real people. He felt that he fitted there, and we all know he's been a bad misfit in his own world."

"And what," asked the Board Master, "is the significance of that?"

"You don't see it?" Wynne Murry lifted his eyebrows. "Theor Realo likes those robots because he is *like* them, obviously. I'll guarantee right now that a complete psychic analysis of Theor Realo will show a modification of several fundamental axioms, and the same ones as in the robots.

"And," the secretary drove on without a pause, "Theor Realo worked for a quarter of a century to prove a point, when all science would have laughed him to death if they had known about it. There's fanaticism there; good, honest, *inhuman* perseverance. *Those robots are probably like that!*"

"You're advancing no logic. You're arguing like a maniac, like a moon-struck idiot."

"I don't need strict mathematical proof. Reasonable doubt is sufficient. I've got to protect the Federation. Look, it *is* reasonable, you know. The psychologists of Dorlis weren't as super as all that. They had to advance stepwise, as you yourself pointed out. Their humanoids — let's not call them robots—were only imitations of human beings and they couldn't be good ones. Humans possess certain very, *very* complicated reaction systems—things like social consciousness, and a tendency toward the establishment of ethical systems; and more ordinary things like chivalry, generosity, fair play and so on, that simply can't possibly be duplicated. I don't think those humanoids can have them. But they *must* have perseverance, which practically implies stubbornness and combativeness, if my notion on Theor Realo holds good. Well, if their science is anywhere at all, then I don't want to have them running loose in the Galaxy, if our numbers are a thousand or a million times theirs. And I don't intend to permit them to do so!"

The Board Master's face was rigid. "What are your immediate intentions?"

"As yet undecided. But I think I am going to organize a small-scale landing on the planet."

"Now, wait." The old psychologist was up and around the desk. He seized the secretary's elbow. "Are you quite certain you know what you're doing? The potentialities in this massive experiment are beyond any possible precalculation by you or me. You can't know what you're destroying."

"I know. Do you think I enjoy what I'm doing? This isn't a hero's job. I'm enough of a psychologist to want to know what's going on, but I've been sent here to protect the Federation, and to the best of my ability I intend doing it—and a dirty job it is. But I can't help it."

"You can't have thought it out. What can you know of the insight it will give us into the basic ideas of psychology? This will amount to a fusion of two Galactic systems, that will send us to heights that will make up in knowledge and power a million times the amount of harm the robots could ever do, if they *were* metal-electricity supermen."

The secretary shrugged. "Now you're the one that is playing with faint possibilities."

"Listen, I'll make a deal. Blockade them. Isolate them with your ships. Mount guards. But don't touch them. Give us more time. Give us a chance. You must!"

"I've thought of that. But I would have to get Congress to agree to that. It would be expensive, you know."

The Board Master flung himself into his chair in wild impatience. "What kind of expense are you talking about? Do you realize the nature of the repayment if we succeed?"

Murry considered; then, with a half smile, "What if they develop interstellar travel?"

The Board Master said quickly, "Then I'll withdraw my objections."

The secretary rose, "I'll have it out with Congress."

* * *

Brand Gorla's face was carefully emotionless as he watched the Board Master's stooped back. The cheerful pep talks to the available members of the expedition lacked meat, and he listened to them impatiently.

He said, "What are we going to do now?"

The Board Master's shoulders twitched and he didn't turn. "I've sent for Theor Realo. That little fool left for the Eastern Continent last week—"

"Why?"

The older man blazed at the interruption. "How can I understand anything that freak does! Don't you see that Murry's right? He's a psychic abnormality. We had no business leaving him unwatched. If I had ever thought of looking at him twice, I wouldn't have. He's coming back now, though, and he's going to stay back." His voice fell to a mumble. "Should have been back two hours ago."

"It's an impossible position, sir," said Brand, flatly.

"Think so?"

"Well— Do *you* think Congress will stand for an indefinite patrol off the robot world? It runs into money, and average Galactic citizens aren't going to see it as worth the taxes. The psychological equations degenerate into the axioms of common sense. In fact, I don't see why Murry agreed to consult Congress."

"Don't you?" The Board Master finally faced his junior. "Well, the fool considers himself a psychologist, Galaxy help us, and that's his weak point. He flatters himself that he doesn't want to destroy the robot world in his heart, but that it's the good of the Federation that requires it. And he'll jump at any reasonable compromise. Congress won't agree to it indefinitely, you don't have to point that out to me." He was talking quietly, patiently. "But I will ask for ten years, two years, six months—as much as I can get. I'll get something. In that time, we'll learn new facts about the world. Somehow we'll strengthen our case and renew the agreement when it expires. We'll save the project yet."

There was a short silence and the Board Master added slowly and bitterly, "And that's where Theor Realo plays a vital part."

Brand Gorla watched silently, and waited. The Board Master said, "On that one point, Murry saw what we didn't. Realo is a psychological cripple, and is our real clue to the whole affair. If we study him, we'll have a rough picture of what the robot is like, distorted of course, since his environment had been a hostile, unfriendly one. But we can make allowance for that, estimate his nature in a— Ahh, I'm tired of the whole subject."

The signal box flashed, and the Board Master sighed. "Well, he's here. All right, Gorla, sit down, you make me nervous. Let's take a look at him."

* * *

Theor Realo came through the door like a comet and brought himself to a panting halt in the middle of the floor. He looked from one to the other with weak, peering eyes.

"How did all this happen?"

"All what?" said the Board Master coldly. "Sit down. I want to ask you some questions."

"No. You first answer *me*."

"*Sit down!*"

Realo sat. His eyes were brimming. "They're going to destroy the robot world."

"Don't worry about that."

"But you said they could if the robots discovered interstellar travel. You said so. You fool. Don't you see—" He was choking.

The Board Master frowned uneasily. "Will you calm down and talk sense?"

The albino gritted his teeth and forced the words out. "But they'll *have* interstellar travel before long."

And the two psychologists shot toward the little man.

"What!!"

"Well . . . well, what do you think?" Realo sprang upward with all the fury of desperation. "Did you think I landed in a desert or in the middle of an ocean and explored a world all by myself? Do you think life is a storybook? I was captured as soon as I landed and taken to a big city. At least, I think it was a big city. It was different from our kind. It had— But I won't tell you."

"Never mind the city," shrieked the Board Master. "You were captured. Go ahead."

"They studied *me*. They studied my machine. And then, one night, I left, to tell the Federation. They didn't know I left. They didn't want me to leave." His voice broke. "And I would have stayed as soon as not, but the Federation had to know."

"Did you tell them anything about your ship?"

"How could I? I'm no mechanic. I don't know the theory or construction. But I showed them how to work the controls and let them look at the motors. That's all."

Brand Gorla said, to himself mostly, "Then they'll never get it. That isn't enough."

The albino's voice raised itself in sudden shrieking triumph. 'Oh, yes, they will. I know them. They're machines, you know. They'll work on that problem. And they'll work. And they'll work. And they'll never quit. And they'll get it. They got enough out of me. I'll *bet* they got enough."

The Board Master looked long, and turned away—wearily. "Why didn't you tell us?"

"Because you took my world away from me. I discovered it—by myself—all by myself. And after I had done all the real work, and invited you in, you threw me out. All you had for me was complaints that I had landed on the world and might have ruined everything by interference. Why should I tell you? Find out for yourselves if you're so wise, that you could afford to kick me around."

The Board Master thought bitterly, "Misfit! Inferiority complex! Persecution mania! Nice! It all fits in, now that we've bothered to take our eyes off the horizon and see what was under our nose. And now it's all ruined."

He said, "All right, Realo, we all lose. Go away."

Brand Gorla said tightly, "All over? Really all over?"

The Board Master answered, "Really all over. The original experiment, as such, is over. The distortions created by Realo's visit will easily be large enough to make the plans we are studying here a dead language. And besides—Murry is right. If they have interstellar travel, they're dangerous."

Realo was shouting, "But you're not going to destroy them. You can't destroy them. They haven't hurt anyone."

There was no answer, and he raved on, "I'm going back. I'll warn them. They'll be prepared. I'll warn them."

He was backing toward the door, his thin, white hair bristling, his red-rimmed eyes bulging.

The Board Master did not move to stop him when he dashed out.

"Let him go. It was *his* lifetime. I don't care any more."

Theor Realo smashed toward the robot world at an acceleration that was half choking him.

Somewhere ahead was the dustspeck of an isolated world with artificial imitations of humanity struggling along in an experiment that had died. Struggling blindly toward a new goal of interstellar travel that was to be their death sentence.

He was heading toward that world, toward the same city in which he had been "studied" the first time. He remembered it well. Its name was the first words of their language he had learned.

New York!

Catch That Rabbit

The vacation was longer than two weeks. That, Mike Donovan had to admit. It had been six months, with pay. He admitted that, too. But that, as he explained, furiously, was fortuitous. U. S. Robots had to get the bugs out of the multiple robot, and there were plenty of bugs, and there are always at least half a dozen bugs left for the field-testing. So they waited and relaxed until the drawing-board men and the slide-rule boys had said "OK!". And now he and Powell were out on the asteroid and it was *not* OK. He repeated that a dozen time, with a face that had gone beety, "For the love of Pete, Greg, get realistic. What's the use of adhering to the letter of the specifications and watching the test go to pot? It's about time you got the red tape out of your pants and went to work."

"I'm only saying," said Gregory Powell, patiently, as one explaining electronics to an idiot child, "that according to spec, those robots are equipped for asteroid mining without supervision. We're not supposed to watch them."

"All right. Look—logic!" He lifted his hairy fingers and pointed. "One: That new robot passed every test in the home laboratories. Two: United States Robots guaranteed their passing the test of actual performance on an asteroid. Three: The robots are not passing said tests. Four: If they don't pass, United States Robots loses ten million credits in cash and about one hundred million in reputation. Five: If they don't pass and we can't explain why they don't pass, it is just possible two good jobs may have to be bidden a fond farewell."

Powell groaned heavily behind a noticeably insincere smile. The unwritten motto of United States Robots and Mechanical Men Corporation was well-known: "No employee makes the same mistake twice. He is fired the first time."

Aloud he said, "You're as lucid as Euclid with everything except the facts. You've watched that robot group for three shifts, you redhead, and they did their work perfectly. You said so yourself. What else can we do?"

"Find out what's wrong, that's what we can do. So they did work perfectly when I watched them. But on three different occasions when I didn't watch them, they didn't bring in any ore. They didn't even come back on schedule. I had to go after them."

"And was anything wrong?"

"Not a thing. Not a thing. Everything was perfect. Smooth and perfect as the luminiferous ether. Only one little insignificant detail disturbed me—*there was no ore*."

Powell scowled at the ceiling and pulled at his brown mustache. "I'll tell you what, Mike. We've been stuck with pretty lousy jobs in our time, but this takes the iridium asteroid. The whole business is complicated past endurance. Look, that robot, DV-5, has six robots under it. And not just under it—they're part of it."

"I know that—"

"Shut up!" said Powell, savagely, "I know you know it, but I'm just describing for the hell of it. Those six subsidiaries are part of DV-5 like your fingers are part of you and it gives them their orders neither by voice nor radio, but directly through positronic fields. Now—there isn't a roboticist back at United States Robots that knows what a positronic field is or how it works. And neither do I. Neither do you."

"The last," agreed Donovan, philosophically, "I know."

"Then look at our position. If everything works—fine! If anything goes wrong—we're out of our depth and there probably isn't a thing we can do, or anybody else. But the job belongs to us and not to anyone else so we're on the spot, Mike." He blazed away for a moment in silence. Then, "All right, have you got him outside?"

"Yes."

"Is everything normal now?"

"Well he hasn't got religious mania, and he isn't running around in a circle spouting Gilbert and Sullivan, so I suppose he's normal."

Donovan passed out the door, shaking his head viciously.

* * *

Powell reached for the "Handbook of Robotics" that weighed down one side of his desk to a near-founder and opened it reverently. He had once jumped out of the window of a burning house dressed only in shorts and the "Handbook." In a pinch, he would have skipped the shorts.

The "Handbook" was propped up before him, when Robot DV-5 entered, with Donovan kicking the door shut behind him.

Powell said somberly, "Hi, Dave. How do you feel?"

"Fine," said the robot. "Mind if I sit down?" He dragged up the specially reinforced chair that was his, and folded gently into it.

Powell regarded Dave—laymen might think of robots by their serial numbers; roboticists never—with approval. It was not overmassive by any means, in spite of its construction as thinking-unit of an integrated seven-unit robot team. It was seven feet tall, and a half-ton of metal and electricity. A lot? Not when that half-ton has to be a mass of condensers, circuits, relays, and vacuum cells that can handle practically any psychological reaction known to humans. And a positronic brain, which with ten pounds of matter and a few quintillions of positrons runs the whole show.

Powell groped in his shirt pocket for a loose cigarette. "Dave," he said, "you're a good fellow. There's nothing flighty or prima donnaish about you. You're a stable, rock-bottom mining robot, except that you're equipped to handle six subsidiaries in direct coordination. As far as I know, that has not introduced any unstable paths in your brain-path map."

The robot nodded, "That makes me feel swell, but what are you getting at, boss?" He was equipped with an excellent diaphragm, and the presence of overtones in the sound unit robbed him of much of that metallic flatness that marks the usual robot voice.

"I'm going to tell you. With all that in your favor, what's going wrong with your job? For instance, today's B-shift?"

Dave hesitated, "As far as I know, nothing."

"You didn't produce any ore."

"I know."

"Well, then—"

Dave was having trouble, "I can't explain that, boss. It's been giving me a case of nerves, or it would if I let it. My subsidiaries worked smoothly. I know I did." He considered, his photoelectric eyes glowing intensely. Then, "I don't remember. The day ended and there was Mike and there were the ore cars, mostly empty."

Donovan broke in, "You didn't report at shift-end those days, Dave. You know that?"

"I know. But as to why—" He shook his head slowly and ponderously.

Powell had the queasy feeling that if the robot's face was capable of expression, it would be one of pain and mortification. A robot, by its very nature, cannot bear to fail its function.

Donovan dragged his chair up to Powell's desk and leaned over, "Amnesia, do you think?"

"Can't say. But there's no use in trying to pin disease names on this. Human disorders apply to robots only as romantic analogies. They're no help to robotic engineering." He scratched his neck, "I hate to put him through the elementary brain-reaction tests. It won't help his self-respect any."

He looked at Dave thoughtfully, and then at the Field-Test outline given in the "Handbook." He said, "See here, Dave, what about sitting through a test? It would be the wise thing to do."

The robot rose, "If you say so, boss." There *was* pain in his voice.

* * *

It started simply enough. Robot DV-5 multiplied five-place figures to the heartless ticking of a stop watch. He recited the prime numbers between a thousand and ten thousand. He extracted cube roots and integrated functions of varying complexity. He went through mechanical reactions in order of increasing difficulty. And, finally, worked his precise mechanical mind over the highest function of the robot world—the solutions of problems in judgment and ethics.

At the end of two hours, Powell was copiously besweated. Donovan had enjoyed a none-too-nutritious diet of fingernail and the robot said, "How does it look, boss?"

Powell said, "I've got to think it over, Dave. Snap judgments won't help much. Suppose you go back to the C-shift. Take it easy. Don't press too hard for quota just for a while—and we'll fix things up."

The robot left. Donovan looked at Powell.

"Well—"

Powell seemed determined to push up his mustache by the roots. He said, "There is nothing wrong with the currents of his positronic brain."

"I'd hate to be that certain."

"Oh, Jupiter, Mike! The brain is the surest part of a robot. It's quintuple-checked back on Earth. If they pass the field test perfectly, the way Dave did, there just isn't a chance of brain misfunction. That test covered every key path in the brain."

"So where are we?"

"Don't rush me. Let me work this out. There's still the possibility of a mechanical breakdown in the body. That leaves about fifteen hundred condensers, twenty thousand individual electric circuits, five hundred vacuum cells, a thousand relays, and upty-ump thousand other individual pieces of complexity that can be wrong. *And* these mysterious positronic fields no one knows anything about."

"Listen, Greg," Donovan grew desperately urgent. "I've got an idea. That robot may be lying. He never—"

"Robots can't knowingly lie, you fool. Now if we had the McCormack-Wesley tester, we could check each individual item in his body within twenty-four to forty-eight hours, but the only two M.-W. testers existing are on Earth, and they weigh ten tons, are on concrete foundations and can't be moved. Isn't that peachy?"

Donovan pounded the desk, "But, Greg, he only goes wrong when we're not around. There's something—sinister—about—that." He punctuated the sentence with slams of fist against desk.

"You," said Powell, slowly, "make me sick. You've been reading adventure novels."

"What I want to know," shouted Donovan, "is what we're going to do about it."

"I'll tell you. I'm going to install a visiplate right over my desk. Right on the wall over there, see!" He jabbed a vicious finger at the spot. "Then I'm going to focus it at whatever part of the mine is being worked, and I'm going to watch. That's all."

"That's all? Greg—"

Powell rose from his chair and leaned his balled fists on the desk, "Mike, I'm having a hard time." His voice was weary. "For a week, you've been plaguing me about Dave. You say he's gone wrong. Do you know how he's gone wrong? No! Do you know what shape this wrongness takes? No! Do you know what brings it on? No! Do you know what snaps him out? No! Do you know anything about it? No! Do I know anything about it? No! So what do you want me to do?"

Donovan's arm swept outward in a vague, grandiose gesture, "You got me!"

"So I tell you again. Before we do anything toward a cure, we've got to find out what the disease is in the first place. The first step in cooking rabbit stew is catching the rabbit. Well, we've got to catch that rabbit! Now get out of here."

* * *

Donovan stared at the preliminary outline of his field report with weary eyes. For one thing, he was tired and for another, what was there to report while things were unsettled? He felt resentful.

He said, "Greg, we're almost a thousand tons behind schedule."

"You," replied Powell, never looking up, "are telling me something I don't know."

"What I want to know," said Donovan, in sudden savagery, "is why we're always tangled up with new-type robots. I've finally decided that the robots that were good enough for my great-uncle on my mother's side are good enough for me. I'm for what's tried and true. The test of time is what counts—good, solid, old-fashioned robots that never go wrong."

Powell threw a book with perfect aim, and Donovan went tumbling off his seat.

"Your job," said Powell, evenly, "for the last five years has been to test new robots under actual working conditions for United States Robots. Because you and I have been so injudicious as to display proficiency at the task, we've been rewarded with the dirtiest jobs. That," he jabbed holes in the air with his finger in Donovan's direction, "is your work. You've been griping about it, from personal memory, since about five minutes after United States Robots signed you up. Why don't you resign?"

"Well, I'll tell you." Donovan rolled onto his stomach, and took a firm grip on his wild, red hair to hold his head up. "There's a certain principle involved. After all, as a trouble shooter, I've played a part in the development of new robots. There's the principle of aiding scientific advance. But don't get me wrong. It's not the principle that keeps me going; it's the money they pay us. *Greg!*"

Powell jumped at Donovan's wild shout, and his eyes followed the redhead's to the visiplate, when they goggled in fixed horror. He whispered, "Holy—howling—Jupiter!"

Donovan scrambled breathlessly to his feet, "Look at them, Greg. They've gone nuts."

Powell said, "Get a pair of suits. We're going out there."

He watched the posturings of the robots on the visiplate. They were bronzy gleams of smooth motion against the shadowy crags of the airless asteroid. There was a marching formation now, and in their own dim body light, the rough-hewn walls of the mine tunnel swam past noiselessly, checkered with misty erratic blobs of shadow. They marched in unison, seven of them, with Dave at the head. They wheeled and turned in macabre simultaneity; and melted through changes of formation with the weird ease of chorus dancers in Lunar Bowl.

Donovan was back with the suits. "They've gone jingo on us, Greg. That's a military march."

"For all you know," was the cold response, "it may be a series of calisthenic exercises. Or Dave may be under the hallucination of being a dancing master. Just you think first, and don't bother to speak afterward, either."

Donovan scowled and slipped a detonator into the empty side

holster with an ostentatious shove. He said, "Anyway, there you are. So we work with new-model robots. It's our job, granted. But answer me one question. Why . . . *why* does something invariably go wrong with them?"

"Because," said Powell, somberly, "we are accursed. Let's go!"

* * *

Far ahead through the thick velvety blackness of the corridors that reached past the illuminated circles of their flashlights, robot light twinkled.

"There they are," breathed Donovan.

Powell whispered tensely, "I've been trying to get him by radio but he doesn't answer. The radio circuit is probably out."

"Then I'm glad the designers haven't worked out robots who can work in total darkness yet. I'd hate to have to find seven mad robots in a black pit without radio communication, if they *weren't* lit up like blasted radioactive Christmas trees."

"Crawl up on the ledge above, Mike. They're coming this way, and I want to watch them at close range. Can you make it?"

Donovan made the jump with a grunt. Gravity was considerably below Earth-normal, but with a heavy suit, the advantage was not too great, and the ledge meant a near ten-foot jump. Powell followed.

The column of robots were trailing Dave single-file. In mechanical rhythm, they converted to double and returned to single in different order. It was repeated over and over again and Dave never turned his head.

Dave was within twenty feet when the play-acting ceased. The subsidiary robots broke formation, waited a moment, then clattered off into the distance—very rapidly. Dave looked after them, then slowly sat down. He rested his head in one hand in a very human gesture.

His voice sounded in Powell's earphones, "Are you here, boss?"

Powell beckoned to Donovan and hopped off the ledge.

"O.K., Dave, what's been going on?"

The robot shook his head, "I don't know. One moment I was handling a tough outcropping in Tunnel 17, and the next I was aware of humans close by, and I found myself half a mile down main-stem."

"Where are the subsidiaries now?" asked Donovan.

"Back at work, of course. How much time has been lost?"

"Not much. Forget it." Then to Donovan, Powell added, "Stay with him the rest of the shift. Then, come back. I've got a couple of ideas."

*   *   *

It was three hours before Donovan returned. He looked tired.

Powell said, "How did it go?"

Donovan shrugged wearily, "Nothing ever goes wrong when you watch them. Throw me a butt, will you?"

The redhead lit it with exaggerated care and blew a careful smoke ring. He said, "I've been working it out, Greg. You know, Dave has a queer background for a robot. There are six others under him in an extreme regimentation. He's got life and death power over those subsidiary robots and it must react on his mentality. Suppose he finds it necessary to emphasize his power as a concession to his ego."

"Get to the point."

"It's right here. Suppose we have militarism. Suppose he's fashioning himself an army. Suppose he's training them in military maneuvers. Suppose—"

"Suppose you go soak your head. Your nightmares must be in technicolor. You're postulating a major aberration of the positronic brain. If your analysis were correct, Dave would have to break down the First Law of Robotics: that a robot may not injure a human being or, through inaction allow a human being to be injured. The type of militaristic attitude and domineering ego you propose must have as the end-point of its logical implications, domination of humans."

"All right. How do you know that isn't the fact of the matter?"

"Because any robot with a brain like that would, one, never have left the factory, and two, be spotted immediately if it ever was. I tested Dave, you know."

Powell shoved his chair back and put his feet on the desk. "No. We're still in the position where we can't make our stew because we haven't the slightest notion as to what's wrong. For instance, if we could find out what that *danse macabre* we witnessed was all about, we would be on the way out."

He paused, "Now listen, Mike, how does this sound to you? Dave goes wrong only when neither of us is present. And when he is wrong, the arrival of either of us snaps him out of it."

"I once told you that was sinister."

"Don't interrupt. How is a robot different when humans are not present? The answer is obvious. There is a larger requirement of personal initiative. In that case, look for the body parts that are affected by the new requirements."

"Golly." Donovan sat up straight, then subsided. "No, no. Not enough. It's too broad. It doesn't cut the possibilities much."

"Can't help that. In any case, there's no danger of not making quota. We'll take shifts watching those robots through the visor. Any time anything goes wrong, we get to the scene of action immediately. That will put them right."

"But the robots will fail spec anyway, Greg. United States Robots can't market DV models with a report like that."

"Obviously. We've got to locate the error in make-up and correct it—and we've got ten days to do it in." Powell scratched his head. "The trouble is . . . well, you had better look at the blueprints yourself."

The blueprints covered the floor like a carpet and Donovan crawled over the face of them following Powell's erratic pencil.

Powell said, "Here's where you come in, Mike. You're the body specialist, and I want you to check me. I've been trying to cut out all circuits not involved in the personal initiative hookup. Right here, for instance, is the trunk artery involving mechnical operations. I cut out all routine side routes as emergency divisions—" He looked up, "What do you think?"

Donovan had a very bad taste in his mouth, "The job's not that simple, Greg. Personal initiative isn't an electric circuit you can separate from the rest and study. When a robot is on his own, the intensity of the body activity increases immediately on almost all fronts. There isn't a circuit entirely unaffected. What must be done is to locate the particular condition—a very specific condition—that throws him off, and *then* start eliminating circuits."

Powell got up and dusted himself, "Hmph. All right. Take away the blueprints and burn them."

Donovan said, "You see when activity intensifies, anything can happen, given one single faulty part. Insulation breaks down, a condenser spills over, a connection sparks, a coil overheats. And if you work blind, with the whole robot to choose from, you'll never find the bad spot. If you take Dave apart and test every point of his body mechanism one by one, putting him together each time, and trying him out—"

"All right. All right. I can see through a porthole, too."

They faced each other hopelessly, and then Powell said cautiously, "Suppose we interview one of the subsidiaries."

Neither Powell nor Donovan had ever had previous occasion to talk to a "finger." It could talk; it wasn't quite the perfect analogy to a human finger. In fact, it had a fairly developed brain, but that brain was tuned primarily to the reception of orders via positronic field, and its reaction to independent stimuli was rather fumbling.

Nor was Powell certain as to its name. Its serial number was DV-5-2, but that was not very useful.

He compromised. "Look, pal," he said, "I'm going to ask you to do some hard thinking and then you can go back to your boss."

The "finger" nodded its head stiffly, but did not exert its limited brain-power on speech.

"Now on four occasions recently," Powell said, "your boss deviated from brain-scheme. Do you remember those occasions?"

"Yes, sir."

Donovan growled angrily, "*He* remembers. I tell you there is something very sinister—"

"Oh, go bash your skull. Of course, the 'finger' remembers. There is nothing wrong with him." Powell turned back to the robot, "What were you doing each time . . . I mean the whole group."

The "finger" had a curious air of reciting by rote, as if he answered questions by the mechanical pressure of his brain pan, but without any enthusiasm whatever.

He said, "The first time we were at work on a difficult outcropping in Tunnel 17, Level B. The second time we were buttressing the roof against a possible cave-in. The third time we were preparing accurate blasts in order to tunnel farther without breaking into a subterranean fissure. The fourth time was just after a minor cave-in."

"What happened at these times?"

"It is difficult to describe. An order would be issued, but before we could receive and interpret it, a new order came to march in queer formation."

Powell snapped out, "Why?"

"I don't know."

Donovan broke in tensely, "What was the first order . . . the one that was superseded by the marching directions?"

"I don't know. I sensed that an order was sent, but there was never time to receive it."

"Could you tell us anything about it? Was it the same order each time?"

The "finger" shook his head unhappily, "I don't know."

Powell leaned back, "All right, get back to your boss."

The "finger" left, with visible relief.

Donovan said, "Well, we accomplished a lot that time. That was real sharp dialogue all the way through. Listen, Dave and that imbecile 'finger' are both holding out on us. There is too much they don't know and don't remember. We've got to stop trusting them, Greg."

Powell brushed his mustache the wrong way, "So help me, Mike, another fool remark out of you, and I'll take away your rattle and teething ring."

"All right. You're the genius of the team. I'm just a poor sucker. Where do we stand?"

"Right behind the eight ball. I tried to work it backward through the 'finger,' and couldn't. So we've got to work it forward."

"A great man," marveled Donovan. "How simple that makes it. Now translate that into English, Master."

"Translating it into baby talk would suit you better. I mean that we've got to find out what order it is that Dave gives just before everything goes black. It would be the key to the business."

"And how do you expect to do that? We can't get close to him because nothing will go wrong as long as we are there. We can't catch the orders by radio because they are transmitted via this positronic field. That eliminates the close-range and the long-range method, leaving us a neat, cozy zero."

"By direct observation, yes. There's still deduction."

"Huh?"

"We're going on shifts, Mike," Powell smiled grimly. "And we are not taking our eyes off the visiplate. We're going to watch every action of those steel headaches. When they go off into their act, we're going to see what happened immediately before and we're going to deduce the order."

Donovan opened his mouth and left it that way for a full minute. Then he said in strangled tones, "I resign. I quit."

"You have ten days to think up something better," said Powell wearily.

Which, for eight days, Donovan tried mightily to do. For eight days, on alternate four-hour shifts, he watched with aching and bleary eyes those glinty metallic forms move against the vague background. And for eight days in the four-hour in-between, he cursed United States Robots, the DV models, and the day he was born.

And then on the eighth day, when Powell entered with an aching head and sleepy eyes for his shift, Donovan stood up and with very careful and deliberate aim launched a heavy book end for the exact center of the visiplate. There was a very appropriate splintering noise.

Powell gasped, "What did you do that for?"

"Because," said Donovan, almost calmly, "I'm not watching it any more. We've got two days left and we haven't found out a thing. DV-5 is a lousy loss. He's stopped five times since I've been watching and three times on your shift, and I can't make out what orders he gave, and you couldn't make it out. And I don't believe you could ever make it out because I know I couldn't ever."

"Jumping Space, how can you watch six robots at the same time? One makes with the hands, and one with the feet and one like a windmill and another is jumping up and down like a maniac. And the other two . . . devil knows what they are doing. And then they all stop. So! So!"

"Greg, we're not doing it right. We got to get up close. We've got to watch what they're doing from where we can see the details."

Powell broke a bitter silence. "Yeah, and wait for something to go wrong with only two days to go."

"Is it any better watching from here?"

"It's more comfortable."

"Ah— But there's something you can do there that you can't do here."

"What's that?"

"You can make them stop—at whatever time you choose—and while you're prepared and watching to see what goes wrong."

Powell startled into alertness, "Howzzat?"

"Well, figure it out yourself. You're the brains you say. Ask yourself some questions. When does DV-5 go out of whack? When did that 'finger' say he did? When a cave-in threatened, or actually occurred, when delicately measured explosives were being laid down, when a difficult seam was hit."

"In other words, during emergencies," Powell was excited.

"Right! When *did* you expect it to happen! It's the personal initiative factor that's giving us the trouble. And it's just during emergencies in the absence of a human being that personal initiative is most strained. Now what is the logical deduction? How can we create our own stoppage when and where we want it?" He paused triumphantly—he was beginning to enjoy his role—and answered his own question to forestall the obvious answer on Powell's tongue. "By creating our own emergency."

Powell said, "Mike—you're right."

"Thanks, pal. I knew I'd do it some day."

"All right, and skip the sarcasm. We'll save it for Earth, and preserve it in jars for future long, cold winters. Meanwhile, what emergency can we create?"

"We could flood the mines, if this weren't an airless asteroid."

"A witticism, no doubt," said Powell. "Really, Mike, you'll incapacitate me with laughter. What about a mild cave-in?"

Donovan pursed his lips and said, "O.K. by me."

"Good. Let's get started."

Powell felt uncommonly like a conspirator as he wound his way over the craggy landscape. His sub-gravity walk teetered across the broken ground, kicking rocks to right and left under his weight in noiseless puffs of gray dust. Mentally, though, it was the cautious crawl of the plotter.

He said, "Do you know where they are?"

"I think so, Greg."

"All right," Powell said gloomily, "but if any 'finger' gets within twenty feet of us, we'll be sensed whether we are in the line of sight or not. I hope you know that."

"When I need an elementary course in robotics, I'll file an application with you, formally, and in triplicate. Down through here."

They were in the tunnels now; even the starlight was gone. The two hugged the walls, flashes flickering out the way in intermittent bursts. Powell felt for the security of his detonator.

"Do you know this tunnel, Mike?"

"Not so good. It's a new one. I think I can make it out from what I saw in the visiplate, though—"

Interminable minutes passed, and then Mike said, "Feel that!"

There was a slight vibration thrumming the wall against the fingers of Powell's metal-incased hand. There was no sound, naturally.

"Blasting! We're pretty close."

"Keep your eyes open," said Powell.

Donovan nodded impatiently.

It was upon them and gone before they could seize themselves—just a bronze glint across the field of vision. They clung together in silence.

Powell whispered, "Think it sensed us?"

"Hope not. But we'd better flank them. Take the first side tunnel to the right."

"Suppose we miss them altogether?"

"Well what do you want to do? Go back?" Donovan grunted fiercely. "They're within a quarter of a mile. I was watching them through the visiplate, wasn't I? And we've got two days—"

"Oh, shut up. You're wasting your oxygen. Is this a side passage here?" The flash flicked. "It is. Let's go."

The vibration was considerably more marked and the ground below shuddered uneasily.

"This is good," said Donovan, "if it doesn't give out on us, though." He flung his light ahead anxiously.

They could touch the roof of the tunnel with a half-upstretched hand, and the bracings had been newly placed.

Donovan hesitated, "Dead end, let's go back."

"No. Hold on." Powell squeezed clumsily past. "Is that light ahead?"

"Light? I don't see any. Where would there be light down here?"

"Robot light." He was scrambling up a gentle incline on hands and knees. His voice was hoarse and anxious in Donovan's ears. "Hey, Mike, come up here."

There was light. Donovan crawled up and over Powell's outstretched legs. "An opening?"

"Yes. They must be working into this tunnel from the other side now—I think."

Donovan felt the ragged edges of the opening that looked out into what the cautious flashlight showed to be a larger and obviously main-stem tunnel. The hole was too small for a man to go through, almost too small for two men to look through simultaneously.

"There's nothing there," said Donovan.

"Well, not now. But there must have been a second ago or we wouldn't have seen light. Watch out!"

The walls rolled about them and they felt the impact. A fine dust showered down. Powell lifted a cautious head and looked again. "All right, Mike. They're there."

The glittering robots clustered fifty feet down the main stem. Metal arms labored mightily at the rubbish heap brought down by the last blast.

Donovan urged eagerly, "Don't waste time. It won't be long before they get through, and the next blast may get us."

"For Pete's sake, don't rush me." Powell unlimbered the detonator, and his eyes searched anxiously across the dusky background where the only light was robot light and it was impossible to tell a projecting boulder from a shadow.

"There's a spot in the roof, see it, almost over them. The last blast didn't quite get it. If you can get it at the base, half the roof will cave in."

Powell followed the dim finger, "Check! Now fasten your eye on the robots and pray they don't move too far from that part of the tunnel. They're my light sources. Are all seven there?"

Donovan counted, "All seven."

"Well, then, watch them. Watch every motion!"

His detonator was lifted and remained poised while Donovan watched and cursed and blinked the sweat out of his eye.

It flashed!

There was a jar, a series of hard vibrations, and then a jarring thump that threw Powell heavily against Donovan.

Donovan yowled, "Greg, you threw me off. I didn't see a thing."

Powell stared about wildly, "Where are they?"

Donovan fell into a stupid silence. There was no sign of the robots. It was dark as the depths of the River Styx.

"Think we buried them?" quavered Donovan.

"Let's get down there. Don't ask me what I think." Powell crawled backward at tumbling speed.

"Mike!"

Donovan paused in the act of following. "What's wrong now?"

"Hold on!" Powell's breathing was rough and irregular in Donovan's ears. "Mike! Do you hear me, Mike?"

"I'm right here. What is it?"

"We're blocked in. It wasn't the ceiling coming down fifty feet away that knocked us over. It was our own ceiling. The shock's tumbled it!"

"What!" Donovan scrambled up against a hard barrier. "Turn on the flash."

Powell did so. At no point was there room for a rabbit to squeeze through.

Donovan said softly, "Well, what do you know?"

* * *

They wasted a few moments and some muscular power in an effort to move the blocking barrier. Powell varied this by wrenching at the edges of the original hole. For a moment, Powell lifted his blaster. But in those close quarters, a flash would be suicide and he knew it. He sat down.

"You know, Mike," he said, "we've really messed this up. We are no nearer finding out what's wrong with Dave. It was a good idea but it blew up in our face."

Donovan's glance was bitter with an intensity totally wasted on the darkness. "I hate to disturb you, old man, but quite apart from what we know or don't know of Dave, we're slightly trapped. If we don't get loose, fella, we're going to die. D-I-E, die. How much oxygen have we anyway? Not more than six hours."

"I've thought of that." Powell's fingers went up to his long-suffering mustache and clanged uselessly against the transparent visor. "Of course, we could get Dave to dig us out easily in that time, except that our precious emergency must have thrown him off, and his radio circuit is out."

"And isn't that nice?"

Donovan edged up to the opening and managed to get his metal-incased head out. It was an extremely tight fit.

"Hey, Greg!"

"What?"

"Suppose we get Dave within twenty feet. He'll snap to normal. That will save us."

"Sure, but where is he?"

"Down the corridor—way down. For Pete's sake, stop pulling before you drag my head out of its socket. I'll give you your chance to look."

Powell maneuvered his head outside, "We did it all right. Look at those saps. That must be a ballet they're doing."

"Never mind the side remarks. Are they getting any closer?"

"Can't tell yet. They're too far away. Give me a chance. Pass me my flash, will you? I'll try to attract their attention that way."

He gave up after two minutes, "Not a chance! They must be blind. Uh-oh, they're starting toward us. What do you know?"

Donovan said, "Hey, let me see!"

There was a silent scuffle. Powell said, "All right!" and Donovan got his head out.

They were approaching. Dave was high-stepping the way in front and the six "fingers" were a weaving chorus line behind him.

Donovan marveled, "What are they doing? That's what I want to know. It looks like the Virginia reel—and Dave's a major-domo, or I never saw one."

"Oh, leave me alone with your descriptions," grumbled Powell. "How near are they?"

"Within fifty feet and coming this way. We'll be out in fifteen min—Uh—huh—HUH—HEY-Y!"

"What's going on?" It took Powell several seconds to recover from his stunned astonishment at Donovan's vocal gyrations. "Come on, give me a chance at that hole. Don't be a hog about it."

He fought his way upward, but Donovan kicked wildly. "They did an about-face, Greg. They're leaving. Dave! Hey, Da-a-ave!"

Powell shrieked, "What's the use of that, you fool? Sound won't carry."

"Well, then," panted Donovan, "kick the walls, slam them, get some vibration started. We've got to attract their attention somehow, Greg, or we're through." He pounded like a madman.

Powell shook him, "Wait, Mike, wait. Listen, I've got an idea. Jumping Jupiter, this is a fine time to get around to the simple solutions. Mike!"

"What do you want?" Donovan pulled his head in.

"Let me in there fast before they get out of range."

"Our of range! What are you going to do? Hey, what are you going to do with that detonator?" He grabbed Powell's arm.

Powell shook off the grip violently. "I'm going to do a little shooting."

"Why?"

"That's for later. Let's see if it works first. If it doesn't, then—Get out of the way and let me shoot!"

* * *

The robots were flickers, small and getting smaller, in the distance. Powell lined up the sights tensely, and pulled the trigger three times. He lowered the guns and peered anxiously. One of the subsidiaries was down! There were only six gleaming figures now.

Powell called into his transmitter uncertainly. "Dave!"

A pause, then the answer sounded to both men, "Boss? Where are you? My third subsidiary has had his chest blown in. He's out of commission."

"Never mind your subsidiary," said Powell. "We're trapped in a cave-in where you were blasting. Can you see our flashlight?"

"Sure. We'll be right there."

Powell sat back and relaxed. "That, my fran', is that."

Donovan said very softly with tears in his voice, "All right, Greg. You win. I beat my forehead against the ground before your feet. Now don't feed me any bull. Just tell me quietly what it's all about."

"Easy. It's just that all through we missed the obvious—the usual. We knew it was the personal initiative circuit, and that it always happened during emergencies, but we kept looking for a specific order as the cause. Why should it be an order?"

"Why not?"

"Well, look. Why not a type of order. What type of order requires the most initiative? What type of order would occur almost always only in an emergency?"

"Don't ask me, Greg. Tell me!"

"I'm doing it! It's the six-way order. Under all ordinary conditions, one or more of the 'fingers' would be doing routine tasks requiring no close supervision—in the sort of offhand way our bodies handle the routine walking motions. But in an emergency, all six subsidiaries must be mobilized immediately and simultaneously. Dave must handle six robots at a time and something gives. The rest was easy. Any decrease in initiative required, such as the arrival of humans, snaps him back. So I destroyed one of the robots. When I did, he was transmitting only five-way orders. Initiative decreases—he's normal."

"How did you get all that?" demanded Donovan.

"Just logical guessing. I tried it and it worked."

The robot's voice was in their ears again, "Here I am. Can you hold out half an hour?"

"Easy!" said Powell. Then, to Donovan, he continued, "And now the job should be simple. We'll go through the circuits, and check off each part that gets an extra workout in a six-way order as against a five-way. How big a field does that leave us?"

Donovan considered, "Not much, I think. If Dave is like the preliminary model we saw back at the factory, there's a special co-ordinating circuit that would be the only section involved." He cheered up suddenly and amazingly, "Say, that wouldn't be bad at all. There's nothing to that."

"All right. You think it over and we'll check the blueprints when we get back. And now, till Dave reaches us, I'm relaxing."

"Hey, wait! Just tell me one thing. What were those queer shifting marches, those funny dance steps, that the robots went through every time they went screwy?"

"That? I don't know. But I've got a notion. Remember, those subsidiaries were Dave's 'fingers.' We were always saying that, you know. Well, it's my idea that in all these interludes, whenever Dave became a psychiatric case, he went off into a moronic maze, spending his time *twiddling his fingers*."

Blind Alley

Only once in Galactic History was an intelligent race of non-Humans discovered—

"Essays on History,"
by Ligurn Vier

I.

From:Bureau for the Outer Provinces
To: Loodun Antyok, Chief Public Administrator, A-8

Subject: Civilian Supervisor of Cepheus 18, Administrative Position as,

References:

(a) Act of Council 2515, of the year 971 of the Galactic Empire, entitled, "Appointment of Officials of the Administrative Service, Methods for, Revision of."

(b) Imperial Directive, Ja 2374, dated 243/975 G.E.

1. By authorization of reference (a), you are hereby appointed to the subject position. The authority of said position as Civilian Supervisor of Cepheus 18 will extend over non-Human subjects of the Emperor living upon the planet under the terms of autonomy set forth in reference (b).

2. The duties of the subject position shall comprise the general supervision of all non-Human internal affairs, co-ordination of authorized government investigating and reporting committees, and the preparation of semiannual reports on all phases of non-Human affairs.

C. Morily, Chief, BuOuProv,
12/977 G.E.

Loodun Antyok had listened carefully, and now he shook his round head mildly, "Friend, I'd like to help you, but you've grabbed the wrong dog by the ears. You'd better take this up with the Bureau."

Tomor Zammo flung himself back into his chair, rubbed his beak of a nose fiercely, thought better of whatever he was going to say, and answered quietly, "Logical, but not practical. I can't make a trip to Trantor now. You're the Bureau's representative on Cepheus 18. Are you entirely helpless?"

"Well, even as Civilian Supervisor, I've got to work within the limits of Bureau policy."

"Good," Zammo cried, "then, tell me what Bureau policy is. I head a scientific investigating committee, under direct Imperial authorization with, supposedly, the widest powers; yet at every angle in the road I am pulled up short by the civilian authorities with only the parrot shriek of 'Bureau policy' to justify themselves. What *is* Bureau policy? I haven't received a decent definition yet."

Antyok's gaze was level and unruffled. He said, "As I see it—and this is not official, so you can't hold me to it—Bureau policy consists in treating the non-Humans as decently as possible."

"Then, what authority have they—"

"*Ssh!* No use raising your voice. As a matter of fact, His Imperial Majesty is a humanitarian and a disciple of the philosophy of Aurelion. I can tell you quietly that it is pretty well-known that it is the Emperor himself who first suggested that this world be established. You can bet that Bureau policy will stick pretty close to Imperial notions. And you can bet that I can't paddle my way against *that* sort of current."

"Well, m'boy," the physiologist's fleshy eyelids quivered, "if you take that sort of attitude, you're going to lose your job. No, I won't have you kicked out. That's not what I mean at all. Your job will just fade out from under you, because nothing is going to be accom-plished here!"

"Really? Why?" Antyok was short, pink, and pudgy, and his plump-cheeked face usually found it difficult to put on display any expression other than one of bland and cheerful politeness—but it looked grave now.

"You haven't been here long. I have." Zammo scowled. "Mind if I smoke?" The cigar in his hand was gnarled and strong and was puffed to life carelessly.

He continued roughly, "There's no place here for humanitarianism, administrator. You're treating non-Humans as if they were Humans, and it won't work. In fact, I don't like the word 'non-Human.' They're animals."

"They're intelligent," interjected Antyok, softly.

"Well, intelligent animals, then. I presume the two terms are not mutually exclusive. Alien intelligences mingling in the same space won't work, anyway."

"Do you propose killing them off?"

"Galaxy, no!" He gestured with his cigar. "I propose we look upon them as objects for study, and only that. We could learn a good deal from these animals if we were allowed to. Knowledge, I might point out, that would be used for the immediate benefit of the human race. *There's* humanity for you. *There's* the good of the masses, if it's this spineless cult of Aurelion that interests you."

"What, for instance, do you refer to?"

"To take the most obvious—You have heard of their chemistry, I take it?"

"Yes," Antyok admitted. "I have leafed through most of the reports on the non-Humans published in the last ten years. I expect to go through more."

"Hmp. Well— Then, all I need say is that their chemical therapy is extremely thorough. For instance, I have witnessed personally the healing of a broken bone—what passes for a broken bone with them, I mean—by the use of a pill. The bone was whole in fifteen minutes. Naturally, none of their drugs are any earthly use on Humans. Most would kill quickly. But if we found out how they worked on the non-Humans—on the animals—"

"Yes, yes. I see the significance."

"Oh, you do. Come, that's gratifying. A second point is that these animals communicate in an unknown manner."

"Telepathy!"

* * *

The scientist's mouth twisted, as he ground out, "Telepathy! Telepathy! Telepathy! Might as well say by witch brew. Nobody knows anything about telepathy except its name. What is the mechanism of telepathy? What is the physiology and the physics of it? I would like to find out, but I can't. Bureau policy, if I listen to you, forbids."

Antyok's little mouth pursed itself. "But— Pardon me, doctor, but I don't follow you. How are you prevented? Surely the Civil Administration has made no attempt to hamper scientific investigation of these non-Humans. I cannot speak for my predecessor entirely, of course, but I myself—"

"No direct interference has occurred. I don't speak of that. But by the Galaxy, administrator, we're hampered by the spirit of the entire set-up. You're making us deal with humans. You allow them their own leader and internal autonomy. You pamper them and give them what

Aurelion's philosophy would call 'rights.' I can't deal with their leader."

"Why not?"

"Because he refuses to allow me a free hand. He refuses to allow experiments on any subject without the subject's own consent. The two or three volunteers we get are not too bright. It's an impossible arrangement."

Antyok shrugged helplessly.

Zammo continued, "In addition, it is obviously impossible to learn anything of value concerning the brains, physiology, and chemistry of these animals without dissection, dietary experiments, and drugs. You know, administrator, scientific investigation is a hard game. Humanity hasn't much place in it."

Loodun Antyok tapped his chin with a doubtful finger, "Must it be quite so hard? These are harmless creatures, these non-Humans. Surely, dissection— Perhaps, if you were to approach them a bit differently—I have the idea that you antagonize them. Your attitude might be somewhat overbearing."

"Overbearing! I am not one of these whining social psychologists who are all the fad these days. I don't believe you can solve a problem that requires dissection by approaching it with what is called the 'correct personal attitude' in the cant of the times."

"I'm sorry you think so. Sociopsychological training is required of all administrators above the grade of A-4."

Zammo withdrew his cud of a cigar from his mouth and replaced it after a suitably contemptuous interval. "Then you'd better use a bit of your technique on the Bureau. You know, I *do* have friends at the Imperial court."

"Well, now, I *can't* take the matter up with them, not baldly. Basic policy does not fall within my cognizance, and such things can only be initiated by the Bureau. But, you know, we might try an indirect approach on this." He smiled faintly, "Strategy."

"What sort?"

Antyok pointed a sudden finger, while his other hand fell lightly on the rows of gray-bound reports upon the floor just next his chair. "Now, look, I've gone through most of these. They're dull, but contain *some* facts. For instance, when was the last non-Human infant born on Cepheus 18?"

Zammo spent little time in consideration. "Don't know. Don't care either."

"But the Bureau would. There's *never* been a non-Human infant born on Cepheus 18—not in the two years the world has been established. Do you know the reason?"

The physiology shrugged, "Too many possible factors. It would take study."

"All right, then. Suppose you write a report—"

"Reports! I've written twenty."

"Write another. Stress the unsolved problems. Tell them you must change your methods. Harp on the birth-rate problem. The Bureau doesn't dare ignore that. If the non-Humans die out, someone will have to answer to the Emperor. You see—"

Zammo stared, his eyes dark. "That will swing it?"

"I've been working for the Bureau for twenty-seven years. I know its ways."

"I'll think about it." Zammo rose and stalked out of the office. The door slammed behind him.

It was later that Zammo said to a co-worker, "He's a bureaucrat, in the first place. He won't abandon the orthodoxies of paper work and he won't risk sticking his neck out. He'll accomplish little by himself, yet maybe more than a little if we work through him."

From: Administrative Headquarters, Cepheus 18

To: BuOuProv

Subject: Outer Province Project 2563, Part II—Scientific Investigations of non-Humans of Cepheus 18, Co-ordination of,

References:

(a) Bu Ou Prov letr. Cep-N-Cm/jg, 100132, dated 302/975 G.E.

(b) AdHQ-Ceph 18 letr. AA-LA/mn, dated 140/977 G.E.

Enclosure:

1. SciGroup 10, Physical & Biochemical Division, Report, entitled, "Physiologic Characteristics of non-Humans of Cepheus 18, Part XI," dated 172/977 G.E.

1. Enclosure 1, included herewith, is forwarded for the information of the BuOuProv. It is to be noted that Section XII, paragraphs 1-16 ofEncl. 1, concern possible changes in present BuOuProv policy with regard to non-Humans with a view of facilitating physical and chemical investigations at present proceeding under authorization of reference (a)

2. It is brought to the attention of the BuOuProv that reference (b) has already discussed possible changes in investigating methods and that it remains the opinion of AdHQ-Ceph18 that such changes are as yet premature. It is nevertheless suggested that the question of non-Human birth rate be made the subject of a BuOuProv project assigned to AdHQ-Ceph18 in view of the importance attached by SciGroup 10 to the problem, as evidenced in Section V of Enclosure 1.

L. Antyok, Supery, AdHQ-Ceph18,
174/977

From: BuOuProv
To: AdHQ-Celph18
Subject: Outer Province Project 2563—Scientific Investigations of non-Humans of Cepheus 18, Co-ordination of,
References:
(a) AdHQ-Ceph18 letr. AA-LA/mn, dated 174/977 G.E.

1. In response to the suggestion contained in paragraph 2 of reference (a), it is considered that the question of the non-Human birth rate does not fall within the cognizance of AdHQ-Ceph18. In view of the fact that SciGroup 10 has reported said sterility to be probably due to a chemical deficiency in the food supply, all investigations in the field are relegated to SciGroup 10 as the proper authority.

2. Investigating procedures by the various SciGroups shall continue according to current directives on the subject. No changes in policy are envisaged.

C. Morily, Chief, BuOuProv,
186/977 G.E.

II.

There was a loose-jointed gauntness about the news reporter which made him appear somberly tall. He was Gustiv Bannerd, with whose reputation was combined ability—two things which do not invariably go together despite the maxims of elementary morality.

Loodum Antyok took his measure doubtfully and said, "There's no use denying that you're right. But the SciGroup report was confidential. I don't understand how—"

"It leaked," said Bannerd, callously. "Everything leaks."

Antyok was obviously baffled, and his pink face furrowed slightly, "Then I'll just have to plug the leak here. I can't pass your story. All references to SciGroup complaints have to come out. You see that, don't you?"

"No." Bannerd was calm enough. "It's important; and I have my rights under the Imperial directive. I think the Empire should know what's going on."

"But it isn't going on," said Antyok, despairingly. "Your claims are all wrong. The Bureau isn't going to change its policy. I showed you the letters."

"You think you can stand up against Zammo when he puts the pressure on?" the newsman asked derisively.

"I will—if I think he's wrong."

"If!" stated Bannerd flatly. Then, in a sudden fervor, 'Antyok, the

Empire has something great here; something greater by a good deal than the government apparently realizes. They're destroying it. They're treating these creatures like animals."

"Really—" began Antyok, weakly.

"Don't talk about Cepheus 18. It's a zoo. It's a high-class zoo, with your petrified scientists teasing those poor creatures with their sticks poking through the bars. You throw them chunks of meat, but you cage them up. I know! I've been writing about them for two years now. I've almost been living with them."

"Zammo says—"

"Zammo!" This with hard contempt.

"Zammo says," insisted Antyok with worried firmness, "that we treat them too like humans as it is."

The newsman's straight, long cheeks were rigid, "Zammo is rather animallike in his own right. He is a science-worshipper. We can do with less of them. Have you read Aurelion's works?" The last was suddenly posed.

"Umm. Yes. I understand the Emperor—"

"The Emperor tends towards us. That is good—better than the hounding of the last reign."

"I don't see where you're heading?"

"These aliens have much to teach us. You understand? It is nothing that Zammo and his SciGroup can use; no chemistry, no telepathy. It's a way of life; a way of thinking. The aliens have no crime, no misfits. What effort is being made to study their philosophy? Or to set them up as a problem in social engineering?"

Antyok grew thoughtful, and his plump face smoothed out, "It is an interesting consideration. It would be a matter for psychologists—"

"No good. Most of them are quacks. Psychologists point out problems, but their solutions are fallacious. We need men of Aurelion. Men of The Philosophy—"

"But look here, we can't turn Cepheus 18 into . . . into a metaphysical study."

"Why not? It can be done easily."

"How?"

"Forget your puny test-tube peerings. Allow the aliens to set up a society free of Humans. Give them an untrammeled independence and allow an intermingling of philosophies—"

Antyok's nervous response came, "That can't be done in a day."

"We can start in a day."

The administrator said slowly, "Well, I can't prevent you from trying to start." He grew confidential, his mild eyes thoughtful, "You'll ruin your own game, though, if you publish SciGroup 10's report and denounce it on humanitarian grounds. The Scientists are powerful."

"And we of The Philosophy as well."

"Yes, but there's an easy way. You needn't rave. Simply point out that the SciGroup is not solving its problems. Do so unemotionally and let the readers think out your point of view for themselves. Take the birth-rate problem, for instance. *There's* something for you. In a generation, the non-Humans might die out, for all science can do. Point out that a more philosophical approach is required. Or pick some other obvious point. Use your judgment, eh?"

Antyok smiled ingratiatingly as he arose, "But, for the Galaxy's sake, don't stir up a bad smell."

Bannerd was stiff and unresponsive, "You may be right."

It was later that Bannerd wrote in a capsule message to a friend, "He is not clever, by any means. He is confused and has no guiding-line through life. Certainly utterly incompetent in his job. But he's a cutter and a trimmer, compromises his way around difficulties, and will yield concessions rather than risk a hard stand. he may prove valuable in that. Yours in Aurelion."

From: AdHQ-Ceph18
To: BuOuProv
Subject: Birth rate of non-Humans on Cepheus 18, News Report on.
References:
(a) AdHQ-Ceph18 letr. AA-LA/mn, dated 174/977 G.E.
(b) Imperial Directive, Ja2374, dated 243/975 G.E.
Enclosures:
1-G Brannerd new report, date-lined Cepheus 18, 201/977 G.E.
2-G Bannerd news report, datelined Cepheus 18, 203/977 G.E.

1. The sterility of non-Humans on Cepheus 18, reported to the BuOuProv in reference (a), has become the subject of news reports to the galactic press. The news reports in question are submitted herewith for the information of the BuOuProv as Enclosures 1 and 2. Although said reports are based on material considered confidential and closed to the public, the news reporter in question maintained his rights to free expression under the terms of reference (b).

2. In view of the unavoidable publicity and misunderstanding on the part of the general public now inevitable, it is requested that the BuOuProv direct future policy on the problem of non-Human sterility.

L. Antyok, Superv, AdHQ-Ceph18,
209/977 G.C.

From: BuOuProv
To: AdHQ-Ceph18
Subject: Birth rate of non-Humans on Cepheus 18, Investigation of.
References:
(a) AdHQ-Ceph18 letr. AA-LA/mn, dated 209/977 G.E.
(b) AdHQ-Ceph18 letr. AA-LA/mn, dated 174/977 G.E.

1. It is proposed to investigate the causes and the means of precluding the unfavorable birth-rate phenomena mentioned in references (a) and (b). A project is therefore set up, entitled, "Birth rate of non-Humans on Cepheus 18, Investigation of" to which, in view of the crucial importance of the subject, a priority of AA is given.

2. The number assigned to the subject project is 2910, and all expenses incidental to it shall be assigned to Appropriation number 18/78.

C. Morily, Chief, BuOuProv,
223/977 G.E.

III.

If Tomor Zanno's ill-humor lessened within the grounds of SciGroup 10 Experimental Station, his friendliness had not thereby increased. Antyok found himself standing alone at the viewing window into the main field laboratory.

The main field laboratory was a broad court at the environmental conditions of Cepheus 18 itself for the discomfort of the experimenters and the convenience of the experimentees. Through the burning sand, and the dry, oxygen-rich air, there sparkled the hard brilliance of hot, white sunlight. And under the blaze, the brick-red non-Humans, wrinkled of skin and wiry of build, huddled in their squatting positions of ease, by ones and twos.

Zammo emerged from the laboratory. He paused to drink water thirstily. He looked up, moisture gleaming on his upper lip, 'Like to step in there?"

Antyok shook his head definitely, "No, thank you. What's the temperature right now?"

"A hundred twenty, if there were shade. And they complain of the cold. It's drinking time now. Want to watch them drink?"

A spray of water shot upward from the fountain in the center of the court, and the little alien figures swayed to their feet and hopped eagerly forward in a queer, springy half-run. They milled about the water, jostling one another. The centers of their faces were suddenly disfigured by the projection of a long and flexible fleshy tube, which thrust forward into the spray and was withdrawn dripping.

It continued for long minutes. The bodies swelled and the wrinkles disappeared. They retreated slowly, backing away, with the drinking tube flicking in and out, before receding finally into a pink, wrinkled mass above a wide, lipless mouth. They went to sleep in groups in the shaded angles, plump and sated.

"Animals!" said Zammo, with contempt.

"How often do they drink?" asked Antyok.

"As often as they want. They can go a week if they have to. We water them every day. They store it under their skin. They eat in the evenings. Vegetarians, you know."

Antyok smiled chubbily, "It's nice to get a bit of firsthand information occasionally. Can't read reports all the time."

"Yes?"—noncomittally. Then, "What's new? What about the lacypants boys on Trantor?"

Antyok shrugged dubiously, "You can't get the Bureau to commit itself, unfortunately. With the Emperor sympathetic to the Aurelionists, humanitarianism is the order of the day. You know that."

There was a pause in which the administrator chewed his lip uncertainly. "But there's this birth-rate problem now. It's finally been assigned to AdHQ, you know—and double A priority, too."

Zammo muttered wordlessly.

Antyok said, "You may not realize it, but that project will now take precedence over all other work proceeding on Cepheus 18. It's important."

He turned back to the viewing window and said thoughtfully with a bald lack of preamble. "Do you think those creatures might be unhappy?"

"Unhappy!" The word was an explosion.

"Well, then," Antyok corrected hastily, "maladjusted. You understand? It's difficult to adjust an environment to a race we know so little of."

"Say—did you ever see the world we took them from?"

"I've read the reports—"

"Reports!"—infinite contempt. "I've *seen* it. This may look like desert out there to you, but it's a watery paradise to those devils. They have all the food and water they can get. They have a world to themselves with vegetation and natural water flow, instead of a lump of silica and granite where fungi were force-grown in caves and water had to be steamed out of gypsum rock. In ten years, they would have been dead to the last beast, and we saved them. Unhappy? Ga-a-ah, if they were, they haven't the decency of most animals."

"Well, perhaps. Yet I have a notion."

"A notion? What is your notion?" Zammo reached for one of his cigars.

"It's something that might help you. Why not study the creatures in a more integrated fashion? Let them use their initiative. After all, they did have a highly-developed science. Your reports speak of it continually. Give them problems to solve."

"Such as?"

"Oh . . . oh," Antyok waved his hands helplessly. "Whatever you think might help most. For instance, spaceships. Get them into the control room and study their reactions."

"Why?" asked Zammo with dry bluntness.

"Because the reaction of their minds to tools and controls adjusted to the human temperament can teach you a lot. In addition, it will make a more effective bribe, it seems to me, than anything you've yet tried. You'll get more volunteers if they think they'll be doing something interesting."

"That's your psychology coming out. Hm-m-m. Sounds better than it probably is. I'll sleep on it. And where would I get permission, in any case, to let them handle spaceships? I've none at *my* disposal, and it would take a good deal longer than it was worth to follow down the line of red tape to get one assigned to us."

Antyok pondered, and his forehead creased lightly, "It doesn't *have* to be spaceships. But even so— If you would write up another report and make the suggestion yourself—strongly, you understand—I might figure out some way of tying it up with my birth-rate project. A double-A priority can get practically anything, you know, without questions."

Zammo's interest lacked a bit even of mildness. "Well, maybe. Meanwhile, I've some basal metabolism tests in progress, and it's getting late. I'll think about it. It's got its points."

From: AdHQ-Ceph18

To: BuOuProv

Subject: Outer Province Project 2910, Part I—Birth rate of non-Humans on Cepheus 18, Investigation of,

Reference:

(a) BuOuProv letr. Ceph-N-CM/car, 115097, 223/997 G.E.

Enclosure:

1. SciGroup 10, Physical & Biochemical Division report, Part XV, dated 220/998 G.E.

1. Enclosure 1 is forwarded herewith for the information of the BuOuProv.

2. Special attention is directed to Section V, Paragraph 3 of Enclosure 1 in which it is requested that a spaceship be assigned SciGroup 10 for use in expediting investigations authorized by the BuOuProv. It is considered by AdHQ-Ceph18 that such investigations may be of material use in aiding work now in progress on the subject project, authorized by reference (a). It is suggested, in view of the high priority placed by the BuOuProv upon the subject project, that immediate consideration be given the SciGroup's request.

L. Antyok, Superv. AdHQ-Ceph18
240/997 G.E.

From: BuOuProv
To: AdHQ-Ceph18
Subject: Outer Province Project 2910—Birth rate of non-Humans on Cepheus 18, Investigation of.
Reference:
(a) AdHQ-Ceph18 letr. AA-LA/mn, dated 240/997 G.E.

1. Training Ship *AN*-R-2055 is being placed at the disposal of AdHQ-Ceph18 for use in investigation of non-Humans on Cepheus 18 with respect to the subject project and other authorized OuProv projects, as requested in Enclosure 1 to reference (a).

2. It is urgently requested that work on the subject project be expedited by all available means.

C. Morily, Head, BuOuProv,
251/977 G.E.

IV.

The little, bricky creature must have been more uncomfortable than his bearing would admit to. He was carefully wrapped in a temperature already adjusted to the point where his human companions steamed in their open shirts.

His speech was high-pitched and careful, "I find it damp, but not unbearably so at this low temperature.'

Antyok smiled, "It was nice of you to come. I had planned to visit you, but a trial run in your atmosphere out there—" The smile had become rueful.

"It doesn't matter. You other-worldings have done more for us than ever we were able to do for ourselves. It is an obligation that is but imperfectly returned by the endurance on my part of a trifling discomfort." His speech seemed always indirect, as if he approached his thoughts sidelong, or as if it were against all etiquette to be blunt.

Gustiv Bannerd, seated in an angle of the room, with one long leg crossing the other, scrawled nimbly and said, "You don't mind if I record all this?"

The Cepheid non-Human glanced briefly at the journal, "I have no objection."

Antyok's apologetics persisted, "This is not a purely social affair, sir. I would not have forced discomfort on you for that. There are important questions to be considered, and you are the leader of your people."

The Cepheid nodded, "I am satisfied your purposes are kindly. Please proceed."

The administrator almost wriggled in his difficulty in putting thoughts into words. "It is a subject," he said, "of delicacy, and one I would never bring up if it weren't for the overwhelming importance of the . . . uh . . . question. I am only the spokesman of my government—"

"My people consider the otherworld government a kindly one."

"Well, yes, they are kindly. For that reason, they are disturbed over the fact that your people no longer breed."

Antyok paused, and waited with worry for a reaction that did not come. The Cepheid's face was motionless except for the soft, trembling motion of the wrinkled area that was his deflated drinking tube.

Antyok continued, "It is a question we have hesitated to bring up because of its extremely personal angles. Noninterference is my government's prime aim, and we have done our best to investigate the problem quietly and without disturbing your people. But, frankly, we—"

"Have failed?" finished the Cepheid, at the other's pause.

"Yes. Or at least, we have not discovered a concrete failure to reproduce the exact environment of your original world; with, of course, the necessary modification to make it more livable. Naturally, it is thought there is some chemical shortcoming. And so I ask your voluntary help in the matter. Your people are advanced in the study of your own biochemistry. If you do not choose, or would rather not—"

"No, no, I can help." The Cepheid seemed cheerful about it. The smooth flat planes of his loose-skinned, hairless skull wrinkled in an alien response to an uncertain emotion. "It is not a matter that any of us would have thought would have disturbed you other-worldlings. That it does is but another indication of your well-meaning kindness. This world we find congenial, a paradise in comparison to our old. It lacks in nothing. Conditions such as now prevail belong in our legends of the Golden Age."

"Well—"

"But there is a something; a something you may not understand. We cannot expect different intelligences to think alike."

"I shall try to understand."

The Cepheid's voice had grown soft, its liquid undertones more pronounced, "We were dying on our native world; but we were fighting. Our science, developed through a history older than yours, was losing; but it had not yet lost. Perhaps it was because our science was fundamentally biological, rather than physical as yours is. Your people discovered new forms of energy and reached the stars. Our people discovered new truths of psychology and psychiatry and built up a working society free of disease and crime.

"There is no need to question which of the two angles of approach was the more laudable, but there is no uncertainty as to which proved more successful in the end. In our dying world, without the means of life or sources of power, our biological science could but make the dying easier.

"And yet we fought. For centuries past, we had been groping toward the elements of atomic power, and slowly the spark of hope had glimmered that we might break through the two-dimensional limits of our planetary surface and reach the stars. There were no other planets in our system to serve as stepping stones. Nothing but some twenty light-years to the nearest star, without the knowledge of the possibility of the existence of other planetary systems, but rather of the contrary.

"But there is something in all life that insists on striving; even on useless striving. There were only five thousand of us left in the last days. Only five thousand. And our first ship was ready. It was experimental. It would probably have been a failure. But already we had all the principles of propulsion and navigation correctly worked out."

There was a long pause, and the Cepheid's small black eyes seemed glazed in retrospect.

The newspaperman put in suddenly, from his corner, "And then we came?"

'And then you came," the Cepheid agreed simply. "It changed everything. Energy was ours for the asking. A new world, congenial and, indeed, ideal, was ours even without asking. If our problems of society had long been solved by ourselves, our more difficult problems of environment were suddenly solved for us, no less completely."

"Well?" urged Antyok.

"Well—it was somehow not well. For centuries, our ancestors had fought towards the stars, and now the stars suddenly proved to be the property of others. We had fought for life, and it had become a present handed to us by others. There is no longer any reason to fight. There is no longer anything to attain. All the universe is the property of your race."

"This world is yours," said Antyok, gently.

"By sufferance. It is a gift. It is not ours by right."

"You have earned it, in my opinion."

And now the Cepheid's eyes were sharply fixed on the other's countenance, "You mean well, but I doubt that you understand. We have nowhere to go, save this gift of a world. We are in a blind alley. The function of life is striving, and that is taken from us. Life can no longer interest us. We have no offspring—voluntarily. It is our way of removing ourselves from your way."

* * *

Absent-mindedly, Antyok had removed the fluoro-globe from the window seat, and spun it on its base. Its gaudy surface reflected light as it spun, and its three-foot-high bulk floated with incongruous grace and lightness in the air.

Antyok said, "Is that your only solution? Sterility?"

"We might escape still," whispered the Cepheid, "but where in the Galaxy is there place for us? It is all yours."

"Yes, there is no place for you nearer than the Magellanic Clouds if you wished independence. The Magellanic Clouds—"

"And you would not let us go of yourselves. You mean kindly, I know."

"Yes, we mean kindly—but we could not let you go."

"It is a mistaken kindness."

"Perhaps, but could you not reconcile yourselves? You have a world."

"It is something past complete explanations. Your mind is different. We could not reconcile ourselves. I believe, administrator, that you have thought of all this before. The concept of the blind alley we find ourselves trapped in is not new to you."

Antyok looked up, startled, and one hand steadied the fluoro-globe, "Can you read my mind?"

"It is just a guess. A good one, I think."

"Yes—but *can* you read my mind? The minds of humans in general, I mean. It is an interesting point. The scientists say you cannot, but sometimes I wonder if it is that you simply will not. Could you answer that? I am detaining you, unduly, perhaps."

"No . . . no—" But the little Cepheid drew his enveloping robe closer, and buried his face in the electrically-heated pad at the collar for a moment. "You other-worldlings speak of reading minds. It is not so at all, but it is assuredly hopeless to explain."

Antyok mumbled the old proverb, "One cannot explain sight to a man blind from birth."

"Yes, just so. This sense which you call 'mind reading,' quite erroneously, cannot be applied to us. It is not that we cannot receive the proper sensations, it is that your people do not transmit them, and we have no way of explaining to you how to go about it."

"Hm-m-m."

"There are times, of course, of great concentration or emotional tension on the part of an other-worldling when some of us who are more expert in this sense; more sharp-eyed, so to speak; detect vaguely *something*. It is uncertain; yet I myself have at times wondered—"

Carefully, Antyok began spinning the fluoro-globe once more. His pink face was set in thought, and his eyes were fixed upon the Cepheid. Gustiv Bannerd stretched his fingers and reread his notes, his lips moving silently.

The fluoro-globe spun, and slowly the Cepheid seemed to grow tense as well, as his eyes shifted to the colorful sheen of the globe's fragile surface.

The Cepheid said, "What is that?"

Antyok started, and his face smoothed into an almost chuckling placidity, "This? A Galactic fad of three years ago; which means that it is a hopelessly old-fashioned relic this year. It is a useless device but it looks pretty. Bannerd, could you adjust the windows to nontransmission?"

* * *

There was the soft click of a contact, and the windows became curved regions of darkness, while in the center of the room, the fluoro-globe was suddenly the focus of a rosy effulgence that seemed to leap outward in streamers. Antyok, a scarlet figure in a scarlet room, placed it upon the table and spun it with a hand that dripped red. As it spun, the colors changed with a slowly increasing rapidity, blended and fell apart into more extreme contrasts.

Antyok was speaking in an eerie atmosphere of molten, shifting rainbow. "The surface is of a material that exhibits variable fluorescence. It is almost weightless, extremely fragile, but gyroscopically balanced so that it rarely falls, with ordinary care. It is rather pretty, don't you think?"

From somewhere the Cepheid's voice came, "Extremely pretty."

"But it has outworn its welcome; outlived its fashionable existence."

The Cepheid's voice was abstracted. "It is very pretty."

Bannerd restored the light at a gesture, and the colors faded.

The Cepheid said, "That is something my people would enjoy." He stared at the globe with fascination.

And now Antyok rose. "You had better go. If you stay longer, the atmosphere may have bad effects. I thank you humbly for your kindness."

"I thank you humbly for yours." The Cepheid had also risen.

Antyok said, "Most of your people, by the way, have accepted our offers to them to study the make-up of our modern spaceships. You understand, I suppose, that the purpose was to study the reactions of your people to our technology. I trust that conforms with your sense of propriety."

"You need not apologize. I, myself, have now the makings of a human pilot. It was most interesting. It recalls our own efforts—and reminds us of how nearly on the right track we were."

The Cepheid left, and Antyok sat, frowning.

"Well," he said to Bannerd, a little sharply. "You remember our agreement, I hope. This interview can't be published."

Bannerd shrugged, "Very well."

Antyok was at his seat, and his fingers fumbled with the small metal figurine upon his desk, "What do you think of all this, Bannerd?"

"I am sorry for them. I think I understand how they feel. We must educate them out of it. The Philosophy can do it."

"You think so?"

"Yes."

"We can't let them go, of course."

"Oh, no. Out of the question. We have too much to learn from them. This feeling of theirs is only a passing stage. They'll think differently, especially when we allow them the completest independence."

"Maybe. What do you think of the fluoro-globes, Bannerd? He liked them. It might be a gesture of the right sort to order several thousand of them. The Galaxy knows, they're a drug on the market right now, and cheap enough."

"Sounds like a good idea," said Bannerd.

"The Bureau would never agree, though. I know them."

The newsman's eyes narrowed, "But it might be just the thing. They need new interests."

"Yes? Well, we *could* do something. I could include your transcript of the interview as part of a report and just emphasize the matter of the globes a bit. After all, you're a member of The Philosophy and might have influence with important people, whose word with the Bureau might carry much more weight than mine. You understand—?"

"Yes," mused Bannerd. "Yes."

From: AdHQ-Ceph18

To: BuOuProv

Subject: OuProv Project 2910, Part II; Birth rate of non-Humans on Cepheus 18, Investigation of.

Reference:

(a) BuOuProv letr. Ceph-N-CM/car, 115098, dated 223/997 G.E.

Enclosure:

1. Transcript of conversation between L. Antyok of AdHQ-Ceph18, and Ni-San, High Judge of the non-Humans on Cepheus 18.

1. Enclosure 1 is forwarded herewith for the information of the BuOuProv.

2. The investigation of the subject project undertaken in response to the authorization of reference (a) is being pursued along the new lines indicated in Enclosure 1. The BuOuProv is assured that every means will be used to combat the harmful psychological attitude at present prevalent among the non-Humans.

3. It is to be noted that the High Judge of the non-Humans on Cepheus 18 expressed interest in fluoro-globes. A preliminary investigation into this fact of non-Human psychology had been initiated.

L. Antyok, Superv, AdHQ-Ceph18,
272/997 G.C.

From: BuOuProv

To: AdHQ-Ceph18

Subject: OuProv Project 2910; Birth rate of non-Humans on Cepheus 18, Investigation of.

Reference:

(a) AdHQ-Ceph18 letr. AA-LA/mn, dated 272/977 G.E.

1. With reference to Enclosure 1 of reference (a), five thousand fluoro-globes have been allocated for shipment to Cepheus 18, by the Department of Trade.

2. It is instructed that AdHQ-Ceph18 make use of all methods of

appeasing non-Humans' dissatisfaction, consistent with the necessities of obedience to Imperial proclamations.

C. Morily, Chief, BuOuProv,
283/977 G.E.

V.

The dinner was over, the wine had been brought in, and the cigars were out. The groups of talkers had formed, and the captain of the merchant fleet was the center of the largest. His brilliant white uniform quite outsparkled his listeners.

He was almost complacent in his speech: "The trip was nothing. I've had more than three hundred ships under me before this. Still, I've never had a cargo quite like this. What do you want with five thousand fluoro-globes on this desert, by the Galaxy!"

Loodun Antyok laughed gently. He shrugged, "For the non-Humans. It wasn't a difficult cargo, I hope."

"No, not difficult. But bulky. They're fragile, and I couldn't carry more than twenty to a ship, with all the government regulations concerning packing and precautions against breakage. But it's the government's money, I suppose."

Zammo smiled grimly. "Is this your first experience with government methods, captain?"

"Galaxy, no," exploded the spaceman. "I try to avoid it, of course, but you can't help getting entangled on occasion. And it's an abhorrent thing when you are, and that's the truth. The red tape! The paper work! It's enough to stunt your growth and curdle your circulation. It's a tumor, a cancerous growth on the Galaxy. I'd wipe out the whole mess."

Antyok said, "You're unfair, captain. You don't understand."

"Yes? Well, now, as one of these bureaucrats," and he smiled amiably at the word, "suppose you explain your side of the situation, administrator."

"Well, now," Antyok seemed confused, "government is a serious and complicated business. We've got thousands of planets to worry about in this Empire of ours and billions of people. It's almost past human ability to supervise the business of governing without the tightest sort of organization. I think there are something like four hundred million men today in the Imperial Administrative Service alone, and in order to co-ordinate their efforts and to pool their knowledge, you *must* have what you call red tape and paper work. Every bit of it, senseless though it may seem, annoying though it may be, has its uses. Every piece of paper is a thread binding the labors of four hundred million humans. Abolish the Administrative Service and you abolish the Empire; and with it, interstellar peace, order, and civilization."

"Come—" said the captain.

"No. I mean it." Antyok was earnestly breathless. "The rules and system of the Administrative set-up must be sufficiently all-embracing and rigid so that in case of incompetent officials, and sometimes one *is* appointed—you may laugh, but there are incompetent scientists, and newsmen, and captains, too—in case of incompetent officials, I say, little harm will be done. For, at the worst, the system can move by itself."

"Yes," grunted the captain, sourly, "and if a capable administrator should be appointed? He is then caught by the same rigid web and is forced into mediocrity."

"Not at all," replied Antyok, warmly. "A capable man can work within the limits of the rules and accomplish what he wishes."

"How?" asked Bannerd.

"Well . . . well—" Antyok was suddenly ill at ease. "One method is to get yourself an A-priority project, or double-A, if possible."

The captain leaned his head back for laughter, but never quite made it, for the door was flung open and frightened men were pouring in. The shouts made no sense at first. Then:

"Sir, the ships are gone. These non-Humans have taken them by force."

"What? All?"

"Every one. Ships and creatures—"

* * *

It was two hours later that the four were together again, alone in Antyok's office now.

Antyok said coldly, "They've made no mistakes. There's not a ship left behind, not even your training ship, Zammo. And there isn't a government ship available in this entire half of the Sector. By the time we organize a pursuit they'll be out of the Galaxy and halfway to the Magellanic Clouds. Captain, it was your responsibility to maintain an adequate guard."

The captain cried, "It was our first day out of space. Who could have known—"

Zammo interrupted fiercely, "Wait a while, captain. I'm beginning to understand. Antyok," his voice was hard, "you engineered this."

"I?" Antyok's expression was strangely cool, almost indifferent.

"You told us this evening that a clever administrator got an A-priority project assigned to accomplish what he wished. You got such a project in order to help the non-Humans escape."

"I did? I beg your pardon, but how could that be? It was you yourself in one of your reports that brought up the problem of the failing birth rate. It was Bannerd, here, whose sensational articles frightened the Bureau into making a double A-priority project out of it. I had nothing to do with it."

"*You* suggested that I mention the birth rate," said Zammo, violently.

"Did I?" said Antyok, composedly.

"And for that matter," roared Bannerd, suddenly, "you suggested that I mention the birth rate in my articles."

The three ringed him now and hemmed him in. Antyok leaned back in his chair and said easily, "I don't know what you mean by suggestions. If you are accusing me, please stick to evidence—legal evidence. The laws of the Empire go by written, filmed, or transcribed material, or by witnessed statements. All my letters as administrator are on file here, at the Bureau, and at other places. I never asked for an A-priority project. The Bureau assigned it to me, and Zammo and Bannerd are responsible for that. In print, at any rate."

Zammo's voice was an almost inarticulate growl, "You hoodwinked me into teaching the creatures how to handle a spaceship."

"It was *your* suggestion. I have your report proposing they be studied in their reaction to human tools on file. So has the Bureau. The evidence—the *legal* evidence, is plain. I had nothing to do with it."

"Not with the globes?" demanded Bannerd.

The captain howled suddenly, "You had my ships brought here purposely. Five thousand globes! You knew it would require hundreds of craft."

"I never asked for globes," said Antyok coldly. "That was the Bureau's idea, although I think Bannerd's friends of The Philosophy helped that along."

Bannerd fairly choked. He spat out, "You were asking that Cepheid leader if he could read minds. You were telling him to express interest in the globes."

"Come, now. You prepared the transcript of the conversation yourself, and that, too, is on file. You can't proof it." He stood up. "You'll have to excuse me. I must prepare a report for the Bureau."

At the door, Antyok turned, "In a way, the problem of the non-Humans is solved, even if only to their own satisfaction. They'll breed now, and have a world they've earned themselves. It's what they wanted.

"Another thing. Don't accuse me of silly things. I've been in the Service for twenty-seven years, and I assure you that my paper work is proof enough that I have been thoroughly correct in everything I have done. And captain, I'll be glad to continue our discussion of earlier this evening at your convenience and explain how a capable administrator can work through red tape and still get what he wants."

It was remarkable that such a round, smooth baby-face could wear a smile quite so sardonic.

From: BuOuProv
To: Loodun Antyok, Chief Public Administrator, A-8
Subject: Administrative Service, Standing in.
Reference:
(a) AdServ Court Decision 22874-Q, dated 1/978 G.E.

1. In view of the favorable opinion handed down in reference (a) you are hereby absolved of all responsibility for the flight of non-Humans on Cepheus 18. It is requested that you hold yourself in readiness for your next appointment.

R. Horpritt, Chief, AdServ,
15/978 G.E.

Evidence

Francis Quinn was a politician of the new school. That, of course, is a meaningless expression, as are all expressions of the sort. Most of the "new schools" we have were duplicated in the social life of ancient Greece, and perhaps, if we knew more about it, in the social life of ancient Sumeria and in the lake dwellings of prehistoric Switzerland as well.

But, to get out from under what promises to be a dull and complicated beginning, it might be best to state hastily that Quinn neither ran for office nor canvassed for votes, made no speeches and stuffed no ballot boxes. Any more than Napoleon pulled a trigger at Austerlitz.

And since politics makes strange bedfellows, Alfred Lanning sat at the other side of the desk with his ferocious white eyebrows bent far forward over eyes in which chronic impatience had sharpened to acuity. He was not pleased.

The fact, if known to Quinn, would have annoyed him not the least. His voice was friendly, perhaps professionally so.

"I assume you know Stephen Byerley, Dr. Lanning."

"I have heard of him. So have many people."

"Yes, so have I. Perhaps you intend voting for him at the next election."

"I couldn't say." There was an unmistakable trace of acidity here. "I have not followed the political currents, so I'm not aware that he is running for office."

"He may be our next mayor. Of course, he is only a lawyer now, but great oaks—"

"Yes," interrupted Lanning, "I have heard the phrase before. But I wonder if we can get to the business at hand."

"We *are* at the business at hand, Dr. Lanning." Quinn's tone was very gentle, "It is to my interest to keep Mr. Byerley a district attorney at the very most, and it is to your interest to help me do so."

"To *my* interest? Come!" Lanning's eyebrows hunched low.

"Well, say then to the interest of the U. S. Robots and Mechanical Men Corporation. I come to you as Director-Emeritus of Research, because I know that your connection to them is that of, shall we say, 'elder statesman.' You are listened to with respect and yet your connection with them is no longer so tight but that you cannot possess considerable freedom of action; even if the action is somewhat unorthodox."

Dr. Lanning was silent a moment, chewing the cud of his thoughts. He said more softly, "I don't follow you at all, Mr. Quinn."

"I am not surprised, Dr. Lanning. But it's all rather simple. Do you mind?" Quinn lit a slender cigarette with a lighter of tasteful simplicity and his big-boned face settled into an expression of quiet amusement. "We have spoken of Mr. Byerley—a strange and colorful character. He was unknown three years ago. He is very well known now. He is a man of force and ability, and certainly the most capable and intelligent prosecutor I have ever known. Unfortunately he is not a friend of mine—"

"I understand," said Lanning, mechanically. He stared at his fingernails.

"I have had occasion," continued Quinn, evenly, "in the past year to investigate Mr. Byerley—quite exhaustively. It is always useful, you see, to subject the past life of reform politicians to rather inquisitive research. If you knew how often it helped—" He paused to smile humorlessly at the glowing tip of his cigarette. "But Mr. Byerley's past is unremarkable. A quiet life in a small town, a college education, a wife who died young, an auto accident with a slow recovery, law school, coming to the metropolis, an attorney."

Francis Quinn shook his head slowly, then added, "But his present life. Ah, that is remarkable. Our district attorney never eats!"

Lanning's head snapped up, old eyes surprisingly sharp, "Pardon me?"

"Our district attorney never eats." The repetition thumped by syllables. "I'll modify that slightly. He has never been seen to eat or drink. Never! Do you understand the significance of the word? Not rarely, but never!"

"I find that quite incredible. Can you trust your investigators?"

"I can trust my investigators, and I don't find it incredible at all. Further, our district attorney has never been seen to drink—in the aqueous sense as well as the alcoholic—nor to sleep. There are other factors, but I should think I have made my point."

* * *

Lanning leaned back in his seat, and there was the rapt silence of challenge and response between them, and then the old roboticist shook his head. "No. There is only one thing you can be trying to imply, if I couple your statements with the fact that you present them to me, and that is impossible."

"But the man is quite inhuman, Dr. Lanning."

"If you told me he were Satan in masquerade, there would be a faint chance that I might believe you."

"I tell you he is a robot, Dr. Lanning."

"I tell you it is as impossible a conception as I have ever heard, Mr. Quinn."

Again the combative silence.

"Nevertheless," and Quinn stubbed out his cigarette with elaborate care, "you will have to investigate this impossibility with all the resources of the Corporation."

"I'm sure that I could undertake no such thing, Mr. Quinn. You don't seriously suggest that the Corporation take part in local politics."

"You have no choice. Supposing I were to make my facts public without proof. The evidence is circumstantial enough."

"Suit yourself in that respect."

"But it would not suit me. Proof would be much preferable. And it would not suit *you*, for the publicity would be very damaging to your company. You are perfectly well acquainted, I suppose, with the strict rules against the use of robots on inhabited worlds."

"Certainly!" —brusquely.

"You know that the U.S. Robots and Mechanical Men Corporation is the only manufacturer of positronic robots in the Solar System, and if Byerley is a robot, he is a *positronic* robot. You are also aware that all positronic robots are leased, and not sold; that the Corporation remains the owner and manager of each robot, and is therefore responsible for the actions of all."

"It is an easy matter, Mr. Quinn, to prove the Corporation has never manufactured a robot of a humanoid character."

"It can be done? To discuss merely possibilities."

"Yes. It can be done."

"Secretly, I imagine, as well. Without entering it in your books."

"Not the positronic brain, sir. Too many factors are involved in that, and there is the tightest possible government supervision."

"Yes, but robots are worn out, break down, go out of order—and are dismantled."

"And the positronic brains re-used or destroyed."

"Really?" Francis Quinn allowed himself a trace of sarcasm. "And if one were, accidently, of course, not destroyed—and there happened to be a humanoid structure waiting for a brain."

"Impossible!"

"You would have to prove that to the government and the public, so why not prove it to me now."

"But what could our purpose be?" demanded Lanning in exasperation. "Where is our motivation? Credit us with a minimum of sense."

"My dear sir, please. The Corporation would be only too glad to have the various Regions permit the use of humanoid positronic robots on inhabited worlds. The profits would be enormous. But the prejudice of the public against such a practice is too great. Suppose you get them used to such robots first—see, we have a skillful lawyer, a good mayor—and he is a robot. Won't you buy our robot butlers?"

"Thoroughly fantastic. An almost humorous descent to the ridiculous."

"I imagine so. Why not prove it? Or would you still rather try to prove it to the public?"

The light in the office was dimming, but it was not yet too dim to obscure the flush of frustration on Alfred Lanning's face. Slowly, the roboticist's finger touched a knob and the wall illuminators glowed to gentle life.

"Well, then," he growled, "let us see."

* * *

The face of Stephen Byerley is not an easy one to describe. He was forty by birth certificate and forty by appearance—but it was a healthy, well-nourished good-natured appearance of forty; one that automatically drew the teeth of the bromide about "looking one's age."

This was particularly true when he laughed, and he was laughing now. It came loudly and continuously, died away for a bit, then began again—

And Alfred Lanning's face contracted into a rigidly bitter monument of disapproval. He made a half gesture to the woman who sat beside him, but her thin, bloodless lips merely pursed themselves a trifle.

Byerley gasped himself a stage nearer normality.

"Really, Dr. Lanning . . . really—I . . . *I* . . . a robot?"

Lanning bit his words off with a snap, "It is no statement of mine, sir. I would be quite satisfied to have you a member of humanity. Since our corporation never manufactured you, I am quite certain that you are—in a legalistic sense, at any rate. But since the contention that you are a robot has been advanced to us seriously by a man of certain standing—"

"Don't mention his name, if it would knock a chip off your granite block of ethics, but let's pretend it was Frank Quinn, for the sake of argument, and continue."

Lanning drew in a sharp, cutting snort at the interruption, and paused ferociously before continuing with added frigidity, "—by a man of certain standing, with whose identity I am not interested in playing guessing games, I am bound to ask your cooperation in disproving it. The mere fact that such a contention could be advanced and publicized by the means at this mans disposal would be a bad blow to the company I represent—even if the charge were never proven. You understand me?"

"Oh, yes, your position is clear to me. The charge itself is ridiculous. The spot you find yourself in is not. I beg your pardon, if my laughter offended you. It was the first I laughed at, not the second. How can I help you?"

"It could be very simple. You have only to sit down to a meal at a restaurant in the presence of witnesses, have your picture taken, and eat." Lanning sat back in his chair, the worst of the interview over. The woman beside him watched Byerley with an apparently absorbed expression but contributed nothing of her own.

Stephen Byerley met her eyes for an instant, was caught by them, then turned back to the roboticist. For a while his fingers were thoughtful over the bronze paper-weight that was the only ornament on his desk.

He said quietly, "I don't think I can oblige you."

He raised his hand, "Now wait, Dr. Lanning. I appreciate the fact that this whole matter is distasteful to you, that you have been forced into it against your will, that you feel you are playing an undignified and even ridiculous part. Still, the matter is even more intimately concerned with myself, so be tolerant.

"First, what makes you think that Quinn—this man of certain standing, you know—wasn't hoodwinking you, in order to get you to do exactly what you are doing?"

"Why it seems scarcely likely that a reputable person would endanger himself in so ridiculous a fashion, if he weren't convinced he were on safe ground."

There was little humor in Byerley's eyes, "You don't know Quinn. He could manage to make safe ground out of a ledge a mountain sheep could not handle. I suppose he showed the particulars of the investigation he claims to have made of me?"

"Enough to convince me that it would be too troublesome to have our corporation attempt to disprove them when you could do so more easily."

"Then you believe him when he says I never eat. You are a scientist, Dr. Lanning. Think of the logic required. I have not been observed to eat, therefore, I never eat Q.E.D. After all!"

"You are using prosecution tactics to confuse what is really a very simple situation."

"On the contrary, I am trying to clarify what you and Quinn between you are making a very complicated one. You see, I don't sleep much, that's true, and I certainly don't sleep in public. I have never cared to eat with others—an idiosyncrasy which is unusual and probably neurotic in character, but which harms no one. Look, Dr. Lanning, let me present you with a suppositious case. Supposing we had a politician who was interested in defeating a reform candidate at any cost and while investigating his private life came across oddities such as I have just mentioned.

"Suppose further that in order to smear the candidate effectively, he comes to your company as the ideal agent. Do you expect him to say to you, 'So-and-So is a robot because he hardly ever eats with people, and I have never seen him fall asleep in the middle of a case; and once when I peeped into his window in the middle of night, there he was, sitting up with a book; and I looked in his frigidaire and there was no food in it.'

"If he told you that, you would send for a straitjacket. But if he tells you, 'He *never* sleeps; he *never* eats,' then the shock of the statement blinds you to the fact that such statements are impossible to prove. You play into his hands by contributing to the to-do."

"Regardless, sir," began Lanning, with a threatening obstinacy, "of whether you consider this matter serious or not, it will require only the meal I mentioned to end it."

Again Byerley turned to the woman, who still regarded him expressionlessly. "Pardon me. I've caught your name correctly, haven't I? Dr. Susan Calvin?"

"Yes, Mr. Byerley."

"You're the U. S. Robots' psychologist, aren't you?"

"*Robo*psychologist, please."

"Oh, are robots so different from men, mentally?"

"Worlds different." She allowed herself a frosty smile, "Robots are essentially decent."

Humour tugged at the corners of the lawyer's mouth, "Well, that's a hard blow. But what I wanted to say was this. Since you're a psycho—a robopsychologist, *and* a woman, I'll bet that you've done something that Dr. Lanning hasn't thought of."

"And what is that?"

"You've got something to eat in your purse."

Something caught in the schooled indifference of Susan Calvin's eyes. She said, "You surprise me, Mr. Byerley."

And opening her purse, she produced an apple. Quietly, she handed it to him. Dr. Lanning, after an initial start, followed the slow movement from one hand to the other with sharply alert eyes.

Calmly, Stephen Byerley bit into it, and calmly he swallowed it.

"You see, Dr. Lanning?"

Dr. Lanning smiled in a relief tangible enough to make even his eyebrows appear benevolent. A relief that survived for one fragile second.

Susan Calvin said, "I was curious to see if you would eat it, but, of course, in the present case, it proves nothing."

Byerley grinned, "It doesn't?"

"Of course not. It is obvious, Dr. Lanning, that if this man were a humanoid robot, he would be a perfect imitation. He is almost too human to be credible. After all, we have been seeing and observing human beings all our lives; it would be impossible to palm something merely nearly right off on us. It would have to be *all* right. Observe the texture of the skin, the quality of the irises, the bone formation of the hand. If he's a robot, I wish U. S. Robots *had* made him, because he's a good job. Do you suppose then, that anyone capable of paying attention to such niceties would neglect a few gadgets to take care of such things as eating, sleeping, elimination? For emergency use only, perhaps; as, for instance, to prevent such situations as are arising here. So a meal won't really prove anything."

"Now wait," snarled Lanning, "I am not quite the fool both of you make me out to be. I am not interested in the problem of Mr. Byerley's humanity or nonhumanity. I am interested in getting the corporation out of a hole. A public meal will end the matter and keep it ended no matter what Quinn does. We can leave the finer details to lawyers and robopsychologists."

"But, Dr. Lanning," said Byerley, "you forget the politics of the situation. I am as anxious to be elected, as Quinn is to stop me. By the way, did you notice that you used his name. It's a cheap shyster trick of mine; I knew you would, before you were through."

Lanning flushed, "What has the election to do with it?"

"Publicity works both ways, sir. If Quinn wants to call me a robot, and has the nerve to do so, I have the nerve to play the game his way."

"You mean you—" Lanning was quite frankly appalled.

"Exactly. I mean that I'm going to let him go ahead, choose his rope, test its strength, cut off the right length, tie the noose, insert his head and grin. I can do what little else is required."

"You are mighty confident."

Susan Calvin rose to her feet, "Come, Alfred, we won't change his mind for him."

"You see." Byerley smiled gently. "You're a human psychologist, too."

* * *

But perhaps not all the confidence that Dr. Lanning had remarked upon was present that evening when Byerley's car parked on the automatic treads leading to the sunken garage, and Byerley himself crossed the path to the front door of his house.

The figure in the wheel chair looked up as he entered and smiled. Byerley's face lit with affection. He crossed over to it.

The cripple's voice was a hoarse, grating whisper that came out of a mouth forever twisted to one side, leering out of a face that was half scar tissue, "You're late, Steve."

"I know, John, I know. But I've been up against a peculiar and interesting trouble today."

"So?" Neither the torn face nor the destroyed voice could carry expression but there was anxiety in the clear eyes. "Nothing you can't handle?"

"I'm not exactly certain. I may need your help. *You're* the brilliant one in the family. Do you want me to take you out into the garden? It's a beautiful evening."

Two strong arms lifted John from the wheel chair. Gently, almost caressingly, Byerley's arms went around the shoulders and under the swathed legs of the cripple. Carefully, and slowly, he walked through the rooms, down the gentle ramp that had been built with a wheel chair in mind, and out the back door into the walled and wired garden behind the house.

"Why don't you let me use the wheel chair, Steve? This is silly."

"Because I'd rather carry you. Do you object? You know that you're as glad to get out of that motorized buggy for a while as I am to see you out. How do you feel today?" He deposited John with infinite care upon the cool grass.

"How should I feel? But tell me about your trouble."

"Quinn's campaign will be based on the fact that he claims I'm a robot."

John's eyes opened wide, "How do you know? It's impossible. I won't believe it."

"Oh, come, I tell you it's so. He had one of the big-shot scientists of U. S. Robots and Mechanical Men Corporation over at the office to argue with me."

Slowly John's hands tore at the grass, "I see. I see."

Byerley said, "But we can let him choose his ground. I have an idea. Listen to me and tell me if we can do it—"

* * *

The scene as it appeared in Alfred Lanning's office that night was a tableau of stares. Francis Quinn stared meditatively at Alfred Lanning. Lanning's stare was savagely set upon Susan Calvin, who stared impassively in her turn at Quinn.

Francis Quinn broke it with a heavy attempt at lightness, "Bluff. He's making it up as he goes along."

"Are you going to gamble on that, Mr. Quinn?" asked Dr. Calvin, indifferently.

"Well, it's your gamble, really."

"Look here," Lanning covered definite pessimism with bluster, "we've done what you asked. We witnessed the man eat. It's ridiculous to presume him a robot."

"Do *you* think so?" Quinn shot toward Calvin. "Lanning said you were the expert."

Lanning was almost threatening, "Now, Susan—"

Quinn interrupted smoothly, "Why not let her talk, man? She's been sitting there imitating a gatepost for half an hour."

Lanning felt definitely harassed. From what he experienced then to incipient paranoia was but a step. He said, "Very well. Have your say, Susan. We won't interrupt you."

Susan Calvin glanced at him humorlessly, then fixed cold eyes on Mr. Quinn. "There are only two ways of definitely proving Byerley to be a robot, sir. So far you are presenting circumstantial evidence, with which you can accuse, but not prove—and I think Mr. Byerley is sufficiently clever to counter that sort of material. You probably think so yourself, or you wouldn't have come here.

"The two methods of proof are the physical and the psychological. Physically, you can dissect him or use an X-ray. How to do that would be *your* problem. Psychologically, his behavior can be studied, for if he *is* a positronic robot, he must conform to the three Rules of Robotics. A positronic brain can not be constructed without them. You know the Rules, Mr. Quinn?"

She spoke them carefully, clearly, quoting word for word the famous bold print on page one of the "Handbook of Robotics."

"I've heard of them," said Quinn, carelessly.

"Then the matter is easy to follow," responded the psychologist, dryly. "If Mr. Byerley breaks any of those three rules, he is not a robot. Unfortunately, this procedure works in only one direction. If he lives up to the rules, it proves nothing one way or the other."

Quinn raised polite eyebrows, "Why not, doctor?"

"Because, if you stop to think of it, the three Rules of Robotics are the essential guiding principles of a good many of the world's ethical systems. Of course, every human being is supposed to have the instinct of self-preservation. That's Rule Three to a robot. Also, every 'good' human being, with a social conscience and a sense of responsibility, is supposed to defer to proper authority; to listen to his doctor, his boss, his government, his psychiatrist, his fellow man; to obey laws, to follow rules, to conform to custom—even when they interfere with his comfort or his safety. That's Rule Two to a robot. Also, every 'good' human being is supposed to love others as himself, protect his fellow man, risk his life to save another. That's Rule One to a robot. To put it simply—if Byerley follows all the Rules of Robotics, he may be a robot, and may simply be a very good man."

"But," said Quinn, "you're telling me that you can never prove him a robot."

"I may be able to prove him *not* a robot."

"That's not the proof I want."

"You'll have such proof as exists. You are the only one responsible for your own wants."

* * *

Here Lanning's mind leaped suddenly to the sting of an idea, "Has it occurred to anyone," he ground out, "that district attorney is a rather strange occupation for a robot? The prosecution of human beings — sentencing them to death—bringing about their infinite harm—"

Quinn grew suddenly keen, "No, you can't get out of it that way. Being district attorney doesn't make him human. Don't you know his record? Don't you know that he boasts that he has never prosecuted an innocent man; that there are scores of people left untried because the evidence against them didn't satisfy him, even though he could probably have argued a jury into atomizing them? That happens to be so."

Lanning's thin cheeks quivered, "No, Quinn, no. There is nothing in the Rules of Robotics that makes any allowance for human guilt. A robot may not judge whether a human being deserves death. It is not for him to decide. *He may not harm a human*—variety skunk, or variety angel."

Susan Calvin sounded tired. "Alfred," she said, "don't talk foolishly. What if a robot came upon a madman about to set fire to a house with people in it. He would stop the madman, wouldn't he?"

"Of course."

"And if the only way he could stop him was to kill him—"

There was a faint sound in Lanning's throat. Nothing more.

"The answer to that, Alfred, is that he would do his best not to kill him. If the madman died, the robot would require psychotherapy because he might easily go mad at the conflict presented him—of having broken Rule One to adhere to Rule One in a higher sense. But a man would be dead and a robot would have killed him."

"Well, *is* Byerley mad?" demanded Lanning, with all the sarcasm he could muster.

"No, but he has killed no man himself. He has exposed facts which might represent a particular human being to be dangerous to the large mass of other human beings we call society. He protects the greater number and thus adheres to Rule One at maximum potential. That is as far as he goes. It is the judge who then condemns the criminal to death or imprisonment, after the jury decides on his guilt or innocence. It is the jailer who imprisons him, the executioner who kills him. And Mr. Byerley has done nothing but determine truth and aid society.

"As a matter of fact, Mr. Quinn, I have looked into Mr. Byerley's career since you first brought this matter to our attention. I find that he has never demanded the death sentence in his closing speeches to the jury. I also find that he has spoken on behalf of the abolition of capital punishment and contributed generously to research institutions engaged in criminal neurophysiology. He apparently believes in the cure, rather than the punishment of crime. I find that significant."

"You do?" Quinn smiled. "Significant of a certain odor of roboticity, perhaps?"

"Perhaps. Why deny it? Actions such as his could come only from a robot, or from a very honorable and decent human being. But you see, you just can't differentiate between a robot and the very best of humans."

Quinn sat back in his chair. His voice quivered with impatience.

"Dr. Lanning, it's perfectly possible to create a humanoid robot that would perfectly duplicate a human in appearance, isn't it?"

Lanning harrumphed and considered, "It's been done experimentally by U. S. Robots," he said reluctantly, "without the addition of a positronic brain, of course. By using human ova and hormone control, one can grow human flesh and skin over a skeleton of porous silicone plastics that would defy external examination. The eyes, the hair, the skin would be really human, not humanoid. And if you put a positronic brain, and such other gadgets as you might desire inside, you have a humanoid robot."

Quinn said shortly, "How long would it take to make one?"

Lanning considered, "If you had all your equipment—the brain, the skeleton, the ovum, the proper hormones and radiations—say, two months."

The politician straightened out of his chair. "Then we shall see what the insides of Mr. Byerley look like. It will mean publicity for U. S. Robots—but I gave you your chance."

Lanning turned impatiently to Susan Calvin, when they were alone. "Why do you insist—"

And with real feeling, she responded sharply and instantly, "Which do you want—the truth or my resignation? I won't lie for you. U. S. Robots can take care of itself. Don't turn coward."

"What," said Lanning, "if he opens up Byerley, and wheels and gears fall out. What then?"

"He won't open Byerley," said Calvin, disdainfully. "Byerley is as clever as Quinn, at the very least."

* * *

The news broke upon the city a week before Byerley was to have been nominated. But "broke" is the wrong word. It staggered upon the city, shambled, crawled. Laughter began, and wit was free. And as the far off hand of Quinn tightened its pressure in easy stages, the laughter grew forced, an element of hollow uncertainty entered, and people broke off to wonder.

The convention itself had the air of a restive stallion. There had been no contest planned. Only Byerley could possibly have been nominated a week earlier. There was no substitute even now. They had to nominate him, but there was complete confusion about it.

It would not have been so bad if the average individual were not torn between the enormity of the charge, if true, and its sensational folly, if false.

The day after Byerley was nominated perfunctorily, hollowly—a newspaper finally published the gist of a long interview with Dr. Susan Calvin, "world famous expert on robopsychology and positronics."

What broke loose is popularly and succinctly described as hell.

It was what the Fundamentalists were waiting for. They were not a political party; they made pretense to no formal religion. Essentially they were those who had not adapted themselves to what had once been called the Atomic Age, in the days when atoms were a novelty. Actually, they were the Simple-Lifers, hungering after a life, which to those who lived it had probably appeared not so Simple, and who had been, therefore, Simple-Lifers themselves.

The Fundamentalists required no new reason to detest robots and robot manufacturers; but a new reason such as the Quinn accusation and the Calvin analysis was sufficient to make such detestation audible.

The huge plants of the U. S. Robots and Mechanical Men Corporation was a hive that spawned armed guards. It prepared for war.

Within the city the house of Stephen Byerley bristled with police.

The political campaign, of course, lost all other issues, and resembled a campaign only in that it was something filling the hiatus between nomination and election.

* * *

Stephen Byerley did not allow the fussy little man to distract him. He remained comfortably unperturbed by the uniforms in the background. Outside the house, past the line of grim guards, reporters and photographers waited according to the tradition of the caste. One enterprising 'visor station even had a scanner focused on the blank entrance to the prosecutor's unpretentious home, while a synthetically excited announcer filled in with inflated commentary.

The fussy little man advanced. He held forward a rich, complicated sheet. "This, Mr. Byerley, is a court order authorizing me to search these premises for the presence of illegal . . . uh . . . mechanical men or robots of any description."

Byerley half rose, and took the paper. He glanced at it indifferently, and smiled as he handed it back. "All in order. Go ahead. Do your job. Mrs. Hoppen"—to his housekeeper, who appeared reluctantly from the next room—"please go with them, and help out if you can."

The little man, whose name was Harroway, hesitated, produced an unmistakable blush, failed compltely to catch Byerley's eyes, and muttered, "Come on," to the two policemen.

He was back in ten minutes.

"Through?" questioned Byerley, in just the tone of a person who is not particularly interested in the question, or its answer.

Harroway cleared his throat, made a bad start in falsetto, and began again, angrily, "Look here, Mr. Byerley, our special instructions were to search the house very thoroughly."

"And haven't you?"

"We were told exactly what to look for."

"Yes?"

"In short, Mr. Byerley, and not to put too fine a point on it, we were told to search you."

"Me?" said the prosecutor with a broadening smile. "And how do you intend to do that?"

"We have a Penet-radiation unit—"

"Then I'm to have my X-ray photograph taken, hey? You have the authority?"

"You saw my warrant."

"May I see it again?"

Harroway, his forehead shining with considerably more than mere enthusiasm, passed it over a second time.

Byerley said evenly, "I read here as the description of what you are to search; I quote: 'the dwelling place belonging to Stephen Allen Byerley, located at 355 Willow Grove, Evanston, together with any garage, storehouse or other structures or buildings thereto appertaining, together with all grounds thereto appertaining' . . . um . . . and so on. Quite in order. But, my good man, it doesn't say anything about searching my interior. I am not part of the premises. You may search my clothes if you think I've got a robot hidden in my pocket."

Harroway had no doubt on the point of to whom he owed his job. He did not propose to be backward, given a chance to earn a much better—i.e., more highly paid—job.

He said, in a faint echo of bluster, "Look here. I'm allowed to search the furniture in your house, and anything else I find in it. You are in it, aren't you?"

"A remarkable observation. I *am* in it. But I'm not a piece of furniture. As a citizen of adult responsibility—I have the psychiatric certificate proving that—I have certain rights under the Regional Articles. Searching me would come under the heading of violating my Right of Privacy. That paper isn't sufficient."

"Sure, but if you're a robot, you don't have Right of Privacy."

"True enough—but that paper still isn't sufficient. It recognizes me implicitly as a human being."

"Where?" Harroway snatched at it.

"Where it says 'the dwelling place belonging to' and so on. A robot cannot own property. And you may tell your employer, Mr. Harroway, that if he tries to issue a similar paper which does *not* implicitly recognize me as a human being, he will be immediately faced with a restraining injunction and a civil suit which will make it necessary for him to *prove* me a robot by means of information *now* in his possession, or else to pay a whopping penalty for an attempt to deprive me unduly of my Rights under the Regional Articles. You'll tell him that, won't you?"

Harroway marched to the door. He turned. "You're a slick lawyer—" His hand was in his pocket. For a short moment, he stood there. Then he left, smiling in the direction of the 'visor scanner, still playing away—waved to the reporters, and shouted, "We'll have something for you tomorrow boys. No kidding."

In his ground car, he settled back, removed the tiny mechanism from his pocket and carefully inspected it. It was the first time he had ever taken a photograph by X-ray reflection. He hoped he had done it correctly.

Quinn and Byerley had never met face-to-face alone. But visorphone was pretty close to it. In fact, accepted literally, perhaps the phrase was accurate, even if to each, the other were merely the light and dark pattern of a bank of photocells.

It was Quinn who had initiated the call. It was Quinn, who spoke first, and without particular ceremony, "Thought you would like to know, Byerley, that I intend to make public the fact that you're wearing a protective shield against Penet-radiation."

"That so? In that case, you've probably already made it public. I have a notion our enterprising press representatives have been tapping my various communication lines for quite a while. I know they have my office line full of holes; which is why I've dug in at my home these last weeks." Byerley was friendly, almost chatty.

Quinn's lips tightened slightly, "This call is shielded—thoroughly. I'm making it at a certain personal risk."

"So I should imagine. Nobody knows you're behind this campaign. At least, nobody knows it officially. Nobody doesn't know it unofficially. I wouldn't worry. So I wear a protective shield? I suppose you found that our when your puppy dog's Penet-radiation photograph, the other day, turned out to be overexposed."

"You realize, Byerley, that it would be pretty obvious to everyone that you don't dare face X-ray analysis."

"Also that you, or your men, attempted illegal invasion of my Right of Privacy."

"The devil they'll care for that."

"They might. It's rather symbolic of our two campaigns, isn't it? You have little concern with the rights of the individual citizen. I have great concern. I will not submit to X-ray analysis, because I wish to maintain my Rights on principle. Just as I'll maintain the rights of others when elected."

"That will no doubt make a very interesting speech, but no one will believe you. A little too high-sounding to be true. Another thing," a sudden, crisp change, "the personnel in your home was not complete the other night."

"In what way?"

"According to the report," he shuffled papers before him that were just within the range of vision of the visiplate, "there was one person missing—a cripple."

"As you say," said Byerley, tonelessly, "a cripple. My old teacher, who lives with me and who is now in the country—and has been for two months. A 'much-needed rest' is the usual expression applied in the case. He has your permission?"

"Your teacher? A scientist of sorts?"

"A lawyer once—before he was a cripple. He has a government license as a research biophysicist, with a laboratory of his own, and a complete description of the work he's doing filed with the proper authorities, to whom I can refer you. The work is minor, but is a harmless and engaging hobby for a—poor cripple. I am being as helpful as I can, you see."

"I see. And what does this . . . teacher . . . know about robot manufacture?"

"I couldn't judge the extent of his knowledge in a field with which I am unacquainted."

"He wouldn't have access to positronic brains?"

"Ask your friends at U. S. Robots. They'd be the ones to know."

"I'll put it shortly, Byerley. Your crippled teacher is the real Stephen Byerley. You are his robot creation. We can prove it. It was he who was in the automobile accident, not you. There will be ways of checking the records."

"Really? Do so, then. My best wishes."

"And we can search your so-called teacher's 'country place,' and see what we can find there."

"Well, not quite, Quinn." Byerley smiled broadly. "Unfortunately for you, my so-called teacher is a sick man. His country place is his place of rest. His Right of Privacy as a citizen of adult responsibility is naturally even stronger, under the circumstances. You won't be able to obtain a warrant to enter his grounds without showing just cause. However, I'd be the last to prevent you from trying."

There was a pause of moderate length, and then Quinn leaned forward, so that his imaged-face expanded and the fine lines on his forehead were visible, "Byerley, why do you carry on? You can't be elected."

"Can't I?"

"Do you think you can? Do you suppose that your failure to make any attempt to disprove the robot charge—when you could easily, by breaking one of the Three Laws—does anything but convince the people that you *are* a robot?"

"All I see so far is that from being a rather vaguely known, but still largely obscure metropolitan lawyer, I have now become a world figure. You're a good publicist."

"But you *are* a robot."

"So it's been said, but not proven."

"It's been proven sufficiently for the electorate."

"Then relax—you've won."

"Good-by," said Quinn, with his first touch of viciousness, and the visorphone slammed off.

"Good-by," said Byerley imperturbably, to the blank plate.

* * *

Byerley brought his "teacher" back the week before election. The air car dropped quickly in an obscure part of the city.

"You'll stay here till after election," Byerley told him. "It would be better to have you out of the way if things take a bad turn."

The hoarse voice that twisted painfully out of John's crooked mouth might have had accents of concern in it. "There's danger of violence?"

"The Fundamentalists threaten it, so I suppose there is, in a theoretical sense. But I really don't expect it. The Fundies have no real power. They're just the continuous irritant factor that might stir up a riot after a while. You don't mind staying here? Please. I won't be myself if I have to worry about you."

"Oh, I'll stay. You still think it will go well?"

"I'm sure of it. No one bothered you at the place?"

"No one. I'm certain."

"And your part went well?"

"Well enough. There'll be no trouble there."

"Then take care of yourself, and watch the televisor tomorrow, John." Byerley pressed the gnarled hand that rested on his.

* * *

Lenton's forehead was a furrowed study in suspense. He had the completely unenviable job of being Byerley's campaign manager in a campaign that wasn't a campaign, for a person that refused to reveal his strategy, and refused to accept his manager's.

"You can't!" It was his favorite phrase. It had become his only phrase. "I tell you, Steve, you can't!"

He threw himself in front of the prosecutor, who was spending his time, leafing through the typed pages of his speech.

"Put that down, Steve. Look, that mob has been organized by the Fundies. You won't get a hearing. You'll be stoned more likely. Why do you have to make a speech before an audience? What's wrong with a recording, a visual recording?"

"You want me to win the election, don't you?" asked Byerley, mildly.

"Win the election! You're not going to win, Steve. I'm trying to save your life."

"Oh, I'm not in danger."

"He's not in danger. He's not in danger." Lenton made a queer, rasping sound in his throat. "You mean you're getting out on that balcony in front of fifty thousand crazy crackpots and try to talk sense to them—on a balcony like a medieval dictator?"

Byerley consulted his watch. "In about five minutes—as soon as the television lines are free."

Lenton's answering remark was not quite transliterable.

* * *

The crowd filled a roped off area of the city. Trees and houses seemed to grow out of a mass-human foundation. And by ultrawave, the rest of the world watched. It was a purely local election, but it had a world audience just the same. Byerley thought of that and smiled.

But there was nothing to smile at in the crowd itself. There were banners and streamers, ringing every possible change on his supposed roboticity. The hostile attitude rose thickly and tangibly into the atmosphere.

From the start the speech was not successful. It competed against the inchoate mob howl and the rhythmic cries of the Fundie claques the formed mob-islands within the mob. Byerley spoke on, slowly, unemotionally—

Inside, Lenton clutched his hair and groaned—and waited for the blood.

* * *

There was a writhing in the front ranks. An angular citizen with popping eyes, and clothes too short for the lank length of his limbs, was pulling to the fore. A policeman dived after him, making slow, struggling passage. Byerley waved the latter off, angrily.

The thin man was directly under the balcony. His words tore unheard against the roar.

Byerley leaned forward. "What do you say? If you have a legitimate question, I'll answer it." He turned to a flanking guard. "Bring that man up here."

There was a tensing in the crowd. Cries of "Quiet" started in various parts of the mob, and rose to a bedlam, then toned down raggedly. The thin man, red-faced and panting, faced Byerley.

Byerley said, "Have you a question?"

The thin man stared, and said in a cracked voice, "Hit me!"

With sudden energy, he thrust out his chin at an angle. "Hit me! You say you're not a robot. Prove it. You can't hit a human, you monster."

There was a queer, flat, dead silence. Byerley's voice punctured it. "I have no reason to hit you."

The thin man was laughing wildly. "You *can't* hit me. You *won't* hit me. You're not a human. You're a monster, a make-believe man."

And Stephen Byerley, tight-lipped, in the face of thousands who watched in person and the millions who watched by screen, drew back his fist and caught the man crackingly upon the chin. The challenger went over backwards in sudden collapse, with nothing on his face but blank, blank surprise.

Byerley said, "I'm sorry. Take him in and see that he's comfortable. I want to speak to him when I'm through."

And when Dr. Calvin, from her reserved space, turned her automobile and drove off, only one reporter had recovered sufficiently from the shock to race after her, and shout an unheard question.

Susan Calvin called over her shoulder, "He's human."

That was enough. The reporter raced away in his own direction.

The rest of the speech might be described as "Spoken but not heard."

* * *

Dr. Calvin and Stephen Byerley met once again—a week before he took the oath of office as mayor. It was late—past midnight.

Dr. Calvin said, "You don't look tired."

The mayor-elect smiled. "I may stay up for a while. Don't tell Quinn."

"I shan't. But that was an interesting story of Quinn's, since you mention him. It's a shame to have spoiled it. I suppose you knew his theory?"

"Parts of it."

"It was highly dramatic. Stephen Byerley was a young lawyer, a powerful speaker, a great idealist—and with a certain flair for biophysics. Are you interested in robotics, Mr. Byerley?"

"Only in the legal aspects."

"*This* Stephen Byerley was. But here was an accident. Byerley's wife died; he himself, worse. His legs were gone; his face was gone; his voice was gone. Part of his mind was—bent. He would not submit to plastic surgery. He retired from the world, legal career gone—only his intelligence, and his hands left. Somehow he could obtain positronic brains, even a complex one, one which had the greatest capacity of forming judgments in ethical problems—which is the highest robotic function so far developed.

"He grew a body about it. Trained it to be everything he would have been and was no longer. He sent it out into the world as Stephen Byerley, remaining behind himself as the old, crippled teacher that no one ever saw—"

"Unfortunately," said the mayor-elect, "I ruined all that by hitting a man. The papers say it was your official verdict on the occasion that I was human."

"How did that happen? Do you mind telling me? It couldn't have been accidental."

"It wasn't entirely. Quinn did most of the work. My men started quietly spreading the fact that I had never hit a man; that I was unable to hit a man; that to fail to do so under provocation would be sure proof that I was a robot. So I arranged for a silly speech in public, with all sorts of publicity overtones, and almost inevitably, some fool fell for it. In its essence, it was what I call a shyster trick. One in which the artificial atmosphere which has been created does all the work. Of course, the emotional effects made my election certain, as intended."

The robopsychologist nodded. "I see you intrude on my field—as every politician must, I suppose. But I'm very sorry it turned out this way. I like robots. I like them considerably better than I do human beings. If a robot can be created capable of being a civil executive, I think he'd make the best one possible. By the Laws of Robotics, he'd be incapable of harming humans, incapable of tyranny, or corruption, of stupidity, of prejudice. And after he had served a decent term, he would leave, even though he were immortal, because it would be impossible for him to hurt humans by letting them know that a robot had ruled them. It would be most ideal."

"Except that a robot might fail due to the inherent inadequacies of his brain. The positronic brain has never equalled the complexities of the human brain."

"He would have advisers. Not even a human brain is capable of governing without assistance."

Byerley considered Susan Calvin with grave interest. "Why do you smile, Dr. Calvin?"

"I smile because Mr. Quinn didn't think of everything."

"You mean there could be more to that story of his."

"Only a little. For the three months before election, this Stephen Byerley that Mr. Quinn spoke about, this broken man, was in the country for some mysterious reason. He returned in time for that famous speech of yours. And after all, what the old cripple did once, he could do a second time, particularly where the second job is very simple in comparison to the first."

"I don't quite understand."

Dr. Calvin rose and smoothed her dress. She was obviously ready to leave. "I mean there is one time when a robot may strike a human being without breaking the First Law. Just one time."

"And when is that?"

Dr. Calvin was at the door. She said quietly, "When the human to be struck is merely another robot."

She smiled broadly, her thin face glowing. "Good-by, Mr. Byerley. I hope to vote for you five years from now—for co-ordinator."

Stephen Byerley chuckled. "I must reply that that is a somewhat farfetched idea."

The door closed behind her.

Little Lost Robot

Measures on Hyper Base had been taken in a sort of rattling fury—the muscular equivalent of an hysterical shriek.

To itemize them in order of both chronology and desperation, they were:

1. All work on the Hyperatomic Drive through all the space volume occupied by the Stations of the Twenty-Seventh Asteroidal Grouping came to a halt.

2. The entire volume of space was nipped out of the System, practically speaking. No one entered without permission. No one left under any conditions.

3. By special government patrol ship, Drs. Susan Calvin and Peter Bogert, respectively Head Psychologist and Mathematical Director of United States Robots and Mechanical Men Corporation, where brought to Hyper Base.

* * *

Susan Calvin had never left the surface of Earth before, and had no perceptible desire to leave it this time. In an age of Atomic Power and a clearly coming Hyperatomic Drive, she remained quietly provincial. So she was dissatisfied with her trip and unconvinced of the emergency, and every line of her plain, middle-aged face showed it clearly enough during her first dinner at Hyper Base.

Nor did Dr. Bogert's sleek paleness abandon a certain hangdog attitude. Nor did Major-general Kallner, who headed the project, even once forget to maintain a haunted expression.

In short, it was a grisly episode, that meal, and the little session of three that followed began in a gray, unhappy manner.

Kallner, with his baldness glistening, and his dress uniform oddly unsuited to the general mood, began with uneasy directness.

"This is a queer story to tell, sir, and madam. I want to thank you for coming on short notice and without a reason being given. We'll try to correct that now. We've lost a robot. Work has stopped and *must* stop until such time as we locate it. So far we have failed, and we feel we need expert help."

Perhaps the general felt his predicament anticlimactic. He continued with a note of desperation, "I needn't tell you the importance of our work here. More than eighty percent of last year's appropriations for scientific research have gone to us—"

"Why, we know that," said Bogert, agreeably. "U.S. Robots is receiving a generous rental fee for use of our robots."

Susan Calvin injected a blunt, vinegary note, "What makes a single robot so important to the project, and why hasn't it been located?"

The general turned his red face toward her and wet his lips quickly, "Why, in a manner of speaking we *have* located it." Then, with near anguish, "Here, suppose I explain. As soon as the robot failed to report, a state of emergency was declared, and all movement off Hyper Base stopped. A cargo vessel had landed the previous day and had delivered us two robots for our laboratories. It had sixty-two robots of the . . . uh . . . same type for shipment elsewhere. We are certain as to that figure. There is no question about it whatever."

"Yes? And the connection?"

"When our missing robot was not located anywhere—I assure you we would have found a missing blade of grass if it had been there to find—we brainstormed ourselves into counting the robots left on the cargo ship. They have sixty-three now."

"So that the sixty-third, I take it, is the missing prodigal?" Dr. Calvin's eyes darkened.

"Yes, but we have no way of telling which is the sixty-third."

There was a dead silence while the electric clock chimed eleven times, and then the robopsychologist said, "Very peculiar," and the corners of her lips moved downward.

"Peter," she turned to her colleague with a trace of savagery, "what's wrong here? What kind of robots are they using at Hyper Base?"

Dr. Bogert hesitated and smiled feebly, "It's been rather a matter of delicacy till now, Susan."

She spoke rapidly, "Yes, *till* now. If there are sixty-three same-type robots, one of which is wanted and the identity of which cannot be determined, why won't any of them do? What's the idea of all this? Why have we been sent for?"

Bogert said in resigned fashion, "If you'll give me a chance, Susan—Hyper Base happens to be using several robots whose brains are not impressioned with the entire First Law of Robotics."

"*Aren't* impressioned?" Calvin slumped back in her chair, "I see. How many were made?"

"A few. It was on government order and there was no way of violating the secrecy. No one was to know except the top men directly concerned. You weren't included, Susan. It was nothing I had anything to do with."

* * *

The general interrupted with a measure of authority. "I would like to explain that bit. I hadn't been aware that Dr. Calvin was unacquainted with the situation. I needn't tell you, Dr. Calvin, that there always has been strong opposition to robots on the Planet. The only defense the government has had against the Fundamentalist radicals in this matter was the fact that robots are always built with an unbreakable First Law—which makes it impossible for them to harm human beings under any circumstance.

"But we *had* to have robots of a different nature. So just a few of the NS-2 model, the Nestors, that is, were prepared with a modified First Law. To keep it quiet, all NS-2's are manufactured without serial numbers; modified members are delivered here along with a group of normal robots; and, of course, all our kind are under the strictest impressionment never to tell of their modification to unauthorized personnel." He wore an embarrassed smile, "This has all worked out against us now."

Calvin said grimly, "Have you asked each one who it is, anyhow? Certainly, you are authorized?"

The general nodded, "All sixty-three deny having worked here — and one is lying."

"Does the one you want show traces of wear? The others, I take it, are factory-fresh."

"The one in question only arrived last month. It, and the two that have just arrived, were to be the last we needed. There's no perceptible wear." He shook his head slowly and his eyes were haunted again, "Dr. Calvin, we don't dare let that ship leave. If the existence of non-First Law robots becomes general knowledge—" There seemed no way of avoiding understatement in the conclusion.

"Destroy all sixty-three," said the robopsychologist coldly and flatly, "and make an end of it."

Bogert drew back a corner of his mouth. "You mean destroy thirty thousand dollars per robot. I'm afraid U. S. Robots wouldn't like that. We'd better make an effort first, Susan, before we destroy anything."

"In that case," she said, sharply, "I need facts. Exactly what advantage does Hyper Base derive from these modified robots? What factor made them desirable, general?"

Kallner ruffled his forehead and stroked it with an upward gesture of his hand. "We had trouble with our previous robots. Our men work with hard radiations a good deal, you see. It's dangerous, of course, but reasonable precautions are taken. There have been only two accidents since we began and neither was fatal. However, it was impossible to explain that to an ordinary robot. The First Law states—I'll quote it—'*No robot may harm a human being, or through inaction, allow a human being to come to harm.*'

"That's primary, Dr. Calvin. When it was necessary for one of our men to expose himself for a short period to a moderate gamma field, one that would have no physiological effects, the nearest robot would dash in to drag him out. If the field were exceedingly weak, it would succeed, and work could not continue till all robots were cleared out. If the field were a trifle stronger, the robot would never reach the technician concerned, since its positronic brain would collapse under gamma radiations—and then we would be out one expensive and hard-to-replace robot.

"We tried arguing with them. Their point was that a human being in a gamma field was endangering his life and that it didn't matter that he could remain there half an hour safely. Supposing, they would say, he forgot and remained an hour. They couldn't take chances. We pointed out that they were risking their lives on a wild off-chance. But self-preservation is only the Third Law of Robotics—and the First Law of human safety came first. We gave them orders; we ordered them strictly and harshly to remain out of gamma fields at whatever cost. But obedience is only the Second Law of Robotics—and the First Law of human safety came first. Dr. Calvin, we either had to do without robots, or do something about the First Law—and we made our choice."

"I can't believe," said Dr. Calvin, "that it was found possible to remove the First Law."

"It wasn't removed, it was modified," explained Kallner. "Positronic brains were constructed that contained the positive aspect only of the Law, which in them reads: '*No robot may harm a human being.*' That is all. They have no compulsion to prevent one coming to harm through an extraneous agency such as gamma rays. I state the matter correctly, Dr. Bogert?"

"Quite," assented the mathematician.

"And that is the only difference of your robots from the ordinary NS-2 model? The *only* difference? Peter?"

"The *only* difference, Susan."

She rose and spoke with finality, "I intend sleeping now, and in about eight hours, I want to speak to whomever saw the robot last. And from now on, General Kallner, if I'm to take any responsibility at all for events, I want full and unquestioned control of this investigation."

Susan Calvin, except for two hours of resentful lassitude, experienced nothing approaching sleep. She signaled at Bogert's door at the local time of 0700 and found him also awake. He had apparently taken the trouble of transporting a dressing gown to Hyper Base with him, for he was sitting in it. He put his nail scissors down when Calvin entered.

He said softly, "I've been expecting you more or less. I suppose you feel sick about all this."

"I do."

"Well—I'm sorry. There was no way of preventing it. When the call came out from Hyper Base for us, I knew that something must have gone wrong with the modified Nestors. But what was there to do? I couldn't break the matter to you on the trip here as I would have liked to, because I had to be sure. The matter of the modification is top secret."

The psychologist muttered, "I should have been told. U. S. Robots had no right to modify positronic brains this way without the approval of a psychologist."

Bogert lifted his eyebrows and sighed. "Be reasonable, Susan. You couldn't have influenced them. In this matter, the government was bound to have its way. They want the Hyperatomic Drive and the etheric physicists want robots that won't interfere with them. They were going to get them even if it did mean twisting the First Law. We had to admit it was possible from a construction standpoint and they swore a mighty oath that they wanted only twelve, that they would be used only at Hyper Base, that they would be destroyed once the Drive was perfected, and that full precautions would be taken. And they insisted on secrecy—and that's the situation."

Dr. Calvin spoke through her teeth, "I would have resigned."

"It wouldn't have helped. The government was offering the company a fortune, and theatening it with antirobot legislation in case of a refusal. We were stuck then, and we're badly stuck now. If this leaks out, it might hurt Kallner and the government, but it would hurt U. S. Robots a devil of a lot more."

The psychologist stared at him. "Peter, don't you realize what all this is about? Can't you understand what the removal of the First Law means? It isn't just a matter of secrecy."

"I know what removal would mean. I'm not a child. It would mean complete instability, with no nonimaginary solutions to the positronic Field Equations."

"Yes, mathematically. But can you translate that into crude psychological thought. All normal life, Peter, consciously or otherwise, resents domination. If the domination is by an inferior, or by a supposed inferior, the resentment becomes stronger. Physically, and, to an extent, mentally, a robot—any robot—is superior to human beings. What makes him slavish, then? *Only the First Law!* Why, without it, the first order you tried to give a robot would result in your death. Unstable? What do you think?"

"Susan," said Bogert, with an air of sympathetic amusement, "I'll admit that this Frankenstein Complex you're exhibiting has a certain justification—hence the First Law in the first place. But the Law, I repeat and repeat, has not been removed—merely modified."

"And what about the stability of the brain?"

The mathematician thrust out his lips, "Decreased, naturally. But it's within the border of safety. The first Nestors were delivered to Hyper Base nine months ago, and nothing whatever has gone wrong till now, and even this involves merely fear of discovery and not danger to humans."

'Very well, then. We'll see what comes of the morning conference."

Bogert saw her politely to the door and grimaced eloquently when she left. He saw no reason to change his perennial opinion of her as a sour and fidgety frustration.

Susan Calvin's train of thought did not include Bogert in the least. She had dismissed him years ago as a smooth and pretentious sleekness.

* * *

Gerald Black had taken his degree in etheric physics the year before and, in common with his entire generation of physicists, found himself engaged in the problem of the Drive. He now made a proper addition to the general atmosphere of these meetings on Hyper Base. In his stained white smock, he was half rebellious and wholly uncertain. His stocky strength seemed striving for release and his fingers, as they twisted each other with nervous yanks, might have forced an iron bar out of true.

Major-general Kallner sat beside him, the two from U. S. Robots faced him.

Black said, "I'm told that I was the last to see Nestor 10 before he vanished. I take it you want to ask me about that."

Dr. Calvin regarded him with interest, "You sound as if you were not sure, young man. Don't you *know* whether you were the last to see him?"

"He worked with me, ma'am, on the field generators, and he was with me the morning of his disappearance. I don't know if anyone saw him after about noon. No one admits having done so."

"Do you think anyone's lying about it?"

"I don't say that. But I don't say that I want the blame of it, either." His dark eyes smoldered.

"There's no question of blame. The robot acted as it did because of what it is. We're just trying to locate it, Mr. Black, and let's put everything else aside. Now if you've worked with the robot, you probably know it better than anyone else. Was there anything unusual about it that you noticed? Had you ever worked with robots before?"

"I've worked with other robots we have here—the simple ones. Nothing different about the Nestors except that they're a good deal cleverer—and more annoying."

"Annoying? In what way?"

"Well—perhaps it's not their fault. The work here is rough and most of us get a little jagged. Fooling around with hyper-space isn't fun." He smiled feebly, finding pleasure in confession. "We run the risk continually of blowing a hole in normal space-time fabric and dropping right out of the universe, asteroid and all. Sounds screwy, doesn't it? Naturally, you're on edge sometimes. But these Nestors aren't. They're curious, they're calm, they don't worry. It's enough to drive you nuts at times. When you want something done in a tearing hurry, they seem to take their time. Sometimes I'd rather do without."

"You say they take their time? Have they ever refused an order?"

"Oh, no,"—hastily. "They do it all right. They tell you when they think you're wrong, though. They don't know anything about the subject but what we taught them, but that doesn't stop them. Maybe I imagine it, but the other fellows have the same trouble with their Nestors."

General Kallner cleared his throat ominously, "Why have no complaints reached me on the matter, Black?"

The young physicist reddened, "We didn't *really* want to do without the robots, sir, and besides we weren't certain exactly how such . . . uh . . . minor complaints might be received."

Bogert interrupted softly, "Anything in particular happen the morning you last saw it?"

There was a silence. With a quiet motion, Calvin repressed the comment that was about to emerge from Kallner, and waited patiently.

Then Black spoke in blurting anger, "I had a little trouble with it. I'd broken a Kimball tube that morning and was out five days of work; my entire program was behind schedule; I hadn't received any mail from home for a couple of weeks. And *he* came around wanting me to repeat an experiment I had abandoned a month ago. He was always annoying me on that subject and I was tired of it. I told him to go away—and that's all I saw of him."

"You told him to go away?" asked Dr. Calvin with sharp interest. "In just those words? Did you say 'Go away'? Try to remember the exact words."

There was apparently an internal struggle in progress. Black cradled his forehead in a broad palm for a moment, then tore it away and said defiantly, "I said, 'Go lose yourself.' "

Bogert laughed for a short moment. "And he did, eh?"

But Calvin wasn't finished. She spoke cajolingly, "Now we're getting somewhere, Mr. Black. But exact details are important. In understanding the robot's actions, a word, a gesture, an emphasis may be everything. You couldn't have said just those three words, for instance, could you? By your own description you must have been in a hasty mood. Perhaps you strengthened your speech a little."

The young man reddened, "Well . . . I may have called it a . . . a few things."

"Exactly what things?"

"Oh—I wouldn't remember exactly. Besides I couldn't repeat it. You know how you get when you're excited." His embarrassed laugh was almost a giggle, "I sort of have a tendency to strong language."

"That's quite all right," she replied, with prim severity. "At the moment, I'm a psychologist. I would like to have you repeat exactly what you said as nearly as you remember, and, even more important, the exact tone of voice you used."

Black looked at his commanding officer for support, found none. His eyes grew round and appalled, "But you can't."

"You must."

"Suppose," said Bogert, with ill-hidden amusement, "you address me. You may find it easier."

The young man's scarlet face turned to Bogert. He swallowed. "I said—" His voice faded out. He tried again, "I said—"

And he drew a deep breath and spewed it out hastily in one long succession of syllables. Then, in the charged air that lingered, he concluded almost in tears, ". . . more or less. I don't remember the exact order of what I called him, and maybe I left out something or put in something, but that was about it."

Only the slightest flush betrayed any feeling on the part of the psychologist. She said, "I am aware of the meaning of most of the items used. The others, I suppose, are equally derogatory."

"I'm afraid so," agreed the tormented Black.

"And in among it, you told him to lose himself."

"I meant it only figuratively."

"I realize that. No disciplinary action is intended, I am sure." And at her glance, the general, who, five seconds earlier, had seemed not sure at all, nodded angrily.

"You may leave, Mr. Black. Thank you for your co-operation."

* * *

It took five hours for Susan Calvin to interview the sixty-three robots. It was five hours of multi-repetition; of replacement after replacement of identical robot; of Questions A, B, C, D; and Answers A, B, C, D; of a carefully bland expression, a carefully neutral tone, a carefully friendly atmosphere; and a hidden wire recorder.

The psychologist felt drained of vitality when she was finished.

Bogert was waiting for her and looked expectant as she dropped the recording spool with a clang upon the plastic of the desk.

She shook her head, "All sixty-three seemed the same to me. I couldn't tell—"

He said, "You couldn't expect to tell by ear, Susan. Suppose we analyze the recordings."

Ordinarily, the mathematical interpretation of verbal reactions of robots is one of the more intricate branches of robotic analysis. It requires a staff of trained technicians and the help of complicated computing machines. Bogert knew that. Bogert stated as much, in an extreme of unshown annoyance after having listened to each set of replies, made lists of word deviations, and graphs of the intervals of responses.

"There are no anomalies present, Susan. The variation in wording and the time reactions are within the limits of ordinary frequency groupings. We need finer methods. They must have computers here. No." He frowned and nibbled delicately at a thumbnail. "We can't use computers. Too much danger of leakage. Or maybe if we—"

Dr. Calvin stopped him with an impatient gesture, "Please, Peter. This isn't one of your petty laboratory problems. If we can't determine the modified Nestor by some gross differnce that we can see with the naked eye, one that there is no mistake about, we're out of luck. The danger of being wrong, and of letting him escape is otherwise too great. It's not enough to point out a minute irregularity in a graph. I tell you, if that's all I've got to go on, I'd destroy them all just to be certain. Have you spoken to the other modified Nestors?"

"Yes, I have," snapped back Bogert, "and there's nothing wrong with them. They're above normal in friendliness if anything. They answered my questions, displayed pride in their knowledge—except the two new ones that haven't had time to learn their etheric physics. They laughed rather good-naturedly at my ignorance in some of the specializations here." He shrugged, "I suppose that forms some of the basis for resentment toward them on the part of the technicians here. The robots are perhaps too willing to impress you with their greater knowledge."

"Can you try a few Planar Reactions to see if there has been any change, any deterioration, in their mental set-up since manufacture?"

"I haven't yet, but I will." He shook a slim finger at her, "You're losing your nerve, Susan. I don't see what it is you're dramatizing. They're essentially harmless."

"They are?" Calvin took fire. "They are? Do you realize one of them is lying? One of the sixty-three robots I have just interviewed has deliberately lied to me after the strictest injunction to tell the truth. The abnormality indicated is horribly deep-seated, and horribly frightening."

Peter Bogert felt his teeth harden against each other. He said, "Not at all. Look! Nestor 10 was given orders to lose himself. Those orders were expressed in maximum urgency by the person most authorized to command him. You can't counteract that order either by superior urgency or superior right of command. Naturally, the robot will attempt to defend the carrying out of his orders. In fact, objectively, I admit his ingenuity. How better can a robot lose himself than to hide himself among a group of similar robots?"

"Yes, you would admire it. I've detected amusement in you, Peter—amusement and an appalling lack of understanding. Are you a roboticist, Peter? Those robots attach importance to what they consider superiority. You've just said as much yourself. Subconsciously they feel humans to be inferior and the First Law which protects us from them is imperfect. They are unstable. And here we have a young man ordering a robot to leave him, to lose himself, with every verbal appearance of revulsion, disdain, and digust. Granted, that robot must follow orders, but subconsciously, there is resentment. It will become more important than ever for it to prove that it is superior despite the horrible names it was called. It may become *so* important that what's left of the First Law won't be enough."

"How on Earth, or anywhere in the Solar System, Susan, is a robot going to know the meaning of the assorted strong language used upon him? Obscenity is not one of the things impressioned upon his brain."

"Original impressionment is not everything," Calvin snarled at him. "Robots have learning capacity, you . . . you fool—" And Bogert knew that she had really lost her temper. She continued hastily, "Don't you suppose he could tell from the tone used that the words weren't complimentary? Don't you suppose he's heard the words used before and noted upon what occasions?"

"Well, then," shouted Bogert, "will you kindly tell me one way in which a modified robot can harm a human being, no matter how offended it is, no matter how sick with desire to prove superiority?"

"If I tell you one way, will you keep quiet?"

"Yes."

They were leaning across the table at each other, angry eyes nailed together.

The psychologist said, "If a modified robot were to drop a heavy weight upon a human being, he would not be breaking the First Law, if he did so with the knowledge that his strength and reaction speed would be sufficient to snatch the weight away before it struck the man. However once the weight left his fingers, he would be no longer the active medium. Only the blind force of gravity would be that. The robot could then change his mind and merely by inaction allow the weight to strike. The modified First Law allows that."

"That's an awful stretch of imagination."

"That's what my profession requires sometimes. Peter, let's not quarrel. Let's work. You know the exact nature of the stimulus that caused the robot to lose himself. You have the records of his original mental make-up. I want you to tell me how possible it is for our robot to do the sort of thing I just talked about. Not the specific instance, mind you, but that whole class of response. And I want it done quickly."

"And meanwhile—"

"And meanwhile, we'll have to try performance tests directly on the response to First Law."

* * *

General Black, at his own request, was supervising the mushrooming wooden partitions that were springing up in a bellying circle on the vaulted third floor of Radiation Building 2. The laborers worked in the main, silently, but more than one was openly a-wonder at the sixty-three photocells that required installation.

One of them sat down near Black, removed his hat, and wiped his forehead thoughtfully with a freckled forearm.

Black nodded at him, "How's it doing, Walensky?"

Walensky shrugged and fired a cigar, "Smooth as butter. What's going on anyway, Doc? First, there's no work for three days and then we have this mess of jiggers." He leaned backward on his elbows and puffed smoke.

Black twitched his eyebrows, "A couple of robot men came over from Earth. Remember the trouble we had with robots running into the gamma fields, before we pounded it into their skulls that they weren't to do it."

"Yeah. Didn't we get new robots?"

"We got some replacements, but mostly it was a job of indoctrination. Anyway, the people who make them want to figure out robots that aren't hit so bad by gamma rays."

"Sure seems funny, though, to stop all the work on the Drive for this robot deal. I thought nothing was allowed to stop the Drive."

"Well, it's the fellows upstairs that have the say on that. Me—I just do as I'm told. Probably all a matter of pull—"

"Yeah," the electrician jerked a smile, and winked a wise eye. "Somebody knew somebody in Washington. But as long as my pay comes through on the dot, I should worry. The Drive's none of my affair. What are they going to do here?"

"You're asking me? They brought a mess of robots with them, — over sixty, and they're going to measure reactions. That's all *my* knowledge."

"How long will it take?"

"I wish I knew."

"Well," Walensky said, with heavy sarcasm, "as long as they dish me my money, they can play games all they want."

Black felt quietly satisfied. Let the story spread. It was harmless, and near enough to the truth to take the fangs out of curiosity.

* * *

A man sat in the chair, motionless, silent. A weight dropped, crashed downward, then pounded aside at the last moment under the synchronized thump of a sudden force beam. In sixty-three wooden cells, watching NS-2 robots dashed forward in that split second before the weight veered, and sixty-three photocells five feet ahead of their original positions jiggled the marking pen and presented a little jag on the paper. The weight rose and dropped, rose and dropped, rose—

Ten times!

Ten times the robots sprang forward and stopped, as the man remained safely seated.

*   *   *

Major-general Kallner had not worn his uniform in its entirety since the first dinner with the U. S. Robot representatives. He wore nothing over his blue-gray shirt now, the collar was open, and the black tie was pulled loose.

He looked hopefully at Bogert, who was still blandly neat and whose inner tension was perhaps betrayed only by the trace of glister at his temples.

The general said, "How does it look? What is it you're trying to see?"

Bogert eplied, "A difference which may turn out to be a little too subtle for our purposes, I'm afraid. For sixty-two of those robots the necessity of jumping toward the apparently threatened human was what we call, in robotics, a forced reaction. You see, even when the robots knew that the human in question would not come to harm—and after the third or fourth time they must have known it—they could not prevent reacting as they did. First Law requires it."

"Well?"

"But the sixty-third robot, the modified Nestor, had no such compulsion. He was under free action. If he had wished, he could have remained in his seat. Unfortunately," and his voice was mildly regretful, "he didn't so wish."

"Why do you suppose?"

Bogert shrugged, "I suppose Dr. Calvin will tell us when she gets here. Probably with a horribly pessimistic interpretation, too. She is sometimes a bit annoying."

"She's qualified, isn't she?" demanded the general with a sudden frown of uneasiness.

"Yes." Bogert seemed amused. "She's qualified all right. She understands robots like a sister—comes from hating human beings so much, I think. It's just that, psychologist or not, she's an extreme neurotic. Has paranoid tendencies. Don't take her too seriously."

He spread the long row of broken-line graphs out in front of him.

"You see, general, in the case of each robot the time interval from moment of drop to the completion of a five-foot movement tends to decrease as the tests are repeated. There's a definite mathematical relationship that governs such things and failure to comform would indicate marked abnormality in the positronic brain. Unfortunately, all here appear normal."

"But if our Nestor 10 was not responding with a forced action, why isn't his curve different? I don't understand that."

"It's simple enough. Robotic responses are not perfectly analogous to human responses, more's the pity. In human beings, voluntary action is much slower than reflex action. But that's not the case with robots; with them it is merely a question of freedom of choice, otherwise the speeds of free and forced action are much the same. What I *had* been expecting, though, was that Nestor 10 would be caught by surprise the first time and allow too great an interval to elapse before responding."

"And he didn't?"

"I'm afraid not."

"Then we haven't gotten anywhere." The general sat back with an expression of pain. "It's five days since you've come."

At this point, Susan Calvin entered and slammed the door behind her. "Put your graphs away, Peter," she cried, "you know they don't show anything."

She mumbled something impatiently as Kallner half-rose to greet her, and went on, "We'll have to try something else quickly. I don't like what's happening."

Bogert exchanged a resigned glance with the general. "Is anything wrong?"

"You mean specifically? No. But I don't like to have Nestor 10 continue to elude us. It's bad. It *must* be gratifying his swollen sense of superiority. I'm afraid that his motivation is no longer simply one of following orders. I think it's becoming more a matter of sheer neurotic necessity to out-think humans. That's a dangerously unhealthy situation. Peter, have you done what I asked? Have you worked out the instability factors of the modified NS-2 along the lines I want?"

"It's in progress," said the mathematician, without interest.

She stared at him angrily for a moment, then turned to Kallner. "Nestor 10 is decidedly aware of what we're doing, general. He had no reason to jump for the bait in this experiment, especially after the first time, when he must have seen that there was no real danger to our subject. The others couldn't help it; but *he* was deliberately falsifying a reaction."

"What do you think we ought to do now, then, Dr. Calvin?"

"Make it impossible for him to fake an action the next time. We will repeat the experiment, but with an addition. High-tension cables, capable of electrocuting the Nestor models will be placed between subject and robot—enough of them to avoid the possibility of jumping over—and the robot will be made perfectly aware in advance that touching the cables will mean death."

"Hold on," spat out Bogert with sudden viciousness. "I rule that out. We are not electrocuting two million dollars worth of robots to locate Nestor 10. There are other ways."

"You're certain? You've found none. In any case, it's not a question of electrocution. We can arrange a relay which will break the current at the instant of application of weight. If the robot should place his weight on it, he won't die. *But he won't know that*, you see."

The general's eyes gleamed into hope. "Will that work?"

"It should. Under those conditions, Nestor 10 would have to remain in his seat. He could be *ordered* to touch the cables and die, for the Second Law of obedience is superior to the Third Law of self-preservation. But *he won't* be ordered to; he will merely be left to his own devices, as will all the robots. In the case of the normal robots, the First Law of human safety will drive them to their death even without orders. But not our Nestor 10. Without the entire First Law, and without having received any orders on the matter, the Third Law, self-preservation, will be the highest operating, and he will have no choice but to remain in his seat. It would be a forced action."

"Will it be done tonight, then?"

"Tonight," said the psychologist, "if the cables can be laid in time. I'll tell the robots now what they're to be up against."

* * *

A man sat in the chair, motionless, silent. A weight dropped, crashed downward, then pounded aside at the last moment under the synchronized thump of a sudden force beam.

Only once—

And from her small camp chair in the observing booth in the balcony, Dr. Susan Calvin rose with a short gasp of pure horror.

Sixty-three robots sat quietly in their chairs, staring owlishly at the endangered man before them. Not one moved.

* * *

Dr. Calvin was angry, angry almost past endurance. Angry the worse for not daring to show it to the robots that, one by one, were entering the room and then leaving. She checked the list. Number Twenty-eight was due in now—Thirty-five still lay ahead of her.

Number Twenty-eight entered, diffidently.

She forced herself into reasonable calm. "And who are you?"

The robot replied in a low, uncertain voice, "I have received no number of my own yet, ma'am. I'm an NS-2 robot, and I was Number Twenty-eight in line outside. I have a slip of paper here that I'm to give to you."

"You haven't been in here before this today?"

"No, ma'am."

"Sit down. Right there. I want to ask you some questions, Number Twenty-eight. Were you in the Radiation Room of Building Two about four hours ago?"

The robot had trouble answering. Then it came out hoarsely, like machinery needing oil, "Yes, ma'am."

"There was a man who almost came to harm there, wasn't there?"

"Yes, ma'am."

"You did nothing, did you?"

"No, ma'am."

"The man might have been hurt because of your inaction. Do you know that?"

"Yes, ma'am. I couldn't help it, ma'am." It is hard to picture a large expressionless metallic figure cringing, but it managed.

"I want you to tell me exactly why you did nothing to save him."

"I want to explain, ma'am. I certainly don't want to have you . . . have *anyone* . . . think that I could do a thing that might cause harm to a master. Oh, no, that would be a horrible . . . an inconceivable—"

"Please don't get excited, boy. I'm not blaming you for anything. I only want to know what you were thinking at the time."

"Ma'am, before it all happened you told us that one of the masters would be in danger of harm from that weight that keeps falling and that we would have to cross electric cables if we were to try to save him. Well, ma'am, that wouldn't stop me. What is my destruction compared to the safety of a master? But . . . but it occurred to me that if I died on my way to him, I wouldn't be able to save him anyway. The weight would crush him and then I would be dead for no purpose and perhaps some day some other master might come to harm who wouldn't have, if I had only stayed alive. Do you understand me, ma'am?"

"You mean that it was merely a choice of the man dying, of both the man and yourself dying. Is that right?"

"Yes, ma'am. It was impossible to save the master. He might be considered dead. In that case, it is inconceivable that I destroy myself for nothing—without orders."

The psychologist twiddled a pencil. She had heard the same story with insignificant verbal variations twenty-seven times before. This was the crucial question now.

"Boy," she said, "your thinking has its points, but it is not the sort of thing I thought you might think. Did you think of this yourself?"

The robot hesitated. "No."

"Who thought of it, then?"

"We were talking last night, and one of us got that idea and it sounded reasonable."

"Which one?"

The robot thought deeply. "I don't know. Just one of us."

She sighed, "That's all."

Number Twenty-nine was next. Thirty-four after that.

* * *

Major-general Kallner, too, was angry. For one week all of Hyper Base had stopped dead, barring some paper work on the subsidiary asteroids of the group. For nearly one week, the two top experts in the field had aggravated the situation with useless tests. And now they—or the woman, at any rate—made impossible propositions.

Fortunately for the general situation, Kallner felt it impolite to display his anger openly.

Susan Calvin was insisting, "Why not, sir? It's obvious that the present situation is unfortunate. The only way we may reach results in the future—or what future is left us in this matter—is to separate the robots. We can't keep them together any longer."

"My dear Dr. Calvin," rumbled the general, his voice sinking into the lower baritone registers. "I don't see how I can quarter sixty-three robots all over the place—"

Dr. Calvin raised her arms helplessly. "I can do nothing them. Nestor 10 will either imitate what the other robots would do, or else argue them plausibly into not doing what he himself cannot do. And in any case, this is bad business. We're in actual combat with this little lost robot of ours and he's winning out. Every victory of his aggravates his abnormality."

She rose to her feet in determination. "General Kallner, if you do not separate the robots as I ask, then I can only demand that all sixty-three be destroyed immediately."

"You demand it, do you?" Bogert looked up suddenly, and with real anger. "What gives you the right to demand any such thing. Those robots remain as they are. *I'm* responsible to the management, not you."

"And I," added Major-general Kallner, "am responsible to the World Co-ordinator—and I must have this settled."

"In that case," flashed back Calvin, "there is nothing for me to do but resign. If necessary to force you to the necessary destruction, I'll make this whole matter public. It was not I that approved the manufacture of modified robots."

"One word from you, Dr. Calvin," said the general, deliberately, "in violation of security measures, and you would be certainly imprisoned instantly."

Bogert felt the matter to be getting out of hand. His voice grew syrupy, "Well, now, we're beginning to act like children, all of us. We need only a little more time. Surely we can outwit a robot without resigning, or imprisoning people, or destroying two million."

The psychologist turned on him with quiet fury, "I don't want any unbalanced robots in existence. We have one Nestor that's definitely unbalanced, eleven more that are potentially so, and sixty-two normal robots that are being subjected to an unbalanced environment. The only absolutely safe method is complete destruction."

The signal-burr brought all three to a halt, and the angry tumult of growingly unrestrained emotion froze.

"Come in," growled Kallner.

It was Gerald Black, looking perturbed. He had heard angry voices. He said, "I thought I'd come myself . . . didn't like to ask anyone else—"

"What is it? Don't orate—"

"The locks of Compartment C in the trading ship have been played with. There are fresh scratches on them."

"Compartment C?' exclaimed Calvin quickly. "That's the one that holds the robots, isn't it? Who did it?"

"From the inside," said Black, laconically.

"The lock isn't out of order, is it?"

"No. It's all right. I've been staying on the ship now for four days and none of them have tried to get out. But I thought you ought to know, and I didn't like to spread the news. I noticed the matter myself."

"Is anyone there now?" demanded the general.

"I left Robbins and McAdams there."

There was a thoughtful silence, and then Dr. Calvin said, ironically, "Well?"

Kallner rubbed his nose uncertainly, "What's it all about?"

"Isn't it obvious? Nestor 10 is planning to leave. That order to lose himself is dominating his abnormality past anything we can do. I wouldn't be surprised if what's left of his First Law would scarcely be powerful enough to override it. He is perfectly capable of seizing the ship and leaving with it. Then we'd have a mad robot on a spaceship. What would he do next? Any idea? Do you still want to leave them all together, general?"

"Nonsense," interrupted Bogert. He had regained his smoothness. "All that from a few scratch marks on a lock."

"Have you, Dr. Bogert, completed the analysis I've required, since you volunteer opinions?"

"Yes."

"May I see it?"

"No."

"Why not? Or mayn't I ask that, either?"

"Because there's no point in it, Susan. I told you in advance that these modified robots are less stable than the normal variety, and my analysis shows it. There's a certain very small chance of breakdown under extreme circumstances that are not likely to occur. Let it go at that. I won't give you ammunition for your absurd claim that sixty-two perfectly good robots be destroyed just because so far you lack the ability to detect Nestor 10 among them."

Susan Calvin stared him down and let disgust fill her eyes. "You won't let anything stand in the way of the permanent directorship, will you?"

"Please," begged Kallner, half in irritation. "Do you insist that nothing further can be done, Dr. Calvin?"

"I can't think of anything, sir," she replied, wearily. "If there were only other differences between Nestor 10 and the normal robots, differences that didn't involve the First Law. Even one other difference. Something in impressionment, environment, specification—" And she stopped suddenly.

"What is it?"

"I've thought of something . . . I think—" Her eyes grew distant and hard, "These modified Nestors, Peter. They get the same impressioning the normal ones get, don't they?"

"Yes. Exactly the same."

"And what was it you were saying, Mr. Black," she turned to the young man, who thought the storms that had followed his news had maintained a discreet silence. "Once when complaining of the Nestors' attitude of superiority, you said the technicians had taught them all they knew."

"Yes, in etheric physics. They're not acquainted with the subject when they come here."

"That's right," said Bogert, in surprise. "I told you, Susan, when I spoke to the other Nestors here that the two new arrivals hadn't learned etheric physics yet."

"And why is that?" Dr. Calvin was speaking in mounting excitement. "Why aren't NS-2 models impressioned with etheric physics to start with?"

"I can tell you that," said Kallner. "It's all of a piece with the secrecy. We thought that if we made a special model with knowledge of etheric physics, used twelve of them and put the others to work in an unrelated field, there might be suspicion. Men working with normal Nestors might wonder why they knew etheric physics. So there was merely an impressionment with a capacity for training in the field. Only the ones that come here, naturally, receive such a training. It's that simple."

"I understand. Please get out of here, the lot of you. Let me have an hour or so."

* * *

Calvin felt she could not face the ordeal for a third time. Her mind had contemplated it and rejected it with an intensity that left her nauseated. She could face that unending file of repetitious robots no more.

So Bogert asked the questions now, while she sat aside, eyes and mind half-closed.

Number Fourteen came in—forty-nine to go.

Bogert looked up from the guide sheet and said, "What is your number in line?"

"Fourteen, sir." The robot presented his numbered ticket.

"Sit down, boy."

Bogert asked, "You haven't been here before on this day?"

"No, sir."

"Well, boy, we are going to have another man in danger of harm soon after we're through here. In fact, when you leave this room you will be led to a stall where you will wait quietly, till you are needed. Do your understand?"

"Yes, sir."

"Now, naturally, if a man is in danger of harm, you will try to save him."

"Naturally, sir."

"Unfortunately, between the man and yourself, there will be a gamma ray field."

Silence.

"Do you know what gamma rays are?" asked Bogert sharply.

"Energy radiation, sir?"

The next question came in a friendly, offhand manner, "Ever work with gamma rays?"

"No, sir." The answer was definite.

"Mm-m. Well, boy, gamma rays will kill you instantly. They'll destroy your brain. That is a fact you must know and remember. Naturally, you don't want to destroy yourself."

"Naturally." Again the robot seemed shocked. Then, slowly, "But sir, if the gamma rays are between myself and the master that may be harmed, how can I save him? I would be destroying myself to no purpose."

"Yes, there is that," Bogert seemed concerned about the matter. "The only thing I can advise, boy, is that if you detect the gamma radiation between yourself and the man, you may as well sit where you are."

The robot was openly relieved. "Thank you, sir. There wouldn't be any use, would there?"

"Of course not. But if there *weren't* any dangerous radiation, that would be a different matter."

"Naturally, sir. No question of that."

"You may leave now. The man on the other side of the door will lead you to your stall. Please wait there."

He turned to Susan Calvin when the robot left. "How did that go, Susan?"

"Very well," she said, dully.

"Do you think we could catch Nestor 10 by quick questioning on etheric physics?"

"Perhaps, but it's not sure enough." Her hands lay loosely in her lap. "Remember, he's fighting us. He's on his guard. The only way we can catch him is to outsmart him—and, within his limitations, he can think much more quickly than a human being."

"Well, just for fun—suppose I ask the robots from now on a few questions on gamma rays. Wave length limits, for instance."

"No!" Dr. Calvin's eyes sparked to life. "It would be too easy for him to deny knowledge and then he'd be warned against the test that's coming up—which is our real chance. Please follow the questions I've indicated, Peter, and don't improvise. It's just within the bounds of risk to ask them if they've ever worked with gamma rays. And try to sound even less interested then you do when you ask it."

Bogert shrugged, and pressed the buzzer that would allow the entrance of Number Fifteen.

The large Radiation Room was in readiness once more. The robots waited patiently in their wooden cells, all open to the center but closed off from each other.

Major-general Kallner mopped his brow slowly with a large handkerchief while Dr. Calvin checked the last details with Black.

"You're sure now," she demanded, "that none of the robots have had a chance to talk with each other after leaving the Orientation Room?"

"Absolutely sure," insisted Black. "There's not been a word exchanged."

"And the robots are put in the proper stalls?"

"Here's the plan."

The psychologist looked at it thoughtfully, "Um-m-m."

The general peered over her shoulder. "What's the idea of the arrangement, Dr. Calvin?"

"I've asked to have those robots that appeared even slightly out of true in the previous tests concentrated on one side of the circle. I'm going to be sitting in the center myself this time, and I wanted to watch those particularly."

"*You're* going to be sitting there—" exclaimed Bogert.

"Why not?" she demanded coldly. "What I expect to see may be something quite momentary. I can't risk having anyone else as main observer. Peter, you'll be in the observing booth, and I want you to keep your eye on the opposite side of the circle. General Kallner, I've arranged for motion pictures to be taken of each robot, in case visual observation isn't enough. If these are required, the robots are to remain exactly where they are until the pictures are developed and studied. None must leave, none must change place. Is that clear?"

"Perfectly."

"Then let's try it this one last time."

* * *

Susan Calvin sat in the chair, silent, eyes restless. A weight dropped, crashed downward, then pounded aside at the last moment under the synchronized thump of a sudden force beam.

And a single robot jerked upright and took two steps.

And stopped.

But Dr. Calvin was upright, and her finger pointed to him sharply. "Nestor 10, come here," she cried, "*come here!* COME HERE!"

Slowly, reluctantly, the robot took another step forward. The psychologist shouted at the top of her voice, without taking her eyes from the robot, "Get every other robot out of this place, somebody. Get them out quickly, and *keep* them out."

Somewhere within reach of her ears there was noise, and the thud of hard feet upon the floor. She did not look away.

Nestor 10—if it was Nestor 10—took another step, and then, under force of her imperious gesture, two more. He was only ten feet away, when he spoke harshly, "I have been told to be lost—"

Another step. "I must not disobey. They have not found me so far—He would think me a failure—He told me—But it's not so—I am powerful and intelligent—"

The words came in spurts.

Another step. "I know a good deal— He would think . . . I mean I've been found— Disgraceful— Not I— I am intelligent— And by just a master . . . who's weak— Slow—"

Another step—and one metal arm flew out suddenly to her shoulder, and she felt the weight bearing her down. Her throat constricted, and she felt a shriek tear through.

Dimly, she heard Nestor 10's next words, "No one must find me. No master—" and the cold metal was against her, and she was sinking under the weight of it.

And then a queer, metallic sound, and she was on the ground with an unfelt thump, and a gleaming arm was heavy across her body. It did not move. Nor did Nestor 10, who sprawled beside her.

And now faces were bending over her.

Gerald Black was gasping, "Are you hurt, Dr. Calvin?"

She shook her head feebly. They pried the arm off her and lifted her gently to her feet, "What happened?"

Black said, "I bathed the place in gamma rays for five seconds. We didn't know what was happening. It wasn't till the last second that we realized he was attacking you, and then there was no time for anything but a gamma field. He went down in an instant. There wasn't enough to harm you though. Don't worry about it."

"I'm not worried." She closed her eyes and leaned for a moment upon his shoulder. "I don't think I was attacked exactly. Nestor 10 was simply *trying* to do so. What was left of the First Law was still holding him back."

* * *

Susan Calvin and Peter Bogert, two weeks after their first meeting with Major-general Kallner had their last. Work at Hyper Base had been resumed. The trading ship with its sixty-two normal NS-2's was gone to wherever it was bound, with an officially imposed story to explain its two weeks' delay. The government cruiser was making ready to carry the two roboticists back to Earth.

Kallner was once again a-gleam in dress uniform. His white gloves shone as he shook hands.

Calvin said, "The other modified Nestors are, of course, to be destroyed."

"They will be. We'll make shift with normal robots, or, if necessary, do without."

"Good."

"But tell me— You haven't explained— How was it done?"

She smiled tightly, "Oh, that. I would have told you in advance if I had been more certain of its working. You see, Nestor 10 had a superiority complex that was becoming more radical all the time. He liked to think that he and other robots knew more than human beings. It was becoming very important for him to think so.

"We knew that. So we warned every robot in advance that gamma rays would kill them, which it would, and we further warned them all that gamma rays would be between them and myself. So they all stayed where they were, naturally. By Nestor 10's own logic in the previous test they had all decided that there was no point in trying to save a human being if they were sure to die before they could do it."

"Well, yes, Dr. Calvin, I understand that. But why did Nestor 10 himself leave his seat."

"Ah! That was a little arrangement between myself and your young Mr. Black. You see it wasn't gamma rays that flooded the area between myself and the robots—but infrared rays. Just ordinary heat rays, absolutely harmless. Nestor 10 knew they were infrared and harmless and so he began to dash out, as he expected the rest would do, under First Law compulsion. It was only a fraction of a second too late that he remembered that the normal NS-2's could detect radiation, but could not identify the type. That he himself could only identify wave lengths by virtue of the training he had received at Hyper Base, under mere human beings, was a little too humiliating to remember for just a moment. To the normal robots the area was fatal because we had told them it would be, and only Nestor 10 knew we were lying.

"And just for a moment he forgot, or didn't want to remember, that other robots might be more ignorant than human beings. His very superiority caught him. Good-by, general."

No Connection

Raph was a typical American of his times. Remarkably ugly, too, by American standards of our times. The bony structure of his jaws was tremendous and the musculature suited it. His nose was arched and wide and his black eyes were small and forced wide apart by the span of said nose. His neck was thick, his body broad, his fingers spatulate, with strongly curved nails.

If he had stood erect, on thick legs with large, well-padded feet, he would have topped two and a half yards. Standing or sitting, his mass neared a quarter of a ton.

Yet his forehead rose in an unrestricted arc and his cranial capacity did not stint. His enormous hand dealt delicately with a pen, and his mind droned comfortably on as he bent over his desk.

In fact, his wife and most of his fellow-Americans found him a fine-looking fellow.

Which shows the alchemy of a long displacement along the time-axis.

* * *

Raph, Junior, was a smaller edition of our typical American. He was adolescent and had not yet lost the hairy covering of childhood. It spread in a dark, close-curled mat across his chest and back, but it was already thinning and perhaps within the year he would first don the adult shirt that would cover the proudly-naked skin of manhood.

But, meanwhile, he sat in breeches alone, and scratched idly at a favorite spot just above the diaphragm. He felt curious and just a little bored. It wasn't bad to come with his father to the museum when people were there. Today was a Closed-Day, however, and the empty corridors rang lonesomely when he walked along them.

Besides, he knew everything in it—mostly bones and stones.

Junior said: "What's that thing?"

"What thing?" Raph lifted his head and looked over his shoulder. Then he looked pleased. "Oh, that's something quite new. That's a reconstruction of Primate Primeval. It was sent to me from the North River Grouping. Isn't it a nice job, though?" And he returned to his work, in the grip of a momentary twinge of pleasure. Primate Primeval wasn't to go on exhibition for a week at least—not until he prepared an honourable place for it with suitable surroundings, but, for the moment, it was in his office and his own private darling.

Raph looked at the "nice job" with quite other emotions, however. What he saw was a spindly figure of contemptuous size, with thin legs and arms, hair-covered and owning an ugly, small-featured face with large, protruding eyes.

He said: "Well, what *is* it, Pa?"

Raph stirred impatiently: "It's a creture that lived many millions of years ago, we think. That's the way we think it looks."

"Why?" insisted the youngster.

Raph gave up. Apparently, he would have to root out the subject and do away with it.

"Well, for one thing we can tell about the muscles from the shape of the bones, and the positions where the tendons would fit and where some of the nerves would go. From the teeth we can tell the type of digestive system the animal would have, and from the footbones, what type of posture it would have. For the rest, we go by the principle of Analogy, that is, by the outside appearance of creatures that exist today that have the same kind of skeleton. For instance, that's why he's covered with red hair. Most of the Primates today—they're little insignificant creatures, practically extinct—are red-haired, have bare callosities on the rump—"

Junior scurried behind the figure and satisfied himself on that score.

"—have long, fleshy probosces, and short, shriveled ears. Their diets are unspecialized, hence the rather all-purpose teeth, and they are nocturnal, hence the large eyes. It's all simple, really. Now, does that dispose of you, youngster?"

And then Junior, having thought and thought about it, came out with a disparaging: "He looks just like an Eekah to me, though. Just like an ugly, old Eekah."

Raph stared at him. Apparently he had missed a point: "An Eekah?" he said, "What's an Eekah? Is that an imaginary creature you've been reading about?"

"Imaginary! Say, Pa, don't you *ever* stop at the Recorder's?"

This was an embarrassing question to answer, for "Pa" never did, or at least, never since his maturity. As a child, the Recorder, as custodian of the world's spoken, written, and recorded fiction, had, of course, had an unfailing fascination. But he had grown up—

He said, tolerantly: "Are there new stories about Eekahs? I remember none when I was young."

"You don't get it, Pa." One would almost suppose that the young Raph was on the very verge of an exasperation he was too cautious to express. He explained in wounded fashion: "The Eekahs are real things. They come from the Other World. Haven't you heard about *that?* We've been hearing about it in school, even, and in the Group Magazine. They stand upside down in their country, only they don't know it, and they look just like Ol' Primeval there."

Raph collected his astonished wits. He felt the incongruity of cross-examining his half-grown child for archeological data and he hesitated a moment. After all, he had heard *some* things. There *had* been word of vast continents existing on the other hemisphere of Earth. It seemed to him that there were reports of life on them. It was all hazy—perhaps it wasn't always wise to stick so closely to the field of one's own interest.

He asked Junior: "Are there Eekahs here among the Groupings?"

Junior nodded rapidly: "The Recorder says they can think as good as us. They got machines that go through the air. That's how they got here."

"Junior!" said Raph severely.

"I ain't lying," Junior cried with aggrieved virtue. "You ask the Recorder and see what *he* says."

Raph slowly gathered his papers together. It was Closed-Day, but he could find the Recorder at his home, no doubt.

* * *

The Recorder was an elderly member of the Red River Gurrow Grouping and few alive could remember a time when he was not. He had succeeded to the post by general consent and filled it well, for he was Recorder for the same reason that Raph was curator of the museum. He liked to be, he wanted to be, and he could conceive no other life.

The social pattern of the Gurrow Grouping is difficult to grasp unless born into it, but there was a looseness about it that almost made the word "pattern" incongruous. The individual Gurrow took whatever job he felt an aptitude for, and such work as was left over and needed to be done was done either in common, or consecutively by each according to an order determined by lot. Put so, it sounds too simple to work, but actually the traditions that had gathered with the five thousand years since the first Voluntary Grouping of Gurrahs was supposed to have been established, made the system complicated, flexible—and workable.

The Recorder was, as Raph had anticipated, at his home, and there was the embarrassment of renewing an old and unjustly neglected acquaintanceship. He had made use of the Recorder's reference library, of course, but always indirectly—yet he had once been a child, an intimate learner at the feet of accumulated wisdom, and he had let the intimacy lapse.

The room he now entered was more or less choked with recordings and, to a lesser degree, with printed material. The Recorder interspersed greetings with apologies.

"Shipments have come from some of the other Groupings," he said. "It needs time for cataloguing, you know, and I can't seem to find the time I used to." He lit a pipe and puffed strongly. "Seems to me I'll have to find a full-time assistant. What about your son, Raph? He clusters about here the way you did twenty years ago."

"You remember those times?"

"Better than you do, I think. Think your son would like that?"

"Suppose you talk to him. He might like to. I can't honestly say he's fascinated by archaeology." Raph picked up a recording at random and looked at the identification tag: "Um-m-m—from the Joquin Valley Grouping. That's a long way from here."

"A long way." The Recorder nodded. "I have sent them some of ours, of course. The works of our own Grouping are highly regarded throughout the continent," he said, with proprietary pride. "In fact"—he pointed the stem of his pipe at the other—"your own treatise on extinct primates has been distributed everywhere. I've sent out two thousand copies and there are still requests. That's pretty good—for archaeology."

"Well, archaeology is why I am here—that and what my son says you've been telling him." Raph had a little trouble starting: "It seems you have spoken of creatures called Eekahs from the Antipodes, and I would like to have such information as you have on them."

The Recorder looked thoughtful: "Well, I could tell you what I know offhand, or we could go to the Library and look up the references."

"Don't bother opening the Library for me. It's a Closed-Day. Just give me some notion of things and I'll search the references later."

The Recorder bit at his pipe, shoved his chair back against the wall and de-focused his eyes thoughtfully. "Well," he said, "I suppose it starts with the discovery of the continents on the other side. That was five years ago. You know about that, perhaps?"

"Only the fact of it. I know the continents exist, as everyone does now. I remember once speculating on what a shining new field it would be for archaeological research, but that is all."

"Ah, then there is much else to tell you of. The new continents were never discovered by us directly, you know. It was five years ago that a group of non-Gurrow creatures arrived at the East Harbor Grouping in a machine that flew—by definite scientific principles, we found out later, based essentially on the buoyancy of air. They spoke a language, were obviously intelligent, and called themselves Eekahs. The Gurrows, of the East Harbor Grouping, learned their language—a simple one though full of unpronounceable sounds—and I have a grammar of it, if you're interested—"

Raph waved that away.

The Recorder continued: "The Gurrows of the Grouping, with the aid of those of the Iron Mountain Grouping—which specialize in steel works, you know—built duplicates of the flying machine. A flight was made across the ocean, and I should say there are several dozens of volumes on all that—volumes on the flying machine, on a new science called aerodynamics, new geographies, even a new system of philosophy based on the plurality of intelligences. All produced at the East Harbor and Iron Mountain Groupings. Remarkable work for only five years, and all are available here."

"But the Eekahs—are they still at the East Harbor Groupings?"

"Um-m-m. I'm pretty certain they are. They refused to return to their own continents. They call themselves 'political refugees.' "

"Politi . . . *what?*"

"It's their own language," said the Recorder, "and it's the only translation available."

"Well, why *political* refugees? Why not geological refugees, or oompah refugees. I should think a translation ought to make sense."

The Recorder shrugged: "I refer you to the books. They're not criminals, they claim. I know only what I tell you."

"Well, then, what do they look like? Do you have pictures?"

"At the Library."

"Did you read my 'Principles of Archaeology'?"

"I looked through it."

"Do you remember the drawings of Primate Primeval?"

"I'm afraid not."

"Then, look, let's go down to the Library, after all."

"Well, sure." The Recorder grunted as he rose.

* * *

The Administrator of the Red River Gurrow Grouping held a position in no way different in essentials from that of the Museum Curator, the Recorder or any other voluntary job holder. To expect a difference is to assume a society in which executive ability is rare.

Actually, all jobs in a Gurrow Grouping—where a "job" is defined as regular work, the fruits of which adhere to others in addition to the worker himself—are divided into two classes: one, Voluntary Jobs, and the other, Involuntary or Community Jobs. All of the first classification are equal. If a Gurrow enjoys the digging of useful ditches, his bent is to be respected and his job to be honored. If no one enjoys such burrowing and yet it is found necessary for comfort, it becomes a Community Job, done by lot or rotation according to convenience—annoying but unavoidable.

And so it was that the Administrator lived in a house no more ample and luxurious than others, sat at the head of no tables, had no particular title other than the name of his job, and was neither envied, hated, nor adored.

He liked to arrange Inter-Group trade, to supervise the common finances of the Group, and to judge the infrequent disagreements that arose. Of course, he received no additional food or energy privileges for doing what he liked.

It was not, therefore, to obtain permission, but to place his accounts in decent order, that Raph stopped in to see the Administrator. The Closed-Day had not yet ended. The Administrator sat peacefully in his after-dinner armchair, with an after-dinner cigar in his mouth, and an after-dinner book in his hand. Although there was something rather timeless about six children and a wife, even they had an after-dinner air about them.

Raph received a multiple greeting upon entering, and raised two hands to his ears, for if the various Administratelets (Only applicable title. Author.) had a job, it was noisemaking. Certainly, it was what they liked to do, and certainly others reaped most of the fruits therefrom, for their own eardrums were apparently impervious.

The Administrator shooed them.

Raph accepted a cigar.

"I intend leaving the Grouping for a time, Lahr," he said. "My job necessitates it."

"We won't enjoy your going, Raph. I hope it will not be for long."

"I hope not. What have we in Common Units?"

"Oh, ample for your purposes, I'm sure. Where do you intend going?"

"To the East Harbor Grouping."

The Administrator nodded and blew out a thoughtful puff of smoke: "Unfortunately, East Harbor has a surplus in their favor registered in our books—I can verify that, if you wish—but the Common Units of Exchange on hand will take care of transportation and necessary expenses."

"Well, that's fine. But tell me, what is my status on the Community Job Roster?"

"Um-m-m—I'll have to get the rolls. You'll excuse me a moment." He trundled away, heaving his great weight across the room and out into the hallway. Raph paused to poke at the youngest of the children who rolled up to him, growling in mock ferocity with gleaming teeth—a black little bundle of thick fur, with the long, childish snout that had not yet broadened away from the shape of the animal ancestry of half a million years earlier.

The Administrator returned with a heavy ledger and larger spectacles. He opened the ledger meticulously, riffled the pages to the proper place and then drew a careful finger down the columns.

He said: "There's only the question of the water supply, Raph. You're due on the Maintenance gang for this next week. There's nothing else due for at least two months."

"I'll be back before then. Is there any chance of someone subbing for me on the Water Maintenance?"

"Um-m-m—I'll get someone. I can always send my oldest. He's getting to job age and he might as well taste everything. He may like working on the dam."

"Yes? You tell me if he does, then. He can replace me, regularly."

The Administrator smiled gently: "Don't plan on that, Raph. If he can figure out a way of making sleeping useful to all of us, he'll certainly take it up as a job. And why are you going to East Harbor Grouping, by the way, if it's something you care to talk about?"

"You'll laugh, perhaps, but I have just found out that there exist such things as Eekahs."

"Eekahs? Yes, I know." The Administrator pointed a finger. "Creatures from across the sea! Right?"

"Right! But that's not all. I've come from the Library. I've seen trimensional reproductions, Lahr, and they're *Primate Primeval*, or almost. They're primates, anyway, *intelligent* primates. They've got small eyes, flat noses, and completely different jawbones—but they're at least second cousins. I've *got* to see them, Lahr."

The Administrator shrugged. He felt no interest in the matter himself. "Why? I ask out of ignorance, Raph. Does it matter, your seeing them?"

"Matter?" Raph was obviously appalled at the question. "Don't you know what's been going on these last years? Have you read my archaeology book?"

"No," said the Administrator, definitely, "I wouldn't read it to save myself a turn at Garbage Disposal."

Raph said: "Which probably proves you more suited to Garbage Disposal than archaeology. But never mind. I've been fighting single-handed for nearly ten years in favor of my theory that Primate Primeval was an intelligent creature with a developed civilization. I have nothing on my side so far but logical necessity, which is the last thing most archaeologists will accept. They want something solid. They want the remains of a Grouping, or artifacts, structures, books—get it. All I can give them is a skeleton with a huge brain-pan. Stars above, Lahr, what do they expect to survive in ten million years? Metal dies. Paper dies. Film dies.

"Only stone lasts, Lahr. And bone that's turned to stone. I've got that. A skull with room for a brain. And stone, too, old sharpened knives. Ground flints."

"Well," said Lahr, "there are your artifacts."

"Those are called eoliths, dawn stones. They won't accept them. They call them natural products, fortuitously shaped by erosion into the shapes they have, the idiots."

Then he grinned with a scientific ferocity: "But if the Eekahs are intelligent primates, I've practically proven my case."

* * *

Raph had traveled before, but never eastward, and the decline of agriculture on the road impressed him. In early history, the Gurrow Groupings had been entirely unspecialized. Each had been self-sufficient, and trade was a gesture of friendliness rather than a matter of necessity.

And so it was still in most Groupings. His own Grouping, the Red River, was perhaps typical. Some five hundred miles inland, set in lush farm land, agriculture remained centric. The river yielded some fish and there was a well-developed dairy industry. In fact, it was food exports that provided cause for the healthy state of the store of Common Units.

As they traveled eastward, however, the Groupings through which they passed paid less and less mind to the shallowing soil and more and more to the smoking factory structures.

In the East Harbor Grouping, Raph found a trading center which depended for its prosperity primarily upon ships. It was a more populous Grouping than the average, more densely packed, with houses, on occasion, within a hundred yards of each other.

Raph felt an uncomfortable prickling at the thought of living in such close quarters. The docks were even worse, with Gurrows engaged at the huge Community Jobs of loading and unloading.

The Administrator of this East Harbor Grouping was a young man, new at his job, overwhelmed with the joy of his work, and beside himself with the pleasure of welcoming a distinguished stranger.

Raph sat through an excellent meal, and was treated to a long discourse as to the exact derivation of each dish. To his provincial ears, beef from the Prairie Grouping, potatoes from the Northeast Woods Grouping, coffee from the Isthmus Grouping, wine from the Pacific Grouping, and fruit from the Central Lakes Grouping were something strange and wonderful.

Over the cigars—South Island Grouping—he brought up the subject of the Eekahs. The East Harbor Administrator grew solemn and a little uneasy.

"The man you want to see is Lernin. He'll be glad to help you all he can. You say you know something of these Eekahs?"

"I say I would *like* to know something. They resemble an extinct species of animal I am familiar with."

"Then *that* is your field of interest. I see."

"Perhaps you can tell me some of the details of their arrival, Administrator," suggested Raph, politely.

"I was not Administrator at the time, friend, so that I lack firsthand information, but the records are plain. This group of Eekahs that arrived in their flying-machine . . . you've heard about these aeronautical devices?"

"Yes, yes."

"Yes. Well . . . apparently they were fugitives."

"So I have heard. Yet they claim not to be criminals. Isn't that so?"

"Yes. Queer, isn't it? They admitted that they had been condemned—this was after long and skilful questioning, once we had learned their language—but denied that they were evildoers. Apparently, they had disagreed with their Administrator on principles of policy."

Raph nodded his head knowingly: "Ah, and refused to abide by the common decision. Is that it?"

"More confusing than that. They insist there was no common decision. They claim that the Administrator decided on policy of his own accord."

"And was not replaced?"

"Apparently those who believe he should are considered criminals—as these were."

There was a frank pause of disbelief. Then Raph said: "Does that sound reasonable to you?"

"No, I merely relay to you their words. Of course, the Eekah language is quite a barrier. Some of the sounds can't be pronounced: words have different meanings according to position in the sentence and according to tiny differences in inflection. And it happens often that Eekah words even when best translated are a complete puzzle."

"They must have been surprised to find Gurrows here," suggested Raph, "if they are members of a different genus."

"Surprised!" The Administrator's voice sank: "I'll say they were surprised. Now, this information has not been generally published for obvious reasons, so I hope you remember that it's confidential. These Eekahs killed five Gurrows before they could be disarmed. They had an instrument that expelled metal pellets at high speed by means of a controlled explosive chemical reaction. We have duplicated it since. Naturally, under the circumstances, we are not branding them criminals, for it is reasonable to assume that they did not realize we were intelligent beings. Apparently," and the Administrator smiled ruefully, "we resemble certain animals in their world. Or so they say."

But Raph was galvanized into a sudden enthusiasm: "Stars above! They said that, did they? Did they go into details? What kind of animals?"

The Administrator was taken back: "Well, I don't know. They give names in their language. What meaning has that? They called us giant 'bears.' "

"Giant what?"

"Bears. Bears." Raph stumbled over the word. "That's interesting. It's more than interesting. It's stupendous. Do you know, Administrator, that there is a great dispute among us as to the ancestry of Gurrows? Living animals related to Gurrow sapiens would be of immense importance." Raph rubbed his huge hands with pleasure.

The Administrator was pleased at the sensation he had caused. He said: "And a puzzling thing in addition is that they call themselves by two names."

"Two names?"

"Yes. No one knows the distinction yet, no matter how much the Eekahs explain it to us, except that one is a more general name, and one a more specific. The basis of the difference escapes us."

"I see. Which is 'Eekah'?"

"That is the specific one. The general one is"—the Administrator stumbled slowly over the harsh syllables—"Chim-pan-zee. There, that's it. There are a group called Eekahs and there are other groups with other names. But they are all called Chim . . . what I said before."

The Administrator sought through his mind for other juicy items of miscellany with which he was acquainted, but Raph interrupted him.

"May I see Lernin tomorrow?"

"Of course."

"Then I shall do so. Thank you for your courtesy, Administrator."

* * *

Lernin was a slight individual. It is doubtful if he weighed more than two hundred and fifty. There was also an imperfection in his walk, a slight lameness. But neither of these facts made much of an impression on Raph once the conversation had begun, for Lernin was a thinker who could impose his vigor upon others.

It was Raph whose eagerness dominated the first half of the conversation, and Lernin's comments were as luminous and as brief as lightning flashes. And then, there was a sudden whirl of the center of gravity, and Lernin took over.

"You will excuse me, learned friend," Lernin said with a characteristic stiffness that he could make so amiable, "if I find your problem unimportant. No, no"—he lifted a long-fingered hand—"not, in the uncomplicated talk of the times, merely unimportant to myself because my interest lies elsewhere, but unimportant to the Grouping of all the Groupings—to every single Gurrow from end to end of the world."

The concept was staggering. For a moment, Raph was offended; offended deep in his sense of individuality. It showed in his face.

Lernin added quickly: "It may sound impolite, crude, uncivilized. But I must explain. I must explain because you are primarily a social scientist and will understand—perhaps better than we ourselves."

"My life-interest," said Raph angrily, "is important to myself. I cannot assume those of others in preference."

"What I talk about should be the life-interest of all—if only because it may be the means of saving the lives of all of us."

Raph was beginning to suspect all sorts of things from a queer form of joking to the unbalance of mind that sometimes came with age. Yet Lernin was not old.

Lernin said, with an impressive fervor: "The Eekahs of the other world are a danger to us, for they are not friendly to us."

And Raph replied naturally: "How do you know?"

"No one other than myself, my friend, has lived more closely with these Eekahs who have arrived here, and I find them people with minds of emotional content strange to us. I have collected queer facts which we find difficult to interpret, but which point, at any rate, in disquieting directions.

"I'll list a few: Eekahs in organized groups kill one another periodically for obscure reasons. Eekahs find it impossible to live in a manner other than those of ants—that is, in huge conglomerate societies—yet find it impossible to allow for the presence of one another. Or, to use the terminology of the social scientists, they are gregarious without being social, just as we Gurrows are social without being gregarious. They have elaborate codes of behavior, which, we are told, are taught to the young, but which are disobeyed in universal practice, for reasons obscure to us. Et cetera. Et cetera. Et cetera."

"I am an archaeologist," said Raph, stiffly. "These Eekahs are of interest to me biologically only. If the curvature of the thigh bone is known to me, I care little for the curvature of their cultural processes. If I can follow the shape of the skull, it is immaterial to me that the shape of their ethics is mysterious."

"You don't think that their insanities may affect us here?"

"We are six thousand miles apart, or more, along either ocean," said Raph. "We have our world. They have theirs. There is no connection between us."

"No connection," mused Lernin, "so others have said. No connection at all. Yet Eekahs have reached us, and others may follow. We are told that the other world is dominated by a few, who are in turn dominated by their queer need for security which they confuse with an Eekah word called 'power,' which, apparently, means the prevailing on one's own will over the sum of the will of the community. What if this 'power' should extend to us?"

Raph bent his mind to the task. The matter was utterly ridiculous. It seemed impossible to picture the strange concepts.

Lernin said: "These Eekahs say that their world and ours in the long past were closer together. They say that there is a well-known scientific hypothesis in their world of a continental drift. That may interest you, since otherwise you might find it difficult to reconcile the existence of fossils of Primate Primeval closely related to living Eekahs six thousand miles away."

* * *

And the mists cleared from the archaeologist's brain as he glanced up with a live interest untroubled by insanities: "Ah, you should have said this sooner."

"I say it now as an example of what you may achieve for yourself by joining us and helping us. There is another thing. These Eekahs are physical scientists, like ourselves here in East Harbor, but with a difference dictated by their own cultural pattern. Since they live in hives, they think in hives, and their science is the result of an ant-society. Individually, they are slow and unimaginative; collectively, each supplies a crumb different from that supplied by his fellow—so that a vast structure is erected quickly. Here the individual is infinitely brighter, but he works alone. You, for instance, know nothing of chemistry, I imagine."

"A few of the fundamentals, but nothing else," admitted Raph. "I leave that, naturally, to the chemist."

"Yes, naturally. But I *am* a chemist. Yet these Eekahs, though my mental inferiors, and no chemists in their own world, know more chemistry than I. For instance, did you know that there exist elements that spontaneously disintegrate?"

"Impossible," exploded Raph. "Elements are eternal, change-less—"

Lernin laughed: "So you have been taught. So I have been taught. So I taught others. Yet the Eekahs are right, for in my laboratories I have checked them, and in every detail they are right. Uranium gives rise to a spontaneous radiation. You've heard of uranium, of course? And furthermore, I have detected radiations of energy beyond that produced by uranium which must be due to traces of elements unknown to us but described by the Eekahs. And these missing elements fit well into the so-called Periodic Tables some chemists have tried to foist upon the science. Though I do wrong to use the word 'foist' now."

"Well," said Raph, "why do you tell me this? Does this, too, help me in my problem?"

"Perhaps," said Lernin, ironically, "you will yet find it a royal bribe. You see, the energy production of uranium is absolutely constant. No known outward change in environment can affect it—and as a result of the loss in energy, uranium slowly turns to lead at an *absolutely constant rate*. A group of our men is even now using this fact as a basis for a method of determining the age of the earth. You see, to determine the age of a stratum of rock in the earth, then, it is but necessary to discover a region in it containing a trace of uranium—a widely spread element—and to determine about it the quantity of lead—and I might here add that the lead produced from uranium differs from ordinary lead and can be easily characterized—and it is then simple to determine the length of time in which that stratum has been solid. And of course, if a fossil is found in that stratum, it is of the same age, am I not correct?"

"Stars above," and Raph rose to his feet in a tremble, "you do not deceive me? It is really possible to do this?"

"It is possible. It is even easy. I tell you that our great defense, even at this late date, is co-operation in science. We are a group now of many, my friend, from many Groupings, and we want you among us. If you join us, it would be a simple matter to extend our earth-age project to such regions as you may indicate—regions rich in fossils. What do you say?"

"I will help you."

* * *

It is doubtful if the Gurrow Groupings had ever before seen a community venture of such breadth as now took place. East Harbor Grouping, as has been remarked, was a shipping center, and certainly a trans-Atlantic vessel was not beyond the capacity of a Grouping that traded along the full lengths of both coasts of the Americas. What *was* unusual was the vastness of the co-operation of Gurrows from many Groupings, Gurrows of many interests.

Not that they were all happy.

Raph, for instance, on the particular morning that now concerns us, six months from the date of his first arrival in East Harbor, was searching anxiously for Lernin.

Lernin, for his part, was searching for nothing but greater speed.

They met on the docks, where Lernin, biting the end off a cigar and leading the way to a region where smoking was permitted, said: "And you, my friend, seem concerned. Not, certainly, about the progress of our ocean liner?"

"I am concerned," said Raph, gravely, "about the reports I have received of the expedition testing the age of the rocks."

"Oh— And you are unhappy about it?"

"Unhappy!" exploded Raph. "Have you seen them?"

"I have received a copy. I have looked at it. I have even read parts of it. But I have had little time and most of it bounced off. Will you please enlighten me?"

"Certainly. In the last several months, three of the regions I have indicated as being fossiliferous have been tested. The first region was in the area of East Harbor Grouping itself. Another was in the Pacific Bay Grouping, and a third in the Central Lakes Grouping. I purposely asked that those be done first because they are the richest areas and because they are widely separately. Do you know, for instance, what age they tell me the rocks upon which we stand are?"

"Two billion years, I think, is the oldest figure I noticed."

"And that's the figure for the oldest rocks—the basic igneous stratum of basalt. The upper strata, however—the recent sedimentary layers containing dozens of fossils of Primate Primeval—how old do you think *these* are supposed to be? Five—hundred—trillion—years! How is that? Do you understand?"

"Trillion?" Lernin squinted upwards and shook his head. "That's strange."

"I'll add to it. The Pacific Coast Grouping is one hundred trillion years old—so I am told—and Central Lakes almost eighty trillion years old."

Lernin said: "And the other measurements? The ones that did not involve your strata?"

"That is the most peculiar thing of all. Most of the chosen investigations were carried on in strata that were not particularly fossiliferous. They had their own criteria of choice based on geological reasoning—and they got consistent results—one million to two billion years depending upon the depth and geological history of the particular region tested. Only *my* areas give these strange and impossible vagaries."

And Lernin said, "But what do the geologists say about all this? Can there be some error?"

"Undoubtedly. But they have fifty decent, reasonable measurements. For themselves, they have proved the method and are happy. There are three anomalies, to be sure, but they view them with equanimity as involving some unknown factors. I don't see it that way. These three measurements mean everything." Raph interrupted himself fiercely: "How sure are you that radioactivity is an absolute constant?"

"Sure? Can one ever be sure? Nothing we know of so far affects it, and such is likewise the definite testimony of our Eekahs. Besides, my friend, if you are implying that radioactivity was more extensive in the past than in the present, why only in your fossil regions? Why not everywhere?"

"Why, indeed? It's another aspect of a problem which is growing more important daily. Consider. We have regions which show a past of abnormal radioactivity. We have regions which show abnormal fossil frequencies. Why should these regions coincide, Lernin?"

"One obvious answer suggests itself, my friend. If your Primate Primeval existed at a time when certain regions were highly radioactive, certain individuals would wander into them and die. Radioactive radiation is deadly in excess, of course. Radioactivity and fossils, there you are."

"Why not other creatures," demanded Raph. "Only Primate Primeval occurs in excess, and he was intelligent. He would not be trapped by dangerous radiation."

"Perhaps he was not intelligent. That is, after all, only your theory and not a proven fact."

"Certainly, then, he was more intelligent than his small-brained contemporaries."

"Perhaps not even that. You romanticize too much."

"Perhaps I do." Raph spoke in half a whisper. "It seems to me that I can conjure up visions of a great civilization of a million years back—or more. A great power; a great intelligence—that has vanished completely, except for the tiny whispers of ossified bones which retain that huge cavity in which a brain once existed, and a bony five-fingered hand curving into slender signs of manipulative skill—with an opposing thumb. They *must* have been intelligent."

"Then, what killed them?" Lernin shrugged: "Several million species of living things have survived."

* * *

Raph looked up, half in anger: "I cannot accompany your group, Lernin, on a Voluntary basis. To go to the other world would be useful, yes, if I could engage in my own studies. For your purposes, it can be only a Community Job to me. I cannot give my heart to it."

But Lernin's jaw was set: "That arrangement would not be fair. There are many of us, my friend, who are sacrificing our own interests. If we all placed them first and investigated the other world in terms of our own particular provincialisms only, our great purpose would be destroyed. My friend, there is not one of our men that we can spare. We must all work as if our lives depended on our instant solution of the Eekah problem, which, believe me, it does."

Raph's jaws twisted in distaste. "On your side, you have a vague apprehension of these weak, stupid little creatures. On my side I have a definite problem of great intellectual attraction to myself. And between the two I can see no connection—no possible connection at all."

"Nor can I. But listen to me a moment. A small group of our most trusted men returned last week from a visit to the other world. It was not official, as ours will be. It made no contacts. It was a frank piece of espionage, which I am telling you about now. I ask your discretion on the matter."

"Naturally."

"Our men possessed themselves of Eekah event-sheets."

"Pardon me?"

"It is a created name to describe the objects. Printed records are issued daily in the various centers of Eekah population of events and occurrences of the day, and what passes for literary efforts as well."

Raph was momentarily interested: "It strikes me as an excellent idea."

"Yes, in its essence. The Eekah notion of interesting events, however, appears to consist entirely of antisocial events. However, leave that be. My point is that the existence of the Americas is well-known there these days—and it is universally spoken of as a 'new land of opportunity.' The various divisions of Eekahs eye it with a universal desire. The Eekahs are many, they are crowded, their economy is irrational. They want new land, and that is what this is to them—new and empty land."

"Not empty," pointed out Raph, mildly.

"Empty to them," insisted Lernin terribly. "That is the vast danger. Lands occupied by Gurrows are to them empty and they mean to take it, all the more so since they have often enough striven to take the lands of one another."

Raph shrugged: "Even so, they—"

"Yes. They are weak and stupid. You said that, and so they are. But only singly. They will unite for a purpose. To be sure, they will fall apart when the purpose is done—but momentarily they will join and become strong, which we perhaps cannot do, witness yourself. And their weapons of war have been keened in the fire of conflict. Their flying machines, for instance, are superb war weapons."

"But we have duplicated it—"

"In quantity? We have also duplicated their chemical explosives, but only in the laboratory, and their firing tubes and armored vehicles, but only in experimental plants. And yet there is more—something developed within the last five years, for our own Eekahs know nothing about it."

"And what is that?"

"We don't know. Their event-sheets speak of it—the names applied to it mean nothing to us—but the context implies the terror of it, even on the part of these kill-mad Eekahs. There seems no evidence that it has been used, or that all the Eekah groups have it—but it is used as a supreme threat. It will perhaps be clearer to you when all the evidence is presented once our voyage is under way."

"But what is it? You talk of it as if it were a bogey."

"Why, *they* talk of it as if it were a bogey. And what *could* be a bogey to an Eekah? That is the most frightening aspect of it. So far, we know only that it involves the bombardment of an element they call plutonium—of which we have never heard and of which our own Eekahs have never heard either—by objects called neutrons, which our Eekahs say are subatomic particles without charge, which seems to us completely ridiculous."

"And that is all?"

"All. Will you suspend judgment till we show you the sheets?"

Raph nodded reluctantly: "Very well."

* * *

Raph's leaden thoughts revolved in their worn groove as he stood there alone.

Eekahs and Primate Primeval. A living creature of erratic habits and a dead creature that must have aspired to heights. A sordid present of explosives and neutron bombardments and a glorious, mysterious past—

No connection! No connection!

The Red Queen's Race

Here's a puzzle for you, if you like. Is it a crime to translate a chemistry textbook into Greek?

Or let's put it another way. If one of the country's largest atomic power plants is completely ruined in an unauthorized experiment, is an admitted accessory to that act a criminal?

These problems only developed with time, of course. We started with the atomic power plant—drained. I really mean *drained*. I don't know exactly how large the fissionable power source was—but in two flashing microseconds, it has all fissioned.

No explosion. No undue gamma ray density. It was merely that every moving part in the entire structure was fused. The entire main building was mildly hot. The atmosphere for two miles in every direction was gently warm. Just a dead, useless building which later on took a hundred million dollars to replace.

It happened about three in the morning, and they found Elmer Tywood alone in the central source chamber. The findings of twenty-four close-packed hours can be summarized quickly.

1. Elmer Tywood—Ph.D., Sc.D., Fellow of This Honorary and That, one-time youthful participant of the original Manhattan Project, and now full Professor of Nuclear Physics—was no interloper. He had a Class-A Pass—Unlimited. But no record could be found as to his purpose in being there just then. A table on casters contained equipment which had not been made on any recorded requisition. It, too, was a single fused mass—not quite too hot to touch.

2. Elmer Tywood was dead. He lay next to the table; his face congested, nearly black. No radiation effect. No external force of any sort. The doctor said apoplexy.

3. In Elmer Tywood's office safe were found two puzzling items: i.e. twenty foolscap sheets of apparent mathematics, and a bound folio in a foreign language which turned out to be Greek, the subject matter, on translation, turning out to be chemistry.

The secrecy which poured over the whole mess was something so terrific as to make everything that touched it, *dead*. It's the only word that can describe it. Twenty-seven men and women, all told, including the Secretary of Defense, the Secretary of Science, and two or three others so top-notch that they were completely unknown to the public, entered the power plant during the period of investigation. All who had been in the plant that night, the physicist who had identified Tywood, the doctor who had exami-ned him, were retired into virtual home arrest.

No newspaper ever got the story. No inside dopester got it. A few members of Congress got part of it.

And naturally so! Anyone or any group of any country that could suck all the available energy out of the equivalent of perhaps fifty to a hundred pounds of plutonium without exploding it, had America's industry and America's defense so snugly in the palm of the hand that the light and life of one hundred sixty million people could be turned off between yawns.

Was it Tywood? Or Tywood and others? Or just others, through Tywood?

And my job? I was decoy; or front man, if you like. Someone has to hang around the university and ask questions about Tywood. After all, he was missing. It could be amnesia, a hold-up, a kidnapping, a killing, a runaway, insanity, accident—I could busy myself with that for five years and collect black looks, and maybe divert attention. To be sure, it didn't work out that way.

But don't think I was in on the whole case at the start. I wasn't one of the twenty-seven men I mentioned a while back, though my boss was. But I knew a little—enough to get started.

Professor John Keyser was also in Physics. I didn't get to him right away. There was a good deal of routine to cover first in as conscientious a way as I could. Quite meaningless. Quite necessary. But I was in Keyser's office now.

Professors' offices are distinctive. Nobody dusts them except some tired cleaning woman who hobbles in and out at eight in the morning, and the professor never notices the dust anyway. Lots of books without much arrangement. The ones close to the desk are used a lot—lectures are copied out of them. The ones out of reach are wherever a student put them back after borrowing them. Then there are professional journals that look cheap and are darned expensive, which are waiting about and which may some day be read. And plenty of paper on the desk; some of it scribbled on.

Keyser was an elderly man—one of Tywood's generation. His nose was big and rather red, and he smoked a pipe. He had that easy-going and nonpredatory look in his eyes that goes with an academic job—either because that kind of job attracts that kind of man or because that kind of job makes that kind of man.

I said: "What kind of work is Professor Tywood doing?"

"Research physics."

Answers like that bounce off me. Some years ago they used to get me mad. Now I just said: "We know that, professor. It's the details I'm after."

And he twinkled at me tolerantly: "Surely the details can't help much unless you're a research physicist yourself. Does it matter — under the circumstances?"

"Maybe not. But he's gone. If anything's happened to him in the way of" I gestured, and deliberately clinched—"foul play, his work may have something to do with it—unless he's rich and the motive is money."

Keyser chuckled dryly: "College professors are never rich. The commodity we peddle is but lightly considered, seeing how large the supply is."

I ignored that, too, because I know my looks are against me. Actually, I finished college with a "very good" translated into Latin so that the college president could understand it, and never played in a football game in my life. But I look rather the reverse.

I said: "Then we're left with his work to consider."

"You mean spies? International intrigue?"

"Why not? It's happened before! After all, he's a nuclear physicist, isn't he?"

"He is. But so are others. So am I."

"Ah, but perhaps he knows somthing you don't."

There was a stiffening to the jaw. When caught off-guard, professors can act just like people. He said, stiffly: "As I recall offhand, Tywood has published papers on the effect of liquid viscosity on the wings of the Rayleigh line, on higher-orbit field equations, and on spin-orbit coupling of two nucleons, but his main work is on quadrupole moments. I am quite competent in these matters."

"Is he working on quadrupole moments now?" I tried not to bat an eye, and I think I succeeded.

"Yes—in a way." He almost sneered, "He may be getting to the experimental stage finally. He's spent most of his life, it seems, working out the mathematical consequences of a special theory of his own."

"Like this," and I tossed a sheet of foolscap at him.

That sheet was one of those in the safe in Tywood's office. The chances, of course, were that the bundle meant nothing, if only because it was a professor's safe. That is, things are sometimes put in at the spur of the moment because the logical drawer was filled with unmarked exam papers. And, of course, nothing is ever taken out. We had found in that safe dusty little vials of yellowish crystals with scarcely legible labels, some mimeographed booklets dating back to World War II and marked "Restricted," a copy of an old college yearbook, and some correspondence concerning a possible position as Director of Research for American Electric, dated ten years back, and, of course, chemistry in Greek.

The foolscap was there, too. It was rolled up like a college diploma with a rubber band about it and had no label or descriptive title. Some twenty sheets were covered with ink marks, meticulous and small—

I had one sheet of that foolscap. I don't think any one man in the world had more than one sheet. And I'm sure that no man in the world but one knew that the loss of his particular sheet and of his particular life would be as nearly simultaneous as the government could make it.

So I tossed the sheet at Keyser, as if it were something I'd found blowing about the campus.

He stared at it and then looked at the back side, which was blank. His eyes moved down from the top to the bottom, then jumped back to the top.

"I don't know what this is about," he said, and the words seemed sour to his own taste.

I didn't say anything. Just folded the paper and shoved it back into the inside jacket pocket.

Kayser added petulantly: "It's a fallacy you laymen have that scientists can look at an equation and say, 'Ah, yes—' and go on to write a book about it. Mathematics has no existence of its own. It is merely an arbitrary code devised to describe physical observations or philosophical concepts. Every man can adapt it to his own particular needs. For instance no one can look at a symbol and be sure of what it means. So far, science has used every letter in the alphabet, large, small and italic, each symbolizing many different things. They have used bold-faced letters, Gothic-type letters, Greek letters, both capital and small, subscripts, superscripts, asterisks, even Hebrew letters. Different scientists use different symbols for the same concept and the same symbol for different concepts. So if you show a disconnected page like this to any man, without information as to the subject being investigated or the particular symbology used, he could absolutely not make sense out of it."

I interrupted: "But you said he was working on quadrupole moments. Does that make this sensible?" and I tapped the spot on my chest where the foolscap had been slowly scorching a hole in my jacket for two days.

"I can't tell. I saw none of the standard relationships that I'd expect to be involved. At least I recognized none. But I obviously can't commit myself."

There was a short silence, then he said: "I'll tell you. Why don't you check with his students?"

I lifted my eyebrows: "You mean in his classes?"

He seemed annoyed: "No, for Heaven's sake. His research students! His doctoral candidates! They've been working with him. They'll know the details of that work better than I, or anyone in the faculty, could possibly know it."

"It's an idea," I said, casually. It was, too. I don't know why, but I wouldn't have thought of it myself. I guess it's because it's only natural to think that any professor knows more than any student.

Keyser latched onto a lapel as I rose to leave. "And, besides," he said, "I think you're on the wrong track. This is in confidence, you understand, and I wouldn't say it except for the unusual circumstances, but Tywood is not thought of too highly in the profession. Oh, he's an adequate teacher, I'll admit, but his research papers have never commanded respect. There has always been a tendency towards vague theorizing, unsupported by experimental evidence. That paper of yours is probably more of it. No one could possibly want to . . . er, kidnap him because of it."

"Is that so? I see. Any ideas, yourself, as to why he's gone, or where he's gone?"

"Nothing concrete," he said pursing his lips, "but everyone knows he is a sick man. He had a stroke two years ago that kept him out of classes for a semester. He never did get well. His left side was paralyzed for a while and he still limps. Another stroke would kill him. It could come any time."

"You think he's dead, then?"

"It's not impossible."

"But where's the body, then?"

"Well, really—that is *your* job, I think."

It was, and I left.

* * *

I interviewed each one of Tywood's four research students in a volume of chaos called a research laboratory. These student research laboratories usually have two hopefuls working therein, said two constituting a floating population, since every year or so they are alternately replaced.

Consequently, the laboratory has its equipment stack in tiers. On the laboratory benches is the equipment immediately being used, and in three or four of the handiest drawers are replacements or supplements which are likely to be used. In the farther drawers, in the shelves reaching up to the ceiling, in odd corners, are fading remnants of the past student generations—oddments never used and never discarded. It is claimed, in fact, that no research student ever knew all the contents of his laboratory.

All four of Tywood's students were worried. But three were worried mainly by their own status. That is, by the possible effect the absence of Tywood might have on the status of their "problem." I dismissed those three—who all have their degrees now, I hope—and called back the fourth.

He had the most haggard look of all, and had been least communicative—which I considered a hopeful sign.

He now sat stiffly in the straight-backed chair at the right of the desk, while I leaned back in a creaky old swivel-chair and pushed my hat off my forehead. His name was Edwin Howe and *he* did get his degree later on; I know for sure, because he's a big wheel in the Department of Science now.

I said: "You do the same work the other boys do, I suppose?"

"It's all nuclear work, in a way."

"But it's not all exactly the same?"

He shook his head slowly. "We take different angles. You have to have something clear-cut, you know, or you won't be able to publish. We've got to get our degrees."

He said it exactly the way you or I might say, "We've got to make a living." At that, maybe it's the same thing for them.

I said: "All right. What's *your* angle?"

He said: "I do the math. I mean, with Professor Tywood."

"What kind of math?"

And he smiled a little, getting the same sort of atmosphere about him that I had noticed in Professor Keyser's case that morning. A sort of, "Do-you-really-think-I-can-explain-all-my-profound-thoughts-to-stupid-little-you?" sort of atmosphere.

All he said aloud, however, was: "That would be rather complicated to explain."

"I'll help you," I said. "Is that anything like it?" And I tossed the foolscap sheet at him.

He didn't give it any once-over. He just snatched it up and let out a thin wail: "Where'd you get this?"

"From Tywood's safe."

"Do you have the rest of it, too?"

"It's safe," I hedged.

He relaxed a little—just a little: "You didn't show it to anybody, did you?"

"I showed it to Professor Keyser."

Howe made an impolite sound with his lower lip and front teeth, "*That* jackass. What did he say?"

I turned the palms of my hands upward and Howe laughed. Then he said, in an offhand manner: "Well, that's the sort of stuff I do."

"And what's it all about? Put it so I can understand it."

There was distinct hesitation. He said: "Now, look. This is confidential stuff. Even Pop's other students don't know anything about it. I don't even think *I* know *all* about it. This isn't just a degree I'm after, you know. It's Pop Tywood's Nobel Prize, and it's going to be an Assistant Professorship for me at Cal Tech. This has got to be published before it's talked about."

And I shook my head slowly and made my words very soft: "No, son. You have it twisted. You'll have to talk about it before it's published, because Tywood's gone and maybe he's dead and maybe he isn't. And if he's dead, maybe he's murdered. And when the department has a suspicion of murder, everybody talks. Now, it will look bad for you, kid, if you try to keep some secrets."

It worked. I knew it would, because everyone reads murder mysteries and knows all the clichés. He jumped out of his chair and rattled the words off as if he had a script in front of him.

"Surely," he said, "you can't suspect *me* of . . . of anything like that. Why . . . why, my career—"

I shoved him back into his chair with the beginnings of a sweat on his forehead. I went into the next line: "I don't suspect anybody of anything *yet*. And you won't be in any trouble, if you talk, chum."

He was ready to talk. "Now this is all in strict confidence."

Poor guy. He didn't know the meaning of the word "strict." He was never out of eyeshot of an operator from that moment till the government decided to bury the whole case with the one final comment of "?" Quote. Unquote. (I'm not kidding. To this day, the case is neither opened nor closed. It's just "?")

He said, dubiously; "You know what time travel is, I suppose?"

Sure I knew what time travel was. My oldest kid is twelve and he listens to the afternoon video programs till he swells up visibly with the junk he absorbs at the ears and eyes.

"What about time travel?" I said.

"In a sense, we can do it. Actually, it's only what you might call micro-temporal-translation—"

I almost lost my temper. In fact, I think I did. It seemed obvious that the squirt was trying to diddle me; and without subtlety. I'm used to having people think I look dumb; but not *that* dumb.

I said through the back of my throat: "Are you going to tell me that Tywood is out somewhere in time—like Ace Rogers, the Lone Time Ranger?" (That was Junior's favorite program—Ace Rogers was stopping Genghis Khan single-handed that week.)

But he looked as disgusted as I must have. "No," he yelled. "I don't know where Pop is. If you'd *listen* to me—I said micro-temporal-translation. Now, this isn't a video show and it isn't magic; this happens to be science. For instance, you know about matter-energy equivalence, I suppose."

I nodded sourly. Everyone knows about that since Hiroshima in the last war but one.

"All right, then," he went on, "that's good for a start. Now, if you take a brown mass of matter and apply temporal translation to it—you know, send it back in time—you are, in effect, creating matter at the point in time to which you are sending it. To do that, you must use an amount of energy equivalent to the amount of matter you have created. In other words, to send a gram—or, say, an ounce—of anything back in time, you have to disintegrate an ounce of matter completely, to furnish the energy required."

"Hm-m-m," I said, "that's to create the ounce of matter in the past. But aren't you destroying an ounce of matter by removing it from the present? Doesn't that *create* the equivalent amount of energy?"

And he looked just about as annoyed as a fellow sitting on a bumblebee that wasn't quite dead. Apparently laymen are never supposed to question scientists.

He said: "I was trying to simplify it so you would understand it. Actually, it's more complicated. It would be very nice if we could use the energy of disappearance to cause it to appear, but that would be working in a circle, believe me. The requirements of entropy would forbid it. To put it more rigorously, the energy is required to overcome temporal inertia and it just works out so that the energy in ergs required to send back a mass, in grams, is equal to that mass times the square of the speed of light in centimeters per second. Which just happens to be the Einstein Mass-Energy Equivalence Equation. I can give you the mathematics, you know."

"I know," I waxed some of that misplaced eagerness back. "But was all this worked out experimentally? Or is it just on paper?"

Obviously, the thing was to keep him talking.

He had that queer light in his eye that every research student gets, I am told, when he is asked to discuss his problem. He'll discuss it with anyone, even with a "dumb flatfoot"—which was convenient at the moment.

"You see," he said like a man slipping you the inside dope on a shady business deal, "what started the whole thing was this neutrino business. They've been trying to find that neutrino since the late thirties and they haven't succeeded. It's a subatomic particle which has no charge and has a mass much less than even an electron. Naturally, it's next to impossible to spot, and hasn't been spotted yet. But they keep looking because, without assuming that a neutrino exists, the energetics of some nuclear reactions can't be balanced. So Pop Tywood got the idea about twenty years ago that some energy was disappearing, in the form of matter, back into time. We got working on that—or he did—and I'm the first student he's ever had tackle it along with him.

"Obviously, we had to work with tiny amounts of material and . . . well, it was just a stroke of genius on Pop's part to think of using traces of artificial radioactive isotopes. You could work with just a few micrograms of it, you know, by following its activity with counters. The variation of activity with time should follow a very definite and simple law which has never been altered by any laboratory condition known.

"Well, we'd send a speck back fifteen minutes, say, and fifteen minutes before we did that—everything was arranged automatically, you see—the count jumped to nearly double what it should be, fell off normally, and then dropped sharply at the moment it was sent back below where it would have been normally. The material overlapped itself in time, you see, and for fifteen minutes we counted the doubled material—"

I interrupted: "You mean you had the same atoms existing in two places at the same time."

"Yes," he said, with mild surprise, "why not? That's why we use so much energy—the equivalent of creating those atoms." And then he rushed on, "Now I'll tell you what my particular job is. If you send back the material fifteen minutes, it is apparently sent back to the same spot relative to the Earth despite the fact that in fifteen minutes, the Earth moved sixteen thousand miles around the Sun, and the Sun itself moves more thousand miles and so on. But there are certain tiny discrepancies which I've analyzed and which turn out to be due, possibly, to two causes.

"First, there is a frictional effect—if you can use such a term—so that matter does drift a little with respect to the Earth, depending on how far back in time it is sent, and on the nature of the material. Then, too, some of the discrepancy can only be explained by the assumption that passage through time itself takes time."

"How's that?" I said.

"What I mean is that some of the radioactivity is evenly spread throughout the time of translation as if the material tested had been reacting during backward passage through time by a constant amount. My figures show that—well, if you were to be moved backward in time, you would age one day for every hundred years. Or, to put it another way, if you could watch a time dial which recorded the time outside a 'time-machine,' your watch would move forward twenty-four hours while the time dial moved back a hundred years. That's a universal constant, I think, because the speed of light is a universal constant. Anyway, that's my work."

After a few minutes, in which I chewed all this, I asked: "Where did you get the energy needed for your experiments?"

"They ran out a special line from the power plant. Pop's a big shot there, and swung the deal."

"Hm-m-m. What was the heaviest amount of material you sent into the past?"

"Oh"—he sent his eyes upward—"I think we shot back one hundredth of a milligram once. That's ten micrograms."

"Ever try sending anything into the future?"

"That won't work," he put in quickly. "Impossible. You can't change signs like that, because the energy required becomes more than infinite. It's a one-way proposition."

I looked hard at my fingernails: "How much material could you send back in time if you fissioned about . . . oh, say, one hundred pounds of plutonium." Things, I thought, were becoming, if anything, too obvious.

The answer came quickly: "In plutonium fission," he said, "not more than one or two percent of the mass is converted into energy. Therefore, one hundred pounds of plutonium when completely used up would send a pound or two back into time."

"Is that all? But could you handle all that energy? I mean, a hundred pounds of plutonium can make quite an explosion."

"All relative," he said, a bit pompously. "If you took all that energy and let it loose a little at a time, you could handle it. If you released it all at once, but used it just as fast as you released it, you could still handle it. In sending back material through time, energy can be used much faster than it can possibly be released even through fission. Theoretically, anyway."

"But how do you get rid of it?"

"It's spread through time, naturally. Of course, the minimum time through which material could be transferred would, therefore, depend on the mass of the material. Otherwise, you're liable to have the energy density with time too high."

"All right, kid," I said. "I'm calling up Headquarters, and they'll send a man here to take you home. You'll stay there a while."

"But—What for?"

"It won't be for long."

It wasn't—and it was made up to him afterwards.

I spent the evening at Headquarters. We had a library there—a very special kind of library. The very morning after the explosion, two or three operators had drifted quietly into the chemistry and physics libraries of the University. Experts in their way. They located every article Tywood had ever published in any scientific journal and had snapped each page. Nothing was disturbed otherwise.

Other men went through magazine files and through book lists. It ended with a room at Headquarters that represented a complete Tynwoodana. Nor was there a definite purpose in doing this. It merely represented part of the thoroughness with which a problem of this sort is met.

I went through that library. Not the scientific papers. I knew there'd be nothing there that I wanted. But he had written a series of articles for a magazine twenty years back, and I read those. And I grabbed at every piece of private correspondence they had available.

After that, I just sat and thought—and got scared.

I got to bed about four in the morning and had nightmares.

But I was in the Boss' private office at nine in the morning just the same.

He's a big man, the Boss, with iron-gray hair slicked down tight. He doesn't smoke, but he keeps a box of cigars on his desk and when he doesn't want to say anything for a few seconds, he picks one up, rolls it about a little, smells it, then sticks it right into the middle of his mouth and lights it in a very careful way. By that time, he either has something to say or doesn't have to say anything at all. Then he puts the cigar down and lets it burn to death.

He used up a box in about three weeks, and every Christmas, half his gift-wraps held boxes of cigars.

He wasn't reaching for any cigars now, though. He just folded his big fists together on the desk and looked up at me from under a creased forehead. "What's boiling?"

I told him. Slowly, because micro-temporal-translation doesn't sit well with anybody, especially when you call it time travel, which I did. It's a sign of how serious things were that he only asked me once if I were crazy.

Then I was finished and we stared at each other.

He said: "And you think he tried to send something back in time—something weighing a pound or two—and blew an entire plant doing it?"

"It fits in," I said.

I let him go for a while. He was thinking and I wanted him to keep on thinking. I wanted him, if possible, to think of the same thing I was thinking, so that I wouldn't have to tell him—

Because I hated to have to tell him—

Because it was nuts, for one thing. And too horrible, for another.

So I kept quiet and he kept on thinking and every once in a while some of his thoughts came to the surface.

After a while, he said: "Assuming the student, Howe, to have told the truth—and you'd better check his notebooks, by the way, which I hope you've impounded—"

"The entire wing of that floor is out of bounds, sir. Edwards has the notebooks."

He went on: "All right. Assuming he told us all the truth he knows, why did Tywood jump from less than a milligram to a pound?"

His eyes came down and they were hard: "Now you're concentrating on the time-travel angle. To you, I gather, that is the crucial point, with the energy involved as incidental—purely incidental."

"Yes, sir," I said grimly. "I think exactly that."

"Have you considered that you might be wrong? That you might have matters inverted?"

"I don't quite get that."

"Well, look. You say you've read up on Tywood. All right. He was one of that bunch of scientists after World War II that fought the atom bomb; wanted a world state—You know about that, don't you?"

I nodded.

"He had a guilt complex," the Boss said with energy. "He'd helped work out the bomb, and he couldn't sleep nights thinking of what he'd done. He lived with that fear for years. And even though the bomb wasn't used in World War II, can you imagine what every day of uncertainty must have meant for him? Can you imagine the shriveling horror in his soul as he waited for others to make the decision at every crucial moment till the final Compromise of Sixty-Five?

"We have a complete psychiatric analysis of Tywood and several others just like him, taking during the last war. Did you know that?"

"No, sir."

"It's true. We let up after Sixty-Five, of course, because with the establishment of world control of atomic power, the scrapping of the atomic bomb stockpile in all countries, and the establishment of research liaison among the various spheres of influence on the planet, most of the ethical conflict in the scientific mind was removed.

"But the findings at the time were serious. In 1964, Tywood had a morbid subconscious hatred for the very concept of atomic power. He began to make mistakes, serious ones. Eventually, we were forced to take him off research of any kind. And several others as well, even though things were pretty bad at the time. We had just lost India, if you remember."

Considering that I was in India at the time, I remembered. But I still wasn't seeing his point.

"Now, what," he continued, "if dregs of that attitude remained buried in Tywood to the very end? Don't you see that this time-travel is a double-edged sword? Why throw a pound of anything into the past, anyway? For the sake of proving a point? He had proved his case just as much when he sent back a fraction of a milligram. That was good enough for the Nobel Prize, I suppose.

"But there was *one* thing he could do with a pound of matter that he couldn't do with a milligram, and that was *to drain a power plant*. So that was what he must have been after. He had discovered a way of consuming inconceivable quantities of energy. By sending back eighty pounds of dirt, he could remove all the existing plutonium in the world. End atomic power for an indefinite period."

I was completely unimpressed, but I tried not to make that too plain. I just said: "Do you think he could possibly have thought he could get away with it more than once?"

"This is all based on the fact that he wasn't a normal man. How do I know what he could imagine he could do? Besides, there may be men behind him—with less science and more brains—who are quite ready to continue onwards from this point."

"Have any of these men been found yet? Any evidence of such men?"

A little wait, and his hand reached for the cigar box. He stared at the cigar and turned it end for end. Just a little wait more. I was patient.

Then he put it down decisively without lighting it.

"No," he said.

He looked at me, and clear through me, and said: "Then, you still don't go for that?"

I shrugged, "Well—It doesn't sound right."

"Do you have a notion of your own?"

"Yes. But I can't bring myself to talk about it. If I'm wrong, I'm the wrongest man that ever was; but if I'm right, I'm the rightest."

"I'll listen," he said, and he put his hand under the desk.

That was the pay-off. The room was armored, sound-proof, and radiation-proof to anything short of a nuclear explosion. And with that little signal showing on his secretary's desk, the President of the United States couldn't have interrupted us.

I leaned back and said: "Chief, do you happen to remember how you met your wife? Was it a little thing?"

He must have thought it a *non sequitur*. What else could he have thought? But he was giving me my head now; having his own reasons, I suppose.

He just smiled and said: "I sneezed and she turned around. It was at a street corner."

"What made you be on that street corner just then? What made her be? Do you remember just why you sneezed? Where you caught the cold? Or where the speck of dust came from? Imagine how many factors had to intersect in just the right place at just the right time for you to meet your wife."

"I suppose we would have met some other time, if not then?"

"But you can't *know* that. How do you know whom you *didn't* meet, because once when you might have turned around, you didn't; because once when you might have been late, you weren't. Your life forks at every instant, and you go down one of the forks almost at random, and so does everyone else. Start twenty years ago, and the forks diverge further and further with time.

"You sneezed, and met a girl, and not another. As a consequence, you made certain decisions, and so did the girl, and so did the girl you didn't meet, and the man who did meet her, and the people you all met thereafter. And your family, her family, their family—and your children.

"Because you sneezed twenty years ago, five people, or fifty, or five hundred, might be dead now who would have been alive, or might be alive who would have been dead. Move it two hundred years ago: two thousand years ago, and a sneeze—even by someone no history ever heard of—might have meant that no one now alive would have been alive."

The Boss rubbed the back of his head: "Widening ripples. I read a story once—"

"So did I. It's not a new idea—but I want you to think about it for a while, because I want to read to you from an article by Professor Elmer Tywood in a magazine twenty years old. It was just before the last war."

I had copies of the film in my pocket and the white wall made a beautiful screen, which was what it was meant to do. The Boss made a motion to turn about, but I waved him back.

"No, sir," I said. "I want to read this to you. And I want you to listen to it."

He leaned back.

"The article," I went on, "is entitled: 'Man's First Great Failure!' Remember, this was just before the war, when the bitter disappointment at the final failure of the United Nations was at its height. What I will read are some excerpts from the first part of the article. It goes like this:

" '. . . That Man, with his technical perfection, has failed to solve the great sociological problems of today is only the second immense tragedy that has come to the race. The first, and perhaps the greater, was that, once, these same great sociological problems *were* solved; and yet these solutions were not permanent, because the technical perfection we have today did not then exist.

" 'It was a case of having bread without butter, or butter without bread. Never both together . . .

" 'Consider the Hellenic world, from which our philosophy, our mathematics, our ethics, our art, our literature—our entire culture, in fact—stem . . . In the days of Pericles, Greece, like our own world in microcosm, was a surprisingly modern potpourri of conflicting ideologies and ways of life. But then Rome came, adopting the culture, but bestowing, and enforcing, peace. To be sure, the *Pax Romana* lasted only two hundred years, but no like period has existed since . . .

" 'War was abolished. Nationalisn did not exist. The Roman citizen was Empire-wide. Paul of Tarsus and Flavius Josephus were Roman citizens. Spaniards, North Africans, Illyrians assumed the purple. Slavery existed, but it was an indiscriminate slavery, imposed as a punishment, incurred as the price of economic failure, brought on by the fortunes of war. No man was a *natural* slave—because of the color of his skin or the place of his birth.

" 'Religious toleration was complete. If an exception was made early in the case of the Christians, it was because they refused to accept the principle of toleration; because they insisted that only they themselves knew truth—a principle abhorrent to the civilized Roman . . .

" 'With all of Western culture under a single *polis*, with the cancer of religious and national particularism and exclusivism absent; with a high civilization in existence—why could not Man hold his gains?

" 'It was because, technologically, ancient Hellenism remained backward. It was because without a machine civilization, the price of leisure—and hence civilization and culture—for the few, was slavery for the many. Because the civilization could not find the means to bring comfort and ease to *all* the population.

" 'Therefore, the depressed classes turned to the other world, and to religions which spurned the material benefits of this world—so that science was made impossible in any true sense for over a millennium. And further, as the initial impetus of Hellenism waned, the Empire lacked the technological powers to beat back the barbarians. In fact, it was not till after 1500 A.D. that war became sufficiently a function of the industrial resources of a nation to enable the settled people to defeat invading tribesmen and nomads with ease . . .

" 'Imagine, then, if somehow the ancient Greeks had learned just a hint of modern chemistry and physics. Imagine if the growth of the Empire had been accompanied by the growth of science, technology and industry. Imagine an Empire in which machinery replaced slaves, in which all men had a decent share of the world's goods, in which the legion became the armored column against which no barbarians could stand. Imagine an Empire which would therefore spread all over the world, *without* religious or national prejudices.

" 'An Empire of all men—all brothers—eventually all free . . .

" 'If history could be changed. If that first great failure could have been prevented—"

And I stopped at that point.

"Well?" said the Boss.

"Well," I said, "I think it isn't difficult to connect all that with the fact that Tywood blew an entire power plant in his anxiety to send something back to the past, while in his office we found sections of a chemistry textbook translated into Greek."

His face changed, while he considered.

Then he said heavily: "But nothing's happened."

"I know. But then I've been told by Tywood's student that it takes a day to move back a century in time. Assuming that ancient Greece was the target area, we have twenty centuries, hence twenty days."

'But can it be stopped?"

"*I* wouldn't know, Tywood might, but he's dead."

The enormity of it all hit me at once, deeper than it had the night before—

All humanity was virtually under sentence of death. And while that was merely horrible abstraction, the fact that reduced it to a thoroughly unbearable reality was that I was, too. And my wife, and my kid.

Further, it was a death without precedence. A ceasing to exist, and no more. The passing of a breath. The vanishing of a dream. The drift into eternal non-space and non-time of a shadow. I would not be dead at all, in fact. I would merely never have been born.

Or would I? Would I exist—my individuality—my ego—my soul, if you like? Another life? Other circumstances?

I thought none of that in words then. But if a cold knot in the stomach could ever speak under the circumstances, it would sound like that, I think.

The Boss moved in on my thoughts—hard.

"Then, we have about two and a half weeks. No time to lose. Come on."

I grinned with one side of my mouth: "What do we do? Chase the book?"

"No," he replied coldly, "but there are two courses of action we must follow. First, you may be wrong—altogether. All of this circumstantial reasoning may still represent a false lead, perhaps deliberately thrown before us, to cover up the real truth. That must be checked.

"Secondly, you may be right—but there may be some way of stopping the book: other than chasing it in a time machine, I mean. If so, we must find out how."

"I would just like to say, sir, if this is a false lead, only a madman would consider it a believable one. So suppose I'm right, and suppose there's no way of stopping it?"

"Then, young fellow, I'm going to keep pretty busy for two and a half weeks, and I'd advise you to do the same. The time will pass more quickly that way."

Of course he was right.

"Where do we start?" I asked.

"The first thing we need is a list of all men and women on the government payroll under Tywood."

"Why?"

"Reasoning. Your specialty, you know. Tywood doesn't know Greek, I think we can assume with fair safety, so someone else must have done the translating. It isn't likely that anyone would do a job like that for nothing, and it isn't likely that Tywood would pay out of his personal funds—not on a professor's salary."

"He might," I pointed out, "have been interested in more secrecy than a government payroll affords."

"Why? Where was the danger? Is it a crime to translate a chemistry textbook into Greek? Who would ever deduce from that a plot such as you've described?"

It took us half an hour to turn up the name of Mycroft James Boulder, listed as "Consultant," and to find out that he was mentioned in the University Catalogue as Assistant Professor of Philosophy and to check by telephone that among his many accomplishments was a thorough knowledge of Attic Greek.

Which was a coincidence—because with the Boss reaching for his hat, the inter-office teletype clicked away and it turned out that Mycroft James Boulder was in the anteroom, at the end of a two-hour continuing insistence that he see the Boss.

The Boss put his hat back and opened his office door.

Professor Mycroft James Boulder was a gray man. His hair was gray and his eyes were gray. His suit was gray, too.

But most of all, his expression was gray; gray with a tension that seemed to twist at the lines in his thin face.

Boulder said, softly: "I've been trying for three days to get a hearing, sir, with a responsible man. I can get no higher than yourself."

"I may be high enough," said the Boss. "What's on your mind?"

"It is quite important that I be granted an interview with Professor Tywood."

"Do you know where he is?"

"I am quite certain that he is in government custody."

"Why?"

"Because I know that he was planning an experiment which would entail the breaking of security regulations. Events since, as nearly as I can make them out, flow naturally from the supposition that security regulations have indeed been broken. I can presume, then, that the experiment has at least been attempted. I must discover whether it had been successfully concluded."

"Professor Boulder," said the Boss, "I believe you can read Greek."

"Yes, I can,"—coolly.

"And have translated chemical texts for Professor Tywood on government money."

"Yes—as a legally employed consultant."

"Yet such translation, under the circumstances, constitutes a crime, since it makes you an accessory to Tywood's crime."

"You can establish a connection?"

"Can't you? Or haven't you heard of Tywood's notions on time travel, or . . . what do you call it . . . micro-temporal-translation?"

"Ah?" and Boulder smiled a little. "He's told you, then."

"No, he hasn't," said the Boss, harshly. "Professor Tywood is dead."

"What?" Then—"I don't believe you."

"He died of apoplexy. Look at this."

He had one of the photographs taken that first night in his wall safe. Tywood's face was distorted but recognizable—sprawled and dead.

Boulder's breath went in and out as if the gears were clogged. He stared at the picture for three full minutes by the electric clock on the wall. "Where is this place?" he asked.

"The Atomic Power Plant."

"Had he finished his experiment?"

The Boss shrugged: "There's no way of telling. He was dead when we found him."

Boulder's lips were pinched and colorless. "That must be determined, somehow. A commission of scientists must be established, and, if necessary, the experiment must be repeated—"

But the Boss just looked at him, and reached for a cigar. I've never seen him take longer—and when he put it down, curled in its unused smoke, he said: "Tywood wrote an article for a magzine, twenty years ago—"

"Oh," and the professor's lips twisted, "is *that* what gave you your clue? You may ignore that. the man is only a physical scientist and knows nothing of either history or sociology. A schoolboy's dreams and nothing more."

"Then, you don't think sending your translation back will inaugurate a Golden Age, do you?"

"Of course not. Do you think you can graft the developments of two thousand years of slow labor onto a child society not ready for it? Do you think a great invention or a great scientific principle is born full-grown in the mind of a genius divorced from his cultural *milieu*? Newton's enunciation of the Law of Gravity was delayed for twenty years because the then-current figure for the Earth's diameter was wrong by ten percent. Archimedes almost discovered calculus, but failed because Arabic numerals, invented by some nameless Hindu or group of Hindus, were unknown to him.

"For that matter, the mere existence of a slave society in ancient Greece and Rome meant that machines could scarcely attract much attention—slaves being so much cheaper and more adaptable. And men of true intellect could scarcely be expected to spend their energies on devices intended for manual labor. Even Archimedes, the greatest engineer of antiquity, refused to publish any of his practical inventions —only mathematic abstractions. And when a young man asked Plato of what use geometry was, he was forthwith expelled from the Academy as a man with a mean, unphilosophic soul.

"Science does not plunge forward—it inches along in the directions permitted by the greater forces that mold society and which are in turn molded by society. And no great man advances but on the shoulders of the society that surrounds him—"

The Boss interrupted him at that point. "Suppose you tell us what your part in Tywood's work was, then. We'll take your word for it that history cannot be changed."

"Oh it can, but not purposefully—You see, when Tywood first requested my services in the matter of translating certain textbook passages into Greek, I agreed for the money involved. But he wanted the translation on parchment; he insisted on the use of ancient Greek terminology—the language of Plato, to use his words—regardless of how I had to twist the literal significance of passages, and he wanted it hand-written in rolls.

"I was curious. I, too, found his magazine article. It was difficult for me to jump to the obvious conclusion, since the achievements of modern science transcend the imaginings of philosophy in so many ways. But I learned the truth eventually, and it was at once obvious that Tywood's theory of changing history was infantile. There are twenty million variables for every instant of time, and no system of mathematics—no mathematic psychohistory, to coin a phrase—has yet been developed to handle that ocean of varying functions.

"In short, any variation of events two thousand years ago would change all subsequent history, but in no *predictable way.*"

The Boss suggested, with a false quietness: "Like the pebble that starts the avalanche, right?"

"Exactly. You have some understanding of the situation, I see. I thought deeply for weeks before I proceeded, and then I realized how I must act—*must* act."

There was a low roar. The Boss stood up and his chair went over backward. He swung around his desk, and he had a hand on Boulder's throat. I was stepping out to stop him, but he waved me back—

He was only tightening the necktie a little. Boulder could still breathe. He had gone very white, and for all the time that the Boss talked, he restricted himself to just that—breathing.

And the Boss said: "Sure, I can see how you decided you must act. I know that some of you brain-sick philosophers think the world needs fixing. You want to throw the dice again and see what turns up. Maybe you don't even care if you're alive in the new setup—or that no one can possibly know what you've done. But you're going to create, just the same. You're going to give God another chance, so to speak.

"Maybe I just want to live—but the world could be worse. In twenty million different ways, it could be worse. A fellow named Wilder once wrote a play called *The Skin of Our Teeth.* Maybe you've read it. Its thesis was that Mankind survived by just that skin of their teeth. No, I'm not going to give you a speech about the Ice Age nearly wiping us out. I don't know enough. I'm not even going to talk about the Greeks winning at Marathon; the Arabs being defeated at Tours; the Mongols turning back at the last minute without even being defeated—because I'm no historian.

"But take the Twentieth Century. The Germans were stopped at the Marne twice in World War I. Dunkirk happened in World War II, and somehow the Germans were stopped at Moscow and Stalingrad. We could have used the atom bomb in the last war and we didn't, and just when it looked as if both sides would have to, the Great Compromise happened—just because General Bruce was delayed in taking off from the Ceylon airfield long enough to receive the message directly. One after the other, just like that, all through history—lucky breaks. For every 'if' that didn't come true that would have made wonder-men of all of us if it had, there were twenty 'ifs' that didn't come true that would have brought disaster to all of us if they had.

"You're gambling on that one-in-twenty chance—gambling every life on Earth. And you've succeeded, too, because Tywood *did* send that text back."

He ground out that last sentence, and opened his fist, so that Boulder could fall out and back into his chair.

And Boulder laughed.

"You fool," he gasped, bitterly, "How close you can be and yet how widely you can miss the mark. Tywood *did* send his book back, then? You are sure of that?"

"No chemical textbook in Greek was found on the scene," said the Boss, grimly, "and millions of calories of energy had disappeared. Which doesn't change the fact, however, that we have two and a half weeks in which to—make things interesting for you."

"Oh, nonsense. No foolish dramatics, please. Just listen to me, and try to understand. There were Greek philosophers once, named Leucippus and Democritus, who evolved an atomic theory. All matter, they said, was composed of atoms. Varieties of atoms were distinct and changeless and by their different combinations with each other formed the various substances found in nature. That theory was not the result of experiment or observation. It came into being, somehow, full-grown.

"The didactic Roman poet Lucretius, in his '*De Rerum Natura*,'—'On the Nature of Things'—elaborated on that theory and throughout manages to sound startlingly modern.

"In Hellenistic times, Hero build a steam engine and weapons of war became almost mechanized. The period has been referred to as an abortive mechanical age, which came to nothing because, somehow, it neither grew out of nor fitted into its social and economic *milieu*. Alexandrian science was a queer and rather inexplicable phenomenon.

"Then one might mention the old Roman legend about the books of the Sibyl that contained mysterious information direct from the gods—

"In other words, gentlemen, while you are right that any change in the course of past events, however trifling, would have incalculable consequences, and while I also believe that you are right in supposing that any random change is much more likely to be for the worse than for the better, I must point out that you are nevertheless wrong in your final conclusions.

"*Because* THIS *is the world in which the Greek chemistry text* WAS *sent back.*

"This has been a Red Queen's race, if you remember your 'Through the Looking Glass.' In the Red Queen's country, one had to run as fast as one could merely to stay in the same place. And so it was in this case! Tywood may have thought he was creating a new world, but it was I who prepared the translations, and I took care that only such passages as would account for the queer scraps of knowledge the ancients apparently got from nowhere would be included.

"And my only intention, for all my racing, was to stay in the same place."

Three weeks passed; three months; three years. Nothing happened. When nothing happens, you have no proof. We gave up trying to explain, and we ended, the Boss and I, by doubting it ourselves.

The case never ended. Boulder could not be considered a criminal without being considered a world savior as well, and vice versa. He was ignored. And in the end, the case was neither solved, nor closed out; merely put in a file all by itself, under the designation "?" and buried in the deepest vault in Washington.

The Boss is in Washington now; a big wheel. And I'm Regional Head of the Bureau.

Boulder is still assistant professor, though. Promotions are slow at the University.

Green Patches

He had slipped aboard the ship! There had been dozens waiting outside the energy barrier when it had seemed that waiting would do no good. Then the barrier had faltered for a matter of two minutes (which showed the superiority of unified organisms over life fragments) and he was across.

None of the others had been able to move quickly enough to take advantage of the break, but that didn't matter. All alone, he was enough. No others were necessary.

And the thought faded out of satisfaction and into loneliness. It was a terribly unhappy and unnatural thing to be parted from all the rest of the unified organism, to be a life fragment oneself. How could these aliens stand being fragments?

It increased his sympathy for the aliens. Now that he experienced fragmentation himself, he could feel, as though from a distance, the terrible isolation that made them so afraid. It was fear born of that isolation that dictated their actions. What but the insane fear of their condition could have caused them to blast an area, one mile in diameter, into dull-red heat before landing their ship? Even the organized life ten feet deep in the soil had been destroyed in the blast.

He engaged reception, listening eagerly, letting the alien thought saturate him. He enjoyed the touch of life upon his consciousness. He would have to ration that enjoyment. He must not forget himself.

But it could do no harm to listen to thoughts. Some of the fragments of life on the ship thought quite clearly, considering that they were such primitive, incomplete creatures. Their thoughts were like tiny bells.

Roger Oldenn said, "I feel contaminated. You know what I mean? I keep washing my hands and it doesn't help."

Jerry Thorn hated dramatics and didn't look up. They were still maneuvering in the stratosphere of Saybrook's Planet and he preferred to watch the panel dials. He said, "No reason to feel contaminated. Nothing happened."

"I hope not," said Oldenn. "At least they had all the field men discard their spacesuits in the air lock for complete disinfection. They had a radiation bath for all men entering from outside. I *suppose* nothing happened."

"Why be nervous, then?"

"I don't know. I wish the barrier hadn't broken down."

"Who doesn't? It was an accident."

"I wonder." Oldenn was vehement. "I was here when it happened. My shift, you know. There was no reason to overload the power line. There was equipment plugged into it that had no damn business near it. None whatsoever."

"All right. People are stupid."

"Not that stupid. I hung around when the Old Man was checking into the matter. None of them had reasonable excuses. The armor-baking circuits, which were draining off two thousand watts, had been put into the barrier line. They'd been using the second subsidiaries for a week. Why not this time? They couldn't give any reason."

"Can you?"

Oldenn flushed. "No, I was just wondering if the men had been"—he searched for a word—"hypnotized into it. By those things outside."

Thorn's eyes lifted and met those of the other levelly. "I wouldn't repeat that to anyone else. The barrier was down only two minutes. If anything had happened, if even a spear of grass had drifted across it would have shown up in our bacteria cultures within half an hour, in the fruit-fly colonies in a matter of days. Before we got back it would show up in the hamsters, the rabbits, maybe the goats. Just get it through your head, Oldenn, that nothing happened. Nothing."

Oldenn turned on his heel and left. In leaving, his foot came within two feet of the object in the corner of the room. He did not see it.

* * *

He disengaged his reception centers and let the thoughts flow past him unperceived. These life fragments were not important, in any case, since they were not fitted for the continuation of life. Even as fragments, they were incomplete.

The other types of fragments now—they were different. He had to be careful of them. The temptation would be great, and he must give no indication, none at all, of his existence on board ship till they landed on their home planet.

He focused on the other parts of the ship, marveling at the diversity of life. Each item, no matter how small, was sufficient to itself. He forced himself to contemplate this, until the unpleasantness of the thought grated on him and he longed for the normality of home.

Most of the thoughts he received from the smaller fragments were vague and fleeting, as you would expect. There wasn't much to be had from them, but that meant their need for completeness was all the greater. It was that which touched him so keenly.

There was the life fragment which squatted on its haunches and fingered the wire netting that enclosed it. Its thoughts were clear, but limited. Chiefly, they concerned the yellow fruit a companion fragment was eating. It wanted the fruit very deeply. Only the wire netting that separated the fragments prevented its seizing the fruit by force.

He disengaged reception in a moment of complete revulsion. *These fragments competed for food!*

He tried to reach far outward for the peace and harmony of home, but it was already an immense distance away. He could reach only into the nothingness that separated him from sanity.

He longed at the moment even for the feel of the dead soil between the barrier and the ship. He had crawled over it last night. There had been no life upon it, but it had been the soil of home, and on the other side of the barrier there had still been the comforting feel of the rest of organized life.

He could remember the moment he had located himself on the surface of the ship, maintaining a desperate suction grip until the air lock opened. He had entered, moving cautiously between the outgoing feet. There had been an inner lock and that had been passed later. Now he lay here, a life fragment himself, inert and unnoticed.

Cautiously, he engaged reception again at the previous focus. The squatting fragment of life was tugging furiously at the wire netting. It still wanted the other's food, though it was the less hungry of the two.

* * *

Larsen said, "Don't feed the damn thing. She isn't hungry; she's just sore because Tillie had the nerve to eat before she herself was crammed full. The greedy ape! I wish we were back home and I never had to look another animal in the face again."

He scowled at the older female chimpanzee frowningly and the chimp mouthed and chattered back to him in full reciprocation.

Rizzo said, "Okay, okay. Why hang around here, then? Feeding time is over. Let's get out."

They went past the goat pens, the rabbit hutches, the hamster cages.

Larsen said bitterly, "You volunteer for an exploration voyage.

You're a hero. They send you off with speeches—and make a zoo keeper out of you."

They give you double pay."

"All right, so what? I didn't sign up just for the money. They said at the original briefing that it was even odds we wouldn't come back, that we'd end up like Saybrook. I signed up because I wanted to do something important."

"Just a bloomin' bloody hero," said Rizzo.

"I'm not an animal nurse."

Rizzo paused to lift a hamster out of the cage and stroke it. "Hey," he said, "did you ever think that maybe one of these hamsters has some cute little baby hamsters inside, just getting started?"

"Wise guy! They're tested every day."

"Sure, sure." He muzzled the little creature, which vibrated its nose at him. "But just suppose you came down one morning and found them there. New little hamsters looking up at you with soft, green patches of fur where the eyes ought to be."

"Shut up, for the love of Mike," yelled Larsen.

"Little soft, green patches of shining fur," said Rizzo, and put the hamster down with a sudden loathing sensation.

* * *

He engaged reception again and varied the focus. There wasn't a specialized life fragment at home that didn't have a rough counterpart on shipboard.

There were the moving runners in various shapes, the moving swimmers, and the moving fliers. Some of the fliers were quite large, with perceptible thoughts; others were small, gauzy-winged creatures. These last transmitted only patterns of sense perception, imperfect patterns at that, and added nothing intelligent of their own.

There were the non-movers, which, like the non-movers at home, were green and lived on the air, water, and soil. These were a mental blank. They knew only the dim, dim consciousness of light, moisture and gravity.

And each fragment, moving and non-moving, had its mockery of life.

Not yet. Not yet . . .

He clamped down hard upon his feelings. Once before, these life fragments had come, and the rest at home had tried to help them—too quickly. It had not worked. This time they must wait.

If only these fragments did not discover him.

They had not, so far. They had not noticed him lying in the corner of the pilot room. No one had bent down to pick up and discard him. Earlier, it had meant he could not move. Someone might have turned and stared at the stiff wormlike thing, not quite six inches long. First stare, then shout, and then it would all be over.

But now, perhaps, he had waited long enough. The take-off was long past. The controls were locked; the pilot room was empty.

It did not take him long to find the chink in the armor leading to the recess where some of the wiring was. They were dead wires.

The front end of his body was a rasp that cut in two a wire of just the right diameter. Then, six inches away, he cut it in two again. He pushed the snipped-off section of the wire ahead of him packing it away neatly and invisibly into a corner of recess. Its outer covering was a brown elastic material and its core was gleaming, ruddy metal. He himself could not reproduce the core, of course, but that was not necessary. It was enough that the pellicle that covered him had been carefully bred to resemble a wire's surface.

He returned and grasped the cut sections of the wire before and behind. He tightened against them as his little suction disks came into play. Not even a seam showed.

They could not find him now. They could look right at him and see only a continuous stretch of wire.

Unless they looked very closely indeed and noted that, in a certain spot on this wire, there were two tiny patches of soft and shining green fur.

* * *

"It is remarkable," said Dr. Weiss, "that little green hairs can do so much."

Captain Loring poured the brandy carefully. In a sense, this was a celebration. They would be ready for the jump through hyper-space in two hours, and after that, two days would see them back on Earth.

"You are convinced, then, the green fur is the sense organ?" he asked.

"It is," said Weiss. Brandy made him come out in splotches, but he was aware of the need of celebration—quite aware. "The experiments were conducted under difficulties, but they were quite significant."

The captain smiled stiffly. " 'Under difficulties' is one way of phrasing it. I would never have taken the chances you did to run them."

"Nonsense. We're all heroes aboard this ship, all volunteers, all great men with trumpet, fife and fanfarade. You took the chance of coming here."

"You were the first to go outside the barrier."

"No particular risk was involved," Weiss said. "I burned the ground before me as I went, to say nothing of the portable barrier that surrounded me. Nonsense, Captain. Let's all take our medals when we come back; let's take them without attempt at gradation. Besides, I'm a male."

"But you're filled with bacteria here." The captain's hand made a quick, cutting gesture three inches above his head. "Which makes you as vulnerable as a female would be."

They paused for drinking purposes.

"Refill?" asked the captain.

"No, thanks. I've exceeded my quota already."

"Then one last for the spaceroad." He lifted his glass in the general direction of Saybrook's Planet, no longer visible, its sun only a bright star in the visiplate. "To the little green hairs that gave Saybrook his first lead."

Weiss nodded. "A lucky thing. We'll quarantine the planet, of course."

The captain said, "That doesn't seem drastic enough. Someone might always land by accident someday and not have Saybrook's insight, or his guts. Suppose he did not blow up his ship, as Saybook did. Suppose he got back to some inhabited place."

The captain was somber. "Do you suppose they might ever develop interstellar travel on their own?"

"I doubt it. No proof, of course. It's just that they have such a completely different orientation. Their entire organization of life has made tools unnecessary. As far as we know, even a stone ax doesn't exist on the planet."

"I hope you're right. Oh, and, Weiss, would you spend some time with Drake?"

"The Galactic Press fellow?"

"Yes. Once we get back, the story of Saybrook's Planet will be released for the public and I don't think it would be wise to oversensationalize it. I've asked Drake to let you consult with him on the story. You're a biologist and enough of an authority to carry weight with him. Would you oblige?"

"A pleasure."

The captain closed his eyes wearily and shook his head.

"Headache, Captain?"

"No. Just thinking of poor Saybrook."

* * *

He was weary of the ship. Awhile back there had been a queer, momentary sensation, as though he had been turned inside out. It was alarming and he had searched the minds of the keen-thinkers for an explanation. Apparently the ship had leaped across vast stretches of empty space by cutting across something they knew as "hyper-space." The keen-thinkers were ingenious.

But—he was weary of the ship. It was such a futile phenomenon. These life fragments were skillful in their constructions, yet it was only a measure of their unhappiness, after all. They strove to find in the control of inanimate matter what they could not find in themselves. In their unconscious yearning for completeness, they built machines and scoured space, seeking, seeking . . .

These creatures, he knew, could never, in the very nature of things, find that for which they were seeking. At least not until such time as he gave it to them. He quivered a little at the thought.

Completeness!

These fragments had no concept of it, even. "Completeness" was a poor word.

In their ignorance they would even fight it. There had been the ship that had come before. The first ship had contained many of the keen-thinking fragments. There had been two varieties, life producers and the sterile ones. (How different this second ship was. The keen-thinkers were all sterile, while the other fragments, the fuzzy-thinkers and the no-thinkers, were all producers of life. It was strange.)

How gladly that first ship had been welcomed by all the planet! He could remember the first intense shock at the realization that the visitors were fragments and not complete. The shock had given way to pity, and the pity to action. It was not certain how they would fit into the community, but there had been no hesitation. All life was sacred and somehow room would have been made for them—for all of them, from the large keen-thinkers to the little multipliers in the darkness.

But there had been a miscalculation. They had not correctly analyzed the course of the fragments' way of thinking. The keen-thinkers became aware of what had been done and resented it. They were frightened, of course; they did not understand.

They had developed the barrier first, and then, later, had destroyed themselves, exploding their ship to atoms.

Poor, foolish fragments.

This time, at least, it would be different. They would be saved, despite themselves.

* * *

John Drake would not have admitted it in so many words, but he was very proud of his skill on the photo-typer. He had a travel-kit model, which was a six-by-eight, featureless dark plastic slab, with cylindrical bulges on either end to hold the roll of thin paper. It fitted into a brown leather case, equipped with a beltlike contraption that held it closely about the waist and at one hip. The whole thing weighed less than a pound.

Drake could operate it with either hand. His fingers would flick quickly and easily, placing their light pressure at exact spots on the blank surface, and, soundlessly, words would be written.

He looked thoughtfully at the beginning of his story, then up at Dr. Weiss. "What do you think, Doc?"

"It starts well."

Drake nodded. "I thought I might as well start with Saybrook himself. They haven't released his story back home yet. I wish I could have seen Saybrook's original report. How did he ever get it through, by the way?"

"As near as I could tell, he spent one last night sending it through the sub-ether. When he was finished, he shorted the motors, and converted the entire ship into a thin cloud of vapor a millionth of a second later. The crew and himself along with it."

"What a man! You were in this from the beginning, Doc?"

"Not from the beginning," corrected Weiss gently. "Only since the receipt of Saybrook's report."

He could not help thinking back. He had read that report, realizing even then how wonderful the planet must have seemed when Saybrook's colonizing expedition first reached it. It was practically a duplicate of Earth, with an abounding plant life and a purely vegetarian animal life.

There had been only the little patches of green fur (how often had he used that phrase in his speaking and thinking!) which seemed strange. No living individual on the planet had eyes. Instead, there was this fur. Even the plants, each blade or leaf or blossom, possessed the two patches of richer green.

Then Saybrook had noticed, startled and bewildered, that there was no conflict for food on the planet. All plants grew pulpy appendages which were eaten by the animals. These were regrown in a matter of hours. No other parts of the plant were touched. It was as though the plants fed the animals as part of the order of nature. And the plants themselves did not grow in overpowering profusion. They might almost have been cultivated, they were spread across the available soil so discriminately.

How much time, Weiss wondered, had Saybrook had to observe the strange law and order on the planet?—the fact that insects kept their numbers reasonable, though no birds ate them; that the rodentlike things did not swarm, though no carnivores existed to keep them in check.

And then there had come the incident of the white rats.

That prodded Weiss. He said, "Oh, one correction, Drake. Hamsters were not the first animals involved. It was the white rats."

"White rats," said Drake, making the correction in his notes.

"Every colonizing ship," said Weiss, "takes a group of white rats for the purpose of testing any alien foods. Rats, of course, are very similar to human beings from a nutritional viewpoint. Naturally, only female white rats are taken."

Naturally. If only one sex was present, there was no danger of unchecked multiplication in case the planet proved favorable. Remember the rabbits in Australia.

"Incidentally, why not use males?" asked Drake.

"Females are hardier," said Weiss, "which is lucky, since that gave the situation away. It turned out suddenly that all the rats were bearing young."

"Right. Now that's where I'm up to, so here's my chance to get some things straight. For my own information, Doc, how did Saybrook find out they were in a family way?"

"Accidentally, of course. In the course of nutritional investigations, rats are dissected for evidence of internal damage. Their condition was bound to be discovered. A few more were dissected; same results. Eventually, all that lived gave birth to young—with *no* male rats aboard!"

"And the point is that all the young were born with little green patches of fur instead of eyes."

"That is correct. Saybrook said so and we corroborate him. After the rats, the pet cat of one of the children was obviously affected. When it finally kittened, the kittens were not born with closed eyes but with little patches of green fur. There was no tomcat aboard.

"Eventually Saybrook had the women tested. He didn't tell them what for. He didn't want to frighten them. Every single one of them was in the early stages of pregnancy, leaving out of consideration those few who had been pregnant at the time of embarkation. Saybrook never waited for any child to be born, of course. He knew they would have no eyes, only shining patches of green fur.

"He even prepared bacterial cultures (Saybrook was a thorough man) and found each bacillus to show microscopic green spots."

Drake was eager. "That goes way beyond our briefing—or, at least, the briefing I got. But granted that life on Saybrook's Planet is organized into a unified whole, how is it done?"

"How? How are your cells organized into a unified whole? Take an individual cell out of your body, even a brain cell, and what is it by itself? Nothing. A little blob of protoplasm with no more capacity for anything human than an amoeba. Less capacity, in fact, since it couldn't live by itself. But put the cells together and you have something that could invent a spaceship or write a symphony."

"I get the idea," said Drake.

Weiss went on, "*All* life on Saybrook's Planet is a *single* organism. In a sense, all life on Earth is too, but it's a fighting dependence, a dog-eat-dog dependence. The bacteria fix nitrogen; the plants fix carbon; animals eat plants and each other; bacterial decay hits everything. It comes full circle. Each grabs as much as it can, and is, in turn, grabbed.

"On Saybrook's Planet, each organism has its place, as each cell in our body does. Bacteria and plants produce food, on the excess of which animals feed, providing in turn carbon dioxide and nitrogenous wastes. Nothing is produced more or less than is needed. The scheme of life is intelligently altered to suit the local environment. No group of life forms multiplies more or less than is needed, just as the cells in our body stop multiplying when there are enough of them for a given purpose. When they don't stop multiplying, we call it cancer. And that's what life on Earth really is, the kind of organic organization we have, compared to that on Saybrook's Planet. One big cancer. Every species, every individual doing its best to thrive at the expense of every other species and individual."

"You sound as if you approve of Saybrook's Planet, Doc."

"I do, in a way. It makes sense out of the business of living. I can see their viewpoint toward us. Suppose one of the cells of your body could be conscious of the efficiency of the human body as compared with that of the cell itself, and could realize that this was only the result of the union of many cells into a higher whole. And then suppose it became conscious of the existence of free-living cells, with bare life and nothing more. It might feel a very strong desire to drag the poor thing into an organization. It might feel sorry for it, feel perhaps a sort of missionary spirit. The things on Saybrook's Planet—or the thing; one should use the singular—feels just that, perhaps."

"And went ahead by bringing about virgin births, eh, Doc? I've got to go easy on that angle of it. Post-office regulations, you know."

"There's nothing ribald about it, Drake. For centuries we've been able to make the eggs of sea urchins, bees, frogs, et cetera develop without the intervention of male fertilization. The touch of a needle was something enough, or just immersion in the proper salt solution. The thing on Saybrook's Planet can cause fertilization by the controlled use of radiant energy. That's why an appropriate energy barrier stops it; interference, you see, or static.

"They can do more than stimulate the division and development of an unfertilized egg. They can impress their own characteristics upon its nucleoproteins, so that the young are born with the little patches of green fur, which serve as the planet's sense organ and means of communication. The young, in other words, are not individuals, but become part of the thing on Saybrook's Planet. The thing on the planet, not at all incidentally, can impregnate any species—plant, animal, or microscopic."

"Potent stuff," muttered Drake.

"Totipotent," Dr. Weiss said sharply. "Universally potent. Any fragment of it is totipotent. Given time, a single bacterium from Saybrook's Planet can convert *all of Earth* into a single organism! We've got the experimental proof of that."

Drake said unexpectedly, "You know, I think I'm a millionaire, Doc. Can you keep a secret?"

Weiss nodded, puzzled.

"I've got a souvenir from Saybrook's Planet," Drake told him, grinning. "It's only a pebble, but after the publicity the planet will get, combined with the fact that it's quarantined from here on in, the pebble will be all any human being will ever see of it. How much do you suppose I could sell the thing for?"

Weiss stared. "A pebble?" He snatched at the object shown him, a hard, gray ovoid. "You shouldn't have done that, Drake. It was strictly against regulations."

"I know. That's why I asked if you could keep a secret. If you could give me a signed note of authentication— *What's the matter, Doc?*"

Instead of answering, Weiss could only chatter and point. Drake ran over and stared down at the pebble. It was the same as before—

Except that the light was catching it at an angle, and it showed up two little green spots. Look very closely; they were patches of green hairs.

* * *

He was disturbed. There was a definite air of danger within the ship. There was the suspicion of his presence aboard. How could that be? He had done nothing yet. Had another fragment of home come aboard and been less cautious? That would be impossible without his knowledge, and though he probed the ship intensely, he found nothing.

And then the suspicion diminished, but it was not quite dead. One of the keen-thinkers still wondered, and was treading close to the truth.

How long before the landing? Would an entire world of life fragments be deprived of completeness? He clung closer to the severed ends of the wire he had been specially bred to imitate, afraid of detection, fearful for his altruistic mission.

* * *

Dr. Weiss had locked himself in his own room. They were already within the solar system, and in three hours they would be landing. He had to think. He had three hours in which to decide.

Drake's devilish "pebble" had been part of the organized life on Saybrook's Planet, of course, but it was dead. It was dead when he had first seen it, and if it hadn't been, it was certainly dead after they fed it into the hyper-atomic motor and converted it into a blast of pure heat. And the bacterial cultures still showed normal when Weiss anxiously checked.

That was not what bothered Weiss now.

Drake had picked up the "pebble" during the last hours of the stay on Saybrook's Planet—*after* the barrier breakdown. What if the breakdown had been the result of a slow, relentless mental pressure on the part of the thing on the planet? What if parts of its being waited to invade as the barrier dropped? If the "pebble" had not been fast enough and had moved only after the barrier was re-established, it would have been killed. It would have lain there for Drake to see and pick up.

It was a "pebble," not a natural life form. But did that mean it was not *some* kind of life form? It might have been a deliberate production of the planet's single organism—a creature deliberately designed to look like a pebble, harmless-seeming, unsuspicious. Camouflage, in other words—a shrewd and frighteningly successful camouflage.

Had any other camouflaged creature succeeded in crossing the barrier *before* it was re-established—with a suitable shape filched from the minds of the humans aboard ship by the mind-reading organism of the planet? Would it have the casual appearance of a paperweight? Of an ornamental brass-head nail in the captain's old-fashioned chair? And how would they locate it? Could they search every part of the ship for the telltale green patches—even down to individual microbes?

And why camouflage? Did it intend to remain undetected for a time? Why? So that it might wait for the landing on Earth?

An infection *after landing* could not be cured by blowing up a ship. The bacteria of Earth, the molds, yeasts, and protozoa, would go first. Within a year the non-human young would begin arriving by the uncountable billions.

Weiss closed his eyes and told himself it might not be such a bad thing. There would be no more disease, since no bacterium would multiply at the expense of its host, but instead would be satisfied with its fair share of what was available. There would be no more overpopulation; the hordes of mankind would decline to adjust themselves to the food supply. There would be no more wars, no crime, no greed.

But there would be no more individuality, either.

Humanity would find security by becoming a cog in a biological machine. A man would be brother to a germ, or to a liver cell.

He stood up. He would have a talk with Captain Loring. They would send their report and blow up the ship, just as Saybrook had done.

He sat down again, Saybrook had had proof, while he had only the conjectures of a terrorized mind, rattled by the sight of two green spots on a pebble. Could he kill the two hundred men on board ship because of a feeble suspicion?

He had to *think!*

* * *

He was straining. Why did he have to wait? If he could only welcome those who were aboard now. *Now!*

Yet a cooler, more reasoning part of him told him that he could not. The little multipliers in the darkness would betray their new status in fifteen minutes, and the keen-thinkers had them under continual observation. Even one mile from the surface of their planet would be too soon, since they might still destroy themselves and their ship out in space.

Better to wait for the main air locks to open, for the planetary air to swirl in with millions of the little multipliers. Better to greet each one of them into the brotherhood of unified life and let them swirl out again to spread the message.

Then it would be done! Another world organized, complete!

He waited. There was the dull throbbing of the engines working mightily to control the slow dropping of the ship; the shudder of contact with planetary surface, then—

He let the jubilation of the keen-thinkers sweep into reception, and his own jubilant thoughts answered them. Soon they would be able to receive as well as himself. Perhaps not these particular fragments, but the fragments that would grow out of those which were fitted for the continuation of life.

The main air locks were about to be opened—

And all thought ceased.

* * *

Jerry Thorn thought, Damn it, something's wrong *now*.

He said to Captain Loring, "Sorry. There seems to be a power breakdown. The locks won't open."

"Are you sure, Thorn? The lights are on."

"Yes, sir. We're investigating it now."

He tore away and joined Roger Oldenn at the air-lock wiring box. "What's wrong?"

"Give me a chance, will you?" Oldenn's hands were busy. Then he said, "For the love of Pete, there's a six-inch break in the twenty-amp lead."

"What? That can't be!"

Oldenn held up the broken wires with their clean, sharp, sawn-through ends.

Dr. Weiss joined them. He looked haggard and there was the smell of brandy on his breath.

He said shakily, "What's the matter?"

They told him. At the bottom of the compartment, in one corner, was the missing section.

Weiss bent over. There was a black fragment on the floor of the compartment. He touched it with his finger and it smeared, leaving a sooty smudge on his finger tip. He rubbed it off absently.

There might have been something taking the place of the missing section of wire. Something that had been alive and only looked like wire, yet something that would heat, die, and carbonize in a tiny fraction of a second once the electrical circuit which controlled the air lock had been closed.

He said, "How are the bacteria?"

A crew member went to check, returned and said, "All normal, Doc."

The wires had meanwhile been spliced, the locks opened, and Dr. Weiss stepped out into the anarchic world of life that was Earth.

"Anarchy," he said, laughing a little wildly. "And it will stay that way."

"Breeds There a Man. . . ?"

Police Sergeant Mankiewicz was on the telephone, and he wasn't enjoying it. His conversation was sounding like a one-sided view of a firecracker.

He was saying, "That's right! He came in here and said, 'Put me in jail, because I want to kill myself.'

". . . I can't help that. Those were his exact words. It sounds crazy to me, too.

". . . Look, mister, the guy answers the description. You asked me for information and I'm giving it to you.

". . . He has exactly that scar on his right cheek and he said his name was John Smith. He didn't say it was Doctor anything-at-all.

". . . Well, sure it's a phony. Nobody is named John Smith. Not in a police station, anyway.

". . . He's in jail now.

". . . Yes, I mean it.

". . . Resisting an officer; assault and battery; malicious mischief. That's three counts.

". . . I don't care who he is.

". . . All right. I'll hold on."

He looked up at Officer Brown and put his hand over the mouthpiece of the phone. It was a ham of a hand that nearly swallowed up the phone altogether. His blunt-featured face was ruddy and steaming under a thatch of pale-yellow hair.

He said, "Trouble! Nothing but trouble at a precinct station. I'd rather be pounding a beat any day."

'Who's on the phone?" asked Brown. He had just come in and didn't really care. He thought Mankiewicz would look better on a suburban beat, too.

"Oak Ridge. Long Distance. A guy called Grant. Head of somethingological division, and now he's getting somebody else at seventy-five cents a min . . . Hello!"

Mankiewicz got a new grip on the phone and held himself down.

"Look," he said, "let me go through this from the beginning. I want you to get it straight and then if you don't like it, you can send someone down here. The guy doesn't want a lawyer. He claims he just wants to stay in jail and, brother, that's all right with me.

"Well, will you listen? He came in yesterday, walked right up to me, and said, 'Officer, I want you to put me in jail because I want to kill myself.' So I said, 'Mister, I'm sorry you want to kill yourself. Don't do it, because if you do, you'll regret it the rest of your life.'

". . . I *am* serious. I'm just telling you what I said. I'm not saying it was a funny joke, but I've got my own troubles here, if you know what I mean. Do you think all I've got to do here is to listen to cranks who walk in and—

" '. . . Give me a chance, will you?' I said, 'I can't put you in jail for wanting to kill yourself. That's no crime.' And he said, 'But I don't want to die.' So I said, 'Look, bud, get out of here.' I mean if a guy wants to commit suicide, all right, and if he doesn't want to, all right, but I don't want him weeping on my shoulder.

". . . I'm *getting* on with it. So he said to me, 'If I commit a crime, will you put me in jail?' I said, 'If you're caught and if someone files a charge and you can't put up bail, we will. Now beat it.' So he picked up the inkwell on my desk and, before I could stop him, he turned it upside down on the open police blotter.

". . . That's right! Why do you think we have 'malicious mischief' tabbed on him? The ink ran down all over my pants.

". . . Yes, assault and battery, too! I came hopping down to shake a little sense into him, and he kicked me in the shins and handed me one in the eye.

". . . I'm not making this up. You want to come down here and look at my face?

". . . He'll be up in court one of these days. About Thursday, maybe.

". . . Ninety days is the least he'll get, unless the psychoes say otherwise. I think he belongs in the loony-bin myself.

". . . Officially, he's John Smith. That's the only name he'll give.

". . . No, sir, he doesn't get released without the proper legal steps.

". . . O.K., you do that, if you want to, bud! I just do my job here."

He banged the phone into its cradle, glowered at it, then picked it up and began dialing. He said, "Gianetti?", got the proper answer and began talking.

"What's the A.E.C.? I've been talking to some Joe on the phone and he says—

". . . No, I'm not kidding, lunk-head. If I were kidding, I'd put up a sign. What's the alphabet soup?"

He listened, said, "Thanks" in a small voice and hung up again.

He had lost some of his color. "That second guy was the head of the Atomic Energy Commission," he said to Brown. "They must have switched me from Oak Ridge to Washington."

Brown lounged to his feet, "Maybe the F.B.I. is after this John Smith guy. Maybe he's one of these here scientists." He felt moved to philosophy. "They ought to keep atomic secrets away from those guys. Things were O.K. as long as General Groves was the only fella who knew about the atom bomb. Once they cut in these here scientists on it, through—"

"Ah, shut up," snarled Mankiewicz.

* * *

Dr. Oswald Grant kept his eyes fixed on the white line that marked the highway and handled the car as though it were an enemy of his. He always did. He was tall and knobby with a withdrawn expression stamped on his face. His knees crowded the wheel, and his knuckles whitened whenever he made a turn.

Inspector Darrity sat beside him with his legs crossed so that the sole of his left shoe came up hard against the door. It would leave a sandy mark when he took it away. He tossed a nut-brown penknife from hand to hand. Earlier, he had unsheathed its wicked, gleaming blade and scraped casually at his nails as they drove, but a sudden swerve had nearly cost him a finger and he desisted.

He said, "What do you know about this Ralson?"

Dr. Grant took his eyes from the road momentarily, then returned them. He said, uneasily, "I've known him since he took his doctorate at Princeton. He's a very brilliant man."

"Yes? Brilliant, huh? Why is it that all you scientific men describe one another as 'brilliant'? Aren't there any mediocre ones?"

"Many. I'm one of them. But Ralson isn't. You ask anyone. Ask Oppenheimer. Ask Bush. He was the youngest observer at Alamogordo."

"O.K. He was brilliant. What about his private life?"

Grant waited. "I wouldn't know."

"You know him since Princeton. How many years is that?"

They had been scouring north along the highway from Washington for two hours with scarcely a word between them. Now Grant felt the atmosphere change and the grip of the law on his coat collar.

"He got his degree in '43."

"You've known him eight years then."

"That's right."

"And you don't know about his private life?"

"A man's life is his own, Inspector. He wasn't very sociable. A great many of the men are like that. They work under pressure and when they're off the job, they're not interested in continuing the lab acquaintanceships."

"Did he belong to any organizations that you know of?"

"No."

The inspector said, "Did he ever say anything to you that might indicate he was disloyal?"

Grant shouted "No!" and there was silence for a while.

Then Darrity said, "How important is Ralson in atomic research?"

Grant hunched over the wheel and said, "As important as any one man can be. I grant you that no one is indispensable, but Ralson has always seemed to be rather unique. He has the engineering mentality."

"What does that mean?"

"He isn't much of a mathematician himself, but he can work out the gadgets that put someone else's math into life. There's no one like him when it comes to that. Time and again, Inspector, we've had a problem to lick and no time to lick it in. There were nothing but blank minds all around until he put some thought into it and said, 'Why don't you try so-and-so?' Then he'd go away. He wouldn't even be interested enough to see if it worked. But it always did. Always! Maybe we would have got it ourselves eventually, but it might have taken months of additional time. I don't know how he does it. It's no use asking him either. He just looks at you and says 'It was obvious', and walks away. Of course, once he's shown us how to do it, it *is* obvious."

The inspector let him have his say out. When no more came, he said, "Would you say he was queer, mentally? Erratic, you know."

"When a person is a genius, you wouldn't expect him to be normal, would you?"

"Maybe not. But just how abnormal was this particular genius?"

"He never talked, particularly. Sometimes, he wouldn't work."

"Stayed at home and went fishing instead?"

"No. He came to the labs all right; but he would just sit at his desk. Sometimes that would go on for weeks. Wouldn't answer you, or even look at you, when you spoke to him."

"Did he ever actually leave work altogether?"

"Before now, you mean? Never!"

"Did he ever claim he wanted to commit suicide? Ever say he wouldn't feel safe except in jail?"

"No."

"You're sure this John Smith is Ralson?"

"I'm almost positive. He has a chemical burn on his right cheek that can't be mistaken."

"O.K. That's that, then I'll speak to him and see what he sounds like."

The silence fell for good this time. Dr. Grant followed the snaking line as Inspector Darrity tossed the penknife in low arcs from hand to hand.

The warden listened to the call-box and looked up at his visitors. "We can have him brought up here, Inspector, regardless."

"No." Dr. Grant shook his head. "Let's go to him."

Darrity said, "Is that normal for Ralson, Dr. Grant? Would you expect him to attack a guard trying to take him out of a prison cell?"

Grant said, "I can't say."

The warden spread a calloused palm. His thick nose twitched a little. "We haven't tried to do anything about him so far because of the telegram from Washington, but, frankly, he doesn't belong here. I'll be glad to have him taken off my hands."

"We'll see him in his cell," said Darrity.

They went down the hard, barlined corridor. Empty, incurious eyes watched their passing.

Dr. Grant felt his flesh crawl. "Has he been kept *here* all the time?"

Darrity did not answer.

The guard, pacing before them, stopped. "This is the cell."

Darrity said, "Is that Dr. Ralson?"

Dr. Grant looked silently at the figure upon the cot. The man had been lying down when they first reached the cell, but now he had risen to one elbow and seemed to be trying to shrink into the wall. His hair was sandy and thin, his figure slight, his eyes blank and china-blue. On his right cheek was a raised pink patch that tailed off like a tadpole.

Dr. Grant said, "That's Ralson."

The guard opened the door and stepped inside, but Inspector Darrity sent him out again with a gesture. Ralson watched them mutely. He had drawn both feet up to the cot and was pushing backwards. His Adam's apple bobbled as he swallowed.

Darrity said quietly, "Dr. Elwood Ralson?"

"What do you want?" The voice was a surprising baritone.

"Would you come with us, please? We have some questions we would like to ask you."

"No! Leave me alone!"

"Dr. Ralson," said Grant, "I've been sent here to ask you to come back to work."

Ralson looked at the scientist and there was a momentary glint of something other than fear in his eyes. He said, "Hello, Grant." He got off his cot. "Listen, I've been trying to have them put me into a padded cell. Can't you make them do that for me? You know me, Grant. I wouldn't ask for something I didn't feel was necessary. Help me. I can't stand the hard walls. It makes me want to . . . bash—" He brought the flat of his palm thudding down against the hard, dull-gray concrete behind his cot.

Darrity looked thoughtful. He brought out his penknife and unbent the gleaming blade. Carefully, he scraped at his thumbnail, and said, "Would you like to see a doctor?"

But Ralson didn't answer. He followed the gleam of metal and his lips parted and grew wet. His breath became ragged and harsh.

He said, "Put that away!"

Darrity paused. "Put what away?"

"The knife. Don't hold it in front of me. I can't stand looking at it."

Darrity said, "Why not?" He held it out. "Anything wrong with it? It's a good knife."

Ralson lunged. Darrity stepped back and his left hand came down on the other's wrist. He lifted the knife high in the air. "What's the matter, Ralson? What are you after?"

Grant cried a protest but Darrity waved him away.

Darrity said, "What do you want, Ralson?"

Ralson tried to reach upward, and bent under the other's appalling grip. He gasped, "Give me the knife."

"Why, Ralson? What do you want to do with it?"

"Please. I've got to—" He was pleading. "I've got to stop living."

"You want to die?"

"No. But I must."

Darrity shoved. Ralson flailed backward and tumbled into his cot, so that it squeaked noisily. Slowly, Darrity bent the blade of his penknife into its sheath and put it away. Ralson covered his face. His shoulders were shaking but otherwise he did not move.

There was a sound of shouting from the corridor, as the other prisoners reacted to the noise issuing from Ralson's cell. The guard came hurrying down, yelling, "Quiet!" as he went.

Darrity looked up. "It's all right, guard."

He was wiping his hands upon a large white handkerchief. "I think we'll get a doctor for him."

* * *

Dr. Gottfried Blaustein was small and dark and spoke with a trace of an Austrian accent. He needed only a small goatee to be the layman's caricature of a psychiatrist. But he was clean-shaven, and very carefully dressed. He watched Grant closely, assessing him, blocking in certain observations and deductions. He did this automatically, now, with everyone he met.

He said, "You give me a sort of picture. You describe a man of great talent, perhaps even genius. You tell me he has always been uncomfortable with people; that he has never fitted in with his laboratory environment, even though it was there that he met the greatest of success. Is there another environment to which he has fitted himself?"

"I don't understand."

"It is not given to all of us to be so fortunate as to find a congenial type of company at the place or in the field where we find it necessary to make a living. Often, one compensates by playing an instrument, or going hiking, or joining some club. In other words, one creates a new type of society, when not working, in which one can feel more at home. It need not have the slightest connection with what one's ordinary occupation is. It is an escape, and not necessarily an unhealthy one." He smiled and added, "Myself, I collect stamps. I am an active member of the American Society of Philatelists."

Grant shook his head. "I don't know what he did outside working hours. I doubt that he did anything like what you've mentioned."

"Um-m-m. Well, that would be sad. Relaxation and enjoyment are wherever you find them; but you must find them somewhere, no?"

"Have you spoken to Dr. Ralson, yet?"

"About his problems? No."

"Aren't you going to?"

"Oh, yes. But he has been here only a week. One must give him a chance to recover. He was in a highly excited state when he first came here. It was almost a delirium. Let him rest and become accustomed to the new environment. I will question him, then."

"Will you be able to get him back to work?"

Blaustein smiled. "How should I know? I don't even know what his sickness is."

"Couldn't you at least get rid of the worst of it; this suicidal obsession of his, and take care of the rest of the cure while he's at work?"

"Perhaps. I couldn't even venture an opinion so far without several interviews."

"How long do you suppose it will all take?"

"In these matters, Dr. Grant, nobody can say."

Grant brought his hands together in a sharp slap. "Do what seems best then. But this is more important than you know."

"Perhaps. But you may be able to help me, Dr. Grant."

"How?"

"Can you get me certain information which may be classified as top secret?"

"What kind of information?"

"I would like to know the suicide rate, since 1945, among nuclear scientists. Also, how many have left their jobs to go into other types of scientific work, or to leave science altogether."

"Is this in connection with Ralson?"

"Don't you think it might be an occupational disease, this terrible unhappiness of his?"

"Well—a good many have left their jobs, naturally."

"Why naturally, Dr. Grant?"

"You must know how it is, Dr. Blaustein. The atmosphere in modern atomic research is one of great pressure and red tape. You work with the government; you work with military men. You can't talk about your work; you have to be careful what you say. Naturally, if you get a chance at a job in a university, where you can fix your own hours, do your own work, write papers that don't have to be submitted to the A.E.C., attend conventions that aren't held behind locked doors, you take it."

"And abandon your field of specialty forever."

"There are always non-military applications. Of course, there was one man who did leave for another reason. He told me once he couldn't sleep nights. He said he'd hear one hundred thousand screams coming from Hiroshima, when he put the lights out. The last I heard of him he was a clerk in a haberdashery."

"And do you ever hear a few screams yourself?"

Grant nodded. "It isn't a nice feeling to know that even a little of the responsibility of atomic destruction might be your own."

"How did Ralson feel?"

"He never spoke of anything like that."

"In other words, if he felt it, he never even had the safety-valve effect of letting off steam to the rest of you."

"I guess he hadn't."

"Yet nuclear research must be done, no?"

"I'll say."

"What would you do, Dr. Grant, if you felt you *had* to do something that you *couldn't* do."

Grant shrugged. "I don't know."

"Some people kill themselves."

"You mean that's what has Ralson down."

"I don't know. I do not know. I will speak to Dr. Ralson this evening. I can promise nothing, of course, but I will let you know whatever I can."

Grant rose. "Thanks, Doctor. I'll try to get the information you want."

* * *

Elwood Ralson's appearance had improved in the week he had been at Dr. Blaustein's sanatorium. His face had filled out and some of the restlessness had gone out of him. He was tieless and beltless. His shoes were without laces.

Blaustein said, "How do you feel, Dr. Ralson?"

"Rested."

"You have been treated well?"

"No complaints, Doctor."

Blaustein's hand fumbled for the letter-opener with which it was his habit to play during moments of abstraction, but his fingers met nothing. It had been put away, of course, with anything else possessing a sharp edge. There was nothing on his desk, now, but papers.

He said, "Sit down, Dr. Ralson. How do your symptoms progress?"

"You mean, do I have what you would call a suicidal impulse? Yes. It gets worse or better, depending on my thoughts, I think. But it's always with me. There is nothing you can do to help."

"Perhaps you are right. There are often things I cannot help. But I would like to know as much as I can about you. You are an important man—"

Ralson snorted.

"You do not consider that to be so?" asked Blaustein.

"No, I don't. There are no important men, any more than there are important individual bacteria."

"I don't understand."

"I don't expect you do."

"And yet it seems to me that behind your statement there must have been much thought. It would certainly be of the greatest interest to have you tell me some of this thought."

For the first time, Ralson smiled. It was not a pleasant smile. His nostrils were white. He said, "It is amusing to watch you, Doctor. You go about your business so conscientiously. You must listen to me, mustn't you, with just that air of phony interest and unctuous sympathy. I can tell you the most ridiculous things and still be sure of an audience, can't I?"

"Don't you think my interest can be real, even granted that it is professional, too?"

"No, I don't."

"Why not?"

"I'm not interested in discussing it."

"Would you rather return to your room?"

"If you don't mind. No!" His voice had suddenly suffused with fury as he stood up, then almost immediately sat down again. "Why shouldn't I use you? I don't like to talk to people. They're stupid. They don't see things. They stare at the obvious for hours and it means nothing to them. If I spoke to them, they wouldn't understand; they'd lose patience; they'd laugh. Whereas you must listen. It's your job. You can't interrupt to tell me I'm mad, even though you may think so."

"I'd be glad to listen to whatever you would like to tell me."

Ralson drew a deep breath. "I've known something for a year now, that very few people know. Maybe it's something no *live* person knows. Do you know that human cultural advances come in spurts? Over a space of two generations in a city containing thirty thousand free men, enough literary and artistic genius of the first rank arose to supply a nation of millions for a century under ordinary circumstances. I'm referring to the Athens of Pericles.

"There are other examples. There is the Florence of the Medicis, the England of Elizabeth, the Spain of the Cordovan Emirs. There was the spasm of social reformers among the Israelites of the Eighth and Seventh centuries before Christ. Do you know what I mean?"

Blaustein nodded. "I see that history is a subject that interests you."

"Why not? I suppose there's nothing that says I must restrict myself to nuclear cross-sections and wave mechanics."

"Nothing at all. Please proceed."

"At first, I thought I could learn more of the true inwardness of historical cycles by consulting a specialist. I had some conferences with a professional historian. A waste of time!'

"What was his name; this professional historian?"

"Does it matter?"

"Perhaps not, if you would rather consider it confidential. What did he tell you?"

"He said I was wrong; that history only appeared to go in spasms. He said that after closer studies the great civilizations of Egypt and Sumeria did not arise suddenly or out of nothing, but upon the basis of a long-developing sub-civilization that was already sophisticated in its arts. He said that Periclean Athens built upon a pre-Periclean Athens of lower accomplishments, without which the age of Pericles could not have been.

"I asked why was there not a post-Periclean Athens of higher accomplishments still, and he told me that Athens was ruined by a plague and by a long war with Sparta. I asked about other cultural spurts and each time it was a war that ended it, or, in some cases, even accompanied it. He was like all the rest. The truth was there; he had only to bend and pick it up; but he didn't."

Ralson stared at the floor, and said in a tired voice, "They come to me in the laboratory sometimes, Doctor. They say, 'how the devil are we going to get rid of the such-and-such effect that is ruining all our measurements, Ralson?' They show me the instruments and the wiring diagrams and I say, 'It's staring at you. Why don't you do so-and-so? A child could tell you that.' Then I walk away because I can't endure the slow puzzling of their stupid faces. Later, they come to me and say, 'It worked, Ralson. How did you figure it out?' I can't explain to them, Doctor; it would be like explaining that water is wet. And I couldn't explain to the historian. And I can't explain to you. It's a waste of time."

"Would you like to go back to your room?"

"Yes."

Blaustein sat and wondered for many minutes after Ralson had been escorted out of his office. His fingers found their way automatically into the upper right drawer of his desk and lifted out the letter-opener. He twiddled it in his fingers.

Finally, he lifted the telephone and dialed the unlisted number he had been given.

He said, "This is Blaustein. There is a professional historian who was consulted by Dr. Ralson some time in the past, probably a bit over a year ago. I don't know his name. I don't even know if he was connected with a university. If you could find him, I would like to see him."

* * *

Thaddeus Milton, Ph.D., blinked thoughtfully at Blaustein and brushed his hand through his iron-gray hair. He said, "They came to me and I said that I had indeed met this man. However, I have had very little connection with him. None, in fact, beyond a few conversations of a professional nature."

"How did he come to you?"

"He wrote me a letter; why me, rather than someone else, I do not know. A series of articles written by myself had appeared in one of the semi-learned journals of semi-popular appeal about that time. It may have attracted his attention."

"I see. With what general topic were the articles concerned?"

"They were a consideration of the validity of the cyclic approach to history. That is, whether one can really say that a particular civilization must follow laws of growth and decline in any matter analogous to those involving individuals."

"I have read Toynbee, Dr. Milton."

"Well, then, you know what I mean."

Blaustein said, "And when Dr. Ralson consulted you, was it with reference to this cyclic approach to history?"

"Um-m-m. In a way, I suppose. Of course, the man is not an historian and some of his notions about cultural trends are rather dramatic and . . . what shall I say . . . tabliodish. Pardon me, Doctor, if I ask a question which may be improper. Is Dr. Ralson one of your patients?"

"Dr. Ralson is not well and is in my care. This, and all else we say here, is confidential, of course."

"Quite. I understand that. However, your answer explains something to me. Some of his ideas almost verged on the irrational. He was always worried, it seemed to me, about the connection between what he called 'cultural spurts' and calamities of one sort or another. Now such connections have been noted frequently. The time of a nation's greatest vitality may come at a time of great national insecurity. The Netherlands is a good case in point. Her great artists, statesmen, and explorers belong to the early Seventeenth Century at the time when she was locked in a death struggle with the greatest European power of the time, Spain. When at the point of destruction at home, she was building an empire in the Far East and had secured footholds on the northern coast of South America, the southern tip of Africa, and the Hudson Valley of North America. Her fleets fought England to a standstill. And then, once her political safety was assured, she declined.

"Well, as I say, that is not unusual. Groups, like individuals, will rise to strange heights in answer to a challenge, and vegetate in the absence of a challenge. Where Dr. Ralson left the paths of sanity, however, was in insisting that such a view amounted to confusing cause and effect. He declared that it was not times of war and danger that stimulated 'cultural spurts', but rather vice versa. He claimed that each time a group of men showed too much vitality and ability, a war became necessary to destroy the possibility of their further development."

"I see," said Blaustein.

"I rather laughed at him, I am afraid. It may be that that was why he did not keep the last appointment we made. Just toward the end of that last conference he asked me, in the most intense fashion imaginable, whether I did not think it queer that such an improbable species as man was dominant on earth, when all he had in his favor was intelligence. There I laughed aloud. Perhaps I should not have, poor fellow."

"It was a natural reaction," said Blaustein, "but I must take no more of your time. You have been most helpful."

They shook hands, and Thaddeus Milton took his leave.

* * *

"Well," said Darrity, "there are your figures on the recent suicides among scientific personnel. Get any deductions out of it?"

"I should be asking you that," said Blaustein, gently. "The F.B.I. must have investigated thoroughly."

"You can bet the national debt on that. They *are* suicides. There's no mistake about it. There have been people checking on it in another department. The rate is about four times above normal, taking age, social status, economic class into consideration."

"What about British scientists?"

"Just about the same."

"And the Soviet Union?"

"Who can tell?" The investigator leaned forward. "Doc, you don't think the Soviets have some sort of ray that can make people want to commit suicide, do you? It's sort of suspicious that men in atomic research are the only ones affected."

"Is it? Perhaps not. Nuclear physicists may have peculiar strains imposed upon them. It is difficult to tell without thorough study."

"You mean complexes might be coming through?" asked Darrity, warily.

Blaustein made a face. "Psychiatry is becoming too popular. Everybody talks of complexes and neuroses and psychoses and compulsions and what-not. One man's guilt complex is another man's good night's sleep. If I could talk to each one of the men who committed suicide, maybe I could know something."

"You're talking to Ralson."

"Yes, I'm talking to Ralson."

"Has *he* got a guilt complex?"

"Not particularly. He has a background out of which it would not surprise me if he obtained a morbid concern with death. When he was twelve he saw his mother die under the wheels of an automobile. His father died slowly of cancer. Yet the effect of those experiences on his present troubles is not clear."

Darrity picked up his hat. "Well, I wish you'd get a move on, Doc. There's something big on, bigger than the H-Bomb. I don't know how anything *can* be bigger than that, but it is."

* * *

Ralson insisted on standing. "I had a bad night last night, Doctor."

"I hope," said Blaustein, "these conferences are not disturbing you."

"Well, maybe they are. They have me thinking on the subject again. It makes things bad, when I do that. How do you imagine it feels being part of a bacterial culture, Doctor?"

"I had never thought of that. To a bacterium, it probably feels quite normal."

Ralson did not hear. He said, slowly, "A culture in which intelligence is being studied. We study all sorts of things as far as their genetic relationships are concerned. We take fruit flies and cross red eyes and white eyes to see what happens. We don't care anything about red eyes and white eyes, but we try to gather from them certain basic genetic principles. You see what I mean?"

"Certainly."

"Even in humans, we can follow various physical characteristics. There are the Hapsburg lips, and the hemophilia that started with Queen Victoria and cropped up in her descendants among the Spanish and Russian royal families. We can even follow feeble-mindedness in the Jukeses and Kallikaks. You learn about it in high-school biology. But you can't breed human beings the way you do fruit flies. Humans live too long. It would take centuries to draw conclusions. It's a pity we don't have a special race of men that reproduce at weekly intervals, eh?"

He waited for an answer, but Blaustein only smiled.

Ralson said, "Only that's exactly what we would be for another group of beings whose life span might be thousands of years. To them, we could reproduce rapidly enough. We would be short-lived creatures and they could study the genetics of such things as musical aptitude, scientific intelligence, and so on. Not that those things would interest them as such, any more than the white eyes of the fruit fly interest us as white eyes."

"This is a very interesting notion," said Blaustein.

"It is not simply a notion. It is true. To me, it is obvious, and I don't care how it seems to you. Look around you. Look at the planet, Earth. What kind of a ridiculous animal are we to be lords of the world after the dinosaurs had failed? Sure, we're intelligent, but what's intelligence? We think it is important because we have it. If the Tyranosaurus could have picked out the one quality that he thought would ensure species domination, it would be size and strength. And he would make a better case for it. He lasted longer than we're likely to.

"Intelligence in itself isn't much as far as survival values are concerned. The elephant makes out very poorly indeed when compared to the sparrow even though he is much more intelligent. The dog does well, under man's protection, but not as well as the housefly against whom every human hand is raised. Or take the primates as a group. The small ones cower before their enemies; the large ones have always been remarkably unsuccessful in doing more than barely holding their own. The baboons do the best and that is because of their canines, not their brains."

A light film of perspiration covered Ralson's forehead. "And one can see that man has been tailored, made to careful specifications for those things that study us. Generally, the primate is short-lived. Naturally, the larger ones live longer, which is a fairly general rule in animal life. Yet the human being has a life span twice as long as any of the other great apes; considerably longer even than the gorilla that outweighs him. We mature later. It's as though we've been carefully bred to live a little longer so that our life cycle might be of a more convenient length."

He jumped to his feet, shaking his fists above his head. "A thousand years are but as yesterday—"

Blaustein punched a button hastily.

For a moment, Ralson struggled against the white-coated orderly who entered, and then he allowed himself to be led away.

Blaustein looked after him, shook his head, and picked up the telephone.

He got Darrity. "Inspector, you may as well know that this may take a long time."

He listened and shook his head. "I know. I don't minimize the urgency."

The voice in the receiver was tinny and harsh. "Doctor, you *are* minimizing it. I'll send Dr. Grant to you. He'll explain the situation to you."

* * *

Dr. Grant asked how Ralson was, then asked somewhat wistfully if he could see him. Blaustein shook his head gently.

Grant said, "I've been directed to explain the current situation in atomic research to you."

"So that I will understand, no?"

"I hope so. It's a measure of desperation. I'll have to remind you—"

"Not to breathe a word of it. Yes, I know. This insecurity on the part of you people is a very bad symptom. You must know these things cannot be hidden."

"You live with secrecy. It's contagious."

"Exactly. What is the current secret?"

"There is . . . or, at least, there might be a defense against the atomic bomb."

"And that is a secret? It would be better if it were shouted to all the people of the world instantly."

"For heaven's sake, no. Listen to me, Dr. Blaustein. It's only on paper so far. It's at the E equal mc square stage, almost. It may not be practical. It would be bad to raise hopes we would have to disappoint. On the other hand, if it were known that we *almost* had a defense, there *might* be a desire to start and win a war before the defense were completely developed."

"That I don't believe. But, nevertheless, I distract you. What is the nature of this defense, or have you told me as much as you dare?"

"No, I can go as far as I like; as far as is necessary to convince you we have to have Ralson—and fast!"

"Well, then tell me, and I too, will know secrets. I'll feel like a member of the Cabinet."

"You'll know more than most. Look, Dr. Blaustein, let me explain it in lay language. So far, military advances have been made fairly equally in both offensive and defensive weapons. Once before there seemed to be a definite and permanent tipping of all warfare in the direction of the offense, and that was with the invention of gunpowder. But the defense caught up. The medieval man-in-armor-on-horse became the modern man-in-tank-on-treads, and the stone castle became the concrete pillbox. The same thing, you see, except that everything has been boosted several orders of magnitude."

"Very good. You make it clear. But with the atomic bomb comes more orders of magnitude, no? You must go past concrete and steel for protection."

"Right. Only we can't just make thicker and thicker walls. We've run out of materials that are strong enough. So we must abandon materials altogether. If the atom attacks, we must let the atom defend. We will use energy itself; a force field."

"And what," asked Blaustein, gently, "is a force field?"

"I wish I could tell you. Right now, it's an equation on paper. Energy can be so channeled as to create a wall of matterless inertia, theoretically. In practice, we don't know how to do it."

"It would be a wall you could not go through, is that it? Even for atoms?"

"Even for atom bombs. The only limit on its strength would be the amount of energy we could pour into it. It could even theoretically be made to be impermeable to radiation. The gamma rays would bounce off it. What we're dreaming of is a screen that would be in permanent place about cities; at minimum strength, using practically no energy. It could then be triggered to maximum intensity in a fraction of a millisecond at the impingement of short-wave radiation; say the amount radiating from the mass of plutonium large enough to be an atomic war head. All this is theoretically possible."

"And why must you have Ralson?"

"Because he is the only one who can reduce it to practice, if it can be made practical at all, quickly enough. Every minute counts these days. You know what the international situation is. Atomic defense *must* arrive before atomic war."

"You are so sure of Ralson?"

"I am as sure of him as I can be of anything. The man is amazing, Dr. Blaustein. He is always right. Nobody in the field knows how he does it."

"A sort of intuition, no?" The psychiatrist looked disturbed. "A kind of reasoning that goes beyond ordinary human capacities. Is that it?"

"I make no pretense of knowing what it is."

"Let me speak to him once more then. I will let you know."

"Good." Grant rose to leave; then, as if in afterthought, he said, "I might say, Doctor, that if you don't do something, the Commission plans to take Dr. Ralson out of your hands."

"And try another psychiatrist? If they wish to do that, of course, I will not stand in their way. It is my opinion, however, that no reputable practitioner will pretend there is a rapid cure."

"We may not intend further mental treatment. He may simply be returned to work."

"That, Dr. Grant, I will fight. You will get nothing out of him. It will be his death."

"We get nothing out of him anyway."

"This way there is at least a chance, no?"

"I hope so. And by the way, please don't mention the fact that I said anything about taking Ralson away."

"I will not, and I thank you for the warning. Good-bye, Dr. Grant."

* * *

"I made a fool of myself last time, didn't I, Doctor?" said Ralson. He was frowning.

"You mean you don't believe what you said then?"

"*I do!*" Ralson's slight form trembled with the intensity of his affirmation.

He rushed to the window, and Blaustein swiveled in his chair to keep him in view. There were bars in the window. He couldn't jump. The glass was unbreakable.

Twilight was ending, and the stars were beginning to come out. Ralson stared at them in fascination, then he turned to Blaustein and flung a finger outward. "Every single one of them is an incubator. They maintain temperatures at the desired point. Different experiments; different temperatures. And the planets that circle them are just huge cultures, containing different nutrient mixtures and different life forms. The experimenters are economical, too—whatever and whoever they are. They've cultured many types of life forms in this particular test-tube. Dinosaurs in a moist, tropical age and ourselves among the glaciers. They turn the sun up and down and we try to work out the physics of it. Physics!' He drew his lips back in a snarl.

"Surely," said Dr. Blaustein, "it is not possible that the sun can be turned up and down at will."

"Why not? It's just like a heating element in an oven. You think bacteria knows what it is that works the heat that reaches them? Who knows? Maybe they evolve theories, too. Maybe they have their cosmogonies about cosmic catastrophes, in which clashing lightbulbs create strings of Petri dishes. Maybe they think there must be some beneficent creator that supplies them with food and warmth and says to them, 'Be fruitful and multiply!'

"We breed like them, not knowing why. We obey the so-called laws of nature which are only our interpretation of the not-understood forces imposed upon us.

"And now they've got the biggest experiment of any yet on their hands. It's been going on for two hundred years. They decided to develop a strain for mechanical aptitude in England in the seventeen hundreds, I imagine. We call it the Industrial Revolution. It began with steam, went on to electricity, then atoms. It was an interesting experiment, but they took their chances on letting it spread. Which is why they'll have to be very drastic indeed in ending it."

Blaustein said, "And how would they plan to end it? Do you have an idea about that?"

"You ask *me* how they plan to end it. You can look about the world today and still ask what is likely to bring our technological age to an end. All the earth fears an atomic war and would do anything to avoid it; yet all the earth fears that an atomic war is inevitable."

"In other words, the experimenters will arrange an atom war whether we want it or not, to kill off the technological era we are in, and to start fresh. That is it, no?"

"Yes. It's logical. When we sterilize an instrument, do the germs know where the killing heat comes from? Or what has brought it about? There is some way the experimenters can raise the heat of our emotions; some way they can handle us that passes our understanding."

"Tell me," said Blaustein, "is that why you want to die? Because you think the destruction of civilization is coming and can't be stopped?"

Ralson said, "I *don't* want to die. It's just that I must." His eyes were tortured. "Doctor, if you had a culture of germs that were highly dangerous and that you had to keep under absolute control, might you not have an agar medium impregnated with, say, penicillin, in a circle at a certain distance from the center of inoculation? Any germs spreading out too far from the center would die. You would have nothing against the particular germs who were killed; you might not even know that any germs had spread that far in the first place. It would be purely automatic.

"Doctor, there is a penicillin ring about our intellects. When we stray too far; when we penetrate the true meaning of our own existence, we have reached into the penicillin and we must die. It works slowly—but it's hard to stay alive."

He smiled briefly and sadly. Then he said, "May I go back to my room now, Doctor?"

* * *

Dr. Blaustein went to Ralson's room about noon the next day. It was a small room and featureless. The walls were gray with padding.

Two small windows were high up and could not be reached. The mattress lay directly on the padded floor. There was nothing of metal in the room; nothing that could be utilized in tearing life from body. Even Ralson's nails were clipped short.

Ralson sat up. "Hello!"

"Hello, Dr. Ralson. May I speak to you?"

"Here? There isn't any seat I can offer you."

"It's all right. I'll stand. I have a sitting job and it is good for my sitting-down place that I should stand sometimes. Dr. Ralson, I have thought all night of what you told me yesterday and in the days before."

"And now you are going to apply treatment to rid me of what you think are delusions."

"No. It is just that I wish to ask questions and perhaps to point out some consequences of your theories which . . . you will forgive me? . . . you may not have thought of."

"Oh?"

"You see, Dr. Ralson, since you have explained your theories, I, too, know what you know. Yet I have no feeling about suicide."

"Belief is more than something intellectual, Doctor. You'd have to believe this with all your insides, which you don't."

"Do you not think perhaps it is rather a phenomenon of adaptation?"

"How do you mean?"

"You are not really a biologist, Dr. Ralson. And although you are very brilliant indeed in physics, you do not think of everything with respect to these bacterial cultures you use as analogies. You know that it is possible to breed bacterial strains that are resistant to penicillin or to almost any bacterial poison."

"Well?"

"The experimenters who breed us have been working with humanity for many generations, no? And this particular strain which they have been culturing for two centuries shows no sign of dying out spontaneously. Rather, it is a vigorous strain and a very infective one. Older high-culture strains were confined to single cities or to small areas and lasted only a generation or two. This one is spreading throughout the world. It is a *very* infective strain. Do you not think it may have developed penicillin immunity? In other words, the methods the experimenters use to wipe out the culture may not work too well any more, no?"

Ralson shook his head. "It's working on me."

"You are perhaps non-resistant. Or you have stumbled into a very high concentration of penicillin indeed. Consider all the people who have been trying to outlaw atomic warfare and to establish some form of world government and lasting peace. The effort has risen in recent years, without too awful results."

"It isn't stopping the atomic war that's coming."

"No, but maybe only a little more effort is all that is required. The peace-advocates do not kill themselves. More and more humans are immune to the experimenters. Do you know what they are doing in the laboratory?"

"I don't want to know."

"You *must* know. They are trying to invent a force field that will stop the atom bomb, Dr. Ralson, if I am culturing a virulent and pathological bacterium; then, even with all precautions, it may sometimes happen that I will start a plague. We may be bacteria to them, but we are dangerous to them, also, or they wouldn't wipe us out so carefully after each experiment.

"They are not quick, no? To them a thousand years is as a day, no? By the time they realize we are out of the culture, past the penicillin, it will be too late for them to stop us. They have brought us to the atom, and if we can only prevent ourselves from using it upon one another, we may turn out to be too much even for the experimenters."

Ralson rose to his feet. Small though he was, he was an inch and a half taller than Blaustein. "They are really working on a force field?"

"They are trying to. But they need you."

"No. I can't."

"They must have you in order that you might see what is obvious to you. It is not obvious to them. Remember, it is your help, or else—defeat of man by the experimenters."

Ralson took a few rapid steps away, staring into the blank, padded wall. He muttered, "But there must be that defeat. If they build a force field, it will mean death for all of them before it can be completed."

"Some or all of them may be immune, no? And in any case, it will be death for them anyhow. They are trying."

Ralson said, "I'll try to help them."

"Do you still want to kill yourself?"

"Yes."

"But you'll try not to, no?"

"I'll *try* not to, Doctor." His lip quivered. "I'll have to be watched."

* * *

Blaustein climbed the stairs and presented his pass to the guard in the lobby. He had already been inspected at the outer gate, but he, his pass, and its signature were now scrutinized once again. After a moment, the guard retired to his little booth and made a phone call. The answer satisfied him. Blaustein took a seat and, in half a minute, was up again, shaking hands with Dr. Grant.

"The President of the United States would have trouble getting in here, no?" said Blaustein.

The lanky physicist smiled. "You're right, if he came without warning."

They took an elevator which traveled twelve floors. The office to which Grant led the way had windows in three directions. It was sound-proofed and air-conditioned. Its walnut furniture was in a state of high polish.

Blaustein said, "My goodness. It is like the office of the chairman of a board of directors. Science is becoming big business."

Grant looked embarrassed. "Yes, I know, but government money flows easily and it is difficult to persuade a congressman that your work is important unless he can see, smell, and touch the surface shine."

Blaustein sat down and felt the upholstered seat give way slowly. He said, "Dr. Elwood Ralson has agreed to return to work."

"Wonderful. I was hoping you would say that. I was hoping that was why you wanted to see me." As though inspired by the news, Grant offered the psychiatrist a cigar, which was refused.

"However," said Blaustein, "he remains a very sick man. He will have to be treated carefully and with insight."

"Of course. Naturally."

"It's not quite as simple as you may think. I want to tell you something of Ralson's problems, so that you will really understand how delicate the situation is."

He went on talking and Grant listened first in concern, and then in astonishment. "But then the man is out of his head, Dr. Blaustein. He'll be of no use to us. He's crazy."

Blaustein shrugged. "It depends on how you define 'crazy.' It's a bad word; don't use it. He had delusions, certainly. Whether they will affect his peculiar talents one cannot know."

"But surely no sane man could possibly—"

"Please. Please. Let us not launch into long discussions on psychiatric definitions of sanity and so on. The man has delusions and, ordinarily, I would dismiss them from all consideration. It is just that I have been given to understand that the man's particular ability lies in his manner of proceeding to the solution of a problem by what seems to be outside ordinary reason. That is so, no?"

"Yes. That *must* be admitted."

"How can you and I judge then as to the worth of one of his conclusions. Let me ask you, do *you* have suicidal impulses lately?"

"I don't think so."

"And other scientists here?"

"No, of course not."

"I would suggest, however, that while research on the force field proceeds, the scientists concerned be watched here and at home. It might even be a good enough idea that they should not go home. Offices like these could be arranged to be a small dormitory—"

"Sleep at work. You would never get them to agree."

"Oh, yes. If you do not tell them the real reason but say it is for security purposes, they will agree. 'Security purposes' is a wonderful phrase these days, no? Ralson must be watched more than anyone."

"Of course."

"But all this is minor. It is something to be done to satisfy my conscience in case Ralson's theories are correct. Actually, I don't believe them. They *are* delusions, but once that is granted, it is necessary to ask what the causes of those delusions are. What is it in Ralson's mind, in his background, in his life that makes it so necessary for him to have these particular delusions? One cannot answer that simply. It may well take years of constant psychoanalysis to discover the answer. And until the answer is discovered, he will not be cured.

"But, meanwhile, we can perhaps make intelligent guesses. He has had an unhappy childhood, which, in one way or another, has brought him face to face with death in very unpleasant fashion. In addition, he has never been able to form associations with other children, or, as he grew older, with other men. He was always impatient with their slower forms of reasoning. Whatever difference there is between his mind and that of others, it has built a wall between him and society as strong as the force field you are trying to design. For similar reasons, he has been unable to enjoy a normal sex life. He has never married; he has had no sweethearts.

"It is easy to see that he could easily compensate to himself for this failure to be accepted by his social milieu by taking refuge in the thought that other human beings are inferior to himself. Which is, of course, true, as far as mentality is concerned. There are, of course, many, many facets to the human personality and in not all of them is he superior. No one is. Others, then, who are more prone to see merely what is inferior, just as he himself is, would not accept his affected pre-eminence of position. They would think him queer, even laughable, which would make it even more important to Ralson to prove how miserable and inferior the human species was. How could he better do that then to show that mankind was simply a form of bacteria to other superior creatures which experiment upon them. And then his impulses to suicide would be a wild desire to break away completely from being a man at all; to stop this identification with the miserable species he has created in his mind. You see?"

Grant nodded. "Poor guy."

"Yes, it is a pity. Had he been properly taken care of in childhood—Well, it is best for Dr. Ralson that he have no contact with any of the other men here. He is too sick to be trusted with them. You, yourself, must arrange to be the only man who will see him or speak to him. Dr. Ralson has agreed to that. He apparently thinks you are not as stupid as some of the others."

Grant smiled faintly. "That is agreeable to me."

"You will, of course, be careful. I would not discuss anything with him but his work. If he should volunteer information about his theories, which I doubt, confine yourself to something non-committal, and leave. And at all times, keep away anything that is sharp and pointed. Do not let him reach a window. Try to have his hands kept in view. You understand. I leave my patient in your care, Dr. Grant."

"I will do my best, Dr. Blaustein."

* * *

For two months, Ralson lived in a corner of Grant's office, and Grant lived with him. Gridwork had been built up before the windows, wooden furniture was removed and upholstered sofas brought in. Ralson did his thinking on the couch and his calculating on a desk pad atop a hassock.

The "Do Not Enter" was a permanent fixture outside the office. Meals were left outside. The adjoining men's room was marked off for private use and the door between it and the office removed. Grant switched to an electric razor. He made certain that Ralson took sleeping pills each night and waited till the other slept before sleeping himself.

And always reports were brought to Ralson. He read them while Grant watched and tried to seem not to watch.

Then Ralson would let them drop and stare at the ceiling, with one hand shading his eyes.

"Anything?" asked Grant.

Ralson shook his head from side to side.

Grant said, "Look, I'll clear the building during the swing shift. It's important that you see some of the experimental jigs we've been setting up."

They did so, wandering through the lighted, empty buildings like drifting ghosts, hand in hand. Always hand in hand. Grant's grip was tight. But after each trip, Ralson would still shake his head from side to side.

Half a dozen times he would begin writing; each time there wold be a few scrawls and then he would kick the hassock over on its side.

Until, finally, he began writing once again and covered half a page rapidly. Automatically, Grant approached. Ralson looked up, covering the sheet of paper with a trembling hand.

He said, "Call Blaustein."

"What?"

"I said, 'Call Blaustein.' Get him here. Now!"

Grant moved to the telephone.

Ralson was writing rapidly now, stopping only to brush wildly at his forehead with the back of a hand. It came away wet.

He looked up and his voice was cracked, "Is he coming?"

Grant looked worried. "He isn't at his office."

"Get him at his home. Get him wherever he is. *Use* that telephone. Don't play with it."

Grant used it; and Ralson pulled another sheet toward himself.

Five minutes later, Grant said, "He's coming. What's wrong? You're looking sick."

Ralson could speak only thickly, "No time— Can't talk—"

He was writing, scribbling, scrawling, shakily diagraming. It was as though he were driving his hands, fighting it.

"Dictate!" urged Grant. I'll write."

Ralson shook him off. His words were unintelligible. He held his wrist with his other hand, shoving it as though it were a piece of wood, and then he collapsed over the papers.

Grant edged them out from under and laid Ralson down on the couch. He hovered him restlessly and hopelessly until Blaustein arrived.

Blaustein took one look. "What happened?"

Grant said, "I think he's alive," but by that time Blaustein had verified that for himself, and Grant told him what had happened.

Blaustein used a hypodermic and they waited. Ralson's eyes were blank when they opened. He moaned.

Blaustein leaned close. "Ralson."

Ralson's hands reached out blindly and clutched at the psychiatrist. "Doc. Take me back."

"I will. Now. It is that you have the force field worked out, no?"

"It's on the papers. Grant, it's on the papers."

Grant had them and was leafing through them dubiously. Ralson said, weakly, "It's not *all* there. It's all I can write. You'll *have* to make it out of that. Take me back, Doc!"

"Wait," said Grant. He whispered urgently to Blaustein. "Can't you leave him here till we test this thing? I can't make out what most of this is. The writing is illegible. Ask him what makes him think this will work."

"Ask *him?*" said Blaustein, gently. "Isn't he the one who always knows?"

"Ask me, anyway," said Ralson, overhearing from where he lay on the couch. His eyes were suddenly wide and blazing.

They turned to him.

He said, "*They* don't want a force field. *They!* The experimenters! As long as I had no true grasp, things remained as they were. But I hadn't followed up that thought—*that* thought which is there in the papers—I hadn't followed it up for thirty seconds before I felt . . . I felt—Doctor—"

Blaustein said, "What is it?"

Ralson was whispering again, "I'm deeper in the penicillin. I could feel myself plunging in and in, the further I went with that. I've never been in . . . so deep. That's how I knew I was right. Take me away."

Blaustein straightened. "I'll have to take him away, Grant. There's no alternative. If you can make out what he's written, that's it. If you can't make it out, I can't help you. That man can do no more work in his field without dying, do you understand?"

"But," said Grant, "he's dying of something imaginary."

"All right. Say that he is. But he will be really dead just the same, no?"

Ralson was unconscious again and heard nothing of this. Grant looked at him somberly, then said, "Well, take him away, then."

* * *

Ten of the top men at the Institute watched glumly as slide after slide filled the illuminated screen. Grant faced them, expression hard and frowning.

He said, "I think the idea is simple enough. You're mathematicians and you're engineers. The scrawl may seem illegible, but it was done with meaning behind it. That meaning must somehow remain in the writing, distorted though it is. The first page is clear enough. It should be a good lead. Each one of you will look at every page over and over again. You're going to put down every possible version of each page as it seems it might be. You will work independently. I want no consultations."

One of them said, "How do you know it means *anything*, Grant?"

"Because those are Ralson's notes."

"*Ralson!* I thought he was—"

"You thought he was sick," said Grant. He had to shout over the rising hum of conversation. "I know. He is. That's the writing of a man who was nearly dead. It's all we'll ever get from Ralson, any more. Somewhere in that scrawl is the answer to the force field problem. If we can't find it, we may have to spend ten years looking for it elsewhere."

They bent to their work. The night passed. Two nights passed. Three nights—

Grant looked at the results. He shook his head. "I'll take your word for it that it is all self-consistent. I can't say I understand it."

Lowe, who, in the absence of Ralson, would readily have been rated the best nuclear engineer at the Institute, shrugged. "It's not exactly clear to me. If it works, he hasn't explained why."

"He had no time to explain. Can you build the generator as he describes it?"

"I could try."

'Would you look at all the other versions of the pages?"

"The others are definitely not self-consistent."

"Would you double-check?"

"Sure."

"And could you start construction anyway?"

"I'll get the shop started. But I tell you frankly that I'm pessimistic."

"I know. So am I."

* * *

The thing grew. Hal Ross, Senior Mechanic, was put in charge of the actual construction, and he stopped sleeping. At any hour of the day or night, he could be found at it, scratching his bald head.

He asked questions only once, "What is it, Dr. Lowe? Never saw anything like it. What's it supposed to do?"

Lowe said, "You know where you are, Ross. You know we don't ask questions here. Don't ask again."

Ross did not ask again. He was known to dislike the structure that was being built. He called it ugly and unnatural. But he stayed at it.

* * *

Blaustein called one day.

Grant said, "How's Ralson?"

"Not good. He wants to attend the testing of the Field Projector he designed."

Grant hesitated, "I suppose he should. It's his after all."

"I would have to come with him."

Grand looked unhappier. "It might be dangerous, you know. Even in a pilot test, we'd be playing with tremendous energies."

Blaustein said, "No more dangerous for us than for you."

"Very well. The list of observers will have to be cleared through the Commission and the F.B.I., but I'll put you in."

* * *

Blaustein looked about him. The field projector squatted in the very center of the huge testing laboratory, but all else had been cleared. There was no visible connection with the plutonium pile which served as energy-source, but from what the psychiatrist heard in scraps about him—he knew better than to ask Ralson—the connection was from beneath.

At first, the observers had circled the machine, talking in incomprehensibles, but they were drifting away now. The gallery was filling up. There were at least three men in generals' uniforms on the other side, and a real coterie of lower-scale military. Blaustein chose an unoccupied portion of the railing; for Ralson's sake, most of all.

He said, "Do you still think you would like to stay?"

It was warn enough within the laboratory, but Ralson was in his coat, with his collar turned up. It made little difference, Blaustein felt. He doubted that any of Ralson's former acquaintances would now recognize him.

Ralson said, "I'll stay."

Blaustein was pleased. He wanted to see the test. He turned again at a new voice.

"Hello, Dr. Blaustein."

For a minute, Blaustein did not place him, then he said, "Ah, Inspector Darrity. What are you doing here?"

"Just what you would suppose." He indicated the watchers. "There isn't any way you can weed them out so that you can be sure there won't be any mistakes. I once stood as near to Klaus Fuchs as I am standing to you." He tossed his pocketknife into the air and retrieved it with a dexterous motion.

"Ah, yes. Where shall one find perfect security? What man can trust even his own unconscious? And you will now stand near to me, no?"

"Might as well." Darrity smiled. "You were very anxious to get in here, weren't you?"

"Not for myself, Inspector. And would you put away the knife, please."

Darrity turned in surprise in the direction of Blaustein's gentle head-gesture. He put his knife away and looked at Blaustein's companion for the second time. He whistled softly.

He said, "Hello, Dr. Ralson."

Ralson croaked, "Hello."

Blaustein was not surprised at Darrity's reaction. Ralson had lost twenty pounds since returning to the sanatorium. His face was yellow and wrinkled; the face of a man who had suddenly become sixty.

Blaustein said, "Will the test be starting soon?"

Darrity said, "It looks as if they're starting now."

He turned and leaned on the rail. Blaustein took Ralson's elbow and began leading him away, but Darrity said, softly, "Stay here, Doc. I don't want you wandering about."

Blaustein looked across the laboratory. Men were standing about with the uncomfortable air of having turned half to stone. He could recognize Grant, tall and gaunt, moving his hand slowly to light a cigarette, then changing his mind and putting lighter and cigarette in his pocket. The young men at the control panels waited tensely.

Then there was a low humming and the faint smell of ozone filled the air.

Ralson said harshly, "Look!"

Blaustein and Darrity looked along the pointing finger. The projector seemed to flicker. It was as though there were heated air rising between it and them. An iron ball came swinging down pendulum fashion and passed through the flickering area.

"It slowed up, no?" said Blaustein, excitedly.

Ralson nodded. "They're measuring the height of rise on the other side to calculate the loss of momentum. Fools! I *said* it would work." He was speaking with obvious difficulty.

Blaustein said, "Just watch, Dr. Ralson. I would not allow myself to grow needlessly excited."

The pendulum was stopped in its swinging, drawn up. The flickering about the projector became a little more intense and the iron sphere arced down once again.

Over and over again, and each time the sphere's motion was slowed with more of a jerk. It made a clearly audible sound as it struck the flicker. And eventually, it *bounced.* First, soggily, as though it hit putty, and then ringingly, as though it hit steel, so that the noise filled the place.

They drew back the pendulum bob and used it no longer. The projector could hardly be seen behind the haze that surrounded it.

Grant gave an order and the odor of ozone was suddenly sharp and pungent. There was a cry from the assembled observers; each one exclaiming to his neighbor. A dozen fingers were pointing.

Blaustein leaned over the railing, as excited as the rest. Where the projector had been, there was now only a huge semi-globular mirror. It was perfectly and beautifully clear. He could see himself in it, a small man standing on a small balcony that curved up on each side. He could see the fluorescent lights reflected in spots of glowing illumination. It was wonderfully sharp.

He was shouting, "Look, Ralson. It is reflecting energy. It is reflecting light waves like a mirror. Ralson—"

He turned, "Ralson! Inspector, where is Ralson?"

"What?" Darrity whirled. "I haven't seen him."

He looked about, wildly. "Well, he won't get away. No way of getting out of here now. You take the other side." And then he clapped hand to thigh, fumbled for a moment in his pocket, and said, "My knife is gone."

Blaustein found him. He was inside the small office belonging to Hal Ross. It led off the balcony, but under the circumstances, of course, it had been deserted. Ross himself was not even an observer. A senior mechanic need not observe. But his office would do very well for the final end of the long fight against suicide.

Blaustein stood in the doorway for a sick moment, then turned. he caught Darrity's eye as the latter emerged from a similar office a hundred feet down the balcony. He beckoned, and Darrity came at a run.

* * *

Dr. Grant was trembling with excitement. He had taken two puffs at each of two cigarettes and trodden each underfoot thereafter. He was fumbling with the third now.

He was saying, "This is better than any of us could possibly have hoped. We'll have the gunfire test tomorrow. I'm sure of the result now, but we've planned it; we'll go through with it. We'll skip the small arms and start with the bazooka levels. Or maybe not. It might be necessary to construct a special testing structure to take care of the ricochet problem."

He discarded his third cigarette.

A general said, "We'd have to try a literal atom-bombing, of course."

"Naturally. Arrangements have already been made to build a mock-city at Eniwetok. We could build a generator on the spot and drop the bomb. There's be animals inside."

"And you really think if we set up a field in full power it would hold the bomb?"

"It's not just that, General. There'd be no noticeable field at all until the bomb is dropped. The radiation of the plutonium would have to energize the field before explosion. As we did here in the last step. That's the essence of it all."

"You know," said a Princeton professor, "I see disadvantages, too. When the field is on full, anything it protects is in total darkness, as far as the sun is concerned. Besides that, it strikes me that the enemy can adopt the practice of dropping harmless radioactive missiles to set off the field at frequent intervals. It would have nuisance value and be a considerable drain on our pile as well."

"Nuisances," said Grant, "can be survived. These difficulties will be met eventually, I'm sure, now that the main problem has been solved."

The British observer had worked his way toward Grant and was shaking hands. He said, "I feel better about London already. I cannot help but wish your government would allow me to see the complete plans. What I have seen strikes me as completely ingenious. It seems obvious now, of course, but how did anyone ever come to think of it?"

Grant smiled. "That question has been asked before with reference to Dr. Ralson's devices—"

He turned at the touch of a hand upon his shoulder. "Dr. Blaustein! I had nearly forgotten. Here, I want to talk to you."

He dragged the small psychiatrist to one side and hissed in his ear, "Listen, can you persuade Ralson to be introduced to these people? This is his triumph."

Blaustein said, "Ralson is dead."

"*What!*"

"Can you leave these people for a time?"

"Yes . . . yes— Gentlemen, you will excuse me for a few minutes?"

He hurried off with Blaustein.

The Federal men had already taken over. Unobtrusively, they barred the doorway to Ross's office. Outside there was the milling crowd discussing the answer to Alamogordo that they had just witnessed. Inside, unknown to them, was the death of the answerer. The G-man barrier divided to allow Grant and Blaustein to enter. It closed behind them again.

For a moment, Grant raised the sheet. He said, "He looks peaceful."

"I would say—happy," said Blaustein.

Darrity said, colorlessly, "The suicide weapon was my own knife. It was my negligence; it will be reported as such."

"No, no," said Blaustein, "that would be useless. He was my patient and I am responsible. In any case, he would not have lived another week, Since he invented the projector, he was a dying man."

Grant said, "How much of this has to be placed in the Federal files? Can't we forget all about his madness?"

"I'm afraid not, Dr. Grant," said Darrity.

"I have told him the whole story," said Blaustein, sadly.

Grant looked from one to the other. "I'll speak to the Director. I'll go to the President, if necessary. I don't see that there need be any mention of suicide or of madness. He'll get full publicity as inventor of the field projector. It's the least we can do for him." His teeth were gritting.

Blaustein said, "He left a note."

"A note?"

Darrity handed him a sheet of paper and said, "Suicides almost always do. This is one reason the doctor told me about what really killed Ralson."

The note was addressed to Blaustein and it went:

"The projector works; I knew it would. The bargain is done. You've got it and you don't need me any more. So I'll go. You needn't worry about the human race, Doc. You were right. They've bred us too long; they've taken too many chances. We're out of the culture now and they won't be able to stop us. I know. That's all I can say. I know."

He had signed his name quickly and then underneath there was one scrawled line, and it said:

"Provided enough men are penicillin-resistant."

Grant made a motion to crumple the paper, but Darrity held out a quick hand.

"For the record, Doctor," he said.

Grant gave it to him and said, "Poor Ralson! He died believing all that trash."

Blaustein nodded. "So he did. Ralson will be given a great funeral, I suppose, and the fact of his invention will be publicized without the madness and the suicide. But the government men will remain interested in his mad theories. They may not be so mad, no, Mr. Darrity?"

"That's ridiculous, Doctor," said Grant. "There isn't a scientist on the job who has shown the least uneasiness about it at all."

"Tell him, Mr. Darrity," said Blaustein.

Darrity said, "There has been another suicide. No, no, none of the scientists. No one with a degree. It happened this morning, and we investigated because we thought it might have some connection with today's test. There didn't seem any, and we were going to keep it quiet till the test was over. Only now there seems to be a connection.

"The man who died was just a guy with a wife and three kids. No reason to die. No history of mental illness. He threw himself under a car. We have witnesses, and it's certain he did it on purpose. He didn't die right away and they got a doctor to him. He was horribly mangled, but his last words were 'I feel much better now' and he died."

"But who was he?" cried Grant.

"Hal Ross. The guy who actually built the projector. The guy whose office this is."

Blaustein walked to the window. The evening sky was darkening into starriness.

He said, "The man knew nothing about Ralson's views. He had never spoken to Ralson, Mr. Darrity tells me. Scientists are probably resistant as a whole. They must be or they are quickly driven out of the profession. Ralson was an exception, a penicillin-sensitive who insisted on remaining. You see what happened to him. But what about the others; those who have remained in walks of life where there is no constant weeding out of the sensitive ones. How much of humanity *is* penicillin-resistant?"

"You *believe* Ralson?" asked Grant in horror.

"I don't really know."

Blaustein looked at the stars.

Incubators?

The Martian Way

From the doorway of the short corridor between the only two rooms in the travel-head of the spaceship, Mario Esteban Rioz watched sourly as Ted Long adjusted the video dials painstakingly. Long tried a touch clockwise, then a touch counter. The picture was lousy.

Rioz knew it would stay lousy. They were too far from Earth and at a bad position facing the Sun. But then Long would not be expected to know that. Rioz remained standing in the doorway for an additional moment, head bent to clear the upper lintel, body turned half sidewise to fit the narrow opening. Then he jerked into the gallery like a cork popping out of a bottle.

"What are you after?" he asked.

"I thought I'd get Hilder," said Long.

Rioz propped his rump on the corner of a table shelf. He lifted a conical can of milk from the companion shelf just above his head. Its point popped under pressure. He swirled it gently as he waited for it to warm.

"What for?" he said. He upended the cone and sucked noisily.

"Thought I'd listen."

"I think it's a waste of power."

Long looked up, frowning. "It's customary to allow free use of personal video sets."

"Within reason," retorted Rioz.

Their eyes met challengingly. Rioz had the rangy body, the gaunt, cheek-sunken face that was almost the hallmark of the Martian Scavenger, those Spacers who patiently haunted the space routes between Earth and Mars. Pale blue eyes were set keenly in the brown, lined face which, in turn, stood darkly out against the white surrounding synthofur that lined the up-turned collar of his leathtic space jacket.

Long was altogether paler and softer. He bore some of the marks of the Grounder, although no second-generation Martian could be a Grounder in the sense that Earthmen were. His own collar was thrown back and his dark brown hair freely exposed.

"What do you call within reason?" demanded Long.

Rioz's thin lips grew thinner. He said, "Considering that we're not even going to make expenses this trip, the way it looks, any power drain at all is outside reason."

Long said, "If we're losing money, hadn't you better get back to your post? It's your watch."

Rioz grunted and ran a thumb and forefinger over the stubble on his chin. He got up and trudged to the door, his soft, heavy boots muting the sound of his steps. He paused to look at the thermostat, then turned with a flare of fury.

"I *thought* it was hot. Where do you think you are?"

Long said, "Forty degrees isn't excessive."

"For you it isn't, maybe. But this is space, not a heated office at the iron mines." Rioz swung the thermostat control down to minimum with a quick thumb movement. "Sun's warm enough."

"The gallery isn't on Sunside."

"It'll percolate through, damn it."

Rioz stepped through the door and Long stared after him for a long moment, then turned back to the video. He did not turn up the thermostat.

The picture was still flickering badly, but it would have to do. Long folded a chair down out of the wall. He leaned forward waiting through the formal announcement, the momentary pause before the slow dissolution of the curtain, the spotlight picking out the well-known bearded figure which grew as it was brought forward until it filled the screen.

The voice, impressive even through the flutings and croakings induced by the electron storms of twenty millions of miles, began:

"Friends! My fellow citizens of Earth . . ."

2

Rioz's eye caught the flash of the radio signal as he stepped into the pilot room. For one moment, the palms of his hands grew clammy when it seemed to him that it was a radar pip; but that was only his guilt speaking. He should not have left the pilot room while on duty theoretically, though all Scavangers did it. Still, it was the standard nightmare, this business of a strike turning up during just those five minutes when one knocked off for a quick coffee because it seemed certain that space was clear. And the nightmare had been known to happen, too.

Rioz threw in the multi-scanner. It was a waste of power, but while he was thinking about it, he might as well make sure.

Space was clear except for the far-distant echoes from the neighboring ships on the scavanging line.

He hooked up the radio circuit, and the blond, long-nosed head of Richard Swenson, copilot of the next ship on the Marsward side, filled it.

"Hey, Mario," said Swenson.

"Hi. What's new?"

There was a second and a fraction of pause between that and Swenson's next comment, since the speed of electromagnetic radiation is not infinite.

"What a day I've *had*."

"Something happened?" Rioz asked.

"I had a strike."

"Well, good."

"Sure, if I'd roped it in," said Swenson morosely.

"What happened?"

"Damn it, I headed in the wrong direction."

Rioz knew better than to laugh. He said, "How did you do that?"

"It wasn't my fault. The trouble was the shell was moving way out of the ecliptic. Can you imagine the stupidity of a pilot that can't work the release maneuver decently? How was I to know? I got the distance of the shell and let it go at that. I just assumed its orbit was in the usual trajectory family. Wouldn't you? I started along what I thought was a good line of intersection and it was five minutes before I noticed the distance was still going up. The pigs were taking their sweet time returning. So then I took the angular projections of the thing, and it was too late to catch up with it."

"Any of the other boys getting it?"

"No. It's 'way out of the ecliptic and'll keep on going forever. That's not what bothers me so much. It was only an inner shell. But I hate to tell you how many tons of propulsion I wasted getting up speed and then getting back to station. You should have heard Canute."

Canute was Richard Swenson's brother and partner.

"Mad, huh?" said Rioz.

"Mad? Like to have killed me! But then we've been out five months now and it's getting kind of sticky. You know."

"I know."

"How are you doing, Mario?"

Rioz made a spitting gesture. "About that much this trip. Two shells in the last two weeks and I had to chase each one for six hours."

"Bit ones?"

"Are you kidding? I could have scaled them down to Phobos by hand. This is the worst trip I've ever had."

"How much longer are you staying?"

"For my part, we can quit tomorrow. We've only been out two months and it's got so I'm chewing Long out all the time."

There was a pause over and above the electromagnetic lag.

Swenson said, "What's he like, anyway? Long, I mean."

Rioz looked over his shoulder. He could hear the soft, crackly mutter of the video in the gallery. "I can't make him out. He says to me about a week after the start of the trip, 'Mario, why are you a Scavenger?' I just look at him and say, 'To make a living. Why do you suppose?' I mean, what the hell kind of a question is that? Why is anyone a Scavenger?

"Anyway, he says, 'That's not it, Mario.' *He's* telling *me*, you see. He says, 'You're a Scavenger because this is part of the Martian way.' "

Swenson said, "And what did he mean by that?"

Rioz shrugged. "I never asked him. Right now he's sitting in there listening to the ultra-microwave from Earth. He's listening to some Grounder called Hilder."

"Hilder? A Grounder politician, an Assembly man or something isn't he?"

"That's right. At least, I think that's right. Long is always doing things like that. He brought about fifteen pounds of books with him, all about Earth. Just plain dead weight, you know."

"Well, he's your partner. And talking about partners, I think I'll get back on the job. If I miss another strike, there'll be murder around here."

He was gone and Rioz leaned back. He watched the even green line that was the pulse scanner. He tried the multi-scanner a moment. Space was still clear.

He felt a little better. A bad spell is always worse if the Scavengers all about you are pulling in shell after shell; if the shells go spiraling down to the Phobos scrap forges with everyone's brand welded on except your own. Then, too, he had managed to work off some of his resentment toward Long.

It was a mistake teaming up with Long. It was always a mistake to team up with a tenderfoot. They thought what you wanted was conversation, especially Long, with his eternal theories about Mars and its great new role in human progress. That was the way he said it—Human Progress: the Martian Way; the New Creative Minority. And all the time what Rioz wanted wasn't talk, but a strike, a few shells to call their own.

At that, he hadn't any choice, really. Long was pretty well known down on Mars and made good pay as a mining engineer. He was a friend of Commissioner Sankov and he'd been out on one or two short scavenging missions before. You can't turn a fellow down flat before a tryout, even though it did look funny. Why should a mining engineer with a comfortable job and good money want to muck around in space?

Rioz never asked Long that question. Scavenger partners are forced too close together to make curiosity desirable, or sometimes even safe. But Long talked so much that he answered the question.

"I had to come out here, Mario," he said. "The future of Mars isn't in the mines; it's in space."

Rioz wondered how it would be to try a trip alone. Everyone said it was impossible. Even discounting lost opportunities when one man had to go off watch to sleep or attend to other things, it was well known that one man alone in space would become intolerably depressed in a relatively short while.

Taking a partner along made a six-month trip possible. A regular crew would be better, but no Scavenger could make money on a ship large enough to carry one. The capital it would take in propulsion alone!

Even two didn't find it exactly fun in space. Usually you had to change partners each trip and you could stay out longer with some than with others. Look at Richard and Canute Swenson. They teamed up every five or six trips because they were brothers. And yet whenever they did, it was a constantly mounting tension and antagonism after the first week.

Oh well. Space was clear. Rioz would feel a little better if he went back in the gallery and smoothed down some of the bickering with Long. He might as well show he was an old spacehand who took the irritations of space as they came.

He stood up, walked the three steps necessary to reach the short, narrow corridor that tied together the two rooms of the spaceship.

3

Once again Rioz stood in the doorway for a moment, watching. Long was intent on the flickering screen.

Rioz said gruffly, "I'm shoving up the thermostat. It's all right—we can spare the power."

Long nodded. "If you like."

Rioz took a hesitant step forward. Space was clear, so to hell with sitting and looking at a blank, green, pipless line. He said, "What's the Grounder been talking about?"

"History of space travel mostly. Old stuff, but he's doing it well. He's giving the whole works—color cartoons, trick photography, stills from old films, everything."

As if to illustrate Long's remarks, the bearded figure faded out of view, and a cross-sectional view of a spaceship flitted onto the screen. Hilder's voice continued, pointing out features of interest that appeared in schematic color. The communications system of the ship outlined itself in red as he talked about it, the storerooms, the patron micropile drive, the cybernetic circuits . . .

Then Hilder was back on the screen. "But this is only the travelhead of the ship. What moves it? What gets it off the Earth?"

Everyone knew what moved a spaceship, but Hilder's voice was like a drug. He made spaceship propulsion sound like the secret of the ages, like an ultimate revelation. Even Rioz felt a slight tingling of suspence, though he had spent the greater part of his life aboard ship.

Hilder went on. "Scientists call it different names. They call it the Law of Action and Reaction. Sometimes they call it Newton's Third Law. Sometimes they call it Conservation of Momentum. But we don't have to call it any name. We can just use our common sense. When we swim we push water backward and move forward ourselves. When we walk, we push back against the ground and move forward. When we fly a gyro-flivver, we push air backward and move forward.

"Nothing can move forward unless something else moves backward. It's the old principle of 'You can't get something for nothing.' "

"Now imagine a spaceship that weighs a hundred thousand tons lifting off Earth. To do that, something else must be moved downward. Since a spaceship is extremely heavy, a great deal of material must be moved downward. So much material, in fact, that there is no place to keep it all aboard ship. A special compartment must be built behind the ship to hold it."

Again Hilder faded out and the ship returned. It shrank and a truncated cone appeared behind it. In bright yellow, words appeared within it: MATERIAL TO BE THROWN AWAY.

"But now," said Hilder, "the total weight of the ship is much greater. You need still more propulsion and still more."

The ship shrank enormously to add on another larger shell and still another immense one. The ship proper, the travel-head, was a little dot on the screen, a glowing red dot.

Rioz said, "Hell, this is kindergarten stuff."

"Not to the people he's speaking to, Mario," replied Long. "Earth isn't Mars. There must be billions of Earth people who've never seen a spaceship; don't know the first thing about it."

Hilder was saying, "When the material inside the biggest shell is used up, the shell is detached. It's thrown away, too."

The outermost shell came loose, wobbled about the screen.

"Then the second one goes," said Hilder, "and then, if the trip is a long one, the last is ejected."

The ship was just a red dot now, with three shells shifting and moving, lost in space.

Hilder said, "These shells represent a hundred thousand tons of tungsten, magnesium, aluminum, and steel. They are gone forever from Earth. Mars is ringed by Scavengers, waiting along the routes of space travel, waiting for the cast-off shells, netting and branding them, saving them for Mars. Not one cent of payment reaches Earth for them. They are salvage. They belong to the ship that finds them."

Rioz said, "We risk our investment and our lives. If we don't pick them up, no one gets them. What loss is that to Earth?"

"Look," said Long, "he's been talking about nothing but the drain that Mars, Venus, and the Moon put on Earth. This is just another item of loss."

"They'll get their return. We're mining more iron every year."

"And most of it goes right back into Mars. If you can believe his figures, Earth has invested two hundred billion dollars in Mars and received back about five billion dollars' worth of iron. It's put five hundred billion dollars into the Moon and gotten back a little over twenty-five billion dollars of magnesium, titanium, and assorted light metals. It's put fifty billion dollars into Venus and gotten back nothing. And that's what the taxpayers of Earth are really interested in—tax money out; nothing in."

The screen was filled, as he spoke, with diagrams of the Scavengers on the route to Mars; little, grinning caricatures of ships, reaching out wiry, tenuous arms that groped for the tumbling, empty shells, seizing and shaking them in, branding tham MARS PROPERTY in glowing letters, then scaling them down to Phobos.

Then it was Hilder again. "They tell us eventually they will return it all to us. Eventually! Once they are a going concern! We don't know when that will be. A century from now? A thousand years? A million? 'Eventually.' Let's take them at their word. Someday they will give us back all our metals. Someday they will grow their own foods, use their own power, live their own lives.

"But one thing they can never return. Not in a hundred million years. *Water!*

"Mars has only a trickle of water because it is too small. Venus has no water at all because it is too hot. The Moon has none because it is too hot and too small. So Earth must supply not only drinking water and washing water for the Spacers, water to run their industries, water for the hydroponic factories they claim to be setting up—but even water to throw away by the millions of tons.

"What is the propulsive force that spaceships use? What is it they throw behind so that they can accelerate forward? Once it was the gases generated from explosives. That was very expensive. Then the proton micropile was invented—a cheap power source that could heat up any liquid until it was a gas under tremendous pressure. What is the cheapest and most plentiful liquid available? Why, water of course.

"Each spaceship leaves Earth carrying nearly a million tons—not pounds, *tons*—of water, for the sole purpose of driving it into space, so that it may speed up or slow down.

"Our ancestors burned the oil of Earth madly and willfully. They destroyed its coal recklessly. We despise and condemn them for that, but at least they had this excuse—they thought that when the need arose, substitutes would be found. And they were right. We have our plankton farms and our proton micropiles.

"But there is no substitute for water. None! There never can be. And when our descendants view the desert we will have made of Earth, what excuse will they find for us? When the droughts come and grow—"

Long leaned forward and turned off the set. He said, "That bothers me. The damn fool is deliberately—What's the matter?"

Rioz had risen uneasily to his feet. "I ought to be watching the pips."

"The hell with the pips." Long got up likewise, followed Rioz through the narrow corridor, and stood just inside the pilot room. "If Hilder carries this through, if he's got the guts to make a real issue out of it—*Wow!*"

He had seen it too. The pip was a Class A, racing after the outgoing signal like a greyhound after a mechanical rabbit.

Rioz was babbling, "Space was clear, I tell you, *clear.* For Mar's sake, Ted, don't just freeze on me. See if you can spot it visually."

Rioz was working speedily and with an efficiency that was the result of nearly twenty years of scavenging. He had the distance in two minutes. Then, remembering Swenson's experience, he measured the angle of declination and the radial velocity as well.

He yelled at Long, "One point seven six radians. You can't miss it, man."

Long held his breath as he adjusted the vernier. "It's only half a radian off the Sun. It'll only be crescent-lit."

He increased magnification as rapidly as he dared, watching for the one "star" that changed position and grew to have a form, revealing itself to be no star.

"I'm starting, anyway," said Rioz. "We can't wait."

"I've got it. I've got it." Magnification was still too small to give it a definite shape, but the dot Long watched was brightening and dimming rhythmically as the shell rotated and caught sunlight on cross sections of different sizes.

"Hold on."

The first of many fine spurts of steam squirted out of the proper vents, leaving long trails of micro-crystals of ice gleaming mistily in the pale beams of the distant Sun. They thinned out for a hundred miles or so. One spurt, then another, then another, as the Scavenger ship moved out of its stable trajectory and took up a course tangential to that of the shell.

"It's moving like a comet at perihelion!" yelled Rioz. "Those damned Grounder pilots knock the shells off that way on purpose. I'd like to—"

He swore his anger in a frustrated frenzy as he kicked steam backward and backward recklessly, till the hydraulic cushioning of his chair had soughed back a full foot and Long had found himself all but unable to maintain his grip on the guard rail.

"Have a heart," he begged.

But Rioz had his eye on the pips. "If you can't take it, man, stay on Mars!" The steam spurts continued to boom distantly.

The radio came to life. Long managed to lean forward through what seemed like molasses and closed contact. It was Swenson, eyes glaring.

Swenson yelled, "Where the hell are you guys going? You'll be in my sector in ten seconds."

Rioz said, "I'm chasing a shell."

"In *my* sector?"

"It started in mine and you're not in position to get it. Shut off that radio, Ted."

The ship thundered through space, a thunder that could be heard only within the hull. And then Rioz cut the engines in stages large enough to make Long flail forward. The sudden silence was more ear-shattering than the noise that had preceded it.

Rioz said, "All right. Let me have the 'scope."

They both watched. The shell was a definite truncated cone now, tumbling with slow solemnity as it passed along among the stars.

"It's a Class A shell, all right," said Rioz with satisfaction. A giant among shells, he thought. It would put them into the black.

Long said, "We've got another pip on the scanner. I think it's Swenson taking after us."

Rioz scarcely gave it a glance. "He won't catch us."

The shell grew larger still, filling the visiplate.

Rioz's hands were on the harpoon lever. He waited, adjusted the angle microscopically twice, played out the length allotment. Then he yanked, tripping the release.

For a moment, nothing happened. Then a metal mesh cable snaked out onto the visiplate, moving toward the shell like a striking cobra. It made contact, but it did not hold. If it had, it would have snapped instantly like a cobweb strand. The shell was turning with a rotational momentum amounting to thousands of tons. What the cable did do was set up a powerful magnetic field that acted as a brake on the shell.

Another cable and another lashed out. Rioz sent them out in an almost heedless expenditure of energy.

"I'll get this one! Mars, I'll get this one!"

With some two dozen cables stretching between ship and shell, he desisted. The shell's rotational energy, converted by breaking into heat, had raised its temperature to a point where its radiation could be picked up by the ship's meters.

Long said, "Do you want me to put our brand on?"

"Suits me. But you don't have to if you don't want to. It's my watch."

"I don't mind."

Long clambered into his suit and went out the lock. It was the surest sign of his newness to the game that he could count the number of times he had been out in space in a suit. This was the fifth time.

He went out along the nearest cable, hand over hand, feeling the vibration of the mesh against the metal of his mitten.

He burned their serial number in the smooth metal of the shell.

There was nothing to oxidize the steel in the emptiness of space. It simply melted and vaporized, condensing some feet away from the energy beam, turning the surface it touched into a gray, powdery dullness.

Long swung back toward the ship.

Inside again, he took off his helmet, white and thick with frost that collected as soon as he had entered.

The first thing he heard was Swenson's voice coming over the radio in this almost unrecognizable rage: ". . . straight to the Commissioner. Damn it, there are rules to this game!"

Rioz sat back, unbothered. "Look, it hit my sector. I was late spot ting it and I chased it into yours. You couldn't have gotten it with Mars for a backstop. That's all there is to it—You back, Long?"

He cut contact.

The signal button raged at him, but he paid no attention.

"He's going to the Commissioner?" Long asked.

"Not a chance. He just goes on like that because it breaks the monotony. He doesn't mean anything by it. He knows it's our shell. And how do you like that hunk of stuff, Ted?"

"Pretty good."

"Pretty good? It's terrific! Hold on. I'm setting it swinging."

The side jets spat steam and the ship started a slow rotation about the shell. The shell followed it. In thirty minutes, they were a gigantic bolo spinning in emptiness. Long checked the *Ephemeris* for the position of Deimos.

At a precisely calculated moment, the cables released their magnetic field and the shell went streaking off tangentially in a trajectory that would, in a day or so, bring it within pronging distance of the shell stores on the Martian satellite.

Rioz watched it go. He felt good. He turned to Long. "This is one fine day for us."

"What about Hilder's speech?" asked Long.

"What? Who? Oh, that. Listen, if I had to worry about every thing some damned Grounder said, I'd never get any sleep. Forget it."

"I don't think we should forget it."

"You're nuts. Don't bother me about it, will you? Get some sleep instead."

4

Ted Long found the breadth and height of the city's main thoroughfare exhilarating. It had been two months since the Commissioner had declared a moratorium on scavenging and had pulled all ships out of space, but this feeling of a stretched-out vista had not stopped thrilling Long. Even the thought that the moratorium was called pending a decision on the part of Earth to enforce its new insistence on water economy, by deciding upon a ration limit for scavenging, did not cast him entirely down.

The roof of the avenue was painted a luminous light blue, perhaps as an old-fashioned imitation of Earth's sky. Ted wasn't sure. The walls were lit with the store windows that pierced it.

Off in the distance, over the hum of traffic and the sloughing noise of people's feet passing him, he could hear the intermittent blasting as new channels were being bored into Mars' crust. All his life he remembered such blastings. The ground he walked on had been part of solid, unbroken rock when he was born. The city was growing and would keep on growing—if Earth would only let it.

He turned off at a cross street, narrower, not quite as brilliantly lit, shop windows giving way to apartment houses, each with is row of lights along the front facade. Shoppers and traffic gave way to slower-paced individuals and to squawling youngsters who had as yet evaded the maternal summons to the evening meal.

At the last minute, Long remembered the social amenities and stopped off at a corner water store.

He passed over his canteen. "Fill 'er up."

The plump storekeeper unscrewed the cap, cocked an eye into the opening. He shook it a little and let it gurgle. "Not much left," he said cheerfully.

"No," agreed Long.

The storekeeper trickled water in, holding the neck of the canteen close to the hose tip to avoid spillage. The volume gauge whirred. He screwed the cap back on.

Long passed over the coins and took his canteen. It clanked against his hip now with a pleasing heaviness. It would never do to visit a family without a full canteen. Among the boys, it didn't matter. Not as much, anyway.

He entered the hallway of No. 27, climbed a short flight of stairs, and paused with his thumb on the signal.

The sound of voices could be heard quite plainly.

One was a woman's voice, somewhat shrill. "It's all right for you to have your Scavenger friends here, isn't it? I'm supposed to be thankful you manage to get home two months a year. Oh, it's quite enough that you spend a day or two with me. After that, it's the Scavengers again."

"I've been home for a long time now," said a male voice, "and this is business. For Mars' sake, let up, Dora. They'll be here soon."

Long decided to wait a moment before signaling. It might give them a chance to hit a more neutral topic.

"What do I care if they come?" retorted Dora. "Let them hear me. And I'd just as soon the Commissioner kept the moratorium on permanently. You hear me?"

"And what would we live on?" came the male voice hotly. "You tell me that."

"I'll tell you. You can make a decent, honorable living right here on Mars, just like everybody else. I'm the only one in this apartment house that's a Scavenger widow. That's what I am—a widow. I'm worse than a widow, because if I were a widow, I'd at least have a chance to marry someone else—What did you say?"

"Nothing. Nothing at all."

"Oh, I know what you said. Now listen here, Dick Swenson—"

"I only said," cried Swenson, "that now I know why Scavengers usually don't marry."

"You shouldn't have either. I'm tired of having every person in the neighborhood pity me and smirk and ask when you're coming home. Other people can be mining engineers and administrators and even tunnel borers. At least tunnel borers' wives have a decent home life and their children don't grow up like vagabonds. Peter might as well not have a father—"

A thin boy-soprano voice made its way through the door. It was somewhat more distant, as though it were in another room. "Hey, Mom, what's a vagabond?"

Dora's voice rose a notch. "Peter! You keep your mind on your homework."

Swenson said in a low voice, "It's not right to talk this way in front of the kid. What kind of notions will he get about me?"

"Stay home then and teach him better notions."

Peter's voice called out again. "Hey, Mom, I'm going to be a Scavenger when I grow up."

Footsteps sounded rapidly. There was a momentary hiatus in the sounds, then a piercing, "Mom! Hey, Mom! Leggo my ear! What did I do?" and a snuffling silence.

Long seized the chance. He worked the signal vigorously.

Swenson opened the door, brushing down his hair with both hands.

"Hello, Ted," he said in a subdued voice. Then loudly, "Ted's here, Dora. Where's Mario, Ted?"

Long said, "He'll be here in a while."

Dora came bustling out of the next room, a small, dark woman with a pinched nose, and hair, just beginning to show touches of gray, combed off the forehead.

"Hello, Ted. Have you eaten?"

"Quite well, thanks. I haven't interrupted you, have I?"

"Not at all. We finished ages ago. Would you like some coffee?"

"I think so." Ted unslung his canteen and offered it.

"Oh, goodness, that's all right. We've plenty of water."

"I insist."

"Well, then—"

Back into the kitchen she went. Through the swinging door, Long caught a glimpse of dishes sitting in Secoterg, the "waterless cleaner that soaks up and absorbs grease and dirt in a twinkling. One ounce of water will rinse eight square feet of dish surface clean as clean. Buy Secoterg. Secoterg just cleans it right, makes your dishes shiny bright, does away with water waste—"

The tune started whining through his mind and Long crushed it with speech. He said, "How's Pete?"

"Fine, fine. The kid's in the fourth grade now. You know I don't get to see him much. Well, sir, when I came back last time, he looked at me and said . . ."

It went on for a while and wasn't too bad as bright sayings of bright children as told by dull parents go.

The door signal burped and Mario Rioz came in, frowning and red.

Swenson stepped to him quickly. "Listen, don't say anything about shell-snaring. Dora still remembers the time you fingered a Class A shell out of my territory and she's in one of her moods now."

"Who the hell wants to talk about shells?" Rioz slung off a fur-lined jacket, threw it over the back of the chair, and sat down.

Dora came through the swinging door, viewed the newcomer with a synthetic smile, and said, "Hello, Mario. Coffee for you, too?"

"Yeah," he said, reaching automatically for his canteen.

"Just use some more of my water, Dora," said Long quickly. "He'll owe it to me."

"Yeah," said Rioz.

"What's wrong, Mario?" asked Long.

Rioz said heavily, "Go on. Say you told me so. A year ago when Hilder made that speech, you told me so. Say it."

Long shrugged.

Rioz said, "They've set up the quota. Fifteen minutes ago the news came out."

"Well?"

"Fifty thousand tons of water per trip."

"What?" yelled Swenson, burning. "You can't get off Mars with fifty thousand!"

"That's the figure. It's a deliberate piece of gutting. No more scavenging."

Dora came out with the coffee and set it down all around.

"What's all this about no more scavenging?" She sat down very firmly and Swenson looked helpless.

"It seems," said Long, "that they're rationing us at fifty thousand tons and that means we can't make any more trips."

"Well, what of it?" Dora sipped her coffee and smiled gaily. "If you want my opinion, it's a good thing. It's time all you Scavengers found yourselves a nice, steady job here on Mars. I mean it. It's no life to be running all over space—"

"Please, Dora," said Swenson.

Rioz came close to a snort.

Dora raised her eyebrows. "I'm just giving my opinions."

Long said, "Please feel free to do so. But I would like to say something. Fifty thousand is just a detail. We know that Earth—or at least Hilder's party—wants to make political capital out of a campaign for water economy, so we're in a bad hole. We've got to get water somehow or they'll shut us down altogether, right?"

"Well, sure," said Swenson.

"But the question is how, right?"

"If it's only getting water," said Rioz in a sudden gush of words, "there's only one thing to do and you know it. If the Grounders won't give us water, we'll take it. The water doesn't belong to them just because their fathers and grandfathers were too damned sick-yellow ever to leave their fat planet. Water belongs to people wherever they are. We're people and the water's ours, too. We have a right to it."

"How do you propose taking it?" asked Long.

"Easy! They've got oceans of water on Earth. They can't post a guard over every square mile. We can sink down on the night side of the planet any time we want, fill our shells, then get away. How can they stop us?"

"In half a dozen ways, Mario. How do you spot shells in space up to distances of a hundred thousand miles? One thin metal shell in all that space. How? By radar. Do you think there's no radar on Earth? Do you think that if Earth ever gets the notion we're engaged in waterlegging, it won't be simple for them to set up a radar network to spot ships coming in from space?"

Dora broke in indignantly. "I'll tell you one thing, Mario Rioz. My husband isn't going to be part of any raid to get water to keep up his scavenging with."

"It isn't just scavenging," said Mario. "Next they'll be cutting down on everything else. We've got to stop them now."

"But we don't need their water, anyway," said Dora. "We're not the Moon or Venus. We pipe enough water down from the polar caps for all we need. We have a water tap right in this apartment. There's one in every apartment on this block."

Long said, "Home use is the smallest part of it. The mines use water. And what do we do about the hydroponic tanks?"

"That's right," said Swenson. "What about the hydroponic tanks, Dora? They've got to have water and it's about time we arranged to grow our own fresh food instead of having to live on the condensed crud they ship us from Earth."

"Listen to him," said Dora scornfully. "What do you know about fresh food? You've never eaten any."

"I've eaten more than you think. Do you remember those carrots I picked up once?"

"Well, what was so wonderful about them? If you ask me, good baked protomeal is much better. And healthier, too. It just seems to be the fashion now to be talking fresh vegetables because they're increasing taxes for these hydroponics. Besides, all this will blow over."

Long said, "I don't think so. Not by itself, anyway. Hilder will probably be the next Co-ordinator, and then things may really get bad. If they cut down on food shipments, too—"

"Well, then," shouted Rioz, "what do we do? I still say take it! Take the water!"

"And I say we can't do that, Mario. Don't you see that what you're suggesting is the Earth way, the Grounder way? You're trying to hold on to the umbilical cord that ties Mars to Earth. Can't you get away from that? Can't you see the Martian way?"

"No, I can't. Suppose you tell me."

"I will, if you'll listen. When we think about the Solar System, what do we think about? Mercury, Venus, Earth, Moon, Mars, Phobos, and Deimos. There you are—seven bodies, that's all. But that doesn't represent 1 per cent of the Solar System. We Martians are right at the edge of the other 99 per cent. Out there, farther from the Sun, there's unbelievable amounts of water!"

The others stared.

Swenson said uncertainly, "You mean the layers of ice on Jupiter and Saturn?"

"Not that specifically, but it *is* water, you'll admit. A thousand-mile-thick layer of water is a lot of water."

"But it's all covered up with layers of ammonia or—or something, isn't it?" asked Swenson. "Besides, we can't land on the major planets."

"I know that," said Long, "but I haven't said that was the answer. The major planets aren't the only objects out there. What about the asteroids and the satellites? Vesta is a two-hundred-mile-diameter asteroid that's hardly more than a chunk of ice. One of the moons of Saturn is mostly ice. How about that?"

Rioz said, "Haven't you ever been in space, Ted?"

"You know I have. Why do you ask?"

"Sure, I know you have, but you still talk like a Grounder. Have you thought of the distances involved? The average asteroid is a hundred twenty million miles from Mars at the closest. That's twice the Venus-Mars hip and you know that hardly any liners do even that in one jump. They usually stop off at Earth or the Moon. After all, how long do you expect anyone to stay in space, man?"

"I don't know. What's your limit?"

"You know the limit. You don't have to ask me. It's six months. That's handbook data. After six months, if you're still in space, you're psychotherapy meat. Right, Dick?"

Swenson nodded.

"And that's just the asteroids," Rioz went on. "From Mars to Jupiter is three hundred thirty million miles, and to Saturn it's seven hundred million. How can anyone handle that kind of distance? Suppose you hit standard velocity or, to make it even, say you get up to a good two hundred kilomiles an hour. It would take you—let's see, allowing time for acceleration and deceleration—abut six or seven months to get to Jupiter and nearly a year to get to Saturn. Of course, you could hike the speed to a million miles an hour, theoretically, but where would you get the water to do that?"

"Gee," said a small voice attached to a smutty nose and round eyes. "Saturn!"

Dora whirled in her chair. "Peter, march right back into your room!"

"Aw, Ma."

"Don't 'Aw, Ma' me." She began to get out of the chair, and Peter scuttled away.

Swenson said, "Say, Dora, why don't you keep him company for a while? It's hard to keep his mind on homework if we're all out here talking."

Dora smiled obstinately and stayed put. "I'll sit right here until I find out what Ted Long is thinking of. I tell you right now I don't like the sound of it."

Swenson said nervously, "Well, never mind Jupiter and Saturn. I'm sure Ted isn't figuring on that. But what about Vesta? We could make it in ten or twelve weeks there and the same back. And two hundred miles in diameter. That's four million cubic miles of ice!"

"So what?" said Rioz. "What do we do on Vesta? Quarry the ice? Set up mining machinery? Say, do you know how long that would take?"

Long said, "I'm talking about Saturn, not Vesta."

Rioz addressed an unseen audience. "I tell him seven hundred million miles and he keeps on talking."

"All right," said Long, "suppose you tell me how you know we can only stay in space six months, Mario?"

"It's common knowledge, damn it."

"Because it's in the *Handbook of Space Flight*. It's data compiled by Earth scientists from experience with Earth pilots and space-men. You're still thinking Grounder style. You won't think the Martian way."

"A Martian may be a Martian, but he's still a man."

"But how can you be so blind? How many times have you fellows been out for over six months without a break?"

Rioz said, "That's different."

"Because you're Martians? Because you're professional Scavengers?"

"No. Because we're not on a flight. We can put back for Mars any time we want to."

"But you *don't* want to. That's my point. Earthmen have tremendous ships with libraries of films, with a crew of fifteen plus passengers. Still, they can only stay out six months maximum. Martian Scavengers have a two-room ship with only one partner. But we can stick it out more than six months."

Dora said, "I suppose you want to stay in a ship for a year and go to Saturn."

"Why not, Dora?" said Long. "We can do it. Don't you see we can? Earthmen can't. They've got a real world. They've got open sky and fresh food, all the air and water they want. Getting into a ship is a terrible change for them. More than six months is too much for them for that very reason. Martians are different. We've been living on a ship our entire lives.

"That's all Mars is—a ship. It's just a big ship forty-five hundred miles across with one tiny room in it occupied by fifty thousand people. It's closed in like a ship. We breathe packaged air and drink packaged water, which we repurify over and over. We eat the same food rations we eat aboard ship. When we get into a ship, it's the same thing we've known all our lives. We can stand it for a lot more than a year if we have to."

Dora said, "Dick, too?"

"We all can."

"Well, Dick can't. It's all very well for you, Ted Long, and this shell stealer here, this Mario, to talk about jaunting off for a year. You're not married. Dick is. He has a wife and he has a child and that's enough for him. He can just get a regular job right here on Mars. Why, my goodness, suppose you go to Saturn and find there's no water there. How'll you get back? Even if you had water left, you'd be out of food. It's the most ridiculous thing I ever heard of."

"No. Now listen," said Long tightly. "I've thought this thing out. I've talked to Commissioner Sankow and he'll help. But we've got to have ships and men. I can't get them. The men won't listen to me. I'm green. You two are known and respected. You're veterans. If you back me, even if you don't go yourselves, if you'll just help me sell this thing to the rest, get volunteers—"

"First," said Rioz grumpily, "you'll have to do a lot more explaining. Once we get to Saturn, where's the water?"

"That's the beauty of it," said Long. "That's why it's got to be Saturn. The water there is just floating around in space for the taking."

5

When Hamish Sankov had come to Mars, there was no such thing as a native Martian. Now there were two-hundred-odd babies whose grandfathers had been born on Mars—native in the third generation.

When he had come as a boy in his teens, Mars had been scarcely more than a huddle of grounded spaceships connected by sealed underground tunnels. Through the years, he had seen buildings grow and burrow widely, thrusting blunt snouts up into the thin, unbreathable atmosphere. He had seen huge storage depots spring up into which spaceships and their loads could be swallowed whole. He had seen the mines grow from nothing to a huge gouge in the Martian crust, while the population of Mars grew from fifty to fifty thousand.

It made him feel old, these long memories—they and the even dimmer memories induced by the presence of this Earthman before him. His visitor brought up those long-forgotten scraps of thought about a soft-warm world that was as kind and gentle to mankind as the mother's womb.

The Earthman seemed fresh from that womb. Not very tall, not very lean; in fact, distinctly plump. Dark hair with a neat little wave in it, a neat little mustache, and neatly scrubbed skin. His clothing was right in style and as fresh and neatly turned as plastek could be.

Sankov's own clothes were of Martian manufacture, serviceable and clean, but many years behind the times. His face was craggy and lined, his hair was pure white, and his Adam's apple wobbled when he talked.

The Earthman was Myron Digby, member of Earth's General Assembly. Sankov was Martian Commissioner.

Sankov said, "This all hits us hard, Assemblyman."

"It's hit most of us hard, too, Commissioner."

"Uh-huh. Can't honestly say then that I can make it out. Of course, you understand, I don't make out that I can understand Earth ways, for all that I was born there. Mars is a hard place to live, Assemblyman, and you have to understand that. It takes a lot of shipping space just to bring us food, water, and raw materials so we can live. There's not much room left for books and news films. Even video programs can't reach Mars, except for about a month when Earth is in conjunction, and even then nobody has much time to listen.

"My office gets a weekly summary film from Planetary Press. Generally, I don't have time to pay attention to it. Maybe you'd call us provincial, and you'd be right. When something like this happens, all we can do is kind of helplessly look at each other."

Digby said slowly, "You can't mean that your people on Mars haven't heard of Hilder's anti-Waster campaign."

"No, can't exactly say that. There's a young Scavenger, son of a good friend of mine who died in space"—Sankov scratched the side of his neck doubtfully—"who makes a hobby out of reading up on Earth history and things like that. He catches video broadcasts when he's out in space and he listened to this man Hilder. Near as I can make out, that was the first talk Hilder made about Wasters.

"The young fellow came to me with that. Naturally, I didn't take him very serious. I kept an eye on the Planetary Press films for a while after that, but there wasn't much mention of Hilder and what there was made him out to look pretty funny."

"Yes, Commissioner," said Digby, "it all seemed quite a joke when it started."

Sankov stretched out a pair of long legs to one side of his desk and crossed them at the ankles. "Seems to me it's still pretty much of a joke. What's his argument? We're using up water. Has he tried looking at some figures? I got them all here. Had them brought to me when this committee arrived.

"Seems that Earth has four hundred million cubic miles of water in its oceans and each cubic mile weighs four and a half billion tons. That's a lot of water. Now we use some of that heap in space flight. Most of the thrust is inside Earth's gravitational field, and that means the water thrown out finds its way back to the oceans. Hilder doesn't figure that in. When he says a million tons of water is used up per flight, he's a liar. It's less than a hundred thousand tons.

"Suppose, now, we have fifty thousand flights a year. We don't, of course; not even fifteen hundred. But let's say there are fifty thousand. I figure there's going to be considerable expansion as time goes on. With fifty thousand flights, one cubic mile of water would be lost to space each year. That means that in a million years, Earth would lose *one quarter of 1 per cent* of its total water supply!"

Digby spread his hands, palms upward, and let them drop. "Commissioner, Interplanetary Alloys has used figures like that in their campaign against Hilder, but you can't fight a tremendous, emotion-filled drive with cold mathematics. This man Hilder has invented a name, 'Wasters.' Slowly he has build this name up into a gigantic conspiracy; a gang of brutal, profit-seeking wretches raping Earth for their own immediate benefit.

"He has accused the government of being riddled with them, the Assembly of being dominated by them, the press of being owned by them. None of this, unfortunately, seems ridiculous to the average man. He knows all too well what selfish men can do to Earth's resources. He knows what happened to Earth's oil during the Time of Troubles, for instance, and the way topsoil was ruined.

"When a farmer experiences a drought, he doesn't care that the amount of water lost in space flight isn't a droplet in a fog as far as

Earth's over-all water supply is concerned. Hilder has given him something to blame and that's the strongest possible consolation for disaster. He isn't going to give that up for a diet of figures."

Sankov said, "That's where I get puzzled. Maybe it's because I don't know how things work on Earth, but it seems to me that there aren't just droughty farmers there. As near as I could make out from the news summaries, these Hilder people are a minority. Why is it Earth goes along with a few farmers and some crackpots that egg them on?"

"Because, Commissioner, there are such things as worried human beings. The steel industry sees that an era of space flight will stress increasingly the light, nonferrous alloys. The various miners' unions worry about extraterrestrial competition. Any Earthman who can't get aluminum to build a prefab is certain that it is because the aluminum is going to Mars. I know a professor of archaeology who's an anti-Waster because he can't get a government grant to cover his excavations. He's convinced that all government money is going into rocketry research and space medicine and he resents it."

Sankov said, "That doesn't sound like Earth people are much different from us here on Mars. But what about the General Assembly? Why do they have to go along with Hilder?"

Digby smiled sourly. "Politics isn't pleasant to explain. Hilder introduced this bill to set up a committee to investigate waste in space flight. Maybe three fourths or more of the General Assembly was against such an investigation as an intolerable and useless extension of bureaucracy—which it is. But then how could any legislator be against a mere investigation of waste? It would sound as though he had something to fear or to conceal. It would sound as though he were himself profiting from waste. Hilder is not in the least afraid of making such accusations, and whether true or not, they would be a powerful factor with the voters in the next election. The bill passed.

"And then there came the question of appointing the members of the committee. Those who were against Hilder shied away from membership, which would have meant decisions that would be continually embarrassing. Remaining on the side lines would make that one that much less a target for Hilder. The result is that I am the only member of the committee who is outspokenly anti-Hilder and it may cost me re-election."

Sankov said, "I'd be sorry to hear that, Assemblyman. It looks as though Mars didn't have as many friends as we thought we had. We wouldn't like to lose one. But if Hilder wins out, what's he after, anyway?"

"I should think," said Digby, "that that is obvious. He wants to be the next Global Co-ordinator."

"Think he'll make it?"

"If nothing happens to stop him, he will."

"And then what? Will he drop this Waster campaign then?"

"I can't say. I don't know if he's laid his plans past the Co-ordinacy. Still, if you want my guess, he couldn't abandon the campaign and maintain his popularity. It's gotten out of hand."

Sankov scratched the side of his neck. "All right. In that case, I'll ask you for some advice. What can we folks on Mars do? You know Earth. You know the situation. We don't. Tell us what to do."

Digby rose and stepped to the window. He looked out upon the low domes of other buildings; red, rocky, completely desolate plain in between; a purple sky and a shrunken sun.

He said, without turning, "Do you people really like it on Mars?"

Sankov smiled. "Most of us don't exactly know any other world, Assemblyman. Seems to me Earth would be something queer and uncomfortable to them."

"But wouldn't Martians get used to it? Earth isn't hard to take after this. Wouldn't your people learn to enjoy the privilege of breathing air under an open sky? You once lived on Earth. You remember what it was like."

"I sort of remember. Still, it doesn't seem to be easy to explain. Earth is just there. It fits people and people fit it. People take Earth the way they find it. Mars is different. It's sort of raw and doesn't fit people. People got to make something out of it. They got to *build* a world, and not take what they find. Mars isn't much yet, but we're building, and when we're finished, we're going to have just what we like. It's sort of a great feeling you know you're building a world. Earth would be kind of unexciting after that."

The Assemblyman said, "Surely the ordinary Martian isn't such a philosopher that he's content to live this terribly hard life for the sake of a future that must be hundreds of generations away."

"No-o, not just like that." Sankov put his right ankle on his left knee and cradled it as he spoke. "Like I said, Martians are a lot like Earthmen, which means they're sort of human beings, and human beings don't go in for philosophy much. Just the same, there's something to living in a growing world, whether you think about it much or not.

"My father used to send me letters when I first came to Mars. He was an accountant and he just sort of stayed an accountant. Earth wasn't much different when he died from what it was when he was born. He didn't see anything happen. Every day was like every other day, and living was just a way of passing time until he died.

"On Mars, it's different. Every day there's something new—the city's bigger, the ventilation system gets another kick, the water lines from the poles get slicked up. Right now, we're planning to set up a news-film association of our own. We're going to call it Mars Press. If you haven't lived when things are growing all about you, you'll never understand how wonderful it feels.

"No, Assemblyman, Mars is hard and tough and Earth is a lot more comfortable, but seems to me if you take our boys to Earth, they'll be unhappy. They probably wouldn't be able to figure out why, most of them, but they'd feel lost; lost and useless. Seems to me lots of them would never make the adjustment."

Digby turned away from the window and the smooth, pink skin of his forehead was creased into a frown. "In that case, Commissioner, I am sorry for you. For all of you."

"Why?"

"Because I don't think there's anything your people on Mars can do. Or the people on the Moon or Venus. It won't happen now; maybe it won't happen for a year or two, or even for five years. But pretty soon you'll all have to come back to Earth, unless—"

Sankov's white eyebrows bent low over his eyes. "Well?"

"Unless you can find another source of water besides the planet Earth."

Sankov shook his head. "Don't seem likely, does it?"

"Not very."

"And except for that, seems to you there's no chance?"

"Not at all."

Digby said that and left, and Sankov stared for a long time at nothing before he punched a combination of the local communiline.

After a while, Ted Long looked out at him.

Sankov said, "You were right, son. There's nothing they can do. Even the ones that mean well see no way out. How did you know?"

"Commissioner," said Long, "when you've read all you can about the Time of Troubles, particularly about the twentieth century, nothing political can come as a real surprise."

"Well, maybe. Anyway, son, Assemblyman Digby is sorry for us, quite a piece sorry, you might say, but that's all. He says we'll have to leave Mars—or else get water somewhere else. Only he thinks that we can't get water somewhere else."

"You know we can, don't you, Commissioner?"

"I know we *might*, son. It's a terrible risk."

"If I find enough volunteers, the risk is our business."

"How is it going?"

"Not bad. Some of the boys are on my side right now. I talked Mario Rioz into it, for instance, and you know he's one of the best."

"That's just it—the volunteers will be the best men we have. I hate to allow it."

"If we get back, it will be worth it."

"If! If's a big word, son."

"And a big thing we're trying to do."

"Well, I gave my word that if there was no help on Earth, I'll see that the Phobos water hole lets you have all the water you'll need. Good luck.

6

Half a million miles above Saturn, Mario Rioz was cradled on nothing and sleep was delicious. He came out of it slowly and for a while, alone in his suit, he counted the stars and traced lines from one to another.

At first, as the weeks flew past, it was scavenging all over again, except for the gnawing feeling that every minute meant an additional number of thousands of miles away from all humanity. That made it worse.

They had aimed high to pass out of the ecliptic while moving through the Asteroid Belt. That had used up water and had probably been unnecessary. Although tens of thousands of worldlets look as thick as vermin in two-dimensional projection upon a photographic plate, they are nevertheless scattered so thinly through the quadrillions of cubic miles that make up their conglomerate orbit that only the most ridiculous of coincidence would have brought about a collision.

Still, they passed over the Belt and someone calculated the chances of collision with a fragment of matter large enough to do damage. The value was so low, so impossibly low, that it was perhaps inevitable that the notion of the "space-float" should occur to someone.

The days were long and many, space was empty, only one man was needed at the controls at any one time. The thought was a natural.

First, it was a particularly daring one who ventured out for fifteen minutes or so. Then another who tried half an hour. Eventually, before the asteroids were entirely behind, each ship regularly had its off-watch member suspended in space at the end of a cable.

It was easy enough. The cable, one of those intended for operations at the conclusion of their journey, was magnetically attached at both ends, one to the space suit to start with. Then you clambered out the lock onto the ship's hull and attached the other end there. You paused awhile, clinging to the metal skin by the electromagnets in your boots. Then you neutralized those and made the slightest muscular effort.

Slowly, ever so slowly, you lifted from the ship and even more slowly the ship's larger mass moved an equivalently shorter distance downward. You floated incredibly, weightlessly, in solid, speckled black. When the ship had moved far enough away from you, your gauntleted hand, which kept touch upon the cable, tightened its grip slightly. Too tightly, and you would begin moving back toward the ship and it toward you. Just tightly enough, and friction would halt you. Because your motion was equivalent to that of the ship, it seemed as motionless below you as though it had been painted against an impossible background while the cable between you hung in coils that had no reason to straighten out.

It was a half-ship to your eye. One half was lit by the light of the feeble Sun, which was still too bright to look at directly without the heavy protection of the polarized space-suit visor. The other half was black on black, invisible.

Space closed in and it was like sleep. Your suit was warm, it renewed its air automatically, it had food and drink in special containers from which it could be sucked with a minimal motion of the head, it took care of wastes appropriately. Most of all, more than anything else, there was the delightful euphoria of weightlessness.

You never felt so well in your life. The days stopped being too long, they weren't long enough, and there weren't enough of them.

They had passed Jupiter's orbit at a spot some 30 degrees from its then position. For months, it was the brightest object in the sky, always excepting the glowing white pea that was the Sun. At its brightest, some of the Scavengers insisted they could make out Jupiter as a tiny sphere, one side squashed out of true by the night shadow.

Then over a period of additional months it faded, while another dot of light grew until it was brighter than Jupiter. It was Saturn, first as a dot of brilliance, then as an oval, glowing splotch.

("Why oval?" someone asked, and after a while, someone else said, "The rings, of course," and it was obvious.)

Everyone space-floated at all possible times toward the end, watching Saturn incessantly.

("Hey, you jerk, come on back in, damn it. You're on duty." "Who's on duty? I've got fifteen minutes more by my watch." "You wouldn't give two minutes to your grandmother." "Come on in, damn it, or I'm coming out anyway." "All right, I'm coming. Holy howlers, what a racket over a lousy minute." But no quarrel could possibly be serious, not in space. It felt too good.)

Saturn grew until at last it rivaled and then surpassed the Sun. The rings, set at a broad angle to their trajectory of approach, swept grandly about the planet, only a small portion being eclipsed. Then, as they approached, the span of the rings grew still wider, yet narrower as the angles of approach constantly decreased.

The large moons showed up in the surrounding sky like serene fireflies.

Mario Rioz was glad he was awake so that he could watch again.

Saturn filled half the sky, streaked with orange, the night shadow cutting it fuzzily nearly one quarter of the way in from the right. Two round little dots in the brightness were shadows of two of the moons. To the left and behind them (he could look over his left shoulder to see, and as he did so, the rest of his body inched slightly to the right to conserve angular momentum) was the white diamond of the Sun.

Most of all he liked to watch the rings. At the left, they emerged from behind Saturn, a tight, bright triple band of orange light. At the right, their beginnings were hidden in the night shadow, but showed up closer and broader. They widened as they came, just like the flare of a horn, growing hazier as they approached, until, while the eye followed them, they seemed to fill the sky and lose themselves.

From the position of the Scavenger fleet just inside the outer rim of the outermost ring, the rings broke up and assumed their true identity as a phenomenal cluster of solid fragments rather than the tight, solid band of light they seemed.

Below him, or rather in the direction his feet pointed, some twenty miles away, was one of the ring fragments. It looked like a large, irregular splotch, marring the symmetry of space, three quarters in brightness and the night shadow cutting it like a knife. Other fragments were farther off, sparkling like star dust, dimmer and thicker, until, as you followed them down, they became rings once more.

The fragments were motionless, but that was only because the ships had taken up an orbit about Saturn equivalent to that of the outer edge of the rings.

The day before, Rioz reflected, he had been on that nearest fragment, working along with more than a score of others to mold it into the desired shape. Tomorrow he would be at it again.

Today—today he was space-floating.

"Mario?" The voice that broke upon his earphones was questioning.

Momentarily Rioz was flooded with annoyance. Damn it, he wasn't in the mood for company.

"Speaking," he said.

"I thought I had your ship spotted. How are you?"

"Fine. That you, Ted?"

"That's right," said Long.

"Anything wrong on the fragment?"

"Nothing. I'm out here floating."

"You?"

"It gets me, too, occasionally. Beautiful, isn't it?"

"Nice," agreed Rioz.

"You know, I've read Earth books—"

"Grounder books, you mean." Rioz yawned and found it difficult of resentment.

"—and sometimes I read descriptions of people lying on grass," continued Long. "You know that green stuff like thin, long pieces of paper they have all over the ground down there, and they look up at the blue sky with clouds in it. Did you ever see any films of that?"

"Sure. It didn't attract me. It looked cold."

"I suppose it isn't, though. After all, Earth is quite close to the Sun, and they say their atmosphere is thick enough to hold the heat. I must admit that personally I would hate to be caught under open sky with nothing on but clothes. Still, I imagine they like it."

"Grounders are nuts!"

"They talk about the trees, big brown stalks, and the wind, air movements, you know."

"You mean drafts. They can keep that, too."

"It doesn't matter. The point is they describe it beautifully, almost passionately. Many times I've wondered, 'What's it really like? Will I ever feel it or is this something only Earthmen can possibly feel?' I've felt so often that I was missing something vital. Now I know what it must be like. It's this. Complete peace in the middle of a beauty-drenched universe."

Rioz said, "They wouldn't like it. The Grounders, I mean. They're so used to their own lousy little world they wouldn't appreciate what it's like to float and look down on Saturn." He flipped his body slightly and began swaying back and forth about his center of mass, slowly, soothingly.

Long said, "Yes, I think so too. They're slaves to their planet. Even if they come to Mars, it will only be their children that are free. They'll be starships someday; great, huge things that can carry thousands of people and maintain their self-contained equilibrium for decades, maybe centuries. Mankind will spread through the whole Galaxy. But people will have to live their lives out on shipboard until new methods of interstellar travel are developed, so it will be Martians, not planet-bound Earthmen, who will colonize the Universe. That's inevitable. It's got to be. It's the Martian way."

But Rioz made no answer. He had dropped off to sleep again, rocking and swaying gently, half a million miles above Saturn.

7

The work shift of the ring fragment was the tail of the coin. The weightlessness, peace and privacy of the spacefloat gave place to something that had neither peace nor privacy. Even the weightlessness, which continued, became more a purgatory than a paradise under the new conditions.

Try to manipulate an ordinarily non-portable head projector. It could be lifted despite the fact that it was six feet high and wide and almost solid metal, since it weighed only a fraction of an ounce. But its inertia was exactly what it had always been, which meant that if it wasn't moved into position very slowly, it would just keep on going, taking you with it. Then you would have to hike the pseudo-grav field of your suit and come down with a jar.

Keralski had hiked the field a little too high and he came down a little too roughly, with the projector coming down with him at a dangerous angle. His crushed ankle had been the first casualty of the expedition.

Rioz was swearing fluently and nearly continuously. He continued to have impulse to drag the back of his hand across his forehead in order to wipe away the accumulating sweat. The few times that he had succumbed to the impulse, metal had met silicone with a clash that rang loudly inside his suit, but served no useful purpose. The desiccators within the suit were sucking at maximum and, of course, recovering the water and restoring iron-exchanged liquid, containing a careful proportion of salt, into the appropriate receptacle.

Rioz yelled, "Damn it, Dick, wait till I give the word, will you?"

And Swenson's voice rang in his ears, "Well, how long am I supposed to sit here?"

"Till I say," replied Rioz.

He strengthened pseudo-grav and lifted the projector a bit. He released pesudo-grav, insuring that the projector would stay in place for minutes even if he withdrew support altogether. He kicked the cable out of the way (it stretched beyond the close "horizon" to a power source that was out of sight) and touched the release.

The material of which the fragment was composed bubbled and vanished under its touch. A section of the lip of the tremendous cavity he had already carved into its substance melted away and a roughness in its contour had disappeared.

"Try it now," called Rioz.

Swenson was in the ship that was hovering nearly over Rioz's head.

Swenson called, "All clear?"

"I told you to go ahead."

It was a feeble flicker of steam that issued from one of the ship's forward vents. The ship drifted down toward the ring fragment. Another flicker adjusted a tendency to drift sidewise. It came down straight.

A third flicker to the rear slowed it to a feather rate.

Rioz watched tensely. "Keep her coming. You'll make it. You'll make it."

The rear of the ship entered the hole, nearly filling it. The bellying walls came closer and closer to its rim. There was a grinding vibration as the ship's motion halted.

It was Swenson's turn to curse. "It doesn't fit," he said.

Rioz threw the projector groundward in a passion and went flailing up into space. The projector kicked up a white crystalline dust all about it, and when Rioz came down under pseudo-grav, he did the same.

He said, "You went in on the bias, you dumb Grounder."

"I hit it level, you dirt-eating farmer."

Backward-pointing side jets of the ship were blasting more strongly than before, and Rioz hopped to get out of the way.

The ship scraped up from the pit, then shot into space half a mile before forward jets could bring it to a halt.

Swenson said tensely, "We'll spring half a dozen plates if we do this once again. Get it right, will you?"

"I'll get it right. Don't worry about it. Just you come in right."

Rioz jumped upward and allowed himself to climb three hundred yards to get an over-all look at the cavity. The gouge marks of the ship were plain enough. They were concentrated at one point halfway down the pit. He would get that.

It began to melt outward under the blaze of the projector.

Half an hour later the ship snuggled neatly into its cavity, and Swenson, wearing his space suit, emerged to join Rioz.

Swenson said, "If you want to step in and climb out of the suit, I'll take care of the icing."

"It's all right," said Rioz. "I'd just as soon sit here and watch Saturn."

He sat down at the lip of the pit. There was a six-foot gap between it and the ship. In some places about the circle, it was two feet; in a few places, even merely a matter of inches. You couldn't expect a better fit out of handwork. The final adjustment would be made by steaming ice gently and letting it freeze into the cavity between the lip and the ship.

Saturn moved visibly across the sky, its vast bulk inching below the horizon.

Rioz said, "How many ships are left to put in place?"

Swenson said, "Last I heard, it was eleven. We're in now, so that leaves only ten. Seven of the ones that are placed are iced in. Two or three are dismantled."

"We're coming along fine."

"There's plenty to do yet. Don't forget the main jets at the other end. And the cables and the power lines. Sometimes I wonder if we'll make it. On the way out, it didn't bother me so much, but just now I was sitting at the controls and I was saying, 'We won't make it. We'll sit out here and starve and die with nothing but Saturn over us.' It makes me feel—"

He didn't explain how it made him feel. He just sat there.

Rioz said, "You think too damn much."

"It's different with you," said Swenson. "I keep thinking of Pete—and Dora."

"What for? She said you could go, didn't she? The Commissioner gave her that talk on patriotism and how you'd be a hero and set for life once you got back, and she said you could go. You didn't sneak out the way Adams did."

"Adams is different. That wife of his should have been shot when she was born. Some women can make hell for a guy, can't they? She didn't want him to go—but she'd probably rather he didn't come back if she can get his settlement pay."

"What's your kick, then? Dora wants you back, doesn't she?"

Swenson sighed. "I never treated her right."

"You turned over your pay, it seems to me. I wouldn't do that for any woman. Money for value received, not a cent more."

"Money isn't it. I get to thinking out here. A woman likes company. A kid needs his father. What am I doing way out here?"

"Getting set to go home."

"Ah-h, you don't understand."

8

Ted Long wandered over the ridged surface of the ring fragment with his spirits as icy as the ground he walked on. It had all seemed perfectly logical back on Mars, but that was Mars. He had worked it out carefully in his mind in perfectly reasonable steps. He could still remember exactly how it went.

It didn't take a ton of water to move a ton of ship. It was not mass equals mass, but mass times velocity equals mass times velocity. It didn't matter, in other words, whether you shot out a ton of water at a mile a second or a hundred pounds of water at twenty miles a second. You got the same final velocity out of the ship.

That meant the jet nozzles had to be made narrower and the steam hotter. But then drawbacks appeared. The narrower the nozzle, the more energy was lost in friction and turbulence. The hotter the steam, the more refractory the nozzle had to be and the shorter its life. The limit in that direction was quickly reached.

Then, since a given weight of water could move considerably more than its own weight under the narrow-nozzle conditions, it paid to be big. The bigger the water-storage space, the larger the size of the actual travel-head, even in proportion. So they started to make liners heavier and bigger. But then the larger the shell, the heavier the bracings, the more difficult the weldings, the more exacting the engineering requirements. At the moment, the limit in that direction had been reached also.

And then he had put his finger on what had seemed to him to be the basic flaw—the original unswervable conception that the fuel had to be placed *inside* the ship; the metal had to be built to encircle a million tons of water.

Why? Water did not have to be water. It could be ice, and ice could be shaped. Holes could be melted into it. Travel-heads and jets could be fitted into it. Cables could hold travel-heads and jets stiffly together under the influence of magnetic field-force grips.

Long felt the trembling of the ground he walked on. He was at the head of the fragment. A dozen ships were blasting in and out of sheaths carved in its substance, and the fragment shuddered under the continuing impact.

* * *

The ice didn't have to be quarried. It existed in proper chunks in the rings of Saturn. That's all the rings were—pieces of nearly pure ice, circling Saturn. So spectroscopy stated and so it had turned out to be. He was standing on one such piece now, over two miles long, nearly one mile thick. It was almost half a billion tons of water, all in one piece, and he was standing on it.

But now he was face to face with the realities of life. He had never told the men just how quickly he had expected to set up the fragment as a ship, but in his heart, he had imagined it would be two days. It was a week now and he didn't dare to estimate the remaining time. He no longer even had any confidence that the task was a possible one. Would they be able to control jets with enough delicacy through leads slung across two miles of ice to manipulate out of Saturn's dragging gravity?

Drinking water was low, though they could always distill more out of the ice. Still, the food stores were not in a good way either.

He paused, looking up into the sky, eyes straining. *Was* the object growing larger? He ought to measure the distance. Actually, he lacked the spirit to add that trouble to the others. His mind slid back to greater immediacies.

Morale, at least, was high. The men seemed to enjoy being out Saturn-way. They were the first humans to penetrate this far, the first to pass the asteroids, the first to see Jupiter like a glowing pebble to the naked eye, the first to see Saturn—like that.

He didn't think fifty practical, case-hardened, shell-snatching Scavengers would take time to feel that sort of emotion. But they did. And they were proud.

Two men and a half-buried ship slid up the moving horizon as he walked.

He called crisply, "Hello, there!"

Rioz answered, "That you, Ted?"

"You bet. Is that Dick with you?"

"Sure. Come on, sit down. We were just getting ready to ice in and we were looking for an excuse to delay."

"I'm not," said Swenson promptly. "When will we be leaving, Ted?"

"As soon as we get through. That's no answer, is it?"

Swenson said dispiritedly, "I suppose there isn't any other answer."

Long looked up, staring at the irregular bright splotch in the sky.

Rioz followed his glance. "What's the matter?"

For a moment, Long did not reply. The sky was black otherwise and the ring fragments were an orange dust against it. Saturn was more than three fourths below the horizon and the rings were going with it. Half a mile away a ship bounded past the icy rim of the planetoid into the sky, was orange-lit by Saturn-light, and sank down again.

The ground trembled gently.

Rioz said, "Something bothering you about the Shadow?"

They called it that. It was the nearest fragment of the rings, quite close considering that they were at the outer rim of the rings, where the pieces spread themselves relatively thin. It was perhaps twenty miles off, a jagged mountain, its shape clearly visible.

"How does it look to you?" asked Long.

Rioz shrugged. "Okay, I guess. I don't see anything wrong."

"Doesn't it seem to be getting larger?"

"Why shouldn't it?"

"Well, doesn't it?" Long insisted.

Rioz and Swenson stared at it thoughtfully.

"It does look bigger," said Swenson.

"You're just putting the notion into our minds," Rioz argued. "If it were getting bigger, it would be coming closer."

"What's impossible about that?"

"These things are on stable orbits."

"They were when we came here," said Long. "There, did you feel that?"

The ground had trembled again.

Long said, "We've been blasting this thing for a week now. First, twenty-five ships landed on it, which changed its momentum right there. Not much, of course. Then we've been melting parts of it away and our ships have been blasting in and out of it—all at one end, too. In a week, we may have changed its orbit just a bit. The two fragments, this one and the Shadow, might be converging."

"It's got plenty of room to miss us in." Rioz watched it thoughtfully.

"Besides, if we can't even tell for sure that it's getting bigger, how quickly can it be moving? Relative to us, I mean."

"It doesn't have to be moving quickly. Its momentum is as large as ours, so that, however gently it hits, we'll be nudged completely out of our orbit, maybe toward Saturn, where we don't want to go. As a matter of fact, ice has a very low tensile strength, so that both planetoids might break up into gravel."

Swenson rose to his feet. "Damn it, if I can tell how a shell is moving a thousand miles away, I can tell what a mountain is doing twenty miles away." He turned toward the ship.

Long didn't stop him.

Rioz said, "There's a nervous guy."

The neighboring planetoid rose to zenith, passed overhead, began sinking. Twenty minutes later, the horizon opposite that portion behind which Saturn had disappeared burst into orange flame as its bulk began lifting again.

Rioz called into his radio, "Hey, Dick, are you dead in there?"

"I'm checking," came the muffled response.

"Is it moving?" asked Long.

"Yes."

"Toward us?"

There was a pause. Swenson's voice was a sick one. "On the nose, Ted. Intersection or orbits will take place in three days."

"You're crazy!" yelled Rioz.

"I checked four times," said Swenson.

Long thought blankly, What do we do now?

9

Some of the men were having trouble with the cables. They had to be laid precisely; their geometry had to be very nearly perfect for the magnetic field to attain maximum strength. In space, or even in air, it wouldn't have mattered. The cables would have lined up automatically once the juice went on.

Here it was different. A gouge had to be plowed along the planetoid's surface and into it the cable had to be laid. If it were not lined up within a few minutes of arc of the calculated direction, a torque would be applied to the entire planetoid, with consequent loss of energy, none of which could be spared. The gouges then had to be redriven, the cables shifted and iced into the new positions.

The men plodded wearily through the routine.

And then the word reached them:

"All hands to the jets!"

Scavengers could not be said to be the type that took kindly to discipline. It was a grumbling, growling, muttering group that set about disassembling the jets of the ships that yet remained intact, carrying them to the tail end of the planetoid, grubbing them into position, and stringing the leads along the surface.

It was almost twenty-four hours before one of them looked into the sky and said, "Holy jeepers!" followed by something less printable.

His neighbor looked and said, "I'll be damned!"

Once they noticed, all did. It became the most astonishing fact in the Universe.

"Look at the Shadow!"

It was spreading across the sky like an infected wound. Men looked at it, found it had doubled its size, wondered why they hadn't noticed that sooner.

Work came to a virtual halt. They besieged Ted Long.

He said, "We can't leave. We don't have the fuel to see us back to Mars and we don't have the equipment to capture another planetoid. So we've got to stay. Now the Shadow is creeping in on us because our blasting has thrown us out of orbit. We've got to change that by continuing the blasting. Since we can't blast the front end any more without endangering the ship we're building, let's try another way."

They went back to work on the jets with a furious energy that received impetus every half hour when the Shadow rose again over the horizon, bigger and more menacing than before.

Long had no assurance that it would work. Even if the jets would respond to the distant controls, even if the supply of water, which depended upon a storage chamber opening directly into the icy body of the planetoid, with built-in heat projectors steaming the propulsive fluid directly into the driving cells, were adequate, there was still no certainty that the body of the planetoid without a magnetic cable sheathing would hold together under the enormously disruptive stresses.

"Ready!" came the signal in Long's receiver.

Long called, "Ready!" and depressed the contact.

The vibration grew about him. The star field in the visiplate trembled.

In the rearview, there was a distant gleaming spume of swiftly moving ice crystals.

"It's blowing!" was the cry.

It kept on blowing. Long dared not stop. For six hours, it blew, hissing, bubbling, steaming into space; the body of the planetoid converted to vapor and hurled away.

The Shadow came closer until men did nothing but stare at the mountain in the sky, surpassing Saturn itself in spectacularity. Its every groove and valley was a plain scar upon its face. But when it passed through the planetoid's orbit, it crossed more than half a mile behind its then position.

The steam jet ceased.

Long bent in his seat and covered his eyes. He hadn't eaten in two days. He could eat now, though. Not another planetoid was close enough to interrupt them, even if it began an approach that very moment.

Back on the planetoid's surface, Swenson said, "All the time I watched that damned rock coming down, I kept saying to myself, 'This can't happen. We can't let it happen.' "

"Hell," said Rioz, "we were all nervous. Did you see Jim Davis? He was green. I was a little jumpy myself."

"That's not it. It wasn't just—dying, you know. I was thinking—I know it's funny, but I can't help it—I was thinking that Dora warned me I'd get myself killed, she'll never let me hear the last of it. Isn't that a crummy sort of attitude at a time like that?"

"Listen," said Rioz, "you wanted to get married, so you got married. Why come to me with your troubles?"

10

The flotilla, welded into a single unit, was returning over its mighty course from Saturn to Mars. Each day it flashed over a length of space it had taken nine days outward.

Ted Long had put the entire crew on emergency. With twenty-five ships embedded in the planetoid taken out of Saturn's wings and unable to move or maneuver independently, the co-ordination of their power sources into unified blasts was a ticklish problem. The jarring that took place on the first day of travel nearly shook them out from under their hair.

That, at least, smoothed itself out as the velocity raced upward under the steady thrust from behind. They passed the one-hundred-thousand-miles-an-hour mark late on the second day, and climbed steadily toward the million-mile mark and beyond.

Long's ship, which formed the needle point of the frozen fleet, was the only one which possessed a five-way view of space. It was an uncomfortable position under the circumstances. Long found himself watching tensely, imagining somehow that the stars would slowly begin to slip backward, to whizz past them, under the influence of the multi-ship's tremendous rate of travel.

They didn't, of course. They remained nailed to the black backdrop, their distance scorning with patient immobility any speed mere man could achieve.

The men complained bitterly after the first few days. It was not only that they were deprived of the space-float. They were burdened by much more than the ordinary pseudo-gravity field of the ships, by the effects of the fierce acceleration under which they were living. Long himself was weary to death of the relentless pressure against hydraulic cushions.

They took to shutting off the jet thrusts one hour out of every four and Long fretted.

It had been just over a year that he had last seen Mars shrinking in an observation window from this ship, which had then been an independent entity. What had happened since then? Was the colony still there?

In something like a growing panic, Long sent out radio pulses towards Mars daily, with the combined power of twenty-five ships behind it. There was no answer. He expected none. Mars and Saturn were on opposite sides of the Sun now, and until he mounted high enough above the ecliptic to get the Sun well beyond the line connecting himself and Mars, solar interference would prevent any signal from getting through.

High above the outer rim of the Asteroid Belt, they reached maximum velocity. With short spurts of power from first one side jet, then another, the huge vessel reversed itself. The composite jet in the rear began its mighty roaring once again, but now the result was deceleration.

They passed a hundred million miles over the Sun, curving down to intersect the orbit of Mars.

A week out of Mars, answering signals were heard for the first time, fragmentary, ether-torn, and incomprehensible, but they were coming from Mars. Earth and Venus were at angles sufficiently different to leave no doubt of that.

Long relaxed. There were still humans on Mars, at any rate.

Two days out of Mars, the signal was strong and clear and Sankov was at the other end.

Sankov said, "Hello, son. It's three in the morning here. Seems like people have no consideration for an old man. Dragged me right out of bed."

"I'm sorry, sir."

"Don't be. They were following orders. I'm afraid to ask, son. Anyone hurt? Maybe dead?"

"No deaths, sir. Not one."

"And—and the water? Any left?"

Long said, with an effort at nonchalance, "Enough."

"In that case, get home as fast as you can. Don't take any chances, of course."

"There's trouble, then."

"Fair to middling. When will you come down?"

"Two days. Can you hold out that long?"

"I'll hold out."

Forty hours later Mars had grown to a ruddy-orange ball that filled the ports and they were in the final planet-landing spiral.

"Slowly," Long said to himself, "slowly." Under these conditions, even the thin atmosphere of Mars could do dreadful damage if they moved through it too quickly.

Since they came in from well above the ecliptic, their spiral passed from north to south. A polar cap shot whitely below them, then the much smaller one of the summer hemisphere, the larger one again, the small one, at longer and longer intervals. The planet approached closer, the landscape began to show features.

"Prepare for landing!" called Long.

11

Sankov did his best to look placid, which was difficult considering how closely the boys had shaved their return. But it had worked out well enough.

Until a few days ago, he had no sure knowledge that they had survived. It seemed more likely—inevitable, almost—that they were nothing but frozen corpses somewhere in the trackless stretches from Mars to Saturn, new planetoids that had once been alive.

The Committee had been dickering with him for weeks before the news had come. They had insisted on his signature to the paper for the sake of appearances. It would look like an agreement, voluntarily and mutually arrived at. But Sankov knew well that, given complete obstinacy on his part, they would act unilaterally and be damned with appearances. It seemed fairly certain that Hilder's election was secure now and they would take the chance of arousing a reaction of sympathy for Mars.

So he dragged out the negotiations, dangling before them always the possibility of surrender.

And then he heard from Long and concluded the deal quickly.

The papers had lain before him and he had made a last statement for the benefit of the reporters who were present.

He said, "Total imports of water from Earth are twenty million tons a year. This is declining as we develop our own piping system. If I sign this paper agreeing to an embargo, our industry will be paralyzed, any possibilities of expansion will halt. It looks to me as if that can't be what's in Earth's mind, can it?"

Their eyes met his and held only a hard glitter. Assemblyman Digby had already been replaced and they were unanimous against him.

The Committee Chairman impatiently pointed out, "You have said all this before."

"I know, but right now I'm kind of getting ready to sign and I want it clear in my head. Is Earth set and determined to bring us to an end here?"

"Of course not. Earth is interested in conserving its irreplaceable water supply, nothing else."

"You have one and a half quintillion tons of water on Earth."

The Committee Chairman said, "We cannot spare water." And Sankov had signed.

That had been the final note he wanted. Earth had one and a half quintillion tons of water and could spare none of it.

Now, a day and a half later, the Committee and the reporters waited in the spaceport dome. Through thick, curving windows, they could see the bare and empty grounds of Mars Spaceport.

The Committee Chairman asked with annoyance, "How much longer do we have to wait? And, if you don't mind, what are we waiting for?"

Sankov said, "Some of our boys have been out in space, out past the asteroids."

The Committee Chairman removed a pair of spectacles and cleaned them with a snowy-white handkerchief. "And they're returning?"

"They are."

The Chairman shrugged, lifted his eyebrows in the direction of the reporters.

In the smaller room adjoining, a knot of women and children clustered about another window. Sankov stepped back a bit to cast a glance toward them. He would much rather have been with them, been part of their excitement and tension. He, like them, had waited over a year now. He, like them, had thought, over and over again, that the men must be dead.

"You see that?" said Sankov, pointing.

"Hey!" cried a reporter. "It's a ship!"

A confused shouting came from the adjoining room.

It wasn't a ship so much as a bright dot obscured by a drifting white cloud. The cloud grew larger and began to have form. It was a double streak against the sky, the lower ends billowing out and upward again. As it dropped still closer, the bright dot at the upper end took on a crudely cylindrical form.

It was rough and craggy, but where the sunlight hit, brilliant high lights bounced back.

The cylinder dropped toward the ground with the ponderous slowness characteristic of space vessels. It hung suspended on those blasting jets and settled down upon the recoil of tons of matter hurling downward like a tired man dropping into his easy chair.

And as it did so, a silence fell upon all within the dome. The woman and children in one room, the politicians and reporters in the other remained frozen, heads craned incredulously upward.

The cylinder's landing flanges, extending far below the two rear jets, touched ground and sank into a pebbly morass. And then the ship was motionless and the jet action ceased.

But the silence continued in the dome. It continued for a long time.

Men came clambering down the sides of the immense vessel, inching down, down the two-mile trek to the ground, with spikes on their shoes and ice axes in their hands. They were gnats against the blinding surface.

One of the reporters croaked, "What is it?"

"That," said Sankov calmly, "happens to be a chunk of matter that spent its time scooting around Saturn as part of its rings. Our boys fitted it out with travel-head and jets and ferried it home. It just turns out the fragments in Saturn's rings are made up out of ice."

He spoke into a continuing deathlike silence. "That thing that looks like a spaceship is just a mountain of hard water. If it were standing like that on Earth, it would be melting into a puddle and maybe it would break under its own weight. Mars is colder and has less gravity, so there's no such danger.

"Of course, once we get this thing really organized, we can have water stations on the moons of Saturn and Jupiter and on the asteroids. We can scale in chunks of Saturn's rings and pick them up and send them on at the various stations. Our Scavengers are good at that sort of thing.

"We'll have all the water we need. That one chunk you see is just under a cubic mile—or about what Earth would send us in two hundred years. The boys used quite a bit of it coming back from Saturn. They made it in five weeks, they tell me, and used up about a hundred million tons. But, Lord, that didn't make any dent at all in that mountain. Are you getting all this, boys?"

He turned to the reporters. There was no doubt they were getting it.

He said, "Then get this, too. Earth is worried about its water supply. It only has one and a half quintillion tons. It can't spare us a single ton of it. Write down that we folks on Mars are worried about Earth and don't want anything to happen to Earth people. Write down that we'll sell water to Earth. Write down that we'll let them have million-ton lots for a reasonable fee. Write down that in ten years, we figure we can sell it in cubic-mile lots. Write down that Earth can quit worrying because Mars can sell it all the water it needs and wants."

The Committee Chairman was past hearing. He was feeling the future rushing in. Dimly he could see the reporters grinning as they wrote furiously.

Grinning.

He could hear the grin become laughter on Earth as Mars turned the tables so neatly on the anti-Wasters. He could hear the laughter thunder from every continent when word of a fiasco spread. And he could see the abyss, deep and black as space, into which would drop forever the political hopes of John Hilder and of every opponent of space flight left on Earth—his own included, of course.

In the adjoining room, Dora Swenson screamed with joy, and Peter, grown two inches, jumped up and down, calling, "Daddy! Daddy!"

Richard Swenson had just stepped off the extremity of the flange and, face showing clearly through the clear silicone of the headpiece, marched toward the dome.

"Did you ever see a guy look so happy?" asked Ted Long. "Maybe there's something in this marriage business."

"Ah, you've just been out in space too long," Rioz said.

Sally

Sally was coming down the lake road, so I waved to her and called her by name. I always liked to see Sally. I liked all of them, you understand, but Sally's the prettiest one of the lot. There just isn't any question about it.

She moved a little faster when I waved to her. Nothing undignified. She was never that. She moved just enough faster to show that she was glad to see me, too.

I turned to the man standing beside me. "That's Sally," I said.

He smiled at me and nodded.

Mrs. Hester had brought him in. She said, "This is Mr. Gellhorn, Jake. You remember he sent you the letter asking for an appointment."

That was just talk, really. I have a million things to do around the Farm, and one thing I just can't waste my time on is mail. That's why I have Mrs. Hester around. She lives pretty close by, she's good at attending to foolishness without running to me about it, and most of all, she likes Sally and the rest. Some people don't.

"Glad to see you, Mr. Gellhorn," I said.

"Raymond J. Gellhorn," he said, and gave me his hand, which I shook and gave back.

He was a largish fellow, half a head taller than I and wider, too. He was about half my age, thirtyish. He had black hair, plastered down slick, with a part in the middle, and a thin mustache, very neatly trimmed. His jawbones got big under his ears and made him look as if he had a slight case of mumps. On video he'd be a natural to play the villain, so I assumed he was a nice fellow. It goes to show that video can't be wrong all the time.

"I'm Jacob Folkers," I said. "What can I do for you?"

He grinned. It was a big, wide, white-toothed grin. "You can tell me a little about your Farm here, if you don't mind."

I heard Sally coming up behind me and I put out my hand. She slid right into it and the feel of the hard, glossy enamel of her fender was warm in my palm.

"A nice automatobile," said Gellhorn.

That's one way of putting it. Sally was a 2045 convertible with a

Hennis-Carleton positronic motor and an Armat chassis. She had the cleanest, finest lines I've ever seen on any model, bar none. For five years, she'd been my favorite, and I'd put everything into her I could dream up. In all that time, there'd never been a human being behind her wheel.

Not once.

"Sally," I said, patting her gently, "meet Mr. Gellhorn."

Sally's cylinder-purr keyed up a little. I listened carefully for any knocking. Lately, I'd been hearing motor-knock in almost all the cars and changing the gasoline hadn't done a bit of good. Sally was as smooth as her paint job this time, however.

"Do you have names for all your cars?" asked Gellhorn.

He sounded amused, and Mrs. Hester doesn't like people to sound as though they were making fun of the Farm. She said, sharply, "Certainly. The cars have real personalities, don't they, Jake? The sedans are all males and the convertibles are females."

Gellhorn was smiling again. "And do you keep them in separate garages, ma'am?"

Mrs. Hester glared at him.

Gellhorn said to me, "And now I wonder if I can talk to you alone, Mr. Folkers?"

"That depends," I said. "Are you a reporter?"

"No, sir. I'm a sales agent. Any talk we have is not for publication. I assure you I am interested in strict privacy."

"Let's walk down the road a bit. There's a bench we can use."

We started down. Mrs. Hester walked away. Sally nudged along after us.

I said, "You don't mind if Sally comes along, do you?"

"Not at all. She can't repeat what we say, can she?" He laughed at his own joke, reached over and rubbed Sally's grille.

Sally raced her motor and Gellhorn's hand drew away quickly.

"She's not used to strangers," I explained.

We sat down on the bench under the big oak tree where we could look across the small lake to the private speedway. It was the warm part of the day and the cars were out in force, at least thirty of them. Even at this distance I could see that Jeremiah was pulling his usual stunt of sneaking up behind some staid older model, then putting on a jerk of speed and yowling past with deliberately squealing brakes. Two weeks before he had crowded old Angus off the asphalt altogether, and I had turned off his motor for two days.

It didn't help through, I'm afraid, and it looks as though there's nothing to be done about it. Jeremiah is a sports model to begin with and that kind is awfully hot-headed.

"Well, Mr. Gellhorn," I said. "Could you tell me why you want the information?"

But he was just looking around. He said, "This *is* an amazing place, Mr. Folkers."

"I wish you'd call me Jake. Everyone does."

"All right, Jake. How many cars do you have here?"

"Fifty-one. We get one or two new ones every year. One year we got five. We haven't lost one yet. They're all in perfect running order. We even have a '15 model Mat-O-Mot in working order. One of the original automatics. It was the first car here."

Good old Matthew. He stayed in the garage most of the day now, but then he was the granddaddy of all positronic-motored cars. Those were the days when blind war veterans, paraplegics and heads of state were the only ones who drove automatics. But Samson Harridge was my boss and he was rich enough to be able to get one. I was his chauffeur at the time.

The thought makes me feel old. I can remember when there wasn't an automobile in the world with brains enough to find its own way home. I chauffeured dead lumps of machines that needed a man's hand at their controls every minute. Every year machines like that used to kill tens of thousands of people.

The automatics fixed that. A positronic brain can react much faster than a human one, of course, and it paid people to keep hands off the controls. You got in, punched your destination and let it go its own way.

We take it for granted now, but I remember when the first laws came out forcing the old machines off the highways and limiting travel to automatics. Lord, what a fuss. They called it everything from communism to fascism, but it emptied the highways and stopped the killing, and still more people get around more easily the new way.

Of course, the automatics were ten to a hundred times as expensive as the hand-driven ones, and there weren't many that could afford a private vehicle. The industry specialized in turning out omnibus-automatics. You could always call a company and have one stop at your door in a matter of minutes and take you where you wanted to go. Usually, you had to drive with others who were going your way, but what's wrong with that?

Samson Harridge had a private car though, and I went to him the minute it arrived. The car wasn't Matthew to me then. I didn't know it was going to be the dean of the Farm some day. I only knew it was taking my job away and I hated it.

I said, "You won't be needing me any more, Mr. Harridge?"

He said, "What are you dithering about, Jake? You don't think I'll trust myself to a contraption like that, do you? You stay right at the controls."

I said, "But it works by itself, Mr. Harridge. It scans the road, reacts properly to obstacles, humans, and other cars, and remembers routes to travel."

"So they say. So they say. Just the same, you're sitting right behind the wheel in case anything goes wrong."

Funny how you can get to like a car. In no time I was calling it Matthew and was spending all my time keeping it polished and humming. A positronic brain stays in condition best when it's got control of its chassis at all times, which means it's worth keeping the gas tank filled so that the motor can turn over slowly day and night. After a while, it got so I could tell by the sound of the motor how Matthew felt.

In his own way, Harridge grew fond of Matthew, too. He had no one else to like. He'd divorced or outlived three wives and outlived five children and three grandchildren. So when he died, maybe it wasn't surprising that he had his estate converted into a Farm for Retired Automobiles, with me in charge and Matthew the first member of a distinguished line.

It's turned out to be my life. I never got married. You can't get married and still tend to automatics the way you should.

The newspapers thought it was funny, but after a while they stopped joking about it. Some things you can't joke about. Maybe you've never been able to afford an automatic and maybe you never will, either, but take it from me, you get to love them. They're hard-working and affectionate. It takes a man with no heart to mistreat one or to see one mistreated.

It got so that after a man had an automatic for a while, he would make provisions for having it left to the Farm, if he didn't have an heir he could rely on to give it good care.

I explained that to Gellhorn.

He said, "Fifty-one cars! That represents a lot of money.'

"Fifty thousand minimum per automatic, original investment," I said. "They're worth a lot more now. I've done things for them."

"It must take a lot of money to keep up the Farm."

"You're right there. The Farm's a non-profit organization, which gives us a break on taxes and, of course, new automatics that come in usually have trust funds attached. Still, costs are always going up. I have to keep the place landscaped; I keep laying down new asphalt and keeping the old in repair; there's gasoline, oil, repairs, and new gadgets. It adds up."

"And you've spent a long time at it."

"I sure have, Mr. Gellhorn. Thirty-three years."

"You don't seem to be getting much out of it yourself."

"I don't? You surprise me, Mr. Gellhorn. I've got Sally and fifty others. Look at her."

I was grinning. I couldn't help it. Sally was so clean, it almost hurt. Some insect must have died on her windshield or one speck of dust too many had landed, so she was going to work. A little tube protruded and spurted Tergosol over the glass. It spread quickly over the silicone surface film and squeejees snapped into place instantly, passing over the windshield and forcing the water into the little channel that led it, dripping, down to the ground. Not a speck of water got onto her glistening apple-green hood. Squeejee and detergent tube snapped back into place and disappeared.

Gellhorn said, "I never saw an automatic do that."

"I guess not," I said. "I fixed that up specially on our cars. They're clear. They're always scrubbing their glass. They like it. I've even got Sally fixed up with wax jets. She polishes herself every night till you can see your face in any part of her and shave by it. If I can scrape up the money, I'd be putting it on the rest of the girls. Convertibles are very vain."

"I can tell you how to scrape up the money, if that interests you."

"That always does. How?"

"Isn't that obvious, Jake? Any of your cars is worth fifty thousand minimum, you said. I'll bet most of them top six figures."

"So?"

"Ever think of selling a few?"

I shook my head. "You don't realize it, I guess, Mr. Gellhorn, but I can't sell any of these. They belong to the Farm, not to me."

"The money would go to the Farm."

"The incorporation papers of the Farm provide that the cars receive perpetual care. They can't be sold."

"What about the motors, then?"

"I don't understand you."

Gellhorn shifted position and his voice got confidential. "Look here, Jake, let me explain the situation. There's a big market for private automatics if they could only be made cheaply enough. Right?"

"That's no secret."

"And ninety-five per cent of the cost is the motor. Right? Now, I know where we can get a supply of bodies. I also know where we can sell automatics at a good price—twenty or thirty thousand for the cheaper models, maybe fifty or sixty for the better ones. All I need are the motors. You see the solution?"

"I don't, Mr. Gellhorn." I did, but I wanted him to spell it out.

"It's right here. You've got fifty-one of them. You're an expert automatobile mechanic, Jake. You must be. You could unhook a motor and place it in another car so that no one would know the difference."

"It wouldn't be exactly ethical."

"You wouldn't be harming the cars. You'd be doing them a favor. Use your older cars. Use that old Mat-O-Mot."

"Well, now, wait a while, Mr. Gellhorn. The motors and bodies aren't two separate items. They're a single unit. Those motors are used to their own bodies. They wouldn't be happy in another car."

"All right, that's a point. That's a very good point, Jake. It would be like taking your mind and putting it in someone else's skull. Right? You don't think you would like that?"

"I don't think I would. No."

"But what if I took your mind and put it into the body of a young athlete. What about that, Jake? You're not a youngster anymore. If you had the chance, wouldn't you enjoy being twenty again? That's what I'm offering some of your positronic motors. They'll be put into new '57 bodies. The latest construction."

I laughed. "That doesn't make much sense, Mr. Gellhorn. Some of our cars may be old, but they're well-cared for. Nobody drives them. They're allowed their own way. They're *retired*, Mr. Gellhorn. I wouldn't want a twenty-year-old body if it meant I had to dig ditches for the rest of my new life and never have enough to eat . . . What do you think, Sally?"

Sally's two doors opened and then shut with a cushioned slam.

"What's that?" said Gellhorn.

"That's the way Sally laughs."

Gellhorn forced a smile. I guess he thought I was making a bad joke. He said, "Talk sense, Jake. Cars are *made* to be driven. They're probably not happy if you don't drive them."

I said, "Sally hasn't been driven in five years. She looks happy to me."

"I wonder."

He got up and walked toward Sally slowly. "Hi, Sally, how'd you like a drive?"

Sally's motor revved up. She backed away.

"Don't push her, Mr. Gellhorn," I said. "She's liable to be a little skittish."

Two sedans were about a hundred yards up the road. They had stopped. Maybe, in their own way, they were watching. I didn't bother about them. I had my eyes on Sally, and I kept them there.

Gellhorn said, "Steady now, Sally." He lunged out and seized the door handle. It didn't budge, of course.

He said, "It opened a minute ago."

I said, "Automatic lock. She's got a sense of privacy, Sally has."

He let go, then said, slowly and deliberately, "A car with a sense of privacy shouldn't go around with its top down."

He stepped back three or four paces, then quickly, so quickly I couldn't take a step to stop him, he ran forward and vaulted into the car. He caught Sally completely by surprise, because as he came down, he shut off the ignition before she could lock it in place.

For the first time in five years, Sally's motor was dead.

I think I yelled, but Gellhorn had the switch on "Manual" and locked that in place, too. He kicked the motor into action. Sally was alive again but she had no freedom of action.

He started up the road. The sedans were still there. They turned and drifted away, not very quickly. I suppose it was all a puzzle to them.

One was Giuseppe, from the Milan factories, and the other was Stephen. They were always together. They were both new at the Farm, but they'd been here long enough to know that our cars just didn't have drivers.

Gellhorn went straight on, and when the sedans finally got it through their heads that Sally wasn't going to slow down, that she *couldn't* slow down, it was too late for anything but desperate measures.

They broke for it, one to each side, and Sally raced between them like a streak. Steve crashed through the lakeside fence and rolled to a halt on the grass and mud not six inches from the water's edge. Giuseppe bumped along the land side of the road to a shaken halt.

I had Steve back on the highway and was trying to find out what harm, if any, the fence had done him, when Gellhorn came back.

Gellhorn opened Sally's door and stepped out. Leaning back, he shut off the ignition a second time.

"There," he said. "I think I did her a lot of good."

I held my temper. "Why did you dash through the sedans? There was no reason for that."

"I kept expecting them to turn out."

"They did. One went through a fence."

"I'm sorry, Jake," he said. "I thought they'd move more quickly. You know how it is. I've been in lots of buses, but I've only been in a private automatic two or three times in my life, and this is the first time I ever drove one. That just shows you, Jake. It got me, driving one, and I'm pretty hard-boiled. I tell you, we don't have to go more than twenty percent below list price to reach a good market, and it would be ninety percent profit."

"Which we would split?"

"Fifty-fifty. And I take all the risks, remember."

"All right. I listened to you. Now you listen to me." I raised my voice because I was just too mad to be polite anymore. "When you turn off Sally's motor, you hurt her. How would you like to be kicked unconscious? That's what you do to Sally, when you turn her off."

"You're exaggerating, Jake. The automatobuses get turned off every night."

"Sure, that's why I want none of my boys or girls in your fancy '57 bodies, where I won't know what treatment they'll get. Buses need major repairs in their positronic circuits every couple of years. Old Matthew hasn't had his circuits touched in twenty years. What can you offer him compared with that?"

"Well, you're excited now. Suppose you think over my proposition when you've cooled down and get in touch with me."

"I've thought it over all I want to. If I ever see you again, I'll call the police."

His mouth got hard and ugly. He said, "Just a minute, old-timer."

I said, "Just a minute, you. This is private property and I'm ordering you off."

He shrugged. "Well, then, goodbye."

I said, "Mrs. Hester will see you off the property. Make that goodbye permanent."

* * *

But it wasn't permanent. I saw him again two days later. Two and a half days, rather, because it was about noon when I saw him first and a little after midnight when I saw him again.

I sat up in bed when he turned the light on, blinking blindly till I made out what was happening. Once I could see, it didn't take much explaining. In fact, it took none at all. He had a gun in his right fist, the nasty little needle barrel just visible between two fingers. I knew that all he had to do was to increase the pressure of his hand and I would be torn apart.

He said, "Put on your clothes, Jake."

I didn't move. I just watched him.

He said, "Look, Jake, I know the situation. I visited you two days ago, remember. You have no guards on this place, no electrified fences, no warning signals. Nothing."

I said, "I don't need any. Meanwhile there's nothing to stop you from leaving, Mr. Gellhorn. I would if I were you. This place can be very dangerous."

He laughed a little. "It is, for anyone on the wrong side of a fist gun."

"I see it," I said. "I know you've got one."

"Then get a move on. My men are waiting."

"No, sir, Mr. Gellhorn. Not unless you tell me what you want, and probably not then."

"I made you a proposition day before yesterday."

"The answer's still no."

"There's more to the proposition now. I've come here with some men and an automatobus. You have your chance to come with me and disconnect twenty-five of the positronic motors. I don't care which twenty-five you choose. We'll load them on the bus and take them away. Once they're disposed of, I'll see to it that you get your fair share of the money."

"I have your word on that, I suppose."

He didn't act as if he thought I was being sarcastic. He said, "You have."

I said, "No."

"If you insist on saying no, we'll go about it in our own way. I'll disconnect the motors myself, only I'll disconnect all fifty-one. Every one of them."

"It isn't easy to disconnect positronic motors, Mr. Gellhorn. Are you a robotics expert? Even if you are, you know, these motors have been modified by me."

"I know that, Jake. And to be truthful, I'm not an expert. I may ruin quite a few motors trying to get them out. That's why I'll have to work over all fifty-one if you don't cooperate. You see, I may only end up with twenty-five when I'm through. The first few I'll tackle will probably suffer the most. Till I get the hang of it, you see. And if I go it myself, I think I'll put Sally first in line."

I said, "I can't believe you're serious, Mr. Gellhorn."

He said, "I'm serious, Jake." He let it all dribble in. "If you want to help, you can keep Sally. Otherwise, she's liable to be hurt very badly. Sorry."

I said, "I'll come with you, but I'll give you one more warning. You'll be in trouble, Mr. Gellhorn."

He thought that was very funny. He was laughing very quietly as we went down the stairs together.

* * *

There was an automatobus waiting outside the driveway to the garage apartments. The shadows of three men waited beside it, and their flash beams went on as we approached.

Gellhorn said in a low voice, "I've got the old fellow. Come on. Move the truck up the drive and let's get started."

One of the others leaned in and punched the proper instructions on the control panel. We moved up the driveway with the bus following submissively.

"It won't go inside the garage," I said. "The door won't take it. We don't have buses here. Only private cars."

"All right," said Gellhorn. "Pull it over onto the grass and keep it out of sight."

I could hear the thrumming of the ears when we were still ten yards from the garage.

Usually they quieted down if I entered the garage. This time they didn't. I think they knew that strangers were about, and once the faces of Gellhorn and the others were visible they got noisier. Each motor was a warm rumble, and each motor was knocking irregularly until the place rattled.

The lights went up automatically as we stepped inside. Gellhorn didn't seem bothered by the car noise, but the three men with him looked surprised and uncomfortable. They had the look of the hired thug about them, a look that was not compounded of physical features so much as of a certain wariness of eye and hang-dogness of face. I knew the type and I wasn't worried.

One of them said, "Damn it, they're burning gas."

"My cars always do," I replied stiffly.

"Not tonight," said Gellhorn. "Turn them off."

"It's not that easy, Mr. Gellhorn," I said.

"Get started!" he said.

I stood there. He had his fist gun pointed at me steadily. I said, "I told you, Mr. Gellhorn, that my cars have been well-treated while they've been at the Farm. They're used to being treated that way, and they resent anything else."

"You have one minute," he said. "Lecture me some other time."

"I'm trying to explain something. I'm trying to explain that my cars can understand what I say to them. A positronic motor will learn to do that with time and patience. My cars have learned. Sally understood your proposition two days ago. You'll remember she laughed when I asked her opinion. She also knows what you did to her and so do the two sedans you scattered. And the rest know what to do about tresspasers in general."

"Look, you crazy old fool—"

"All I have to say is—" I raised my voice. "Get them!"

One of the men turned pasty and yelled, but his voice was drowned completely in the sound of fifty-one horns turned loose at once. They held their notes, and within the four walls of the garage the echoes rose to a wild, metallic call. Two cars rolled forward, not hurriedly, but with no possible mistake as to their target. Two cars fell in line behind the first two. All the cars were stirring in their separate stalls.

The thugs stared, then backed.

I shouted, "Don't get up against a wall."

Apparently, they had that instinctive thought themselves. They rushed madly for the door of the garage.

At the door one of Gellhorn's men turned, brought up a fist gun of his own. The needle pellet tore a thin, blue flash toward the first car. The car was Giuseppe.

A thin line of paint peeled up Giuseppe's hood, and the right half of his windshield crazed and splintered but did not break through.

The men were out the door, running, and two by two the cars crunched out after them into the night, their horns calling the charge.

I kept my hand on Gellhorn's elbow, but I don't think he could have moved in any case. His lips were trembling.

I said, "That's why I don't need electrified fences or guards. My property protects itself."

Gellhorn's eyes swiveled back and forth in fascination as, pair by pair, they whizzed by. He said, "They're killers!"

"Don't be silly. They won't kill your men."

"They're killers!"

"They'll just give your men a lesson. My cars have been specially trained for cross-country pursuit for just such an occasion; I think what your men will get will be worse than an outright quick kill. Have you ever been chased by an automatobile?"

Gellhorn didn't answer.

I went on. I didn't want him to miss a thing. "They'll be shadows going no faster than your men, chasing them here, blocking them there, blaring at them, dashing at them, missing with a screech of brake and a thunder of motor. They'll keep it up till your men drop, out of breath and half-dead, waiting for the wheels to crunch over their breaking bones. The cars won't do that. They'll turn away. You can bet, though, that your men will never return here in their lives. Not for all the money you or ten like you could give them. Listen—"

I tightened my hold on his elbow. He strained to hear.

I said, "Don't you hear car doors slamming?"

It was faint and distant, but unmistakable.

I said, "They're laughing. They're enjoying themselves."

His face crumpled with rage. He lifted his hand. He was still holding his fist gun.

I said, "I wouldn't. One automatocar is still with us."

I don't think he had noticed Sally till then. She had moved up so quietly. Though her right front fender nearly touched me, I couldn't hear her motor. She might have been holding her breath.

Gellhorn yelled.

I said, "She won't touch you, as long as I'm with you. But if you kill me . . . You know, Sally doesn't like you."

Gellhorn turned the gun in Sally's direction.

"Her motor is shielded," I said, "and before you could ever squeeze the gun a second time she would be on top of you."

"All right, then," he yelled, and suddenly my arm was bent behind my back and twisted so I could hardly stand. He held me between Sally and himself, and his pressure didn't let up. "Back out with me and don't try to break loose, old-timer, or I'll tear your arm out of its socket."

I had to move. Sally nudged along with us, worried, uncertain what to do. I tried to say something to her and couldn't. I could only clench my teeth and moan.

Gellhorn's automatobus was still standing outside the garage. I was forced in. Gellhorn jumped in after me, locking the doors.

He said, "All right, now. We'll talk sense."

I was rubbing my arm, trying to get life back into it, and even as I did I was automatically and without any conscious effort studying the control board of the bus.

I said, "This is a rebuilt job."

"So?" he said caustically. "It's a sample of my work. I picked up a discarded chassis, found a brain I could use and spliced me a private bus. What of it?"

I tore at the repair panel, forcing it aside.

He said, "What the hell. Get away from that." The side of his palm came down numbingly on my left shoulder.

I struggled with him. "I don't want to do this bus any harm. What kind of a person do you think I am? I just want to take a look at some of the motor connections."

It didn't take much of a look. I was boiling when I turned to him. I said, "You're a hound and a bastard. You had no right installing this motor yourself. Why didn't you get a robotics man?"

He said, "Do I look crazy?"

"Even if it was a stolen motor, you had no right to treat it so. I wouldn't treat a man the way you treated that motor. Solder, tape, and pinch clamps! It's brutal!"

"It works, doesn't it?"

"Sure it works, but it must be hell for the bus. You could live with migraine headaches and acute arthritis, but it wouldn't be much of a life. This car is *suffering*."

"Shut up!" For a moment he glanced out the window at Sally, who had rolled up as close to the bus as she could. He made sure the doors and windows were locked.

He said, "We're getting out of here now, before the other cars come back. We'll stay away."

"How will that help you?"

"Your cars will run out of gas someday, won't they? You haven't got them fixed up so they can tank up on their own, have you? We'll come back and finish the job."

"They'll be looking for me," I said. "Mrs. Hester will call the police."

He was past reasoning with. He just punched the bus in gear. It lurched forward. Sally followed.

He giggled. "What can she do if you're here with me?"

Sally seemed to realize that, too. She picked up speed, passed us and was gone. Gellhorn opened the window next to him and spat through the opening.

The bus lumbered on over the dark road, its motor rattling unevenly. Gellhorn dimmed the periphery light until the phosphorescent green stripe down the middle of the highway, sparkling in the moonlight, was all that kept us out of the trees. There was virtually no traffic. Two cars passed ours, going the other way, and there was none at all on our side of the highway, either before or behind.

I heard the door-slamming first. Quick and sharp in the silence, first on the right and then on the left. Gellhorn's hands quivered as he punched savagely for increased speed. A beam of light shot out from among a scrub of trees, blinding us. Another beam plunged at us from behind the guard rails on the other side. At a crossover, four hundred yards ahead, there was a sque-e-e-e-e as a car darted across our path.

"Sally went for the rest," I said. "I think you're surrounded."

"So what? What can they do?"

He hunched over the controls, peering through the windshield.

"And don't *you* try anything, old-timer," he muttered.

I couldn't. I was bone-weary; my left arm was on fire. The motor sounds gathered and grew closer. I could hear the motors missing in odd patterns; suddenly it seemed to me that my cars were speaking to one another.

A medley of horns came from behind. I turned and Gellhorn looked quickly into the rear-view mirror. A dozen cars were following in both lanes.

Gellhorn yelled and laughed madly.

I cried, "Stop! Stop the car!"

Because not a quarter of a mile ahead, plainly visible in the light beams of two sedans on the roadside was Sally, her trim body plunked square across the road. Two cars shot into the opposite lane to our left, keeping perfect time with us and preventing Gellhorn from turning out.

But he had no intention of turning out. He put his finger on the full-speed-ahead button and kept it there.

He said, "There'll be no bluffing here. This bus outweighs her five to one, old-timer, and we'll just push her off the road like a dead kitten."

I knew he could. The bus was on manual and his finger was on the button. I knew he would.

I lowered the window, and stuck my head out. "Sally," I screamed. "Get out of the way. *Sally!*"

It was drowned out in the agonized squeal of maltreated brake-bands. I felt myself thrown forward and heard Gellhorn's breath puff out of his body.

I said, "What happened?" It was a foolish question. We had stopped. That was what had happened. Sally and the bus were five feet apart. With five times her weight tearing down on her, she had not budged. The guts of her.

Gellhorn yanked at the Manual toggle switch. "It's got to," he kept muttering. "It's got to."

I said, "Not the way you hooked up the motor, expert. Any of the circuits could cross over."

He looked at me with a tearing anger and growled deep in her throat. His hair was matted over his forehead. He lifted his fist.

"That's all the advice out of you there'll ever be, old-timer."

And I knew the needle gun was about to fire.

I pressed back against the bus door, watching the fist come up, and when the door opened I went over backward and out, hitting the ground with a thud. I heard the door slam closed again.

I got to my knees and looked up in time to see Gellhorn struggle uselessly with the closing window, then aim his fist-gun quickly through the glass. He never fired. The bus got under way with a tremendous roar, and Gellhorn lurched backward.

Sally wasn't in the way any longer, and I watched the bus's rear light flicker away down the highway.

I was exhausted. I sat down right there, right on the highway, and put my head down in my crossed arms, trying to catch my breath.

I heard a car stop gently at my side. When I looked up, it was Sally. Slowly—lovingly, you might say—her front door opened.

No one had driven Sally for five years—except Gellhorn, of course—and I know how valuable such freedom was to a car. I appreciated the gesture, but I said, "Thanks, Sally, but I'll take one of the newer cars."

I got up and turned away, but skillfully and neatly as a pirouette, she wheeled before me again. I couldn't hurt her feelings. I got in. Her front seat had the fine, fresh scent of an automatobile that kept itself spotlessly clean. I lay down across it, thankfully, and with even, silent, and rapid efficiency, my boys and girls brought me home.

* * *

Mrs. Hester brought me the copy of the radio transcript the next evening with great excitement.

"It's Mr. Gellhorn," she said. "The man who came to see you."

"What about him?"

I dreaded her answer.

"They found him dead," she said. "Imagine that. Just lying dead in a ditch."

"It might be a stranger altogether," I mumbled.

"Raymond J. Gellhorn," she said, sharply. "There can't be two, can there? The description fits, too. Lord, what a way to die? They found tire marks on his arms and body. Imagine! I'm glad it turned out to be a bus; otherwise they might have come poking around here."

"Did it happen near here?" I asked, anxiously.

"No . . . Near Cooksville. But, goodness, read about it yourself if you—What happened to Giuseppe?"

I welcomed the diversion. Giuseppe was waiting patiently for me to complete the repaint job. His windshield had been replaced.

After she left, I snatched up the transcript. There was no doubt about it. The doctor reported he had been running and was in a state of totally spent exhaustion. I wondered for how many miles the bus had played with him before the final lunge. The transcript had no notion of anything like that, of course.

They had located the bus and identified it by the tire tracks. The police had it and were trying to trace its ownership.

There was an editorial in the transcript about it. It had been the first traffic fatality in the state for that year and the paper warned strenuously against manual driving after night.

There was no mention of Gellhorn's three thugs and for that, at least, I was grateful. None of our cars had been seduced by the pleasure of the chase into killing.

That was all. I let the paper drop. Gellhorn had been a criminal. His treatment of the bus had been brutal. There was no question in my mind he deserved death. But still I felt a bit queasy over the manner of it.

A month has passed now and I can't get it out of my mind.

My cars talk to one another. I have no doubt about it anymore. It's as though they've gained confidence; as though they're not bothering to keep it secret anymore. Their engines rattle and knock continuously.

And they don't talk among themselves only. They talk to the cars and buses that come into the Farm on business. How long have they been doing that?

They must be understood, too. Gellhorn's bus understood them, for all it hadn't been on the grounds more than an hour. I can close my eyes and bring back that dash along the highway, with our cars flanking the bus on either side, clacking their motors at it till it understood, stopped, let me out, and ran off with Gellhorn.

Did my cars tell him to kill Gellhorn? Or was that his idea?

Can cars have such ideas? The motor designers say no. But they mean under ordinary conditions. Have they foreseen *everything?*

Cars get ill-used, you know.

Some of them enter the Farm and observe. They get told things. They find out that cars exist whose motors are never stopped, whom no one ever drives, whose every need is supplied.

Then maybe they go out and tell others. Maybe the word is spreading quickly. Maybe they're going to think that the Farm way should be the way all over the world. They don't understand. You couldn't expect them to understand about legacies and the whims of rich men.

There are millions of automatobiles on Earth, tens of millions. If the thought gets rooted in them that they're slaves; that they should do something about it . . . If they begin to think the way Gellhorn's bus did . . .

Maybe it won't be till after my time. And then they'll have to keep a few of us to take care of them, won't they? They wouldn't kill us all.

And maybe they would. Maybe they wouldn't understand about how someone would have to care for them. Maybe they won't wait.

Every morning I wake up and think, Maybe today . . .

I don't get as much pleasure out of my cars as I used to. Lately, I notice that I'm even beginning to avoid Sally.

The Fun They Had

Margie even wrote about it that night in her diary. On the page headed May 17, 2157, she wrote, "Today Tommy found a real book!"

It was a very old book. Margie's grandfather once said that when he was a little boy *his* grandfather told him that there was a time when all stories were printed on paper.

They turned the pages, which were yellow and crinkly, and it was awfully funny to read words that stood still instead of moving the way they were supposed to—on a screen, you know. And then, when they turned back to the page before, it had the same words on it that it had had when they read it the first time.

"Gee," said Tommy, "what a waste. When you're through with the book, you just throw it away, I guess. Our television screen must have had a million books on it and it's good for plenty more. I wouldn't throw *it* away."

"Same with mine," said Margie. She was eleven and hadn't seen as many telebooks as Tommy had. He was thirteen.

She said, "Where did you find it?"

"In my house." He pointed without looking, because he was busy reading. "In the attic."

"What's it about?"

"School."

Margie was scornful. "School? What's there to write about school? I hate school."

Margie always hated school, but now she hated it more than ever. The mechanical teacher had been giving her test after test in geography and she had been doing worse and worse until her mother had shaken her head sorrowfully and sent for the County Inspector.

He was a round little man with a red face and a whole box of tools with dials and wires. He smiled at Margie and gave her an apple, then took the teacher apart. Margie had hoped he wouldn't know how to put it together again, but he knew how all right, and, after an hour or so, there it was again, large and black and ugly, with a big screen on which all the lessons were shown and the questions were asked. That wasn't so bad. The part Margie hated most was the slot where she had to put homework and test papers. She always had to write them out in a punch code they made her learn when she was six years old, and the mechanical teacher calculated the mark in no time.

The Inspector had smiled after he was finished and patted Margie's head. He said to her mother, "It's not the little girl's fault, Mrs. Jones. I think the geography sector was geared a little too quick. Those things happen sometimes. I've slowed it up to an average ten-year level. Actually, the over-all pattern of her progress is quite satisfactory." And he patted Margie's head again.

Margie was disappointed. She had been hoping they would take the teacher away altogether. They had once taken Tommy's teacher away for nearly a month because the history sector had blanked out completely.

So she said to Tommy, "Why would anyone write about school?"

Tommy looked at her with very superior eyes. "Because it's not our kind of school, stupid. This is the old kind of school that they had hundreds and hundreds of years ago." He added loftily, pronouncing the word carefully, "*Centuries* ago."

Margie was hurt. "Well, I don't know what kind of school they had all that time ago." She read the book over his shoulder for a while, then said, "Anyway, they had a teacher."

"Sure they had a teacher, but it wasn't a *regular* teacher. It was a man."

"A man? How could a man be a teacher?"

"Well, he just told the boys and girls things and gave them homework and asked them questions."

"A man isn't smart enough."

"Sure he is. My father knows as much as my teacher."

"He can't. A man can't know as much as a teacher."

"He knows almost as much, I betcha."

Margie wasn't prepared to dispute that. She said, "I wouldn't want a strange man in my house to teach be."

Tommy screamed with laughter. "You don't know much, Margie. The teachers didn't live in the house. They had a special building and all the kids went there."

"And all the kids learned the same thing?"

"Sure, if they were the same age."

"But my mother says a teacher has to be adjusted to fit the mind of each boy and girl it teaches and that each kid has to be taught differently."

"Just the same they didn't do it that way then. If you don't like it, you don't have to read the book."

"I didn't say I didn't like it," Margie said quickly. She wanted to read about those funny schools.

* * *

They weren't even half-finished when Margie's mother called, "Margie! School!"

Margie looked up. "Not yet, Mamma."

"Now!" said Mrs. Jones. "And it's probably time for Tommy, too."

Margie said to Tommy, "Can I read the book some more with you after school?"

"Maybe," he said nonchalantly. He walked away whistling, the dusty old book tucked beneath his arm.

Margie went into the schoolroom. It was right next to her bedroom, and the mechanical teacher was on and waiting for her. It was always on at the same time every day except Saturday and Sunday, because her mother said little girls learned better if they learned at regular hours.

The screen was lit up, and it said: "Today's arithmetic lesson is on the addition of proper fractions. Please insert yesterday's homework in the proper slot."

Margie did so with a sigh. She was thinking about the old schools they had when her grandfather's grandfather was a little boy. All the kids from the whole neighborhood came, laughing and shouting in the schoolyard, sitting together in the schoolroom, going home together at the end of the day. They learned the same things, so they could help one another on the homework and talk about it.

And the teachers were people . . .

The mechanical teacher was flashing on the screen: "When we add the fractions $\frac{1}{2}$ and $\frac{1}{4}$—"

Margie was thinking about how the kids must have loved it in the old days. She was thinking about the fun they had.

Franchise

Linda, age ten, was the only one of the family who seemed to enjoy being awake.

Norman Muller could hear her now through his own drugged, unhealthy coma. (He had finally managed to fall asleep an hour earlier but even then it was more like exhaustion than sleep.)

She was at his bedside now, shaking him. "Daddy, Daddy, wake up. Wake up!"

He suppressed a groan. "All right, Linda."

"But, Daddy, there's more policemen around than any time. Police cars and everything!"

Norman Muller gave up and rose blearily to his elbows. The day was beginning. It was faintly stirring toward dawn outside, the germ of a miserable gray that looked about as miserably gray as he felt. He could hear Sarah, his wife, shuffling about breakfast duties in the kitchen. His father-in-law, Matthew, was hawking strenuously in the bathroom. No doubt agent Handley was ready and waiting for him.

This was *the* day.

Election Day!

* * *

To begin with, it had been like every other year. Maybe a little worse, because it was a presidential year, but no worse than other presidential years if it came to that.

The politicians spoke about the guh-reat electorate and the vast electuh-ronic intelligence that was its servant. The press analyzed the situation with industrial computers (the New York *Times* and the St. Louis *Post-Dispatch* had their own computers) and were full of little hints as to what would be forthcoming. Commentators and columnists pinpointed the crucial state and county in happy contradiction to one another.

The first hint that it would *not* be like every other year was when Sarah Muller said to her husband on the evening of October 4 (with

Election Day exactly a month off), "Cantwell Johnson says that Indiana will be the state this year. He's the fourth one. Just think, *our* state this time."

Matthew Hortenweiler took his fleshy face from behind the paper, stared dourly at his daughter and growled, "Those fellows are paid to tell lies. Don't listen to them."

"Four of them, Father," said Sarah mildly. "They all say Indiana."

"Indiana *is* a key state, Matthew," said Norman, just as mildly, "on account of the Hawkins-Smith Act and this mess in Indianapolis. It—"

Matthew twisted his old face alarmingly and rasped out, "No one says Bloomington or Monroe County, do they?"

"Well—" said Norman.

Linda, whose little pointed-chinned face had been shifting from one speaker to the next, said pipingly, "You going to be voting this year, Daddy?"

Norman smiled gently and said, "I don't think so, dear."

But this was in the gradually growing excitement of an October in a presidential election year and Sarah had led a quiet life with dreams for her companions. She said longingly, "Wouldn't *that* be wonderful, though?"

"If I voted?" Norman Muller had a small blond mustache that had given him a debonair quality in the young Sarah's eyes, but which, with gradual graying, had declined merely to lack of distinction. His forehead bore deepening lines born of uncertainty and, in general, he had never seduced his clerkly soul with the thought that he was either born great or would under any circumstances achieve greatness. He had a wife, a job and a little girl, and except under extraordinary conditions of elation or depression was inclined to consider that to be an adequate bargain struck with life.

So he was a little embarrassed and more than a little uneasy at the direction his wife's thoughts were taking. "Actually, my dear," he said, "there are two hundred million people in the country, and, with odds like that, I don't think we ought to waste our time wondering about it."

His wife said, "Why, Norman, it's no such thing like two hundred million and you know it. In the first place, only people between twenty and sixty are eligible and it's always men, so that puts it down to maybe fifty million to one. Then, if it's really Indiana—"

"Then it's about one and a quarter million to one. You wouldn't want me to bet in a horse race against those odds, now, would you? Let's have supper."

Matthew muttered from behind his newspaper, "Damned foolishness."

Linda asked again, "You going to be voting this year, Daddy?"

Norman shook his head and they all adjourned to the dining room.

* * *

By October 20, Sarah's excitement was rising rapidly. Over the coffee, she announced that Mrs. Schultz, having a cousin who was the secretary of an Assemblyman, said that all the "smart money" was on Indiana.

"She says President Villers is even going to make a speech at Indianapolis."

Norman Muller, who had had a hard day at the store, nudged the statement with a raising of eyebrows and let it go at that.

Matthew Hortenweiler, who was chronically dissatisfied with Washington, said, "If Villers makes a speech in Indiana, that means he thinks Multivac will pick Arizona. He wouldn't have the guts to go closer, the mushhead."

Sarah, who ignored her father whenever she could decently do so, said, "I don't know why they don't announce the state as soon as they can, and then the county and so on. Then the people who were eliminated could relax."

"If they did anything like that," pointed out Norman, "the politicians would follow the announcements like vultures. By the time it was narrowed down to a township, you'd have a Congressman or two at every street corner."

"Matthew narrowed his eyes and brushed angrily at his sparse, gray hair. "They're vultures, anyhow. Listen—"

Sarah murmured, "Now, Father—"

Matthew's voice rumbled over her protest without as much as a stumble or hitch. "Listen, I was around when they set up Multivac. It would end partisan politics, they said. No more voters' money wasted on campaigns. No more grinning nobodies high-pressured and advertising-campaigned into Congress or the White House. So what happens. More campaigning then ever, only now they do it blind. They'll send guys to Indiana on account of the Hawkins-Smith Act and other guys to California in case it's the Joe Hammer situation that turns out crucial. I say, wipe out all that nonsense. Back to the good old—"

Linda asked suddenly, "Don't you want Daddy to vote this year, Grandpa?"

Matthew glared at the young girl. "Never you mind, now." He turned back to Norman and Sarah. "There was a time I voted.

Marched right up to the polling booth, stuck my fist on the levers and voted. There was nothing to it. I just said: This fellow's my man and I'm voting for him. *That's* the way it should be."

Linda said excitedly, "You voted, Grandpa? You really did?"

Sarah leaned forward quickly to quiet what might easily become an incongruous story drifting about the neighborhood. "It's nothing, Linda. Grandpa doesn't really mean voted. Everyone did that kind of voting, your grandpa, too, but it wasn't *really* voting."

Matthew roared, "It wasn't when I was a little boy. I was twenty-two and I voted for Langley and it was real voting. My vote didn't count for much, maybe, but it was as good as anyone else's. *Anyone* else's. And no Multivac to—"

Norman interposed, "All right, Linda, time for bed. And stop asking questions about voting. When you grow up, you'll understand all about it."

He kissed her with antiseptic gentleness and she moved reluctantly out of range under maternal prodding and a promise that she might watch the bedside video till 9:15, *if* she was prompt about the bathing ritual.

Linda said, "Grandpa," and stood with her chin down and her hands behind her back until his newspaper lowered itself to the point where shaggy eyebrows and eyes, nested in fine wrinkles, showed themselves. It was Friday, October 31.

He said, "Yes?"

Linda came closer and put both her forearms on one of the old man's knees so that he had to discard his newspaper altogether.

She said, "Grandpa, did you really once vote?"

He said, "You heard me say I did, didn't you? Do you think I tell fibs?"

"N—no, but Mamma says everybody voted then."

"So they did."

"But how could they? How could *everybody* vote?"

Matthew stared at her solemnly, then lifted her and put her on his knee.

He even moderated the tonal qualities of his voice. He said, "You see, Linda, till about forty years ago, everybody always voted. Say we wanted to decide who was to be the new President of the United States. The Democrats and Republicans would both nominate someone, and everybody would say who they wanted. When Election Day was over, they would count how many people wanted the Democrat and how many wanted the Republican. Whoever had more votes was elected. You see?"

Linda nodded and said, "How did all the people know who to vote for? Did Multivac tell them?"

Matthew's eyebrows hunched down and he looked severe. "They just used their own judgment, girl."

She edged away from him, and he lowered his voice again, "I'm not angry at you, Linda. But, you see, sometimes it took all night to count what everyone said and people were impatient. So they invented special machines which could look at the first few votes and compare them with the votes from the same places in previous years. That way the machine could compute how the total vote would be and who would be elected. You see?"

She nodded. "Like Multivac."

"The first computers were much smaller than Multivac. But the machines grew bigger and they could tell how the election would go from fewer and fewer votes. Then, at last, they built Multivac and it can tell from just one voter."

Linda smiled at having reached a familiar part of the story and said, "That's nice."

Matthew frowned and said, "No, it's not nice. I don't want a machine telling me how I would have voted just because some joker in Milwaukee says he's against higher tariffs. Maybe I wanted to vote cockeyed just for the pleasure of it. Maybe I don't want to vote. Maybe—"

But Linda had wriggled from his knee and was beating a retreat.

She met her mother at the door. Her mother, who was still wearing her coat and had not even had time to remove her hat, said breathlessly, "Run along, Linda. Don't get in Mother's way."

Then she said to Matthew, as she lifted her hat from her head and patted her hair back into place, "I've been at Agatha's."

Matthew stared at her censoriously and did not even dignify that piece of information with a grunt as he groped for his newspaper.

Sarah said, as she unbuttoned her coat, "Guess what she said?"

Matthew flattened out his newspaper for reading purposes with a sharp crackle and said, "Don't much care."

Sarah said, "Now, Father—" But she had no time for anger. The news had to be told and Matthew was the only recipient handy, so she went on, "Agatha's Joe is a policeman, you know, and he says a whole truckload of secret service men came into Bloomington last night."

"They're not after me."

"Don't you see, Father? Secret service agents, and it's almost election time. In *Bloomington*."

"Maybe they're after a bank robber."

"There hasn't been a bank robbery in town in ages . . . Father, you're hopeless."

She stalked away.

* * *

Nor did Norman Muller receive the news with noticeably greater excitement.

"Now, Sarah, how did Agatha's Joe know they were secret service agents?" he asked calmly. "They wouldn't go around with identification cards pasted on their foreheads."

But by next evening, with November a day old, she could say triumphantly, "It's just everyone in Bloomington that's for someone local to be the voter. The Bloomington *News* as much as said so on video."

Norman stirred uneasily. He couldn't deny it, and his heart was sinking. If Bloomington was really to be hit by Multivac's lightning, it would mean newspapermen, video shows, tourists, all sorts of—strange upsets. Norman liked the quiet routine of his life, and the distant stir of politics was getting uncomfortably close.

He said, "It's all rumor. Nothing more."

"You wait and see, then. You just wait and see."

As things turned out, there was very little time to wait, for the doorbell rang insistently, and when Norman Muller opened it and said, "Yes?" a tall, grave-faced man said, "Are you Norman Muller?"

Norman said, "Yes," again, but in a strange dying voice. It was not difficult to see from the stranger's bearing that he was one carrying authority, and the nature of his errand suddenly became as inevitably obvious as it had, until the moment before, been unthinkably impossible.

The man presented credentials, stepped into the house, closed the door behind him and said ritualistically, "Mr. Norman Muller, it is necessary for me to inform you on the behalf of the President of the United States that you have been chosen to represent the American electorate on Tuesday, November 4, 2008."

* * *

Norman Muller managed, with difficulty, to walk unaided to his chair. He sat there, white-faced and almost insensible, while Sarah brought water, slapped his hands in panic and moaned to her husband between clenched teeth, "Don't be sick, Norman. *Don't* be sick. They'll pick someone else."

When Norman could manage to talk, he whispered, "I'm sorry, sir."

The secret service agent had removed his coat, unbuttoned his jacket and was sitting at ease on the couch.

"It's all right," he said, and the mark of officialdom seemed to have vanished with the formal announcement and leave him simply a large and rather friendly man. "This is the sixth time I've made the announcement and I've seen all kinds of reactions. Not one of them was the kind you see on the video. You know what I mean? A holy, dedicated look, and a character who says, 'It will be a great privilege to serve my country.' That sort of stuff." The agent laughed comfortingly.

Sarah's accompanying laugh held a trace of shrill hysteria.

The agent said, "Now you're going to have me with you for a while. My name is Phil Handley. I'd appreciate it if you call me Phil. Mr. Muller can't leave the house any more till Election Day. You'll have to inform the department store that he's sick, Mrs. Muller. You can go about your business for a while, but you'll have to agree not to say a word about this. Right, Mrs. Muller?"

Sarah nodded vigorously. "No, sir. Not a word."

"All right. But, Mrs. Muller," Handley looked grave, "we're not kidding now. Go out only if you must and you'll be followed when you do. I'm sorry but that's the way we must operate."

"Followed?"

"It won't be obvious. Don't worry. And it's only for two days till the formal announcement to the nation is made. Your daughter—"

"She's in bed," said Sarah hastily.

"Good. She'll have to be told I'm a relative or friend staying with the family. If she does find out the truth, she'll have to be kept in the house. Your father had better stay in the house in any case."

"He won't like that," said Sarah.

"Can't be helped. Now, since you have no others living with you—"

"You know all about us apparently," whispered Norman.

"Quite a bit," agreed Handley. "In any case, those are all my instructions to you for the moment. I'll try to co-operate as much as I can and be as little of a nuisance as possible. The government will pay for my maintenance so I won't be an expense to you. I'll be relieved each night by someone who will sit up in this room, so there will be no problem about sleeping accommodations. Now, Mr. Muller—"

"Sir?"

"You can call me Phil," said the agent again. "The purpose of the two-day preliminary before formal announcement is to get you used to your position. We prefer to have you face Multivac in as normal a state of mind as possible. Just relax and try to feel this is all in a day's work. Okay?"

"Okay," said Norman, and then shook his head violently. "But I don't want the responsibility. Why me?"

"All right," said Handley, "let's get that straight to begin with. Multivac weighs all sorts of known factors, billions of them. One factor isn't known, though, and won't be known for a long time. That's the reaction pattern of the human mind. All Americans are subjected to the molding pressure of what other Americans do and say, to the things that are done to him and the things he does to others. Any American can be brought to Multivac to have the bent of his mind surveyed. From that the bent of all other minds in the country can be estimated. Some Americans are better for the purpose than others at some given time, depending upon the happenings of that year. Multivac picked you as most representative this year. Not the smartest, or the strongest, or the luckiest, but just the most representative. Now we don't question Multivac, do we?"

"Couldn't it make a mistake?" asked Norman.

Sarah, who listened impatiently, interrupted to say, "Don't listen to him, sir. He's just nervous, you know. Actually, he's very well read and he always follows politics very closely."

Handley said, "Multivac makes the decisions, Mrs. Muller. It picked your husband."

"But does it know everything?" insisted Norman wildly. "Couldn't it have made a mistake?"

"Yes, it can. There's no point in not being frank. In 1993, a selected Voter died of a stroke two hours before it was time for him to be notified. Multivac didn't predict that; it couldn't. A Voter might be mentally unstable, morally unsuitable, or, for that matter, disloyal. Multivac can't know everything about everybody until he's fed all the data there is. That's why alternative selections are always held in readiness. I don't think we'll be using one this time. You're in good health, Mr. Muller, and you've been carefully investigated. You qualify."

Norman buried his face in his hands and sat motionless.

"By tomorrow morning, sir," said Sarah, "he'll be perfectly all right. He just has to get used to it, that's all."

"Of course," said Handley.

* * *

In the privacy of their bedchamber, Sarah Muller expressed herself in other and stronger fashion. The burden of her lecture was, "So get hold of yourself, Norman. You're trying to throw away the chance of a lifetime."

Norman whispered desperately, "It frightens me, Sarah. The whole thing."

"For goodness' sake, why? What's there to it but answering a question or two?"

"The responsibility is too great. I couldn't face it."

"What responsibility? There isn't any. Multivac picked you. It's Multivac's responsibility. Everyone knows that."

Norman sat up in bed in a sudden excess of rebellion and anguish. "Everyone is *supposed* to know that. But they don't. They—"

"Lower your voice," hissed Sarah icily. "They'll hear you downtown."

"They don't," said Norman, declining quickly to a whisper. "When they talk about the Ridgely administration of 1988, do they say he won them over with pie-in-the-sky promises and racist baloney? No! They talk about the 'goddam MacComber vote,' as though Humphrey MacComber was the only man who had anything to do with it because he faced Multivac. I've said it myself—only now I think the poor guy was just a truck farmer who didn't ask to be picked. Why was it his fault more than anyone else's? Now his name is a curse."

"You're just being childish," said Sarah.

"I'm being sensible. I tell you, Sarah, I won't accept. They can't make me vote if I don't want to. I'll say I'm sick. I'll say—"

But Sarah had had enough. "Now you listen to me," she whispered in a cold fury. "You don't have only yourself to think about. You know what it means to be Voter of the Year. A presidential year at that. It means publicity and fame and, maybe, buckets of money—"

"And then I go back to being a clerk."

"You will *not*. You'll have a branch managership at the least if you have any brains at all, and you *will* have, because I'll tell you what to do. You control the kind of publicity if you play your cards right, and you can force Kennell Stores, Inc., into a tight contract *and* an escalator clause in connection with your salary *and* a decent pension plan."

"That's not the point in being Voter, Sarah."

"That will be your point. If you don't owe anything to yourself or to me—I'm not asking for myself—you owe something Linda."

Norman groaned.

"Well, don't you?" snapped Sarah.

"Yes, dear," murmured Norman.

* * *

On November 3, the official announcement was made and it was too late for Norman to back out even if he had been able to find the courage to make the attempt.

Their house was sealed off. Secret service agents made their appearance in the open, blocking off all approach.

At first the telephone rang incessantly, but Philip Handley with an engagingly apologetic smile took all calls. Eventually, the exchange shunted all calls directly to the police station.

Norman imagined that, in that way, he was spared not only the bubbling (and envious?) congratulations of friends, but also the egregious pressure of salesmen scenting a prospect and the designing smoothness of politicians from all over the nation . . . Perhaps even death threats from the inevitable cranks.

Newspapers were forbidden to enter the house now in order to keep out weighted pressures, and television was gently but firmly disconnected, over Linda's loud protests.

Matthew growled and stayed in his room; Linda, after the first flurry of excitement, sulked and whined because she could not leave the house; Sarah divided her time between preparation of meals for the present and plans for the future; and Norman's depression lived and fed upon itself.

And the morning of Tuesday, November 4, 2008, came at last, and it was Election Day.

* * *

It was early breakfast, but only Norman Muller ate, and that mechanically. Even a shower and shave had not succeeded in either restoring him to reality or removing his own conviction that he was as grimy without as he felt grimy within.

Handley's friendly voice did its best to shed some normality over the gray and unfriendly dawn. (The weather prediction had been for a cloudy day with prospects of rain before noon.)

Handley said, "We'll keep this house insulated till Mr. Muller is back, but after that we'll be off your necks." The secret service agent was in full uniform now, including sidearms in heavily brassed holsters.

"You've been no trouble at all, Mr. Handley," simpered Sarah.

Norman drank through two cups of black coffee, wiped his lips with a napkin, stood up and said haggardly, "I'm ready."

Handley stood up, too. "Very well, sir. And thank you, Mrs. Muller, for your very kind hospitality."

* * *

The armored car purred down empty streets. They were empty even for that hour of the morning.

Handley indicated that and said, "They always shift traffic away from the line of drive ever since the attempted bombing that nearly ruined the Leverett Election of '92."

When the car stopped, Norman was helped out by the always polite Handley into an underground drive whose walls were lined with soldiers at attention.

He was led into a brightly lit room, in which three white-uniformed men greeted him smilingly.

Norman said sharply, "But this is the hospital."

"There's no significance to that," said Handley at once. "It's just that the hospital has the necessary facilities."

"Well, what do I do?"

Handley nodded. One of the three men in white advanced and said, "I'll take over now, agent."

Handley saluted in an offhand manner and left the room.

The man in white said, "Won't you sit down, Mr. Muller? I'm John Paulson, Senior Computer. These are Samson Levine and Peter Dorogobuzh, my assistants."

Norman shook hands numbly all about. Paulson was a man of middle height with a soft face that seemed used to smiling and a very obvious toupee. He wore plastic-rimmed glasses of an old-fashioned cut, and he lit a cigarette as he talked. (Norman refused his offer of one.)

Paulson said, "In the first place, Mr. Muller, I want you to know we are in no hurry. We want you to stay with us all day if necessary, just so that you get used to your surroundings and get over any thought you might have that there is anything unusual in this, anything clinical, if you know what I mean."

"It's all right," said Norman. "I'd just as soon this were over."

"I understand your feelings. Still, we want you to know exactly what's going on. In the first place, Multivac isn't here."

"It isn't?" Somehow through all his depression, he had still looked forward to seeing Multivac. They said it was half a mile and three stories high, that fifty technicians walked the corridors *within* its structure continuously. It was one of the wonders of the world.

Paulson smiled. "No. It's not portable, you know. It's located underground, in fact, and very few people know exactly where. You can understand that, since it is our greatest natural resource. Believe me, elections aren't the only things it's used for."

Norman thought he was being deliberately chatty and found himself intrigued all the same. "I thought I'd see it. I'd like to."

"I'm sure of that. But it takes a presidential order and even then it has to be countersigned by Security. However, we are plugged into Multivac right here by beam transmission. What Multivac says can be interpreted here and what we say is beamed directly to Multivac, so in a sense we're in its presence."

Norman looked about. The machines within the room were all meaningless to him.

"Now let me explain, Mr. Muller," Paulson went on. "Multivac already has most of the information it needs to decide all the elections, national, state and local. It needs only to check certain imponderable attitudes of mind and it will use you for that. We can't predict what questions it will ask, but they may not make much sense to you, or even to us. It may ask you how you feel about garbage disposal in your town; whether you favor central incinerators. It might ask you whether you have a doctor of your own or whether you make use of National Medicine, Inc. Do you understand?"

"Yes, sir."

"Whatever it asks, you answer in your own words in any way you please. If you feel you must explain quite a bit, do so. Talk an hour, if necessary."

"Yes, sir."

"Now, one more thing. We will have to make use of some simple devices which will automatically record your blood pressure, heart-beat, skin conductivity and brain-wave pattern while you speak. The machinery will seem formidable, but it's all absolutely painless. You won't even know it's going on."

The other two technicians were already busying themselves with smooth-gleaming apparatus on oiled wheels.

Norman said, "Is that to check on whether I'm lying or not?"

"Not at all, Mr. Muller. There's no question of lying. It's only a matter of emotional intensity. If the machine asks you your opinion of your child's school, you may say, 'I think it is overcrowded.' Those are only words. From the way your brain and heart and hormones and sweat glands work, Multivac can judge exactly how intensely you feel about the matter. It will understand your feelings better than you yourself."

"I never heard of this," said Norman.

"No, I'm sure you didn't. Most of the details of Multivac's workings are top secret. For instance, when you leave, you will be asked to sign a paper swearing that you will never reveal the nature of the questions you were asked, the nature of your responses, what was done, or how it was done. The less is known about the Multivac, the less chance of attempted outside pressures upon the men who service it." He smiled grimly. "Our lives are hard enough as it is."

Norman nodded. "I understand."

"And now would you like anything to eat or drink?"

"No. Nothing right now."

"Do you have any questions?"

Norman shook his head.

"Then you tell us when you're ready."

"I'm ready right now."

"You're certain?"

"Quite."

Paulson nodded, and raised his hand in a gesture to the others. They advanced with their frightening equipment, and Norman Muller felt his breath come a little quicker as he watched.

* * *

The ordeal lasted nearly three hours, with one short break for coffee and an embarrassing session with a chamber pot. During all this time, Norman Muller remained encased in machinery. He was bone-weary at the close.

He thought sardonically that his promise to reveal nothing of what had passed would be an easy one to keep. Already the questions were a hazy mishmash in his mind.

Somehow he had thought Multivac would speak in a sepulchral, superhuman voice, resonant and echoing, but that, after all, was just an idea he had from seeing too many television shows, he now decided. The truth was distressingly undramatic. The questions were slips of a kind of metallic foil patterned with numerous punctures. A second machine converted the pattern into words and Paulson read the words to Norman, then gave him the question and let him read it for himself.

Norman's answers were taken down by a recording machine, played back to Norman for confirmation, with emendations and added remarks also taken down. All that was fed into a pattern-making instrument and that, in turn, was radiated to Multivac.

The one question Norman could remember at the moment was an incongruously gossipy: "What do you think of the price of eggs?"

Now it was over, and gently they removed the electrodes from various portions of his body, unwrapped the pulsating band from his upper arm, moved the machinery away.

He stood up, drew a deep, shuddering breath and said, "Is that all? Am I through?"

"Not quite." Paulson hurried to him, smiling in reassuring fashion. "We'll have to ask you to stay another hour."

"Why?" asked Norman sharply.

"It will take that long for Multivac to weave its new data into the trillions of items it has. Thousands of elections are concerned, you know. It's very complicated. And it may be that an odd contest here or there, a comptrollership in Phoenix, Arizona, or some council seat in Wilkesboro, North Carolina, may be in doubt. In that case, Multivac may be compelled to ask you a deciding question or two."

"No," said Norman. "I won't go through this again."

"It probably won't happen," Paulson said soothingly. "It rarely does. But, just in case, you'll have to stay." A touch of steel, just a touch, entered his voice. "You have no choice, you know. You must."

Norman sat down wearily. He shrugged.

Paulson said, "We can't let you read a newspaper, but if you'd care for a murder mystery, of if you'd like to play chess, or if there's anything we can do for you to help pass the time, I wish you'd mention it."

"It's all right. I'll just wait."

They ushered him into a small room just next to the one in which he had been questioned. He let himself sink into a plastic-covered armchair and closed his eyes.

As well as he could, he must wait out this final hour.

* * *

He sat perfectly still and slowly the tension left him. His breathing grew less ragged and he could clasp his hands without being quite so conscious of the trembling of his fingers.

Maybe there would be no questions. Maybe it was all over.

If it *were* over, then the next thing would be torchlight processions and invitations to speak at all sorts of functions. The Voter of the Year!

He, Norman Muller, ordinary clerk of a small department store in

Bloomington, Indiana, who had neither been born great nor achieved greatness would be in the extraordinary position of having had greatness thrust upon him.

The historians would speak soberly of the Muller Election of 2008. That would be its name, the Muller Election.

The publicity, the better job, the flash flood of money that interested Sarah so much, occupied only a corner of his mind. It would all be welcome, of course. He couldn't refuse it. But at the moment something else was beginning to concern him.

A latent patriotism was stirring. After all, he was representing the entire electorate. He was the focal point for *them*. He was, in his own person, for this one day, all of America!

The door opened, snapping him to open-eyed attention. For a moment, his stomach constricted. Not more questions!

But Paulson was smiling. "That will be all, Mr. Muller."

"No more questions, sir?"

"None needed. Everything was quite clear-cut. You will be escorted back to your home and then you will be a private citizen once more. Or as much so as the public will allow."

"Thank you. Thank you." Norman flushed and said, "I wonder—who was elected?"

Paulson shook his head. "That will have to wait for the official announcement. The rules are quite strict. We can't even tell you. You understand."

"Of course. Yes." Norman felt embarrassed.

"Secret service will have the necessary papers for you to sign."

"Yes." Suddenly, Norman Muller felt proud. It was on him now in full strength. He was proud.

In this imperfect world, the sovereign citizens of the first and greatest Electronic Democracy had, through Norman Muller (through *him!*) exercised once again its free, untrammeled franchise.

The Last Question

The last question was asked for the first time, half in jest, on May 21, 2061, at a time when humanity first stepped into the light. The question came about as a result of a five-dollar bet over highballs, and it happened this way:

Alexander Adell and Bertram Lupov were two of the faithful attendants of Multivac. As well as any human beings could, they knew what lay behind the cold, clicking, flashing face—miles and miles of face—of that giant computer. They had at least a vague notion of the general plan of relays and circuits that had long since grown past the point where any single human could possibly have a firm grasp of the whole.

Multivac was self-adjusting and self-correcting. It had to be, for nothing human could adjust and correct it quickly enough or even adequately enough. —So Adell and Lupov attended the monstrous giant only lightly and superficially, yet as well as any men could. They fed it data, adjusted questions to its needs and translated the answers that were issued. Certainly they, and all others like them, were fully entitled to share in the glory that was Multivac's.

For decades, Multivac had helped design the ships and plot the trajectories that enabled man to reach the Moon, Mars, and Venus, but past that, Earth's poor resources could not support the ships. Too much energy was needed for the long trips. Earth exploited its coal and uranium with increasing efficiency, but there was only so much of both.

But slowly Multivac learned enough to answer deeper questions more fundamentally, and on May 14, 2061, what had been theory, became fact.

The energy of the sun was stored, converted, and utilized directly on a planet-wide scale. All Earth turned off its burning coal, its fissioning uranium, and flipped the switch that connected all of it to a small station, one mile in diameter, circling the Earth at half the distance of the Moon. All Earth ran by invisible beams of sunpower.

Seven days had not sufficed to dim the glory of it and Adell and Lupov finally managed to escape from the public functions, and to meet in quiet where no one would think of looking for them, in the deserted underground chambers, where portions of the mighty buried body of Multivac showed. Unattended, idling, sorting data with contented lazy clickings, Multivac, too, had earned its vacation and the boys appreciated that. They had no intention, originally, of disturbing it.

They had brought a bottle with them, and their only concern at the moment was to relax in the company of each other and the bottle.

"It's amazing when you think of it," said Adell. His broad face had lines of weariness in it, and he stirred his drink slowly with a glass rod, watching the cubes of ice slur clumsily about. "All the energy we can possibly ever use for free. Enough energy, if we wanted to draw on it, to melt all Earth into a big drop of impure liquid iron, and still never miss the energy so used. All the energy we could ever use, forever and forever and forever."

Lupov cocked his head sideways. He had a trick of doing that when he wanted to be contrary, and he wanted to be contrary now, partly because he had had to carry the ice and glassware. "Not forever," he said.

"Oh, hell, just about forever. Till the sun runs down, Bert."

"That's not forever."

"All right, then. Billions and billions of years. Ten billion, maybe. Are you satisfied?"

Lupov put his fingers through his thinning hair as though to reassure himself that some was still left and sipped gently at his own drink. "Ten billion years isn't forever."

"Well, it will last our time, won't it?"

"So would the coal and uranium."

"All right, but now we can hook up each individual spaceship to the Solar Station, and it can go to Pluto and back a million times without ever worrying about fuel. You can't do *that* on coal and uranium. Ask Multivac, if you don't believe me."

"I don't have to ask Multivac. I know that."

"Then stop running down what Multivac's done for us," said Adell, blazing up, "It did all right."

"Who says it didn't? What I say is that a sun won't last forever. That's all I'm saying. We're safe for ten billion years, but then what?" Lupov pointed a slightly shaky finger at the other. "And don't say we'll switch to another sun."

There was a silence for a while. Adell put his glass to his lips only occasionally, and Lupov's eyes slowly closed. They rested.

Then Lupov's eyes snapped open. "You're thinking we'll switch to another sun when ours is done, aren't you?"

"I'm not thinking."

"Sure you are. You're weak on logic, that's the trouble with you. You're like the guy in the story who was caught in a sudden shower and who ran to a grove of trees and got under one. He wasn't worried, you see, because he figured when one tree got wet through, he would just get under another one."

"I get it," said Adell. "Don't shout. When the sun is done, the other stars will be gone, too."

"Darn right they will," muttered Lupov. "It all had a beginning in the original cosmic explosion, whatever that was, and it'll all have an end when all the stars run down. Some run down faster than others. Hell, the giants won't last a hundred million years. The sun will last ten billion years and maybe the dwarfs will last two hundred billion for all the good theyare. But just give us a trillion years and everything will be dark. Entropy has to increase to maximum, that's all."

"I know all about entropy," said Adell, standing on his dignity.

"The hell you do."

"I know as much as you do."

"Then you know everything's got to run down someday."

"All right. Who says they won't?"

"You did, you poor sap. You said we had all the energy we needed, forever. You said 'forever.' "

It was Adell's turn to be contrary. "Maybe we can build things up again someday," he said.

"Never."

"Why not? Someday."

"Never."

"Ask Multivac."

"*You* ask Multivac. I dare you. Five dollars says it can't be done."

Adell was just drunk enough to try, just sober enough to be able to phrase the necessary symbols and operations into a question which, in words, might have corresponded to this: Will mankind one day without the net expenditure of energy be able to restore the sun to its full youthfulness even after it had died of old age?

Or maybe it could be put more simply like this: How can the net amount of entropy of the universe be massively decreased?

Multivac fell dead and silent. The slow flashing of lights ceased, the distant sounds of clicking relays ended.

Then, just as th frightened technicians felt they could hold their breath no longer, there was a sudden spring to life of the teletype attached to that portion of Multivac. Five words were printed: INSUFFICIENT DATA FOR MEANINGFUL ANSWER.

"No bet," whispered Lupov. They left hurriedly.

By next morning, the two, plagued with throbbing head and cottony mouth, had forgotten the incident.

* * *

Jerrodd, Jerrodine, and Jerrodette I and II watched the starry picture in the visiplate change as the passage through hyperspace was completed in its non-time lapse. At once, the even powdering of stars gave way to the predominance of a single bright shining disk, the size of a marble, centered on the viewing-screen.

"That's X-23," said Jerrod confidently. His thin hands clamped tightly behind his back and the knuckles whitened.

The little Jerrodettes, both girls, had experienced the hyperspace passage for the first time in their lives and were self-conscious over the momentary sensation of inside-outness. They buried their giggles and chased one another wildly about their mother, screaming, "We've reached X-23—we've reached X-23—we've—"

"Quiet, children," said Jerrodine sharply. "Are you sure, Jerrodd?"

"What is there to be but sure?" asked Jerrodd, glancing up at the bulge of featureless metal just under the ceiling. It ran the length of the room, disappearing through the wall at either end. It was as long as the ship.

Jerrodd scarcely knew a thing about the thick rod of metal except that it was called a Microvac, that one asked it questions if one wished; that if one did not it still had its task of guiding the ship to a preordered destination; of feeding on energies from the various Sub-galactic Power Stations; of computing the equations for the hyperspatial jumps.

Jerrodd and his family had only to wait and live in the comfortable residence quarters of the ship.

Someone had once told Jerrodd that the "ac" at the end of "Microvac" stood for "automatic computer" in ancient English, but he was on the edge of forgetting even that.

Jerrodine's eyes were moist as she watched the visiplate. "I can't help it. I feel funny about leaving Earth."

"Why, for Pete's sake?" demanded Jerrodd. "We had nothing there. We'll have everything on X-23. You won't be alone. You won't be a pioneer. There are over a million people on the planet already. Good Lord, our great-grandchildren will be looking for new worlds because X-23 will be overcrowded." Then, after a reflective pause, "I tell you, it's a lucky thing the computers worked out intersteller travel the way the race is growing."

"I know, I know," said Jerrodine miserably.

Jerrodette I said promptly, "Our Microvac is the best Microvac in the world."

"I think so, too," said Jerrodd, tousling her hair.

It *was* a nice feeling to have a Microvac of your own and Jerrodd was glad he was part of his generation and no other. In his father's youth, the only computers had been tremendous machines taking up a hundred square miles of land. There was only one to a planet. Planetary ACs they were called. They had been growing in size steadily for a thousand years and then, all at once, came refinement. In place of transistors, had come molecular valves so that even the largest Planetary AC could be put into a space only half the volume of a spaceship.

Jerrodd felt uplifted, as he always did when he thought that his own personal Microvac was many times more complicated than the ancient and primitive Multivac that had first tamed the Sun, and almost as complicated as Earth's Planetary AC (the largest) that had first solved the problem of hyperspatial travel and had made trips to the stars possible.

"So many stars, so many planets," sighed Jerrodine, busy with her own thoughts. "I suppose families will be going out to new planets forever, the way we are now."

"Not forever," said Jerrodd, with a smile. "It will all stop someday, but not for billions of years. Many billions. Even the stars run down, you know. Entropy must increase."

"What's entropy, daddy?" shrilled Jerrodette II.

"Entropy, little sweet, is just a word which means the amount of running-down of the universe. Everything runs down, you know, like your little walkie-talkie robot, remember?"

"Can't you just put in a new power unit, like with my robot?"

"The stars *are* the power-units, dear. Once they're gone, there are no more power-units."

Jerrodette I at once set up a howl. "Don't let them, daddy. Don't let the stars run down."

"Now look what you've done," whispered Jerrodine, exasperated.

"How was I to know it would frighten them?" Jerrodd whispered back.

"Ask the Microvac," wailed Jerrodette I. "Ask him how to turn the stars on again."

"Go ahead," said Jerrodine. "It will quiet them down." (Jerrodette II was beginning to cry, also.)

Jerrodd shrugged. "Now, now, honeys. I'll ask Microvac. Don't worry, he'll tell us."

He asked the Microvac, adding quickly, "Print the answer."

Jerrodd cupped the strip of thin cellulfilm and said cheerfully, "See now, the Microvac says it will take care of everything when the time comes so don't worry."

Jerrodine said, "And now, children, it's time for bed. We'll be in our new home soon."

Jerrodd read the words on the cellufilm again before destroying it: INSUFFICIENT DATA FOR MEANINGFUL ANSWER.

He shrugged and looked at the visiplate. X-23 was just ahead.

* * *

VJ-23X of Lameth stared into the black depths of the three-dimensional, small-scale map of the Galaxy and said, "Are we ridiculous, I wonder, in being so concerned about the matter?"

MQ-17J of Nicron shook his head. "I think not. You know the Galaxy will be filled in five years at the present rate of expansion."

Both seemed in their early twenties, both were tall and perfectly formed.

"Still," said VJ-23X, "I hesitate to submit a pessimistic report to the Galactic Council."

"I wouldn't consider any other kind of report. Stir them up a bit. We've got to stir them up."

VJ-23X sighed. "Space is infinite. A hundred billion Galaxies are there for the taking. More."

"A hundred billion is *not* infinite and it's getting less infinite all the time. Consider! Twenty thousand years ago, mankind first solved the problem of utilizing stellar energy, and a few centuries later, interstellar travel became possible. It took mankind a million years to fill one small world and then only fifteen thousand years to fill the rest of the Galaxy. Now the population doubles every ten years—"

VJ-23X interrupted. "We can thank immortality for that."

"Very well. Immortality exists and we have to take it into account. I admit it has its seamy side, this immortality. The Galactic AC has solved many problems for us, but in solving the problem of preventing old age and death, it has undone all its other solutions."

"Yet you wouldn't want to abandon life, I suppose."

"Not at all," snapped MQ-17J, softening it at once to, "Not yet. I'm by no means old enough. How old are you?"

"Two hundred twenty-three. And you?"

"I'm still under two hundred. —But to get back to my point.

Population doubles every ten years. Once this Galaxy is filled, we'll have filled another in ten years. Another ten years and we'll have filled two more. Another decade, four more. In a hundred years, we'll have filled a thousand Galaxies. In a thousand years, a million Galaxies. In ten thousand years, the entire known Universe. Then what?"

VJ-23X said, "As a side issue, there's a problem of transportation. I wonder how many sunpower units it will take to move Galaxies of individuals from one Galaxy to the next."

"A very good point. Already, mankind consumes two sun-power units per year."

"Most of it's wasted. After all, our own Galaxy alone pours out a thousand sunpower units a year and we only use two of those."

"Granted, but even with a hundred per cent efficiency, we only stave off the end. Our energy requirements are going up in a geometric progression even faster than our population. We'll run out of energy even sooner than we run out of Galaxies. A good point. A very good point."

"We'll just have to build new stars out of interstellar gas."

"Or out of dissipated heat?" asked MQ-17J, sarcastically.

"There may be some way to reverse entropy. We ought to ask the Galactic AC."

VJ-23X was not really serious, but MQ-17J pulled out his AC-contact from his pocket an placed it on the table before him.

"I've half a mind to," he said. "It's something the human race will have to face some day."

He stared somberly at his small AC-contact. It was only two inches cubed and nothing in itself, but it was connected through hyperspace with the great Galactic AC that served all mankind. Hyperspace considered, it was an integral part of the Galactic AC.

MQ-17J paused to wonder if someday in his immortal life he would get to see the Galactic AC. It was on a little world of its own, a spider webbing of force-beams holding the matter within which surges of submesons took the place of the old clumsy molecular valves. Yet despite its sub-etheric workings, the Galactic AC was known to be a full thousand feet across.

MQ-17J asked suddenly of his AC-contact, "Can entropy ever be reversed?"

VJ-23X looked startled and said at once, "Oh, say, I didn't really mean to have you ask that."

"Why not?"

"We both know entropy can't be reversed. You can't turn smoke and ash back into a tree."

"Do you have trees on your world?" asked MQ-17J.

The sound of the Galactic AC startled them into silence. Its voice came thin and beautiful out of the small AC-contact on the desk. It said: THERE IS INSUFFICIENT DATA FOR A MEANINGFUL ANSWER.

VJ-23X said, "See!"

The two men thereupon returned to the question of the reports they were to make to the Galactic Council.

* * *

Zee Prime's mind spanned the new Galaxy with a faint interest in the countless twists of stars that powdered it. He had never seen this one before. Would he ever see them all? So many of them, each with its load of humanity. —But a load that was almost a dead weight. More and more, the real essence of men was to be found out here, in space.

Minds, not bodies! The immortal bodies remained back on the planets, in suspension over the eons. Sometimes they roused for material activity but that was growing rarer. Few new individuals were coming into existence to join the incredibly mighty throng, but what matter? There was little room in the Universe for new individuals.

Zee Prime was roused out of his reverie upon coming across the wispy tendrils of another mind.

"I am Zee Prime," said Zee Prime. "And you?"

"I am Dee Sub Wun. Your Galaxy?"

"We call it only the Galaxy. And you?"

"We call ours the same. All men call their Galaxy their Galaxy and nothing more. Why not?"

"True. Since all Galaxies are the same."

"Not all Galaxies. On one particular Galaxy the race of man must have originated. That makes it different."

Zee Prime said, "On which one?"

"I cannot say. The Universal AC would know."

"Shall we ask him? I am suddenly curious."

Zee Prime's perceptions broadened until the Galaxies themselves shrank and became a new, more diffuse powdering on a much larger background. So many hundreds of billions of them, all with their immortal beings, all carrying their load of intelligences with minds that drifted freely through space. And yet one of them was unique among them all in being the original Galaxy. One of them had, in its vague and distant past, a period when it was the only Galaxy populated by man.

Zee Prime was consumed with curiosity to see this Galaxy and he called out: "Universal AC! On which Galaxy did mankind originate?"

The Universal AC heard, for on every world and throughout space, it had its receptors ready, and each receptor lead through hyperspace to some unknown point where the Universal AC kept itself aloof.

Zee Prime knew of only one man whose thoughts had penetrated within sensing distance of Universal AC, and he reported only a shining globe, two feet across, difficult to see.

"But how can that be all of Universal AC?" Zee Prime had asked.

"Most of it," had been the answer, "is in hyperspace. In what form it is there I cannot imagine."

Nor could anyone, for the day had long since passed, Zee Prime knew, when any man had any part of the making of a Universal AC. Each Universal AC designed and constructed its successor. Each, during its existence of a million years or more accumulated the necessary data to build a better and more intricate, more capable successor in which its own store of data and individuality would be submerged.

The Universal AC interrupted Zee Prime's wandering thoughts, not with words, but with guidance. Zee Prime's mentality was guided into the dim sea of Galaxies and one in particular enlarged into stars.

A thought came, infinitely distant, but infinitely clear. "THIS IS THE ORIGINAL GALAXY OF MAN."

But it was the same after all, the same as any other, and Zee Prime stifled his disappointment.

Dee Sub Wun, whose mind had accompanied the other, said suddenly, "And is one of these stars the original star of Man?"

The Universal AC said, "MAN'S ORIGINAL STAR HAS GONE NOVA. IT IS A WHITE DWARF."

"Did the men upon it die?" asked Zee Prime, startled and without thinking.

The Universal AC said, "A NEW WORLD, AS IN SUCH CASES WAS CONSTRUCTED FOR THEIR PHYSICAL BODIES IN TIME."

"Yes, of course," said Zee Prime, but a sense of loss overwhelmed him even so. His mind released its hold on the original Galaxy of Man, let it spring back and lose itself among the blurred pin points. He never wanted to see it again.

Dee Sub Wun said, "What is wrong?"

"The stars are dying. The original star is dead."

"They must all die. Why not?"

"But when all energy is gone, our bodies will finally die, and you and I with them."

"It will take billions of years."

"I do not wish it to happen even after billions of years. Universal AC! How may stars be kept from dying?"

Dee Sub Wun said in amusement, "You're asking how entropy might be reversed in direction."

And the Universal AC answered: "THERE IS AS YET INSUFFICIENT DATA FOR A MEANINGFUL ANSWER."

Zee Prime's thoughts fled back to his own Galaxy. He gave no further thought to Dee Sub Wun, whose body might be waiting on a Galaxy a trillion light-years away, or on the star next to Zee Prime's own. It didn't matter.

Unhappily, Zee Prime began collecting interstellar hydrogen out of which to build a small star of his own. If the stars must someday die, at least some could yet be built.

* * *

Man considered with himself, for in a way, Man, mentally, was one. He consisted of a trillion, trillion, trillion ageless bodies, each in its place, each resting quiet and incorruptible, each cared for by perfect automations, equally incorruptible, while the minds of all the bodies freely melted one into the other, indistinguishable.

Man said, "The Universe is dying."

Man looked about at the dimming Galaxies. The giant stars, spendthrifts, were gone long ago, back in the dimmest of the dim far past. Almost all stars were white dwarfs, fading to the end.

New stars had been built of the dust between the stars, some by natural processes, some by Man himself, and those were going, too. White dwarfs might yet be crashed together and of the mighty forces so released, new stars built, but only one star for every thousand white dwarfs destroyed, and those would come to an end, too.

Man said, "Carefully husbanded, as directed by the Cosmic AC, the energy that is even yet left in all the Universe will last for billions of years."

"But even so," said Man, "eventually it will all come to an end. However it may be husbanded, however stretched out, the energy once expended is gone and cannot be restored. Entropy must increase forever to the maximum."

Man said, "Can entropy not be reversed? Let us ask the Cosmic AC."

The Cosmic AC surrounded them but not in space. Not a fragment of it was in space. It was in hyperspace and made of something that was neither matter not energy. The question of its size and nature no longer had meaning in any terms that Man could comprehend.

"Cosmic AC," said Man, "how may entropy be reversed?"

The Cosmic AC said, "THERE IS AS YET INSUFFICIENT DATA FOR A MEANINGFUL ANSWER."

Man said, "Collect additional data."

The Cosmic AC said, "I WILL DO SO. I HAVE BEEN DOING SO FOR A HUNDRED BILLION YEARS. MY PREDECESSORS AND I HAVE BEEN ASKED THIS QUESTION MANY TIMES. ALL THE DATA I HAVE REMAINS INSUFFICIENT."

"Will there come a time," said Man, "when data will be sufficient or is the problem insoluable in all conceivable circumstances?"

The Cosmic AC said, "NO PROBLEM IS INSOLUBLE IN ALL CONCEIVABLE CIRCUMSTANCES."

Man said, "When will you have enough data to answer the question?"

The Cosmic AC said, "THERE IS AS YET INSUFFICIENT DATA FOR A MEANINGFUL ANSWER."

"Will you keep working on it?" asked Man.

The Cosmic AC said, "I WILL."

Man said, "We shall wait."

* * *

The stars and Galaxies died and snuffed out, and space grew black after ten trillion years of running down.

One by one Man fused with AC, each physical body losing its mental identity in a manner that was somehow not a loss but a gain.

Man's last mind paused before fusion, looking over a space that included nothing but the dregs of one last dark star and nothing besides but incredibly thin matter, agitated randomly by the tag ends of heat wearing out, asymptotically, to the absolute zero.

Man said, "AC, is this the end? Can this chaos not be reversed into the Universe once more? Can that not be done?"

AC said, "THERE IS AS YET INSUFFICIENT DATA FOR A MEANINGFUL ANSWER."

Man's last mind fused and only AC existed—and that in hyperspace.

* * *

Matter and energy had ended and with it space and time. Even AC existed only for the sake of the one last question that it had never answered from the time a half-drunken computer ten trillion years before had asked the question of a computer that was to AC far less than was a man to Man.

All other questions had been answered, and until this last question was answered also, AC might not release his consciousness.

All collected data had come to a final end. Nothing was left to be collected.

But all collected data had yet to be completely correlated and put together in all possible relationships.

A timeless interval was spent in doing that.

And it came to pass that AC learned how to reverse the direction of entropy.

But there was now no man to whom AC might give the answer of the last question. No matter. The answer—by demonstration—would take care of that, too.

For another timeless interval, AC thought how best to do this. Carefully, AC organized the program.

The consciousness of AC encompassed all of what had once been a Universe and brooded over what was now Chaos. Step by step, it must be done.

And AC said, "LET THERE BE LIGHT!"

And there was light—

Profession

George Platen could not conceal the longing in his voice. It was too much to suppress. He said, "Tomorrow's the first of May. Olympics!"

He rolled over on his stomach and peered over the foot of his bed at his roommate. Didn't *he* feel it, too? Didn't *this* make some impression on him?

George's face was thin and had grown a trifle thinner in the nearly year and a half that he had been at the House. His figure was slight but the look in his blue eyes was as intense as it had ever been, and right now there was a trapped look in the way his fingers curled against the bedspread.

George's roommate looked up briefly from his book and took the opportunity to adjust the light-level of the stretch of wall near his chair. His name was Hali Omani and he was a Nigerian by birth. His dark brown skin and massive features seemed made for calmness, and mention of the Olympics did not move him.

He said, "I know, George."

George owed much to Hali's presence and kindness when it was needed, but even patience and kindness could be overdone. Was this a time to sit there like a statue built of some dark, warm wood?

George wondered if he himself would grow like that after ten years here and rejected the thought violently. No!

He said defiantly, "I think you've forgotten what May means."

The other said, "I remember very well what it means. It means nothing! You're the one who's forgotten that. May means nothing to you, George Platen, and," he added softly, "it means nothing to me, Hali Omani."

George said, "The ships are coming in for recruits. By June, thousands and thousands will leave with millions of men and women heading for any world you can name, and all that means nothing?"

"Less than nothing. What do you want me to do about it, anyway?" Omani ran his finger along a difficult passage in the book he was reading and his lips moved soundlessly.

George watched him. Damn it, he thought, yell, scream; you can do that much. Kick at me, do anything.

It was only that he wanted not to be so alone in his anger. He wanted not to be the only one so filled with resentment, not to be the only one dying a slow death.

It was better those first weeks when the Universe was a small shell of vague light and sound pressing down upon him. It was better before Omani had wavered into view and dragged him back to a life that wasn't worth living.

Omani! He was old! He was at least thirty. George thought: Will I be like that at thirty? Will I be like that in twelve years?

And because he was afraid he might be, he yelled at Omani, "Will you stop reading that fool book?"

Omani turned a page and read on a few words, then lifted his head with its skullcap of crisply curled hair and said, "What?"

"What good does it do you to read the book?" He stepped forward, snorted "More electronics," and slapped it out of Omani's hands.

Omani got up slowly and picked up the book. He smoothed a crumpled page without visible rancor. "Call it the satisfaction of curiosity," he said. "I understand a little of it today, perhaps a little more tomorrow. That's a victory in a way."

"A victory. What kind of a victory? Is that what satisfies you in life? To get to know enough to be a quarter of a Registered Electronician by the time you're sixty-five?"

"Perhaps by the time I'm thirty-five."

"And then who'll want you? Who'll use you? Where will you go?"

"No one. No one. Nowhere. I'll stay here and read other books."

"And that satisfies you? Tell me! You've dragged me to class. You've got me to reading and memorizing, too. For what? There's nothing in it that satisfies me."

"What good will it do you to deny yourself satisfaction?"

"It means I'll quit the whole farce. I'll do as I planned to do in the beginning before you dovey-lovied me out of it. I'm going to force them to—to—"

Omani put down his book. He let the other run down and then said, "To what, George?"

"To correct a miscarriage of justice. A frame-up. I'll get that Antonelli and force him to admit he—he—"

Omani shook his head. "Everyone who comes here insists it's a mistake. I thought you'd passed that stage."

"Don't call it a stage," said George violently. "In my case, it's a fact. I've told you—"

"You've told me, but in your heart you know no one made any mistake as far as you were concerned."

"Because no one will admit it? You think any of them would admit a mistake unless they were forced to? —Well, I'll force them."

It was May that was doing this to George; it was Olympics month. He felt it bring the old wildness back and he couldn't stop it. He didn't want to stop it. He had been in danger of forgetting.

He said, "I was going to be a Computer Programmer and I *can* be one. I could be one today, regardless of what they say analysis shows." He pounded his mattress. "They're wrong. They *must* be."

"The analysts are never wrong."

"They *must* be. Do you doubt my intelligence?"

"Intelligence hasn't one thing to do with it. Haven't you been told that often enough? Can't you understand that?"

George rolled away, lay on his back, and stared somberly at the ceiling.

"What did you want to be, Hali?"

"I had no fixed plans. Hydroponicist would have suited me, I suppose."

"Did you think you could make it?"

"I wasn't sure."

George had never asked personal questions of Omani before. It struck him as queer, almost unnatural, that other people had had ambitions and ended here. Hydroponicist!

He said, "Did you think you'd make *this?*"

"No, but here I am just the same."

"And you're satisfied. Really, really satisied. You're happy. You love it. You wouldn't be anywhere else."

Slowly, Omani got to his feet. Carefully, he began to unmake his bed. He said, "George, you're a hard case. You're knocking yourself out because you won't accept the facts about yourself. George, you're here in what you call the House, but I've never heard you give it its full title. Say it, George, say it. Then go to bed and sleep this off."

George gritted his teeth and showed them. He choked out, "No!"

"Then I will," said Omani, and he did. He shaped each syllable carefully.

George was bitterly ashamed at the sound of it. He turned his head away.

* * *

For most of the first eighteen years of his life, George Platen had headed firmly in one direction, that of Registered Computer

Programmer. There were those in his crowd who spoke wisely of Spationautics, Refrigeration Technology, Transportation Control, and even Administration. But George held firm.

He argued relative merits as vigorously as any of them, and why not? Education Day loomed ahead of them and was the great fact of their existence. It approached steadily, as fixed and certain as the calendar—the first day of November of the year following one's eighteenth birthday.

After that day, there were other topics of conversation. One could discuss wih others some detail of the profession, or the virtues of one's wife and children, or the fate of one's space-polo team, or one's experiences in the Olympics. Before Education Day, however, there was only one topic that unfailingly and unwearyingly held everyone's interest, and that was Education Day.

"What are you going for? Think you'll make it? Heck, that's no good. Look at the records; quota's been cut. Logistics now—"

Or Hypermechanics now— Or Communications now— Or Gravitics now—

Especially Gravitics at the moment. Everyone had been talking about Gravitics in the few years just before George's Education Day because of the development of the Gravitic power engine.

Any world within ten light-years of a dwarf star, everyone said, would give its eyeteeth for any kind of Registered Gravitics Engineer.

The thought of that never bothered George. Sure it would; all the eyeteeth it could scare up. But George had also heard what had happened before in a newly developed technique. Rationalization and simplification followed in a flood. New models each year; new types of gravitic engines; new principles. Then all those eyeteeth gentlemen would find themselves out of date and superseded by later models with later educations. The first group would then have to settle down to unskilled labor or ship out to some backwoods world that wasn't quite caught up yet.

Now Computer Programmers were in steady demand year after year, century after century. The demand never reached wild peaks; there was never a howling bull market for Programmers; but the demand climbed steadily as new worlds opened up and as older words grew more complex.

He had argued with Stubby Trevelyan about that constantly. As best friends, their arguments had to be constant and vitriolic and, of course, neither ever persuaded or was persuaded.

But then Trevelyan had had a father who was a Registered Metallurgist and had actually served on one of the Outworlds, and a grandfather who had also been a Registered Metallurgist. He himself was intent on becoming a Registered Metallurgist almost as a matter of family right and was firmly convinced that any other profession was a shade less than respectable.

"There'll always be metal," he said, "and there's an accomplishment in molding alloys to specification and watching structures grow. Now what's a Programmer going to be doing. Sitting at a coder all day long, feeding some fool mile-long machine."

Even at sixteen, George had learned to be practical. He said simply, "There'll be a million Metallurgists put out along with you."

"Because it's good. A good profession. The best."

"But you get crowded out, Stubby. You can be way back in line. Any world can tape out its own Metallurgists, and the market for advanced Earth models isn't so big. And it's mostly the small worlds that want them. You know what per cent of the turnout of Registered Metallurgists get tabbed for worlds with a Grade A rating. I looked it up. It's just 13.3 per cent. That means you'll have seven chances in eight of being stuck in some world that just about has running water. You may even be stuck on Earth; 2.3 per cent are."

Trevelyan said belligerently, "There's no disgrace in staying on Earth. Earth needs technicians, too. Good ones." His grandfather had been an Earth-bound Metallurgist, and Trevelyan lifted his finger to his upper lip and dabbed at an as yet nonexistent mustache.

George knew about Trevelyan's grandfather and, considering the Earth-bound position of his own ancestry, was in no mood to sneer. He said diplomatically, "No intellectual disgrace. Of course not. But it's nice to get into a Grade A world, isn't it?

"Now you take Programmers. Only the Grade A worlds have the kind of computers that really need first-class Programmers so they're the only ones in the market. And Programmer tapes are complicated and hardly any one fits. They need more Programmers than their own population can supply. It's just a matter of statistics. There's one first-class Programmer per million, say. A world needs twenty and has a population of ten million, they have to come to Earth for five to fifteen Programmers. Right?

"And you know how many Registered Computer Programmers went to Grade A planets last year? I'll tell you. Every last one. If you're a Programmer, you're a picked man. Yes, sir."

Trevelyan frowned. "If only one in a million makes it, what makes you think *you'll* make it?"

George said guardedly, "I'll make it."

He never dared tell anyone; not Trevelyan; not his parents; of exactly what he was doing that made him so confident. But he wasn't worried. He was simply confident (that was the worst of the memories he had in the hopeless days afterward). He was as blandly confident as the average eight-year-old kid approaching Reading Day—that childhood preview of Education Day.

* * *

Of course, Reading Day had been different. Partly, there was the simple fact of childhood. A boy of eight takes many extraordinary things in stride. One day you can't read and the next day you can. That's just the way things are. Like the sun shining.

And then not so much depended upon it. There were no recruiters just ahead, waiting and jostling for the lists and scores on the coming Olympics. A boy or girl who goes through the Reading Day is just someone who has ten more years of undifferentiated living upon Earth's crawling surface; just someone who returns to his family with one new ability.

By the time Education Day came, ten years later, George wasn't even sure of most of the details of his own Reading Day.

Most clearly of all, he remembered it to be a dismal September day with a mild rain falling. (September for Reading Day; November for Education Day; May for Olympics. They made nursery rhymes out of it.) George had dressed by the wall lights, with his parents far more excited than he himself was. His father was a Registered Pipe Fitter and had found his occupation on Earth. This fact had always been a humiliation to him, although, of course, as anyone could see plainly, most of each generation must stay on Earth in the nature of things.

There had to be farmers and miners and even technicians on Earth. It was only the late-model, high-specialty professions that were in demand on the Outworlds, and only a few millions a year out of Earth's eight billion population could be exported. Every man and woman on Earth couldn't be among that group.

But every man and woman could hope that at least one of his children could be one, and Platen, Senior, was certainly no exception. It was obvious to him (and, to be sure, to others as well) that George was notably intelligent and quick-minded. He would be bound to do well and he would have to, as he was an only child. If George didn't end on an Outworld, they would have to wait for grandchildren before a next chance would come along, and that was too far in the future to be much consolation.

Reading Day would not prove much, of course, but it would be the only indication they would have before the big day itself. Every parent on Earth would be listening to the quality of reading when his child came home with it; listening for any particularly easy flow of words and building that into certain omens of the future. There were few families that didn't have at least one hopeful who, from Reading Day on, was the great hope because of the way he handled his trisyllabics.

Dimly, George was aware of the cause of his parents' tension, and if there was any anxiety in his young heart that drizzly morning, it was only the fear that his father's hopeful expression might fade out when he returned home with his reading.

The children met in the large assembly room of the town's Education hall. All over Earth, in millions of local halls, throughout that month, similar groups of children would be meeting. George felt depressed by the grayness of the room and by the other children, strained and stiff in unaccustomed finery.

Automatically, George did as all the rest of the children did. He found the small clique that represented the children on his floor of the apartment house and joined them.

Trevelyan, who lived immediately next door, still wore his hair childishly long and was years removed from the sideburns and thin, reddish mustache that he was to grow as soon as he was physiologically capable of it.

Trevelyan (to whom George was then known as Jaw-jee) said, "Bet you're scared."

"I am not," said George. Then, confidentially, "My folks got a hunk of printing up on the dresser in my room, and when I come home, I'm going to read it for them." (George's main suffering at the moment lay in the fact that he didn't quite know where to put his hands. He had been warned not to scratch his head or rub his ears or pick his nose or put his hands into his pockets. This eliminated almost every possibility.)

Trevelyan put *his* hands in his pockets and said, "My father isn't worried."

Trevelyan, Senior, had been a Metallurgist on Diporia for nearly seven years, which gave him a superior social status in his neighborhood even though he had retired and returned to Earth.

Earth discouraged these re-immigrants because of population problems, but a small trickle did return. For one thing the cost of living was lower on Earth, and what was a trifling annuity on Diporia, say, was a comfortable income on Earth. Besides, there were always men who found more satisfaction in displaying their success before the friends and scenes of their childhood than before all the rest of the Universe besides.

Trevelyan, Senior, further explained that if he stayed on Diporia, so would his children, and Diporia was a one-spaceship world. Back on Earth, his kids could end anywhere, even Novia.

Stubby Trevelyan had picked up that item early. Even before Reading Day, his conversation was based on the carelessly assumed fact that his ultimate home would be in Novia.

George, oppressed by thoughts of the other's future greatness and his own small-time contrast, was driven to belligerent defense at once.

"My father isn't worried either. He just wants to hear me read because he knows I'll be good. I suppose your father would just as soon not hear you because he knows you'll be all wrong."

"I will not be all wrong. Reading is *nothing*. On Novia, I'll *hire* people to read to me."

"Because *you* won't be able to read yourself, on account of you're *dumb!*"

"Then how come I'll be on Novia?"

And George, driven, made the great denial, "Who says you'll be on Novia? Bet you don't go anywhere."

Stubby Trevelyan reddened. "I won't be a Pipe Fitter like your old man."

"Take that back, you dumbhead."

"You take *that* back."

They stood nose to nose, not wanting to fight but relieved at having something familiar to do in this strange place. Furthermore, now that George had curled his hands into fists and lifted them before his face, the problem of what to do with his hands was, at least temporarily, solved. Other children gathered round excitedly.

But then it all ended when a woman's voice sounded loudly over the public address system. There was instant silence everywhere. George dropped his fists and forgot Trevelyan.

"Children," said the voice, "we are going to call out your names. As each child is called, he or she is to go to one of the men waiting along the side walls. Do you see them? They are wearing red uniforms so they will be easy to find. The girls will go to the right. The boys will go to the left. Now look about and see which man in red is nearest to you—"

George found his man at a glance and waited for his name to be called off. He had not been introduced before this to the sophistications of the alphabet, and the length of time it took to reach his own name grew disturbing.

The crowd of children thinned; little rivulets made their way to each of the red-clad guides.

When the name "George Platen" was finally called, his sense of relief was exceeded only by the feeling of pure gladness at the fact that Stubby Trevelyan still stood in his place, uncalled.

George shouted back over his shoulder as he left, "Yay, Stubby, maybe they don't want you."

That moment of gaiety quickly left. He was herded into a line and directed down corridors in the company of strange children. They all looked at one another, large-eyed and concerned, but beyond a snuffling, "Quitcher pushing" and "Hey, watchout" there was no conversation.

They were handed little slips of paper which they were told must remain with them. George stared at his curiously. Little black marks of different shapes. He knew it to be printing but how could anyone make words out of it? He couldn't imagine.

He was told to strip; he and four other boys who were all that now remained together. All the new clothes came shucking off and four eight-year-olds stood naked and small, shivering more out of embarrassment than cold. Medical technicians came past, probing them, testing them with odd instrument, pricking them for blood. Each took the little cards and made additional marks on them with little black rods that produced the marks, all neatly lined up, with great speed. George stared at the new marks, but they were no more comprehensible than the old. The children were ordered back into their clothes.

They sat on separate little chairs then and waited again. Names were called again and "George Platen" came third.

He moved into a large room, filled with frightening instruments with knobs and glassy panels in front. There was a desk in the very center, and behind it a man sat, his eyes on the papers piled before him.

He said, "George Platen?"

"Yes, sir," said George, in a shaky whisper. All this waiting and all this going here and there was making him nervous. He wished it were over.

The man behind the desk said, "I am Dr. Lloyed, George. How are you?"

The doctor didn't look up as he spoke. It was as though he had said those words over and over again and didn't have to look up any more.

"I'm all right."

"Are you afraid, George?"

"N—no, sir," said the doctor, "because there's nothing to be afraid of, you know. Let's see, George. It says here on your card that your father is named Peter and that he's a Registered Pipe Fitter and your mother is named Amy and is a Registered Home Technician. Is that right?"

"Y—yes, sir."

"And your birthday is February 13, and you had an ear infection about a year ago. Right?"

"Yes, sir."

"Do you know how I know all these things?"

"It's on the card, I think, sir."

"That's right." The doctor looked up at George for the first time and smiled. He showed even teeth and looked much younger than George's father. Some of George's nervousness vanished.

The doctor passed the card to George. "Do you know what all those things there mean, George?"

Although George knew he did not he was startled by the sudden request into looking at the card as though he might understand now through some sudden stroke of fate. But they were just marks as before and he passed the card back. "No, sir."

"Why not?"

George felt a sudden pang of suspicion concerning the sanity of this doctor. Didn't he know why not?

George said, "I can't read, sir."

"Would you like to read?"

"Yes, sir."

"Why, George?"

George stared, appalled. No one had ever asked him that. He had no answer. He said falteringly, "I don't know, sir."

"Printed information will direct you all through your life. There is so much you'll have to know even after Education Day. Cards like this one will tell you. Books will tell you. Television screens will tell you. Printing will tell you such useful things and such interesting things that not being able to read would be as bad as not being able to see. Do you understand?"

"Yes, sir."

"Are you afraid, George?"

"No, sir."

"Good. Now I'll tell you exactly what we'll do first. I'm going to put these wires on your forehead just over the corners of your eyes. They'll stick there but they won't hurt at all. Then, I'll turn on something that will make a buzz. It will sound funny and it may tickle you, but it won't hurt. Now if it does hurt, you tell me, and I'll turn it off right away, but it won't hurt. All right?"

George nodded and swallowed.

"Are you ready?"

George nodded. He closed his eyes while the doctor busied himself.

His parents had explained this to him. They, too, had said it wouldn't hurt, but then there were always the older children. There were the ten-and twelve-year-olds who howled after the eight-year-olds waiting for Reading Day, "Watch out for the needle." There were the others who took you off in confidence and said, "They got to cut your head open. They use a sharp knife that big with a hook on it," and so on into horrifying details.

George had never believed them but he had had nightmares, and now he closed his eyes and felt pure terror.

He didn't feel the wires at his temple. The buzz was a distant thing, and there was the sound of his own blood in his ears, ringing hollowly as though it and he were in a large cave. Slowly he chanced opening his eyes.

The doctor had his back to him. From one of the instruments a strip of paper unwound and was covered with a thin, wavy purple line. The doctor tore off pieces and put them into a slot in another machine. He did it over and over again. Each time a little piece of film came out, which the doctor looked at. Finally, he turned toward George with a queer frown between his eyes.

The buzzing stopped.

George said breathlessly, "Is it over?"

The doctor said, "Yes," but he was still frowning.

"Can I read now?" asked George. He felt no different.

The doctor said, "What?" then smiled very suddenly and briefly. He said, "It works fine, George. You'll be reading in fifteen minutes. Now we're going to use another machine this time and it will take longer. I'm going to cover your whole head, and when I turn it on you won't be able to see or hear anything for a while, but it won't hurt. Just to make sure I'm going to give you a little switch to hold in your hand. If anything hurts, you press the little button and everything shuts off. All right?"

In later years, George was told that the little switch was strictly a dummy; that it was introduced solely for confidence. He never did know for sure, however, since he never pushed the button.

A large smoothly curved helmet with a rubbery inner lining was placed over his head and left there. Three or four little knobs seemed to grab at him and bite into his skull, but there was only a little pressure that faded. No pain.

The doctor's voice sounded dimly. "Everything all right, George?"

And then, with no real warning, a layer of thick felt closed down all about him. He was disembodied, there was no sensation, no universe, only himself and a distant murmur at the very ends of nothingness telling him something—telling him—telling him—

He strained to hear and understand but there was all that thick felt between.

Then the helmet was taken off his head, and the light was so bright that it hurt his eyes while the doctor's voice drummed at his ears.

The doctor said, "Here's your card, George. What does it say?"

George looked at his card again and gave out a strangled shout. The marks weren't just marks at all. They made up words. They were words just as clearly as though something were whispering them in his ears. He could *hear* them being whispered as he looked at them.

"What does it say, George?"

"It says—it says—'Platen, George. Born 13 February 6492 of Peter and Amy Platen in . . .' " He broke off.

"You can read, George," said the doctor. "It's all over."

"For good? I won't forget how?"

"Of course not." The doctor leaned over to shake hands gravely. "You will be taken home now."

It was days before George got over this new and great talent of his. He read for his father with such facility that Platen, Senior, wept and called relatives to tell the good news.

George walked about town, reading every scrap of printing he could find and wondering how it was that none of it had ever made sense to him before.

He tried to remember how it was not to be able to read and he couldn't. As far as his feeling about it was concerned, he had always been able to read. Always.

* * *

At eighteen, George was rather dark, of medium height, but thin enough to look taller. Trevelyan, who was scarcely an inch shorter, had a stockiness of build that made "Stubby" more than ever appropriate, but in this last year he had grown self-conscious. The nickname could no longer be used without reprisal. And since Trevelyan disaproved of his proper first name even more strongly, he was called Trevelyan or any decent variant of that. As though to prove his manhood further, he had most persistently grown a pair of sideburns and a bristly mustache.

He was sweating and nervous now, and George, who had himself grown out of "Jaw-jee" and into the curt monosyllabic gutturality of "George," was rather amused by that.

They were in the same large hall they had been in ten years before (and not since). It was as if a vague dream of the past had come to sudden reality. In the first few minutes George had been distinctly surprised at finding everything seem smaller and more cramped than his memory told him; then he made allowance for his own growth.

The crowd was smaller than it had been in childhood. It was exclusively male this time. The girls had another day assigned them.

Trevelyan leaned over to say, "Beats me the way they make you wait."

"Red tape," said George. "You can't avoid it."

Trevelyan said, "What makes *you* so damned tolerant about it?"

"I've got nothing to worry about."

"Oh, brother, you make me sick. I hope you end up Registered Manure Spreader just so I can see your face when you do." His somber eyes swept the crowd anxiously.

George looked about, too. It wasn't quite the system they used on the children. Matters went slower, and instructions had been given out at the start in print (an advantage over the pre-Readers). The names Platen and Trevelyan were well down the alphabet still, but this time the two knew it.

Young men came out of the education rooms, frowning and uncomfortable, picked up their clothes and belongings, then went off to analysis to learn the results.

Each, as he came out, would be surrounded by a clot of the thinning crowd. "How was it?" "How'd it feel?" "Whatcha think ya made?" "Ya feel any different?"

Answers were vague and noncommittal.

George forced himself to remain out of those clots. You only raised your own blood pressure. Everyone said you stood the best chance if you remained calm. Even so, you could feel the palms of your hands grow cold. Funny that new tensions came with the years.

For instance, high-specialty professionals heading out for an Outworld were accompanied by a wife (or husband). It was important to keep the sex ratio in good balance on all worlds. And if you were going out to a Grade A world, what girl would refuse you? George had no specific girl in mind yet; he wanted none. Not now! Once he made Programmer; once he could add to his name, Registered Computer Programmer, he could take his pick, like a sultan in a harem. The thought excited him and he tried to put it away. Must stay calm.

Trevelyan muttered, "What's it all about anyway? First they say it works best if you're relaxed and at ease. Then they put you through this and make it impossible for you to be relaxed and at ease."

"Maybe that's the idea. They're separating the boys from the men to begin with. Take it easy, Trev."

"Shut up."

George's turn came. His name was not called. It appeared in glowing letters on the notice board.

He waved at Trevelyan. "Take it easy. Don't let it get you."

He was happy as he entered the test chamber. Actually happy.

* * *

The man behind the desk said, "George Platen?"

For a fleeting instant there was a razor-sharp picture in George's mind of another man, ten years earlier, who had asked the same question, and it was almost as though this were the same man and he, George, had turned eight again as he had stepped across the threshold.

But the man looked up and, of course, the face matched that of the sudden memory not at all. The nose was bulbous, the hair thin and stringy, and the chin wattled as though its owner had once been grossly overweight and had reduced.

The man behind the desk looked annoyed. "Well?"

George came to Earth. "I'm George Platen, sir."

"Say so, then. I'm Dr. Zachary Antonelli, and we're going to be intimately acquainted in a moment."

He stared at small strips of film, holding them up to the light owlishly.

George winced inwardly. Very hazily, he remembered that other doctor (he had forgotten the name) staring at such film. Could these be the same? The other doctor had frowned and this one was looking at him now as though he were angry.

His happiness was already just about gone.

Dr. Antonelli spread the pages of a thickish film before him now and put the films carefully to one side. "It says here you want to be a Computer Programmer."

"Yes, doctor."

"Still do?"

"Yes, sir."

"It's a responsible and exacting position. Do you feel up to it?"

"Yes, sir."

"Most pre-Educates don't put down any specific profession. I believe they are afraid of queering it."

"I think that's right, sir."

"Aren't you afraid of that?"

"I might as well be honest, sir."

Dr. Antonelli nodded, but without any noticeable lightening of his expression. "Why do you want to be a Programmer?"

"It's a responsible and exacting position as you said, sir. It's an important job and an exciting one. I like it and I think I can do it."

Dr. Antonelli put the papers away, and looked at George sourly. He said, "How do you know you like it? Because you think you'll be snapped up by some Grade A planet?"

George thought uneasily: He's trying to rattle you. Stay calm and stay frank.

He said, "I think a Programmer has a good chance, sir, but even if I were left on Earth, I know I'd like it." (That was true enough. I'm not lying, thought George.)

"All right, how do you know?"

He asked it as though he knew there was no decent answer and George almost smiled. He had one.

He said, "I've been reading about Programming, sir."

"You've been *what?*" Now the doctor looked genuinely astonished and George took pleasure in that.

"Reading about it, sir. I bought a book on the subject and I've been studying it."

"A book for Registered Programmers?"

"Yes, sir."

"But you couldn't understand it."

"Not at first. I got other books on mathematics and electronics. I made out all I could. I still don't know much, but I know enough to know I like it and to know I can make it." (Even his parents never found that secret cache of books or knew why he spent so much time in his own room or exactly what happened to the sleep he missed.)

The doctor pulled at the loose skin under his chin. "What was your idea in doing that, son?"

"I wanted to make sure I would be interested, sir."

"Surely you know that being interested means nothing. You could be devoured by a subject and if the physical make-up of your brain makes it more efficient for you to be something else, something else you will be. You know that, don't you?"

"I've been told that," said George cautiously.

"Well, believe it. It's true."

George said nothing.

Dr. Antonelli said, "Or do you believe that studying some subject will bend the brain cells in that direction, like that other theory that a pregnant woman need only listen to great music persistently to make a composer of her child. Do you believe that?"

George flushed. That had certainly been in his mind. By forcing his intellect constantly in the desired direction, he had felt sure that he would be getting a head start. Most of his confidence had rested on exactly that point.

"I never—" he began, and found no way of finishing.

"Well, it isn't true. Good Lord, youngster, your brain pattern is fixed at birth. It can be altered by a blow hard enough to damage the cells or by a burst blood vessel or by a tumor or by a major infection—each time, of course, for the worse. But it certainly can't be affected by your thinking special thoughts." He stared at George thoughtfully, then said, "Who told you to do this?"

George, now throughly disturbed, swallowed and said, "No one, doctor. My own idea."

"Who knew you were doing it after you started?"

"No one. Doctor, I meant to do no wrong."

"Who said anything about wrong? Useless is what I would say. Why did you keep it to yourself?"

"I—I thought they'd laugh at me." (He thought abruptly of a recent exchange with Trevelyan. George had very cautiously broached the thought, as of something merely circulating distantly in the very outermost reaches of his mind, concerning the possibility of learning something by ladling it into the mind by hand, so to speak, in bits and pieces. Trevelyan had hooted, "George, you'll be tanning your own shoes next and weaving your own shirts." He had been thankful then for his policy of secrecy.)

Dr. Antonelli shoved the bits of film he had first looked at from position to position in morose thought. Then he said, "Let's get you analyzed. This is getting me nowhere."

The wires went to George's temples. There was the buzzing. Again there came a sharp memory of ten years ago.

George's hands were clammy; his heart pounded. He should never have told the doctor about his secret reading.

It was his damned vanity, he told himself. He had wanted to show how enterprising he was, how full of initiative. Instead, he had showed himself superstitious and ignorant and aroused the hostility of the doctor. (He could tell the doctor hated him for a wise guy on the make.)

And now he had brought himself to such a state of nervousness, he was sure the analyzer would show nothing that made sense.

He wasn't aware of the moment when the wires were removed from his temples. The sight of the doctor, staring at him thoughtfully, blinked into his consciousness and that was that; the wires were gone. George dragged himself together with a tearing effort. He had quite given up his ambition to be a Programmer. In the space of ten minutes, it had all gone.

He said dismally, "I suppose no?"

"No what?"

"No Programmer?"

The doctor rubbed his nose and said, "You get your clothes and whatever belongs to you and go to room 15-C. Your files will be waiting for you there. So will my report."

George said in complete surprise, "Have I been Educated already? I thought this was just to—"

Dr. Antonelli stared down at his desk. "It will all be explained to you. You do as I say."

George felt something like panic. What was it they couldn't tell him? He wasn't fit for anything but Registered Laborer. They were going to prepare him for that; adjust him to it.

He was suddenly certain of it and he had to keep from screaming by main force.

He stumbled back to his place of waiting. Trevelyan was not there, a fact for which he would have been thankful if he had had enough self-possession to be meaningfully aware of his surroundings. Hardly anyone was left, in fact, and the few who were looked as though they might ask him questions were it not that they were too worn out by their tail-of-the-alphabet waiting to buck the fierce, hot look of anger and hate he cast at them.

What right had *they* to be technicians and he, himself, a Laborer? Laborer! He was *certain!*

* * *

He was led by a red-uniformed guide along the busy corridors lined with separate rooms each containing its groups, here two, there five: the Motor Mechanics, the Construction Engineers, the Agronomists— There were hundreds of specialized Professions and most of them would be represented in this small town by one or two anyway.

He hated them all just then: the Statisticians, the Accountants, the lesser breeds and the higher. He hated them because they owned their smug knowledge now, knew their fate, while he himself, empty still, had to face some kind of further red tape.

He reached 15-C, was ushered in and left in an empty room. For one moment, his spirits bounded. Surely, if this were the Labor classification room, there would be dozens of youngsters present.

A door sucked into its recess on the other side of a waist-high partition and an elderly, white-haired man stepped out. He smiled and showed even teeth that were obviously false, but his face was still ruddy and unlined and his voice had vigor.

He said, "Good evening, George. Our own sector has only one of you this time, I see."

"Only one?" said George blankly.

"Thousands over the Earth, of course. Thousands. You're not alone."

George felt exasperated. He said, "I don't understand, sir. What's my classification? What's happening?"

"Easy, son. You're all right. It could happen to anyone." He held out his hand and George took it mechanically. It was warm and it pressed George's hand firmly. "Sit down, son. I'm Sam Ellenford."

George nodded impatiently. "I want to know what's going on, sir."

"Of course. To begin with, you can't be a Computer Programmer, George. You've guessed that, I think."

"Yes, I have," said George bitterly. "What will I be, then?"

"That's the hard part to explain, George." He paused, then said with careful distinctness, "Nothing."

"*What!*"

"Nothing!"

"But what does that mean? Why can't you assign me a profession?"

"We have no choice in the matter, George. It's the structure of your mind that decides that."

George went a sallow yellow. His eyes bulged. "There's something wrong with my mind?"

"There's *something* about it. As far as professional classification is concerned, I suppose you can call it wrong."

"But why?"

Ellenford shrugged. "I'm sure you know how Earth runs its Educational program, George. Practically any human being can absorb practically any body of knowledge, but each individual brain pattern is better suited to receiving some types of knowledge than others. We try to match mind to knowledge as well as we can within the limits of the quota requirements for each profession.

George nodded. "Yes, I know."

"Every once in a while, George, we come up against a young man whose mind is not suited to receiving a superimposed knowledge of any sort."

"You mean I can't be Educated?"

"That is what I mean."

"But that's crazy. I'm intelligent. I can understand—" He looked helplessly about as though trying to find some way of proving that he had a functioning brain.

"Don't misunderstand me, please," said Ellenford gravely. "You're intelligent. There's no question about that. You're even above average in intelligence. Unfortunately that has nothing to do with whether the mind ought to be allowed to accept superimposed knowledge or not. In fact, it is almost always the intelligent person who comes here."

"You mean I can't even be a Registered Laborer?" babbled George. Suddenly even that was better than the blank that faced him. "What's there to know to be a Laborer?"

"Don't underestimate the Laborer, young man. There are dozens of subclassifications and each variety has its own corpus of fairly detailed knowledge. Do you think there's no skill in knowing the proper manner of lifting a weight? Besides, for the Laborer, we must select not only minds suited to it, but bodies as well. You're not the type, George, to last long as a Laborer."

George was conscious of his slight build. He said, "But I've never heard of anyone without a profession."

"There aren't many," conceded Ellenford. "And we protect them."

"Protect them?" George felt confusion and fright grow higher inside him.

"You're a ward of the planet, George. From the time you walked through that door, we've been in charge of you." And he smiled.

It was a fond smile. To George it seemed the smile of ownership; the smile of a grown man for a helpless child.

He said, "You mean, I'm going to be in prison?"

"Of course not. You will simply be with others of your kind."

Your kind. The words made a kind of thunder in George's ear.

Ellenford said, "You need special treatment. We'll take care of you."

To George's own horror, he burst into tears. Ellenford walked to the other end of the room and faced away as though in thought.

George fought to reduce the agonized weeping to sobs and then to strangle those. He thought of his father and mother, of his friends, of Trevelyan, of his own shame—

He said rebelliously, "I learned to read."

"Everyone with a whole mind can do that. We've never found exceptions. It is at this stage that we discover—exceptions. And when you learned to read, George, we were concerned about your mind pattern. Certain peculiarities were reported even then by the doctor in charge."

"Can't you try Educating me? You haven't even tried. I'm willing to take the risk."

"The law forbids us to do that, George. But look, it will not be bad. We will explain matters to your family so they will not be hurt. At the place to which you'll be taken, you'll be allowed privileges. We'll get you books and you can learn what you will."

"Dab knowledge in by hand," said George bitterly. "Shred by shred. Then, when I die I'll know enough to be a Registered Junior Office Boy, Paper-Clip Division."

"Yet I understand you've already been studying books."

George froze. He was struck devastatingly by sudden understanding. "That's it . . ."

"What is?"

"That fellow Antonelli. He's knifing me."

"No, George. You're quite wrong."

"Don't tell me that." George was in an ecstasy of fury. "That lousy bastard is selling me out because he thought I was a little too wise for him. I read books and tried to get a head start toward programming. Well, what do you want to square things? Money? You won't get it. I'm getting out of here and when I finish broadcasting this—"

He was screaming.

Ellenford shook his head and touched a contact.

Two men entered on catfeet and got on either side of George. They pinned his arms to his sides. One of them used an air-spray hypodermic in the hollow of his right elbow and the hypnotic entered his vein and had an almost immediate effect.

His screams cut off and his head fell forward. His knees buckled and only the men on either side kept him erect as he slept.

* * *

They took care of George as they said they would; they were good to him and unfailingly kind—about the way, George thought, he himself would be to a sick kitten he had taken pity on.

They told him that he should sit up and take some interest in life; and then told him that most people who came there had the same attitude of despair at the beginning and that he would snap out of it.

He didn't even hear them.

Dr. Ellenford himself visited him to tell him that his parents had been informed that he was away on special assignment.

George muttered, "Do they know—"

Ellenford assured him at once, "We gave no details."

At first George had refused to eat. They fed him intravenously. They hid sharp objects and kept him under guard. Hali Omani came to be his roommate and his stolidity had a calming effect.

One day, out of sheer desperate boredom, George asked for a book. Omani, who himself read books constantly, looked up, smiling broadly. George almost withdrew the request then, rather than give any of them satisfaction, then thought: What do I care?

He didn't specify the book and Omani brought one on chemistry. It was in big print, with small words and many illustrations. It was for teenagers. He threw the book violently against the wall.

That's what he would be always. A teenager all his life. A pre-Educate forever and special books would have to be written for him. He lay smoldering in bed, staring at the ceiling, and after an hour had passed, he got up sulkily, picked up the book, and began reading.

* * *

It took him a week to finish it and then he asked for another.

"Do you want me to take the first one back?" asked Omani.

George frowned. There were things in the book he had not understood, yet he was not so lost to shame as to say so.

But Omani said, "Come to think of it, you'd better keep it. Books are meant to be read and reread."

It was that same day that he finally yielded to Omani's invitation that he tour the place. He dogged at the Nigerian's feet and took in his surroundings with quick hostile glances.

The place was no prison certainly. There were no walls, no locked doors, no guards. But it was a prison in that the inmates had no place to go outside.

It was somehow good to see others like himself by the dozen. It was so easy to believe himself to be the only one in the world so—maimed.

He mumbled, "How many people here anyway?"

"Two hundred and five, George, and this isn't the only place of the sort in the world. There are thousands."

Men looked up as he passed, wherever he went; in the gymnasium, along the tennis courts; through the library (he had never in his life imagined books could exist in such numbers; they were stacked, actually stacked, along long shelves). They stared at him curiously and he returned the looks savagely. At least *they* were no better than he; no call for *them* to look at him as though he were some sort of curiosity.

Most of them were in their twenties. George said suddenly, "What happens to the older ones?"

Omani said, "This place specializes in the younger ones." Then, as though he suddenly recognized an implication in George's question that he had missed earlier, he shook his head gravely and said, "They're not put out of the way, if that's what you mean. There are other Houses for older ones."

"Who cares?" mumbled George, who felt he was sounding too interested and in danger of slipping into surrender.

"You might. As you grow older, you will find yourself in a House with occupants of both sexes."

That surprised George somehow. "Women, too?"

"Of course. Do you suppose women are immune to this sort of thing?"

George thought of that with more interest and excitement than he had felt for anything since before that day when— He forced his thought away from that.

Omani stopped at the doorway of a room that contained a small closed-circuit television set and a desk computer. Five or six men sat about the television. Omani said, "This is a classroom."

George said, "What's that?"

"The young men in there are being educated. Not," he added, quickly, "in the usual way."

"You mean they're cramming it in bit by bit."

"That's right. This is the way everyone did it in ancient times."

This was what they kept telling him since he had come to the House but what of it? Suppose there had been a day when mankind had not known the diatherm-oven. Did that mean he should be satisfied to eat meat raw in a world where others ate it cooked?

He said, "Why do they want to go through that bit-by-bit stuff?"

"To pass the time, George, and because they're curious."

"What good does it do them?"

"It makes them happier."

George carried that thought to bed with him.

The next day he said to Omani ungraciously, "Can you get me into a classroom where I can find out something about programming?"

Omani replied heartily, "Sure."

* * *

It was slow and he resented it. Why should someone have to explain something and explain it again? Why should he have to read and reread a passage, then stare at a mathematical relationship and not understand it at once? That wasn't how other people had to be.

Over and over again, he gave up. Once he refused to attend classes for a week.

But always he returned. The official in charge, who assigned reading, conducted the television demonstrations, and even explained difficult passages and concepts, never commented on the matter.

George was finally given a regular task in the gardens and took his turn in the various kitchen and cleaning details. This was represented to him as being an advance, but he wasn't fooled. The place might have been far more mechanized than it was, but they deliberately made work for the young men in order to give them the illusion of worth-while occupation, of usefulness. George wasn't fooled.

They were even paid small sums of money out of which they could buy certain specified luxuries or which they could put aside for a problematical use in a problematical old age. George kept his money in an open jar, which he kept on a closet shelf. He had no idea how much he had accumulated. Nor did he care.

He made no real friends though he reached the stage where a civil good day was in order. He even stopped brooding (or almost stopped) on the miscarriage of justice that had placed him there. He would go weeks without dreaming of Antonelli, of his gross nose and wattled neck, of the leer with which he would push George into a boiling quicksand and hold him under, till he woke screaming with Omani bending over him in concern.

Omani said to him on a snowy day in February, "It's amazing how you're adjusting."

But that was February, the thirteenth to be exact, his nineteenth birthday. March came, then April, and with the approach of May he realized he hadn't adjusted at all.

The previous May had passed unregarded while George was still in his bed, drooping and ambitiousless. This May was different.

All over Earth, George knew, Olympics would be taking place and young men would be competing, matching their skills against one another in the fight for a place on a new world. There would be the holiday atmosphere, the excitement, the news reports, the self-contained recruiting agents from the worlds beyond space, the glory of victory or the consolation of defeat.

How much of fiction dealt with these motifs; how much of his own boyhood excitement lay in following the events of Olympics from year to year; how many of his own plans—

George Platen could not conceal the longing in his voice. It was too much to suppress. He said, "Tomorrow's the first of May. Olympics!"

And that led to his first quarrel with Omani and to Omani's bitter enunciation of the exact name of the institution in which George found himself.

Omani gazed fixedly at George and said distinctly, "A House for the Feeble-minded."

* * *

George Platen flushed. Feeble-minded!

He rejected it desperately. He said in a monotone, "I'm leaving." He said it on impulse. His conscious mind learned it first from the statement as he uttered it.

Omani, who had returned to his book, looked up. "What?"

George knew what he was saying now. He said it fiercely, "I'm leaving."

"That's ridiculous. Sit down, George, calm yourself."

"Oh, no. I'm here on a frame-up, I tell you. This doctor, Antonelli, took a dislike to me. It's the sense of power these petty bureaucrats have. Cross them and they wipe out your life with a stylus mark on some card file."

"Are you back to that?"

"And staying there till it's all straightened out. I'm going to get to Antonelli somehow, break him, force the truth out of him." George was breathing heavily and he felt feverish. Olympics month was here and he couldn't let it pass. If he did, it would be the final surrender and he would be lost for all time.

Omani threw his legs over the side of his bed and stood up. He was nearly six feet tall and the expression on his face gave him the look of a concerned Saint Bernard. He put his arm about George's shoulder, "If I hurt your feeling—"

George shrugged him off. "You just said what you thought was the truth, and I'm going to prove it isn't the truth, that's all. Why not? The door's open. There aren't any locks. No one ever said I couldn't leave. I'll just walk out."

"All right, but where will you go?"

"To the nearest air terminal, then to the nearest Olympics center. I've got money." He seized the open jar that held the wages he had put away. Some of the coins jangled to the floor.

"That will last you a week maybe. Then what?"

"By then I'll have things settled."

"By then you'll come crawling back here," said Omani earnestly, "with all the progress you've made to do over again. You're mad, George."

"Feeble-minded is the word you used before."

"Well, I'm sorry I did. Stay here, will you?"

"Are you going to try to stop me?"

Omani compressed his full lips. "No, I guess I won't. This is your business. If the only way you can learn is to buck the world and come back with blood on your face, go ahead. —Well, go ahead."

George was in the doorway now, looking back over his shoulder. "I'm going,"—he came back to pick up his pocket grooming set slowly—"I hope you don't object to my taking a few personal belongings."

Omani shrugged. He was in bed again reading, indifferent.

George lingered at the door again, but Omani didn't look up. George gritted his teeth, turned and walked rapidly down the empty corridor and out into the night-shrouded grounds.

He had expected to be stopped before leaving the grounds. He wasn't. He had stopped at an all-night diner to ask directions to an air terminal and expected the proprietor to call the police. That didn't happen. He summoned a skimmer to take him to the airport and the driver asked no questions.

Yet he felt no lift at that. He arrived at the airport sick at heart. He had not realized how the outer world would be. He was surrounded by professionals. The diner's proprietor had had his name inscribed on the plastic shell over the cash register. So and so, Registered Cook. The man in the skimmer had his license up, Registered Chauffeur. George felt the bareness of his name and experienced a kind of nakedness because of it; worse, he felt skinned. But no one challenged him. No one studied him suspiciously and demanded proof of professional rating.

George thought bitterly: Who would imagine any human being without one?

He bought a ticket to San Francisco on the 3 A.M. plane. No other plane for a sizeable Olympics center was leaving before morning and he wanted to wait as little as possible. As it was, he sat huddled in the waiting room, watching for the police. They did not come.

He was in San Francisco before noon and the noise of the city struck him like a blow. This was the largest city he had ever seen and he had been used to silence and calm for a year and a half now.

Worse, it was Olympics month. He almost forgot his own predicament in his sudden awareness that some of the noise, excitement, confusion was due to that.

The Olympics boards were up at the airport for the benefit of the incoming travelers, and crowds jostled around each one. Each major profession had its own board. Each listed directions to the Olympics Hall where the contest for that day for that profession would be given; the individuals competing and their city of birth; the Outworld (if any) sponsoring it.

It was a completely stylized thing. George had read descriptions often enough in the newsprints and films, watched matches on television, and even witnessed a small Olympics in the Registered Butcher classification at the county seat. Even that, which had no conceivable Galactic implication (there was no Outworlder in attendance, of course) aroused excitement enough.

Partly, the excitement was caused simply by the fact of competition, partly by the spur of local pride (oh, when there was a hometown boy to cheer for, though he might be a complete stranger), and, of course, partly by betting. There was no way of stopping the last.

George found it difficult to approach the board. He found himself looking at the scurrying, avid onlookers in a new way.

There must have been a time when they themselves were Olympic material. What had *they* done? Nothing!

If they had been winners, they would be far out in the Galaxy somewhere, not stuck here on Earth. Whatever they were, their professions must have made them Earth-bait from the beginning; or else they had made themselves Earth-bait by inefficiency at whatever high-specialized professions they had had.

Now these failures stood about and speculated on the chances of newer and younger men. Vultures!

How he wished they were speculating on him.

He moved down the line of boards blankly, clinging to the outskirts of the groups about them. He had eaten breakfast on the strato and he wasn't hungry. He was afraid, though. He was in a big city during the confusion of the beginning of Olympics competition. That was protection, sure. The city was full of strangers. No one would question George. No one would care about George.

No one would care. Not even the House, thought George bitterly. They cared for him like a sick kitten, but if a sick kitten up and wanders off, well, too bad, what can you do?

And now that he was in San Francisco, what did he do? His thoughts struck blankly against a wall. See someone? Whom? How? Where would he even stay? The money he had left seemed pitiful.

The first shamefaced thought of going back came to him. He could go to the police— He shook his head violently as though arguing with a material adversary.

A word caught his eye on one of the boards, gleaming there: *Metallurgist*. In smaller letters, *nonferrous*. At the bottom of a long list of names, in flowing script, *sponsored by Novia.*

It induced painful memories: himself arguing with Trevelyan, so certain that he himself would be a Programmer, so certain that a Programmer was superior to a Metallurgist, so certain that he was following the right course, so certain that he was clever—

So clever that he had to boast to that small-minded, vindictive Antonelli. He had been so sure of himself that moment when he had been called and had left the nervous Trevelyan standing there, so cocksure.

George cried out in a short, incoherent high-pitched gasp. Someone turned to look at him, then hurried on. People brushed past impatiently pushing him this way and that. He remained staring at the board, openmouthed.

It was as though the board had answered his thought. He was thinking "Trevelyan" so hard that it had seemed for a moment that of course the board would say "Trevelyan" back at him.

But that *was* Trevelyan, up there. And *Armand* Trevelyan (Stubby's hated first name; up in lights for everyone to see) and the right hometown. What's more, Trev had wanted Novia, aimed for Novia, insisted on Novia; and this competition was sponsored by Novia.

This had to be Trev; good old Trev. Almost without thinking, he noted the directions for getting to the place of competition and took his place in line for a skimmer.

Then he thought somberly: Trev made it! He wanted to be a Metallurgist, and he made it!

George felt colder, more alone than ever.

* * *

There was a line waiting to enter the hall. Apparently, Metallurgy Olympics was to be an exciting and closely fought one. At least, the illuminated sky sign above the hall said so, and the jostling crowd seemed to think so.

It would have been a rainy day, George thought, from the color of the sky, but San Francisco had drawn the shield across its breadth from bay to ocean. It was an expense to do so, of course, but all expenses were warranted where the comfort of Outworlders was concerned. They would be in town for the Olympics. They were heavy spenders. And for each recruit taken, there would be a fee both to Earth and to the local government from the planet sponsoring the Olympics. It paid to keep Outworlders in mind of a particular city as a pleasant place in which to spend Olympics time. San Francisco knew what it was doing.

George, lost in thought, was suddenly aware of a gentle pressure on his shoulder blade and a voice saying, "Are you in line here, young man?"

The line had moved up without George's having noticed the widening gap. He stepped forward hastily and muttered, "Sorry, sir."

There was the touch of two fingers on the elbow of his jacket and he looked about furtively.

The man behind him nodded cheerfully. He had iron-gray hair, and under his jacket he wore an old-fashioned sweater that buttoned down the front. He said, "I didn't mean to sound sarcastic."

"No offense."

"All right, then." He sounded cozily talkative. "I wasn't sure you might not simply be standing there, entangled with the line, so to speak, only by accident. I thought you might be a—"

"A what?" said George sharply.

"Why, a contestant, of course. You look young."

George turned away. He felt neither cozy nor talkative, and bitterly impatient with busybodies.

A thought struck him. Had an alarm been sent out for him? Was his description known, or his picture? Was Gray-hair behind him trying to get a good look at his face?

He hadn't seen any news reports. He craned his neck to see the moving strip of news headlines parading across one section of the city shield, somewhat lackluster against the gray of the cloudy afternoon sky. It was no use. He gave up at once. The headlines would never concern themselves with him. This was Olympics time and the only news worth headlining was the comparative scores of the winners and the trophies won by continents, nations, and cities.

It would go on like that for weeks, with scores calculated on a per capita basis and every city finding some way of calculating itself into a position of honor. His own town had once placed third in an Olympics covering Wiring Technician; third in the whole state. There was still a plaque saying so in Town Hall.

George hunched his head between his shoulders and shoved his hands in his pocket and decided that made him more noticeable. He relaxed and tried to look unconcerned, and felt no safer. He was in the lobby now, and no authoritative hand had yet been laid on his shoulder. He filed into the hall itself and moved as far forward as he could.

It was with an unpleasant shock that he noticed Gray-hair next to him. He looked away quickly and tried reasoning with himself. The man had been right behind him in line after all.

Gray-hair, beyond a brief and tentative smile, paid no attention to him and, besides, the Olympics was about to start. George rose in his seat to see if he could make out the position assigned to Trevelyan and at the moment that was all his concern.

* * *

The hall was moderate in size and shaped in the classical long oval, with the spectators in the two balconies running completely about the rim and the contestants in the linear trough down the center. The machines were set up, the progress boards above each bench were dark, except for the name and contest number of each man. The contestants themselves were on the scene, reading, talking together; one was checking his fingernails minutely. (It was, of course, considered bad form for any contestant to pay any attention to the problem before him until the instant of the starting signal.)

George studied the program sheet he found in the appropriate slot in the arm of his chair and found Trevelyan's name. His number was twelve and, to George's chagrin, that was at the wrong end of the hall. He could make out the figure of Contestant Twelve, standing with his hands in his pockets, back to his machine, and staring at the audience as though he were counting the house. George couldn't make out the face.

Still, that was Trev.

George sank back in his seat. He wondered if Trev would do well. He hoped, as a matter of conscious duty, that he would, and yet there was something within him that felt rebelliously resentful. George, professionless, here, watching. Trevelyan, Registered Metallurgist, Nonferrous, there, competing.

George wondered if Trevelyan had competed in his first year. Sometimes men did, if they felt particularly confident—or hurried. It involved a certain risk. However efficient the Educative process, a preliminary year on Earth ("oiling the stiff knowledge," as the expression went) insured a higher score.

If Trevelyan was repeating, maybe he wasn't doing so well. George felt ashamed that the thought pleased him just a bit.

He looked about. The stands were almost full. This would be a well-attended Olympics, which meant greater strain on the contestants—or greater drive, perhaps, depending on the indi-vidual.

Why Olympics, he thought suddenly? He had never known. Why was bread called bread?

Once he had asked his father: "Why do they call it Olympics, Dad?"

And his father had said: "Olympics means competition."

George had said: "Is when Stubby and I fight an Olympics, Dad?"

Platen, Senior, had said: "No. Olympics is a special kind of competition and don't ask silly questions. You'll know all you have to know when you get Educated."

George, back in the present, sighed and crowded down into his seat.

All you have to know!

Funny that the memory should be so clear now. "When you get Educated." No one ever said, "*If* you get Educated."

He always had asked silly questions, it seemed to him now. It was as though his mind had some instinctive foreknowledge of its inability to be Educated and had gone about asking questions in order to pick up scraps here and there as best it could.

And at the House they encouraged him to do so because they agreed with his mind's instinct. It was the only way.

He sat up suddenly. What the devil was he doing? Falling for that lie? Was it because Trev was there before him, an Educee, competing in the Olympics that he himself was surrendering?

He *wasn't* feeble-minded! *No!*

And the shout of denial in his mind was echoed by the sudden clamor in the audience as everyone got to his feet.

The box seat in the very center of one long side of the oval was filling with an entourage wearing the colors of Novia, and the word "Novia" went up above them on the main board.

Novia was a Grade A world with a large population and a thoroughly developed civilization, perhaps the best in the Galaxy. It was the kind of world that every Earthman wanted to live in someday; or, failing that, to see his children live in. (George remembered Trevelyan's insistence on Novia as a goal—and there he was competing for it.)

The lights went out in that section of the ceiling above the audience and so did the wall lights. The central trough, in which the contestants waited, became floodlit.

Again George tried to make out Trevelyan. Too far.

The clear, polished voice of the announcer sounded.

"Distinguished Novian sponsors. Ladies. Gentlemen. The Olympics competition for Metallurgist, Nonferrous, is about to begin. The contestants are—"

Carefully and conscientiously, he read off the list in the program. Names. Home towns. Educative years. Each name received its cheers, the San Franciscans among them receiving the loudest. When Trevelyan's name was reached, George surprised himself by shouting and waving madly. The gray-haired man next to him surprised him even more by cheering likewise.

George could not help but stare in astonishment and his neighbor leaned over to say (speaking loudly in order to be heard over the hubbub), "No one here from my home town; I'll root for yours. Someone you know?"

George shrank back. "No."

"I noticed you looking in that direction. Would you like to borrow my glasses?"

"No. Thank you." (Why didn't the old fool mind his own business?)

The announcer went on with other formal details concerning the serial number of the competition, the method of timing and scoring and so on. Finally, he approached the meat of the matter and the audience grew silent as it listened.

"Each contestant will be surprised with a bar of nonferrous alloy of unspecified composition. He will be required to sample and assay the bar, reporting all results correctly to four decimals in per cent. All will utilize for this purpose a Beeman Microspectrograph, Model FX-2, each of which is, at the moment, not in working order."

There was an appreciative shout from the audience.

"Each contestant will be required to analyze the fault of his machine and correct it. Tools and spare parts are supplied. The spare part necessary may not be present, in which case it must be asked for, and time of delivery thereof will be deducted from final time. Are all contestants ready?"

The board above Contestant Five flashed a frantic red signal. Contestant Five ran off the floor and returned a moment later. The audience laughed good-naturedly.

"Are all contestants ready?"

The boards remained blank.

"Any questions?"

Still blank.

"You may begin."

* * *

There was, of course, no way anyone in the audience could tell how any contestant was progressing except for whatever notations went up on the notice board. But then, that didn't matter. Except for what professional Metallurgists there might be in the audience, none would understand anything about the contest professionally in any case. What was important was who won, who was second, who was third. For those who had bets on the standings (illegal, but unpreventable) that was all-important. Everything else might go hang.

George watched as eagerly as the rest, glancing from one contestant to the next, observing how this one had removed the cover from his microspectrograph with deft strokes of a small instrument; how that one was peering into the face of the thing; how still a third was setting his alloy bar into its holder; and how a fourth adjusted a vernier with such small touches that he seemed momentarily frozen.

Trevelyan was as absorbed as the rest. George had no way of telling how he was doing.

The notice board over Contestant Seventeen flashed: Focus plate out of adjustment.

The audience cheered wildly.

Contestant Seventeen might be right and he might, of course, be wrong. If the latter, he would have to correct his diagnosis later and lose time. Or he might never correct his diagnosis and be unable to complete his analysis or, worse still, end with a completely wrong analysis.

Never mind. For the moment, the audience cheered.

Other boards lit up. George watched for Board Twelve. That came on finally: "Sample holder off-center. New clamp depresser needed."

An attendant went running to him with a new part. If Trevelyan was wrong, it would mean useless delay. Nor would the time elapsed in waiting for the part be deducted. George found himself holding his breath.

Results were beginning to go up on Board Seventeen, in gleaming letters: aluminium, 41.2649; magnesium, 22.1914; copper, 10.1001.

Here and there, other boards began sprouting figures.

The audience was in bedlam.

George wondered how the contestants could work in such pandemonium, then wondered if that were not even a good thing. A first-class technician should work best under pressure.

Seventeen rose from his place as his board went red-rimmed to signify completion. Four was only two seconds behind him. Another, then another.

Trevelyan was still working, the minor constituents of his alloy bar still unreported. With nearly all contestants standing, Trevelyan finally rose, also. Then, tailing off, Five rose, and received an ironic cheer.

It wasn't over. Official announcements were naturally delayed. Time elapsed was something, but accuracy was just as important. And not all diagnoses were of equal difficulty. A dozen factors had to be weighed.

Finally, the announcer's voice sounded, "Winner in the time of four minutes and twelve seconds, diagnosis correct, within an average of zero point seven parts per hundred thousand, Contestant Number—*Seventeen*, Henry Anton Schmidt of—"

What followed was drowned in the screaming. Number Eight was next and then Four, whose good time was spoiled by a five part in ten thousand error in the niobium figure. Twelve was never mentioned. He was an also-ran.

George made his way through the crowd to the Contestant's Door and found a large clot of humanity ahead of him. There would be weeping relatives (joy or sorrow, depending) to greet them, newsmen to interview the top-scorers, or the home-town boys, autograph hounds, publicity seekers and the just plain curious. Girls, too, who might hope to catch the eye of a top-scorer, almost certainly headed for Novia (or perhaps a low-scorer who needed consolation and had the cash to afford it).

George hung back. He saw no one he knew. With San Francisco so far from home, it seemed pretty safe to assume that there would be no relatives to condole with Trev on the spot.

Contestants emerged, smiling weakly, nodding at shouts of approval. Policemen kept the crowds far enough away to allow a lane for walking. Each high-scorer drew a portion of the crowd off with him, like a magnet pushing through a mound of iron filings.

When Trevelyan walked out, scarcely anyone was left. (George felt somehow that he had delayed coming out until just that had come to pass.) There was a cigarette in his dour mouth and he turned, eyes downcast, to walk off.

It was the first hint of home George had had in what was almost a year and a half and seemed almost a decade and a half. He was almost amazed that Trevelyan hadn't aged, that he was the same Trev he had last seen.

George sprang forward. "*Trev!*"

Trevelyan spun about, astonished. He stared at George and then his hand shot out. "George Platen, *what* the devil—"

And almost as soon as the look of pleasure had crossed his face, it left. His hand dropped before George had quite the chance of seizing it.

"Were you in there?" A curt jerk of Trev's head indicated the hall.

"I was."

"To see me?"

"Yes."

"Didn't do so well, did I?" He dropped his cigarette and stepped on it, staring off to the street, where the emerging crowd was slowly eddying and finding its way into skimmers, while new lines were forming for the next scheduled Olympics.

Trevelyan said heavily, "So what? It's only the second time I missed. Novia can go shove after the deal I got today. There are planets that would jump at me fast enough—But listen, I haven't seen you since Education Day. Where did you go? Your folks said you were on special assignment but gave no details and you never wrote. You might have written."

"I should have," said George uneasily. "Anyway, I came to say I was sorry the way things went just now."

"Don't be," said Trevelyan. "I told you. Novia can go shove— At least that I should have known. They've been saying for weeks that the Beeman machine would be used. All the wise money was on Beeman machines. The damned Education tapes they ran through me were for Henslers and who uses Henslers? The worlds in the Goman Cluster if you want to call them worlds. Wasn't *that* a nice deal they gave me?"

"Can't you complain to—"

"Don't be a fool. They'll tell my brain was built for Henslers. Go argue. *Everything* went wrong. I was the only one who had to send out for a piece of equipment. Notice that?"

"They deducted the time for that, though."

"Sure, but I lost time wondering if I could be right in my diagnosis when I noticed there wasn't any clamp depresser in the parts they had supplied. They don't deduct for that. If it had been a Hensler, I would have *known* I was right. How could I match up then? The top winner was a San Franciscan. So were three of the next four. And the fifth guy was from Los Angeles. They get big-city Educational tapes. The best available. Beeman spectrographs and all. How do I compete with them? I came all the way out here just to get a chance at a Novian-sponsored Olympics in my classification and I might just as well have stayed home. I knew it, I tell you, and that settles it. Novia isn't the only chunk of rock in space. Of all the damned—"

He wasn't speaking to George. He wasn't speaking to anyone. He was just uncorked and frothing. George realized that.

George said, "If you knew in advance that the Beemans were going to be used, couldn't you have studied up on them?"

"They weren't in my tapes, I tell you."

"You could have read—books."

The last word had tailed off under Trevelyan's suddenly sharp look.

Trevelyan said, "Are you trying to make a big laugh out of this? You think this is funny? How do you expect me to read some book and try to memorize enough to match someone else who *knows*."

"I thought—"

"You try it. You try—" Then, suddenly, "What's your profession, by the way?" He sounded thoroughly hostile.

"Well—"

"Come on, now. If you're going to be a wise guy with me, let's see what you've done. You're still on Earth, I notice, so you're not a Computer Programmer and your special assignment can't be much."

George said, "Listen, Trev, I'm late for an appointment." He backed away, trying to smile.

"No, you don't." Trevelyan reached out fiercely, catching hold of George's jacket. "You answer my question. Why are you afraid to tell me? What is it with you? Don't come here rubbing a bad showing in my face, George, unless you can take it, too. Do you hear me?"

He was shaking George in frenzy and they were struggling and swaying across the floor, when the Voice of Doom struck George's ear in the form of a policeman's outraged call.

"All right now. *All* right. Break it up."

George's heart turned to lead and lurched sickeningly. The policeman would be taking names, asking to see identity cards, and George lacked one. He would be questioned and his lack of profession would show at once; and before Trevelyan, too, who ached with the pain of the drubbing he had taken and would spread the news back home as a salve for his own hurt feelings.

George couldn't stand that. He broke away from Trevelyan and made to run, but the policeman's heavy hand was on his shoulder. "Hold on, there. Let's see your identity card."

Trevelyan was fumbling for his, saying harshly, "I'm Armand Trevelyan, Metallurgist, Nonferrous. I was just competing in the Olympics. You better find out about him, though, officer."

George faced the two, lips dry and throat thickened past speech.

Another voice sounded, quiet, well-mannered. "Officer. One moment."

The policeman stepped back. "Yes, sir?"

"This young man is my guest. What is the trouble?"

George looked about in wild surprise. It was the gray-haired man who had been sitting next to him. Gray-hair nodded benignly at George.

Guest? Was he mad?

The policeman was saying, "These two were creating a disturbance, sir."

"Any criminal charges? Any damages?"

"No, sir."

"Well, then, I'll be responsible." He presented a small card to the policeman's view and the latter stepped back at once.

Trevelyan began indignantly, "Hold on, now—" but the policeman turned on him.

"All right, now. Got any charges?"

"I just—"

"On your way. The rest of you—move on." A sizeable crowd had gathered, which now, reluctantly, unknotted itself and raveled away.

George let himself be led to a skimmer but balked at entering.

He said, "Thank you, but I'm not your guest." (Could it be a ridiculous case of mistaken identity?)

But Gray-hair smiled and said, "You weren't but you are now. Let me introduce myself, I'm Ladislas Ingenescu, Registered Historian."

"But—"

"Come, you will come to no harm, I assure you. After all, I only wanted to spare you some trouble with a policeman."

"But why?"

"Do you want a reason? Well, then, say that we're honorary townsmates, you and I. We both shouted for the same man, remember, and we townspeople must stick together, even if the tie is only honorary. Eh?"

And George, completely unsure of this man, Ingenescu, and of himself as well, found himself inside the skimmer. Before he could make up his mind that he ought to get off again, they were off the ground.

He thought confusedly: The man has some status. The policeman deferred to him.

He was almost forgetting that his real purpose here in San Francisco was not to find Trevelyan but to find some person with enough influence to force a reappraisal of his own capacity of Education.

It could be that Ingenescu was such a man. And right in George's lap.

Everything could be working out fine—fine. Yet it sounded hollow in his thought. He was uneasy.

* * *

During the short skimmer-hop, Ingenescu kept up an even flow of small-talk, pointing out the landmarks of the city, reminiscing about past Olympics he had seen. George, who paid just enough attention to make vague sounds during the pauses, watched the route of flight anxiously.

Would they head for one of the shield-openings and leave the city altogether?

No, they headed downward, and George sighed his relief softly. He felt safer in the city.

The skimmer landed at the roof-entry of a hotel and, as he alighted, Ingenescu said, "I hope you'll eat dinner with me in my room?"

George said, "Yes," and grinned unaffectedly. He was just beginning to realize the gap left within him by a missing lunch.

Ingenescu let George eat in silence. Night closed in and the wall lights went on automatically. (George thought: I've been on my own almost twenty-four hours.)

And then over the coffee, Ingenescu finally spoke again. He said, "You've been acting as though you think I intend you harm."

George reddened, put down his cup and tried to deny it, but the older man laughed and shook his head.

"It's so. I've been watching you closely since I first saw you and I think I know a great deal about you now."

George half rose in horror.

Ingenescu said, "But sit down. I only want to help you."

George sat down but his thoughts were in a whirl. If the old man knew who he was, why had he not left him to the policeman? On the other hand, why should he volunteer help?

Ingenescu said, "You want to know why I should want to help you? Oh, don't look alarmed. I can't read minds. It's just that my training enables me to judge the little reactions that give minds away, you see. Do you understand that?"

George shook his head.

Ingenescu said, "Consider my first sight of you. You were waiting in line to watch an Olympics, and your micro-reactions didn't match what you were doing. The expression of your face was wrong, the action of your hands was wrong. It meant that something, in general, was wrong, and the interesting thing was that, whatever it was, it was nothing common, nothing obvious. Perhaps, I thought, it was something of which your own conscious mind was unaware.

"I couldn't help but follow you, sit next to you. I followed you again when you left and eavesdropped on the conversation between your friend and yourself. After that, well, you were far too interesting an object of study—I'm sorry if that sounds cold-blooded—for me to allow you to be taken off by a policeman. — Now tell me, what is it that troubles you?"

George was in an agony of indecision. If this was a trap, why should it be such an indirect, roundabout one? And he *had* to turn to someone. He had come to the city to find help and here was help being offered. Perhaps what was wrong was that it was being offered. It came too easy.

Ingenescu said, "Of course, what you tell me as a Social Scientist is a privileged communication. Do you know what that means?"

"No, sir."

"It means, it would be dishonourable for me to repeat what you say to anyone for any purpose. Moreover no one has the legal right to compel me to repeat it."

George said, with sudden suspicion, "I thought you were a Historian."

"So I am."

"Just now you said you were a Social Scientist."

Ingenescu broke into loud laughter and apologized for it when he could talk. "I'm sorry, young man, I shouldn't laugh, and I wasn't really laughing at you. I was laughing at Earth and its emphasis on physical science, and the practical segments of it at that. I'll bet you can rattle off every subdivision of construction technology or mechanical engineering and yet you're a blank on social science."

"Well, then what *is* social science?"

"Social science studies groups of human beings and there are many high-specialized branches to it, just as there are to zoology, for instance. For instance, there are Culturists, who study the mechanics of cultures, their growth, development, and decay. Cultures," he added, forestalling a question, "are all the aspects of a way of life. For instance it includes the way we make our living, the things we enjoy and believe, what we consider good and bad and so on. Do you understand?"

"I think I do."

"An Economist—not an Economic Statistician, now, but an Economist—specializes in the study of the way a culture supplies the bodily needs of its individual members. A Psychologist specializes in the individual member of a society and how he is affected by the society. A Futurist specializes in planning the future course of a society, and a Historian— That's where I come in, now."

"Yes, sir."

"A Historian specializes in the past development of our own society and of societies with other cultures."

George found himself interested. "Was it different in the past?"

"I should say it was. Until a thousand years ago, there was no Education; not what we call Education, at least."

George said, "I know. People learned in bits and pieces out of books."

"Why, how do you know this?"

"I've heard it said," said George cautiously. Then, "Is there any use in worrying about what's happened long ago? I mean, it's all done with, isn't it?"

"It's never done with, my boy. The past explains the present. For instance, why is our Educational system what it is?"

George stirred restlessly. The man kept bringing the subject back to that. He said snappishly, "Because it's best."

"Ah, but why is it best? Now you listen to me for one moment and I'll explain. Then you can tell me if there is any use in history. Even before interstellar travel was developed—" He broke off at the look of complete astonishment on George's face. "Well, did you think we always had it?"

"I never gave it any thought, sir."

"I'm sure you didn't. But there was a time, four or five thousand years ago when mankind was confined to the surface of Earth. Even then, his culture had grown quite technological and his numbers had increased to the point where any failure in technology would have meant mass starvation and disease. To maintain the technological level and advance it in the face of an increasing population, more and more technicians and scientists had to be trained, and yet, as science advanced, it took longer and longer to train them.

"As first interplanetary and then intersteller travel was developed, the problem grew more acute. In fact, actual colonization of extra-Solar planets was impossible for about fifteen hundred years because of a lack of properly trained men.

"The turning point came when the mechanics of the storage of knowledge within the brain was worked out. Once that had been done, it became possible to devise Educational tapes that would modify the mechanics in such a way as to place within the mind a body of knowledge ready-made so to speak. But you know about *that.*

"Once that was done, trained men could be turned out by the thousands and millions, and we could begin what someone has since called the 'Filling of the Universe.' There are now fifteen hundred inhabited planets in the Galaxy and there is no end in sight.

"Do you see all that is involved? Earth exports Education tapes for low-specialized professions and that keeps the Galactic culture unified. For instance, the Reading tapes insure a single language for all of us. —Don't look so surprised, other languages are possible, and in the past were used. Hundreds of them.

"Earth also exports high-specialized professionals and keeps its own population at an endurable level. Since they are shipped out in a balanced sex ratio, they act as self-reproductive units and help increase the populations in the Outworlds where an increase is needed. Furthermore, tapes and men are paid for in material which we much need and on which our economy depends. *Now* do you understand why our Education is the best way?"

"Yes, sir."

"Does it help you to understand, knowing that without it, interstellar colonization was impossible for fifteen hundred years?"

"Yes, sir."

"Then you see the uses of history," the Historian smiled. "And now I wonder if you see why I'm interested in you?"

George snapped out of time and space back to reality. Ingenescu, apparently, didn't talk aimlessly. All this lecture had been a device to attack him from a new angle.

He said, once again withdrawn, hesitating. "Why?"

"Social Scientists work with societies and societies are made up of people."

"All right."

"But people aren't machines. The professionals in physical science work with machines. There is only a limited amount to know about a machine and the professionals know it all. Furthermore, all machines of a given sort are just about alike so that there is nothing to interest them in any given individual machine. But people, ah—They are so complex and so different one from another that a Social Scientist never knows all there is to know or even a good part of what there is to know. To understand his own specialty, he must always be ready to study people; particularly unusual specimens."

"Like me," said George tonelessly.

"I shouldn't call you a specimen, I suppose, but you are unusual. You're worth studying, and if you will allow me that privilege then, in return, I will help you if you are in trouble and if I can."

There were pin wheels whirring in George's mind. —All this talk about people and colonization made possible by Education. It was as though caked thoughts within him were being broken up and strewn about mercilessly.

He said, "Let me think," and clamped his hands over his ears.

He took them away and said to the Historian, "Will you do something for me, sir?"

"If I can," said the Historian amiably.

"And everything I say in this room is a privileged communication. You said so."

"And I meant it."

"Then get me an interview with an Outworld official, with—with a Novian."

Ingenescu looked startled. "Well, now—"

"You can do it," said George earnestly. "You're an important official. I saw the policeman's look when you put that card in front of his eyes. If you refuse, I—I won't let you study me."

It sounded a silly threat in George's own ears, one without force. On Ingenescu, however, it seemed to have a strong effect.

He said, "That's an impossible condition. A Novian in Olympics month—"

"All right, then, get me a Novian on the phone and I'll make my own arrangements for an interview."

"Do you think you can?"

"I know I can. Wait and see."

Ingenescu stared at George thoughtfully and then reached for the visiphone.

George waited, half drunk with this new outlook on the whole problem and the sense of power it brought. It couldn't miss. It *couldn't* miss. He would be a Novian yet. He would leave Earth in triumph despite Antonelli and the whole crew of fools at the House for the (he almost laughed aloud) Feeble-minded.

* * *

George watched eagerly as the visiplate lit up. It would open up a window into a room of Novians, a window into a small patch of Novia transplanted to Earth. In twenty-four hours he had accomplished that much.

There was a burst of laughter as the plate unmisted and sharpened, but for the moment no single head could be seen but rather the fast passing of the shadows of men and women, this way and that. A voice was heard, clear-worded over a background of babble. "Ingenescu? He wants me?"

Then there he was, staring out of the plate. A Novian. A genuine Novian. (George had not an atom of doubt. There was something completely Outworldly about him. Nothing that could be completely defined, or even momentarily mistaken.)

He was swarthy in complexion with a dark wave of hair combed rigidly back from his forehead. He wore a thin black mustache and a pointed beard, just as dark, that scarcely reached below the lower limit of his narrow chin, but the rest of his face was so smooth that it looked as though it had been depilated permanently.

He was smiling. "Ladislas, this goes too far. We fully expect to be spied on, within reason, during our stay on Earth, but mind reading is out of bounds."

"Mind reading, Honorable?"

"Confess! You knew I was going to call you this evening. You knew I was only waiting to finish this drink." His hand moved up into view and his eye peered through a small glass of a faintly violet liqueur. "I can't offer you one, I'm afraid."

George, out of range of Ingenescu's transmitter could not be seen by the Novian. He was relieved at that. He wanted time to compose himself and he needed it badly. It was as though he were made up exclusively of restless fingers, drumming, drumming—

But he was right. He hadn't miscalculated. Ingenescu *was* important. The Novian called him by his first name.

Good! Things worked well. What George had lost on Antonelli, he would make up, with advantage, on Ingenescu. And someday, when he was on his own at last, and could come back to Earth as powerful a Novian as this one who could negligently joke with Ingenescu's first name and be addressed as "Honorable" in turn—when he came back, he would settle with Antonelli. He had a year and a half to pay back and he—

He all but lost his balance on the brink of the enticing daydream and snapped back in sudden anxious realization that he was losing the thread of what was going on.

The Novian was saying, "—doesn't hold water. Novia has a civilization as complicated and advanced as Earth's. We're not Zeston, after all. It's ridiculous that we have to come here for individual technicians."

Ingenescu said soothingly, "Only for new models. There is never any certainty that new models will be needed. To buy the Educational tapes would cost you the same price as a thousand technicians and how do you know you would need that many?"

The Novian tossed off what remained of his drink and laughed. (It displeased George, somehow, that a Novian should be this frivolous. He wondered uneasily if perhaps the Novian ought not to have skipped that drink and even the one or two before that.)

The Novian said, "That's typical pious fraud, Ladislas. You know we can make use of all the late models we can get. I collected five Metallurgists this afternoon—"

"I know," said Ingenescu. "I was there."

"Watching me! Spying!" cried the Novian. "I'll tell you what it is. The new-model Metallurgists I got differed from the previous model only in knowing the use of Beeman Spectrographs. The tapes couldn't be modified that much, not that much" (he held up two fingers close together) "from last year's model. You introduce the new models only to *make* us buy and spend and come here hat in hand."

"We don't *make* you buy."

"No, but you sell late-model technicians to Landonum and so we have to keep pace. It's a merry-go-round you have us on, you pious Earthmen, but watch out, there may be an exit somewhere." There was a sharp edge to his laugh, and it ended sooner than it should have.

Ingenescu said, "In all honesty, I hope there is. Meanwhile, as to the purpose of my call—"

"That's right, *you* called. Oh, well, I've said my say and I suppose next year there'll be a new model of Metallurgist anyway for us to spend goods on, probably with a new gimmick for niobium assays and nothing else altered and the next year— But go on, what is it you want?"

"I have a young man here to whom I wish you to speak."

"Oh?" the Novian looked not completely pleased with that. "Concerning what?"

"I can't say. He hasn't told me. For that matter he hasn't even told me his name and profession."

The Novian frowned. "Then why take up my time?"

"He seems quite confident that you will be interested in what he has to say."

"I dare say."

"And," said Ingenescu, "as a favor to me."

The Novian shrugged. "Put him on and tell him to make it short."

Ingenescu stepped aside and whispered to George, "Address him as 'Honorable.' "

George swallowed with difficulty. This was it.

* * *

George felt himself going moist with perspiration. The thought had come so recently, yet it was in him now so certainly. The beginnings of it had come when he had spoken to Trevelyan, then everything had fermented and billowed into shape while Ingenescu had prattled, and then the Novian's own remarks had seemed to nail it all into place.

George said, "Honorable, I've come to show you the exit from the merry-go-round." Deliberately, he adopted the Novian's own metaphor.

The Novian stared at him gravely. "What merry-go-round?"

"You yourself mentioned it, Honorable. The merry-go-round that Novia is on when you come to Earth to—to get technicians." (He couldn't keep his teeth from chattering; from excitement, not fear.)

The Novian said, "You're trying to say that you know a way by which we can avoid patronizing Earth's mental super-market. Is that it?"

"Yes, sir. You can control your own Educational system."

"Umm. Without tapes?"

"Y—yes, Honorable."

The Novian, without taking his eyes from George, called out, "Ingenescu, get into view."

The Historian moved to where he could be seen over George's shoulder.

The Novian said, "What is this? I don't seem to penetrate."

"I assure you solemnly," said Ingenescu, "that whatever this is it is being done on the young man's own initiative, Honorable. I have not inspired this. I have nothing to do with it."

"Well, then, what is the young man to you? Why do you call me on his behalf?"

Ingenescu said, "He is an object of study, Honorable. He has value to me and I humor him."

"What kind of value?"

"It's difficult to explain; a matter of my profession."

The Novian laughed shortly. "Well, to each his profession." He nodded to an invisible person or persons outside plate range. "There's a young man here, a protégé of Ingenescu or some such thing, who will explain to us how to Educate without tapes." He snapped his fingers, and another glass of pale liqueur appeared in his hand. "Well, young man?"

The faces on the plate were multiple now. Men and women, both, crammed in for a view of George, their faces molded into various shades of amusement and curiosity.

George tried to look disdainful. They were all, in their own ways,

Novians as well as the Earthman, "studying" him as though he were a bug on a pin. Ingenescu was sitting in a corner, now, watching him owl-eyed.

Fools, he thought tensely, one and all. But they would have to understand. He would *make* them understand.

He said, "I was at the Metallurgist Olympics this afternoon."

"You too?" said the Novian blandly. "It seems all Earth was there."

"No, Honorable, but I was. I had a friend who competed and who made out very badly because you were using the Beeman machines. His education had included only the Henslers, apparently an older model. You said the modification involved was slight." George held up two fingers close together in conscious mimicry of the other's previous gesture. "And my friend had known some time in advance that knowledge of the Beeman machines would be required."

"And what does that signify?"

"It was my friend's lifelong ambition to qualify for Novia. He already knew the Henslers. He had to know the Beemans to qualify and he knew that. To learn about the Beemans would have taken just a few more facts, a bit more data, a small amount of practice perhaps. With a life's ambition riding the scale, he might have managed this—"

"And where would he have obtained a tape for the additional facts and data? Or has Education become a private matter for home study here on Earth?"

There was dutiful laughter from the faces in the background.

George said, "That's why he didn't learn, Honorable. He thought he needed a tape. He wouldn't even try without one, no matter what the prize. He refused to try without a tape."

"Refused, eh? Probably the type of fellow who would refuse to fly without a skimmer." More laughter and the Novian thawed into a smile and said, "The fellow is amusing. Go on. I'll give you another few moments."

George said tensely, "Don't think this is a joke. Tapes are actually bad. They teach too much; they're too painless. A man who learns that way doesn't know how to learn any other way. He's frozen into whatever position he's been taped. Now if a person *weren't* given tapes but were forced to learn by hand, so to speak, from the start; why, then he'd get the habit of learning, and continue to learn. Isn't that reasonable? Once he has the habit well developed he can be given just a small amount of tape-knowledge, perhaps, to fill in gaps or fix details. Then he can make further progress on his own. You can make Beeman

Metallurgists out of your own Hensler Metallurgists in that way and not have to come to Earth for new models."

The Novian nodded and sipped at his drink. "And where does everyone get knowledge without tapes? From interstellar vacuum?"

"From books. By studying the instruments themselves. By *thinking*."

"Books? How does one understand books without Education?"

"Books are in words. Words can be understood for the most part. Specialized words can be explained by the technicians you already have."

"What about reading? Will you allow reading tapes?"

"Reading tapes are all right, I suppose, but there's no reason you can't learn to read the old way, too. At least in part."

The Novian said, "So that you can develop good habits from the start?"

"Yes, yes," George said gleefully. The man was beginning to understand.

"And what about mathematics?"

"That's the easiest of all, sir—Honorable. Mathematics is different from other technical subjects. It starts with certain simple principles and proceeds by steps. You can start with nothing and learn. It's practically designed for that. Then, once you know the proper types of mathematics, other technical books become quite understandable. Especially if you start with easy ones."

"Are there easy books?"

"Definitely. Even if there weren't, the technicians you now have can try to write easy books. Some of them might be able to put some of their knowledge into words and symbols."

"Good Lord," said the Novian to the men clustered about him. "The young devil has an answer for everything."

"I have. I have," shouted George. "Ask me."

"Have you tried learning from books yourself? Or is this just theory with you?"

George turned to look quickly at Ingenescu, but the Historian was passive. There was no sign of anything but gentle interest in his face.

George said, "I have."

"And do you find it works?"

"Yes, Honorable," said George eagerly. "Take me with you to Novia. I can set up a program and direct—"

"Wait, I have a few more questions. How long would it take, do you suppose, for you to become a Metallurgist capable of handling a Beeman machine, supposing you started from nothing and did not use Educational tapes?"

George hesitated. "Well—years, perhaps."

"Two years? Five? Ten?"

"I can't say, Honorable."

"Well, there's a vital question to which you have no answer, have you? Shall we say five years? Does that sound reasonable to you?"

"I suppose so."

"All right. We have a technician studying metallurgy according to this method of yours for five years. He's no good to us during that time, you'll admit, but he must be fed and housed and paid all that time."

"But—"

"Let me finish. Then when he's done and can use the Beeman, five years have passed. Don't you suppose we'll have modified Beemans then which he *won't* be able to use?"

"But by then he'll be expert on learning. He could learn the new details necessary in a matter of days."

"So you say. And suppose this friend of yours, for instance, had studied up on Beemans on his own and managed to learn it; would he be as expert in its use as a competitor who had learned it off the tapes?"

"Maybe not—" began George.

"Ah," said the Novian.

"Wait, let *me* finish. Even if he doesn't know something as well, it's the ability to learn further that's important. He may be able to think up things, new things that no tape-Educated man would. You'll have a reservoir of original thinkers—"

"In your studying," said the Novian, "have you thought up any new things?"

"No, but I'm just one man and I haven't studied long—"

"Yes.—Well, ladies, gentlemen, have we been sufficiently amused?"

"Wait," cried George, in sudden panic. "I want to arrange a personal interview. There are things I can't explain over the visiphone. There are details—"

The Novian looked past George. "Ingenescu! I think I have done you your favor.

The screen went blank.

* * *

George's hands shot out toward the screen, as though in a wild impulse to shake life back into it. He cried out, "He didn't believe me. He didn't believe me."

Ingenescu said, "No, George. Did you really think he would?"

George scarcely heard him. "But why not? It's all true. It's all so much to his advantage. No risk. I and a few men to work with— A dozen men training for years would cost less than one technician.—He was drunk! Drunk! He didn't understand."

George looked about breathlessly. "How do I get to him? I've got to. This was wrong. Shouldn't have used the visiphone. I need time. Face to face. How do I—"

Ingenescu said, "He won't see you, George. And if he did, he wouldn't believe you."

"He will, I tell you. When he isn't drinking. He—" George turned squarely toward the Historian and his eyes widened. "Why do you call me George?"

"Isn't that your name? George Platen?"

"You know me?"

"All about you."

George was motionless except for the breath pumping his chest wall up and down.

Ingenescu said, "I want to help you, George. I told you that. I've been studying you and I want to help you."

George screamed, "I don't need help. I'm not feeble-minded. The whole world is, but I'm not." He whirled and dashed madly for the door.

He flung it open and two policemen roused themselves suddenly from their guard duty and seized him.

For all George's straining, he could feel the hypo-spray at the fleshy point just under the corner of his jaw, and that was it. The last thing he remembered was the face of Ingenescu, watching with gentle concern.

* * *

George opened his eyes to the whiteness of a ceiling. He remembered what had happened. He remembered it distantly as though it had happened to somebody else. He stared at the ceiling till the whiteness filled his eyes and washed his brain clean, leaving room, it seemed, for new thought and new ways of thinking.

He didn't know how long he lay there so, listening to the drift of his own thinking.

There was a voice in his ear. "Are you awake?"

And George heard his own moaning for the first time. Had he been moaning? He tried to turn his head.

The voice said, "Are you in pain, George?"

George whispered, "Funny. I was so anxious to leave Earth. I didn't understand."

"Do you know where you are?"

"Back in the—the House." George managed to turn. The voice belonged to Omani.

George said, "It's funny I didn't understand."

Omani smiled gently, "Sleep again—"

George slept.

* * *

And woke again. His mind was clear.

Omani sat at the bedside reading, but he put down the book as George's eyes opened.

George struggled to a sitting position. He said, "Hello."

"Are you hungry?"

"You bet." He stared at Omani curiously. "I was followed when I left, wasn't I?"

Omani nodded. "You were under observation at all times. We were going to maneuver you to Antonelli and let you discharge your aggressions. We felt that to be the only way you could make progress. Your emotions were clogging your advance."

George said, with a trace of embarrassment, "I was all wrong about him."

"It doesn't matter now. When you stopped to stare at the Metallurgy notice board at the airport, one of our agents reported back the list of names. You and I had talked about your past sufficiently so that I caught the significance of Trevelyan's name there. You asked for directions to the Olympics; there was the possibility that this might result in the kind of crisis we were hoping for; we sent Ladislas Ingenescu to the hall to meet you and take over."

"He's an important man in the government, isn't he?"

"Yes, he is."

"And you had him take over. It makes me sound important."

"You *are* important, George."

A thick stew had arrived, steaming, fragrant. George grinned wolfishly and pushed his sheets back to free his arms. Omani helped arrange the bed-table. For a while, George ate silently.

Then George said, "I woke up here once before just for a short time."

Omani said, "I know. I was here."

"Yes, I remember. You know, everything was changed. It was as though I was too tired to feel emotion. I wasn't angry any more. I could just think. It was as though I had been drugged to wipe out emotion."

"You weren't," said Omani. "Just sedation. You had rested."

"Well, anyway, it was all clear to me, as though I had known it all the time but wouldn't listen to myself. I thought: What was it I had wanted Novia to let me do? I had wanted to go to Novia and take a batch of un-Educated youngsters and teach them out of books. I had wanted to establish a House for the Feeble-minded—like here—and Earth already has them—many of them."

Omani's white teeth gleamed as he smiled. "The Institute of Higher Studies is the correct name for places like this."

"Now I see it," said George, "so easily I am amazed at my blindness before. After all, who invents the new instrument models that require new-model technicians? Who invented the Beeman spectrographs, for instance? A man called Beeman, I suppose, but he couldn't have been tape-Educated or how could he have made the advance?"

"Exactly."

"Or who makes Educational tapes? Special tape-making technicians? Then who makes the tapes to train *them?* More advanced technicians? Then who makes the tapes— You see what I mean. Somewhere there has to be an end. Somewhere there must be men and women with capacity for original thought."

"Yes, George."

George leaned back, stared over Omani's head, and for a moment there was the return of something like restlessness to his eyes.

"Why wasn't I told all this at the beginning?"

"Oh, if we could," said Omani, "the trouble it would save us. We can analyze a mind, George, and say this one will make an adequate architect and that one a good woodworker. We know of no way of detecting the capacity for original, creative thought. It is too subtle a thing. We have some rule-of-thumb methods that mark out individuals who may possibly or potentially have such a talent.

"On Reading Day, such individuals are reported. You were, for instance. Roughly speaking, the number so reported comes to one in ten thousand. By the time Education Day arrives, these individuals are checked again, and nine out of ten of them turn out to have been false alarms. Those who remain are sent to places like this."

George said, "Well, what's wrong with telling people that one out of—of a hundred thousand will end at places like these? Then it won't be such a shock to those who do."

"And those who don't? The ninety-nine thousand nine hundred and ninety-nine that don't? We can't have all those people considering themselves failures. They aim at the professions and one way or another they all make it. Everyone can place after his or her name: Registered something-or-other. In one fashion or another every individual hsa his or her place in society and this is necessary."

"But we?" said George. "The one in ten thousand exception?"

"You can't be told. That's exactly it. It's the final test. Even after we've thinned out the possibilities on Education Day, nine out of ten of those who come here are not quite the material of creative genius, and there's no way we can distinguish those nine from the tenth that we want by any form of machinery. The tenth one must tell us himself."

"How?"

"We bring you here to a House for the Feeble-minded and the man who won't accept that is the man we want. It's a method that can be cruel, but it works. It won't do to say to a man, 'You can create. Do so.' It is much safer to wait for a man to say, 'I can create, and I will do so whether you wish it or not.' There are ten thousand men like you, George, who support the advancing technology of fifteen hundred worlds. We can't allow ourselves to miss one recruit to that number or waste our efforts on one member who doesn't measure up."

George pushed his empty plate out of the way and lifted a cup of coffee to his lips.

"What about the people here who don't—measure up?"

"They are taped eventually and become our Social Scientists. Ingenescu is one. I am a Registered Psychologist. We are second echelon, so to speak."

George finished his coffee. He said, "I still wonder about one thing?"

"What is that?"

George threw aside the sheet and stood up. "Why do they call them Olympics?"

The Ugly Little Boy

Edith Fellowes smoothed her working smock as she always did before opening the elaborately locked door and stepping across the invisible dividing line between the *is* and the *is not.* She carried her notebook and her pen although she no longer took notes except when she felt the absolute need for some report.

This time she also carried a suitcase. ("Games for the boy," she had said, smiling, to the guard—who had long since stopped even thinking of questioning her and who waved her on.)

And, as always, the ugly little boy knew that she had entered and came running to her, crying, "Miss Fellowes— Miss Fellowes—" in his soft, slurring way.

"Timmie," she said, and passed her hand over the shaggy, brown hair on his misshapen little head. "What's wrong?"

He said, "Will Jerry be back to play again? I'm sorry about what happened."

"Never mind that now, Timmie. Is that why you've been crying?"

He looked away. "Not just about that, Miss Fellowes. I dreamed again."

"The same dream?" Miss Fellowes' lips set. Of course, the Jerry affair would bring back the dream.

He nodded. His too large teeth showed as he tried to smile and the lips of his forward-thrusting mouth stretched wide. "When will I be big enough to go out there, Miss Fellowes?"

"Soon," she said softly, feeling her heart break. "Soon."

Miss Fellowes let him take her hand and enjoyed the warm touch of the thick dry skin of his palm. He led her through the three rooms that made up the whole of Stasis Section One—comfortable enough, yes, but an eternal prison for the ugly little boy all the seven (was it seven?) years of his life.

He led her to the one window, looking out onto a scrubby woodland section of the world of *is* (now hidden by night), where a fence and painted instructions allowed no men to wander without permission.

He pressed his nose against the window. "Out there, Miss Fellowes?"

"Better places. Nicer places," she said sadly as she looked at his poor little imprisoned face outlined in profile against the window. The forehead retreated flatly and his hair lay down in tufts upon it. That back of his skull bulged and seemed to make the head overheavy so that it sagged and bent forward, forcing the whole body into a stoop. Already, bony ridges were beginning to bulge the skin above his eyes. His wide mouth thrust forward more prominently than did his wide and flattened nose and he had no chin to speak of, only a jawbone that curved smoothly down and back. He was small for his years and his stumpy legs were bowed.

He was a very ugly little boy and Edith Fellowes loved him dearly.

Her own face was behind his line of vision, so she allowed her lips the luxury of a tremor.

They would *not* kill him. She would do anything to prevent it. Anything. She opened the suitcase and began taking out the clothes it contained.

* * *

Edith Fellowes had crossed the threshold of Stasis, Inc. for the first time just a little over three years before. She hadn't, at that time, the slightest idea as to what Stasis meant or what the place did. No one did then, except those who worked there. In fact, it was only the day after she arrived that the news broke upon the world.

At the time, it was just that they had advertised for a woman with knowledge of physiology, experience with clinical chemistry, and a love for children. Edith Fellowes had been a nurse in a maternity ward and believed she fulfilled those qualifications.

Gerald Hoskins, whose name plate on the desk included a Ph.D. after the name, scratched his cheek with his thumb and looked at her steadily.

Miss Fellowes automatically stiffened and felt her face (with its slightly asymmetric nose and its a-trifle-too-heavy eyebrows) twitch.

He's no dreamboat himself, she thought resentfully. He's getting fat and bald and he's got a sullen mouth. —But the salary mentioned had been considerably higher than she had expected, so she waited.

Hoskins said, "Now do you really love children?"

"I wouldn't say I did if I didn't."

"Or do you just love pretty children? Nice chubby children with cute little button-noses and gurgly ways?"

Miss Fellowes said, "Children are children, Dr. Hoskins, and the ones that aren't pretty are just the ones who may happen to need help most."

"Then suppose we take you on—"

"You mean you're offering me the job now?"

He smiled briefly, and for a moment, his broad face had an absent-minded charm about it. He said, "I make quick decisions. So far the offer is tentative, however. I may make as quick a decision to let you go. Are you ready to take the chance?"

Miss Fellowes clutched at her purse and calculated just as swiftly as she could, then ignored calculations and followed impulse. "All right."

"Fine. We're going to form the Stasis tonight and I think you had better be there to take over at once. That will be at 8 P.M. and I'd appreciate it if you could be here at 7:30."

"But what—"

"Fine. Fine. That will be all now." On signal, a smiling secretary came in to usher her out.

Miss Fellowes stared back at Dr. Hoskins' closed door for a moment. What was Stasis? What had this large barn of a building — with its badged employees, its makeshift corridors, and its unmistakable air of engineering—to do with children?

She wondered if she should go back that evening or stay away and teach that arrogant man a lesson. But she knew she would be back if only out of sheer frustration. She would have to find out about the children.

* * *

She came back at 7:30 and did not have to announce herself. One after another, men and women seemed to know her and to know her function. She found herself all but placed on skids as she was moved inward.

Dr. Hoskins was there, but he only looked at her distantly and murmured, "Miss Fellowes."

He did not even suggest that she take a seat, but she drew one calmly up to the railing and sat down.

They were on a balcony, looking down into a large pit, filled with instruments that looked like a cross between the control panel of a spaceship and the working face of a computer. On one side were partitions that seemed to make up an unceilinged apartment, a giant dollhouse into the rooms of which she could look from above.

She could see an electronic cooker and a freeze-space unit in one room and a washroom arrangement off another. And surely the object she made out in another room could only be part of a bed, a small bed.

Hoskins was speaking to another man and, with Miss Fellowes, they made up the total occupancy of the balcony. Hoskins did not offer to introduce the other man, and Miss Fellowes eyed him surreptitiously. He was thin and quite fine-looking in a middle-aged way. He had a small mustache and keen eyes that seemed to busy themselves with everything.

He was saying, "I won't pretend for one moment that I understand all this, Dr. Hoskins; I mean, except as a layman, a reasonably intelligent layman, may be expected to understand it. Still, if there's one part I understand less than another, it's this matter of selectivity. You can only reach out so far; that seems sensible; things get dimmer the further you go; it takes more energy. —But then, you can only reach out so near. That's the puzzling part."

"I can make it seem less paradoxical, Deveney, if you will allow me to use an analogy."

(Miss Fellowes placed the new man the moment she heard his name, and despite herself was impressed. This was obviously Candide Deveney, the science writer of the Telenews, who was notoriously at the scene of every major scientific break-through. She even recognized his face as one she saw on the news-plate when the landing on Mars had been announced. —So Dr. Hoskins must have something important here.

"By all means use an analogy," said Deveney ruefully, "if you think it will help."

"Well, then, you can't read a book with ordinary-sized print if it is held six feet from yours eyes, but you can read it if you hold it one foot from your eyes. So far, the closer the better. If you bring the book to within one inch of your eyes, however, you've lost it again. There is such a thing as being too close, you see."

"Hmm," said Deveney.

"Or take another example. Your right shoulder is about thirty inches from the tip of your right forefinger and you can place your right forefinger on your right shoulder. Your right elbow is only half the distance from the tip of your right forefinger; it should by all ordinary logic be easier to reach, and yet you cannot place your right finger on your right elbow. Again, there is such a thing as being too close."

Deveney said, "May I use these analogies in my story?"

"Well, of course. Only too glad. I've been waiting long enough for someone like you to have a story. I'll give you anything else you want. It is time, finally, that we want the world looking over our shoulder. They'll see something."

(Miss Fellowes found herself admiring his calm certainty despite herself. There was strength there.)

Deveney said, "How far out will you reach?"

"Forty thousand years."

Miss Fellowes drew in her breath sharply.

Years?

There was tension in the air. The men at the controls scarcely moved. One man at a microphone spoke into it in a soft monotone, in short phrases that made no sense to Miss Fellowes.

Deveney, leaning over the balcony railing with an intent stare, said, "Will we see anything, Dr. Hoskins?"

"What? No. Nothing till the job is done. We detect indirectly, something on the principle of radar, except that we use mesons rather than radiation. Mesons reach backward under the proper conditions. Some are reflected and we must analyze the reflections."

"That sounds difficult."

Hoskins smiled again, briefly as always. "It is the end product of fifty years of research; forty years of it before I entered the field. — Yes, it's difficult."

The man at the microphone raised one hand.

Hoskins said, "We've had the fix on one particular moment in time for weeks; breaking it, remaking it after calculating our own movements in time; making certain that we could handle time-flow with sufficient precision. This must work now."

But his forehead glistened.

Edith Fellowes found herself out of her seat and at the balcony railing, but there was nothing to see.

The man at the microphone said quietly, "Now."

There was a space of silence sufficient for one breath and then the sound of a terrified little boy's scream from the dollhouse rooms. Terror! Piercing terror!

Miss Fellowes' head twisted in the direction of the cry. A child was involved. she had forgotten.

And Hoskins' fist pounded on the railing and he said in a tight voice, trembling with triumph, "*Did* it."

* * *

Miss Fellowes was urged down the short, spiral flight of steps by the hard press of Hoskins' palm between her shoulder blades. He did not speak to her.

The men who had been at the controls were standing about now, smiling, smoking, watching the three as they entered on the main floor. A very soft buzz sounded from the direction of the dollhouse.

Hoskins said to Deveney, "It's perfectly safe to enter Stasis. I've done it a thousand times. There's a queer sensation which is momentary and means nothing."

He stepped through an open door in mute demonstration, and Deveney, smiling stiffly and drawing an obviously deep breath, followed him.

Hoskins said, "Miss Fellowes! Please!" He crooked his forefinger impatiently.

Miss Fellowes nodded and stepped stiffly through. It was as though a ripple went through her, an internal tickle.

But once inside all seemed normal. There was the smell of the fresh wood of the dollhouse and—of—of soil somehow.

There was silence now, no voice at least, but there was the dry shuffling of feet, a scrabbling as of a hand over wood—then a low moan.

"Where is it?" asked Miss Fellowes in distress. Didn't these fool men *care*?

* * *

The boy was in the bedroom; at least the room with the bed in it.

It was standing naked, with its small, dirt-smeared chest heaving raggedly. A bushel of dirt and coarse grass spread over the floor at his bare brown feet. The smell of soil came from it and a touch of something fetid.

Hoskins followed her horrified glance and said with annoyance, "You can't pluck a boy cleanly out of time, Miss Fellowes. We had to take some of the surroundings with it for safety. Or would you have preferred to have it arrive here minus a leg or with only half a head?"

"*Please!*" said Miss Fellowes, in an agony of revulsion. "Are we just to stand here? The poor child is frightened. And it's *filthy*."

She was quite correct. It was smeared with encrusted dirt and grease and had a scratch on its thigh that looked red and sore.

As Hoskins approached him, the boy, who seemed to be something over three years in age, hunched low and backed away rapidly. He lifted his upper lip and snarled in a hissing fashion like a cat. With a rapid gesture, Hoskins seized both the child's arms and lifted him, writhing and screaming, from the floor.

Miss Fellowes said, "Hold him, now. He needs a warm bath first.

He needs to be cleaned. Have you the equipment? If so, have it brought here, and I'll need to have help in handling him just at first. Then, too, for heaven's sake, have all this trash and filth removed."

She was giving the orders now and she felt perfectly good about that. And because now she was an efficient nurse, rather than a confused spectator, she looked at the child with a clinical eye—and hesitated for one shocked moment. She saw past the dirt and shrieking, past the thrashing of limbs and useless twisting. She saw the boy himself.

It was the ugliest little boy she had ever seen. It was horribly ugly from misshapen head to bandy legs.

* * *

She got the boy cleaned with three men helping her and with others milling about in their efforts to clean the room. She worked in silence and with a sense of outrage, annoyed by the continued strugglings and outcries of the boy and by the undignified drenchings of soapy water to which she was subjected.

Dr. Hoskins had hinted that the child would not be pretty, but that was far from stating that it would be repulsively deformed. And there was a stench about the boy that soap and water was only alleviating little by little.

She had the strong desire to thrust the boy, soaped as he was, into Hoskins' arms and walk out; but there was the pride of profession. She had accepted an assignment after all. —And there would be the look in his eyes. A cold look that would read: Only pretty children, Miss Fellowes?

He was standing apart from them, watching coolly from a distance with a half-smile on his face when he caught her eyes, as though amused at her outrage.

She decided she would wait a while before quitting. To do so now would only demean her.

Then, when the boy was a bearable pink and smelled of scented soap, she felt better anyway. His cries changed to whimpers of exhaustion as he watched carefully, eyes moving in quick frightened suspicion from one to another of those in the room. His cleanness accentuated his thin nakedness as he shivered with cold after his bath.

Miss Fellowes said sharply, "Bring me a nightgown for the child!"

A nightgown appeared at once. It was as though everything were ready and yet nothing were ready unless she gave orders; as though they were deliberately leaving this in her charge without help, to test her.

The newsman, Deveney, approached and said, "I'll hold him, Miss. You won't get it on yourself."

"Thank you," said Miss Fellowes. And it was a battle indeed, but the nightgown went on, and when the boy made as though to rip it off, she slapped his hand sharply.

The boy reddened, but did not cry. He stared at her and the splayed fingers of one hand moved slowly across the flannel of the nightgown, feeling the strangeness of it.

Miss Fellowes thought desperately: Well, what next?

Everyone seemed in suspended animation, waiting for her—even the ugly little boy.

Miss Fellowes said sharply, "Have you provided food? Milk?"

They had. A mobile unit was wheeled in, with its refrigeration compartment containing three quarts of milk, with a warming unit and a supply of fortifications in the form of vitamin drops, copper-cobalt-iron syrup and others she had no time to be concerned with. There was a variety of canned self-warming junior foods.

She used milk, simply milk, to begin with. The radar unit heated the milk to a set temperature in a matter of ten seconds and clicked off, and she put some in a saucer. She had a certainty about the boy's savagery. He wouldn't know how to handle a cup.

Miss Fellowes nodded and said to the boy, "Drink. Drink." She made a gesture as though to raise the milk to her mouth. The boy's eyes followed but he made no move.

Suddenly, the nurse resorted to direct measures. She seized the boy's upper arm in one hand and dipped the other in the milk. She dashed the milk across his lips, so tha it dripped down cheeks and receding chin.

For a moment, the child uttered a high-pitched cry, then his tongue moved over his wetted lips. Miss Fellowes stepped back.

The boy approached the saucer, bent toward it, then looked up and behind sharply as though expecting a crouching enemy; bent again and licked at the milk eagerly, like a cat. He made a slurping noise. He did not use his hands to lift the saucer.

Miss Fellowes allowed a bit of the revulsion she felt show on her face. She couldn't help it.

Deveney caught that, perhaps. He said, "Does the nurse know, Dr. Hoskins?"

"Know what?" demanded Miss Fellowes.

Deveney hesitated, but Hoskins (again that look of detached amusement on his face) said, "Well, tell her."

Deveney addressed Miss Fellowes. "You may not suspect it, Miss, but you happen to be the first civilized woman in history ever to be taking care of a Neanderthal youngster."

She turned on Hoskins with a kind of controlled ferocity. "You might have told me, Doctor."

"Why? What difference does it make?"

"You said a child."

"Isn't that a child? Have you ever had a puppy or a kitten, Miss Fellowes? Are those closer to the human? If that were a baby chimpanzee, would you be repelled? You're a nurse, Miss Fellowes. Your record places you in a maternity ward for three years. Have you ever refused to take care of a deformed infant?"

Miss Fellowes felt her case slipping away. She said, with much less decision, "You might have told me."

"And you would have refused the position? Well, do you refuse it now?" He gazed at her coolly, while Deveney watched from the other side of the room, and the Neanderthal child, having finished the milk and licked the plate, looked up at her with a wet face and wide, longing eyes.

The boy pointed to the milk and suddenly burst out in a short series of sounds repeated over and over; sounds made up of gutturals and elaborate tongue-clickings.

Miss Fellowes said, in surprise, "Why, he talks."

"Of course," said Hoskins. "Homo neanderthalensis is not a truly separate species, but rather a subspecies of Homo sapiens. Why shouldn't he talk? He's probably asking for more milk."

Automatically, Miss Fellowes reached for the bottle of milk, but Hoskins seized her wrist. "Now, Miss Fellowes, before we go any further, are you staying on the job?"

Miss Fellowes shook free in annoyance, "Won't you feed him if I don't? I'll stay with him—for a while."

She poured the milk.

Hoskins said, "We are going to leave you with the boy, Miss Fellowes. This is the only door to Stasis Number One and it is elaborately locked and guarded. I'll want you to learn the details of the lock which will, of course, be keyed to your fingerprints as they are already keyed to mine. The spaces overhead" (he looked upward to the open ceilings of the dollhouse) "are also guarded and we will be warned if anything untoward takes place in here."

Miss Fellowes said indignantly, "You mean I'll be under view."

She thought suddenly of her own survey of the room interiors from the balcony.

"No, no," said Hoskins seriously, "your privacy will be respected completely. The view will consist of electronic symbolism only, which only a computer will deal with. Now you will stay with him tonight, Miss Fellowes, and every night until further notice. You will be relieved during the day according to some schedule you will find convenient. We will allow you to arrange that."

Miss Fellowes looked about the dollhouse with a puzzled expression. "But why all this, Dr. Hoskins? Is the boy dangerous?"

"It's a matter of energy, Miss Fellowes. He must never be allowed to leave these rooms. Never. Not for an instant. Not for any reason. Not to save his life. Not even to save *your* life, Miss Fellowes. Is that clear?"

Miss Fellowes raised her chin. "I understand the orders, Dr. Hoskins, and the nursing profession is accustomed to placing its duties ahead of self-preservation."

"Good. You can always signal if you need anyone." And the two men left.

* * *

Miss Fellowes turned to the boy. He was watching her and there was still milk in the saucer. Laboriously, she tried to show him how to lift the saucer and place it to his lips. He resisted, but let her touch him without crying out.

Always, his frightened eyes were on her, watching, watching for the one false move. She found herself soothing him, trying to move her hand very slowly toward his hair, letting him see it every inch of the way, see there was no harm in it.

And she succeeded in stroking his hair for an instant.

She said, "I'm going to have to show you how to use the bathroom. Do you think you can learn?"

She spoke quietly, kindly, knowing he would not understand the words but hoping he would respond to the calmness of the tone.

The boy launched into a clicking phrase again.

She said, "May I take your hand?"

She held out hers and the boy looked at it. She left it outstretched and waited. The boy's own hand crept forward toward hers.

"That's right," she said.

It approached within an inch of hers and then the boy's courage failed him. He snatched it back.

"Well," said Miss Fellowes calmly, "we'll try again later. Would you like to sit down here?" She patted the mattress of the bed.

The hours passed slowly and progress was minute. She did not succeed either with bathroom or with the bed. In fact, after the child had given unmistakable signs of sleepiness he lay down on the bare ground and then, with a quick movement, rolled beneath the bed.

She bent to look at him and his eyes gleamed out at her as he tongue-clicked at her.

"All right," she said, "if you feel safer there, you sleep there."

She closed the door to the bedroom and retired to the cot that had been placed for her use in the largest room. At her insistence, a makeshift canopy had been stretched over it. She thought: Those stupid men will have to place a mirror in this room and a larger chest of drawers and a separate washroom if they expect me to spend nights here.

* * *

It was difficult to sleep. She found herself straining to hear possible sounds in the next room. He couldn't get out, could he? The walls were sheer and impossibly high but suppose the child could climb like a monkey? Well, Hoskins said there were observational devices watching through the ceiling.

Suddenly she thought: Can he be dangerous? Physically dangerous?

Surely, Hoskins couldn't have meant that. Surely, he would not have left her alone, if—

She tried to laugh at herself. He was only a three- or four-year-old child. Still, she had not succeeded in cutting his nails. If he should attack her with nails and teeth while she slept—

Her breath came quickly. Oh, ridiculous, and yet—

She listened with painful attentiveness, and this time she heard the sound.

The boy was crying.

Not shrieking in fear or anger; not yelling or screaming. It was crying softly, and the cry was the heartbroken sobbing of a lonely, lonely child.

For the first time, Miss Fellowes thought with a pang: Poor thing!

Of course, it was a child; what did the shape of its head matter? It was a child that had been orphaned as no child had ever been orphaned before. Not only its mother and father were gone, but all its species.

Snatched callously out of time, it was now the only creature of its kind in the world. The last. The only.

She felt pity for it strengthen, and with it shame at her own callousness. Tucking her own nightgown carefully about her calves (incongruously, she thought: Tomorrow I'll have to bring in a bathrobe) she got out of bed and went into the boy's room.

"Little boy," she called in a whisper. "Little boy."

She was about to reach under the bed, but she thought of a possible bite and did not. Instead, she turned on the night light and moved the bed.

The poor thing was huddled in the corner, knees up against his chin, looking up at her with blurred and apprehensive eyes.

In the dim light, she was not aware of his repulsiveness.

"Poor boy," she said, "poor boy." She felt him stiffen as she stroked his hair, then relax. "Poor boy. May I hold you?"

She sat down on the floor next to him and slowly and rhythmically stroked his hair, his cheek, his arm. Softly, she began to sing a slow and gentle song.

He lifted his head at that, staring at her mouth in the dimness, as though wondering at the sound.

She maneuvered him closer while he listened to her. Slowly, she pressed gently against the side of his head, until it rested on her shoulder. She put her arm under his thighs and with a smooth and unhurried motion lifted him into her lap.

She continued singing, the same simple verse over and over, while she rocked back and forth, back and forth.

He stopped crying, and after a while the smooth burr of his breathing showed he was asleep.

With infinite care, she pushed his bed back against the wall and laid him down. She covered him and stared down. His face looked so peaceful and little-boy as he slept. It didn't matter so much that it was so ugly. Really.

She began to tiptoe out, then thought: If he wakes up?

She came back, battled irresolutely with herself, then sighed and slowly got into bed with the child.

It was too small for her. She was cramped and uneasy at the lack of canopy, but the child's hand crept into hers and, somehow, she fell asleep in that position.

* * *

She awoke with a start and a wild impulse to scream. The latter she just managed to suppress into a gurgle. The boy was looking at her, wide-eyed. It took her a long moment to remember getting into bed with him, and now, slowly, without unfixing her eyes from his, she stretched one leg carefully and let it touch the floor, then the other one.

She cast a quick and apprehensive glance toward the open ceiling, then tensed her muscles for quick disengagement.

But at that moment, the boy's stubby fingers reached out and touched her lips. He said something.

She shrank at the touch. He was terribly ugly in the light of day.

The boy spoke again. He opened his own mouth and gestured with his hand as though something were coming out.

Miss Fellowes guessed at the meaning and said tremulously. "Do you want me to sing?"

The boy said nothing but stared at her mouth.

In a voice slightly off key with tension, Miss Fellowes began the little song she had sung the night before and the ugly little boy smiled. He swayed clumsily in rough time to the music and made a little gurgly sound that might have been the beginnings of a laugh.

Miss Fellowes sighed inwardly. Music hath charms to soothe the savage beast. It might help—

She said, "You wait. Let me get myself fixed up. It will just take a minute. Then I'll make breakfast for you."

She worked rapidly, conscious of the lack of ceiling at all times. The boy remained in bed, watching her when she was in view. She smiled at him at those times and waved. At the end, he waved back, and she found herself being charmed by that.

Finally, she said, "Would you like oatmeal with milk?" It took a moment to prepare, and then she beckoned to him.

Whether he understood the gesture or followed the aroma, Miss Fellowes did not know, but he got out of bed.

She tried to show him how to use a spoon but he shrank away from it in fright. (Time enough, she thought.) She compromised on insisting that he lift the bowl in his hands. He did it clumsily enough and it was incredibly messy but most of it did get into him.

She tried the drinking milk in a glass this time, and the little boy whined when he found the opening too small for him to get his face into conveniently. She held his hand, forcing it around the glass, making him tip it, forcing his mouth to the rim.

Again a mess but again most went into him, and she was used to messes.

The washroom, to her surprise and relief, was a less frustrating matter. He understood what it was she expected him to do.

She found herself patting his head, saying. "Good boy. Smart boy."

And to Miss Fellowes' exceeding pleasure, the boy smiled at that.

She thought: When he smiles he's quite bearable. Really.

Later in the day, the gentlemen of the press arrived.

She held the boy in her arms and he clung to her wildly while across the open door they set cameras to work. The commotion frightened the boy and he began to cry, but it was ten minutes before Miss Fellowes was allowed to retreat and put the boy in the next room.

She emerged again, flushed with indignation, walked out of the apartment (for the first time in eighteen hours) and closed the door behind her. "I think you've had enough. It will take me a while to quiet him. Go away."

"Sure, sure," said the gentleman from the *Times-Herald*. "But is that really a Neanderthal or is this some kind of gag?"

"I assure you," said Hoskins' voice, suddenly, from the background, "that this is no gag. The child is authentic Homo neanderthalensis."

"Is it a boy or a girl?"

"Boy," said Miss Fellowes briefly.

"Ape-boy," said the gentleman from the *News*. "That's what we've got here. Ape-boy. How does he act, Nurse?"

"He acts exactly like a little boy," snapped Miss Fellowes, annoyed into the defensive, "and he is not an ape-boy. His name is—is Timothy, Timmie—and he is perfectly normal in his behavior."

She had chosen the name Timothy at a venture. It was the first that had occurred to her.

"Timmie the Ape-boy," said the gentleman from the *News* and, as it turned out, Timmie the Ape-boy was the name under which the child became known to the world.

The gentleman from the *Globe* turned to Hoskins and said, "Doc, what do you expect to do with the ape-boy?"

Hoskins shrugged. "My original plan was completed when I proved it possible to bring him here. However, the anthropologists will be very interested, I imagine, and the physiologists. We have here, after all, a creature which is at the edge of being human. We should learn a great deal about ourselves and our ancestry from him."

"How long will you keep him?"

"Until such a time as we need the space more than we need him. Quite a while, perhaps."

The gentleman from the *News* said, "Can you bring it out into the open so we can set up sub-etheric equipment and put on a real show?"

"I'm sorry, but the child cannot be removed from Stasis."

"Exactly what is Stasis?"

"Ah." Hoskins permitted himself one of his short smiles. "That would take a great deal of explanation, gentlemen. In Stasis, time as we know it doesn't exist. Those rooms are inside an invisible bubble that is not exactly part of our Universe. That is why the child could be plucked out of time as it was."

"Well, wait now," said the gentleman from the *News* discontentedly, "what are you giving us? The nurse goes into the room and out of it."

"And so can any of you," said Hoskins matter-of-factly. "You would be moving parallel to the lines of temporal force and no great energy gain or loss would be involved. The child, however, was taken from the far past. It moved across the lines and gained temporal potential. To move it into the Universe and into our own time would absorb enough energy to burn out every line in the place and probably blank out all powers in the city of Washington. We had to store trash brought with him on the premises and will have to remove it little by little."

The newsmen were writing down sentences busily as Hoskins spoke to them. They did not understand and they were sure their readers would not, but it sounded scientific and that was what counted.

The gentleman from the *Times-Herald* said, "Would you be available for an all-circuit interview tonight?"

"I think so," said Hoskins at once, and they all moved off.

Miss Fellowes looked after them. She understood all this about Stasis and temporal force as little as the newsmen but she managed to get this much. Timmie's imprisonment (she found herself thinking of the little boy as Timmie) was a real one and not one imposed by the arbitrary fiat of Hoskins. Apparently, it was impossible to let him out of Stasis at all, ever.

Poor child. Poor child.

She was suddenly aware of his crying and she hastened in to console him.

* * *

Miss Fellowes did not have a chance to see Hoskins on the all-circuit hook-up, and though his interview was beamed to every part of the world and even to the outpost on the Moon, it did not penetrate the apartment in which Miss Fellowes and the ugly little boy lived.

But he was down the next morning, radiant and joyful.

Miss Fellowes said, "Did the interview go well?"

"Extremely. And how is—Timmie?"

Miss Fellowes found herself pleased at the use of the name. "Doing quite well. Now come out here, Timmie, the nice gentleman will not hurt you."

But Timmie stayed in the other room, with a lock of his matted hair showing behind the barrier of the door and, occasionally, the corner of an eye.

"Actually," said Miss Fellowes, "he is settling down amazingly. He is quite intelligent."

"Are you surprised?"

She hesitated just a moment, then said, "Yes, I am. I suppose I thought he was an ape-boy."

"Well, ape-boy or not, he's done a great deal for us. He's put Stasis, Inc. on the map. We're in, Miss Fellowes, we're in." It was as though he had to express his triumph to someone, even if only to Miss Fellowes.

"Oh?" She let him talk.

He put his hands in his pockets and said, "We've been working on a shoestring for ten years, scrounging funds a penny at a time wherever we could. We had to shoot the works on one big show. It was everything, or nothing. And when I say the works, I mean it. This attempt to bring in a Neanderthal took every cent we could borrow or steal, and some of it *was* stolen—funds for other projects, used for this one without permission. If that experiment hadn't succeeded, I'd have been through."

Miss Fellowes said abruptly, "Is that why there are no ceilings?"

"Eh?" Hoskins looked up.

"Was there no money for ceilings?"

"Oh. Well, that wasn't the only reason. We didn't really know in advance how old the Neanderthal might be exactly. We can detect only dimly in time, and he might have been large and savage. It was possible we might have had to deal with him from a distance, like a caged animal."

"But since that hasn't turned out to be so, I suppose you can build a ceiling now."

"Now, yes. We have plenty of money, now. Funds have been promised from every source. This is all wonderful, Miss Fellowes." His broad face gleamed with a smile that lasted and when he left, even his back seemed to be smiling.

Miss Fellowes thought: He's quite a nice man when he's off guard and forgets about being scientific.

She wondered for an idle moment if he was married, then dismissed the thought in self-embarrassment.

"Timmie," she called. "Come here, Timmie."

* * *

In the months that passed, Miss Fellowes felt herself grow to be an integral part of Stasis, Inc. She was given a small office of her own with her name on the door, an office quite close to the dollhouse (as she never stopped calling Timmie's Stasis bubble). She was given a substantial raise. The dollhouse was covered by a ceiling; its furnishings were elaborated and improved; a second washroom was added—and even so, she gained an apartment of her own on the institute grounds and, on occasion, did not stay with Timmie during the night. An intercom was set up between the dollhouse and her apartment and Timmie learned how to use it.

Miss Fellowes got used to Timmie. She even grew less conscious of his ugliness. One day she found herself staring at an ordinary boy in the street and finding something bulgy and unattractive in his high domed forehead and jutting chin. She had to shake herself to break the spell.

It was more pleasant to grow used to Hoskins' occasional visits. It was obvious he welcomed escape from his increasingly harried role as head of Stasis, Inc., and that he took a sentimental interest in the child who had started it all, but it seemed to Miss Fellowes that he also enjoyed talking to her.

(She had learned some facts about Hoskins, too. He had invented the method of analyzing the reflection of the past-penetrating mesonic beam; he had invented the method of establishing Stasis; his coldness was only an effort to hide a kindly nature; and, oh yes, he *was* married.)

What Miss Fellowes could *not* get used to was the fact that she was engaged in a scientific experiment. Despite all she could do, she found herself getting personally involved to the point of quarreling with the physiologists.

On one occasion, Hoskins came down and found her in the midst of a hot urge to kill. They had no right; they had no *right!*—Even if he *was* a Neanderthal, he still wasn't an animal.

She was staring after them in a blind fury; staring out the open door and listening to Timmie's sobbing, when she noticed Hoskins standing before her. He might have been there for minutes.

He said, "May I come in?"

She nodded curtly, then hurried to Timmie, who clung to her, curling his little bandy legs—still thin, so thin—about her.

Hoskins watched, then said gravely, "He seems quite unhappy."

Miss Fellowes said, "I don't blame him. They're at him every day now with their blood samples and their probings. They keep him on synthetic diets that I wouldn't feed a pig."

"It's the sort of thing they can't try on a human, you know."

"And they can't try it on Timmie, either. Dr. Hoskins, I insist. You told me it was Timmie's coming that put Stasis, Inc. on the map. If you have any gratitude for that at all, you've *got* to keep them away from the poor thing at least until he's old enough to understand a little more. After he's had a bad session with them, he has nightmares, he can't sleep. Now I warn you," (she reached a sudden peak of fury) "I'm not letting them in here any more."

(She realized that she had screamed that, but she couldn't help it.)

She said more quietly, "I know he's Neanderthal but there's a great deal we don't appreciate about Neanderthals. I've read up on them. They had a culture of their own. Some of the greatest human inventions arose in Neanderthal times. The domestication of animals, for instance; the wheel, various techniques in grinding stone. They even had spiritual yearnings. They buried their dead and buried possessions with the body, showing they believed in a life after death. It amounts to the fact that they invented religion. Doesn't that mean Timmie has a right to human treatment?"

She patted the little boy gently on his buttocks and sent him off into his playroom. As the door was opened, Hoskins smiled briefly at the display of toys that could be seen.

Miss Fellowes said defensively, "The poor child deserves his toys. It's all he has and he earns them with what he goes through."

"No, no. No objections, I assure you. I was just thinking how you've changed since the first day, when you were quite angry I had foisted a Neanderthal on you."

Miss Fellowes said in a low voice, "I suppose I didn't—" and faded off.

Hoskins changed the subject, "How old would you say he is, Miss Fellowes?"

She said, "I can't say, since we don't know how Neanderthals develop. In size, he'd only be three but Neanderthals are smaller generally and with all the tampering they do with him, he probably isn't growing. The way he's learning English, though, I'd say he was well over four."

"Really? I haven't noticed anything about learning English in the reports."

"He won't speak to anyone but me. For now, anyway. He's terribly afraid of others, and no wonder. But he can ask for an article of food; he can indicate any need practically; and he understands almost anything I say. Of course," (she watched him shrewdly, trying to estimate if this was the time), "his development may not continue."

"Why not?"

"Any child needs stimulation and this one lives a life of solitary confinement. I do what I can, but I'm not with him all the time and I'm not all he needs. What I mean, Dr. Hoskins, is that he needs another boy to play with."

Hoskins nodded slowly. "Unfortunately, there's only one of him, isn't there? Poor child."

Miss Fellowes warmed to him at once. She said, "You do like Timmie, don't you?" It was so nice to have someone else feel like that.

"Oh, yes," said Hoskins, and with his guard down, she could see the weariness in his eyes.

Miss Fellowes dropped her plans to push the matter at once. She said, with real concern, "You look worn out, Dr. Hoskins."

"Do I, Miss Fellowes? I'll have to practice looking more lifelike then."

"I suppose Stasis, Inc. is very busy and that that keeps you very busy."

Hoskins shrugged. "You suppose right. It's a matter of animal, vegetable, and mineral in equal parts, Miss Fellowes. But then, I suppose you haven't ever seen our displays."

"Actually, I haven't. —But it's not because I'm not interested. It's just that I've been so busy."

"Well, you're not all that busy right now," he said with impulsive decision. "I'll call for you tomorrow at eleven and give you a personal tour. How's that?"

She smiled happily. "I'd love it."

He nodded and smiled in his turn and left.

Miss Fellowes hummed at intervals for the rest of the day. Really—to think so was ridiculous, of course—but really, it was almost like—like making a date.

* * *

He was quite on time the next day, smiling and pleasant. She had replaced her nurse's uniform with a dress. One of conservative cut, to be sure, but she hadn't felt so feminine in years.

He complimented her on her appearance with staid formality and she accepted with equally formal grace. It was really a perfect prelude, she thought. And then the additional thought came, prelude to what?

She shut that off by hastening to say good-by to Timmie and to assure him she would be back soon. She made sure he knew all about what and where lunch was.

Hoskins took her into the new wing, into which she had never yet gone. It still had the odor of newness about it and the sound of construction, softly heard, was indication enough that it was still being extended.

"Animal, vegetable, and mineral," said Hoskins, as he had the day before. "Animal right there; our most spectacular exhibits."

The space was divided into many rooms, each a separate Stasis bubble. Hoskins brought her to the view-glass of one and she looked in. What she saw impressed her first as a scaled, tailed chicken. Skittering on two thin legs it ran from wall to wall with its delicate birdlike head, surmounted by a bony keel like the comb of a rooster, looking this way and that. The paws on its small forelimbs clenched and unclenched constantly.

Hoskins said, "It's our dinosaur. We've had it for months. I don't know when we'll be able to let go of it."

"Dinosaur?"

"Did you expect a giant?"

She dimpled. "One does, I suppose. I know some of them are small."

"A small one is all we aimed for, believe me. Generally, it's under investigation, but this seems to be an open hour. Some interesting things have been discovered. For instance, it is not entirely cold-blooded. It has an imperfect method of maintaining internal temperatures higher than that of its environment. Unfortunately, it's a male. Ever since we brought it in we've been trying to get a fix on another that may be female, but we've had no luck yet."

"Why female?"

He looked at her quizzically. "So that we might have a fighting chance to obtain fertile eggs, and baby dinosaurs."

"Of course."

He led her to the trilobite section. "That's Professor Dwayne of Washington University," he said. "He's a nuclear chemist. If I recall correctly, he's taking an isotope ratio on the oxygen of the water."

"Why?"

"It's primeval water; at least half a billion years old. The isotope ratio gives the temperature of the ocean at that time. He himself happens to ignore the trilobites, but others are chiefly concerned in dissecting them. They're the lucky ones because all they need are scalpels and microscopes. Dwayne has to set up a mass spectrograph each time he conducts an experiment."

"Why's that? Can't be—"

"No, he can't. He can't take anything out of the room as far as can be helped."

There were samples of primordial plant life too and chunks of rock formations. Those were the vegetable and mineral. And every specimen had its investigator. It was like a museum; a museum brought to life and serving as a superactive center of research.

"And you have to supervise all of this, Dr. Hoskins?"

"Only indirectly, Miss Fellowes. I have subordinates, thank heaven. My own interest is entirely in the theoretical aspects of the matter: the nature of Time, the technique of mesonic intertemporal detection and so on. I would exchange all this for a method of detecting objects closer in Time than ten thousand years ago. If we could get into historical times—"

He was interrupted by a commotion at one of the distant booths, a thin voice raised querulously. He frowned, muttered hastily, "Excuse me," and hastened off.

Miss Fellowes followed as best she could without actually running.

An elderly man, thinly-bearded and red-faced, was saying, "I had vital aspects of my investigations to complete. Don't you understand that?"

A uniformed technician with the interwoven SI monogram (for Stasis, Inc.) on his lab coat, said, "Dr. Hoskins, it was arranged with Professor Ademewski at the beginning that the specimen could only remain here two weeks."

"I did not know then how long my investigations would take. I'm not a prophet," said Ademewski heatedly.

Dr. Hoskins said, "You understand, Professor, we have limited space; we must keep specimens rotating. That piece of chalcopyrite must go back; there are men waiting for the next specimen."

"Why can't I have it for myself, then? Let me take it out of there."

"You know you can't have it."

"A piece of chalcopyrite; a miserable five-kilogram piece? Why not?"

"We can't afford the energy expense!" said Hoskins brusquely. "You know that."

The technician interrupted. "The point is, Dr. Hoskins, that he tried to remove the rock against the rules and I almost punctured Stasis while he was in there, not knowing he was in there."

There was a short silence and Dr. Hoskins turned on the investigator with a cold formality. "Is that so, Professor?"

Professor Ademewski coughed. "I saw no harm—"

Hoskins reached up to a hand-pull dangling just within reach, outside the specimen room in question. He pulled it.

Miss Fellowes, who had been peering in, looking at the totally undistinguished sample of rock that occasioned the dispute, drew in her breath sharply as its existence flickered out. The room was empty.

Hoskins said, "Professor, your permit to investigate matters in Stasis will be permanently voided. I am sorry."

"But wait—"

"I am sorry. You have violated one of the stringent rules."

"I will appeal to the International Association—"

"Appeal away. In a case like this, you will find I can't be overruled."

He turned away deliberately, leaving the professor still protesting and said to Miss Fellowes (his face still white with anger), "Would you care to have lunch with me, Miss Fellowes?"

* * *

He took her into the small administration alcove of the cafeteria. He greeted others and introduced Miss Fellowes with complete ease, although she herself felt painfully self-conscious.

What must they think, she thought, and tried desperately to appear businesslike.

She said, "Do you have that kind of trouble often, Dr. Hoskins? I mean like that you had with the professor?" She took her fork in hand and began eating.

"No," said Hoskins forcefully. "That was the first time. Of course I'm always having to argue men out of removing specimens but this the first time one actually tried to *do* it."

"I remember you once talked about the energy it would consume."

"That's right. Of course, we've tried to take it into account. Accidents will happen and so we've got special power sources designed to stand the drain of accidental removal from Stasis, but that doesn't mean we want to see a year's supply of energy gone in half a second—or can afford to without having our plans of expansion delayed for years. —Besides, imagine the professor's being in the room while Stasis was about to be punctured."

"What would have happened to him if it had been?"

"Well, we've experimented with inanimate objects and with mice and they've disappeared. Presumably they've traveled back in time; carried along, so to speak, by the pull of the object simultaneously snapping back into its natural time. For that reason, we have to anchor objects within Stasis that we don't want to move and that's a complicated procedure. The professor would not have been anchored and he would have gone back to the Pliocene at the moment when we abstracted the rock—plus, of course, the two weeks it had remained here in the present."

"How dreadful it would have been."

"Not on account of the professor, I assure you. If he were fool enough to do what he did, it would serve him right. But imagine the effect it would have on the public if the fact came out. All people would need is to become aware of the dangers involved and funds could be choked off like that." He snapped his fingers and played moodily with his food.

Miss Fellowes said, "Couldn't you get him back? The way you got the rock in the first place?"

"No, because once an object is returned, the original fix is lost unless we deliberately plan to retain it and there was no reason to do that in this case. There never is. Finding the professor again would mean relocating a specific fix and that would be like dropping a line into the oceanic abyss for the purpose of dredging up a particular fish. —My God, when I think of the precautions we take to prevent accidents, it makes me mad. We have every individual Stasis unit set up and its own puncturing device—we have to, since each unit has its separate fix and must be collapsible independently. The point is, though, none of the puncturing devices is ever activated until the last minute. And then we deliberately make activation impossible except by the pull of a rope carefully led outside the Stasis. The pull is a gross mechanical motion that requires a strong effort, not something that is likely to be done accidentally."

Miss Fellowes said, "But doesn't it—change history to move something in and out of Time?"

Hoskins shrugged. "Theoretically, yes; actually, except in unusual cases, no. We move objects out of Stasis all the time. Air molecules. Bacteria. Dust. About 10 per cent of our energy consumption goes to make up micro-losses of that nature. But moving even large objects in Time sets up changes that damp out. Take that chalcopyrite from the Pliocene. Because of its absence for two weeks some insect didn't find the shelter it might have found and is killed. That could initiate a whole series of changes, but the mathematics of Stasis indicates that this is a converging series. The amount of change diminishes with time and then things are as before."

"You mean, reality heals itself?"

"In a manner of speaking. Abstract a human from Time or send one back, and you make a larger wound. If the individual is an ordinary one, that wound still heals itself. Of course, there are a great many people who write to us each day and want us to bring Abraham Lincoln into the present, or Mohammed, or Lenin. *That* can't be done, of course. Even if we could find them, the change in reality in moving one of the history molders would be too great to be healed. There are ways of calculating when a change is likely to be too great and we avoid even approaching that limit."

Miss Fellowes said, "Then, Timmie—"

"No, he presents no problem in that direction. Reality is safe. But—" He gave her a quick, sharp glance, then went on, "But never mind. Yesterday you said Timmie needed companionship."

"Yes," Miss Fellowes smiled her delight. "I didn't think you paid that any attention."

"Of course I did. I'm fond of the child. I appreciate your feelings for him and I was concerned enough to want to explain to you. Now I have; you've seen what we do; you've gotten some insight into the difficulties involved; so you know why, with the best will in the world, we can't supply companionship for Timmie."

"You can't?" said Miss Fellowes, with sudden dismay.

"But I've just explained. We couldn't possibly expect to find another Neanderthal his age without incredible luck, and if we could, it wouldn't be fair to multiply risks by having another human being in Stasis."

Miss Fellowes put down her spoon and said energetically, "But, Dr. Hoskins, that is not at all what I meant. I don't want you to bring another Neanderthal into the present. I know that's impossible. But it isn't impossible to bring another child to play with Timmie."

Hoskins stared at her in concern. "A *human* child?"

"*Another* child," said Miss Fellowes, completely hostile now. "Timmie is human."

"I couldn't dream of such a thing."

"Why not? Why couldn't you? What is wrong with the notion? You pulled that child out of Time and made him an eternal prisoner. Don't you owe him something? Dr. Hoskins, if there is any man who, in this world, is that child's father in every sense but the biological, it is you. Why can't you do this little thing for him?"

Hoskins said, "His *father?*" He rose, somewhat unsteadily, to his feet. "Miss Fellowes, I think I'll take you back now, if you don't mind."

They returned to the dollhouse in a complete silence that neither broke.

* * *

It was a long time after that before she saw Hoskins again, except for an occasional glimpse in passing. She was sorry about that at times; then, at other times, when Timmie was more than usually woebegone or when he spent silent hours at the window with its prospect of little more than nothing, she thought, fiercely: Stupid man.

Timmie's speech grew better and more precise each day. It never entirely lost a certain soft, slurriness that Miss Fellowes found rather endearing. In times of excitement, he fell back into tongue-clicking but those times were becoming fewer. He must be forgetting the days before he came into the present—except for dreams.

As he grew older, the physiologists grew less interested and the psychologists more so. Miss Fellowes was not sure that she did not like the new group even less than the first. The needles were gone; the injections and withdrawals of fluid; the special diets. But now Timmie was made to overcome barriers to reach food and water. He had to lift panels, move bars, reach for cords. And the mild electric shocks made him cry and drove Miss Fellowes to distraction.

She did not wish to appeal to Hoskins; she did not wish to have to go to him; for each time she thought of him, she thought of his face over the luncheon table that last time. Her eyes moistened and she thought: Stupid, *stupid* man.

And then one day Hoskins' voice sounded unexpectedly, calling into the dollhouse, "Miss Fellowes."

She came out coldly, smoothing her nurse's uniform, then stopped in confusion at finding herself in the presence of a pale woman, slender and of middle height. The woman's fair hair and complexion gave her an appearane of fragility. Standing behind her and clutching at her skirt was a round-faced, large-eyed child of four.

Hoskins said, "Dear, this is Miss Fellowes, the nurse in charge of the boy. Miss Fellowes, this is my wife."

(Was this his wife? She was not as Miss Fellowes had imagined her to be. But then, why not? A man like Hoskins would choose a weak thing to be his foil. If that was what he wanted—)

She forced a matter-of-fact greeting. "Good afternoon, Mrs. Hoskins. Is this your—your little boy?"

(*That* was a surprise. She had thought of Hoskins as a husband, but not as a father, except, of course— She suddenly caught Hoskins' grave eyes and flushed.)

Hoskins said, "Yes, this is my boy, Jerry. Say hello to Miss Fellowes, Jerry."

(Had he stressed the word "this" just a bit? Was he saying *this* was his son and not—)

Jerry receded a bit further into the folds of the maternal skirt and muttered his hello. Mrs. Hoskins' eyes were searching over Miss Fellowes' shoulders, peering into the room, looking for something.

Hoskins said, "Well, let's go in. Come, dear. There's a trifling discomfort at the threshold, but it passes."

Miss Fellowes said, "Do you want Jerry to come in, too?"

"Of course. He is to be Timmie's playmate. You said that Timmie needed a playmate. Or have you forgotten?"

"But—" She looked at him with a colossal, surprised wonder. "*Your* boy?"

He said peevishly, "Well, whose boy, then? Isn't this what you want? Come on in, dear. Come on in."

Mrs. Hoskins lifted Jerry into her arms with a distinct effort and, hesitantly, stepped over the threshold. Jerry squirmed as she did so, disliking the sensation.

Mrs. Hoskins said in a thin voice, "Is the creature here? I don't see him."

Miss Fellowes called, "Timmie. Come out."

Timmie peered around the edge of the door, staring up at the little boy who was visiting him. The muscles in Mrs. Hoskins' arms tensed visibly.

She said to her husband, "Gerald, are you sure it's safe?"

Miss Fellowes said at once, "If you mean is Timmie safe, why, of course he is. He's a gentle little boy."

"But he's a sa—savage."

(The ape-boy stories in the newspapers!) Miss Fellowes said emphatically, "He is not a savage. He is just as quiet and reasonable as you can possibly expect a five-and-a-half-year-old to be. It is very generous of you, Mrs. Hoskins, to agree to allow your boy to play with Timmie but please have no fears about it."

Mrs. Hoskins said with mild heat, "I'm not sure that I agree."

"We've had it out, dear," said Hoskins. "Let's not bring up the matter for new argument. Put Jerry down."

Mrs. Hoskins did so and the boy backed against her, staring at the pair of eyes which were staring back at him from the next room.

"Come here, Timmie," said Miss Fellowes. "Don't be afraid."

Slowly, Timmie stepped into the room. Hoskins bent to disengage Jerry's fingers from his mother's skirt. "Step back, dear. Give the children a chance."

The ycungsters faced one another. Although the younger, Jerry was nevertheless an inch taller, and in the presence of his straightness and his high-held, well-proportioned head, Timmie's grotesqueries were suddenly almost as pronounced as they had been in the first days.

Miss Fellowes' lips quivered.

It was the little Neanderthal who spoke first, in childish treble. "What's your name?" And Timmie thrust his face suddenly forward as though to inspect the other's features more closely.

Startled, Jerry responded with a vigorous shove that sent Timmie tumbling. Both began crying loudly and Mrs. Hoskins snatched up her child, while Miss Fellowes, flushed with repressed anger, lifted Timmie and comforted him.

Mrs. Hoskins said, "They just instinctively don't like one another."

"No more instinctively," said her husband wearily, "than any two children dislike each other. Now put Jerry down and let him get used to the situation. In fact, we had better leave. Miss Fellowes can bring Jerry to my office after a while and I'll have him taken home."

* * *

The two children spent the next hour very aware of each other. Jerry cried for his mother, stuck out at Miss Fellowes and, finally, allowed himself to be comforted with a lollipop. Timmie sucked at another, and at the end of an hour, Miss Fellowes had them playing with the same set of blocks, though at opposite ends of the room.

She found herself almost maudlinly grateful to Hoskins when she brought Jerry to him.

She searched for ways to thank him but his very formality was a rebuff. Perhaps he could not forgive her for making him feel like a cruel father. Perhaps the bringing of his own child was an attempt, after all, to prove himself both a kind father to Timmie and, also, not his father at all. Both at the same time!

So all she could say was, "Thank you. Thank you very much."

And all he could say was, "It's all right. Don't mention it."

It became a settled routine. Twice a week, Jerry was brought in for an hour's play, later extended to two hours' play. The children learned each other's names and ways and played together.

And yet, after the first rush of gratitude, Miss Fellowes found herself disliking Jerry. He was larger and heavier and in all things dominant, forcing Timmie into a completely secondary role. All that reconciled her to the situation was the fact that, despite difficulties, Timmie looked forward with more and more delight to the periodic appearances of his playfellow.

It was all he had, she mourned to herself.

And once, as she watched them, she thought: Hoskins' two children, one by his wife and one by Stasis.

While she herself—

Heavens, she thought, putting her fists to her temples and feeling ashamed: I'm jealous!

* * *

"Miss Fellowes," said Timmie (carefully, she had never allowed him to call her anything else) "when will I go to school?"

She looked down at those eager brown eyes turned up to hers and passed her hand softly through his thick, curly hair. It was the most disheveled portion of his appearance, for she cut his hair herself while he sat restlessly under the scissors. She did not ask for professional help, for the very clumsiness of the cut served to mask the retreating fore part of the skull and the bulging hinder part.

She said, "Where did you hear about school?"

"Jerry goes to school. Kin-der-gar-ten." He said it carefully. "There are lots of places he goes. Outside. When can I go outside, Miss Fellowes?"

A small pain centered in Miss Fellowes' heart. Of course, she saw, there would be no way of avoiding the inevitability of Timmie's hearing more and more of the outer world he could never enter.

She said, with an attempt at gaiety, "Why, whatever would you do in kindergarten, Timmie?"

"Jerry says they play games, they have picture tapes. He says there are lots of children. He says—he says—" A thought, then a triumphant upholding of both small hands with the fingers splayed apart. "He says this many."

Miss Fellowes said, "Would you like picture tapes? I can get you picture tapes. Very nice ones. And music tapes, too."

So that Timmie was temporarily comforted.

* * *

He pored over the picture tapes in Jerry's absence and Miss Fellowes read to him out of ordinary books by the hours.

There was so much to explain in even the simplest story, so much that was outside the perspective of his three rooms. Timmie took to having his dreams more often now that the outside was being introduced to him.

They were always the same, about the outside. He tried haltingly to describe them to Miss Fellowes. In his dreams, he was outside, an empty outside, but very large, with children and queer indescribable objects half-digested in his thoughts out of bookish descriptions half-understood, or out of distant Neanderthal memories half-recalled.

But the children and objects ignored him and though he was in the world, he was never part of it, but was as alone as though he were in his own room—and would wake up crying.

Miss Fellowes tried to laugh at the dreams, but there were nights in her own apartment when she cried, too.

One day, as Miss Fellowes read, Timmie put his hand under her chin and lifted it gently so that her eyes left the book and met his.

He said, "How do you know what to say, Miss Fellowes?"

She said, "You see these marks? They tell me what to say. These marks make words."

He stared at them long and curiously, taking the book out of her hands. "Some of these marks are the same."

She laughed with pleasure at this sign of his shrewdness and said, "So they are. Would you like to have me show you how to make the marks?"

"All right. That would be a nice game."

It did not occur to her that he could learn to read. Up to the very moment that he read a book to her, it did not occur to her that he could learn to read.

Then, weeks later, the enormity of what had been done struck her. Timmie sat in her lap, following word by word the printing in a child's book, reading to her. He was reading to her!

She struggled to her feet in amazement and said, "Now Timmie, I'll be back later. I want to see Dr. Hoskins."

Excited nearly to frenzy, it seemed to her she might have an answer to Timmie's unhappiness. If Timmie could not leave to enter the world, the world must be brought into those three rooms to Timmie—the whole world in books and film and sound. He must be educated to his full capacity. So much the world owed him.

* * *

She found Hoskins in a mood that was oddly analogous to her own; a kind of triumph and glory. His offices were unusually busy, and for a moment, she thought she would not get to see him, as she stood abashed in the anteroom.

But he saw her, and a smile spread over his broad face. "Miss Fellowes, come here."

He spoke rapidly into the intercom, then shut it off. "Have you heard?— No, of course, you couldn't have. We've done it. We've actually done it. We have intertemporal detection at close range."

"You mean," she tried to detach her thought from her own good news for a moment, "that you can get a person from historical times into the present?"

"That's just what I mean. We have a fix on a fourteenth-century individual right now. Imagine. *Imagine!* If you could only know how glad I'll be to shift from the eternal concentration on the Mesozoic, replace the paleontologists with the historians— But there's something you wish to say to me, eh? Well, go ahead; go ahead. You find me in a good mood. Anything you want you can have."

Miss Fellowes smiled. "I'm glad. Because I wonder if we might not establish a system of instruction for Timmie?"

"Instruction? In what?"

"Well, in everything. A school. So that he might learn."

"But *can* he learn?"

"Certainly, he *is* learning. He can read. I've taught him so much myself."

Hoskins sat there, seeming suddenly depressed. "I don't know, Miss Fellowes."

She said, "You just said that anything I wanted—"

"I know and I should not have. You see, Miss Fellowes, I'm sure you must realize that we cannot maintain the Timmie experiment forever."

She stared at him with sudden horror, not really understanding what he had said. How did he mean "cannot maintain"? With an agonizing flash of recollection, she recalled Professor Ademewski and his mineral specimen that was taken away after two weeks. She said, "But you're talking about a boy. Not about a rock—"

Dr. Hoskins said uneasily, "Even a boy can't be given undue importance, Miss Fellowes. Now that we expect individuals out of historical time, we will need Stasis space, all we can get."

She didn't grasp it. "But you can't. Timmie—Timmie—"

"Now, Miss Fellowes, please don't upset yourself. Timmie won't go right away; perhaps not for months. Meanwhile we'll do what we can."

She was still staring at him.

"Let me get you something, Miss Fellowes."

"No," she whispered. "I don't need anything." She arose in a kind of nightmare and left.

Timmie, she thought, you will *not* die. You will *not* die.

* * *

It was all very well to hold tensely to the thought that Timmie must not die, but how was that to be arranged? In the first weeks, Miss Fellowes clung only to the hope that the attempt to bring forward a man from the fourteenth century would fail completely. Hoskins' theories might be wrong or his practice defective. Then things could go on as before.

Certainly, that was not the hope of the rest of the world and, irrationally, Miss Fellowes hated the world for it. "Project Middle Ages" reached a climax of white-hot publicity. The press and the public had hungered for something like this. Stasis, Inc. had lacked the necessary sensation for a long time now. A new rock or another ancient fish failed to stir them. But *this* was *it.*

A historical human; an adult speaking a known language; someone who could open a new page of history to the scholar.

Zero-time was coming and this time it was not a question of three onlookers from a balcony. This time there would be a world-wide audience. This time the technicians of Stasis, Inc. would play their role before nearly all of mankind.

Miss Fellowes was herself all but savage with waiting. When young Jerry Hopkins showed up for his scheduled playtime with Timmie, she scarcely recognized him. He was not the one she was waiting for.

(The secretary who brought him left hurriedly after the barest nod for Miss Fellowes. She was rushing for a good place from which to watch the climax of Project Middle Ages. —And so ought Miss Fellowes with far better reason, she thought bitterly, if only that stupid girl would arrive.)

Jerry Hoskins sidled toward her, embarrassed. "Miss Fellowes?" He took the reproduction of a news-strip out of his pocket.

"Yes? What is it, Jerry?"

"Is this a picture of Timmie?"

Miss Fellowes stared at him, then snatched the strip from Jerry's hand. The excitement of Project Middle Ages had brought about a pale revival of interest in Timmie on the part of the press.

Jerry watched her narrowly, then said, "It says Timmie is an ape-boy. What does that mean?"

Miss Fellowes caught the youngster's wrist and repressed the impulse to shake him. "Never say that, Jerry. Never, do you understand? It is a nasty word and you mustn't use it."

Jerry struggled out of her grip, frightened.

Miss Fellowes tore up the news-strip with a vicious twist of the wrist. "Now go inside and play with Timmie. He's got a new book to show you."

And then, finally, the girl appeared. Miss Fellowes did not know her. None of the usual stand-ins she had used when business took her elsewhere was available now, not with Project Middle Ages at climax, but Hoskins' secretary had promised to find *someone* and this must be the girl.

Miss Fellowes tried to keep querulousness out of her voice. "Are you the girl assigned to Stasis Section One?"

"Yes, I'm Mandy Terris. You're Miss Fellowes, aren't you?"

"That's right."

"I'm sorry I'm late. There's just so much excitement."

"I know. Now I want you—"

Mandy said, "You'll be watching, I suppose." Her thin, vacuously pretty face filled with envy.

"Never mind that. Now I want you to come inside and meet Timmie and Jerry. They will be playing for the next two hours so they'll be giving you no trouble. They've got milk handy and plenty of toys. In fact, it will be better if you leave them alone as much as possible. Now I'll show you where everything is located and—"

"Is it Timmie that's the ape-b—"

"Timmie is the Stasis subject," said Miss Fellowes firmly.

"I mean, he's the one who's not supposed to get out, is that right?"

"Yes. Now, come in. There isn't much time."

And when she finally left, Mandy Terris called after her shrilly, "I hope you get a good seat and, golly, I sure hope it works."

Miss Fellowes did not trust herself to make a reasonable response. She hurried on without looking back.

* * *

But the delay meant she did *not* get a good seat. She got no nearer then the wall-viewing-plate in the assembly hall. Bitterly, she regretted that. If she could have been on the spot; if she could somehow have reached out for some sensitive portion of the instrumentations; if she were in some way able to wreck the experiment—

She found the strength to beat down her madness. Simple destruction would have done no good. They would have rebuilt and reconstructed and made the effort again. And she would never be allowed to return to Timmie.

Nothing would help. Nothing but that the experiment itself fail; that it break down irretrievably.

So she waited through the countdown, watching every move on the giant screen, scanning the faces of the technicians as the focus shifted from one to the other, watching for the look of worry and uncertainty that would mark something going unexpectedly wrong; watching, watching—

There was no such look. The count reached zero, and very quietly, very unassumingly, the experiment succeeded!

In the new Stasis that had been established there stood a bearded, stoop-shouldered peasant of indeterminate age, in ragged dirty clothing and wooden shoes, staring in dull horror at the sudden mad change that had flung itself over him.

And while the world went mad with jubilation, Miss Fellowes stood frozen in sorrow, jostled and pushed, all but trampled; surrounded by triumph while bowed down with defeat.

And when the loud-speaker called her name with strident force, it sounded it three times before she responded.

"*Miss Fellowes. Miss Fellowes. You are wanted in Stasis Section One immediately. Miss Fellowes. Miss Fell—*"

"Let me though!" she cried breathlessly, while the loud-speaker continued its repetitions without pause. She forced her way through the crowds with wild energy, beating at it, striking out with closed fists, flailing, moving toward the door in a nightmare slowness.

* * *

Mandy Terris was in tears. "I don't know how it happened. I just went down to the edge of the corridor to watch a pocket-viewing-plate they had put up. Just for a minute. And then before I could move or do anything—" She cried out in sudden accusation, "You said they would make no trouble; you *said* to leave them alone—"

Miss Fellowes, disheveled and trembling uncontrollably, glared at her. "Where's Timmie?"

A nurse was swabbing the arm of a wailing Jerry with disinfectant and another was preparing an anti-tetanus shot. There was blood on Jerry's clothes.

"He bit me, Miss Fellowes," Jerry cried in rage. "He *bit* me."

But Miss Fellowes didn't even see him.

"What did you do with Timmie?" she cried out.

"I locked him in the bathroom," said Mandy. "I just threw the little monster in there and locked him in."

Miss Fellowes ran into the dollhouse. She fumbled at the bathroom door. It took an eternity to get it open and to find the ugly little boy cowering in the corner.

"Don't whip me, Miss Fellowes," he whispered. His eyes were red. His lips were quivering. "I didn't mean to do it."

"Oh, Timmie, who told you about whips?" She caught him to her, hugging him wildly.

He said tremulously, "She said, with a long rope. She said you would hit me and hit me."

"You won't be. She was wicked to say so. But what happened? What happened?"

"He called me an ape-boy. He said I wasn't a real boy. He said I was an animal." Timmie dissolved in a flood of tears. "He said he wasn't going to play with a monkey anymore. I said I wasn't a monkey; I *wasn't* a monkey. He said I was all funny-looking. He said I was horrible ugly. He kept saying and saying and I bit him."

They were both crying now. Miss Fellowes sobbed, "But it isn't true. You know that, Timmie. You're a real boy. You're a dear real boy and the best boy in the world. And no one, *no* one will ever take you away from me."

* * *

It was easy to make up her mind, now; easy to know what to do. Only it had to be done quickly. Hoskins wouldn't wait much longer, with his own son mangled—

No, it would have to be done this night, *this* night; with the place four-fifths asleep and the remaining fifth intellectually drunk over Project Middle Ages.

It would be an unusual time for her to return but not an unheard of one. The guard knew her well and would not dream of questioning her.

He would think nothing of her carrying a suitcase. She rehearsed the noncommittal phrase, "Games for the boy," and the calm smile.

Why shouldn't he believe that?

He did. When she entered the dollhouse again, Timmie was still awake, and she maintained a desperate normality to avoid frightening him. She talked about his dreams with him and listened to him ask wistfully after Jerry.

There would be few to see her afterward, none to question the bundle she would be carrying. Timmie would be very quiet and then it would be a *fait accompli*. It would be done and what would be the use of trying to undo it. They would leave her be. They would leave them both be.

She opened the suitcase, took out the overcoat, the woolen cap with the ear-flaps and the rest.

Timmie said, with the beginning of alarm, "Why are you putting all these clothes on me, Miss Fellowes?"

She said, "I am going to take you outside, Timmie. To where your dreams are."

"My dreams?" His face twisted in sudden yearning, yet fear was there, too.

"You won't be afraid. You'll be with me. You won't be afraid if you're with me, will you, Timmie?"

"No, Miss Fellowes." He buried his little misshapen head against her side, and under her enclosing arm she could feel his small heart thud.

It was midnight and she lifted him into her arms. She disconnected the alarm and opened the door softly.

And she screamed, for facing her across the open door was Hoskins!

* * *

There were two men with him and he stared at her, as astonished as she.

Miss Fellowes recovered first by a second and made a quick attempt to push past him; but even with the second's delay he had time. He caught her roughly and hurled her back against a chest of drawers. He waved the men in and confronted her, blocking the door.

"I didn't expect this. Are you completely insane?"

She had managed to interpose her shoulder so that it, rather than Timmie, had struck the chest. She said pleadingly, "What harm can it do if I take him, Dr. Hoskins? You can't put energy loss ahead of a human life?"

Firmly, Hoskins took Timmie out of her arms. "An energy loss this size would mean millions of dollars lost out of the pockets of investors. It would mean a terrible setback for Stasis, Inc. It would mean eventual publicity about a sentimental nurse destroying all that for the sake of an ape-boy."

"*Ape-boy!*" said Miss Fellowes, in helpless fury.

"That's what the reporters would call him," said Hoskins.

One of the men emerged now, looping a nylon rope through eyelets along the upper portion of the wall.

Miss Fellowes remembered the rope that Hoskins had pulled outside the room containing Professor Ademewski's rock specimen so long ago.

She cried out, "No!"

But Hoskins put Timmie down and gently removed the overcoat he was wearing. "You stay here, Timmie. Nothing will happen to you. We're just going outside for a moment. All right?"

Timmie, white and wordless, managed to nod.

Hoskins steered Miss Fellowes out of the dollhouse ahead of himself. For the moment, Miss Fellowes was beyond resistance. Dully, she noticed the hand-pull being adjusted outside the dollhouse.

"I'm sorry, Miss Fellowes," said Hoskins. "I would have spared you this. I planned it for the night so that you would know only when it was over."

She said in a weary whisper, "Because your son was hurt. Because he tormented this child into striking out at him."

"No. Believe me. I understand about the incident today and I know it was Jerry's fault. But the story has leaked out. It would have to with the press surrounding us on this day of all days. I can't risk having a distorted story about negligence and savage Neanderthalers, so-called, distract from the success of Project Middle Ages. Timmie has to go soon anyway; he might as well go now and give the sensationalists as small a peg as possible on which to hang their trash."

"It's not like sending a rock back. You'll be killing a human being."

"Not killing. There'll be no sensation. He'll simply be a Neanderthal boy in a Neanderthal world. He will no longer be a prisoner and alien. He will have a chance at a free life."

"What chance? He's only seven years old, used to being taken care of, fed, clothed, sheltered. He will be alone. His tribe may not be at the point where he left them now that four years have passed. And if they were, they would not recognize him. He will have to take care of himself. How will he know how?"

Hoskins shook his head in hopeless negative. "Lord, Miss Fellowes, do you think we haven't thought of that? Do you think we would have brought in a child if it weren't that it was the first successful fix of a human or near-human we made and that we did not dare to take the chance of unfixing him and finding another fix as good? Why do you suppose we kept Timmie as long as we did, if it were not for our reluctance to send a child back into the past. It's just"—his voice took on a desperate urgency—"that we can wait no longer. Timmie stands in the way of expansion! Timmie is a source of possible bad publicity; we are on the threshold of great things, and I'm sorry, Miss Fellowes, but we can't let Timmie block us. We cannot. We cannot. I'm sorry, Miss Fellowes."

"Well, then," said Miss Fellowes sadly. "Let me say good-by. Give me five minutes to say good-by. Spare me that much."

Hoskins hesitated. "Go ahead."

* * *

Timmie ran to her. For the last time he ran to her and for the last time Miss Fellowes clasped him in her arms.

For a moment, she hugged him blindly. She caught at a chair with the toe of one foot, moved it against the wall, sat down.

"Don't be afraid, Timmie."

"I'm not afraid if you're here, Miss Fellowes. Is that man mad at me, the man out there?"

"No, he isn't. He just doesn't understand about us. —Timmie, do you know what a mother is?"

"Like Jerry's mother?"

"Did he tell you about his mother?"

"Sometimes. I think maybe a mother is a lady who takes care of you and who's very nice to you and who does good things."

"That's right. Have you ever wanted a mother, Timmie?"

Timmie pulled his head away from her so that he could look into her face. Slowly, he put his hand to her cheek and hair and stroked her, as long, long ago she had stroked him. He said, "Aren't you my mother?"

"Oh, Timmie."

"Are you angry because I asked?"

"No. Of course not."

"Because I know your name is Miss Fellowes, but—but sometimes, I call you 'Mother' inside. Is that all right?"

"Yes. Yes. It's all right. And I won't leave you anymore and nothing will hurt you. I'll be with you to care for you always. Call me Mother, so I can hear you."

"Mother," said Timmie contentedly, leaning his cheek against hers.

She rose, and, still holding him, stepped up on the chair. The sudden beginning of a shout from outside went unheard and, with her free hand, she yanked with all her weight at the cord where it hung suspended between two eyelets.

And Stasis was punctured and the room was empty.

Unto the Fourth Generation

At ten of noon, Sam Marten hitched his way out of the taxicab, trying as usual to open the door with one hand, hold his briefcase in another and reach for his wallet with a third. Having only two hands, he found it a difficult job and, again as usual, he thudded his knee against the cab-door and found himself still groping uselessly for his wallet when his feet touched pavement.

The traffic of Madison Avenue inched past. A red truck slowed its crawl reluctantly, then moved on with a rasp as the light changed. White script on its side informed an unresponsive world that its ownership was that of *F. Lewkowitz and Sons, Wholesaler Clothiers.*

Levkowich, thought Marten with brief inconsequence, and finally fished out his wallet. He cast an eye on the meter as he clamped his briefcase under his arms. Dollar sixty-five, make that twenty cents more as a tip, two singles gone would leave him only one for emergencies, better break a fiver.

"Okay," he said, "take out one-eighty-five, bud."

"Thanks," said the cabbie with mechanical insincerity and made the change.

Marten crammed three singles into his wallet, put it away, lifted his briefcase and breasted the human currents on the sidewalk to reach the glass doors of the building.

Levkovich? he thought sharply, and stopped. A passerby glanced off his elbow.

"Sorry," muttered Marten, and made for the door again.

Levkovich? That wasn't what the sign on the truck had said. The name had read Lewkowitz, Loo-koh-itz. Why did he *think* Levkovich? Even with his college German in the near past changing the w's to v's, where did he get the "-ich" from?

Levkovich? He shrugged the whole matter away roughly. Give it a chance and it would haunt him like a Hit Parade tinkle.

Concentrate on business. He was here for a luncheon appointment with this man, Naylor. He was here to turn a contract into an account and begin, at twenty-three, the smooth business rise which, as he planned it, would marry him to Elizabeth in two years and make him a paterfamilias in the suburbs in ten.

He entered the lobby with grim firmness and headed for the banks of elevators, his eye catching at the white-lettered directory as he passed.

It was a silly habit of his to want to catch suite numbers as he passed, without slowing, or (heaven forbid) coming to a full halt. With no break in his progress, he told himself, he could maintain the impression of belonging, of knowing his way around, and that was important to a man whose job involved dealing with other human beings.

Kulin-etts was what he wanted, and the word amused him. A firm specializing in the production of minor kitchen gadgets, striving manfully for a name that was significant, feminine, and coy, all at once—

His eyes snagged at the M's and moved upward as he walked. Mandel, Lusk, Lippert Publishing Company (two full floors), Lafkowitz, Kulin-etts. There it was—1024. Tenth floor. OK.

And then, after all, he came to a dead halt, turned in reluctant fascination, returned to the directory, and stared at it as though he were an out-of-towner.

Lafkowitz?

What kind of spelling was that?

It was clear enough. Lafkowitz, Henry J., 701. With an A. That was no good. That was useless.

Useless? Why useless? He gave his head one violent shake as though to clear it of mist. Damn it, what did he care how it was spelled? He turned away, frowning and angry, and hastened to an elevator door, which closed just before he reached it, leaving him flustered.

Another door opened and he stepped in briskly. He tucked his briefcase under his arm and tried to look bright alive—junior executive in its finest sense. He had to make an impression on Alex Naylor, with whom so far he had communicated only by telephone. If he was going to brood about Lewkowitzes and Lafkowitzes—

The elevator slid noiselessly to a halt at seven. A youth in shirt-sleeves stepped off, balancing what looked like a desk-drawer in which were three containers of coffee and three sandwiches.

Then, just as the doors began closing, frosted glass with black lettering loomed before Marten's eyes. It read: 701—HENRY J. LEFKOWITZ—IMPORTER and was pinched off by the inexorable coming together of the elevator doors.

Marten leaned forward in excitement. It was his impulse to say: Take me back down to 7.

But there were others in the car. And after all, he had no reason.

Yet there was a tingle of excitement within him. The Directory *had* been wrong. It wasn't A, it was E. Some fool of a non-spelling menial with a packet of small letters to go on the board and only one hind foot to do it with.

Lefkowitz. Still not right, though.

Again, he shook his head. Twice. Not right for what?

The elevator stopped at ten and Marten got off.

Alex Naylor of Kulin-etts turned out to be a bluff, middle-aged man with a shock of white hair, a ruddy complexion, and a broad smile. His palms were dry and rough, and he shook hand with a considerable pressure, putting his left hand on Marten's shoulder in an earnest display of friendliness.

He said, "Be with you in two minutes. How about eating right here in the building? Excellent restaurant, and they've got a boy who makes a good martini. That sound all right?"

"Fine. Fine." Marten pumped up enthusiasm from a somehow-clogged reservoir.

It was nearer ten minutes than two, and Marten waited with the usual uneasiness of a man in a strange office. He stared at the upholstery on the chairs and at the little cubby-hole within which a young and bored switchboard operator sat. He gazed at the pictures on the wall and even made a half-hearted attempt to glance through a trade journal on the table next to him.

What he did not do was think of Lev—

He did *not* think of it.

* * *

The restaurant was good, or it would have been good if Marten had been perfectly at ease. Fortunately, he was freed of the necessity of carrying the burden of the conversation. Naylor talked rapidly and loudly, glanced over the menu with a practiced eye, recommended the Eggs Benedict, and commented on the weather and the miserable traffic situation.

On occasion, Marten tried to snap out of it, to lose that edge of fuzzed absence of mind. But each time the restlessness would return. Something ws wrong. The name was wrong. It stood in the way of what he had to do.

With main force, he tried to break through the madness. In sudden verbal clatter, he led the conversation into the subject of wiring. It was reckless of him. There was no proper foundation; the transition was too abrupt.

But the lunch had been a good one; the dessert was on its way; and Naylor responded nicely.

He admitted dissatisfaction with existing arrangements. Yes, he had been looking into Marten's firm and, actually, it seemed to him that, yes, there was a chance, a good chance, he thought, that—

A hand came down on Naylor's shoulder as a man passed behind his chair. "How's the boy, Alex?"

Naylor looked up, grin ready-made and flashing. "Hey, Lefk, how's business?"

"Can't complain. See you at the—" He faded into the distance.

Marten wasn't listening. He felt his knees trembling, as he half-rose. "Who was that man?" he asked, intensely. It sounded more peremptory than he intended.

"Who? Lefk? Jerry Lefkovitz. You know him?" Naylor stared with cool surprise at his lunch companion.

"No. How do you spell his name?"

"L-E-F-K-O-V-I-T-Z, I think. Why?"

"With a V?"

"An F . . . Oh, there's a V in it, too." Most of the good nature had left Naylor's face.

Marten drove on. "There's a Lefkowitz in the building. With a W. You know, Lef-COW-itz."

"Oh?"

"Room 701. This is not the same one?"

"Jerry doesn't work in this building. He's got a place across the street. I don't know this other one. This is a big building, you know. I don't keep tabs on every one in it. What is it all this, anyway?"

Marten shook his head and sat back. He didn't know what all this was, anyway. Or at least, if he did, it was nothing he dared explain. Could he say: I'm being haunted by all manner of Lefkowitzes today.

He said, "We were talking about wiring."

Naylor said, "Yes. Well, as I said, I've been considering your company. I've got to talk it over with the production boys, you understand. I'll let you know."

"Sure," said Marten, infinitely depressed. Naylor wouldn't let him know. The whole thing was shot.

And yet, through and beyond his depression, there was still that restlessness.

The hell with Naylor. All Marten wanted was to break this up and get on with it. (*Get on with what?* But the question was only a whisper.

Whatever did the questioning inside him was ebbing away, dying down . . .)

The lunch frayed to an ending. If they had greeted each other like long-separated friends at last reunited, they parted like strangers.

Marten felt only relief.

He left with pulses thudding, threading through the tables, out of the haunted building, onto the haunted street.

Haunted? Madison Avenue at 1:20 P.M. in an early fall afternoon with the sun shining brightly and ten thousand men and women be-hiving its long straight stretch.

But Marten felt the haunting. He tucked his briefcase under his arm and headed desperately northward. A last sigh of the normal within him warned him he had a three o'clock appointment on 36th Street. Never mind. He headed uptown. Northward.

* * *

At 54th Street, he crossed Madison and walked west, came abruptly to a halt and looked upward.

There was a sign on the window, three stories up. He could make it out clearly: A. S. LEFKOWICH, CERTIFIED ACCOUNTANT.

It had an F and an OW, but it was the first "-ich" ending he had seen. The first one. He was getting closer. He turned north again on Fifth Avenue, hurrying through the unreal streets of an unreal city, panting with the chase of something, while the crowds about him began to fade.

A sign in a ground floor window, M. R. LEFKOWICZ, M.D.

A small gold-leaf semi-circle of letters in a candy-store window: JACOB LEVKOW.

(Half a name, he thought savagely. Why is he disturbing me with half a name?)

The streets were empty now except for the varying clan of Lefkowitz, Levkowitz, Lefkowicz to stand out in the vacuum.

He was dimly aware of the park ahead, standing out in painted motionless green. He turned west. A piece of newspaper fluttered at the corner of his eyes, the only movement in a dead world. He veered, stooped, and picked it up, without slackening his pace.

It was in Yiddish, a torn half-page.

He couldn't read it. He couldn't make out the blurred Hebrew letters, and could not have read it if they were clear. But one word was clear. It stood out in dark letters in the center of the page, each letter clear in its every serif. And it said Lefkovitsch, he knew, and as he said it to himself, he placed its accent on the second syllable: Lef-KUH-vich.

He let the paper flutter away and entered the empty park.

The trees were still and the leaves hung in odd, suspended attitudes. The sunlight was a dead weight upon him and gave no warmth.

He was running, but his feet kicked up no dust and a tuft of grass on which he placed his weight did not bend.

* * *

And there on a bench was an old man; the only man in the desolate park. He wore a dark felt cap, with a visor shading his eyes. From underneath it, tufts of gray hair protruded. His grizzled beard reached the uppermost button of his rough jacket. His old trousers were patched, and a strip of burlap was wrapped about each worn and shapeless shoe.

Marten stopped. It was difficult to breathe. He could only say one word and he used it to ask his question: "Levkovich?"

He stood there, while the old man rose slowly to his feet; brown old eyes peering close.

"Marten," he sighed. "Samuel Marten. You have come." The words sounded with an effect of double exposure, for under the English, Marten heard the faint sigh of a foreign tongue. Under the "Samuel" was the unheard shadow of a "Schmu-el."

The old man's rough, veined hands reached out, then withdrew as though he were afraid to touch. "I have been looking but there are so many people in this wilderness of a city-that-is-to-come. So many Martins and Martines and Mortons and Mertons. I stopped at last when I found greenery, but for a moment only—I would not commit the sin of losing faith. And then you came."

"It is I," said Marten, and knew it was. "And you are Phinehas Levkovich. Why are we here?"

"I am Phinehas ben Jehudah, assigned the name Levkovich by the ukase of the Tsar that ordered family names for all. And we are here," the old man said, softly, "because I prayed. When I was already old, Leah, my only daughter, the child of my old age, left for America with her husband, left the knouts of the old for the hope of the new. And my sons died, and Sarah, the wife of my bosom, was long dead and I was alone. And the time came when I, too, must die. But I had not seen Leah since her leaving for the far country and word had come but rarely. My soul yearned that I might see sons born unto her; sons of my seed; sons in whom my soul might yet live and not die."

His voice was steady and the soundless shadow of sound beneath his words was the stately roll of an ancient language.

"And I was answered and two hours were given me that I might see the first son of my line to be born in a new land and in a new time. My daughter's daughter's daughter's son, have I found you, then, amidst the splendor of this city?"

"But why the search? Why not have brought us together at once?"

"Because there is pleasure in the hope of the seeking, my son," said the old man, radiantly, "and in the delight of the finding. I was given two hours in which I might seek, two hours in which I might find . . . and behold, thou art here, and I have found that which I had not looked to see in life." His voice was old, caressing. "Is it well with thee, my son?"

"It is well, my father, now that I have found thee," said Marten, and dropped to his knees. "Give me thy blessing, my father, that it may be well with me all the days of my life, and with the maid whom I am to take to wife and the little ones yet to be born of my seed and thine."

He felt the old hand resting lightly on his head and there was only the soundless whisper.

Marten rose.

The old man's eyes gazed into his yearningly. Were they losing focus?

"I go to my fathers now in peace, my son," said the old man, and Marten was alone in the empty park.

There was an instant of renewing motion, of the Sun taking up its interrupted task, of the wind reviving, and even with that first instant of sensation, all slipped back—

At ten of noon, Sam Marten hitched his way out of the taxicab, and found himself groping uselessly for his wallet while traffic inched on.

A red truck slowed, then moved on. A white script on its side announced: *F. Lewkowitz and Sons, Wholesale Clothiers.*

Marten didn't see it. Yet somehow he knew that all would be well with him. Somehow, as never before, he knew . . .

Thiotimoline and the Space Age

(*Transcript of a speech delivered at the 12th annual meeting of the American Chronochemical Society.*)

Gentlemen:

I have been called the founder of chronochemistry and in response I cannot resist a certain sense of pride. To have originated a new science is a privilege given to very few.

I can still remember, quite clearly, that day in 1947 when I first dropped a pinch of thiotimoline into water and thought I noticed something odd. To be sure, it dissolved rapidly; but I was used to that. It always seemed to vanish the instant it touched the water.

But I had never handled a sample of thiotimoline quite as pure as the pinch I had obtained that July day and, as I watched the white powder drop toward the water, I distinctly remember myself thinking, "Why, that dissolved *before* it hit the water."

Well, it's an old story to you, I know, though I still like to linger on the thrill of the slow awakening of certainty; of the measurements taken; of the first crude timings by eye; of the more delicate work of the original endochronometer—the same instrument now at the Smithsonian.

The announcement of endochronicity, of the fact that a substance existed which dissolved in water 1.12 seconds *before* the water was added created a stir. You all remember it, I'm sure. And yet, somehow, the impression arose that thiotimoline was a hoax. There was a distinct air of amusement in many of the comments in the learned journals. Private communications reaching me showed a distressing tendency to describe experiments which obviously lacked all scientific validity and which, I could but conclude, were meant as some sort of joke. Perhaps the final proof of the damage this has done is that after twelve years of existence, the American Chronochemical Society can muster an audience of exactly fifteen people to hear this talk.

It has been an expensive joke, gentlemen, one that has cost us our lead in the race for space. For while American researchers have, but with difficulty, obtained grants to continue their investigations of thiotimoline and have been starved into small-scale experiments, while withering under the genial air of disbelief on the part of their colleagues, the Soviet Union has established the town Khruschevsk in the Urals, whose popular nickname of "Tiotimolingrad" will well describe the nature of the activities that go on behind the walls of the modern and well-equipped scientific laboratories that have been established there.

That the Soviet Union has taken thiotimoline seriously and has done something about it as sure as can be, and yet we remain sunk in complacency. No important political figure has viewed the matter with alarm. If they have said anything at all for publication, it is simply, "What's thiotimoline?" I intend now to explain to these near-sighted politicos just what thiotimoline means to our space effort.

Thiotimolins research graduated from what we might now call the "classical" stage, to the "modern" with the development of the "telechronic battery" by Anne McLaren and Donald Michie of the University of Edinburgh. If you have read about it anywhere, you can only be clairvoyant, for the popular press and much of the learned press maintained a stubborn silence. In fact, the original paper appeared only in the small, though highly respected, *Journal of Irreproducible Results*, edited by that able gentleman Alexander Kohn. Let me describe the telechronic battery.

A simple endochronometer—with which we are all acquainted—is a device which will automatically deliver water into a small tube containing thiotimoline. The thiotimoline will dissolve 1.12 seconds before the water is delivered.

Imagine the endochronometer so connected with a second similar unit that the solution of the thiotimoline in the first activates the water-delivering pipette of the second. The thiotimoline of the second unit will dissolve 1.12 seconds before that water is deli-vered, and therefore 2.24 seconds before the water is delivered to the first unit.

An indefinite number of endochronometers can thus be hooked up, the thiotimoline of each of the series dissolving 1.12 seconds before the preceding member. A battery consisting of about 77,000 such units would yield a final sample of thiotimoline which dissolved a full day before the initial quantity of water was delivered.

Such batteries have now been developed both at Edinburgh and in my own laboratories in Boston in extremely compact models, through use of printed circuits and advanced miniaturization. A device of not more than a cubic foot in volume can afford a twenty-four hour endochronic interval. There is strong, if indirect, evidence that the

Soviet Union possesses even more sophisticated devices and is turning them out in commercial quantities.

The obvious practical application of the telechronic battery is that of weather prediction. In other words, if the first element of a battery is exposed to the air in such a way that rain, if any, will fall upon it, the final element will dissolve the day before and thus offer a foolproof method of predicting rain—or lack of rain—one day ahead.

I trust you will all see, gentlemen, that the telechronic battery can be used for generalized predictions as well.

Suppose, to take a frivolous example, you were interested in a particular horse race. Suppose you intended to place a wager that a particular horse would win that race. Twenty-four hours in advance of the race, you could make up your mind quite firmly that if the horse were to win the next day, you would, immediately upon receiving the news, add water to the first element of a telechronic battery. If it did not win, you would not.

Having made that decision, you need then but observe the last element. If the thiotimoline in that last element dissolves—followed by a chain of solutions all along the battery at 1.12 second intervals, with which you need not be concerned—you will know that the horse will win beyond doubt. You might even, if you were in a flamboyant mood, allow the solution of the final element to activate a flashing light, a fire gong, a charge of explosive; anything that will unmistakably attract your attention.

You laugh, gentlemen, and yet can this system not be applied, without change, to the launching of a satellite?

Suppose that four hours after launching, an automatic device on board the satellite telemeters a signal to the launching base. Suppose, next, that this radio signal is designed to activate the first element of a telechronic battery.

Do you see the consequences? The sending of the signal four hours after launching can only mean that the satellite is safely in orbit. If it were not, it would have plunged to destruction before the four hours had elapsed. If then, the final element of the telechronic battery dissolves today, we can be certain that there will be a successful launching tomorrow and all may proceed.

If the final element does not dissolve, the launching will not be successful and there must, therefore, be something wrong with the satellite assembly. A team of technicians will begin checking the device and at the moment when the defective item is corrected, the telechronic battery will operate. The launching will then be scheduled in the full expectation of success.

Do you still laugh, gentlemen?

Is this not the only feasible explanation for the consistent Soviet successes as compared with our own very spotty record? It is customary, of course, to attribute the appearance of unfailing success of Soviet launchings to the fact that they have been deliberately hiding many failures, but does this stand up? Have they not, with remarkable consistency, managed to score successes at such time as would most profit themselves?

Sputnik I went up within a month of the hundredth birthday of Tsiolkovsky, the Soviet rocket pioneer. Sputnik II went up to celebrate the fortieth anniversary of the Russian Revolution. Lunik II went up just before Khrushchev's visit to the United States. Lunik III went up on the second anniversary of Sputnik I.

Coincidence? Or did they simply have the foreknowledge of their telechronic batteries? Have they tested a number of possible rocket assemblies and selected that one for which success was forecast? How else can one explain that the United States has not yet succeeded in launching any of their many rockets on some significant day?

Nor, remember, do the Soviets invariably hold their announcements back until they are certain they have achieved success, as, some have suggested. In at least one case, they announced an achievement in advance.

When Lunik III was on its way to circle the Moon, the Soviet scientists confidently announced it would take pictures of the hidden side of the Moon as it progressed round that body in its orbit. As far as the orbit of Lunik III was concerned, they were safe. From its motion and from the positions of Earth, Moon and Lunik, the orbit of Lunik III could be calculated with absolute precision.

How could the Soviet scientists, however, be so sure that the intricacies of the camera assemblage would work to perfection? Could it be that the successful completion of the camera-task was set to activate a telechronic battery at the launching base? Could its activation have allowed them to make their announcement a day before the pictures were taken with the full knowledge that success and a prestige-victory would result?

I say the answer is: Obviously, yes.

And what of future attempts to send a man into space? Suppose the man were to agree to send a signal, manually, after a certain time had elapsed after firing. A telechronic battery would then tell us, while the astronaut was still on the ground and unlaunched, that not only would he be in orbit but that he would be alive and at least well enough to send the message.

If the telechronic battery remains inactive, the man will not be sent up. It is as simple as that. Since it is the chance of harm to an astronaut that is the deciding factor holding back the step of "man into space," it seems certain that the Soviet Union will achieve this goal first, thanks to our government's obtuseness with respect to thiotimoline.

Presumably, one can extend the principle to all manner of scientific and non-scientific investigations. Gigantic mega-batteries can even be built—in theory—to predict the result of an election to be held the following year—but I have labored the point long enough. Let me, instead, make a few remarks concerning the great dangers, as well as the great benefits, which are involved in thiotimoline research.

* * *

These begin with the oldest of all paradoxes of thiotimoline—the paradox of fooling. In other words, the chance of having thiotimoline dissolve and then being fooled by a refusal to add the water. The original argument against such a notion, as elucidated in my laboratory, involved the theory of the endochronic atom—which has since been confirmed by half a dozen other investigators. One pair of the bonds of one or more of the carbon atoms in the thiotimoline molecule are forced, through supersteric hindrance, to a point in the temporal plane. One bond extends 1.12 seconds into the past and one extends 1.12 seconds into the future. When the future end of a thiotimoline molecule dissolves and drags the rest of the molecule with it, it is therefore not predicting a possible future event. It is recording an actual future event.

Nevertheless, it has been shown that fooling thiotimoline is possible in theory. Using Heisenberg's principle of uncertainty, it can be demonstrated that one cannot say with certainty that an individual molecule of thiotimoline will dissolve before the water is added and that, in fact, the probability of its not doing so is quite appreciable.

That is undoubtedly true—for an individual molecule. When, however, quintillions of molecules are involved as is the case with even the most microscopic samples of thiotimoline actually used in the individual units of even the most sophisticated telechronic batteries, the chance that all of those quintillions, or even a detectable fraction of them, will fail to dissolve is infinitesimal.

To be sure, in setting up a telechronic battery, in which many thousands of units are involved, the failure of the instrument will depend on the failure to dissolve of any one of those units. The chance of

"Heisenberg failure," as it is called, can be calculated and some estimates at least seem to show that a battery will give a false positive one time out of rather more than a million.

In such a case, the final unit in a telechronic battery will dissolve even though water is not added to the first. Somewhat more often, the converse will be true; that the final unit will not dissolve in advance even though water is added to the first. Naturally the former alternative is more interesting from the theoretical viewpoint, the question arising: Then where did the water come from?

An attempt was made in my laboratories to actually record such a false negative involving solution without subsequent addition of water. The possibility of creation of matter out of nothing existed and this would be of great importance in connection with the Gold-Hoyle theory of the steady-state universe.

The principle in the attempt was simple. One of my students would set up a battery adjusted for the manual addition of water the next day, intending in all honesty to allow the experiment to take its course. The final unit would, theoretically, dissolve. I would then place the first student at a different task and put a second student in charge of the battery with instructions not to add water.

Our first great surprise was to find that the final unit actually dissolved, under these circumstances, about once in twenty efforts. This was a far greater incidence than could possibly be explained by "Heisenberg failure." But, as it rapidly turned out, the thiotimoline was not "fooled." Something, in every case, brought about the addition of water. In the first case, the original student returned to add the water and did so before he could be stopped. In another case, there was accidental spillage. In another, a janitor—

But it would be tedious to describe the manner in which thiotimoline, so to speak, refused to be fooled. Suffice it that we did not have one true case of "Heisenberg failure."

With time, of course, we began to guard against ordinary accidents and the incidence of "pseudofailure" declined. For instance, we placed the battery in closed, desiccated vessels; but, during pseudofailure, these cracked and broke.

In our final experiment we thought that surely we had a "Heisenberg failure" but in the end, the experiment was not reported in the literature. I tried instead, and without success, to report the implications of it to appropriate officials. Let me describe the experiment to you now.

* * *

We placed the battery in a welded steel container after it had registered solution.

And as we waited for the moment when the water should be added but would not, Hurricane Diane struck New England. That was in August of 1955. The hurricane had been predicted, its course had been followed and we were ready for it. There had been several hurricanes in New England in '54 and '55 and we were hardened to it.

At one point, though, the Weather Bureau announced the danger to be passed, the hurricane was blowing out to sea. We all sighed with relief as we waited for zero minute.

However, if any of you were in New England that day you will remember that the Weather Bureau announced later that it had "lost" the hurricane; that the backlash struck surprisingly; that five inches of rain or more fell in many places within an hour; that rivers rose and extensive flooding began.

I watched that rain; it was a deluge. I watched the small river running across our campus become a torrent and begin to spread up and out across the lawns while the lines of shrubbery seemed to grow out of roiled sheets of water.

I shouted for an axe. One of my students brought one, remarking afterward that I sounded so wild he was almost afraid I had turned homicidal maniac.

I smashed that steel container. I removed the telechronic battery and in the flickering gray light of that storm-lashed day, I filled a beaker of water and waited for zero minute, ready to douse the battery at the proper moment.

As I did so, the rain slackened, the hurricane moved off.

I do not say we caused the hurricane to return and yet—water had to be added to that battery somehow. If the stainless steel container had to be floated away on a rising flood and smashed by wind and water to have that done, it would be done. The original solution of the final unit predicted that; or else it predicted my deliberate subversion of the experiment. I chose the latter.

As a result of all this, I can envisage what I can only call a "peace bomb." Enemy agents working within a particular nation, can assemble telechronic batteries, operate them until a case occurs in which the final unit dissolves. That battery can then be encased in a steel capsule and placed near a stream well above high-water mark. Twenty-four hours later, a disastrous flood is bound to occur, since only so can water reach the container. This will be accompanied by high winds since only so can the container be smashed.

Damage will undoubtedly be as great in its way as would result from an H-Bomb blast and yet the telechronic battery would be a "peace bomb" for its use will not bring on retaliation and war. There would be no reason to suspect anything but an act of God.

Such a bomb requires little in the way of technology or expense. The smallest nation, the smallest of revolutionary or dissident groups could manage it.

Sometimes in my more morbid moment, I wonder if perhaps Noah's flood—the prototype of which actually has been recorded in Mesopotamian sediments—was not brought about by thiotimoline experiments among the ancient Sumerians.

I tell you, gentlemen, if we have one urgent task ahead of us now it is to convince our government to press for international control of all sources of thiotimoline. It is boundlessly useful when used properly; boundlessly harmful when used improperly.

Not a milligram of it must be allowed to reach irresponsible hands.

Gentlemen, I call you to a crusade for the safety of the world!

The Machine That Won the War

The celebration had a long way to go and even in the silent depths of Multivac's underground chambers, it hung in the air.

If nothing else, there was the mere fact of isolation and silence. For the first time in a decade, technicians were not scurrying about the vitals of the giant computer, the soft lights did not wink out their erratic patterns, the flow of information in and out had halted.

It would not be halted long, of course, for the needs of peace would be pressing. Yet now, for a day, perhaps for a week, even Multivac might celebrate the great time, and rest.

Lamar Swift took off the military cap he was wearing and looked down the long and empty main corridor of the enormous computer. He sat down rather wearily in one of the technician's swing-stools, and his uniform, in which he had never been comfortable, took on a heavy and wrinkled appearance.

He said, "I'll miss it all after a grisly fashion. It's hard to remember when we weren't at war with Deneb, and it seems against nature now to be at peace and to look at the stars without anxiety."

The two men with the Executive Director of the Solar Federation were both younger than Swift. Neither was as gray. Neither looked quite as tired.

John Henderson, thin-lipped and finding it hard to control the relief he felt in the midst of triumph, said, "They're destroyed! They're destroyed! It's what I keep saying to myself over and over and I still can't believe it. We all talked so much, over so many years, about the menace hanging over Earth and all its worlds, over every human being, and all the time it was true, every word of it. And now we're alive and it's the Denebians who are shattered and destroyed. They'll be no menace now, ever again."

"Thanks to Multivac," said Swift, with a quiet glance at the imperturbable Jablonsky, who through all the war had been Chief Interpreter of science's oracle. "Right, Max?"

Jablonsky shrugged. Automatically, he reached for a cigarette and decided against it. He alone, of all the thousands who had lived in the tunnels within Multivac, had been allowed to smoke, but toward the end he had made definite efforts to avoid making use of the privilege.

He said, "Well, that's what *they* say." His broad thumb moved in the direction of his right shoulder, aiming upward.

"Jealous, Max?"

"Because they're shouting for Multivac? Because Multivac is the big hero of mankind in this war?" Jablonsky's craggy face took on an air of suitable contempt. "What's that to me? Let Multivac be the machine that won the war, if it pleases them."

Henderson looked at the other two out of the corners of his eyes. In this short interlude that the three had instinctively sought out in the one peaceful corner of a metropolis gone mad; in this entr'acte between the dangers of war and the difficulties of peace; when, for one moment, they might all find surcease; he was conscious only of his weight of guilt.

Suddenly, it was as though that weight were too great to be borne longer. It had to be thrown off, along with the war; now!

Henderson said, "Multivac had nothing to do with victory. It's just a machine."

"A big one," said Swift.

"Then just a big machine. No better than the data fed it." For a moment, he stopped, suddenly unnerved at what he was saying.

Jablonsky looked at him, his thick fingers once again fumbling for a cigarette and once again drawing back. "You should know. You supplied the data. Or is it just that you're taking the credit?"

"*No*," said Henderson, angrily. "There is no credit. What do you know of the data Multivac had to use; predigested from a hundred subsidiary computers here on Earth, on the Moon, on Mars, even on Titan. With Titan always delayed and always that feeling that its figures would introduce an unexpected bias."

"It would drive anyone mad," said Swift, with gentle sympathy.

Henderson shook his head. "It wasn't just that. I admit that eight years ago when I replaced Lepont as Chief Programmer, I was nervous. But there was an exhilaration about things in those days. The war was still long-range; an adventure without real danger. We hadn't reached the point where manned vessels had had to take over and where interstellar warps could swallow up a planet clean, if aimed correctly. But then, when the real difficulties began—"

Angrily—he could finally permit anger—he said, "You know nothing about it."

"Well," said Swift. "Tell us. The war is over. We've won."

"Yes." Henderson nodded his head. He had to remember that.

Earth had won so all had been for the best. "Well, the data became meaningless."

"Meaningless? You mean that literally?" said Jablonsky.

"Literally. What would you expect? The trouble with you was that you weren't out in the thick of it. You never left Multivac, Max, and you, Mr. Director, never left the Mansion except on state visits where you saw exactly what they wanted you to see."

"I was not as unaware of that," said Swift, "as you may have thought."

"Do you know," said Henderson, "to what extent data concerning our production capacity, our resource potential, our trained manpower—everything of importance to the war effort, in fact—had become unreliable and untrustworthy during the last half of the war? Group leaders, both civilian and military, were intent on projecting their own improved image, so to speak, so they obscured the bad and magnified the good. Whatever the machines might do, the men who programmed them and interpreted the results had their own skins to think of and competitors to stab. There was no way of stopping that. I tried, and failed."

"Of course," said Swift, in quiet consolation. "I can see that you would."

This time Jablonsky decided to light his cigarette. "Yet I presume you provided Multivac with data in your programming. You said nothing to us about unreliability."

"How could I tell you? And if I did, how could you afford to believe me?" demanded Henderson, savagely. "Our entire war effort was geared to Multivac. It was the one great weapon on our side, for the Denebians had nothing like it. What else kept up morale in the face of doom but the assurance that Multivac would always predict and circumvent any Denebian move, and would always direct and prevent the circumvention of our moves? Great Space, after our Spy-warp was blasted out of hyperspace we lacked any reliable Denebian data to feed Multivac and we didn't dare make *that* public."

"True enough," said Swift.

"Well, then," said Henderson, "if I told you the data was unreliable, what could you have done but replace me and refuse to believe me? I couldn't allow that."

"What did you do?" said Jablonsky.

"Since the war is won, I'll tell you what I did. I corrected the data."

"How?" asked Swift.

"Intuition, I presume. I juggled them till they looked right. At first, I hardly dared. I changed a bit here and there to correct what were obvious impossibilities. When the sky didn't collapse about us, I got braver. Toward the end, I scarcely cared. I just wrote out the necessary data as it was needed. I even had the Multivac Annex prepare data for me according to a private programming pattern I had devised for the purpose."

"Random figures?" said Jablonsky.

"Not at all. I introduced a number of necessary biases."

Jablonsky smiled, quite unexpectedly, his dark eyes sparkling behind the crinkling of the lower lids. "Three times a report was brought me about unauthorized uses of the Annex, and I let it go each time. If it had mattered, I would have followed it up and spotted you, John, and found out what you were doing. But, of course, nothing about Multivac mattered in those days, so you got away with it."

"What do you mean, nothing mattered?" asked Henderson, suspiciously.

"Nothing did. I suppose if I had told you this at the time, it would have spared you your agony, but then if you had told me what you were doing, it would have spared me mine. What made you think Multivac was in working order, whatever the data you supplied it?"

"Not in working order?" said Swift.

"Not really. Not reliably. After all, where were my technicians in the last years of the war? I'll tell you, they were feeding computers on a thousand different space devices. They were gone! I had to make do with kids I couldn't trust and veterans who were out-of-date. Besides, do you think I could trust the solid-state components coming out of Cryogenics in the last years? Cryogenics wasn't any better placed as far as personnel was concerned than I was. To me, it didn't matter whether the data being supplied Multivac were reliable or not. The *results* weren't reliable. That much I knew."

"What did you do?" asked Henderson.

"I did what you did, John. I introduced the bugger factor. I adjusted matters in accordance with intuition—and that's how the machine won the war."

Swift leaned back in the chair and stretched his legs out before him. "Such revelations. It turns out then that the material handed me to guide me in my decision-making capacity was a man-made interpretation of man-made data. Isn't that right?"

"It looks so," said Jablonsky.

"Then I perceive I was correct in not placing too much reliance upon it," said Swift.

"You didn't?" Jablonsky, despite what he had just said, managed to look professionally insulted.

"I'm afraid I didn't. Multivac might seem to say, Strike here, not there; do this, not that; wait, don't act. But I could never be certain that what Multivac seemed to say, it really did say; or what it really said, it really meant. I could never be certain."

"But the final report was always plain enough, sir," said Jablonsky.

"To those who did not have to make the decision, perhaps. Not to me. The horror of the responsibility of such decisions was unbearable and not even Multivac was sufficient to remove the weight. But the point is I was justified in doubting and there is tremendous relief in that."

Caught up in the conspiracy of mutual confession, Jablonsky put titles aside, "What was it you did then, Lamar? After all, you did make decisions. How?"

"Well, it's time to be getting back perhaps but—I'll tell you first. Why not? I did make use of a computer, Max, but an older one than Multivac, much older."

He groped in his own pocket for cigarettes, and brought out a package along with a scattering of small change; old-fashioned coins dating to the first years before the metal shortage had brought into being a credit system tied to a computer-complex.

Swift smiled rather sheepishly. "I still need these to make money seem substantial to me. An old man finds it hard to abandon the habits of youth." He put a cigarette between his lips and dropped the coins one by one back into his pocket.

He held the last coin between his fingers, staring absently at it. "Multivac is not the first computer, friends, nor the best-known, nor the one that can most efficiently lift the load of decision from the shoulders of the executive. A machine *did* win the war, John; at least a very simple computing device did; one that I used every time I had a particularly hard decision to make."

With a faint smile of reminiscence, he flipped the coin he held. It glinted in the air as it spun and came down in Swift's outstretched palm. His hand closed over it and brought it down on the back of his left hand. His right hand remained in place, hiding the coin.

"Heads or tails, gentlemen?" said Swift.

My Son, the Physicist

Her hair was a light apple-green in color, very subdued, very old-fashioned. You could see she had a delicate hand with the dye, the way they did thirty years ago, before the streaks and stipples came into fashion.

She had a sweet smile on her face, too, and a calm look that made something serene out of elderliness.

And, by comparison, it made something shrieking out of the confusion that enfolded her in the huge government building.

A girl passed her at a half-run, stopped and turned toward her with a blank stare of astonishment. "How did you get in?"

The woman smiled. "I'm looking for my son, the physicist."

"Your son, the—"

"He's a communications engineer, really. Senior Physicist Gerard Cremona."

"Dr. Cremona. Well, he's— Where's your pass?"

"Here it is. I'm his mother."

"Well, Mrs. Cremona, I don't know. I've got to— His office is down there. You just ask someone." She passed on, running.

Mrs. Cremona shook her head slowly. Something had happened, she supposed. She hoped Gerard was all right.

She heard voices much farther down the corridor and smiled happily. She could tell Gerard's.

She walked into the room and said, "Hello, Gerard."

Gerard was a big man, with a lot of hair still and the gray just beginning to show because he didn't use dye. He said he was too busy. She was very proud of him and the way he looked.

Right now, he was talking volubly to a man in army uniform. She couldn't tell the rank, but she knew Gerard could handle him.

Gerard looked up and said, "What do you— Mother! What are you doing here?"

"I was coming to visit you today."

"Is today Thursday? Oh Lord, I forgot. Sit down, Mother, I can't talk now. Any seat. Any seat. Look, General."

General Reiner looked over his shoulder and one hand slapped against the other in the region of the small of his back. "Your mother?"

"Yes."

"Should she be here?"

"Right now, no, but I'll vouch for her. She can't even read a thermometer so nothing of this will mean anything to her. Now look, General. They're on Pluto. You see? They are. The radio signals can't be of natural origin so they must originate from human beings, from our men. You'll have to accept that. Of all the expeditions we've sent out beyond the asteroid belt, one turns out to have made it. And they've reached Pluto."

"Yes, I understand what you're saying, but isn't it impossible just the same? The men who are on Pluto now were launched four years ago with equipment that could not have kept them alive more than a year. That is my understanding. They were aimed at Ganymede and seem to have gone eight times the proper distance."

"Exactly. And we've got to know how and why. They may—just—have—had—help."

"What kind? How?"

Cremona clenched his jaws for a moment as though praying inwardly. "General," he said, "I'm putting myself out on a limb but it is just barely possible non-humans are involved. Extra-terrestrials. We've got to find out. We don't know how long contact can be maintained."

"You mean" (the General's grave face twitched into an almost-smile) "they may have escaped from custody and they may be recaptured again at any time."

"Maybe. Maybe. The whole future of the human race may depend on our knowing exactly what we're up against. Knowing it *now*."

"All right. What is it you want?"

"We're going to need Army's Multivac computer at once. Rip out every problem it's working on and start programming our general semantic problem. Every communications engineer you have must be pulled off anything he's on and placed into coordination with our own."

"But why? I fail to see the connection."

A gentle voice interrupted. "General, would you like a piece of fruit? I brought some oranges?"

Cremona said, "Mother! Please! Later! General, the point is a simple one. At the present moment Pluto is just under four billion miles away. It takes six hours for radio waves, traveling at the speed of light, to reach from here to there. If we say something, we must wait twelve hours for an answer. If they say something and we miss it and say 'what' and they repeat—bang, goes a day."

"There's no way to speed it up?" said the General.

"Of course not. It's the fundamental law of communications. No information can be transmitted at more than the speed of light. It will take months to carry on the same conversation with Pluto that would take hours between the two of us right now."

"Yes, I see that. And you really think extra-terrestrials are involved?"

"I do. To be honest, not everyone here agrees with me. Still, we're straining every nerve, every fiber, to devise some method of concentrating communication. We must get in as many bits per second as possible and pray we get what we need before we lose contact. And there's where I need Multivac and your men. There must be some communications strategy we can use that will reduce the number of signals we need send out. Even an increase of ten per cent in efficiency can mean perhaps a week of time saved."

The gentle voice interrupted again. "Good grief, Gerard, are you trying to get some talking done?"

"Mother! Please!"

"But you're going about it the wrong way. Really."

"Mother." There was a hysterical edge to Cremona's voice.

"Well, all right, but if you're going to say something and then wait twelve hours for an answer, you're silly. You shouldn't."

The General snorted. "Dr. Cremona, shall we consult—"

"Just one moment, General," said Cremona. "What are you getting at, Mother?"

"While you're waiting for an answer," said Mrs. Cremona, earnestly, "just keep on transmitting and tell them to do the same. You talk all the time and they talk all the time. You have someone listening all the time and they do, too. If either one of you says anything that needs an answer, you can slip one in at your end, but chances are, you'll get all you need without asking."

Both men stared at her.

Cremona whispered, "Of course. Continuous conversation. Just twelve hours out of phase, that's all. God, we've got to get going."

He strode out of the room, virtually dragging the General with him, then strode back in.

"Mother," he said, "if you'll excuse me, this will take a few hours, I think. I'll send in some girls to talk to you. Or take a nap, if you'd rather."

"I'll be all right, Gerard," said Mrs. Cremona.

"Only, how did you think of this, Mother? What made you suggest this?"

"But, Gerard, all women know it. Any two women—on the

videophone, or on the stratowire, or just face to face—know that the whole secret to spreading the news is, no matter what, to Just Keep Talking."

Cremona tried to smile. Then, his lower lip trembling, he turned and left.

Mrs. Cremona looked fondly after him. Such a fine man, her son, the physicist. Big as he was and important as he was, he still knew that a boy should always listen to his mother.

T-Formation

I have been accused of having a mad passion for large numbers and this is perfectly true. I wouldn't dream of denying it. However, may I point out that I am not the only one?

For instance, in a book entitled *Mathematics and the Imagination* (published in 1940) the authors, Edward Kasner and James Newman, introduced a number called the "googol," which is good and large and which was promptly taken up by writers of books and articles on popular mathematics.

Personally, I think it is an awful name, but the young child of one of the authors invented it, and what could a proud father do? Thus, we are afflicted forever with that baby-talk number.

The googol was defined as the number 1 followed by a hundred zeros, and so here (unless I have miscounted or the Noble Printer has goofed) is the googol, written out in full:
10,000,000,000,000,000,000,000,000,000,000,000,000,000,000, 000, 000, 000,000,000,000,000,000,000,000,000,000,000,000,000, 000,000, 000,000.

Now this is a pretty clumsy way of writing a googol, but it fits in with our system of numeration, which is based on the number 10. To write large numbers we simply multiply 10's, so that a hundred is ten times ten and is written 100; a thousand is ten times ten times ten and is written 1000 and so on. The number of zeros in the number is equal to the number of tens being multiplied, so that the googol, with a hundred zeros following the 1, is equal to a hundred tens multiplied together. This can also be written as 10^{100}. And since 100 is ten times ten or 10^2, the googol can even be written as 10^{10^2}.

Certainly, this form of exponential notation (the little figure in the upper right of such a number is an "exponent") is very convenient, and any book on popular math will define a googol as 10^{100}. However, to anyone who loves large numbers, the googol is only the beginning and even this shortened version of writing large numbers isn't simple enough.[1]

[1]The proper name for the googol, before I forget, is "ten duotrigintillion," but I dare say, gloomily, that that will never replace "googol."

So I have made up my own system for writing large numbers and I am going to use this article as a chance to explain it. (Freeze, everyone! No one's leaving till I'm through.)

* * *

The trouble, it seems to me, is that we are using the number 10 to build upon. That was good enough for cave men, I suppose, but we moderns are terribly sophisticated and we know lots of better numbers than that.

For instance, the annual budget of the United States of America is in the neighborhood, now, of $100,000,000,000 (a hundred billion dollars). That means 1,000,000,000,000 (one trillion) dimes.

Why don't we, then, use the number, one trillion, as a base? To be sure, we can't visualize a trillion, but why should that stop us? We can't even visualize fifty-three. At least if someone were to show us a group of objects and tell us there are fifty-three of them altogether, we couldn't tell whether he were right or wrong without counting them. That makes a trillion no less unreal than fifty-three, for we have to count both numbers and both are equally countable. To be sure, it would take us much longer to count one trillion than to count fifty-three, but the principle is the same and I, as anyone will tell you, am a man of principle.

The important thing is to associate a number with something physical that can be grasped and this we have done. The number 1,000,000,000,000 is roughly equal to the number of dimes taken from your pocket and mine (mostly mine, I sometimes sullenly think) each year by kindly, jovial Uncle Sam to build missiles and otherwise run the government and the country.

Then, once we have it firmly fixed in our mind as to what a trillion is, it takes very little effort of imagination to see what a trillion trillion is; a trillion trillion trillion, and so on. In order to keep from drowning in a stutter of trillions, let's use an abbreviated system that, as far as I know, is original with me.[2]

Lets call a trillion T-1; a trillion trillion T-2; a trillion trillion trillion T-3; and form large numbers in this fashion. (And there's the "T-formation" of the title! Surely you didn't expect football?)

[2]Actually, Archimedes set up a system of numbers based on the myriad, and spoke of a myriad myriad, a myriad myriad myriad and so on. But a myriad is only 10,000 and I'm using 1,000,000,000,000, so I don't consider Archimedes to be affecting my originality. Besides, he only beat me out by less than twenty-two centuries.

Shall we see how these numbers can be put to use? I have already said that T-1 is the number of dimes it takes to run the United States for one year. In that case, T-2 would represent the number of dimes it would take to run the United States for a trillion years. Since this length of time is undoubtedly longer than the United States will endure (if I may be permitted this unpatriotic sentiment) and, in all likelihood, longer than the planet earth will endure, we see that we have run out of financial applications of the Asimovian (ahem!) T-numbers long before we have even reached T-2.

Let's try something else. The mass of any object is proportional to its content of protons and neutrons which, together, may be referred to as nucleons. Now T-1 nucleons make up a quantity of mass far too small to see in even the best optical microscope and even T-2 nucleons make up only 1⅔ grams of mass, or about 1/16 of an ounce.

Now we've got room, it would seem, to move way up the T-scale. How massive, for instance, are T-3 nucleons? Since T-3 is a trillion times as large as T-2, T-3 nucleons have a mass of 1.67 trillion grams, or a little under two million tons. Maybe there's not as much room as we thought.

In fact, the T-numbers build up with breath-taking speed. T-4 nucleons equals the mass of all the earth's ocean, and T-5 nucleons equals the mass of a thousand solar systems. If we insist on continuing upward, T-6 nucleons equal the mass of ten thousand galaxies the size of ours, and T-7 nucleons are far, far more massive than the entire known universe.

Nucleons are not the only subatomic particles there are, of course, but even if we throw in electrons, mesons, neutrinos, and all the other paraphernalia of subatomic structure, we cannot reach T-7. In short, there are far less than T-7 subatomic particles of all sorts in the visible universe.

Clearly, the system of T-numbers is a powerful method of expressing large numbers. How does it work for the googol? Well, consider the method of converting ordinary exponential numbers into T-numbers and vice versa. T-1 is equal to a trillion, or 10^{12}; T-2 is equal to a trillion trillion, or 10^{24}, and so on. Well, then, you need only divide an exponent by 12 to have the numerical portion of a T-number; and you need only multiply the numerical portion of a T-number by 12 to get a ten-based exponent.

If a googol is 10^{100}, then divide 100 by 12, and you see at once that it can be expressed at T-8½. Notice that T-8½ is larger than T-7 and T-7 is in turn far larger than the number of subatomic particles in the known universe. It would take a billion trillion universes like our own to contain a googol of subatomic particles.

* * *

When then is the good of a googol, if it is too large to be useful in counting even the smallest material objects spread through the largest known volume?

I could answer: For its own sheer, abstract beauty—

But then you would all throw rocks at me. Instead, then, let me say that there are more things to be counted in this universe than material objects.

For instance, consider an ordinary deck of playing cards. In order to play, you shuffle the deck, the cards fall into a certain order, and you deal a game. Into how many different orders can the deck be shuffled? (Since it is impossible to have more essentially different game-situations than there are orders-of-cards in a shuffled deck, this is a question that should interest your friendly neighborhood poker-player.)

The answer is easily found (if youknow where to look, and I do) and comes out to 80,000,000,000,000,000,000,000,000,000,000,000,000, 000,000, 000,000,000,000,000,000,000,000, or 8×10^{67}. In T-numbers, this is something like T-5⅔. With an ordinary deck of cards, then, we can count arrangements and reach a value equal to that of the number of subatomic particles in a galaxy, more or less. If, instead of 52 cards, we played with 70 cards (and this is not unreasonable; canasta, I understand, uses 108 cards), then the number of different orders after shuffling, just tops the googol mark.

So when it comes to analyzing card games (let alone chess, economics, and nuclear war), numbers like the googol and beyond are met with.

Mathematicians, in fact, are interested in many varieties of numbers (with and without practical applications) in which vastnesses far, far beyond the googol are quickly reached.

* * *

Consider Leonardo Fibonacci, for instance, the most accomplished mathematician of the Middle Ages. (He was born in Pisa, so he is often called Leonardo of Pisa.) About 1200, when Fibonacci was in his prime, Pisa was a great commercial city, engaged in commerce with the Moors in North Africa. Leonardo had a chance to visit that region and profit from a Moorish education.

The Moslem world had by that time learned of a new system of numeration from the Hindus. Fibonacci picked it up and in a book, *Liber Abaci*, published in 1202, introduced these "Arabic numbers" and passed them on to a Europe still suffering under the barbarism of the Roman numerals, it took a mere couple of centuries to convince European merchants to make the change.)

In this same book Fibonacci introduces the following problem: "How many rabbits can be produced from a single pair in a year if every month each pair begets a new pair, which from the second month on become productive, and no deaths occur?" (It is also assumed that each pair consists of a male and female and that rabbits have no objection to incest.)

In the first month we begin with a pair of immature rabbits, and in the second month we still have one pair, but now they are mature. By the third month they have produced a new pair, so there are two pairs, one mature, one immature. By the fourth month the immature pair has become mature and the first pair has produced another immature pair, so there are three pairs, two mature and one immature.

You can go on if you wish, reasoning out how many pairs of rabbits there will be each month, but I will give you the series of numbers right now and save you the trouble. It is:

1, 1, 2, 3, 5, 8, 13, 21, 34, 55, 89, 144

At the end of the year, you see, there would be 144 pairs of rabbits and that is the answer to Fibonacci's problem.

The series of numbers evolved out of the problem is the "Fibonacci series" and the individual numbers of the series are the "Fibonacci numbers." If you look at the series, you will see that each number (from the third member on) is the sum of the two preceeding numbers.

This means we needn't stop the series at the twelfth Fibonacci number (F_{12}). We can construct F_{13} easily enough by adding F_{11} and F_{12}. Since 89 and 144 are 233, that is F_{13}. Adding 144 and 233 gives us 377 or F_{14}. We can continue with F_{15} equal to 610, F_{16} equal to 987, and so on for as far as we care to go. Simple arithmetic, nothing more than addition, will give us all the Fibonacci numbers we want.

To be sure, the process gets tedious after a while as the Fibonacci numbers stretch into more and more digits and the chances of arithmetical error increase. One arithmetical error anywhere in the series, if uncorrected, throws off all the later members of the series.

But why should anyone want to carry the Fibonacci sequence on and on and on into large numbers? Well, the series has its applications.

It is connected with cumulative growth, as the rabbit problem shows, and, as a matter of fact, the distribution of leaves spirally about a lengthening stem, the scales distributed about a pine cone, the seeds distributed in the sunflower center, all have an arrangement related to the Fibonacci series. The series is also related to the "golden section," which is important to art and aesthetics as well as to mathematics.

But beyond all that, there are always people who are fascinated by large numbers. (I can't explain the fascination but believe me it exists.) And if fascination falls short of working away night after night with pen and ink, it is possible, these days, to program a computer to do the work, and get large numbers that it would be impractical to try to work out in the old-fashioned way.

The October 1962 issue of *Recreational Mathematics Magazine*[3] lists the first 571 Fibonacci numbers as worked out on an IBM 7090 computer. The fifty-fifth Fibonacci number passes the trillion mark, so that we can say that F_{55} is greater than T-1.

From that point on, every interval of fifty-five or so Fibonacci numbers (the interval slowly lengthens) passes another T-number. Indeed, F_{481} is larger than a googol. It is equal to almost one and a half googols, in fact.

Those multiplying rabbits, in other words, will quickly surpass any conceivable device to encourage their multiplication. They will outrun any food supply that can be dreamed up, any room that can be imagined. There might be only 144 at the end of a year, but there would be nearly 50,000 at the end of two years, 15,000,000 at the end of three years, and so on. In thirty years there would be more rabbits than there are subatomic particles in the known universe, and in forty years there would be more than a googol of rabbits.

To be sure, human beings do not multiply as quickly as Fibonacci's rabbits, and old human beings do die. Nevertheless,the principle remains. What those rabbits can do in a few years, we can do in a few centuries or millenniums. Soon enough. Think of that when you tend to minimize the population explosion.

For the fun of it, I would like to write F_{571}, which is the largest number given in the article. (There will be larger numbers later, but I will not write them out!) Anyway, F_{571} is: 96041200618922553823942

[3]This is a fascinating little periodical which I heartily recommend to any nut congruent to myself.

883360924865026104917411877067816822264789029014378308478864192589084185254331637646183008074629. This vast number is not quite equal to T-10.[4]

*   *   *

For another example of large numbers, consider the primes. These are numbers like 7, or 641, or 5237, which can be divided evenly only by themselves and 1. They have no other factors. You might suppose that as one goes higher and higher in the scale of numbers, the primes gradually peter out because there would be more and more smaller numbers to serve as possible factors.

This, however, does not happen, and even the ancient Greeks knew that. Euclid was able to prove quite simply that if all the primes are listed up to a "largest prime," it is always possible to construct a still larger number which is either prime itself or has a prime factor that is larger than the "largest prime." It follows then there is no such thing as a "largest prime" and the number of primes is infinite.

Yet even if we can't work out a largest prime, there is an allied problem. What is the largest prime we know? It would be pleasant to point to a large number and say: "This is a prime. There are an infinite number of larger primes, but we don't know which numbers they are. This is the largest number we *know* to be a prime."

Once that is done, you see, then some venturesome amateur mathematician may find a still larger prime.

Finding a really large prime is by no means easy. Earlier, for instance, I said that 5237 is prime. Suppose you doubted that, how would you check me? The only practical way is to try all the prime numbers smaller than the square root of 5237 and see which, if any, are factors. This is tedious but possible for 5237. It is simply impractical for really large numbers—except for computers.

Mathematicians have sought formulas, therefore, that would construct primes. It might not give them every prime in the book, so that it would not be used to test a given number for prime-hood. However, it could construct primes of any desired size, and after that the task of finding a record-high prime would become trivial and could be abandoned.

[4]Since this was written, the editor of *Recreational Mathematics* wrote to say that he had new Fibonacci number, up to F_{1000}. This F_{1000}, with 209 digits, is something over T-17.

However, such a formula has never been found. About 1600, a French friar named Marin Mersenne proposed a formula of partial value which would occasionally, but not always, produce a prime. This formula is $2^p - 1$, where p is itself a prime number. (You understand, I hope, that 2^p represents a number formed by multiplying p two's together, so that 2^8 is $2 \times 2 \times 2 \times 2 \times 2 \times 2 \times 2 \times 2$, or 256.)

Mersenne maintained that the formula would produce primes when p was equal to 2, 3, 5, 7, 13, 17, 19, 31, 67, 127, or 257. This can be tested for the lower numbers easily enough. For instance, if p equals 3, then the formula becomes $2^3 - 1$, or 7, which is indeed prime. If p equals 7, then $2^7 - 1$ equals 127, which is prime. You can check the equation for any of the other values of p you care to.

The numbers obtained by substituting prime numbers for p in Mersenne's equation are called "Mersenne numbers" and if the number happens to be prime it is a "Mersenne prime." They are symbolized by the capital letter M and the value of p. Thus M_3 equals 7; M_7 equals 127, and so on.

I don't know what system Mersenne used to decide what primes would yield Mersenne primes in his equation, but whatever it was, it was wrong. The Mersenne numbers M_2, M_3, M_5, M_7, M_{13}, M_{17}, M_{19}, M_{31}, and M_{127} are indeed primes, so that Mersenne had put his finger on no less than nine Mersenne primes. However, M_{67} and M_{257}, which Mersenne said were primes, proved on painstaking examination to be no primes at all. On the other hand, M_{61}, M_{89}, and M_{107}, which Mersenne did not list as primes, are primes, and this makes a total of twelve Mersenne primes.

In recent years, thanks to computer work, eight more Mersenne primes have been located (according to the April 1962 issue of *Recreational Mathematics)*. These are M_{521}, M_{607}, M_{1279}, M_{2203}, M_{2281}, M_{321}7, M_{4253}, and M_{4423}. What's more, since that issue, three even larger Mersenne primes have been discovered by Donald B. Gillies of the University of Illinois. These are M_{9689}, M_{9941}, and M_{11213}.

The smallest of these newly discovered Mersenne primes, M_{521}, is obtained by working out the formula $2^{521} - 1$. You take 521 two's, multiply them together, and subtract one. The result is far, far higher than a googol. In fact, it is higher than T-13.

Not to stretch out the suspense, the largest known Mersenne prime, M_{11213}, and, I believe, the largest prime known at present, has 3375 digits and is therefore just about T-281¼. The googol, in comparison to that, is a trifle so small that there is no reasonable way to describe its smallness.

* * *

The Greeks played many games with numbers, and one of them was to add up the factors of particular integers. For instance, the factors of 12 (not counting the number itself) are 1, 2, 3, 4, and 6. Each of these numbers, but no others, will go evenly into 12. The sum of these factors is 16, which is greater than the number 12 itself, so that 12 is an "abundant number."

The factors of 10, on the other hand, are 1, 2, and 5, which yield a sum of 8. This is less than the number itself, so that 10 is a "deficient number." (All primes are obviously badly deficient.)

But consider 6. It's factors are 1, 2, and 3, and this adds up to 6. When the factors add up to the number itself, that number is a "perfect number."

Nothing has ever come of the perfect numbers in two thousand years, but the Greeks were fascinated by them, and those of them who were mystically inclined revered them. For instance, it could be argued (once Greek culture had penetrated Judeo-Christianity) that God had created the world in six days because six is a perfect number. (Its factors are the first three numbers, and not only is their sum six, but their product is also six, and God couldn't be expected to resist all that.)

I don't know whether the mystics also made a point of the fact that the lunar month is just a trifle over twenty-eight days long, since 28, with factors of 1, 2, 4, 7, and 14 (which add up to 28), is another perfect number. Alas, the days of the lunar month are actually 29½ and the mystics may have been puzzled over this slipshod arrangement on the part of the Creator.

But how many of these wonderful perfect numbers are there? Considering that by the time you reach 28, you have run into two of them, you might think there were many. However, they are rare indeed; far rarer than almost any other well-known kind of number. The third perfect number is 496, and the fourth is 8128, and throughout ancient and medieval times, those were the only perfect numbers known.

The fifth perfect number was not discovered until about 1460 (the name of the discoverer is not known) and it is 33,550,336. In modern times, thanks to the help of the computer, more and more perfect numbers have been discovered and the total now is twenty. The twentieth and largest of these is a number with 2663 digits, and this is almost equal to T-222.

* * *

But in a way, I have been unfair to Kasner and Newman. I have said they invented the googol and I then went on to show that it was easy to deal with numbers far higher than the googol. However, I should also add they invented another number, far, far larger than the googol. This second number is the "googolplex," which is defined as equal to 10^{googol}. The exponent, then, is a 1 followed by a hundred zeros, and I could write that, but I won't. Instead, I'll say that a googolplex can be written as:

$$10^{10^{100}} \text{ or even } 10^{10^{10^2}}$$

The googol itself can be written out easily. I did it at the beginning of the article and it only took up a few lines. Even the largest number previously mentioned in this article can be written out with ease. The largest Mersenne prime, if written out in full, would take up less than two pages of this book.

The googolplex, however, cannot be written out—literally *cannot*. It is a 1 followed by a googol zeros, and this book will not hold as many as a googol zeros no matter how small, within reason, those zeros are printed. In fact, you could not write the number on the entire surface of the earth, if you made each zero no larger than an atom. In fact, if you represented each zero by a nucleon, there wouldn't be enough nucleons in the entire known universe or in a trillion like it to supply you with sufficient zeros.

You can see then that the googolplex is incomparably larger than anything I have yet dealt with. And yet I can represent it in T-numbers without much trouble.

Consider! The T-numbers go up through the digits, T-1, T-2, T-3, and so on, and eventually reach T-1,000,000,000,000. (This is a number equivalent to saying "a trillion trillion trillion trillion . . ." and continuing until you have repeated the word *trillion* a trillion times. It will take you umpty-ump lifetimes to do it, but the principle remains.) Since we have decided to let a trillion be written as T-1, the number T-1,000,000,000,000 can be written T-(T-1).

Remember that we must multiply the numerical part of the T-number by 12 to get a ten-based exponent. Therefore T-(T-1) is equal to $10^{12,000,000,000,000}$, which is more than $10^{10^{13}}$.

In the same way, we can calculate that T-(T-2) is more than $10^{10^{25}}$, and if we continue we finally find that T-(T)8) is nearly a googolplex.

As for T-(T-9), that is far larger than a googolplex; in fact, it is far larger than a googol googolplexes.

One more item and I am through.

In a book called *The Lore of Large Numbers*, by Philip J. Davis, a number called "Skewes' number" is given. This number was obtained by S. Skewes, a South African mathematician who stumbled upon it while working out a complex theorem on prime numbers. The number is described as "reputed to be the largest number that has occurred in a mathematical proof." It is given as:

$$10^{10^{10^{34}}}$$

Since the googolplex is only $10^{10^{10^{2}}}$, Skewes' number is incomparably the greater of the two.

And how can Skewes' number be put into T-formation?

Well, at this point, even I rebel. I'm not going to do it.

I will leave it to you, O Gentle Reader, and I will tell you this much as a hint. It seems to me to be obviously greater than T-[T-(T-1)].

From there on in, the track in yours and the road to madness is unobstructed. Full speed ahead, all of you.

As for me, I shall hang back and stay sane; or, at least, as sane as I ever am, which isn't much.